STINGER

Cody stepped through the doorway of the empty house. Suddenly he was tumbling forward, falling through the darkness. His mouth opened in a cry of terror as he realized that the room had no floor, that he was crashing through the roof of Hell . . .

Something whammed underneath his right arm. He had the sense to grab hold of it before he slid off. He gripped both hands to a swaying thing that felt like a horizontal length of pipe. Dirt and stones cascaded into the darkness beneath him. He didn't hear them hit bottom . . .

Minutes passed. "Help me!" he shouted. Panic gnawed at his guts. The chill of shocked nerves and blood-drained muscles began to spread through his shoulders.

And then he heard something that made the hairs stir at the nape of his neck. It was a furtive, scuttling sound; a moist sound.

Cody held his breath. Something was moving in the darkness below . . .

Books by Robert R. McCammon

Baal
Bethany's Sin
Blue World
Mine
The Night Boat
Stinger
Swan Song
They Thirst
The Wolf's Hour

Published by POCKET BOOKS

Most Pocket Books are available at special quantity discounts for bulk purchases for sales promotions, premiums or fund raising. Special books or book excerpts can also be created to fit specific needs.

For details write the office of the Vice President of Special Markets, Pocket Books, 1230 Avenue of the Americas, New York, New York 10020.

STINGER

ROBERT R. McCAMMON

POCKET BOOKS

New York   London   Toronto   Sydney   Tokyo   Singapore

For John and Therese

An *Original* Publication of POCKET BOOKS

POCKET BOOKS, a division of Simon & Schuster
1230 Avenue of the Americas, New York, NY 10020

ISBN: 0-671-73776-7

First Pocket Books printing April 1988

10 9 8 7 6 5

POCKET and colophon are registered trademarks of
Simon & Schuster.

Cover art by Rowena Morrill

Printed in the U.S.A.

The motorcycle roared out of Bordertown, carrying the blond boy and dark-haired girl away from the horror behind them.

Smoke and dust whirled into the boy's face; he smelled blood and his own scared sweat, and the girl trembled as she clung to him. The bridge was ahead of them, but the motorcycle's headlight was smashed out and the boy was steering by the dim violet glow that filtered through the smoke clouds. The air was hot, heavy, and smelled burnt: the odor of a battleground.

The tires gave a slight bump. They were on the bridge, the boy knew. He cut his speed slightly as the bridge's concrete sides narrowed, and swerved to avoid a hubcap that must have fallen off one of the cars that had just raced to the Inferno side. The thing that both he and the girl had just seen still clawed at their minds, and the girl looked back with tears in her eyes and her brother's name on her lips.

Almost across, the boy thought. We're gonna make it! We're gonna—

Something rose up from the smoke directly in front of them.

The boy instinctively hit the brakes, started to swerve the machine, but knew there wasn't enough time. The motorcycle smacked into the figure, then skidded out of control. The boy lost his grip, felt the girl go off the motorcycle too, and then he seemed to turn head over heels in midair and slid in a fury of friction burns.

He lay curled up, gasping for breath. Must've been the Mumbler, he thought as he struggled to stay conscious. The Mumbler . . . crawled up on the bridge . . . and gave us a whack.

He tried to sit up. Not enough strength yet. His left arm was hurting, but he could move the fingers and that was a good sign. His ribs felt like splintered razors, and he wanted to sleep, just close his eyes and let go . . . but if he did that, he was sure he would never awaken again.

He smelled gasoline. Motor's tank ruptured, he realized. About two seconds later there was a *whump!* of fire and orange light flickered. Pieces of metal clattered down around him. He got up on his knees, his lungs hitching, and in the firelight could see the girl lying on her back about six feet away, her arms and legs splayed like those of a broken doll. He crawled to her. There was blood on her mouth from a split lower lip and a blue bruise on the side of her face. But she was breathing, and when he spoke her name her eyelids fluttered. He tried to cradle her head, but his fingers found a lump on her skull and he thought he'd better not move her.

And then he heard footsteps—two boots: one clacking, one sliding.

He looked up, his heart hammering. Someone was lurching toward them from the Bordertown side. Rivulets of gasoline burned on the bridge, and the thing strode on through the streams of flame, the cuffs of its jeans catching fire. It was hunchbacked, a grotesque mockery of a human being, and as it got nearer the boy could see a grin of needles.

He crouched protectively over the girl. The clacking boot and dragging boot closed in. The boy started to rise to fight it off, but pain shot through his ribs, stole his breath, and hobbled him. He fell back to his side, wheezing for air.

The hunchbacked, grinning thing reached them, and

stood staring down. Then it bent lower, and a hand with metal, saw-edged fingernails slid over the girl's face.

The boy's strength was gone. The metal nails were about to crush the girl's head, about to rip the flesh off her skull. It would happen in a heartbeat, and the boy knew that on this long night of horror there was only one chance to save her life. . . .

1
Dawn

The sun was rising, and as the heat shimmered in phantom waves the night things crept back to their holes.

The purple light took on a tint of orange. Muted gray and dull brown gave way to deep crimson and burnt amber. Stovepipe cactus and knee-high sagebrush grew violet shadows, and slabs of rough-edged boulders glowed as scarlet as Apache warpaint. The colors of morning mingled and ran along gullies and cracks in the rugged land, sparkling bronze and ruddy in the winding trickle of the Snake River.

As the light strengthened and the alkali odor of heat drifted up from the desert floor, the boy who'd slept under the stars opened his eyes. His muscles were stiff, and he lay for a minute or two looking up at the cloudless sky as it flooded with gold. He thought he remembered dreaming —something about his father, the drunken voice bellowing his name over and over again, distorting it with each repetition until it sounded more like a curse—but he wasn't sure. He didn't usually have good dreams, especially not those in which the old man capered and grinned.

He sat up and drew his knees to his chest, resting his sharp chin between them, and watched the sun explode over the series of jagged ridges that lay far to the east beyond Inferno and Bordertown. The sunrise always reminded him of music, and today he heard the crash and bluster of an Iron Maiden guitar solo, full-throttle and wailing. He liked sleeping out here, even though it took awhile for his muscles to unkink, because he liked to be alone, and he liked the desert's early colors. In another couple of hours, when the sun really started getting hot, the desert would turn the hue of ashes, and you could almost hear the air sizzle. If you didn't find shade at midday, the Great Fried Empty would cook a person's brains to twitching cinders.

But for right now it was fine, while the air was still soft and everything—if just for a short while—held the illusion of beauty. At a time like this he could pretend he'd awakened a long, long way from Inferno.

He was sitting on the flat surface of a boulder as big as a pickup truck, one of a jumble of huge rocks wedged together and known locally as the Rocking Chair because of its curved shape. The Rocking Chair was marred by a barrage of spray-painted graffiti, rude oaths and declarations like RATTLERS BITE JURADO'S COCK obscuring the remnants of pictographs etched there by Indians three hundred years ago. It sat atop a ridge stubbled with cactus, mesquite, and sagebrush, and rose about a hundred feet from the desert's surface. It was the boy's usual roost when he slept out here, and from this vantage point he could see the edges of his world.

To the north lay the black, razor-straight line of Highway 67, which came out of the Texas flatlands, became Republica Road for two miles as it sliced along Inferno's side, crossed the Snake River Bridge, and passed mangy Bordertown; then it became Highway 67 again as it disappeared south toward the Chinati Mountains and the Great Fried Empty. For as far as the boy could see, both north and south, no cars moved on Highway 67, but a few vultures were circling something dead—an armadillo, jackrabbit, or snake—that lay on the roadside. He wished them a good breakfast as they swooped down to feast.

To the east of the Rocking Chair lay the flat, intersecting streets of Inferno. The blocky, adobe-style buildings of the central "business district" stood around the small rectangle of Preston Park, which held a white-painted bandstand, a collection of cacti planted by the Board of Beautification, and a life-size white marble statue of a donkey. The boy shook his head, took a pack of Winstons from the inside pocket of his faded denim jacket, and lit the first cigarette of the day with a Zippo lighter; it was his dumb luck, he mused, to have spent his life in a town named after a jackass. Then again, the statue was probably a pretty fair likeness of Sheriff Vance's mother too.

The wooden and stone houses along Inferno's streets threw purple shadows over the gritty yards and heat-cracked concrete. Multicolored plastic flags drooped over Mack Cade's used-car lot on Celeste Street. The lot was surrounded by an eight-foot-tall chainlink fence topped with barbed wire, and a big red sign trumpeted TRADE WITH CADE THE WORKINGMAN'S FRIEND. The boy figured that every one of those cars were chopshop specials; the best junker on the lot couldn't make five hundred miles, but Cade was making a killing off the Mexicans. Anyway, selling used cars was just pocket change to Cade, whose real business lay elsewhere.

Further east, where Celeste Street crossed Brazos Street at the edge of Preston Park, the windows of the Inferno First Texas Bank glowed orange with the sun's fireball. Its three floors made it the tallest structure in Inferno, not counting the looming gray screen of the StarLite Drive-in off to the northeast. Used to be, you could sit up here on the Rocking Chair and see the movies for free, make up your own dialogue, do a little zooming and freaking around, and have a real scream. But times do change, the boy thought. He drew on his cigarette and puffed a couple of smoke rings. The drive-in shut down last summer, the concession building a nest for snakes and scorpions. About a mile north of the StarLite was a small cinder-block building with a roof like a brown scab. The boy could see that the gravel parking lot was empty, but round about noontime it would start filling up. The Bob Wire Club was the only place in town making money anymore. Beer and whiskey were mighty potent painkillers.

The electric sign in front of the bank spelled out 5:57 in

6

lightbulbs, then abruptly changed to display the present temperature: 78°F. Inferno's four stoplights all blinked caution yellow, and not one of them was in sync with another.

He didn't know if he felt like going to school today or not. Maybè he'd just go for a ride in the desert and keep going until the road trailed out, or maybe he'd wander over to the Warp Room and try to beat his best scores on Gunfighter and Galaxian. He looked way east, across Republica Road toward the W. T. Preston High School and the Inferno Community Elementary School, two long, low-slung brick buildings that made him think of prison movies. They faced each other over a common parking lot, and behind the high school was a football field, the meager grass of autumn long burned away. No new grass would be planted, and there would be no more games on that field. Anyway, the boy thought, the Preston High Patriots had only won twice during the season and had come in dead last in Presidio County, so who gave a flying fuck?

He'd skipped school yesterday, and tomorrow—Friday, May 25—was the last day for the seniors. The ordeal of finals was over, and he would graduate with the rest of his class if he finished his manual-arts project. So maybe he ought to be a choirboy today, go to school like he was supposed to, or at least check in to see what the action was. Maybe Tank, Bobby Clay Clemmons, or somebody would want to go somewhere and zoom, or maybe one of the Mexican bastards needed a nitro lesson. If that was so, he'd be real happy to oblige.

His pale gray eyes narrowed behind a screen of smoke. Looking down on Inferno like this disturbed him, made him feel antsy and mean, like he had an itch he couldn't scratch. He'd decided it must be because there were so many dead-end streets in Inferno. Cobre Road, which intersected Republica and ran west along the Snake River's gulley, continued for about eight more miles—but only past more failure: the copper mine and the Preston Ranch, as well as a few other struggling old spreads. The strengthening sunlight did not make Inferno any prettier; it only exposed all the

7

scars. The town was scorched and dusty and dying, and Cody Lockett knew that by this time next year there'd be nobody left. Inferno would dry up and blow away; already a lot of the houses were empty, the people who'd lived in them packed up and gone for greener pastures.

Travis Street ran north and south, and divided Inferno into its east and west sections. The east section was mostly wooden houses that would not hold paint and that, in the middle of summer, would become ovens of misery. The west section, where the shopowners and "upper class" lived, was predominantly white stone and adobe houses, and in the yards were an occasional sprout of wildflowers. But it was clearing out fast: every week saw more businesses shutting down; amid the wildflowers bloomed FOR SALE signs. And at the northern end of Travis Street, across a parking lot strewn with tumbleweeds, stood a two-story red-brick apartment building, its first-floor windows covered with sheet metal. The building had been constructed back in the late fifties—in the boomtown years—but now it was a warren of empty rooms and corridors that the Renegades, the gang of which Cody Lockett was president, had taken over and made into their fortress. Any member of el Culebra de Cascabel—the Rattlesnakes, a gang of Mexican kids over in Bordertown—was meat to be fried if he or she was caught on 'Gade territory after dark. And 'Gade territory was everything north of the Snake River Bridge.

That was how it had to be. Cody knew the Mexicans would stomp you if you let them. They'd take your money and your job and they'd spit in your face while they were doing it. So they had to be kept in their place, and knocked back if they got out of line. That was what Cody's old man had drilled into his head, day after day, year after year. Wetbacks, Cody's father said, were like dogs that had to be kicked every so often just so they'd know who the masters were around here.

But sometimes, when Cody slowed down and thought about it, he didn't see what harm the Mexicans did. They were out of work, same as everybody else. Still, Cody's father said the Mexicans had ruined the copper mine. Said they fouled everything they touched. Said they'd ruined the state of Texas, and they were going to ruin this country before they were through. Gonna be screwin' white women in the streets before long, the elder Lockett had warned. Gotta kick 'em down and make 'em taste dust.

Sometimes Cody believed it; sometimes he didn't. It depended on his mood. Things were bad in Inferno, and he knew things were bad inside himself too. Maybe it was easier to kick Mexican ass than to let yourself think too much, he reasoned. Anyway, it all boiled down to keeping the Rattlers out of Inferno after sunset, a responsibility that had been passed down to Cody through the six other 'Gade presidents before him.

Cody stood up and stretched. The sunlight shone in his curly, sandy-blond hair, which was cropped close on the sides and left shaggy on top. A small silver skull hung from the hole in his left earlobe. He cast a long, lean shadow; he stood six feet, was rangy and fast, and looked as mean as rusty barbed wire. His face was made up of hard angles and ridges, nothing soft about it at all, his chin and nose sharp, and even his thick blond eyebrows bristling and angry. He could outstare a sidewinder and give a jackrabbit a good foot race, and when he walked he took long strides as if he were trying to stretch his legs free of Inferno's boundaries.

He'd turned eighteen on the fifth of March and he had no idea what he was going to do with the rest of his life. The future was a place he avoided thinking about, and beyond a week from Sunday, when he would graduate with the sixty-three other seniors, the world was a patchwork of shadows. His grades weren't good enough for college, and there wasn't enough money for technical school. The old man drank everything he earned at the bakery and most of what Cody brought home from the Texaco station too. But Cody knew he could keep the job pumping gas and working on cars for as long as he wanted. Mr. Mendoza, who owned the place, was the only good Mexican he knew—or cared to know.

Cody's gaze shifted to the south, across the river toward the small houses and buildings of Bordertown, the Mexican section. Over there, the four narrow, dusty streets had no names, just numbers, and all of them but Fourth Street were dead ends. The steeple of the Sacrifice of Christ Catholic Church, its cross glinting with orange sunlight, was Bordertown's highest point.

Fourth Street led west into Mack Cade's auto junkyard —a two-acre maze of car hulks, heaps of parts and discarded tires, enclosed workshops and concrete pits, all surrounded by a nine-foot-tall sheet-metal fence and another foot of vicious concertina wire atop that. Cody could see the flare of welding torches through the windows of a workshop, and a lug-nut gun squealed. Three tractor-trailer trucks were parked in there, awaiting cargo. Cade kept shifts working around the clock, and his business had bought him a huge modernistic adobe mansion with a swimming pool and a tennis court about two miles south of Bordertown and that much closer to the border of Mexico. Cade had offered Cody a job working in the autoyard, but Cody knew what the man was dealing in, and he wasn't yet ready for that kind of dead end.

He turned toward the west, and his shadow lay before him. His gaze followed the dark line of Cobre Road. Three miles away was the huge red crater of the Preston Copper Mining Company, rimmed with gray like an ulcerous wound. Around the crater stood empty office buildings, storage sheds, the aluminum-roofed refinery building, and abandoned machinery. Cody thought they looked like what was left of dinosaurs after the desert sun had melted their skins away. Cobre Road kept going past the crater in the direction of the Preston Ranch, following the power poles to the west.

He looked down again at the quiet town—population about nineteen hundred and slipping fast—and could imagine he heard the clocks ticking in the houses. Sunlight was creeping around curtains and through blinds to streak the walls with fire. Soon those alarm clocks would go off, shocking the sleepers into another day; those with jobs would get dressed and leave their houses, running before the electric prod of time, to their work either in the remaining stores of Inferno or up north in Fort Stockton and Pecos. And at the end of the day, Cody thought, they would all return to those little houses, and they would watch the flickering tube and fill up the empty spaces as best they could until those bastard clocks whispered sleep. That was the way it would be, day after day, from now until the last door shut and the last car pulled out—and then nothing would live here but the desert, growing larger and shifting over the streets.

"So what do I care?" Cody said, and exhaled cigarette smoke through his nostrils. He knew there was nothing for him here; there never had been. The whole freaking town, he told himself, might've been a thousand miles from civilization except for the telephone poles, the stupid American and even stupider Mexican TV shows, and the chattering bilingual voices that floated through the radios. He looked north along Brazos, past more houses and the white stone Inferno Baptist Church. Just before Brazos ended stood an ornate wrought-iron gate and fence enclosing Joshua Tree Hill, Inferno's cemetery. It was shaded by thin, wind-sculpted Joshua trees, but it was more of a bump than a hill. He stared for a moment toward the tombstones and old monuments, then returned his attention to the houses; he couldn't see much difference.

"Hey, you freakin' zombies!" he shouted on impulse. *"Wake up!"* His voice rolled over Inferno, leaving the sound of barking dogs behind it.

"I'm not gonna be like you," he said, the cigarette clamped in a corner of his mouth, "I swear to God I'm not."

He knew to whom he was speaking, because as he said the words he was staring down at a gray wooden house near where a street called Sombra crossed Brazos. He figured the old man didn't even know he hadn't come home last night, wouldn't have cared anyway. All his father needed was a bottle and a place to sleep it off.

Cody glanced at Preston High. If that project wasn't finished today, Odeale might give him some grief, might even screw up his graduation. He couldn't stand for some bow-tied sonofabitch to watch over his shoulder and tell him what to do, so he'd purposefully slowed his work to a snail's pace. Today, though, he had to finish it; he knew he could've built a roomful of furniture in the six weeks it had taken him to do one lousy tie rack.

The sun had a fierce glare now. Already the bright hues of the desert were fading. A truck was coming down Highway 67, its headlights still on, bringing the morning newspapers from Odessa. A dark blue Chevy backed out of a driveway on Bowden Street, and a woman in a robe waved to her husband from the front porch. Somebody opened their back door and let out a yellow cat, which promptly chased a rabbit into a thicket of cactus. On the side of Republica Road, the buzzards were plucking at their breakfast and other birds of prey were slowly circling in the sullen air above.

Cody took one last pull at his cigarette and then flicked it off the Rocking Chair. He decided he could do with something to eat before school. There were usually stale doughnuts in the house, and those would do.

He turned his back on Inferno and climbed carefully down the rocks to the ridge below. Nearby stood the red Honda 250cc motorcycle he'd salvaged from parts bought at Cade's junkyard two years ago. Cade had given him a good deal, and Cody was smart enough not to ask questions. The ID numbers on the Honda's engine had been filed off, just as they were removed from most of the engines and body parts Mack Cade sold.

As he approached the motorcycle, a slight movement beside his right cowboy boot snagged his attention. He stopped.

His shadow had fallen across a small brown scorpion that crouched on a flat rock. As Cody watched, the scorpion's segmented stinger arced up and struck at the air. The scorpion stood its ground, and Cody lifted his boot to smash the little bastard to eternity.

But he paused an instant before his boot came down. The

12

insect was only about three inches long from head to barb, and Cody knew he could crush it in a heartbeat but he admired its courage. There it was, fighting a giant shadow for a piece of rock in a burning desert. It didn't have too much sense, Cody mused, but it had more than its share of guts. Anyway, there was too much death in the air today, and Cody decided not to add to it.

"It's all yours, *amigo,*" he said, and as he walked past, the scorpion jabbed its stinger at his departing shadow.

Cody swung one leg over the motorcycle and settled himself in the patched leather seat. The dual chrome exhausts were full of dings, the red paint had mottled and faded, the engine sometimes burned oil and had a mind of its own, but the machine got Cody where he wanted to go. Out on Highway 67, once he was far beyond Inferno, he could coax the engine up to seventy, and there were few things he enjoyed better than its husky growl and the wind hissing past his ears. It was at times like that, when he was alone and depending on no one but himself, that Cody felt the most free. Because he knew depending on people freaked your head. In this life, you were alone and you'd better learn to like it.

He took a pair of leather aviator's goggles off the handlebars and slipped them on, put the key in the ignition and brought his weight down on the kick starter. The engine backfired a gout of oily smoke and vibrated as if unwilling to wake up—then the machine came to life under him like a loyal, if sometimes headstrong, mustang, and Cody drove down the ridge's steep slope toward Aurora Street, a trail of yellow dust rising behind him. He didn't know what shape his father would be in today, and he was already toughening himself for it. Maybe he could get in and out without the old man even knowing.

Cody glanced at the straight line of Highway 67, and he vowed that very soon, maybe right after Graduation Day, he was going to hit that damned road and keep on riding, following the telephone poles north, and he would never look back at what he was leaving.

STINGER

I'm not gonna be like you, he swore.

But inside he feared that every day he saw a little more of his old man's face looking back at him from the mirror.

He throttled up, and the rear tire left a black scrawl as he shot along Aurora Street.

The sun lay hot and red in the east, and another day had begun in Inferno.

2
The Great Fried Empty

Jessie Hammond awakened, as was her habit, about three seconds before the alarm clock buzzed on the bedside table. As it went off she reached out, her eyes still closed, and popped the alarm button down with the flat of her hand. She sniffed the air, could smell the inviting aromas of bacon and freshly brewed coffee. "Breakfast's on, Jess!" Tom called from the kitchen.

"Two more minutes." She burrowed her head into the pillow.

"Big minutes or little ones?"

"Tiny ones. Minuscule." She rolled over to find a better position and caught his clean, pleasantly musky scent on the other pillow. "You smell like a puppy," she said sleepily.

"Pardon?"

"What?" She opened her eyes to the bright streamers of sunlight that hit the opposite wall through the window blinds and immediately shut them again.

"How about some lizard eyeballs in your eggs today?" Tom asked. He and Jessie had stayed up until well after one in the morning, talking and sharing a bottle of Blue Nun. But he'd always been a quick starter and enjoyed cooking breakfast, while Jessie took a little longer to get her spark plugs going even on the best of days.

"Make mine rare," she answered, and tried seeing again. The early light was already glary, promising another scorcher. The past week had been one ninety-degree day after the next, and the Odessa weatherman on Channel 19 had said today might break the hundred mark. Jessie knew that meant trouble. Animals weren't acclimated to such heat so soon. Horses would get sluggish and go off their feed, dogs would be surly and snap without cause, and cats would have major spells of claw-happy craziness. Stock animals got unruly too, and bulls were downright dangerous. But it was also rabies season, and her worst fear was that somebody's pet would go chasing after an infected jackrabbit or prairie dog, be bitten, and bring rabies back into the community. All the domesticated animals she could think of had already been given their boosters, but there were always a few folks who didn't bring their pets in for the treatment. It might be a good idea, she decided, to get in the pickup truck today and drive around to some of the small communities near Inferno—like Klyman, No Trees, and Notch Fork—to spread the antirabies gospel.

"'Morning." Tom was standing over her, offering her coffee in a blue clay mug. "This'll get you started."

She sat up and took the mug. The coffee, as usual whenever Tom made it, was ebony and ominous. The first sip puckered her mouth; the second brooded on her tongue for a while, and the third sent the caffeine charging through her system. She needed it too. She'd never been a morning person, but as the only veterinarian within a forty-mile radius she'd learned a long time ago that the ranchers and farmers were up long before the sun first blushed the sky. "Smooth," she managed to say.

"Always is." Tom smiled slightly, walked over to the window, and pushed aside the blinds. Red fire hit his face and glowed in the lenses of his eyeglasses. He looked east, along Celeste Street toward Republica Road and Preston High School—"the Hotbox," he called it, because the air conditioning broke down so often. His smile began to fade.

She knew what he was thinking. They'd talked about it

last night, and many nights before that one. The Blue Nun eased, but it did not heal.

"Come here," she said, and motioned him to the bed.

"Bacon'll get cold," he answered. His accent was the unhurried drawl of east Texas, whereas Jessie's was west Texas's gritty twang.

"Let it freeze."

Tom turned away from the window, could feel the hot stripes of sun across his bare back and shoulders. He wore his faded and comfortable khaki trousers, but he hadn't yet pulled on his socks and shoes. He passed under the bedroom's lazily revolving ceiling fan, and Jessie leaned over in her pale blue, oversized shirt and patted the edge of the bed. When he sat down, she began massaging his shoulders with her strong brown hands. Already his muscles were as tight as piano wire.

"It's going to work out," she told him, her voice calm and deliberate. "This isn't the end of the world."

He nodded, said nothing. The nod wasn't very convincing. Tom Hammond was thirty-seven years old, stood a bit over six feet, was slim and in pretty good shape except for a little potbelly that resisted sit-ups and jogging. His light brown hair was receding to show what Jessie called a "noble forehead," and his tortoiseshell-framed glasses gave him the look of an intelligent if slightly dismayed schoolteacher. Which was exactly what he was: Tom had been a social studies teacher at Preston High for eleven years. And now, with the impending death of Inferno, that was coming to an end. Eleven years of the Hotbox. Eleven years of watching the faces change. Eleven years, and still he hadn't defeated his worst enemy. It was still there, and it would always be there, and every day for eleven years he'd seen it working against him.

"You've done everything you could," Jessie said. "You know you have."

"Maybe. Maybe not." One corner of his mouth angled downward in a bitter smile, and his eyes were pinched with frustration. A week from tomorrow, when school closed, he and the other teachers would have no job. His résumés had brought in only one offer from the state of Texas—a field job, running literacy exams on immigrants who followed the melon crops. Still, he knew that most of the other teachers hadn't landed jobs yet either, but that didn't make the pill any sweeter going down. He'd gotten a nice letter stamped with the state seal of Texas that told him the education budget had been cut for the second year in a row and at present there was a freeze on the hiring of teachers. Of course, since he'd been in the system so long, his name would be put on the waiting list of applicants, thank you and keep this letter for your files. It was the same letter many of his colleagues had received, and the only file it went into was circular.

But he knew that, eventually, another position would come his way. Running the exams on the migrant workers wouldn't be so bad, really, but it would require a lot of time on the road. What had chewed at him day and night for the past year was the memory of all the students who'd passed through his social studies class—hundreds of them, from red-haired American sons to copper-skinned Mexicans to Apache kids with eyes like bullet holes. Hundreds of them: doomed freight, passing through the badlands on tracks already warped. He'd checked; over an eleven-year period with a senior class averaging about seventy to eighty kids, only three hundred and six of them had enrolled as freshmen in either a state or technical college. The rest had just drifted away or set roots in Inferno to work at the mine, drink their wages, and raise a houseful of babies who would probably repeat the pattern. Only now there was no mine, and the pull of drugs and crime in the big cities was stronger. It was stronger, as well, right here in Inferno. And for eleven years he'd seen the faces come and go: boys with knife scars and tattoos and forced laughter, girls with scared eyes and gnawed fingernails and the secret twitches of babies already growing in their bellies.

Eleven years, and tomorrow was his final day. After the senior class walked out at last period, it would be over. And what haunted him, day after day, was the realization that he could recall maybe fifteen kids who'd escaped the Great Fried Empty. That was what they called the desert between Inferno and the Mexican border, but Tom knew it was a state of mind too. The Great Fried Empty could suck the brains out of a kid's skull and replace it with dope smoke, could burn out the ambition and dry up the hope, and what almost killed Tom was the fact that he'd fought it for eleven years but the Great Fried Empty had always been winning.

Jessie kept massaging, but Tom's muscles had tensed. She knew what must be going through his mind. It was the same thing that had slowly burned his spirit to a cinder.

Tom stared at the bars of fire on the wall. "I wish I had three more months. Just three." He had a sudden, startling image of the day he and Jessie had graduated together from the University of Texas, walking out into a flood of sunlight and ready to take on the world. It seemed like a hundred years ago. He'd been thinking a lot about Roberto Perez lately, could not get the boy's face out of his mind, and he knew why. "Roberto Perez," he said. "Do you remember me talking about him?"

"I think so."

"He was in my senior class six years ago. He lived in Bordertown, and his grades weren't very high, but he asked questions. He wanted to know. But he held himself back from doing too well on tests, because that wouldn't be cool." His bitter smile surfaced again. "The day he graduated, Mack Cade was waiting for him. I saw him get into Cade's Mercedes. They drove off. Roberto's brother told me later that Cade got the boy a job up in Houston. Good money, but it wasn't exactly clear what the job was. Then one day Roberto's brother came to me and said I ought to know: Roberto had been killed in a Houston motel. Cocaine deal went bad. He got both barrels of a shotgun in his stomach. But the Perez family didn't blame Cade. Oh, no. Roberto sent home a lot of money. Cade gave Mr. Perez a new Buick. Sometimes I drive by the Perez house after school; the Buick's up on concrete blocks in the front yard."

He stood up abruptly, went to the window, and pulled the blinds aside again. He could feel the heat out there, gathering power and shimmering off the sand and concrete. "There are two boys in my last-period class who remind me of Perez. Neither one of them ever made higher than a C-minus on a test, but I see it in their faces. They listen; something sinks in. But they both do just enough to get by, and no more. You probably know their names: Lockett and Jurado." He glanced at her.

Jessie had heard Tom mention the names before, and she nodded.

"Neither of them took the college entrance exams," Tom continued. "Jurado laughed in my face when I suggested it. Lockett looked at me like I fell out of a dog's ass. But their last day is tomorrow, and they'll graduate a week from Sunday, and that'll be it. Cade'll be waiting. I know it."

"You've done what you could," Jessie said. "Now it's up to them."

"Right." He stood for a moment framed in crimson light, as if on the rim of a blast furnace. "This town," he said softly. "This damned, godforsaken town. Nothing can grow here. I swear to God, I'm beginning to believe there's more use for a vet than there is for a teacher."

She tried for a smile, but wasn't very successful. "You take care of your beasts, I'll take care of mine."

"Yeah." He summoned up a wan smile. He walked to the bed, cupped his hand to the back of Jessie's head, his fingers disappearing into her dark brown, short-cut hair, and kissed her forehead. "I love you, doc." He let his head rest against hers. "Thanks for listening to me."

"I love *you*," she answered, and put her arms around him. They stayed that way for a minute, until Jessie said, "Lizard eyeballs?"

"Yep!" He straightened up. His face was more relaxed now, but his eyes were still troubled and Jessie knew that, however good a teacher he was, Tom thought of himself as a failure. "I guess they're good and cold by now. Come and get 'em!"

Jessie got out of bed and followed her husband through the short hallway into the kitchen. In this room also, a ceiling fan was turning, and Tom had pulled up the blinds

20

on the west-facing windows. The light in that direction was still tinged with violet, but the sky was turning bright blue over Rocking Chair Ridge. Tom had already fixed all four of the breakfast plates—each with bacon, scrambled eggs (no lizard eyeballs today), and toast—and they were waiting on the little circular table in the corner. "Let's go, sleepy-heads!" Tom called toward the kids' rooms, and Ray answered with an unenthusiastic grunt.

Jessie went to the refrigerator and liberally doused milk into her muscular coffee while Tom switched on the radio to catch the six-thirty news from KOAX in Fort Stockton. Stevie bounded into the kitchen. "It's horsie day, Mama!" she said. "We get to go see Sweetpea!"

"We sure do." It amazed her that anybody could be so full of energy in the morning, even a six-year-old child. Jessie poured a glass of orange juice for Stevie while the little girl, clad in her University of Texas nightshirt, climbed into her chair. She sat perched on the edge, swinging her legs and chewing at a piece of toast. "How'd you sleep?"

"Good. Can I ride Sweetpea today?"

"Maybe. We'll see what Mr. Lucas has to say." Jessie was scheduled to drive out to the Lucas place, about six miles west of Inferno, and give their golden palomino Sweetpea a thorough checkup this morning. Sweetpea was a gentle horse that Tyler Lucas and his wife Bess had raised from a colt, and Jessie knew how much Stevie looked forward to their trip.

"Eat your breakfast, cowgirl," Tom said. "Gotta be strong to stay on a bronco."

They heard the television snap on in the front room and the channels being clicked around. Rock music pounded through the speaker on MTV. In back of the house was a satellite dish that picked up about three hundred channels, bringing all parts of the world through the air to Inferno. "No TV!" Tom called, jarred by the noise. "Come on to breakfast!"

"Just one minute!" Ray pleaded, as he always did. He was a TV addict, particularly drawn to the scantily clad models in the videos on MTV.

"Now!"

The television set was clicked off, and Ray Hammond walked into the kitchen. He was fourteen years old, beanpole thin and gawky—looks just like me when I was that age, Tom thought—and wore eyeglasses that slightly magnified his eyes: not much, but enough to earn him the nickname of X Ray from the kids at school. He yearned for contacts and a build like Arnold Schwarzenegger; the first had been promised to him when he turned sixteen, and the second was a fever dream that no number of push-ups could accomplish. His hair was light brown, cropped close except for a few orange-dyed spikes on top that neither his father nor mother could talk him out of, and he was the proud possessor of a wardrobe of paisley-patterned shirts and tie-dyed jeans that made Tom and Jessie think the sixties had come back full vengeful circle. Right now, though, he wore only bright red pajama bottoms, his chest sunken and sallow.

"'Morning, alien," Jessie said.

"'Morning, 'lien," Stevie parroted.

"Hi." Ray plopped down in a chair and yawned hugely. "Juice." He held out a hand.

"Please and thank you." Jessie poured him a glass, gave it to him, and watched as he put it down the awesome hatch. For a boy who only weighed around a hundred and fifteen pounds in a soaking wet suit, he could eat and drink faster than a horde of hungry Cowboy linebackers. He began digging into his eggs and bacon.

There was purpose in Ray's all-out attack on his plate. He'd had a dream about Belinda Sonyers, the blond fox who sat on the next row in his freshman English class, and the details were still percolating. If he got a hard-on here at the table with his folks, he would be in danger of serious embarrassment; so he concentrated on the food, which seemed the second-best thing to sex. Not that he knew, of course. The way his zits were popping up, he could forget about girls for the next thousand years. He stuffed his mouth full of toast.

"Where's the fire?" Tom asked.

Ray almost gagged, but he got the toast down and attacked the eggs because the gauzy porno dream was making his pencil twitch again. After a week from tomorrow, though, he could forget about Belinda Sonyers and all the other foxes who paraded down the halls of Preston High; the school would be shut down, the doors locked, and the dreams would be just so much red-hot dust. But at least it would be summer, and that was okay too. Still, with the whole town closing down, summer was going to be about as much fun as cleaning out the attic.

Jessie and Tom sat down to breakfast, and Ray got his thoughts under rein again. Stevie, the red highlights in her auburn hair shining in the sunlight, ate her food knowing that cowgirls did have to be strong to ride broncos—but Sweetpea was a nice horse, who wouldn't dream of bucking and throwing her. Jessie glanced at the clock on the wall —one of those goofy plastic things shaped like a cat's head, with eyeballs that ticked back and forth to mark the passing seconds; it was quarter to seven, and she knew Tyler Lucas was an early riser and would already be waiting for her to show up. Of course she didn't expect to find anything wrong with Sweetpea, but the horse was getting on in years and the Lucases treated it like a household pet.

After breakfast, as Tom and Ray cleared away the plates, Jessie helped Stevie get dressed in a pair of jeans and a white cotton shirt with the Jetsons pictured on its front. Then she returned to her own bedroom and pulled off her nightshirt, exposing the tight, lithe body of a woman who enjoyed working outdoors; she had a "Texas tan"—arms brown to the shoulders, a deeply bronzed face, and the rest of her body almost ivory in contrast. She heard the TV click on; Ray was grabbing some more of the tube before he and his father left for school—but that was all right, because Ray was an avid reader as well and his brain pulled in information like a sponge. And the way he wore his hair and his taste in clothes were no causes for alarm, either; he was a good boy, a lot shier than he let on, and he was simply doing what he could to get along with his peers. She knew about his nickname, and she remembered that it was sometimes tough to be young.

The harsh desert sun had added lines to Jessie's face, but she possessed a strong, natural beauty that required no aid from jars and tubes. Anyway, she knew, vets weren't expected to win beauty pageants. They were expected to be available at all hours and to work damned hard, and Jessie did not disappoint. Her hands were brown and sturdy, and the things she'd had to grab with them during her thirteen years as a veterinarian would've made most women swoon. Gelding a vicious stallion, delivering a stillborn calf jammed in a cow's birth canal, removing a nail from the trachea of a five-hundred-pound prize boar—all those were operations she'd performed successfully, as well as hundreds of other tasks ranging from treating a canary's injured beak to operating on a Doberman's infected jaw. But she was up to the task; working with animals was all she'd ever wanted to do, even as a child when she used to bring home every stray dog and cat off the streets of her neighborhood in Fort Worth. She'd always been a tomboy, and growing up with three brothers had taught her to roll with the punches —but she gave as good as she got too, and she could vividly recall knocking her oldest brother's front tooth out with a football when she was nine years old. He laughed about it now, whenever they spoke on the phone, and he kidded her that the ball might've sailed to the Gulf if his mouth hadn't been in the way.

She walked into the bathroom to sprinkle on some baby powder and brush the taste of coffee and Blue Nun from her mouth. She quickly ran her hands through her short, dark brown hair. Flecks of gray were creeping back from the temples. The march of time, she thought. Not as startling as watching your kids grow up, of course; it seemed like only yesterday that Stevie was a baby and Ray was in third grade. The years were flying, that was for sure. She went to the closet, pulled out a pair of her well-worn and comfortable jeans and a red T-shirt, put them on and then a pair of white socks and her sneakers. She got her sunglasses and a baseball cap, stopped in the kitchen to fill up two canteens because you never knew what might happen in the desert, and took her veterinary satchel from its place on the upper shelf of the hall closet. Stevie was hopping around like a jumping bean on a hot griddle, eager to get going.

"We're heading off," Jessie told Tom. "See you about four." She leaned over and kissed him, and he planted a kiss on Stevie's cheek. "Be careful, cowgirls!" he said. "Take care of your mama."

"I will!" Stevie clutched her mother's hand, and Jessie paused to take a smaller-sized baseball cap off the hat tree near the front door and put it on Stevie's head. "See you later, Ray!" she called, and he answered, "Check six!" from his own room. Check six? she thought as she and Stevie went out into the already-searing sunlight. Whatever happened to a simple *'Bye, Mom*? Nothing made her feel more like a fossil, at thirty-four, than not understanding her own son's language.

They walked along the stone path that led from the house past the small building next door; it was fashioned of rough white stone, and set out near the street was a little sign that read INFERNO ANIMAL HOSPITAL and, beneath that, *Jessica Hammond, DVM.* Parked at the curb, behind Tom's white Civic, was her dusty, sea-green Ford pickup truck; in a rack across the rear window, where most everybody else carried their rifles, was an extendable-wire restraining noose that Jessie had fortunately only had to use a few times.

In another moment Jessie was driving west on Celeste Street, and Stevie was tucked behind her seat belt but hardly able to stand the confinement. She was fragile in appearance, her features as delicate as a porcelain doll's, but Jessie knew full well that Stevie had an intense curiosity and wasn't shy about going after what she wanted; the child already had an appreciation of animals and enjoyed traveling to the various farms and ranches with her mother, no matter how bone-jarring the trip. Stevie—Stephanie Marie, after Tom's grandmother just as Ray had been named after Jessie's grandfather—was usually a quiet child, and seemed to be absorbing the world through her large green eyes, which were just a few shades lighter than Jessie's. Jessie had enjoyed having her around and helping at the animal hospital, but Stevie would start first grade next September —wherever they happened to end up. Because after the schools in Inferno closed and the exodus continued, the rest of Inferno's stores and shops would shut down, and the few remaining spreads would dry up; there would be no work for Jessie, just as there would be none for Tom, and their only choice would be to pull up roots and hit the road.

She drove past Preston Park on her left, the Ringwald Drug Store, Quik-Check Grocery, and the Ice House on her right. She crossed Travis Street, almost crunching one of Mrs. Stellenberg's big tomcats as it darted in front of the truck, and followed narrow Circle Back Road as it ran along the foot of Rocking Chair Ridge and then, true to its name, circled back to connect with Cobre Road. She paused at the blinking yellow light before she turned west and put the pedal to the metal.

The desert's bittersweet tang blew through the open windows in the blessed breeze. Stevie's hair danced around her shoulders. Jessie figured this was the coolest it was likely to be all day, and they might as well enjoy it. Cobre Road took them past the chainlink fence and the iron gates of the Preston Copper Mine. The gates were padlocked, but the fence was in such bad shape an arthritic old man could've climbed over. Crudely lettered signs said DANGER! NO TRESPASSING! Beyond the gates was the huge crater where a red mountain rich with copper ore had once cast its shadow. In the last months of the mine's existence, the dynamite blasts had gone off like clockwork out here, and Jessie understood from Sheriff Vance that there were still some charges in the crater that had been unexploded and left behind, but no one was crazy enough to go down in there and pull them out. Jessie knew that sooner or later the mine would be exhausted, but nobody had expected the veins of ore to fail with such startling finality. From the moment the jackhammers and bulldozers had scraped against worthless rock, Inferno had been doomed.

With a bump and shudder, the pickup's tires passed over

the railroad tracks that ran north and south from the mining complex. Stevie leaned toward the window, her back already getting damp. She caught sight of a group of prairie dogs atop the mound of their nest, standing motionless on their hind legs. A jackrabbit burst from its cover of cactus and shot across the road, and way up in the sky a vulture was slowly circling. "How're you doing?" Jessie asked her.

"Fine." Stevie strained against the seat belt, the wind blowing into her face. The sky was as blue as a Smurf, and it looked like it went on forever—maybe even a hundred miles. Something struck her that she'd been meaning to ask: "How come Daddy's so sad?"

Of course Stevie had felt it, Jessie thought. There was no way for her not to. "He's not sad, exactly. It's because of school closing. You remember, we talked about that?"

"Yes. But it closes every year."

"Well, it's not going to open up again. Because of that, more people are going to move away."

"Like Jenny did?"

"Right." Jenny Galvin was a little girl who'd lived a few houses up the street from them, and she and her parents had moved just after Christmas. "Mr. Bonner's going to close the Quik-Check store in August. By that time, I expect most everybody'll be gone."

"Oh." Stevie mulled that over for a moment. The Quik-Check store was where everybody bought food. "And we'll be gone too," she said finally.

"Yes. Us too."

Then that meant Mr. and Mrs. Lucas would be leaving, Stevie realized. And Sweetpea: what would happen to Sweetpea? Would they just set him free to run wild, or would they pack him up in a horse box, or would they get on him and ride away? That was a puzzle worth thinking about, but she'd seen the end of something and it gave her a sad feeling down near her heart—the same kind of feeling that she figured her daddy must know.

The land was cut by gullies and covered with wild thatches of sagebrush and towers of stovepipe cactus. A blacktopped highway left Cobre Road about two miles past the copper mine and shot northwestward under a white granite arch with PRESTON embedded in tarnished copper letters. Jessie looked to her right, could see the big hacienda way up at the blacktop's end, shimmering in the rising heatwaves as they sped past. Good luck to you too, Jessie thought, envisioning the woman who was probably sleeping in that house on cool silk sheets. The sheets and the house might be all Celeste Preston had left, and those wouldn't last very much longer, either.

They went on, following the road that carved across the desert. Stevie stared out the window, her face composed and thoughtful under the cap's brim. Jessie shifted in her seat to get her T-shirt unstuck. The turnoff to the Lucas place was about a half mile ahead.

Stevie heard a high humming noise and thought a mosquito was at her ear. She flipped her hand against her ear, but the humming remained and it was getting louder and higher. In another few seconds it had turned painful, like the jabbing of a needle in both ears. "Mama?" she said, wincing. "My ears hurt!"

A sharp, prickling pain had hit Jessie's eardrums as well. Not only that: the fillings in her back teeth were aching. She opened her mouth, working her lower jaw. "Ow!" she heard Stevie say. "What is it, Mama?"

"I don't know, hon—" Suddenly the truck's engine died. Just died, without a stutter or gasp. They were coasting, and Jessie gave it more gas but she'd filled the truck up yesterday and the fuel tank couldn't be empty. Her eardrums were really hurting now—pulsing to a high, painful tone like a far-off, distant wail. Stevie pressed her hands to her ears, and bright tears had come to her eyes. "What is it, Mama?" she asked again, panic quavering in her voice. "What is it?"

Jessie shook her head. The noise was getting louder. She turned the ignition key and pumped the accelerator; still the engine wouldn't fire. She heard the crackle of static electricity in her hair, and she caught sight of her wristwatch: the digital display had gone mad, the hours flickering past at runaway speed. This'll be some story to tell Tom, she thought as she flinched in a cocoon of ear-piercing noise, and she reached out to grasp Stevie's hand.

The child's head jerked to the right; her eyes widened, and she screamed, "Mama!"

She'd seen what was coming, and now Jessie did too. She slammed on the brake, her hands fighting the wheel.

What looked like a flaming locomotive was hurtling through the air, burning parts flying off behind it and spinning away. It passed over Cobre Road, about fifty feet over the desert and maybe forty yards in front of Jessie's truck; she could make out a cylindrical form, glowing red-hot and surrounded by flames, and as the truck went off the road the object passed with a shriek that deafened Jessie and prevented her from hearing her own scream. She saw the rear of the object explode in yellow and violet flames, flinging pieces off in all directions; something came at the truck in a blur, and there was a *wham!* of metal being struck and the pickup shuddered right down to its frame.

A front tire blew. The truck kept going over rocks and through stands of cactus before Jessie got it stopped, her palms sweat-slick on the wheel. The ringing in her ears still kept her from hearing, but she saw Stevie's frantic, tear-streaked face and she said, as calmly as she could, "Hush, now. It's over. It's all over. Hush, now."

Steam was shooting from around the truck's crumpled hood. Jessie looked to her left, saw the flaming object pass over a low ridge and disappear from sight. My God! she thought, stunned. What was it?

In the next instant there was a roaring that penetrated even through Jessie's aural murk. The pickup's cab filled with whirling dust. Jessie grasped Stevie's hand, and the little girl's fingers clamped shut.

There was dust in Jessie's mouth and in her eyes, and her cap had blown out the window. When she got her vision cleared again, she saw three gray-green helicopters, flying in a tight V formation about thirty or forty feet above the desert, following the flaming object toward the southwest.

They too went over the ridge and out of sight. Up in the blue, the contrails of several jets also tracked to the southwest.

The dust settled. Jessie began to get her hearing back; Stevie was sobbing, holding on to her mother's hand for dear life. "It's over," Jessie said, and heard her own raspy voice. "All over." She felt like crying herself, but mothers didn't do such things. The engine ticked like a rusty heart, and Jessie found herself staring at a geyser of steam that rose from a small round hole right in the center of the pickup's hood.

3
Queen of Inferno

"Christ's drawers, what a racket!" the white-haired woman wearing a pink silk sleep mask cried out, sitting up in her canopied bed. The entire house seemed to be vibrating with noise, and she angrily pulled the mask off to reveal eyes the color of arctic ice. "Tania! Miguel!" she shouted in a voice made husky by too many unfiltered cigarettes. "Get in here!" She reached for the bell cord beside her bed and started yanking it. Down in the depths of the Preston mansion, the bell clamored for the servants' attention.

But the horrendous, roaring noise was gone now; it had only lasted a few seconds, but long enough to shock her awake. She threw the covers back, got out of bed, and strode to the balcony doors like a tornado on legs. When she flung them open, the heat almost sucked the breath right out of her lungs. She went out, squinting toward Cobre Road with one hand warding off the glare. She was fifty-three years old, but even without glasses her vision was sharp enough to see what had passed dangerously near the house: three helicopters, racing away toward the southwest and raising a storm of dust beneath them. They vanished behind that dust after a few more seconds, and Celeste Preston was so mad she could've spat nails.

Stout, moon-faced Tania came to the balcony doors. She was braced for the onslaught. *"Sí,* Señora Preston?"

"Where were you? I thought we were bein' bombed! What the hell's goin' on?"

"I don't know, señora. I think—"

"Oh, just get me a drink!" she snapped. "My nerves are shot!"

Tania retreated into the house for her mistress's first drink of the day. Celeste stood on the high balcony, its floor a mosaic of red Mexican clay tiles, and grasped the ornate wrought-iron railing. From this vantage point she could see the estate's stables, the corral, and the riding track —useless, of course, since all the horses had been auctioned off. The blacktopped driveway circled a large bed of what had once been peonies and daisies, now burned brown since the sprinkler system was inoperative. Her lemon-yellow gown was sticking to her back; the sweat and heat rekindled her fury. She returned to the cooler temperature of the bedroom, picked up the pink telephone, and punched the numbers with a manicured fingernail.

"Sheriff's office," a drawling voice answered. A boy's voice. "Deputy Chaffin speak—"

"Put Vance on the phone," she interrupted.

"Uh . . . Sheriff Vance is on patrol right now. Is this—"

"Celeste Preston. I want to know who's flyin' helicopters over my property at"—her eye located the clock on the white bedstand—"at seven-twelve in the mornin'! The bastards almost took my roof off!"

"Helicopters?"

"Clean the wax out of your ear, boy! You heard me! Three helicopters! If they'd been any closer, they could've folded my damn sheets! What's goin' on?"

"Uh . . . I don't know, Mrs. Preston." The deputy's voice sounded more alert now, and Celeste imagined him sitting at attention behind his desk. "I can get Sheriff Vance over the radio for you, if you want."

"I want. Tell him to get out here pronto." She hung up before he could reply. Tania had come in and offered the woman a Bloody Mary on one of the last sterling silver trays. Celeste took it, stirred up the hot peppers with a celery stick, and took most of it down in a couple of swallows. Tania had added more Tabasco than usual today, but Celeste didn't wince. "Who do I have to jaw with today?" She ran the glass's frosty rim over her high, lined forehead.

"No one. Your schedule's clear."

"Thank God and jingle my spurs! Bunch of damned bloodsuckers gonna let me rest a spell, huh?"

"You have appointments with Mr. Weitz and Mr. O'Connor on Monday morning," Tania reminded her.

"That's Monday. I might be dead by then." She finished off her drink and plunked the glass back on the silver tray. The thought of returning to bed entered her mind, but she was too keyed up now. The last six months had been one legal headache after another, not to mention the damage done to her soul. Sometimes she felt like God's punching bag, and she knew she'd done a lot of down-and-dirty things in her life, but she was paying for her sins in spades.

"Is there anything else?" Tania asked, her dark eyes steady and impassive.

"No, that's it." But Celeste changed her mind before Tania could reach the massive, polished redwood door. "Wait a minute. Hold on."

"Yes, señora?"

"I didn't mean to jump down your throat awhile ago. It's just . . . you know, times bein' what they are."

"I understand, señora."

"Good. Listen, anytime you and Miguel want to unlock the bar for yourselves, might as well go ahead." She shrugged. "Ain't no sense lettin' the liquor go to waste."

"I'll remember that, Mrs. Preston."

Celeste knew she wouldn't. Neither Tania nor her husband drank, and anyway somebody had to stay clearheaded around here, if just to keep the human vultures away. Her flinty gaze locked with Tania's. "You know, in thirty-four years you've always called me either 'Mrs. Preston' or 'señora.' Haven't you once wanted to call me 'Celeste'?"

Tania hesitated. Shook her head. "Not once, señora."

Celeste laughed; it was the hearty laughter of a woman who was no stranger to the hard life, who once had been proud of the rodeo dirt under her fingernails and knew that winning and losing were two sides of the same coin. "You're a card, Tania! I know you've never liked me worth a buzzard's fart, but you're all right." Her smile faded. "I appreciate your stayin' on these last few months. You didn't have to."

"Mr. Preston was always very kind to us. We wanted to repay the debt."

"You have." Her eyes narrowed slightly. "But tell me one thing, and tell me true: would the first Mrs. Preston have handled this shit mess any better?"

The other woman's expression was flat and without emotion. "No," she said finally. "The first Mrs. Preston was a beautiful, gracious woman—but she didn't have your courage."

Celeste grunted. "Yeah, and she wasn't crazy, either. That's why she hightailed it out of this hellhole forty years ago!"

Tania abruptly veered back to familiar ground: "Will there be anything else, señora?"

"Nope. But I'm expectin' the sheriff pretty soon, so listen up."

Her back straight and stiff, Tania left the bedroom. Her footsteps clicked away on the oak floor in the long corridor outside.

Celeste listened, realizing how empty a house without furniture sounded. There were a few pieces left, of course, like the bed and her dressing table and the dining-room table downstairs, but not much. She walked across the room, took a thin black cheroot from a silver filigreed case. The French crystal lighter had already gone to the auction house, so Celeste lit her cigar with a pack of matches that advertised the Bob Wire Club on Highway 67. Then she went out again to the balcony, where she exhaled the pungent smoke and lifted her face toward the brutal sun.

Going to be another god-awful hot one, she thought. But

she'd lived through worse. And would again. All this tangled-up mess with the lawyers, the state of Texas, and the Internal Revenue Service was going to pass like a cloud in a high wind, and then she'd get on with her life.

"My life," she said, and the lines around her mouth etched deep. She'd come a long way from a bayside shack in Galveston, she mused. Now she was standing on the balcony of a thirty-six-room Spanish-style hacienda on a hundred acres of land—even if the house was without furniture and the land was rocky desert. In the garage was a canary-yellow Cadillac, the last of the six cars. On the mansion's walls were empty spaces where Miro, Rockwell, and Dali paintings used to hang; those were among the first to be auctioned, along with the French antique furniture and Wint's collection of almost a thousand stuffed rattlesnakes.

Her bank account was frozen tighter than an Eskimo's balls, but a regiment of Dallas lawyers was working on the problem and she knew that any day now she'd get a call from that office with the seven names; they'd say, "Mrs. Preston? Good news, hon! We've tracked down the missing funds, and the IRS has agreed to take their back taxes in monthly payments. You're out of the woods! Yes, ma'am, old Wint took care of you after all!"

Old Wint, Celeste knew, had been slicker than owl shit. He'd danced around government safety regulations and tax codes, corporate laws and bank presidents like a Texas whirlwind, and the stroke that had kicked him out of this world on the second day of December, at the age of eighty-seven, had left her to pay the band.

She looked east, toward Inferno and the mine. Over sixty years ago, Winter Thedford Preston had come south from Odessa with a mule called Inferno, searching for gold in the scrub lands. The gold had eluded him, but he'd found a crimson mountain that the Mexicali Indians had told him was made of sacred, healing dust. Wint had a knack for metallurgy—though his formal education had ended at the seventh grade—and his nose had not picked up the scent of sacred dust but of rich copper ore. Wint had started his mining company with a single clapboard shack, fifty or so Mexicans and Indians, a couple of trucks, and a whole lot of shovels. The first day of digging had turned up a dozen skeletons, and it was then that Wint realized the Mexicalis had been burying their dead in the mountain for over a hundred years.

And then one day a Mexican with a pickax had uncovered a sparkling vein of high-grade ore a hundred feet wide. That was the first of many. The new Texas companies that were stringing telephone wires, electric lines, and water pipes across the state came knocking at Wint's door. And just beyond the mountain of ore a few tents sprang up, then clapboard and adobe houses, followed by stone structures, churches, and schools. Dirt roads were covered with gravel, then pavement. Celeste recalled that Wint had told her he'd looked over his shoulder one day and seen a town where there used to be tumbleweeds. The townspeople, most of them mine workers, had elected him mayor, and under the influence of tequila Wint had christened the town Inferno and vowed to build a statue of his faithful old mule at its center.

But, though there'd been plenty of fits and starts, Inferno had never grown much beyond a one-mule town. It was too hot and dusty, too far from the big cities, and when the water pipeline ruptured, people got thirsty in a mighty big hurry. The copper mine had remained the only real industry. But folks kept coming in, the Ice House plugged into the pipeline and froze water into blocks, the church bells rang on Sunday mornings, the shopkeepers made money, the telephone company strung lines and trained operators, the high school lettered the football and basketball teams, and a concrete bridge replaced the shaky wooden one that spanned the Snake River. The first nails were driven into the boards of Bordertown. Walt Travis was elected sheriff, and in his third month was shot dead on the street that was thereafter named for him. The next man stuck with the job until he was beaten within a finger of St. Peter's handshake and woke up on a northbound train. Gradually, year after year, Inferno sank its roots. But just as gradually, the Preston Copper Mining Company was chewing away the red mountain where the dead Indians of a hundred years slept.

Celeste Street used to be called Pearl Street, after Wint's first wife. Between wives, it was known as Nameless Street. Such was the power of Wint Preston's influence.

She took one last pull on the cheroot, crushed it out on the railing, and flicked it into space. "We had some high old times, didn't we?" she said softly. But they'd fought like cats and dogs too, ever since Celeste had met him when she was singing with a cowboy band at a little dive in Galveston. Celeste hadn't minded; she had a holler like a cement mixer and could cuss Satan into church. The truth was that she'd fallen in love with Wint over the years, in spite of his womanizing and drinking and gambling. In spite of the fact that he kept her in the dark about his business affairs for more than thirty years. And when the machines had begun scraping bottom less than three years ago and frantic dynamiting uncovered no new veins, Wint Preston had seen his dream dying. What Celeste realized now was that Wint had gone nutty; he'd started pulling money out of his accounts, selling his stocks and bonds and gathering cash in a maniacal frenzy. But what he'd done with almost eight million dollars remained a mystery. Maybe he'd opened up new accounts under false names; maybe he'd put all that cash into tin boxes and buried them in the desert. In any case, the money of a lifetime was gone, and when the IRS had swooped down demanding a huge chunk of back taxes and penalties, there was nothing to pay with.

The lawyers had the mess now. Celeste knew full well that she was simply a caretaker, en route back to the dives of Galveston.

She saw the sheriff's blue-and-gray patrol car turning off Cobre Road and coming slowly along the blacktop. She gripped the railing with both hands and waited, a tough one-hundred-and-ten-pound figure backed by a hollow three-thousand-ton house. She stood without moving as the car made the driveway's circle and stopped.

The car's door opened, and a man who more than doubled her weight got out in sweat-saving slow motion. The back of his pale blue shirt was drenched, as was the sweatband of his beige cowboy hat. His belly flopped over his jeans, and he wore a gunbelt and lizard-skin boots.

"You took your damned time, didn't you?" Celeste called sharply. "If the house had been on fire, I'd be standin' in ashes right now!"

Sheriff Ed Vance stopped, looked up, and found her on the balcony. He was wearing sunglasses with mirrored lenses, just like his favorite bad-ass in the movie *Cool Hand Luke*. Last night's dinner of enchiladas and refried beans gurgled in his bulging belly. He showed his teeth in a tight grin. "If the house had been on fire," he said, his drawl as sugary as hot molasses, "I hope you would've had the good sense to call the fire department, Miz Preston." She said nothing, just stared holes through him. "Deputy Chaffin gave me a call," he continued. "Said you was gettin' buzzed by helicopters." He made a big show of inspecting the cloudless sky. "Nary a one around here."

"There were three. They flew over my property, and I've never heard such a noise in all my life. I want to know where they came from and what's goin' on."

He shrugged his thick shoulders. "Don't seem like much is goin' on anywhere, if you ask me. Seems like a pretty peaceful day." His grin widened; now it was more of a grimace. "Up till now, that is."

"They went that way." Celeste pointed toward the southwest.

"Well, maybe if I hurry I can head 'em off at the pass. Just what is it you expect me to *do,* Miz Preston?"

"I *expect* you to earn your pay, Sheriff Vance!" she replied coldly. "That means bein' on top of what goes on around here! I'm tellin' you that three helicopters almost knocked me out of my bed, and I want to know who they belonged to! Does that spell it out any clearer for you?"

"A mite." The grimace remained locked on his square, heavily jowled face. "'Course, they're probably in Mexico by now."

"I don't care if they're in Timbuktu! Those damned things could've crashed into my house!" Vance's obstinacy and slowness infuriated her; if it had been her decision, Vance would never have been reelected sheriff, but he'd ingratiated himself to Wint over the years and had easily beaten the Hispanic candidate. She saw clear through him, though, and knew that Mack Cade pulled his strings; and, like it or not, she realized Mack Cade was now Inferno's ruling power.

"Better calm down. Take a nerve pill. That's what my ex-wife used to do when—"

"She saw you?" Celeste interrupted.

He laughed, hollowly and without mirth. "No call to get nasty, Miz Preston. Don't suit a lady like you." Showed your true stripe, didn't you, bitch? he thought. "So what is it you're sayin'?" he prodded. "You want to file a disturbin' the peace charge against some unknown persons in three helicopters, point of origin unknown and destination unknown?"

"That's right. Is it too much of a job for you?"

Vance grunted. He couldn't wait for the woman to be tossed out on her ass; then he was going to start digging up those cashboxes old Wint must've hidden. "I think I can handle it."

"I hope you can. That's what you're paid for."

Lady, he thought, it sure ain't *you* who writes my ticket! "Miz Preston," he said quietly, as if speaking to a retarded child, "you'd best get on inside now, out of this hot sun. You don't want your brain gettin' baked. Wouldn't want you to have a stroke now, would we?" He gave her his best, most innocent smile.

"Just do it!" she snapped, and then she turned away from the railing and stalked back into the house.

"Yes, ma'am!" Vance gave a mock salute and got behind the wheel again, his wet shirt immediately leeching to the seat. He started the engine and drove away from the hacienda, back to Cobre Road. The knuckles of his large, hairy hands were white on the steering wheel. He turned left, toward Inferno, and as he picked up speed he shouted out the open window, "I ain't your god-damned monkey!"

4
The Visitor

"I guess this means we walk," Jessie had said while Celeste Preston was waiting on her balcony for Sheriff Vance. Her nerves had calmed down somewhat, and Stevie was no longer crying, but Jessie had gotten the truck's hood opened and seen at once that a flat tire was the least of their problems.

The engine had been pierced by the same object that had put a hole in the hood; metal had been flayed open like a flower, and whatever had passed through had driven itself right into the depths of the engine block. There was no sign of what it had been, but there was a smell of scorched iron and charred rubber and the engine was hissing steam from its wound. The truck would do no more traveling for quite some time—possibly the thing was ready for Cade's junkyard. "Damn!" Jessie said, staring at the engine, and instantly regretted it because Stevie would remember the word and spring it on her when she least expected it.

Stevie was looking at the direction the fiery thing and the helicopters had disappeared in, her face covered with dust except for the drying tracks of tears. "What was it, Mama?" she asked, her green eyes wide and watchful.

"I don't know. Something big, for sure." Like a tractor-trailer truck flying through the air and on fire, Jessie thought. Damnedest thing she'd ever seen in her life. It might've been an airplane about to crash, but it hadn't had any wings. Maybe a meteor, but it had looked metallic. Whatever it had been, the helicopters had been chasing it down like hounds after a fox.

"There's part of it," Stevie said, and pointed.

Jessie looked. On the ground about forty feet away, in the midst of chopped-down cactus, was a piece of something sticking up from the sand. Jessie walked toward it, with Stevie right behind. The fragment was the size of a manhole cover, a strange hue of dark, wet-looking blue green. Its edges were smoking, and Jessie felt the heat coming off it before she got within fifteen feet. In the air there was a sweet odor that reminded her of the smell of burning plastic, but the stuff had a metallic sheen. Just to the right was another chunk of the material, this one shaped like a tube, and more smaller pieces lay nearby, smoke rising from all of them. She said, "Stay here" to Stevie and approached the first fragment a little closer, but its heat was intense and she had to stop again. Its surface was covered with small markings arrayed in a circular pattern, a series of Japanese-like symbols and short wavy lines.

"It's hot," Stevie said, standing right beside her mother.

So much for obedience, Jessie thought, but this was not the time for discipline. She took her child's hand. Whatever had passed this way and thrown pieces off in its passage was unlike anything Jessie had ever seen before, and she could still feel the static electricity that had crackled through her hair. She glanced at her wristwatch: the digits had all returned to zeros, flashing erratically. In the blue sky, the jet contrails all aimed toward the southwest. The sun was beginning to beat down on her unprotected skull, and she searched for her cap. It was a red speck about seventy yards on the other side of Cobre Road, blown there by the helicopters' rotors. Too far to walk when they should be going in the opposite direction, toward the Lucas place. They had their canteens, thank God, and at least the sun was still low. There was no need to stand around gawking; they had to get moving.

"Let's go," Jessie said. Stevie resisted her for just a couple of seconds, still looking at the manhole-sized piece of whatever it was, and then allowed herself to be tugged along. Jessie went back to the truck to get her satchel, which contained her wallet and driver's license as well as a few veterinary instruments. Stevie stood gazing up at the contrails. "The planes sure are high," she said, more to herself than to her mother. "I'll bet they're a hundred miles—"

She heard something that stopped her voice.

Music, she thought. But not music. Now it was gone. She listened carefully, heard only the noise of steam from the broken engine.

Then there it was again, and Stevie thought she knew what the sound was but she couldn't exactly remember. Music, but not music. Not like the kind Ray listened to.

Gone again.

Now slowly, softly returning.

"We've got a ways to go," Jessie told her. The child nodded absently. "You ready?"

Stevie knew what it was: it hit her quick and clear. On the front porch of the Galvin house, before Jenny had moved away, hung a pretty thing that sounded like a lot of little bells ringing when the wind stirred it. *Wind chimes,* she remembered Jenny's mother saying when Stevie had asked what it was. That was the music she was hearing, but no wind was blowing and there weren't any wind chimes around, anyway.

"Stevie?" Jessie asked. The little girl was just staring at nothing. "What is it?"

"Can you hear that, Mama?"

"Hear what?" Nothing but the damned engine spouting.

"That," Stevie insisted. The sound was fading in and out again, but it seemed to be coming from a certain direction. "Hear it?"

"No," Jessie's voice was careful. Did she hit her head? Jessie wondered. Oh Lord, if she's got a concussion . . . !

Stevie took a few steps toward the blue-green smoking thing out in the cactus. The wind-chimes noise immediately weakened to a whisper. Not that way, she thought, and stopped.

"Stevie? You okay, honey?"

"Yes ma'am." She looked around, walked in another direction. Still the sound was very faint. Not that way, either.

Jessie was getting spooked. "It's too hot to play games. We've got to go. Come on, now."

Stevie walked toward her mother. Stopped abruptly. Took another step, then two more.

Jessie approached her, took off the child's cap, and ran her fingers through the hair. There was no knot, no sign of a bruise on the forehead either. Stevie's eyes were a little shiny and her cheeks were flushed, but Jessie figured that was just from the heat and excitement. She hoped. There was no sign of injury that she could see. Stevie was staring past her. "What is it?" Jessie asked. "What do you hear?"

"The music," she explained patiently. She had figured out where it was coming from, though she knew also that such a thing couldn't be. "It's singing," she said, as the clear strong notes swept over her again. She pointed. "From there."

Jessie saw where she was pointing to. The pickup truck. Its torn-up engine, the hood still raised. She guessed the noise of steam and bubbling fluids from gashed cables might be construed as a weird kind of music, yes, but . . .

"It's singing," Stevie repeated.

Jessie knelt down, checking her daughter's eyes. They were not bloodshot, the pupils looked to be fine. Checked her pulse. A little fast, but otherwise okay. "Do you feel all right?"

That was her mama's doctor voice, Stevie thought. She nodded. The wind-chimes sound was coming from the truck; she was certain of it. But why couldn't her mother hear? The fragile music pulled at her, and she wanted to walk the rest of the way to the truck and keep searching until she found where the wind chimes were hidden, but her mother had hold of her hand and was pulling her away. With each step, the music faded just a little more.

"No! I want to stay!" Stevie protested.

"Stop this foolishness, now. We've got to get to the Lucas place before it gets really hot out here. Stop dragging your feet!" Jessie was trembling. The events of the past few minutes were catching up to her. Whatever that thing had been, it could've easily smashed them to atoms. Stevie'd had flights of fantasy before, but this was certainly neither the time nor the place. "Stop dragging!" she ordered, and finally the little girl was walking under her own power.

Ten more steps, and the wind-chimes music was a whisper. Five more, a sigh. Another five, a memory.

But it had penetrated deep in Stevie's mind, and she could not let it go.

They walked away, following the dirt road to the Lucas place. Stevie kept looking back at the pickup truck until it was a dusty dot, and only when it was out of sight did she remember that they were on their way to see Sweetpea.

5

Bordertown

"Day of reckonin'!" Vance said as the patrol car sped east on Cobre Road. A belch rose from his gut like thunder. "Yes sir, day of reckonin's comin' right soon!" Celeste Preston was going to be out on her rear end before long. Miss High-and-Mighty was going to wish she could get a job swabbing spittoons at the Bob Wire Club, if he had anything to say about it.

The car was moving past the remnants of the mine. Back in March, a couple of kids had climbed over the fence, gone down into the crater, and gotten themselves blown to flyspecks when they found some undetonated dynamite left in drill holes in the rock. In the mine's final weeks, the blasting had been as constant as doom's clockwork, and Vance figured more live sticks were probably down there, but nobody was dumb enough to go dig them out. What was the use, anyway?

He reached to the dash and lifted the radio's microphone. "Hey there, Danny boy! Come on back to me, hear?"

The speaker crackled as Danny Chaffin responded. "Yes, sir?"

"Get on the horn and call around to . . . uh, let's see here a minute." Vance flipped down the visor, took the county map that was clipped to it, and unfolded it on the seat beside him. He let the car have its own mind for a few seconds and it weaved toward the right shoulder, scaring the sense out of an armadillo. "Call around to Rimrock and Presidio airstrips. Ask 'em if they're flyin' any choppers this mornin'. Prissy Preston's in an uproar 'cause her hair got mussed."

"Ten-four."

"Hold on," Vance added. "Might as well go out of the county too. Call up to Midland and Big Spring airports. Hell, call Webb Air Force Base too. That oughta do it."

"Yes sir."

"I'm gonna take a swing through Bordertown and then I'll be on in. Any more calls?"

"No sir. Quiet as a whore in church."

"You got Whale Tail on your mind there, boy? Better quit drillin' that thang 'fore you fall in!" Vance laughed. The idea of Danny getting it on with Sue "Whale Tail" Mullinax tickled him giddy. Whale Tail was about twice the kid's size; she was a waitress at the Brandin' Iron Cafe on Celeste Street, and he knew about ten guys who'd dipped their wicks into her flame. So why not the boy too?

Danny didn't answer. Vance knew talking about Whale Tail like that got his goat, because Danny Chaffin was a moon-eyed kid, wet as oceans behind the ears, and didn't realize Whale Tail was stringing him along. He'd learn. "Check ya later, Danny boy," Vance said, and returned the mike to its cradle. Rocking Chair Ridge was coming up on the left, and along Cobre Road the houses and buildings of Inferno shimmered in the harsh light.

It was too early for trouble in Bordertown, Vance knew. But then again, you never could tell what might set off those Mexicans. *"Hispanics,"* Vance muttered, and shook his head. They had brown skin, black eyes and hair, they lived on tortillas and enchiladas, and they jabbered south-of-the-border lingo; to Vance, that made them Mexicans, no matter where they'd been born or what fancy name you called them. Mexicans, pure and simple.

Nestled in its slot underneath the dashboard was a Remington pump shotgun, and beneath the passenger seat was a Louisville Slugger. That ole baseball bat was just made to bash wetback skulls, Vance mused. Especially the skull of one smart-ass punk who thought he called the shots over there. Sooner or later, he knew, Mr. Louisville was going to meet Rick Jurado, and then—*boom!*—Jurado was going to be the first wetback in outer space.

He drove past Preston Park to Republica Road, turned right at Xavier Mendoza's Texaco station, and headed across the Snake River bridge onto the dusty streets of Bordertown. He decided to drive over to the Jurado house, on Second Street, maybe sit in front and see if anything needed correcting.

Because after all, Vance told himself, correcting was the sheriff's job. By this time next year he'd no longer be a sheriff, so he might as well do as much correcting as he could. He winced at the thought of Celeste Preston ordering him around like a shoeshine boy, and he put his foot down on the accelerator.

He stopped the car in front of a brown clapboard house on Second Street. Parked at the curb was the boy's banged-up black '78 Camaro, and along the street were other junkers that even Mack Cade wouldn't take. Laundry drooped on backyard lines and chickens pecked around some of the grassless yards. The land and houses belonged to a citizens' committee of Mexican-Americans, and the nominal rent went back into the town's fund, but Vance was the law here as well as across the bridge. The houses, most of which dated from the early fifties, were clapboard and stucco structures that all looked to be in need of painting or repair, but the Bordertown fund couldn't keep up with the work. It was a shantytown, the narrow streets sifted with yellow dust and the hulks of old cars, washing machines and other junk standing around like the perpetual monuments of poverty. The majority of Bordertown's thousand or so inhabitants had labored at the copper mine, and when that shut down the skilled ones had gone elsewhere. The others held on desperately to what little they had.

Two weeks ago, a couple of empty houses at the end of

Third Street had caught fire, but the Inferno Volunteer Fire Department had kept the blaze from spreading. Scraps of gasoline-soaked rags had been found in the ashes. Just last weekend, Vance had broken up a fight between a dozen Renegades and Rattlesnakes in Preston Park. Things were heating up again, the same as last summer, but this time Vance meant to bottle up the trouble before any citizens of Inferno got hurt.

He watched a red bantam rooster strutting across the street in front of his car. He hit the horn, and the rooster jumped up in the air and lost three feathers. "Little bastard!" Vance said, reaching into his breast pocket for his pack of Luckies.

But before he got a cigarette out, he caught a movement from the corner of his eye. He looked to his right, at the Jurado house, and he saw the boy standing in the doorway.

They stared at each other. Time ticked past. Then Vance's hand moved as if it had a wit of its own, and he pressed the horn again. The wail echoed along Second Street, stirring up the neighborhood dogs to a frenzy of barks and wails.

The boy didn't move. He was wearing black jeans and a blue-striped short-sleeved shirt, and he was holding the screen door open with one arm. The other hung at his side, the fist clenched.

Vance hit the horn once more, let it moan for about six long seconds. Now the dogs were really raising hell. A man peered from a doorway three houses up. Two children emerged onto the porch of another house and stood watching until a woman urged them back inside. As the noise died away, Vance heard the sound of shouted, Spanish cursing —all that lingo sounded like cursing to him—from a house across the street. And then the boy let the screen door shut as he came down the sagging porch steps to the curb. Come on, li'l rooster! Vance thought. Come on, just *start* some trouble!

The boy stopped right in front of the patrol car.

He stood about five-nine, his brown arms muscular, his jet-black hair combed back from his forehead. Against the dark bronze of his face his eyes were ebony—except they were the eyes of an old man who has seen too much, not the eyes of an eighteen-year-old. They held a cold rage—like that of a wild animal catching a hunter's scent. Around both wrists he wore black leather bracelets studded with small squares of metal; his belt was also made of studded leather. He stared through the windshield at Sheriff Vance, and neither of them moved.

Finally, the boy walked slowly around the car and stood several feet from Vance's open window. "You got a problem, man?" he asked, his voice a mixture of Mexico's stately cadence and west Texas's earthy snarl.

"I'm on patrol," Vance answered.

"You patrollin' in front of my house? On my street?"

Smiling thinly, Vance took off his sunglasses. His eyes were deep-set, light brown, and seemed too small for his face. "I wanted to drive over and see you, Ricky. Wanted to say good mornin'."

"*Buenos días.* Anythin' else? I'm gettin' ready for school."

Vance nodded. "Graduatin' senior, huh? Prob'ly got your future all lined up, right?"

"I'll make out okay."

"I'll bet you will. Prob'ly wind up sellin' drugs on the street, is more like it. Good thing you're a real tough *hombre,* Ricky. You might even learn to enjoy prison life."

"If I get there first," Rick said, "I'll make sure the fags know you're on your way."

Vance's smile fractured. "What's that supposed to mean, smart-ass?"

The boy shrugged, looking along Second Street at nothing in particular. "You're gonna take a fall, man. Sooner or later, the state cops are gonna latch Cade, and you'll be next. 'Cept you'll be the one holdin' his shitbag, and he'll be long gone 'cross the border." He stared at Vance. "Cade doesn't need a number two. Aren't you smart enough to figure that out yet?"

Vance sat very still. His heart was beating hard, and rough memories were being stirred at the back of his brain. He couldn't stomach Rick Jurado—not only because Jurado was the leader of the Rattlesnakes, but on a deeper, more instinctive level. When Vance was a kid living in El Paso with his mother, he'd had to walk home from grammar school across a dusty hellhole called Cortez Park. His mother worked at a laundry in the afternoons, and their house was only four blocks from school, but for him it was a nerve-twisting journey across a brutal no-man's-land. The Mexican kids hung out in Cortez Park, and there was a big eighth-grader named Luis who had the same black, fathomless eyes as Rick Jurado. Eddie Vance had been fat and slow, and the Mexican kids could run like panthers; the awful day came when they'd surrounded him, chattering and hollering, and when he'd started crying that only made it worse. They'd thrown him down and scattered his books while other gringo kids watched but were too scared to interfere; and the one named Luis had pulled his pants down, right off his struggling butt and legs, and then they'd held him while Luis stripped off Eddie's Fruit-of-the-Looms. The underpants had been wrapped around Vance's face like a feedbag, and as the half-naked fat boy ran home the Mexican kids had screamed with laughter and jeered, *"Burro! Burro! Burro!"*

From then on, Eddie Vance had walked more than a mile out of his way to avoid crossing Cortez Park, and in his mind he'd murdered that Mexican boy named Luis a thousand times. And now here was Luis again, only this time his name was Rick Jurado. This time he was older, he spoke English better, and he was no doubt a lot smarter —but, though Vance was approaching his fifty-fourth birthday, the fat little boy inside him would've recognized those cunning eyes anywhere. It was Luis all right, just wearing a different face.

And the truth was that Vance had never met a Mexican who didn't remind him, in some way, of those jeering kids in Cortez Park almost forty years ago.

"What're you starin' at, man?" Rick challenged. "Have I got two heads?"

The sheriff's trance snapped. Rage flooded through him. "I'd just as soon get out of this car and break your neck, you little shit-ass wetback."

"You won't." But the boy's body had tensed for either flight or fight.

Take it easy! Vance warned himself. He wasn't ready for this kind of trouble, not right here in the middle of Bordertown. He abruptly put his sunglasses back on and worked his knuckles. "Some of your boys have been driftin' into Inferno after dark. That won't do, Ricky."

"Last I heard, it was a free country."

"It's free for Americans." Though he knew Jurado had been born at the Inferno Clinic on Celeste Street, Vance knew also that the boy's father and mother had been illegals. "You let your gang punks go over—"

"The Rattlers isn't a gang, man. It's a club."

"Yeah, right. You let your *club* punks go over the bridge after dark and there'll be trouble. I won't stand for it. I don't want any Rattler across the bridge at night. Do I make myself—"

"Bull*shit*," Rick interrupted. He gestured angrily toward Inferno. "What about the 'Gades, man? Do they own the fuckin' town?"

"No. But your boys are askin' for a fight, lettin' themselves be seen where they shouldn't be. I want it to stop."

"It'll stop," Rick said. "When the 'Gades stop makin' raids over here, breakin' out people's windows and spray-paintin' their cars. They raise hell on *my* streets, and we're not even supposed to cross the bridge without gettin' spanked! What about that fire? How come Lockett's not in jail?"

"Because there's no proof he or any of the Renegades set it. All we've got are a few bits of burned-up rags."

"Man, you *know* they set it!" Rick shouted. "They could've burned down the whole town!" He shook his head disgustedly. "You're a chickenshit, Vance! Big sheriff, huh? Well, you listen up! My men are watchin' the streets at night, and I swear to God we'll cut the balls off any 'Gade we catch! *Comprende?*"

Anger reddened Vance's cheeks. He was looking into the face of Luis again, and standing on the battlefield of Cortez Park. Deep down, his stomach was squeezed with a fat kid's fear. "I don't think I like your tone of voice, boy! I'll take care of the Renegades! You just keep your punks on this side of the bridge after dark, you got it?"

Rick Jurado suddenly walked a few feet away, bent down, and picked something up. Vance saw it was the red rooster. The Mexican boy approached the car, held the rooster over the windshield, and gave a quick, strong squeeze with his hands. The rooster squawked and flapped, and a grayish-white blob fell from its rear end onto the windshield and oozed down the glass.

"There's my answer," the boy said defiantly. "Chickenshit for a chickenshit."

Vance was out of the car before the white line reached the hood. Rick took two strides back, dropped the rooster, and tensed himself to meet the onrushing storm. The rooster let out a strangled crowing as it darted for the cover of a yucca bush.

Even as he knew he was touching a match to dynamite, Vance reached out to grab the boy's collar; but Rick was way too fast for him, and easily dodged aside. Vance clutched at empty air, and again the vision of Luis and Cortez Park whirled around him. He bellowed with fury, drawing his fist back to strike at his tormentor.

But before the blow could fall, a screen door slammed and a boy's voice called out in Spanish, "Hey, Ricardo! You need some help?" The voice was followed immediately by a sharp *crack!* that froze the sheriff's fist in midair.

He looked across the street, where a rail-thin Mexican kid wearing chinos, combat boots, and a black T-shirt stood on the front steps of a rundown house. "You need some help, man?" he asked again, this time in English, and then he reared his right hand back and quickly snapped it forward in a smooth, blurred motion.

The bullwhip he was holding popped like a firecracker going off, its tip flicking up a cigarette butt from the gutter. Shreds of tobacco whirled.

The moment stretched. Rick Jurado watched Vance's face, could see the rage and cowardice fighting on it; then he saw Vance blink, and he knew which had won. The sheriff's fist opened. His arm came down to his side, and he clasped it like a broken wing.

"No, Zarra," Rick said, his voice calm now. "Everythin's steady, man."

"Jus' checkin'." Carlos "Zarra" Alhambra wrapped the bullwhip around his right arm and sat on the porch steps, his gangly legs stretched out before him.

Vance saw two more Mexican boys walking in his direction along Second Street. Down where the street dead-ended in a tangle of boulders and sagebrush, another boy stood at the curb, watching the sheriff. In his hand was a tire iron.

"You got anythin' else to say?" Rick prodded.

Vance sensed the many eyes on him from the windows of the crummy houses. He knew there was no way to win here; all Bordertown was a big Cortez Park. Vance glanced uneasily at the punk with the bullwhip, knowing that Zarra Alhambra could snap out a lizard's eyeballs with that damned thing. He pointed a thick finger into Rick's face. "I'm warnin' you! No Rattlers in Inferno after dark, you hear?"

"Eh?" Rick cupped a hand behind his ear.

Across the street, Zarra laughed. "You remember!" Vance said, and then he got into the patrol car. *"You remember, smart-ass!"* he shouted once the door was shut. The streak down his windshield infuriated him, and he switched on the wipers. The streak became a smear. His face burned as their laughter reached him. He put the car in reverse and backed rapidly along Second Street to Republica Road, swerved the car around, and roared over the bridge into Inferno.

"Big lawman!" Zarra hooted. He stood up. "I shoulda popped his fat butt, huh?"

"Not this time." Rick's heartbeat was slowing down now; it had been racing during his confrontation with Vance, but he hadn't dared show even a shadow of fear. "Next time you can pop him real good. You can bust his balls."

"Alllll*right!* Wreckage, man!" Zarra thrust his left fist up in a power salute, the symbol of the Rattlesnakes.

"Wreckage." Rick returned the salute halfheartedly. He saw Chico Magellas and Petey Gomez approaching, jaunty and strutting as if they walked on a street of gold instead of cracked concrete, on their way to the corner to catch the school bus. "Later," he told Zarra, and he went back up the steps into the brown house.

Inside, drawn shades cut the sunlight. The gray wallpaper was faded beige where the sun had burned it, and on the walls hung framed paintings of Jesus against black velvet backgrounds. The house smelled of onions, tortillas, and beans. Floorboards creaked as if in pain under Rick's footsteps. He walked through a short hallway to a door near the kitchen and tapped lightly on it. There was no answer. He waited a few seconds and tapped again, much louder.

"I'm awake, Ricardo," the feeble voice of an old woman replied in Spanish.

Rick had been holding his breath. Now he let it go. One morning, he knew, he was going to come to this door and knock, and there would be no answer. But not this morning. He opened the door and looked into the small bedroom, where the shades were drawn and an electric fan stirred the heavy air. In this room there was an odor like violets on the edge of decay.

Under the sheet on the bed lay the thin figure of an elderly woman, her white hair spread like a lace fan on the pillow, her brown face a mass of deep cracks and wrinkles.

"I'm leaving for school, Paloma." Rick's voice was gentle and articulate now, very much different from the street inflections of a moment before. "Can I get you anything?"

"No, *gracias.*" The old woman slowly sat up and tried to adjust her pillow with a skinny hand, but Rick was quickly there to help. "Are you working today?" she asked.

"*Sí.* I'll be home about six." He worked three afternoons a week at the Inferno Hardware Store, and would have worked longer hours if Mr. Luttrell let him. But jobs were hard to come by, and his grandmother needed to be watched over. Someone from the volunteer committee at the church brought her a boxed lunch every day, Mrs. Ramirez from next door came over to check on her from time to time and Father LaPrado often stopped by, but Rick didn't like leaving her alone so much. At school, he was tormented by the fear that she might fall and break her hip or back, and lie suffering in this awful house until he came home. But they had to have the money from his stockboy job, and that was all there was to it.

"What was that noise I heard?" she asked. "A horn blowing. It woke me up."

"Nothing. Just somebody passing by."

"I heard shouting. There's too much noise on this street. Too much trouble. Someday we'll live on a quiet street, won't we?"

"We will," he replied, and he stroked his grandmother's thin white hair with the same hand that had delivered a power salute.

She reached up, grasping his hand. "You be a good boy today, Ricardo. You do good at school, *sí?*"

"I'll try." He looked into her face. The cataracts on her eyes were pale gray, and she could hardly see at all. She was seventy-one years old, had fought off the effects of two minor strokes, and still had most of her own teeth. Her hair had turned white at an early age, and that was where her name—*Paloma,* the dove—came from. Her real name was peasant Mexican, almost unpronounceable even to his tongue. "I want you to be careful today," he said. "Do you want the shades up?"

She shook her head. "Too bright. But I'll be fine when I have my operation. Then I'll see everything—better than *you,* even!"

"You already see everything better than me." He bent over and kissed her forehead. Again he caught that odor of decaying violets.

Her fingers found one of the leather bracelets. "These things again? Why do you wear these things?"

"No reason. It's just the style." He pulled his hand away.

"The style. *Sí.*" Paloma smiled faintly. "And who sets that style, Ricardo? Probably somebody you don't know and wouldn't like anyway." She tapped her skull. "You use this. You live your own style, not somebody else's."

"It's hard to do."

"I know. But that's how you become your own man, instead of an echo." Paloma turned her head toward the window. The harsh edges of light that crept around the shade made her head ache. "Your mother . . . now she's the stylish one," Paloma said softly.

Rick was caught off guard. It had been a long time since Paloma had mentioned his mother. He waited, but she said nothing else. "It's almost eight. I'd better go."

"Yes. You'd better go on. You don't want to be late, Mr. Senior."

"I'll be home at six," he told her, and then he went to the door; but before he left the room he glanced quickly back at the frail form on the bed and he said, as he did every morning before he went to school, "I love you."

And she answered, as she always did, "Double love back to you."

Rick closed the bedroom door behind him. As he walked through the hallway again, he realized that his grandmother's wish of double love had been enough for him when he was a child; but beyond this house, out in the world where the sun beat down like a sledgehammer and mercy was a coward's word, a wish of double love from a dying old woman would not protect him.

Every step he took brought a subtle change to his face. His eyes lost their softness, took on a hard, cold glare. His mouth tightened, became a grim and bitter line. He stopped before he reached the door and plucked a white fedora with a snakeskin band from its wall hook. He put the hat on before a discolored mirror, tilting it to the proper angle of cool. Then he slid his hand into his jeans pocket and felt the silver switchblade there. Its handle was of green jade and had an embedded cameo of Jesus Christ, and Rick recalled the day he'd snatched that blade—the Fang of Jesus—out of a box where a rattler lay coiled.

He had the mean, ass-kicking look in his eyes now, and he was ready to go.

Once he stepped through that door, the Rick Jurado who cared for his Paloma would be left behind, and the Rick Jurado who was president of the Rattlesnakes would emerge. She had never seen that face, and sometimes he was thankful for the cataracts—but that was how it had to be, if he wanted to survive against Lockett and the Renegades. He dared not let the mask fall, but sometimes he forgot which was the mask and which was the man.

He drew in a deep breath and left the house. Zarra was waiting by the car and flipped him a freshly rolled joint. Rick caught it, tucking it away for later. Being wrecked—or at least pretending to be—was the only way to get through the day.

Rick slid behind the wheel. Zarra got into the passenger side, and the Camaro's engine thundered as Rick turned the key. He put on a pair of black-framed sunglasses and, his transformation complete, he drove away.

6

Black Sphere

It was after nine when a brown pickup truck pulled up alongside Jessie Hammond's wrecked vehicle. Jessie got out, and so did the driver. Bess Lucas was a wiry, gray-haired woman of fifty-eight, with bright blue eyes in a heart-shaped, attractive face. She was wearing jeans, a pale green blouse, and a straw cowboy hat, and she winced as she looked into the mangled engine.

"Lord!" she said. "Nothin' left but scrap in there, for sure!" The engine had cooled down and was silent now. A pool of oil shimmered beneath the truck. "What the hell tore it up this way?"

"I don't know. Like I said, a piece of whatever passed by hit the hood. Like these over here." Jessie walked toward the blue-green fragments, which had ceased smoking. Still, a melting-plastic reek hung in the air.

Bess and Tyler had heard the noise too, and the furniture in their house had danced for a few seconds. When they'd gone outside, they'd seen a lot of dust in the air but no sign of helicopters or anything like what Jessie had described. Bess shook her head and clucked at the engine. The hole in it was the size of a child's fist. She followed Jessie away from the pickup. "Say this thing just shot by, with no warnin'? Where'd it go?"

"That way." Jessie pointed to the southwest. Their view was obstructed by the ridge, but Jessie noted the new contrails of jets in the sky. She reached the fragment that was embedded in the sand and covered with the strange markings. Heat was still radiating off it, enough for Jessie to feel it in her cheeks.

"What's that writin' on there?" Bess asked. "Greek?"

"I don't think so." She knelt down, getting as close as she dared. Where the object had dug into the earth, the sand had been burned into clumps of glass, and blackened cactus lay scattered about.

"Ain't that a sight?" Bess had seen the glass clumps too. "Must've been mighty hot, huh?"

Jessie nodded and stood up.

"Hell of a thing when you're mindin' your own business and you get wrecked right in broad daylight." Bess gazed around at the desolate land. "Maybe it's gettin' too crowded out here, huh?"

Jessie hardly heard her. She was staring at the blue-green fragment. It certainly was not part of a meteor or from any aircraft she'd ever seen, either. Possibly it was part of a satellite? But the markings surely weren't English, nor Russian. What other countries had satellites in orbit? She recalled that space junk had fallen over northern Canada some years ago, and more recently in Australia's outback; she remembered how people had joked about being hit by falling fragments after NASA had announced that a malfunctioned satellite was on the way down, and taken to wearing hardhats to deflect several tons of metal.

But if this material before her was metal, it was the weirdest kind of metal she'd ever seen.

"Here they come," Bess said. Jessie looked up, saw the two figures on horseback approaching. Tyler was letting Sweetpea go at an easy canter, and Stevie was hanging on behind.

Jessie walked back to the truck, leaned over, and peered into the hole that had plowed down through the engine block. Whatever had pierced the engine couldn't be seen in that oily mess of ripped metal and cables. Had it gone all the way through, or was it still lodged in there somewhere? She could see Tom's face when she told him that a falling spacecraft had crossed their path and smashed hell out of—

She stopped. *Spacecraft*. A word she'd been dancing around in her mind. *Spacecraft*. Well, a satellite was a spacecraft, wasn't it? But she couldn't fool herself; she knew what she'd meant. A spacecraft, like from outer space. Far, far outer space.

Christ! she thought, and almost laughed. I've got to get my hat before my brain boils! But her gaze skittered back to the blue-green thing stuck in the sand, and at the other pieces lying nearby. Stop it! she told herself. Just because you don't recognize any of it doesn't mean it's from outer space, for God's sake! You've been watching too many sci-fi flicks off that satellite dish late at night!

Tyler and Stevie, astride the big golden palomino, had almost reached them. A large-boned man in his early sixties, with a leathery, seamed face and a mane of white hair tucked up under a battered Confederate army cap, Tyler got off Sweetpea and then effortlessly lifted Stevie down. He came over to the truck to have a look, and his first reaction was a short, sharp whistle. "You can scratch off an engine," he said. "'Fraid even Mendoza can't patch up that hole." They'd telephoned Xavier Mendoza at his Texaco station before they'd left the house, and he'd promised to be out within a half hour to tow the pickup truck in.

"Pieces of somethin' lyin' all over the place," Bess told him. She motioned around. "Ever see the like?"

"Nope, never have." Tyler was retired from a job with Texas Power, and wrote fairly successful western novels about a bounty hunter named Bart Justice. Bess was content to spend her time compiling sketches of desert flowers and plants, and both of them treated Sweetpea like an overgrown puppy.

"Neither have I," Jessie admitted. She saw Stevie coming closer. The little girl's eyes were wide and entranced again, but Jessie had checked her over thoroughly at the house and found no injuries. "Stevie?" she said softly.

The little girl was pulled by the wind-chimes noise. It was

a lovely, soothing music, and she had to find out where it was coming from. She started to walk past her mother, but Jessie grasped her shoulder before she reached the truck. "Don't get in that oil," Jessie said tensely. "It'll ruin your clothes."

Tyler had on dungarees and didn't mind getting dirty. He was curious about what had put a hole that size through the pickup's hood and engine, and he reached into the mess and started feeling around. "Watch out you don't cut your hand, Ty!" Bess warned, but he grunted and kept on with what he was doing. "You got a flashlight, doc?" he asked.

"Yes. Just a minute." There was a pencil flashlight in her vet bag. "Stay out of Mr. Lucas's way," she told Stevie, who nodded vacantly. Jessie retrieved the bag from the truck's interior, found the little flashlight, and gave it to Tyler. He flicked it on, aiming the light into the hole. "Lordy, what a mess!" he said. "Whatever it was, it went right through the engine block. Knocked the valves all to pieces."

"Can you see what it might've been?"

He moved the light around. "Nope. Must've been hard as a cannonball and movin' like a bat out of hell, though." He glanced up at Stevie. "Oops. Forgive my French, honey." He returned his attention to the beam of light. "Well, I'd say it got pulverized in there somewhere. Doc, you sure are lucky it didn't go through the firewall or hit the gas tank."

"I know."

He straightened up and flicked the light off. "Guess you've got insurance, huh? With the Dodger?"

"Right." Dodge Creech had an Texas Pride Auto and Life Insurance office on the second floor of the bank building in Inferno. "I don't know exactly how to describe the accident to him, though. I'm not sure anything like this is covered in my collision insurance."

"Ol' Dodger'll find a way. He can talk the tears out of a stone."

"It's still in there, Mama," Stevie said softly. "I can hear it singing."

Tyler and Bess looked at her, then at each other. "I think Stevie's a little shaken up," Jessie explained. "It's all right, hon. We're going to be on our way home as soon as Mr. Mendoza—"

"It's still in there," the child repeated. This time her voice was firm. "Can't you hear it?"

"No," Jessie replied. "And neither do you. I want you to stop playacting, *now.*"

Stevie didn't answer; she just kept staring at the truck, trying to figure out exactly where the music was coming from. "Stevie?" Bess said. "Come on over here and let's give Sweetpea his sugar, okay?" She dug into her pocket and brought out a few sugar cubes, and the palomino strode toward her in anticipation of a treat. "Sweets for the sweet," Bess said, giving the horse a couple of cubes. "Come on, Stevie! You give him one, okay?"

Normally, Stevie would have jumped at the chance to feed Sweetpea his sugar—but she shook her head, unwilling to be pulled away from the wind-chimes music. She took a step nearer the truck before Jessie could stop her.

"Looky here," Tyler said. He bent down beside the flat right front tire. There was a blister in the metal of the wheel well's fender. He clicked the light on again and shone it up into the wheel well. "Somethin's lodged in here. Looks like it's burned to the metal."

"What is it?" Jessie asked. Then: "Stevie! Don't get too close!"

"Not very big. Haven't got a hammer on you, do you?" When Jessie shook her head, Tyler gave the blister a knock with his fist, but the object wouldn't come loose. He reached up into the wheel well, and Bess said, "Be careful, Ty!"

"Thing's slick with oil. Stuck tight, I'm tellin' you." He grasped it and gave a yank, but his hand slipped off. He wiped his palm on his dungarees and tried again.

"That oil'll *never* come out!" Bess fretted, but she came closer to watch.

Tyler's shoulder muscles strained with the effort. He kept working. "It moved. I think," he said. "Hold on, I'm gonna give it my best." His fingers tightened around it, and he yanked again with as much strength as he could muster.

The object resisted him for a few seconds longer—and

then it popped out from its indentation in the fender and he had it firmly in his hand. It was perfectly round, and he drew it out like a pearl that had been nestled inside an oyster's shell.

"Here it is." He stood up, his hand and arm black with grime. "Doc, I believe this is what did the damage."

It was, indeed, a cannonball. Except it was the size of Stevie's fist, black as ebony and looked to be smooth and unmarked.

"Must've hit the tire, too," Tyler said. He frowned. "I swear, that's the damnedest thing!" This time he didn't bother to apologize for his French. "It's the right size to have made that hole, but . . ."

"But what?" Jessie asked.

He bounced it up and down in his palm. "There's hardly any weight to it. Thing feels about as tough as a soap bubble." He began wiping away the oil and dirt from its surface on his dungarees, but underneath the black was just more black. "Want to see it?" He offered it to Jessie.

She hesitated. It was only a small black ball, but Jessie suddenly wanted no part of it. She wanted to tell Tyler to put it back where it had been, or just to throw it as far as he could and let it be forgotten.

"Take it, Mama," Stevie said. She was smiling. "That's what's singing."

Jessie had a sensation of slow dizziness, as if she were about to pass out. The sun was getting to her, pounding through her skull. But she extended her hand, and Tyler put the ebony ball into it.

The sphere was as cool as if it had just come from a refrigerator. Her fingers were shocked by its chill. But the truly amazing thing was its weight—about three ounces, she figured. She ran a finger across the smooth surface. Was it glass or plastic? "No way!" she said. "This can't be what hit the truck! It's too fragile!"

"You got me," Tyler agreed. "But it was sure tough enough to knock a blister in the metal and not crack to pieces."

Jessie tried to squeeze the thing, but it wouldn't give. Harder than it appears, she thought. A whole hell of a lot harder. Looks like a perfect sphere, tooled by a machine that left no marks. And why is it so cool? It went through a hot engine and now it's exposed to the direct sun, but it's still cool.

"Thing looks like a big ol' buzzard's egg," Bess remarked. "I wouldn't give you two cents for it."

Jessie glanced at Stevie; the child was staring fixedly at the sphere, and Jessie had to ask the question: "Do you still hear it singing?"

She nodded, took a step forward and lifted both hands. "Can I hold it, Mama?"

Tyler and Bess were watching. Jessie paused, turning the ball over and over. There was no mark on it anywhere, no crack, not even a scuff. She held it up to the sun to try to see into it, but the thing was utterly opaque. It must've had a hell of a velocity when it hit us, Jessie thought—but what was it made of? And what *was* it?

"*Please,* Mama!" Stevie hopped up and down impatiently.

It didn't seem particularly threatening. It was still strangely cool, yes, but her hand felt all right. "Don't drop it," Jessie cautioned. "Be very, very careful. Okay?"

"Yes ma'am."

Reluctantly, Jessie gave it to her. Stevie cradled it in both hands. She now *felt* the wind-chimes music as well as heard it; the notes seemed to sigh through her bones—a beautiful sound, but kind of sad too. Like a song of lost things. It made her feel like she knew what her daddy was feeling, like her heart was a tear, and all things she knew and loved were soon to be gone, left a long, long way behind; so far behind you couldn't even see them if you stood on top of the highest mountain in the world. The sadness sank deep, but the beauty of the notes entranced her. Her expression was caught between crying and wonder.

Jessie saw. "What is it?"

Stevie shook her head. She didn't want to talk, wanted

only to listen. The notes soared through her bones and made colors spark in her brain. They were colors unlike any she'd ever seen before.

And suddenly the music stopped. Just like that.

"Here comes Mendoza." Tyler motioned toward the bright blue wrecker approaching along Cobre Road.

Stevie shook the sphere. The music did not return.

"Give it to me, hon. I'll take care of it." Jessie reached out, but Stevie retreated. "Stevie! Come on, now!" The little girl turned and ran about thirty feet away, still with the ebony sphere in her hands. Jessie pressed down her anger and decided to deal with the child when they got home. Right now, they had enough to worry about.

Xavier Mendoza, a husky white-haired man with a large white mustache, pulled the wrecker off Cobre Road and got it situated to hook Jessie's pickup. He stepped out to have a look at the damage, and his first reaction was *"Ai! Caramba!"*

Stevie walked a little further away, still shaking the black ball, trying to wake up the music. It occurred to her that it must be broken, and maybe if she shook it hard enough, the wind chimes inside might work again. The next time she shook it, she thought she heard it slosh faintly, as if it might be filled with water. And it didn't seem as cool as it had been a minute before. Maybe it was getting warmer, or maybe that was just the sun.

She rotated it between her palms. "Wake up, wake up!" she wished.

With a jolt, she realized the black ball had changed. She could see her fingerprints on it, and the prints of her palms, outlined in electric blue. She pressed her index finger on a black place; the fingerprint held, then slowly began to vanish as if drawn down into the depths. She drew a little smiling face on it with her fingernail; it too stayed there in a startling blue a hundred times more blue than the sky. She drew a heart, then a little house with four stick figures; all the pictures held for about five or six seconds before they melted away. She looked up and started to call for her mother to come see.

But before the words could come out there was a roaring behind her that almost scared her out of her skin, and she was engulfed in whirling dust.

A gray-green helicopter circled over the wrecker and Jessie's truck. Jessie knew it must have come speeding out of nowhere—maybe from beyond that ridge to the southwest—and now it made slow, steady turns above them. Sweetpea neighed and reared, and Bess grabbed his reins to settle him down. The dust spun around them, making Mendoza curse a blue streak in Spanish.

The helicopter made a few more rotations and then turned again toward the southwest; it picked up speed and zoomed away.

"Damned fool!" Tyler Lucas shouted. "I'll kick your butt!"

Jessie saw her daughter standing in the road. Stevie walked toward her and showed her the sphere. "It went all black again," Stevie said, her face coated with dust. "Know what?" The little girl's voice was low, as if confiding a secret. "I think it was about to wake up—but I think it got scared."

What would the world be without a child's imagination? Jessie thought. She was about to demand the sphere back, but she didn't see any harm in letting Stevie hold it; they'd hand it over to Sheriff Vance as soon as they got to town, anyway. "Don't drop it!" she repeated, and then turned away to watch Mendoza at work.

"Yes ma'am." Stevie walked off a few paces and kept shaking the black ball, but neither the wind-chimes music nor its brilliant blue returned. "Don't be dead!" she told it; there was no response. It was just black through and through; she could see her own face reflected on its glossy surface.

Deep down, in the center of the blackness, something might have shifted—a cautious, slow stirring; an ancient thing, contemplating the shine of light that touched it through the murk. Then it was still again, pondering and gathering strength.

Mendoza got the truck hooked to the wrecker. Jessie

thanked Tyler and Bess for their help, and she and Stevie climbed into the wrecker with Mendoza. They drove away toward Inferno, the black sphere still clutched firmly between Stevie's hands.

To the southwest and almost out of sight, a single helicopter followed.

7
Nasty in Action

The bell shrilled for change of classes, and in another moment the quiet halls of Preston High were tumultuous. The central air conditioning was still broken, the bathrooms reeked of cigarette and marijuana smoke, but the rowdy shouts and laughter underscored a joyful abandon.

Much of the laughter, though, had a false ring. All the students knew this was Preston High's final year; even if Inferno was a hot and hellish place, it was still home, and home was a hard place to leave.

They were walking histories of the struggles that had preceded them, their features a mirror of the tribes and races that had come up from Mexico and down from the heartland to carve a home in the Texas desert: here the sleek black hair and sharp cheekbones of the Navajo; the high forehead and ebony glare of the Apache; the aquiline nose and sculpted profile of the conquistador; there the blond, brown, or red hair of frontiersmen and pioneers, the wiry builds of bronco busters, and the long, confident strides of easterners who'd come to Texas seeking their fortunes long before the first shot had fired at a mission called the Alamo.

It was all there in the faces and bones, in the walks and expressions and speech of the students changing classes. A hundred years of showdowns, cattle drives, and saloon brawls moved through the hallways. But their ancestors, even the buckskinned Indian fighters and the warpainted braves who'd sliced off their scalps, might have moaned in their graves if they'd been able to see current fashions from the Happy Hunting Ground. Some of the boys had their heads shaved to a military stubble, some had hair twisted into spikes and tinted with outrageous colors, some wore crewcuts with long tails of hair hanging down their backs. Many of the girls had hair cropped just as severely as the boys' and dyed even more garishly, some wore sleek Princess Di cuts, and some sported manes swept back and frozen with gel, then decorated with feathers in an unconscious tribute to their Indian heritage.

They wore a mixed assemblage of jumpsuits, overalls in military camouflage patterns, madras-plaid shirts with buckskin fringe, T-shirts that exalted bands like the Hooters, the Beastie Boys, and the Dead Kennedys, paisley surfer tees in electric hues that slam-danced the eyeballs, tie-dyed khaki trousers, faded and patched jeans, pegged pants with Day-Glo stripes, combat boots, hand-painted sneakers, penny loafers, gladiator sandals, and plain old flipflops carved out of used tires. There'd been a dress code at the beginning of the year, but the principal of Preston High—a short Hispanic man named Julius Rivera and known as Little Caesar by the student body—had gradually let the code go when it was apparent there would be no reprieve for the school. Students in Presidio County would be bussed thirty miles to the high school in Marfa, and in September Little Caesar would be teaching a sophomore geometry class at Northbrook High in Houston.

The seconds ticked past on the clocks, and the young descendants of gunfighters, ranch hands, and Indian chiefs continued to their next classes.

Ray Hammond was digging his English text from his locker in B Section. His mind was on getting to his next class, way at the end of C Section, and he didn't see what was coming up behind him.

As he brought the book out, a size-ten foot in a scuffed

combat boot suddenly kicked it from his hand. The book opened—notes, page markers, and obscene doodlings sailing into the air—and slammed against the wall, barely missing two girls at the water fountain.

Ray looked up, his eyes wide and startled behind his glasses. He saw then that doom had finally come for him. A hand clenched the front of his shirt and lifted him up on the toes of his sneakers.

"Hey, fuckmeat," a slurred, thickly accented voice growled, "you're in my way, man." The boy who'd spoken was about sixty pounds heavier than his captive and stood more than four inches taller; he was a junior named Paco LeGrande, and he had bad teeth and acne pocks on a grinning, vulpine face. A tattooed rattlesnake crawled across one thick forearm. Paco's eyes were red and unfocused, and Ray knew the boy had been puffing a little too much weed in the bathroom this morning. He usually timed his visits to the locker so as to miss Paco, who had the one right next door, but the inevitable had caught up with him. Paco was fueled and high and ready to give somebody a nitro lesson.

"Hey, X Ray!" Another Hispanic boy was standing behind Paco. His name was Ruben Hermosa, and he was shorter and not nearly as heavy as Paco but his eyes were also aflame. "Hey, don't shit in your pants, *amigo!*"

Ray heard his paisley shirt ripping. He was barely balanced on his toes, and his heart was pounding in his skinny chest but he kept his expression spaceman cool. Other kids were moving back, getting out of danger's way, and there wasn't a Renegade in sight. Paco balled up a tremendous, scarred fist.

"You don't want to break the rules, Paco," Ray said, as calmly as he could manage. "No trouble in school, man."

"Fuck the rules! And fuck school! And fuck you, you little four-eyed piece of—"

A home economics book with a smiling cartoon family on its blue cover whacked into the side of Paco's head with a noise like a gunshot. The blow rocked him, and Ray wrenched free as Paco's grip weakened. He scrabbled across the green linoleum to the base of the water fountain.

"A wetback prick with no balls shouldn't talk about fuckin'," a girl's smoky voice said. "It'll give you ideas you can't do anything about."

Ray knew that voice. Nasty stepped between him and the two Rattlers. She was a senior, and she stood almost six feet tall; her platinum-blond hair was swept back in a Mohawk, the sides shaven to the scalp. Nancy Slattery wore skintight khakis that clung to her rear and her long, strong legs; a hot-pink cotton shirt accentuated the flare of her athletic shoulders. She was lithe and quick, had run track last year for Preston High, and on both wrists she wore a handcuff for a bracelet. Three or four cheap gold chains sparkled around each ankle, above the size-seven bowling shoes she'd swiped from the Bowl-a-Rama in Fort Stockton. Nasty had gotten her name from her initiation into the Renegades, Ray had heard; she'd drunk down what was in a cup the guys had spat their tobacco chews into. And smiled through brown teeth.

"Get up, X Ray," Nasty told him. "These fags won't bother you."

"You watch your mouth, bitch!" Paco roared. "I'll knock the piss outta you!"

Ray stood up, started gathering his notes together. He saw with a jolt of horror that his idle drawing of a huge penis attacking an equally huge vagina had slid under the right sandal of a blond junior fox named Melanie Paulin.

"I'll piss in a glass for you, Paco Fago," Nasty replied, and a few of the onlookers laughed. She just missed being pretty: her chin was a shade too sharp, her two front teeth were chipped, and her nose had been broken when she fell during a track meet. Her dark green eyes glowered under peroxided brows. But Ray thought Nasty, who sat a few seats away from him in study hall, was a smash fox.

"Come on, man!" Ruben urged. "We gotta get to class! Forget it!"

"Yeah, Paco Fago. Better run 'fore you get spanked." She

saw the flare of red in Paco's eyes and knew she'd pushed too far, but she didn't give a shit; she thrived on the smell of danger like other girls desired Giorgio. "Come on," she said, beckoning with one finger. Her nails were polished black. "Come and get it, Paco Fago."

Paco's face darkened like a storm cloud. He started toward her, both fists clenched. Ruben yelled, "Don't, man!" but it was much too late.

"Fight! Fight!" somebody shouted, and Ray scooped up the incriminating drawing as Melanie Paulin backed away. He gave Nasty room; he'd seen what she had done to a Mexican girl in a wild fight after school, and he had no doubt about what she was going to do now.

Nasty waited. Paco was almost upon her. Nasty smiled slightly.

Paco took one more step.

One of Nasty's bowling shoes came up in a vicious kick with all of her hundred and sixteen pounds behind it. The shoe connected squarely with Paco's crotch, and afterward no one remembered which was louder: the sound of the shoe smacking home or Paco's garbled scream. Paco bent double, clutching at himself; in no hurry, Nasty grabbed his hair, crunched her knee up into his nose, and then slammed his face into the nearest locker door. Blood splattered, and Paco's knees buckled like wet cardboard.

She helped him to the floor by kicking his feet out from under him. He lay stretched out, his nose a purple lump. It was all done in about five seconds. Ruben was already backing away from Nasty, his hands upraised in supplication.

"What's going on here?"

The onlookers scattered like chickens before a Mack truck. Mrs. Geppardo, a white-haired history teacher with cocked eyeballs, advanced on Nasty. "My God!" She drew up short when she saw the carnage. Paco was stirring now, trying dazedly to sit up. "Who did this? I want an answer right this minute!"

Nasty looked around; her sharp gaze struck everyone with deaf-dumb-and-blind disease, a common ailment at Preston High.

"Did you see this, young man?" Mrs. Geppardo demanded of Ray, who instantly took off his glasses and began cleaning them on his shirt. "Mr. Hermosa!" she called shrilly, but he took off at a run. Nasty knew that by the end of fourth period every Rattler in school would have heard about this, and they wouldn't like it. Tough shit, she thought, and waited for Mrs. Geppardo's cock eyes to find her.

"Miss *Slattery.*" She spoke the name as if it were something catching. "I think you're at the bottom of this, young lady! I can read you like a book!"

"Really?" Nasty asked, all innocence. "Then read this." She turned and bent over to show Mrs. Geppardo that her tight trousers had split along the rear seam—and Nasty, as Ray and everyone else saw, wore no underwear.

He almost fainted. A roar of hellacious laughter and whooping filled the hallway. Ray fumbled with his glasses and almost dropped them. When he got them on, he could see the small butterfly tattoo on her right cheek.

"Oh . . . Lord!" Mrs. Geppardo's face reddened like a chili pepper about to pop its pods. "You straighten up this instant!"

Nasty obeyed, swiveling gracefully around like a fashion model. The entire hallway was now in chaos, as more students flooded out of the classrooms and teachers valiantly tried to stem the tide. Standing with his English book under his arm and his glasses on crooked, Ray wondered if Nasty would marry him for one night.

"You're going to the office right this minute!" Mrs. Geppardo grabbed for Nasty's arm but the girl dodged her.

"No, I'm not," Nasty said firmly. "I'm goin' home and change pants, that's what I'm gonna do." She stepped over Paco LeGrande with one long stride and walked purposefully to the doors of B Section, her cheeks hanging out and a chorus of howls and laughter following her.

"I'll suspend you! I'll put you on report!" Mrs. Geppardo shook a vengeful finger.

But Nasty stopped at the door and fixed the woman with a stare that would've knocked a buzzard dead. "No, you won't. It's too much trouble. Anyhow, all I've done is split my britches." She gave Ray a quick wink that made him feel like he'd just been knighted by Guinevere, though her language was anything but courtly. "Don't get shit on your shoes, boy," she told him, and went out the doors and into the light that glowed like molten gold in her Mohawk.

"You'll wind up in women's prison!" Mrs. Geppardo sputtered—but the door was swinging shut, and Nasty was gone. She whirled on the gawkers: *"Get back to your rooms!"* The windows almost rattled in their frames. A half second later, the tardy bell rang and there was a new stampede.

Ray felt drunk with lust. The image of Nasty's exposed rear might remain in his mind until he was ninety years old and rears didn't matter anymore. His rod was straining; it was something he had no control over, as if that part of himself held all the brains and the rest was just useless appendage. Sometimes he thought he'd been zapped by an alien Sex Beam or something, because he just couldn't get it off his mind—though he was likely to be a virgin forever, judging how most girls reacted to him. Lord, it was a rough life!

"What are you standing there for?" Mrs. Geppardo's face thrust into his. "Are you asleep?"

He didn't know which eye to look into. "No, ma'am."

"Then get to wherever you're going! *Now!*"

He closed his locker, snapped the lock, and hurried off along the hall. But before he turned the corner he heard Mrs. Geppardo say, "What's wrong with you, you hoodlum? Can't you walk?"

Ray looked back. Paco was on his feet, his face gray; he was still clutching his groin, and he staggered toward the history teacher.

"We're going to see the nurse, young man." She took his arm. "I've never seen such a sight in all my—"

Paco suddenly lurched forward, and belched forth his breakfast onto the front of Mrs. Geppardo's flower-print dress.

Ray ran, instinctively ducking his head as another scream shook the windows.

8
Danny's Question

Danny Chaffin, a somber-faced young man of twenty-two whose father, Vic, owned the Ice House, had just finished telling Sheriff Vance that his calls had turned up nothing about helicopters when they both heard the metallic chattering of rotors.

They ran out of the office and were caught in the teeth of a dust storm. "Christ A'mighty!" Vance shouted—because he'd seen the dark shape of the helicopter descending right in Preston Park. Red Hinton, passing by in his pickup truck on Celeste Street, almost swerved into the front window of Ida Younger's House of Beauty. Mavis Lockridge emerged from the Boots 'n Plenty shoestore, shielding her face with a scarf. People peered out the windows of the bank building, and Vance knew the elderly loungers who sat around in front of the Ice House catching breezes were probably running for their lives.

He strode toward the park, Danny right behind him. The fierce wind and the whirling dust died down after a few more seconds, but the helicopter's rotors continued to slowly turn. Now more people were coming out of the stores, and Vance figured the unholy racket was going to draw everybody in town. Dogs were barking fit to bust. As the dust settled, Vance could see the gray-green paint job on the helicopter and also pick out some lettering: WEBB AFB.

"I thought you called Webb!" Vance snapped at Danny.

"I did! They said they weren't flyin' any 'copters over this way!"

"Well, they lied through their teeth! Hold on, here comes somebody!" He saw two figures approaching, both of them tall and lean. Vance and Danny met them just shy of the mule's statue.

One of them, a young man who looked like he spent all his time indoors, wore a dark blue air-force uniform and a cap with an officer's insignia. The second man, older, with a black crewcut going gray at the temples, was tanned and fit looking, and he was dressed in well-worn jeans and a beige knit shirt. A pilot remained at the helicopter's controls. Vance said to the officer, "What can I do for—"

"We need to talk," the man in blue jeans spoke up. He spoke crisply, accustomed to taking control. He wore aviator-style sunglasses, and behind them his eyes had already noted Vance's badge. "You're the sheriff here, right?"

"That's right. Sheriff Ed Vance." He held out his hand. "Pleased to meet—"

"Sheriff, where can we speak in private?" the young officer asked. The other man did not meet Vance's grip, and Vance blinked with confusion and then let his hand drop.

"Uh . . . my office. This way." He led them across the park, sweat already surfacing on the back of his shirt and ringing his armpits.

When they were inside the office, the younger air-force man took a notebook from his trouser pocket and flipped it open. "The mayor here is Johnny Brett?"

"Yeah." Vance saw other names written in the notebook too—among them his own. He realized somebody had done a lot of homework on Inferno. "He's the fire chief too."

"He needs to be present. Will you call him, please?"

"Do it," Vance said to Danny, and settled himself in his chair behind his desk. These men were giving him the creeps; their backs were as straight as iron rods, and they looked to be holding themselves at attention just standing there. "Brett's office is in the bank buildin'," Vance offered. "He's probably already seen all the commotion." There was no reaction from either of them. "Mind lettin' me know what this is all about, gents?"

The older man walked to the door that led to the cell block and peered through its glass inset; there were only three cells, all empty. "We need your help with something, Sheriff." His accent was less Texan than midwestern. He removed his sunglasses, showing deep-set eyes that were a cool, clear pale gray. "Sorry to make such a dramatic entrance." He smiled, and his face and body relaxed. "Sometimes we air-force folks kind of play it to the hilt and beyond."

"Sure, I understand." He didn't, really. "No harm done."

"Mayor Brett's on his way over," Danny reported, hanging up the phone.

"Sheriff, about how many people live here?" the younger officer asked; he had taken off his cap, revealing close-cropped light brown hair. His eyes were about the same color, and he had a spill of freckles across his nose and cheeks. Vance figured he was no older than twenty-five, while the other man was maybe in his early forties.

"Close to two thousand, I reckon," he answered. "About another five or six hundred in Bordertown. That's across the river."

"Yes sir. No newspaper here?"

"Used to have one. It shut up shop a couple of years ago." He angled around in his chair to watch the older man approach the glass-fronted gun cabinet, which held two shotguns, a pair of Winchester repeating rifles, a hogleg Colt .45 in a calfskin gunbelt, and a Snubnose .38 in a shoulder holster along with boxes of the appropriate ammunition.

"You've got quite an arsenal here," the man said. "Do you ever have to use all this firepower?"

"Never can tell when you'll have need of it. One of the shotguns'll pump out tear-gas shells." His voice swelled with fatherly pride, since he'd fought the town council tooth and nail for the funds to buy it. "Livin' with Mexicans so close, you got to be ready for anythin'."

"I see," the man said.

Johnny Brett came in, puffing from his sprint. He was a barrel-chested man of forty-nine who had once been a shift foreman on the rock crushers at the copper mine, and he carried with him a sense of harried weariness. He had eyes like those of an often-kicked hound dog, and he was fully aware of Mack Cade's power in the community; he was on Cade's payroll, just as Vance was. He nodded nervously at the two air-force men and, clearly out of his depth, waited for them to speak.

"I'm Colonel Matt Rhodes," the older man told him, "and this is my aide, Captain David Gunniston. I apologize for dropping in as we did, but this can't wait." He looked at his watch. "About three hours ago, a seven-ton meteor entered earth's atmosphere and struck approximately fifteen miles south-southwest of your town. We tracked it down on radar and we thought most of it would burn up. It didn't." He glanced at both the sheriff and mayor in turn. "So we've got a visitor from deep space lying not too far from here, and that means we have a security problem."

"A meteor!" Vance grinned excitedly. "You're joshin'!"

Colonel Rhodes fixed him with a steady, level gaze. "I never josh," he said coolly. "Here's the kicker: our friend's putting out some heat. It's radioactive, and—"

"Lord!" Brett gasped.

"—and the radiation will probably move across this area," Rhodes continued. "Which is not to say that it poses an immediate threat to anybody, but it'd be best for people to stay indoors as much as possible."

"Day as hot as this is, most folks'll stay indoors for sure," Vance said, and frowned. "Uh . . . will this stuff cause cancer?"

"I don't think the radiation levels will be critically high in this area. Our weather forecaster says the winds will take most of it to the south, over the Chinati Mountains. But we've got to ask your help in something else, gentlemen.

The air force has to get our visitor out of this area and to a secured location. I'll be in charge of the transfer." His gaze ticked to a clock on the wall. "At fourteen hundred hours —that's two o'clock—I'm expecting two tractor-trailer trucks. One of them will be hauling a crane, and the other will be marked 'Allied Van Lines.' They'll have to pass through your town in order to reach the impact position. Once there, my crew will start the process of breaking up the meteor to get it loaded and moved out. If all goes as planned, we'll be gone by twenty-four hundred hours."

"Twelve midnight," Danny said; he'd wanted to join the army before his father had talked him out of it, and he knew military time.

"Right. So what I have to ask of you gentlemen is to help with the security arrangements," Rhodes went on. "Webb's gotten all sorts of calls from people who saw the meteor pass over Lubbock, Odessa, and Fort Stockton—but of course it was too high for them to tell what it was, and they're reporting seeing a UFO." He smiled again, and pulled nervous smiles from the deputy, sheriff, and mayor. "Par for the course, isn't it?"

"Sure is!" Vance agreed. "Betcha them flying-saucer nuts are comin' out of the woodwork!"

"Yes." The colonel's smile slipped just a fraction, but none of them noticed. "They are. Anyway, we don't want civilians interfering with the work, and we sure as hell don't need the press prowling around. The air force doesn't want to be responsible for any news hound getting a dose of radiation. Sheriff, can you and the mayor keep a tight lid on this situation for us?"

"Yes sir!" Vance said heartily. "Just tell us what we need to do!"

"Firstly, I want you to discourage any sightseers. Of course, we'll have our own security perimeter set up on-site, but I don't want anyone coming out there to gawk. Secondly, I want you to emphasize the radiation danger; not that it's necessarily true, but it wouldn't hurt to scare people a little bit. Keeps them from getting underfoot, right?"

"Right," Vance agreed.

"Thirdly, I don't want any media people anywhere near that site." The colonel's eyes were chilly again. "We'll be patrolling with our 'copters, but if you get any calls from the media I want you to handle them. Webb's not giving out any information. I want you to play dumb too. As I say, we don't need civilians in the area. Clear?"

"Clear as glass."

"Good. Then I think that does it. Gunny, do you have any questions?"

"Just one, sir." Gunniston turned another page in his notebook. "Sheriff Vance, who owns a light green pickup truck marked 'Inferno Animal Hospital'? The license is Texas six-two—"

"Dr. Jessie," Vance told him. "Jessica Hammond, I mean. She's the vet." Gunniston produced a pen and wrote the name down. "Why?"

"We saw the truck being towed in the area of the meteor's impact," Colonel Rhodes said. "It was taken to the Texaco station a couple of streets over. Dr. Hammond probably saw the object go past, and we wanted to check on her."

"She's real nice. Smart lady too. I'm tellin' you, she's not afraid to do anything a man vet wouldn't—"

"Thanks." Gunniston returned the pen and notebook to his pocket. "We'll take it from here."

"Sure thing. You fellas need some more help, you just ask."

Rhodes and Gunniston were moving toward the door, their business done. "We will," Rhodes said. "Again, sorry about all the commotion."

"Don't worry about it. Hell, you gave everybody somethin' to jaw about at the dinner table!"

"Not much jawing, I hope."

"Oh. Right. Don't you worry about a thing. You can count on Ed Vance, yes sir!"

"I know we can. Thank you, Sheriff." Rhodes shook Vance's hand, and for an instant the sheriff thought his knuckles were going to explode. Then Rhodes released him and Vance was left with a sickly smile on his face as the two air-force officers left the building and strode out into the hot white light.

"Wow." Vance massaged his aching fingers. "Fella don't look as strong as he is."

"Man, wait'll I tell Doris about this!" Mayor Brett's voice was shaking and thrilled. "I met a real colonel! Lordy, she won't believe a word of it!"

Danny walked to a window and peered out through the blind; he watched the two men moving away, heading toward Republica Road. He frowned thoughtfully and picked at a hangnail. "Object," he said.

"Huh? You say somethin', Danny boy?"

"Object." Danny turned toward Vance and Brett. He had sorted out what bothered him. "That colonel said Dr. Hammond probably saw the 'object' go past. How come he didn't say 'meteor'?"

Vance paused. His face was blank, his thought processes unhurried. "Same thing, ain't it?" he finally asked.

"Yes sir. I guess. I just wonder why he put it that way."

"Well, you ain't paid to wonder, Danny boy. We've got our orders from the United States Air Force, and we'll do just what Colonel Rhodes says do."

Danny nodded and returned to his desk.

"Met a real air-force colonel!" Mayor Brett said. "Lordy, I'd better get back to my office in case people call and want to know what all the ruckus is. Think that'd be a good idea?" Vance agreed that it would be, and Johnny Brett hurried out the door and just about ran to the bank building, where the electric sign spelled out 87°F. at ten-nineteen.

9

Tic-Tac-Toe

Jessie had seen the helicopter come down in Preston Park as Xavier Mendoza pulled the wrecker into his Texaco station and cut the engine. While Mendoza and his daytime helper, a lean and sullen young Apache named Sonny Crowfield, labored to unhook the pickup and get it into a garage stall, Stevie walked away a few paces with the ebony sphere between her hands; she had no interest in the helicopter, or what its presence might mean.

A Buick that had once been bright red, now faded to a pinkish cast by the sun, slid off Republica Road and pulled up to the garage stalls. "Howdy, doc!" the man at the wheel called; he got out, and Jessie's eyes were bombarded by Dodge Creech's green-and-orange plaid sport jacket. He strode jauntily toward her, his fat round face split by a grin that was all blinding-white caps. One glance at the pickup stopped him in his tracks. "Gag a maggot! That ain't a wreck, it's a *carcass!*"

"It's pretty bad, all right."

Creech looked into the mangled engine and gave a low, trilling whistle. "Rest in peace," he said. "Or pieces, I might say." His laugh was a strangled cackle, like a chicken struggling to squeeze out a square egg. He recovered quickly when he saw that Jessie did not share his humor. "Sorry. I know this truck put in a lot of miles for you. Lucky nobody got hurt—uh—you and Stevie *are* okay, right?"

"I'm fine." Jessie glanced over at her daughter; Stevie had found a slice of shadow at the building's far corner, and looked to be intently examining the black ball. "Stevie's . . . been shaken up, but she's okay. No injuries, I mean."

"Glad to hear that, surely am." Creech dug a lemon-yellow paisley handkerchief from the breast pocket of his jacket and mopped the moisture off his face. His slacks were almost the same shade of yellow, and he wore two-tone yellow-on-white shoes. He owned a closetful of polyester suits in a garish rainbow of colors, and though he read *Esquire* and *GQ* avidly, his fashion sense remained as raucous as a Saturday night rodeo. His wife, Ginger, had sworn she would divorce him if he wore his iridescent red suit to church again. He believed in the power of a man's image, he often told her—and anyone who would listen; if you were scared to make people notice you, he said, you might as well sink on down and let the ground swallow you whole. He was a big, fleshy man in his early forties who always offered a quick smile and a handshake, and he'd sold some form of insurance to almost all the residents of Inferno. In his broad, ruddy-cheeked face his eyes were as blue as a baby's blanket, and he was bald except for a fringe of red hair and a little red tuft atop his forehead that he kept meticulously combed.

He touched the gaping hole in the pickup's engine. "Looks like a cannon hit you, doc. Want to tell me what happened?"

Jessie began; she registered Stevie standing nearby, then focused all her attention on telling Dodge Creech the story.

Stevie, comfortable in the cool shadow, was watching the black ball do magic. Her fingerprints had begun to appear in vivid blue again; it was a color that reminded her of pictures of the ocean, or of that swimming pool at the motel in Dallas where they'd spent last summer vacation. She drew a cactus with her fingernail, watched as the blue picture slowly melted away. She drew scrawls and swirls and circles, and all the patterns drifted down into the ball's dark center.

This is even better than fingerpaints! she thought. You didn't have to clean anything up, and there wasn't any way to spill the paints—except there was only one color, but that was okay, because it sure was pretty.

Stevie had an idea; she drew a little grid across the black ball and began to fill it with *X*s and *O*s. Tic-tac-toe, she knew the game was called. Her daddy was very good at it, and had been teaching her. She filled in all the *X*s and *O*s herself, finding that the *O*s linked up across the bottom row; the grid melted away, and Stevie drew another one. *X*s won this time, in a diagonal line. Time for a third grid, as this one melted away as well. Again, *X*s won. She remembered that her daddy said the middle space was the most important, so she started an *O* there and, indeed, the *O*s won.

"What'cha got there, kid?"

Stevie looked up, startled. Sonny Crowfield was staring at her; his black hair hung to his shoulders, and his eyes were black under thick black brows. "What is it?" he asked, wiping his greasy hands on a rag. "A toy?"

She nodded and said nothing.

He grunted. "Looks like a piece of shit to me." He sneered, and then Mendoza called him and he returned to the garage.

"You're a piece of shit," she said to Crowfield's back —but not too loudly, because she knew *shit* was not a nice word. And then she looked back at the black ball, and she caught her breath with a gasp.

Another blue-lined grid had been drawn in it. The grid was full of *X*s and *O*s, and *X* had won the game across the top row.

It slowly faded away, back into the depths.

She had not drawn that grid. And she did not draw the one that began to appear, the lines precise and as thin as if sketched with a razor, on the surface of the black ball.

Stevie felt her fingers loosen. She almost dropped the ball, but she remembered her mother saying not to. The tic-tac-toe grid was complete in another couple of seconds, and the *X*s and *O*s began to appear. She started to call for her mama, but Jessie was still talking to Dodge Creech; Stevie watched the grid's spaces being filled—and then, on an impulse, she put an *X* in one of them as soon as the ball's inner finger had finished an *O*.

There was no further response. The grid slowly vanished.

A few seconds ticked past; the ball remained solidly black.

I broke it, Stevie thought sadly. It's not going to play anymore!

But something moved down in the depths of the sphere—a brief burst of blue that quickly faded. The razor-sharp lines of another grid began to come up, and Stevie watched as an *O* appeared in the center space. Then there was a pause; Stevie's heart jumped, because she realized whatever was inside the black ball was inviting her to play. She chose a space on the bottom row and drew an *X*. An *O* appeared in the upper left, and there was another pause for Stevie to decide on her move.

The game ended quickly, with a diagonal of *O*s from upper left to lower right.

Another grid appeared as soon as the last vanished, and again an *O* was drawn in the center space. Stevie frowned; whatever it was, it already knew the game too well. But she bravely made her move and lost even faster than before.

"Stevie? Show Mr. Creech what hit us."

She jumped. Her mother and Dodge Creech were standing nearby, but neither of them had seen what she was doing. She thought Mr. Creech's coat looked like somebody had sewn it while they had their finger stuck in an electric socket. "Can I take a gander, hon?" he asked, smiling, and held out his hand.

Stevie hesitated. The ball was cool and utterly black again, all the traces of the grids gone. She didn't want to give it up to that big, stranger's hand. But her mother was watching, expecting her to obey, and she knew she'd already disobeyed far too much today. She gave him the black ball—and as soon as her fingers left it and Mr. Creech had it in his hand, she heard the sigh of the wind chimes singing to her again.

"This did the damage?" Creech blinked slowly, weighing the object in his palm. "Doc, you sure about that?"

"As sure as I can be. I know it's light, but it's the right size; like I said, it was lodged up in the wheel well after it went through the engine."

"I just can't see how somethin' like this could've busted through metal. Feels like glass, kinda. Or wet plastic." He ran his fingers over the smooth surface; Stevie noted that they left no blue fingerprints. The wind-chimes music was insistent, yearning, and Stevie thought, It needs me. "So this is what blew out of the thing that went by, huh?" Dodge Creech held it up to the sun, could see nothing inside it. "Never seen the like of this before. Any idea what it *is?"*

"None," Jessie said. "I expect whoever came down in that helicopter might know. Three of them were following it."

"I don't rightly know what to put in my report," Creech admitted. "I mean, you're covered for collision and injuries and all, but I don't think Texas Pride'll understand that a plastic baby bowlin' ball tore a hole smack dab through a pickup's engine. What're you plannin' on doin' with it?"

"Turning it over to Vance, just as soon as we can get over there."

"Well, I'll be glad to take you. I don't think your pickup's goin' anywhere."

"Mama?" Stevie asked. "What'll the sheriff do with it?"

"I don't know. Maybe send it somewhere to try to figure out what it is. Maybe try to break it open."

The wind-chimes music pulled at her. She thought that the black ball was begging her to take it again; of course she couldn't understand why Mr. Creech or her mother didn't hear the wind chimes too, or what exactly was making the music, but she heard it as the call of a playmate. Try to break it open, she thought, and flinched inside. Oh, no. Oh, no, that wouldn't be right. Because whatever was in the black ball would be hurt if it was cracked open, like a turtle would be hurt if its shell was broken. Oh, no! She looked up imploringly at her mother. "Do we *have* to give it away? Can't we just take it home and keep it?"

"Hon, I'm afraid we can't." Jessie touched the child's cheek. "I'm sorry, but we've got to give it to the sheriff. Okay?"

Stevie didn't answer. Mr. Creech was holding the black ball down at his side in a loose grip. "Well," Mr. Creech said, "why don't we head on over and see Vance right now?" He started to turn away to walk to his car.

The music pained her and gave her courage. She'd never done anything like what streaked through her mind to do; such a thing was a sure invitation to a spanking, but she knew she would have only one chance. Later she could explain why she'd done it, and later always seemed a long way off.

Mr. Creech took one step toward his car. And then Stevie darted forward, past her mother, and plucked the black ball from Dodge Creech's hand; the wind-chimes music stopped as her fingers curled around the ball, and Stevie knew she'd done the right thing.

"Stevie!" Jessie cried out, shocked. "Give that back to—"

But the little girl was running, clutching the black ball close. She ran around the corner of Mendoza's gas station, from shadow into sunlight, narrowly missed ramming into the trash dumpster, and kept going between two cacti as tall as Mr. Creech.

"Stevie!" Jessie came around the corner, saw the little girl running across somebody's backyard, heading toward Brazos Street. "Come back here this *minute!*" Jessie called, but Stevie didn't stop and she knew the child wasn't going to. Stevie ran along a wire-mesh fence, turned a corner, and had reached Brazos; she disappeared from sight. *"Stevie!"* Jessie tried again, but it was no use.

"I do believe she wants to keep that thing, don't you?" Creech asked, standing behind Jessie.

"I don't know what's gotten into her! I swear, she's been acting crazy ever since we got hit! Dodge, I'm sorry about this. I don't—"

"Forget about it." He grunted and shook his head. "Little lady can fly when she wants to, can't she?"

"She's probably heading home. Dammit!" She was almost too stunned to speak. "Will you give me a ride to the house?"

"Sure thing. Come on."

They hurried back around the corner to Creech's Buick —and two men, one in the uniform of an air-force officer, were standing beside it. "Dr. Hammond?" the man with a black crewcut said, stepping forward. "We need to talk."

10
Blue Void

Still cradling the black ball, Stevie reached the house and paused to search beneath the bay window for the white rock that opened to reveal an extra house key tucked away inside. She was out of breath, still shaking from being chased by a dog as she ran along Brazos Street; the dog, a big Doberman, had snarled and leaped at her, but it had been chained to a pole in the yard and the chain had snapped it back. She hadn't even stopped to thumb her nose at it, because she knew her mother and Mr. Creech would be coming after her.

She found the white stone and the key and got into the house. The air conditioning chilled the perspiration on her skin, and she walked into the kitchen, pulled a chair over to stand on, got a Flintstones glass from the cupboard, and poured herself a glass of cold water from a pitcher in the refrigerator. The black ball was still cool, and she rubbed it over her cheeks and forehead.

She listened for the sound of Mr. Creech's car pulling up out front. It wasn't there yet, but it would be soon.

"They want to break you open," she said to her playmate inside the ball. "I don't think that would be very nice, do you?"

Of course it didn't answer. It might know how to play tic-tac-toe, but it had no voice except for the singing.

Stevie took the ball into her room. Should she try to hide it somewhere? she wondered. Surely her mother wouldn't make her give it up after she'd explained about the music, and how the black ball had a playmate deep inside it. She thought of places to hide it: under her bed, in the closet, in her chest of drawers, in her toychest. No, none of those seemed safe enough. Mr. Creech's car wasn't there yet; she still had time to find a good hiding place.

She was mulling it over when the telephone rang. It kept on ringing, and Stevie decided to answer it since, at the moment, she was the lady of the house. She picked it up. "'Lo?"

"Young lady, you're in for a spanking!" Jessie's voice was mock furious, but genuinely relieved. "You could've been killed, hit by a car or something!"

"I'm all right." Better not to say anything about the dog, she decided.

"I'd like to know just what you think you're doing! I'm getting pretty tired of the way you've been acting today!"

"I'm sorry," Stevie said in a small voice. "But I heard the singing again, and I had to get it away from Mr. Creech 'cause I don't want it to get broken."

"That's not for us to decide. Stevie, I'm surprised at you! You've never done anything like this before!"

Stevie's eyes burned with tears. Hearing her mama speak this way was worse than a spanking; her mama could not hear the singing and would not understand about the playmate. "I won't do it again, Mama," she promised.

"I'm very disappointed in you. I thought I'd taught you better manners. Now I want you to listen to me: I'm still at Mr. Mendoza's, but I'm going to be home soon. I want you to stay there. Do you hear me?"

"Yes ma'am."

"All right." Jessie paused; she was mad, but not mad enough to hang up and leave it like this. "You frightened me by running off like that. You could've gotten hurt. Do you understand why I'm upset?"

"Yes. 'Cause I was bad."

"Because you were wrong," Jessie corrected. "But we'll talk about it when I get home. I love you very much, Stevie, and that's why I got so angry. Do you see?"

She said, "Yes. And I love you too, Mama. I'm sorry."

"Okay. You just stay there, and I'll see you later. 'Bye."

"'Bye." They hung up at about the same time, and at the Texaco station Jessie turned to Colonel Rhodes and said, "Meteor my *ass.*"

Stevie's tears dried. She returned to her room with the black ball, which was showing blotches of blue on its surface. Now the idea of hiding it bothered her, but she didn't want it broken to pieces, either. She'd been bad—no, *wrong*—enough for one day; but what was she to do? She crossed her room and looked out her window at the sun-washed street, trying to figure out what was the right thing: to hide the black ball, in disobedience of her mother, or give it up and let it be broken open. Her mind reached a dead end beyond which she could not think, and in the next moment she decided to entertain her playmate as well as possible before Mr. Creech's car arrived.

She wandered over to her collection of glass figurines on a table. Within the black ball there was a line of blue, like an eyelid beginning to open. She said, "Ballerina," and pointed to the dancing glass figure, her favorite. Then: "Horse. This one is like Sweetpea, only Sweetpea's a real horse and this is made of glass. Sweetpea is a pal . . . a pal . . ." She still had trouble with some words. "A 'mino," she said, giving up the struggle. She pointed to the next: "Mouse. Do you know what a mouse is? It eats cheese and doesn't like cats."

At the center of the black sphere, there were little crack-lings of blue like fireworks going off.

Stevie picked her Raggedy Ann doll off the bed. "This is Annie Laredo. Say hello, Annie. Say we're glad you came to visit today. Annie's a rodeo girl," she told the black ball, and then, continuing around the room, came to her bulletin board. On it were construction-paper cutouts that her father had helped her put up. She pointed to the first. "A . . . B . . . C . . . D . . . E . . . F . . . G . . . that's the alphabet.

Know what the alphabet is?" Something struck her as very important. "You don't even know my name!" she said, and held the ball up before her face. She watched the stirrings of color at its center, like beautiful fish swimming inside an aquarium. "It's Stevie. I know how to spell it. S-T-E-V-I-E: Stevie. That's me."

Also on the bulletin board were pictures of animals and insects clipped from magazines. Stevie lifted the ball so her playmate could see, and touched each picture as she said the names: "Lion . . . that's from the jungle. Ost . . . ostr . . . that's a big bird. Dolphin"—she pronounced it *daufin*— "and those swim in the ocean. Eagle . . . that flies really high. Grasshopper . . . those jump a lot." She came to the final picture. "Scor . . . scorp . . . a stinger," she said, and touched it too, though it was her least favorite and her father had put it up as a reminder not to walk barefoot outside.

What resembled tiny bolts of lightning curled up from the sphere's center and danced across its inner surface; they connected briefly with Stevie's fingers, and a cold tingling shot through her hand all the way to her elbow before it subsided. The sensation startled her, but it wasn't painful; she watched the lightning bolts arc and pulse inside the ball, as its center of brilliant blue continued to grow.

More entranced than scared, Stevie held the ball between both hands. The lightning bolts curled out and touched her hands, and for a few seconds she thought she heard her hair crackle like Rice Krispies.

She thought that just maybe she should put it down now. There was a storm inside the black ball, and the storm was getting worse. It occurred to her that her playmate might not have liked something she showed it on her bulletin board.

She took two steps toward the bed, intending to gently put the ball down and wait for her mother to get home.

But she didn't make it another step.

The black ball suddenly burst into an incandescent, frightening blue. She started to open her fingers and drop it, but the movement was too late.

The tiny lightning bolts shot from its surface, intertwined through her fingers, continued up her arms and shoulders, wrapped like smoke around her throat, and leapt up her nostrils, into her widened eyeballs, cocooning her head and piercing through her skull. There was no pain, but in her ears was a low murmur like distant thunder, or a steady and powerful voice unlike anything she'd ever heard. Her hair jumped with sparks, her head rocking back and her mouth opening in a soft, stunned exhalation: *"Oh."*

She smelled an odor of burning. *My hair's on fire!* she thought wildly, and tried to put it out with her hands but they would no longer obey. She wanted to scream and tears were in her eyes, but the thunder voice in her head swelled up and crashed over her senses; she felt herself lifted up as if by waves, pulled down again into a blue swirling place where there was no bottom nor top. It was cool here, and quiet, far from the storm that raged somewhere else. The blue void closed around her, held her firmly, continued to draw her deeper. Only she was no longer in her skin; she seemed to be made of light, and weighed as much as a feather in the wind. It was not a fearsome thing, and she was amazed that she was not afraid—or, at least, not crying. She did not fight it, because fighting seemed a bad thing. It was a good thing to drift down in this blue place, and to rest. To rest, and to dream; because she was certain this was a place where dreams lived, and they would find her if she did not try to fight.

She slept, as the blue currents folded around her, and the first dreams came in the shape of Sweetpea, her mother and father already astride the golden horse and urging her to join them for a long day where there was no sadness, only pure blue sky and sunshine.

Stevie's body fell backward, hitting the floor on its right shoulder. The ball, blue and pulsing, jarred loose from the frozen hands and rolled under the bed, where it slowly turned to ebony again.

11
Transformation

"I don't know what kind of bullshit you're trying to throw," Jessie said, "but it was no meteor. You know that as well as I do."

Matt Rhodes smiled faintly and lit a cigarette. He was sitting across from Jessie in a back booth at the Brandin' Iron Cafe on Celeste Street, a small but tidy place with, appropriately, branding irons adorning the walls, red-checked tablecloths, and red vinyl seats. The specialty was the Big Beef Burger, the meat patty seared with the Brandin' Iron's private Double X brand; the remnants of a burger lay on the plate in front of Rhodes. "Okay, Dr. Hammond," he said when he'd gotten the cigarette going. "Tell me what it was, then."

She shrugged. "How am I supposed to know? I'm not in the air force."

"No, but you seemed to have seen the object clearly enough. Come on, give me your opinion."

Sue Mullinax, a big-hipped, big-boned blond woman who wore way too much makeup and had gentle, childlike brown eyes, came over with a coffeepot and poured another cup for both of them. Ten years ago, Sue had been head cheerleader at Preston High. As she walked away, she left the scent of Giorgio in her wake. "It was a machine," Jessie ventured when Sue was out of earshot. "A secret kind of airplane, maybe. Like one of those Stealth bombers——"

Rhodes laughed, cigarette smoke bursting from his nostrils. "Lady, you read too many spy novels! Anyway, everybody and his Aunt Nellie knows about the Stealth by now; it's sure as hell not a secret anymore."

"If not a Stealth, then something just as important," she went on, undaunted. "I saw a piece of it, covered with symbols. They could've been Japanese, I guess. Or maybe a combination of Japanese and Russian. I'm sure they weren't English. Want to tell me about that?"

The man's smile faded. He looked out the window, showing her a hawklike profile. Not far away, the helicopter still stood in the middle of Preston Park, drawing a crowd. Captain Gunniston sat at the counter, drinking a cup of coffee and warding off questions from Cecil Thorsby, the balloon-bellied cook and owner. "I think we're back to my original inquiry," the colonel said after another moment. "I'd like to know what damaged your pickup truck."

"And *I* want to know what fell." She'd decided not to tell him about the black ball until she got some answers; Stevie seemed to be safe with it, and there was no hurry to give it up.

He sighed, stared at her through slightly slitted, hard eyes. "Lady, I don't know who you think you are, but——"

"Doctor," Jessie said. "I'm a doctor. I wish you'd stop patronizing me."

Rhodes nodded. "Doctor it is." Change tactics, he thought. She wasn't as dumb as lumber, like the sheriff and mayor. "Okay. If I told you what it was, you'd have to sign a lot of top-security forms, probably even have to make the trip to Webb. The red tape's enough to make a strong man cry, but after it's wrapped around your neck, you're sworn not to reveal anything on penalty of a *very* long free room and board courtesy of Uncle Sam." He hesitated to let that image sink in. "Is that what you want, Dr. Hammond?"

"I want to hear the truth. Not bullshit. I want to hear it now, and then I'll tell you what I know."

He worked the knuckles of one hand and tried his best to

look unutterably grim. "We snared a Soviet helicopter a few months ago. The pilot flew it to Japan and defected. The chopper's bristling with weaponry, infrareds and sensors, and it's got a laser targeting system we've been wanting to get our hands on for a long time." He smoked his cigarette down a little further. No one else was in the cafe but Gunniston, Cecil, and Sue Mullinax, but the colonel kept his voice just above a whisper. "The technicians were running tests on the equipment at Holloman AFB in New Mexico—but there was trouble. Evidently one of the technicians who'd gotten through security was a deep-cover agent, and he grabbed the chopper and took off. Holloman asked us to help catch him, because he looked to be heading to the Gulf. Probably was going to be met by Soviet fighters from Cuba. Anyway, we shot him down. No other choice. The chopper was going to pieces just as he crossed your path; now we've got to pick them up and get out before the press comes hunting us." He stabbed his cigarette into an ashtray. "That's it. You might read the whole story in *Time* next week if we don't keep the lid on."

Jessie watched him carefully. He was intent on crushing all signs of life from his cigarette. She said, "I didn't see any rotors."

"Jesus!" Rhodes's voice was a little too loud, and both Cecil and Gunniston looked over at their booth. "I've told you what I know, la—*Dr.* Hammond. Take it or leave it, but remember this: you're withholding information from the United States government, and that can get you and your entire family in some real hot water."

"I don't care to be threatened."

"I don't care to play games! Now: did a piece of the machine hit your truck? What exactly happened?"

Jessie finished her coffee, taking her time about it. She'd seen no rotors; how could it have been a helicopter? Still, it had all been so fast. Maybe she didn't remember what she'd seen, or maybe the rotors had already been blown off. Rhodes was waiting for her to speak, and she knew she had to tell him: "Yes," she said. "The truck got hit. A piece of the thing went right through our engine; you saw the hole. It was a black sphere, about so big." She showed him with her hands. "It shot out of the thing and came straight at us. But the really weird part is that the sphere only seems to weigh a few ounces, and it's made out of either glass or plastic but there isn't a scratch on it. I don't know anything about Russian technology, but if they could create a floor wax that tough, we need to get our hands on—"

"Just a minute, please." Rhodes had leaned forward. "A black sphere. You actually picked it up? Wasn't it hot?"

"No. It was cool—which was strange, because the other pieces were still smoking."

"Did this sphere have symbols on it too?"

She shook her head. "No, it was unmarked."

"Okay." There was a quaver of excitement in his voice. "So you left the sphere near where your truck was?"

"No. We brought it with us."

Colonel Rhodes's eyes widened.

"My daughter's got it right now. Over at my house." She didn't like the amazed expression on his face, or the pulse that beat at his temple. "Why? What is it? Some kind of compu—"

"Gunny!" Rhodes got to his feet, and at once Gunniston was off the counter stool and standing as well. "Pay the man!" He took Jessie's elbow, but she pulled away. He took it again, his grip firm. "Dr. Hammond, will you escort us to your house, please? As quickly as possible?"

They left the Brandin' Iron, and outside Jessie wrenched angrily away. Rhodes did not try to grasp her arm again but he stayed right at her side, with Gunniston a few paces behind. They went around Preston Park, avoiding the gawkers who were pestering Jim Taggart, the 'copter pilot. Jessie's heart was pounding, and she quickened her pace to what was almost a run; the two men stayed with her. "What's inside the sphere?" she asked Rhodes, but he did not—or could not—answer. "It's not going to explode, is it?" Again, no reply.

At the house Jessie was glad to see that Stevie had remembered to relock the door—she was learning responsibility—but at the same time had to spend a few precious seconds fumbling with her keys. She got the right one into the lock and opened the door. Rhodes and Gunniston followed her inside, and the captain closed the door firmly behind them.

"Stevie!" Jessie called. "Where are you?"

Stevie didn't answer.

White light streamed between the window blinds and gridded the walls. "Stevie!" Jessie strode into the kitchen. The cat-faced clock ticked, and the air conditioning hissed and labored. A chair had been left near the counter; a cupboard was open, an empty glass in the sink. Thirsty from all that running, she thought. But Stevie wouldn't have left the house again, would she? If she had . . . oh, was she going to be in for trouble! Jessie went through the den—nothing disturbed in there—and into the hallway that led to the bedrooms. Rhodes and Gunniston were right behind her. "Stevie!" Jessie called again, really getting jittery now. Where could she have gone?

She was almost to the door of Stevie's bedroom when two hands thrust out along the floor, the fingers grasping at the beige carpet.

Jessie abruptly stopped, and Rhodes bumped into her.

They were Stevie's hands, of course. Jessie watched the sinews move in them as the fingers dug at the carpet for traction, and then Stevie's head came into view— her auburn hair damp with sweat, her face puffy and moist, droplets of sweat sparkling on her cheeks. The hands pulled Stevie's body further into the hallway, muscles twitching in her bare arms. She continued, inch by inch, into the hall, and Jessie's hand flew to her mouth. Stevie's legs trailed behind her, the sneaker gone from the left foot, as if the child might be paralyzed from the waist down.

"Ste—" Jessie's voice cracked.

The child stopped crawling. Her head slowly, slowly lifted, and Jessie saw her eyes: lifeless, like the painted eyes of a doll.

Stevie trembled, drew one leg beneath her with what appeared to be painful effort, and began to try to stand.

"Back up," Jessie heard Rhodes say; he grasped her arm and pulled her back when she didn't move.

Stevie had the other leg under her. She wavered, a drop of sweat falling from her chin. Her face was emotionless, composed, remote. And her eyes: a doll's eyes, yes—but now Jessie could see a flicker in them like lightning: a fierceness, a mighty determination that she'd never seen before. She thought, crazily, That's not Stevie.

But the little girl's body was rising to its feet. The face remained remote, but when the body had finally reached its full height, what might have been a quick smile of accomplishment darted across the mouth.

One foot moved forward, as if balancing on a tightwire. The second, sneakerless foot followed—and suddenly Stevie trembled again and the body fell forward. Jessie didn't have time to catch her daughter; Stevie toppled to the carpet on her face, her hands writhing in midair as if they no longer knew quite what to do.

She lay face down, the breath hitching in her body.

"Is she . . . is she *retarded?*" Gunniston asked.

Jessie pulled free from Colonel Rhodes and bent down beside her daughter. The body was shaking, muscles twitching in the shoulders and back. Jessie touched her arm—and felt a shock travel through her hand that left the nerves jangling and raw; she instantly pulled her hand back, before the shock wave reached her shoulder. Stevie's skin was damp and unnaturally cool, much as the black sphere had been. The child's head lifted, the eyes staring into hers without recognition, and Jessie saw blood creeping from Stevie's nostrils where she'd banged against the floor.

It was too much for her, and she came close to fainting. The hallway elongated and twisted like a funhouse's corridor; but then somebody was helping Jessie to her feet. It was Rhodes, his breath smelling of a cigarette, and this time she didn't fight him. "Where's the sphere?" she heard him ask. She shook her head. "She's out of it, Colonel," Gunniston said. "Jesus, what's wrong with the kid?"

"Check her room out. Maybe the sphere's in there—but for God's sake, be careful!"

"Right." Gunniston stepped around Stevie's body and entered the bedroom.

Jessie's legs sagged. "Call an ambulance . . . call Dr. McNeil."

"We will. Take it easy, now. Come on." He helped her out of the hallway and into the den, where he guided her to a chair. She settled into it, sick and dizzy. "Listen to me, Dr. Hammond." Rhodes's voice was low and calm. "Did you bring anything else back from the site except the sphere?"

"No."

"Anything else about it that you haven't told me? Could you see anything inside it?"

"No. Nothing. Oh God . . . I've got to call my husband."

"Just sit still for a few minutes." He restrained her from getting up, which wasn't too hard since her muscles felt like wet spaghetti. "Who found the sphere, and how?"

"Tyler Lucas found it. He lives out there. Wait. Wait." There *was* something she hadn't told him, after all. "Stevie said . . . she said she heard it singing."

"Singing?"

"Yes. Only I couldn't hear anything. I thought . . . you know, the wreck had shaken her up." Jessie ran a hand over her forehead; she felt feverish, everything spinning out of control. She looked up into Rhodes's face and saw that his tan had paled. "What's going on? There wasn't a Russian helicopter, was there?" He hesitated a second too long, and Jessie said, "Tell me, dammit!"

"No," he answered promptly. "There wasn't."

She thought she was about to throw up, and she kept one hand pressed against her forehead as if in anticipation of another shock. "The sphere. What is it?"

"I don't know." He lifted a hand before she could protest. "I swear to God I don't. But . . ." His face tightened; he fought against telling her, but to hell with regulations; she had to know. "I think you brought back a fragment from a spacecraft. An extraterrestrial spacecraft. That's what came down this morning. That's what we were chasing."

She stared at him.

"It caught fire in the atmosphere," he went on. "Our

radars picked it up, and we figured its point of impact. Only it veered toward Inferno, as if . . . the pilot was trying to make it closer to town before he crashed. The craft started going to pieces. There's not much left, just a mangle of stuff that's too hot for anybody to get close to. Anyway, the sphere is part of it—and I want to find out exactly what it is, and why that didn't burn up too."

She couldn't speak. But this was the truth; she saw it in his face. "You didn't answer Gunny's question," Rhodes said. "Is your little girl mentally retarded? Does she have epilepsy? Any other condition?"

Condition, Jessie thought. What a diplomatic way of asking if Stevie was out of her mind. "No. She's never had any—" Jessie stopped, because Stevie was lurching out of the hallway on rubbery legs, her arms dangling at her sides. Her head swiveled slowly from right to left and back again, and she came into the room without speaking. Jessie stood up, ready to catch her if the child stumbled again, but Stevie's legs were working better now. Still, she walked strangely—putting one foot precisely in front of the other as if treading on a skyscraper's ledge. Jessie stood up, and Stevie stopped with one foot poised in the air.

"Where's the black ball, honey? What'd you do with it?"

Stevie stared at her, her head cocked slightly to one side. Then, with slow grace, the other foot touched the floor and she continued on, gliding more than walking; she approached a wall and stood before it, seemingly absorbed by the pattern of sunlight on the paint.

"Not in there, Colonel." Gunniston walked into the den. "I checked the closet, the chest of drawers, under the bed, the toybox—everything." He glanced uneasily at the little girl. "Uh . . . what do we do now, sir?"

Stevie turned, a motion as precise and sharp as a dancer's. Her gaze fixed on Gunniston and stayed there, then moved to Rhodes, finally latching on to Jessie. Jessie's heart fluttered; her daughter's expression revealed only a clinical curiosity, but neither emotion nor recognition. It was how a vet might look at an unfamiliar animal. Stevie began that strange gliding walk again, her knees still wobbly, and she went to a series of framed photographs on a shelf at the bookcase. She looked at each in turn: one of Jessie and Tom alone, one of the family taken on vacation in Galveston a couple of years ago, one of Ray and herself on horseback at the state fair, two more of Tom's and Jessie's parents. Her fingers twitched, but she didn't attempt to use her hands. She moved past the bookcase and the television set, halted again to gaze at a wall-mounted painting of the desert that Bess Lucas had done—a painting she'd seen a hundred times, Jessie thought—and then she continued a few steps more to the doorway between the den and kitchen. She stopped; her right arm lifted, as if battling gravity, and she used her elbow to feel the doorframe.

"I don't really know," Rhodes replied finally. He sounded as if all the breath had been punched out of him. "Honest to God, I don't."

"I do!" Jessie shouted. "My daughter needs a doctor!" She started toward the telephone. The Inferno Health Clinic was a small white stone building a couple of blocks away, and Dr. Earl Lee—Early—McNeil had been Inferno's resident physician for almost forty years. He was a crusty hell-raiser who smoked black cigars, drove a red dune buggy, and drank straight tequila at the Bob Wire Club, but he knew his business and he'd know how to help Stevie too. She picked up the receiver and started to dial.

A finger came down on the disconnect button.

"Let's wait just a minute, Dr. Hammond," Rhodes told her. "Okay? Let's talk about—"

"Get your hand off the phone. *Now,* damn you!"

"Colonel?" Gunniston said.

"Please." Rhodes grasped the receiver. "Let's don't bring anyone else into this yet, not until we know what we're dealing—"

"I said I'm calling Dr. McNeil!" Jessie was furious, close either to tears or to slapping him across the face.

"She's moving again, Colonel," Gunniston told him, and this time both Rhodes and Jessie broke off their argument.

Stevie was gliding to another wall, crisscrossed with sunlight. She stopped before it, stood, and stared. She lifted her right hand, turning it back and forth as if she'd never seen a hand before; the fingers wiggled. Then she touched her bloody nose with her thumb and regarded the blood for a few seconds. Looked at the wall again. Her hand moved forward, and her thumb drew a vertical line of blood on the beige wall. Her thumb went back for more blood, drew a second vertical line a few inches to the right of the first.

More blood. A horizontal line cut the two verticals.

"What the *hell* . . . ?" Rhodes breathed, stepping forward.

A second horizontal line formed a neat grid on the wall. Stevie's blood-smeared thumb went to the center space, and made a small, precise *O*.

Her head turned. She looked at Rhodes and glided back from the wall, one foot placed behind the other.

"Your pen," Rhodes said to Gunniston. "Give me your pen. Hurry!"

The captain gave it over. Rhodes clicked the point out and walked to the wall. He drew an *X* in the lower right space.

Stevie stuck her thumb up a nostril and drew a red *O* in the center left space.

Jessie watched the game of tic-tac-toe in tortured silence. Her gut was churning and a scream pounded against her gritted teeth. This creature with a bleeding nose wore Stevie's skin, but it was not Stevie. And if that were so, what had happened to her daughter? Where was Stevie's mind, her voice, her soul? Jessie's hands clenched into fists, and she thought for a terrible second that the scream was going to escape and when that happened it would be all over. She trembled, praying that the nightmare would snap like a bad heat spell and she would be in bed with Tom calling that breakfast was ready. Dear God, dear God, dear God . . .

Stevie—or the thing that masqueraded as Stevie—blocked the colonel's win. In the next move, Rhodes blocked Stevie's win.

Stevie stared at Rhodes for a moment, looked again at the grid, then back to Rhodes. The face rippled, unfamiliar muscles working. A smile moved across the mouth, but the lips were stiff and unresponsive. She laughed—a *whuff!* of air forced through the vocal cords. The smile broadened, pushing the lips aside to show Stevie's teeth. The face, beaming, became almost the face of a child again.

Rhodes cautiously returned the smile and nodded his head. Stevie's head nodded, with more deliberate effort. Still smiling, she turned away and glided into the hall with her slow wirewalker's gait.

Rhodes's palms were sweating. "Well," he said, his voice tense and raspy, "I believe we've got a situation here, don't you, Gunny?"

"I'd say so, sir." Gunniston's spit-and-polish veneer was cracking. His heart boomed and his knees shook, because he'd realized the same thing as Colonel Rhodes: the little girl was either totally freaked out, or she was no longer truly a little girl. And why or how something like that could be was far beyond his logical, four-square mind.

They heard a voice—an exhalation of breath that made a voice, a weirdly chirring sound like wind through reeds: "Ahhhhhh. Ahhhhhh. Ahhhhhh."

Jessie was the first one to Stevie's room. Stevie—not-Stevie—was standing before the bulletin board; her—its —right hand was extended, the finger pointing to the construction-paper alphabet letters. "Ahhhhhh. Ahhhhhh," the voice continued, trying to grasp a remembered sound. The face contorted with the effort of enunciation. Then: "Ahhhh*A*. A. A." Pointed to the next letter. "Beeeee. Ceeeee. Deeeee. Eeeeee. Effff. Geeeee." There was consternation over the next.

"H," Jessie said softly.

"Chah. Achah. H." The head turned, eyes questioning.

My God, Jessie thought. She grasped the doorframe to keep from falling. An alien with a Texas accent, wearing my little girl's skin and hair and clothes. She was about to choke on a scream. "Where's my daughter?" she said. Her eyes brimmed. "Give her back to me."

What appeared to be a little girl was waiting, pointing to the next letter.

"Give her back to me," Jessie repeated. She lunged forward before Rhodes could stop her. "Give her back!" she shouted, and then Jessie had the figure's cool arm and was spinning it around, looking into the face that used to be her daughter's. *"Give her back!"* Jessie lifted her hand and slapped the face hard across the cheek.

The Stevie-creature staggered back, its knees almost collapsing. It kept its backbone straight and rigid, but its head bobbed from side to side for a few seconds like one of those absurd kewpie dolls that nod in the rear windshields of cars. It blinked, perhaps registering pain, and Jessie watched, newly horrified, as the red blotch of her palm came up on Stevie's skin.

Because it was still her daughter's flesh, even though something else had crawled inside it. Still her daughter's face, hair, and body. The not-Stevie touched the red palmprint on her cheek and swiveled toward the alphabet letters again; she pointed insistently at the next.

"I," Colonel Rhodes offered.

"Iyah," the creature said. The finger moved.

"J." Rhodes glanced quickly at Gunniston as the letter was laboriously repeated. "I think it's figured out the sounds are the base of our language. Jesus, Gunny! What have we got here?"

The captain shook his head. "I wouldn't care to guess, sir."

Jessie stared at the back of Stevie's head. The hair was the same as it had always been, only wet with sweat. And in it were flecks of . . . what were they? Her fingers touched the hair, and picked out a small piece of something pink, like cotton candy. Insulation, she realized. What were pink bits of insulation doing in Stevie's hair? She let the piece drift to the floor, her mind clogged and beginning to skip tracks. Her face had gone gray with shock.

"Take her out, Gunny," Rhodes commanded, and Gunniston led Jessie from the bedroom before she passed out.

"K," Rhodes continued, responding to the moving finger.

"Kah. K," the creature managed to say.

Outside, the two trucks—one hauling a crane and the other marked ALLIED VAN LINES—turned off Republica Road and passed by Preston Park on Cobre Road, heading for the desert site where something that had once been a machine had burned to a blue-green ooze.

12

What Makes the Wheels Turn

The three o'clock bell rang. "Lockett and Jurado!" Tom Hammond called out. "You two stay in your seats. The rest of you can take off."

"Hey, man!" Rick Jurado already had his white fedora on and had started out of his desk at the back left corner of the sweltering classroom. "I didn't do anythin'!"

"I didn't say you did. Just stay seated."

Other kids were gathering their books and leaving. Cody Lockett suddenly stood up from his desk at the room's right rear corner. "Hell with this! I'm goin'!"

"Sit down, Lockett!" Tom rose from his own desk. "I just want to talk to the both of you, that's all."

"You can talk to my south end while I'm headed north," Cody answered, and the group of Renegades who sat protectively around him broke into laughter. "Class is over, and I'm gettin' out." He strode toward the door, with the others following.

Tom stepped into his path. The boy kept coming, as if he were going to try to slam right through. Tom stayed where he was, braced for the impact, and Cody stopped about three feet short of a collision. Right behind him was a hulking two-hundred-pound senior who always wore a beat-up football helmet painted in mottled camouflage colors; his name was Joe Taylor, but Tom had never heard any of the others call him any name but "Tank." And right now Tank was staring holes through him with deep-socketed black eyes in a craggy face only a mother could love—a demented mother, at that. Cody said, "You movin', or not?"

Tom hesitated. Rick Jurado had settled back into his seat, smiling thinly. Around him sat several Hispanic and Indian kids who belonged to the Rattlesnakes. The other seniors who weren't members of either "club" had already hurried out, and Tom was alone with the beasts. I've started this, he thought; I've got to finish it. He looked directly into Cody Lockett's haughty gray eyes and said, "Not."

Cody chewed on his lower lip. He couldn't read the teacher's face, but he knew he hadn't done anything wrong. Lately. "You can't flunk me. I've already passed the final."

"Just sit down and hear me out. Okay?"

"Hey, I'll hear you out, man!" Rick called. He hooked an empty desk toward him and propped both feet atop it, leaning back with his arms crossed. "Lockett don't understan' no English no how, Mr. Hammon'," he said, deliberately thickening his accent.

"Shut your face, spitball," Tank rumbled.

At once several Rattlesnakes were on their feet; a skinny, curly-haired boy sitting next to Rick leapt up. He wore a red bandanna around his forehead and five or six small cruci-fixes on chains around his neck. "Fuck you, fat boy!" he shouted in a thin, reedy voice.

"Your mother and sister." Tank showed him a middle finger.

The Hispanic boy almost flung himself over the rows of desks to get at Tank, who outweighed him by at least seventy pounds—but Rick's hand shot out and grasped his wrist. "Easy, easy," he said quietly, his smile still in place and his gaze aimed at Cody. "Hang back, *muchachos*. Pequin, you settle down, man."

Pequin, whose real name was Pedro Esquimelas, was

trembling with fury, but he allowed himself to be restrained. He sat down, muttering obscenities in gutter Spanish; the other Rattlers—among them Chris Torrez, Diego Montana, and Len Redfeather—remained standing and ready for trouble. Tom could hear disaster knocking at the door; if he didn't keep control of this, the classroom could erupt into a battlefield. But at least Pequin had quieted. Tom knew the boy had a fiery temper that got him into a fight almost every day; his nickname was appropriate, because a *pequin* was a small chile pepper that would make the devil reach for Pepto-Bismol.

"How about it?" Tom asked Cody.

The boy shrugged. In his locker was the tie rack he'd finally finished; he wanted to get that home and work a couple of hours for Mr. Mendoza, but otherwise he wasn't in a hurry. "If I stay, they stay." He nodded at his entourage —six tough 'Gades: Will Latham, Mike Frackner, Bobby Clay Clemmons, Davy Summers, and Tank.

"Okay. Just sit down."

Cody sauntered back to his desk. The others followed his lead. Tank leaned one massive shoulder against the cinderblock wall and cleaned his fingernails with an unbent gem clip.

"I'm gettin' old waitin', *amigo,*" Rick announced.

Tom walked to his desk and sat on its edge. On the blackboard behind him was the outline of a Robert E. Howard *Conan* story he'd asked them to read for a discussion of laws in a barbarian culture. Very few had done it. "Tomorrow's your last day of school," he began. "I wanted to—"

"Oh, *madre!*" Rick moaned and pulled the fedora down over his eyes. Pequin put his head on his desk and snored noisily. The 'Gades watched in stony silence.

Tom's shirt was wet, sticking to his back and shoulders. The fan was only blowing hot air around. Tank suddenly burped; it was like a howitzer going off, and brought laughter from the 'Gades and silence from the Rattlers. Tom tried again: "I wanted to tell you that—" but his voice snagged. None of them were even looking at him. They didn't give a shit, had already retreated behind masks of boredom. Dammit to hell! he thought. I might as well try to lasso the damned moon as get them to listen! But he was mad now—mad at their bored poses, mad at whoever was supposed to fix the screwed-up air conditioners, mad at himself for being so stupid. He felt the walls closing in on him, a rivulet of sweat running down his neck; a surge of anger grew and swelled, thrashed mightily—then broke its bounds and rushed through him.

His hand reacted to it first. He picked up the *Governments in Transition* textbook from his desk and threw it with all his strength across the room.

It whacked against the back wall like a gunshot. Pequin jumped and lifted his head. Rick Jurado slowly pushed the fedora up off his eyes. Tank stopped cleaning his nails, and Cody Lockett's gaze sharpened.

Tom's face had reddened. "So that gets your attention, huh? A loud noise and a little destruction? Does that make the wheels turn?"

"Yeah," Cody answered. "You should've thrown that fuckin' book against the wall the first day of class."

"Tough guys—and girl," Tom said, glancing at Maria Navarre, who sat with the Rattlers. "Real tough. Lockett, you and Jurado have got a lot in common—"

Rick snorted with derision.

"A lot in common," Tom continued. "Both of you have outdone each other acting tough and stupid so you can impress the losers sitting around you right now. I've seen your tests. I know the difference between bullshitting and holding back. Both of you could've done a whole hell of a lot better if you'd—"

"Man, you've got runnin' off at the mouth!" Cody interrupted.

"Maybe so." Rivers of sweat were flowing from Tom's armpits. He had to keep going. "I know both of you could've done a lot better. But you pretend you're dumb, or bored—or just fucked up." The use of that word cemented their attention. "I say you're both cowards."

There was a long silence. Lockett and Jurado's expressions were blank. "Well?" Tom prodded. "Come on! I can't believe two tough guys like you can't come up with some sharp—"

"Yeah, I've got somethin' to say." Cody stood up. "Class dismissed."

"Okay, go ahead! Get out! At least Jurado has the guts to stay and listen!"

Cody smiled coldly. "You're walkin' a mighty fine wire, mister," he said. "I'll sit and listen to your shit durin' school hours, but when that bell rings it's *my* time." He shook his head, and his skull earring threw a red glint of sunlight. "Man, who do you think you are? You think you know all the answers, and you can just spout 'em out? Mister, you don't know a jackdamn thing about me!"

"I know you listen in class, whether you want anybody to know it or not. I know you're a lot smarter than you let on—"

"Forget that! Just forget it! When you walk in my shoes, you can preach to me! Until then you can go straight to hell!" There was a murmur of assent from the other Renegades.

Someone applauded. Tom looked over at Rick Jurado, who was slowly clapping his hands. "Hey, Lockett!" he taunted. "You gonna be an actor, man? You oughta win an award or somethin'!"

"You don't like it?" Cody's tone was chilling, but his eyes burned. "You know what you can do about it, motherfuck."

Rick's clapping stopped. His body had tensed, his legs about to spring him from his desk. "Maybe I do, Lockett. Maybe I'll come burn your fuckin' house down like your people've been burnin' ours."

"Cut the threats," Tom said.

"Yeah, make me laugh!" Cody jeered, ignoring the teacher. "We didn't burn any houses. Hell, you burned 'em yourself so you could holler that *we* did it!"

"You come across that bridge at night, *hombre*," Rick said quietly, "and we'll give you a real hot fiesta." A savage grin hung on his lip. "Understand, shitkicker?"

"I'm shakin'!" In truth, no 'Gade—as far as Cody knew —had set fire to those houses in Bordertown.

"Okay, hold it!" Tom demanded. "Why don't you two forget that gang crap?"

They glared at him as if he were the most useless insect to ever crawl from a hole. "Man," Rick said, "you're way off base. About that and all this school shit too." He looked at Tom with bored eyes. "At least I hung in and finished. I know a lot who didn't."

"And what happened to them?"

"Some of 'em got rich, dealin' coke. Some of 'em got dead too." He shrugged. "Some of 'em went into other things."

"Like working for Mack Cade? That's not much of a future, and neither is prison."

"Neither is crawlin' every day to a job you hate and kissin' ass to keep it." Now Rick had had enough, and he stood up. "People in this town kissed old man Preston's ass for about fifty years. Where'd it get them?"

Tom started to reply, but the wheels of logic in his brain froze up. He had nothing to counter the question with.

"Don't have all the answers, do you?" Rick continued. "See, you live in a nice house, on a nice street. You don't have to listen to somebody tellin' you where you can and can't walk, like you were a dog on a short leash. You don't know what it's like to have to fight for everything you've got, or ever will have."

"That's not the point. I'm talking about your educa—"

"That is the fuckin' point!" Rick yelled, startling Tom into silence. He trembled, clenched his fists, and waited out the anger. "That is the point," he repeated tautly. "Not school. Not books written by dead men. Not kissin' ass every day until you learn to like the taste. The point is to fight until you get what you want."

"So tell me what you want."

"What I want." Rick smiled bitterly. "I want *respect.* I want to walk any street I please—even your street, Mr. Hammond. In the middle of the night, if I want to, without the sheriff slammin' me up against his car. I want a future without somebody ridin' my ass from dawn to sundown. I want to know that tomorrow's gonna be better than today. Can you give me those things?"

"I can't," Tom said. "You can give them to yourself. The first thing is not to give up your mind. You do that and you lose everything, no matter how tough you think you are."

"More words." Rick sneered. "They don't mean shit. Well, you read your dead men's books. Teach 'em if you want to. But don't pretend they really matter, man, because only *this* matters." He lifted his clenched fist, the knuckles scarred from other battles. He turned toward Cody Lockett. "You! Listen up! Your whore hurt one of my men today. Hurt him real bad. And I got a visit this mornin' from that other whore, the one with the badge. You got a deal with Vance? You payin' him to let you burn down our houses?"

"You're crazy as hell." Cody had about as much use for Sheriff Vance as a coyote had for a sidewinder.

"I owe you some pain, Lockett. For Paco LeGrande," Rick went on. "And I'm tellin' you that any of my people who cross that damned bridge better be left alone."

"They come over at night, they're askin' to be stomped. We'll be real glad to oblige."

"Man, you're not the fuckin' king around here!" Rick shouted, and before he could think about it he picked up the desk in front of him and flung it aside. At once all the Rattlers and Renegades were on their feet, separated only by the imaginary line that divided the classroom. "We'll go where we please!"

"Not across the bridge at night," Cody warned. "Not into 'Gade territory."

"Okay, settle down." Tom stepped between them. He felt like an utter fool for having thought this would do any good. "Fighting isn't going to—"

"Shut up!" Rick snapped. "You're out of this, man!" He kept staring at Cody. "You want a war? You keep pushin' it."

"Hey!" Oh, Christ! Tom thought. "I don't want to hear any of that—"

Tank started to lunge at Rick Jurado, but Cody grasped his arm. He figured the Rattlers were carrying blades, like all wetbacks did. Anyway, he didn't like the odds and this wasn't the time or place. "Big man," Cody said. "Big talk."

"I'll let my boot talk to your ass!" Rick threatened; he kept his tough mask on, but inside he didn't want a showdown just yet. He didn't like the odds and, anyway, he figured all the 'Gades were packing knives. His own blade was in his locker, and he didn't allow any of the other Rattlers to bring knives to school.

"Let's get it on right *now!*" Pequin whooped. Rick restrained the urge to bash him in the mouth. Pequin liked to start fights, but he rarely finished them.

"You call it, Jurado," Cody challenged, and almost winced when Tank started making a clucking chicken noise to goad the Rattlers.

"There's not going to be any fighting!" Tom shouted, but he knew they weren't listening. "You hear me? If I see any trouble in the parking lot, I'm going up to the office and call the sheriff! Got it?"

"Fuck the sheriff!" Bobby Clay Clemmons bellowed. "We'll whip his ass too!"

The moment stretched. Cody was ready for the Rattlers to make the first move, and he was measuring a blow to Jurado's solar plexus; but Rick stood rock-steady, awaiting the attack that he knew was coming.

A figure limped into the doorway. Abruptly halted. "Oh! Red says stop!"

Cody glanced over his shoulder, but he already knew who it was from the high, childlike voice. The man in the doorway wore a faded gray uniform, carried a mop, and pushed a combination bucket and wringer. He was in his early sixties, his moon-shaped face ravaged by deep lines and brown age spots, his white hair cropped so close to the scalp it looked like a fine layer of sand. At his left temple there was an unmistakable indentation in his head. The little name tag on his custodian's uniform said "Sarge."

"Sorry, Mr. Hammond. Didn't know anybody was still

here. Green says go!" He started to leave, favoring a right leg that folded up at the knee joint like an accordian.

"No! Wait!" Tom called. "We're just clearing out. Aren't we?" he asked Rick and Cody.

The only sound was Pequin cracking his knuckles.

Cody took the initiative. "You want a nitro lesson, you know where to find me. Anytime, anyplace. But you're gonna stay off 'Gade territory after dark." Before the other boy could reply, Cody turned his back and stalked to the door. Tank stood watchful guard while the Renegades followed, then he left as well.

Rick started to shout a profanity, but checked it. This wasn't the time; it would come, but not now.

Pequin hollered it for him: "Fuck you, assholes!"

"Hey!" Sarge Dennison scowled. "Mama'll wash out that dirty mouth!" He glared reproachfully at Pequin, then dipped the mop in his bucket and went to work.

"It's been a real rush, Mr. Hammond," Rick told him. "Maybe next time we can all come over to your house for milk and cookies."

Tom's heart was still racing, but he made the effort to at least appear composed. "Just remember what I said. You're too smart to throw your life a—"

Rick gathered saliva and spat on the linoleum. Sarge stopped mopping, his expression a deuce of righteous anger and bewilderment. "You just wait!" Sarge said. "Scooter'll chew your legs off!"

"I'm real scared." Everybody knew Sarge was crazy, but Rick liked him. And he kind of admired Mr. Hammond for what he'd just tried to do, but he sure as hell wasn't going to cut the teacher any slack. That just wasn't how things were done. "Let's haul," he told the other Rattlers, and they left the classroom chattering in Spanish, laughing and beating on lockers with an overspill of nervous energy. In the corridor, Rick whacked Pequin on the back of his head a little too roughly to be just jiving, but Pequin grinned anyway, showing a silver tooth at the front of his mouth.

Tom stood listening to their noise recede along the hall

like a wave washing toward a distant shore. He did not belong to their world, and he felt incredibly stupid. Worse than that: he felt old. Damn, what a fiasco! I almost stirred up a gang war! he thought.

"Settle down, boy. They're gone now," Sarge said as he mopped the floor.

"Pardon?"

"Just talkin' to Scooter." Sarge nodded toward an empty corner. "He gets jumpy around them guys."

Tom nodded. Sarge returned to work, his wrinkled face a study of concentration. As Tom understood, "Sarge" Dennison had been hurt as a young soldier in the last months of World War II, and the shock had left him with the mind of a child. He'd been on the custodial staff for over fifteen years, and he lived in a small adobe house at the end of Brazos Street, across from the Inferno Baptist Church. The ladies of the Sisterhood Club brought him home-cooked dinners and kept watch over him so he wouldn't wander the streets in his pajamas, but otherwise he was pretty self-sufficient. The matter of Scooter, though, was something quite different: Sarge would look at you as if you were deranged if you didn't agree that a dog—of uncertain breed—was curled up in an empty corner, perched in a chair, or sitting at his feet. Sure there's a Scooter! Sarge would say, pointing to the fact that Scooter was fast and shy and often didn't want to be seen but that food left in Scooter's dish on the front porch in the evening would be gone by first light. The ladies of the Sisterhood Club had long ago stopped trying to tell Sarge there was no Scooter, because he cried too easily.

"They're not so tough," Sarge said, swabbing up Jurado's spit. "Those guys, I mean. They're just actin' is all."

"Maybe so." That was no consolation, though. Tom was jangled to the core. It was three-fifteen, and Ray would be waiting at the car. He opened the top drawer of his desk and got his keys. For some reason he thought of the car keys that must be somewhere in the Perez house, and he wondered if Mr. Perez ever held them and weighed them against the life of his son. He felt the swift current of time passing, and he knew that at this moment vultures were circling over the Great Fried Empty. He closed his drawer. "See you tomorrow, Sarge."

"Green says go," Sarge said, and Tom walked out of the sun-streaked classroom.

13

Cody's House

As he swerved the motorcycle onto Brazos, Cody felt his gut clench: an instinctive reaction, like the tightening of muscles before a punch landed. His house wasn't very far, standing near the corner of Brazos and Sombra. His rear tire tossed dust from the gutter, and on her front porch the Cat Lady, a broom in her gnarled hands, shouted, "Slow down, you germ!"

He had to smile. The Cat Lady—the widow Mrs. Stellenberg, her real name was—always stood out there sweeping about this time of day, and she always shouted the same thing as Cody sped past. It was a game they played. The Cat Lady had no family but for her dozen or so felines; they multiplied so fast Cody couldn't keep count, but the things sneaked all over the neighborhood and wailed like babies at night.

His heart was beating harder. His house—weathered gray clapboard, the shutters closed at every window—was coming up on the right. Parked at the curb was his father's junker, an old dark brown Chevy with rusted bumpers and a bashed-in passenger door. A layer of dust lay on the car, and Cody immediately saw that it was in exactly the same position it had been in this morning, both the right side tires pinched on the curb. Which meant that his father had either

walked to work at the Inferno Bake Shoppe or that he just
hadn't gone at all. And if the old man had been alone in that
stifling house all day, there could be a fierce storm brewing
between the walls.

Cody drove the motorcycle up over the curb, past the
Fraziers' house, and onto his small front yard. The only
thing growing there was a clump of needle-tipped yucca,
and even that was going brown. He stopped the motorcycle
at the foot of the porch's concrete steps and cut the engine;
it died with a clatter that he knew was bound to alert the old
man.

He got off and unzipped his denim jacket. Held inside it
was his manual-arts project. It was no ordinary tie rack: it
was about sixteen inches long, cut from a piece of rosewood,
sanded and smoothed until its surface felt like cool velvet.
Squares of white plastic had been painstakingly streaked
with silver paint to resemble mother-of-pearl and inserted
into the wood to form a beautiful checkerboard pattern. The
edges had been shaped and scalloped; two more pieces of
inlaid rosewood were jointed in place to hold the wooden
dowel from which the ties would hang, and the entire piece
was carefully polished again. Mr. Odeale, the shop teacher,
had said it was a good-looking work but couldn't understand why Cody had been so slow with it. Cody detested
anyone watching over his shoulder; a C was all he could
hope for, but as long as he passed he didn't care.

He enjoyed working with his hands, though he'd pretended that manual arts was sheer drudgery. As president of
the 'Gades, he was expected by his people to show a healthy
disdain for most everything, especially if it had to do with
school. But his hands seemed to figure out things before his
head did; woodworking was a snap for him, and so was
fixing the cars at Mr. Mendoza's Texaco station. He'd been
meaning to put aside time to tune up his Honda, but he
figured it was kind of like the story of the shoemaker's kids
who went barefoot. Anyway, he'd get around to it one of
these afternoons.

He removed his goggles and slipped them into a pocket.
His hair was wild and tangled and full of dust. He didn't

want to climb those cracked concrete steps and go through that front door; but it was the house he lived in, and he knew he had to.

In and out, he thought as he took the first step. In and out.

The screen door's hinges shrieked like a scalded cat. Cody pushed on through the flimsy wooden door into the gloom. Captured heat almost sucked the breath from his lungs, and he left the inner door open so some of it could drift out. Already he smelled the sour reek of the old man's Kentucky Gent bourbon.

An electric fan whirred in the front room, moving heavy air around. On the table before the stained sofa was a scatter of playing cards, an ashtray overflowing with cigarette butts, and a dirty glass. The door to his father's bedroom was shut. He stopped to open two of the windows, then started for the door to his own room with the tie rack clutched under his arm.

But before he reached that door he heard the other one squeak open. His legs turned heavy. And then there came the voice, raspy as a warped saw blade and ominously slurred: "What're you doin' sneakin' around in here?"

Cody didn't reply. He kept going, and the voice shouted, "Stop and answer me, boy!"

His knees locked. He stopped, his head lowered and his gaze fixed on one of the blue roses in the threadbare rug.

The old man's footsteps creaked on the tired floor. Coming nearer. The smell of Kentucky Gent was stronger. That and body odor. And, of course, Aqua Velva; the old man slapped that stuff all over his face, neck, and underarms and called it washing. The footsteps halted.

"So what it is?" the old man asked. "You didn't want me to hear you?"

"I . . . thought you were sleepin'," Cody said. "I didn't want to wake you u—"

"Bullshit and double bullshit. Who told you to open those windows? I don't like that goddamned sun in here."

"It's hot. I thought—"

"You're too dumb to think." The footsteps moved again.

The shutters were slammed, cutting the light to a dusty gray haze. "I don't like the sun," the old man said. "It gives you skin cancer."

It had to be ninety degrees in the house. Sweat crawled under Cody's clothes. The footsteps came toward him once more, and Cody felt his skull earring being tugged. He looked up into his father's face.

"Why don't you get one of these in your other ear?" Curt Lockett asked. His eyes were muddy gray, sunken into nests of wrinkles in a square-jawed, bony face. "Then everybody would know you were a whole queer instead of just half a queer."

Cody pulled his head away, and his father let him go. "You been to school today?" Curt asked.

"Yes sir."

"You kick a wetback's ass today?"

"Almost did," Cody replied.

"Almost ain't doin'." Curt ran the back of his hand across his dry lips and walked to the sofa. The springs squalled when he flopped down. He had the same wiry build as his son, the same wide shoulders and lean hips. His hair was dark brown, shot through with gray and thinning on top, and he wore it combed back in a stiff Vitalis-frozen pompadour. Cody's curly blond hair came from his mother, who had died giving him birth in an Odessa hospital. Curt Lockett was only forty-two, but his need for Kentucky Gent and long nights at the Bob Wire Club had aged him by at least ten years. He had heavy bags of flesh beneath his eyes, and deep lines carved his face on either side of a narrow, chiseled nose. He was dressed in his favorite outfit: no shoes or socks, jeans with patched knees, and a flaming-red shirt with pictures of cowboys lassoing steers embroidered on the shoulders. The shirt was open, showing his thin, sallow chest. He took a pack of Winstons from his pocket and lit a cigarette with a match. Cody watched the flame waver as his father's fingers shook. "Wetbacks gonna take over this earth," Curt announced as he exhaled a lungful of smoke. "Take everythin' and want more. Ain't no way to stop 'em but kick 'em in the ass. Ain't that right?"

Cody was a second late in answering. "Ain't that *right?*" Curt repeated.

"Yes sir." Cody started for his room but his father's voice stopped him again.

"Whoa! I didn't say you could go nowhere. I'm talkin' to you, boy." He took another long pull from the cigarette. "You goin' to work today?"

Cody nodded.

"Good. I need me some smokes. Think that old wetback'll give you a carton?"

"Mr. Mendoza's okay," Cody told him. "He's not like the other ones."

Curt was silent. He drew the cigarette from his mouth and stared at the burning end. "They're all the same," he said quietly. "All of 'em. If you think different, Mendoza's got you foxed, boy."

"Mr. Mendoza's always been—"

"What's this *Mister* Mendoza bullshit?" Curt glared across the room at his son. Damn the boy! he thought. He's got rocks for brains! "I say they're all alike, and that finishes it. Are you gonna get me the smokes or not?"

Cody shrugged, his head lowered. But he could feel his father watching him, and he had to say, "I will."

"All right, then. We're settled." He returned the cigarette to the corner of his mouth, and the ash glowed red as he inhaled. "What's that thing?"

"What thing?"

"That thing. Right there." Curt jabbed a finger at him. "Under your arm. What's that?"

"Nothin'."

"I ain't gone blind *yet,* boy! I asked you what it was!"

Cody slowly took the tie rack from under his arm. His palms were wet. Sweat trickled down his neck, and he longed for a breath of fresh air. He had trouble looking at his father, as if his eyes couldn't bear the sight; and whenever he was close to the old man, something inside him felt dead, heavy, ready to be buried. But whatever that dead thing was, it sometimes gave a surprising kick, and the gravediggers would not come to dispose of it. "Just a tie rack," he explained. "I made it at school."

"Lordy Mercy." Curt whistled, stood up, and came toward Cody, who retreated a pace before he caught himself. "Hold that up so I can see it." Curt reached out, and Cody let him touch it. His father's nicotine-stained fingers caressed the smooth rosewood and the simulated mother-of-pearl squares. *"You* made this? Who helped you?"

"Nobody."

"I swear, that's a fine piece of work! Them edges are smoother 'n free pussy! How long it take you to do this?"

Cody wasn't used to being praised by the old man, and it made him even more jittery. "I don't know. Awhile, I guess."

"A tie rack." Curt grunted and shook his head. "That beats all. I never knew you had it in you to do somethin' like this, boy. Who taught you?"

"I just learned. Kind of hit-and-miss."

"Pretty thing. I swear it is. I like those little silver squares. Makes it fancy, don't it?"

Cody nodded. And bolstered by his father's interest, he dared to step over the line that they had drawn between them a long time ago, over nights of shouting, cold silence, drunken brawls, and curses. Cody's heart was pounding. "Do you really like it?"

"Sure do."

Cody held it toward his father. His hands were trembling. "I made it for you," he said.

Curt Lockett stared at him, his face slack. His haggard eyes moved to the tie rack, to his son's face, and back again. Slowly, he reached out with both hands and took the tie rack, and Cody let him have it. "Lordy Mercy." Curt's voice was soft and respectful as he drew the tie rack to his chest. "Lordy Mercy. This is better than you could buy at a store, ain't it?"

"Yes sir." The dead thing deep inside Cody suddenly twitched.

Curt's fingers played over the wood. He had the scarred,

rough hands of a man who had dug ditches, laid pipes, and mortared bricks since he was thirteen years old. He cradled the tie rack like a child, and he went back to the sofa and sat down. "This is mighty fine," Curt whispered. "Mighty fine." Cobwebs of smoke from the burning cigarette drifted past his face.

"I used to do carpentry," he said, his eyes focused on nothing. "Long time back. Took the jobs that came along. Your mama used to pack a lunch for me, and she'd say, 'Curt, you do me proud today,' and I'd answer, 'I will, Treasure.' That's what I called your mama: Treasure. Oh, she was a pretty thing. You could look at her and believe in miracles. She was so pretty . . . so pretty. Treasure. That's what I called your mama." His eyes glistened, and he bowed his head with both hands curled around the tie rack.

Cody heard his father make a choking sound, and the thing inside him kicked at his heart. He'd seen his old man cry drunk tears before, but this was different. These tears smelled of hurt instead of whiskey. He didn't know if he could handle the sight or not. He wavered, and then he took a step toward the old man. The second step came easier, and the third was easier still. He lifted his hand to touch the old man's shoulder.

Curt's body shook. He wheezed like he was having a choking fit; and then he suddenly lifted his head, and Cody saw that even though his father's eyes were wet, the old man was laughing. His laughter got harder and harsher, until it boomed from his throat like the snarl of a wild beast.

"You're the damnedest fool!" Curt managed to say, snorting with laughter. "The damnedest fool! You know I ain't got no ties!"

Cody's outstretched hand clenched into a fist. He drew it back against his side.

"Not a one!" Curt hollered, and his head rocked back as the choked laughter spilled out. Tears ran through the cracks around his eyes. "Lordy Mercy, what a fool I've raised!"

Cody stood very still. A pulse beat at his temple. His lips were tight, and they hid his gritted teeth.

"Why the hell didn't you make me a *footstool*, boy? I coulda used a footstool! How the hell am I gonna use a tie rack when I don't own no ties!"

The boy let his father's laughter go on for another thirty seconds or so. And finally Cody said, clearly and firmly, "You didn't go to the bakery today, did you?"

The laughter gurgled to a halt like a clogged drain backing up. Curt coughed a few times, his eyes still watery, and crushed his cigarette out on the burn-scarred tabletop. "Naw. What the fuck is it to you?"

"I'll tell you what it is to me," Cody answered. His spine was rigid, and his eyes looked like scorched holes. "I'm tired of takin' up your slack. I'm tired of workin' at the gas station and watchin' you piss the money down the toi—"

"You watch your mouth!" Curt stood up, one hand gripping the tie rack and the other cocked into a fist.

Cody flinched but did not retreat. His guts were full of fire and fury, and he had to get it all out. "You heard me! I'm not coverin' for you anymore! I'm not callin' that freakin' bakery and tell 'em you're too sick to work! Hell, they *know* you're a drunk! Everybody knows you're not worth a piss-ant's damn!"

Curt bellowed and swung at his son, but Cody was faster by far. The man's fist plowed through empty air.

"Yeah, try to hit me!" Cody backpedaled out of range. "Come on, you old bastard! Just try to hit me!"

Curt lurched forward, tripped, and stumbled over the table. Hollering with rage, he went down onto the floor in a flurry of playing cards and ashes.

"Come on! Come on!" Cody urged wildly, and he started running to the windows and flinging the shutters open. Searing white sunlight flooded the room, exposing the dirty rug, the cracked walls, the beat-up secondhand furniture. The sunlight fell upon the man who was trying to stagger to his feet at the center of the room, and he threw his hand over his eyes and screamed, "Get out! Get out of my house, you little fuck!" He flung the tie rack in Cody's direction. It whacked against the wall and fell to the floor.

Cody didn't look at it. "I'll go," he said, his chest heaving but his voice cold now, his eyes as muddy as his father's as he watched the old man shield his face from the sun. "Sure, I'll go. But I'm not coverin' for you anymore. If you lose the job, it's your ass."

"I'm a man!" Curt shouted. "You can't talk to me like that! I'm a man!"

Now it was Cody's turn to laugh—a bitter, wounded sound. Inside him the weight of the dead thing had gotten heavier. "You just remember." He turned toward the door to get out.

"Boy!" Curt's voice boomed. Cody paused. "You'd better be glad your mama's dead, boy," Curt seethed. "'Cause if she was still alive, she'd hate you as much as I do."

Cody was instantly out the door; it slammed shut like a trap at his back. He sprinted down the steps to his motorcycle and drew the desert air into his lungs to clear his head, because for a second there he'd felt like his brain was being squeezed inside a small box and one more ounce of pressure would've made it blow. "You people crazy over there?" Stan Frazier called from his own porch, his gut hanging over the belt of his trousers. "What's all the hollerin' about?"

"Kiss my ass!" Cody flipped the man a bird as he got onto the Honda and kickstarted it. Frazier's face turned crimson; he wobbled down the steps after Cody, but the boy accelerated so rapidly that the motorcycle's front wheel reared up and the rear tire shot sand into the air. Cody tore across the yard and swerved onto Brazos Street, spinning the red Honda around in a skidding turn that left its signature on the pavement.

Inside the house, Curt stood up and squinted. He stumbled forward, hurriedly closed the shutters again. He felt better when the light was sealed away; he remembered that his father had died with the brown blotches of skin cancer all over his face and arms while the deeper, darker cancer ate his insides away, and that memory was never far from his nightmares. "Damn kid," he muttered. Shouted it: *"Damn kid!"* If he'd talked to his old man the way that kid spoke to him, he'd be six feet under; as it was, his back and legs still carried a few scarred welts, some of his old man's best swings with a shaving strop.

He walked to the screen door, could smell the exhaust of Cody's motorcycle lingering in the air. "Lockett!" It was Frazier's voice. "Hey, Lockett! I wanna talk to you!" Curt closed the inner door and turned the latch. Now the only light came through cracks in the shutters, and the heat settled. He liked to sweat; it cleared the poisons out of a man's system.

There was enough light for Curt to see the tie rack on the floor. He picked it up. One end of the little wooden dowel had split and come loose and one of the perfectly carved edges was a splintered ruin, but other than that it was okay. Curt had never known the boy could do such work. It reminded him of what his own hands used to do, back when he was young and tough and he had Treasure at his side.

That was long before Curt had been sitting in a hospital waiting room, and a doctor with a Mexican name had come to tell him that he had a son. But—and Curt could still feel the pressure of the Mexican doctor's hand on his shoulder —would he please come back to the office? There was something else, something very important, that needed to be talked about.

It was because Treasure had been so frail. Because her body was giving everything to the baby. Odds were ten thousand to one, the Mexican doctor had said. Sometimes a woman's body was so tired and worn out that the shock of childbirth was too much. Complications set in—but, señor, your wife has blessed you with a healthy little boy. Under the circumstances, they both might have died, and for this baby's life you can give thanks to God.

There had been forms to sign. Curt couldn't read very well; Treasure had done all the reading. So he just pretended, and scrawled where his name was supposed to be.

Curt's hand clenched the tie rack, and he almost smashed it against the wall again. It was just like Cody, he realized. What damned good was a kid without a mother? And what damned good was a tie rack without a tie? But he didn't smash it, because it was a pretty thing. He took it with him into his bedroom, where the bed was rumpled and the clothes were dirty and four empty bottles of Kentucky Gent were lined up atop the chest of drawers.

Curt switched on the overhead light and sat down on his bed. He retrieved the half bottle of Kentucky Gent with its trademark happy colonel on the label from the floor and unscrewed the cap. His elbow bent, his mouth accepted, and the taste of life shocked his throat.

But he felt so much better with whiskey inside him. Already stronger. His mind already clearer. He could reason things out again, and after a few more swallows he decided he wasn't going to let Cody get away with talking uppity. Hell, no! He was a man, by God! And it was high time he cut that damn kid down a few pegs.

His gaze wandered to the framed photograph on the little table next to the bed. The picture was sun-faded, many-times-creased, stained with either whiskey or coffee, he couldn't remember. It showed a seventeen-year-old girl in a blue-striped dress, her blond hair boiling in thick curls around her shoulders and aglow with sunlight. She was smiling and making an okay sign for Curt, who'd snapped the photo with an Instamatic four days before they were married. Even then the kid had been growing inside her, Curt thought. Less than nine months later, she would be dead. Why he'd kept the kid he didn't know, but his sister had helped him out before she got married for the third time and moved to Arizona. The kid was part of Treasure, and maybe that was why he'd decided to raise Cody himself. That was the name they'd already decided on if the kid was a boy.

He ran a finger over the sunlit hair. "It's not right," he said softly. "It's not right that I got old."

Swig by swig, the half bottle died. The burn pulsed in his gut, like the center of a volcano that demanded more sacrifices. When he realized the bottle was gone, he remembered that there was another up on the closet's shelf. He got up, stumbled to the closet—howdy there, legs!—and reached up for it, groping amid old shirts, socks, and a couple of cowboy hats to where he'd stashed the juice. He didn't trust the damn kid not to pour the stuff down the drain when his back was turned.

He had to stretch way up to the dusty rear of the shelf before his fingers found the familiar shape. "There y'are! Gotcha, didn't I?" He pulled it free, dislodging a leather belt, a ragged blue shirt, and something else that fell to the floor at his feet.

Curt's cocked grin fractured.

It was a necktie, white with red-and-blue circles all over it.

"Lordy Mercy," Curt whispered.

At first he couldn't place the thing. But then he thought he recalled buying it to wear when the federal safety boys had toured the copper mine and he was an assistant foreman on the railroad loading dock. Long time back, before a Mexican took his job away from him. Curt leaned over to get it, staggered, lost his balance, and fell to the floor on his side. He realized he still had the tie rack gripped in his other hand, and he carefully set the Kentucky Gent aside, righted himself, and picked up the necktie. From it wafted a stale hint of Vitalis.

He had to concentrate to steady his hand; he looped the tie around the tie rack's dowel. It looked real pretty against the smooth wood and the silver squares. A thrill coursed through him, and he wanted Cody to see this. The boy was in the other room; Curt had heard him come in just a minute ago, when the screen door's hinges squealed. "Cody!" he shouted, trying to get up. He finally got his legs under himself and was able to stand. He stumbled to the bedroom door. "Cody, looky here! Looky what I—"

He almost fell through the door into the front room. But Cody was not there, and the only noise was the fan's sluggish stuttering. "Cody?" he asked, the tie trailing from the tie rack in his hand. There was no answer, and Curt rubbed the side of his head with numb fingers. He remembered having a fight with Cody. That was yesterday, wasn't it? Oh, Lord! he thought, speared by panic. I'd better get to the bakery or Mr. Nolan'll skin me! But he was very tired, and his legs were unsteady; he thought he might be coming down with the flu. Missing one day at the bakery wouldn't hurt anything; those cakes, pies, and rolls would get baked whether he was there or not and, anyway, there wasn't much business.

Cody'll cover for me, Curt decided. Always has before. He's a good ol' kid.

Mighty thirsty, he thought. Mighty, mighty thirsty! And cradling the tie rack with its single ugly tie against his chest, he staggered back into the bedroom, where time folded and refolded and the happy colonel held dominion.

14

Daufin's Desire

"What do you mean, she's changed?" Tom blinked, his senses whirling. He looked at Jessie, who was leaning against the doorframe with her arms crossed and hands cupping her elbows. She stared at a place on the floor, her eyes dark and distant, her attention turned inward. "Jessie, what's he talking about?"

"I don't mean your daughter's changed physically." Matt Rhodes was trying to speak in a calm and comforting voice, but he didn't know how successful he was being since his own insides seemed to be tangled into twitching knots. He'd pulled a chair up so that he was only a few feet from where Tom Hammond sat on the sofa, directly facing the man. Ray, just as shocked as his father at coming home and finding two air-force officers, was sitting in a chair to the left. White stripes of sunlight painted the living-room walls. "Physically, she's the same," Rhodes emphasized. "It's just . . . well, there's been a mental change."

"A mental change," Tom repeated, the words as heavy as stones.

"The object that crossed your wife's path this morning," Rhodes said, "might have come from anywhere in space. All we know about it is that it entered the atmosphere, caught fire, and crashed. Now: this other thing that came out of

133

it—the black sphere—has to be found. Captain Gunniston and I have gone through the house pretty thoroughly; we've searched everywhere we figure she could've reached, but she could barely crawl when we got here, so we can't figure how she disposed of it. Your daughter did have it when Mrs. Hammond called here around ten-thirty."

Tom closed his eyes, because the room had started to revolve. When he opened them, the colonel was still there. "This black sphere. What is it?"

"We don't know that, either. As I said, your daughter seemed to hear something from it that no one else could—a singing, she called it. Could've been an aural beacon, maybe tuned in some way to your child's brain waves or something; like I said, we don't know. But, Captain Gunniston and I both agree that . . ." He paused, trying to think of a way to say this. There was no way but to plow straight ahead. "We both agree that there's been a transference."

Tom just stared at him.

"A mental transference," Rhodes said. "Your daughter . . . isn't who she appears to be. She still looks like a little girl, but she's not. Whatever's in your den, Mr. Hammond, is not human."

"Oh," Tom said softly, as if the wind had been punched out of him.

"We think the transference was caused by the black sphere. Why that happened, or how, we don't know. We're dealing with things here that are pretty damned strange —which I guess is the understatement of the year, huh?" He smiled tensely. Tom's expression remained blank. "There's a reason I'm here," the colonel continued. "When the object started coming down, and the tracking computer verified that it wasn't a meteor or a malfunctioning satellite, I was called onto special duty. I've worked for over six years with the Bluebook Project—investigating UFO sightings, talking to witnesses, going to close-encounter sites all over the country. So I've had experience with UFO phenomena."

Tom took his glasses off and cleaned the lenses on his shirt. It seemed very important to him that the lenses be spotless. Jessie was still lost in her thoughts, but Ray suddenly broke out of his own trance and said, "You mean . . . you've seen a *real* flying saucer? Like from another planet?"

"Yes, I have," Rhodes answered without hesitation; this whole incident was going to be a new chapter in the security procedures book anyway, so he figured he might as well tell the truth. "Ninety percent of what's reported are meteor fragments, ball lightning, pranks, that kind of thing. But the ten percent is something else entirely. An ETV —extraterrestrial vehicle—crashed in Vermont three years ago. We got samples of the metal and parts of alien bodies. Another one came down in Georgia last summer—but it was a totally different design, and the pilot was a different life form from the Vermont incident." I'm revealing national secrets to a kid with orange spikes in his hair! he realized. But Ray was paying rapt attention, while Tom had mentally checked out and was still scrubbing his glasses. "So, considering all the sightings of differently shaped ETVs, we've concluded that Earth is near . . . well, a superhighway in space. A corridor from one part of the galaxy to another, maybe. Some of the ETVs, like our cars, they break down; they get sucked into Earth's atmosphere, and they crash."

"Wow," Ray whispered, his eyes huge behind his glasses.

For revealing that information without authority, Rhodes knew he could get life in prison, but the circumstances warranted explanation and—besides—nobody ever believed such stories anyway unless they'd had a personal close encounter. He returned his gaze to Tom. "My crew is cleaning up the crash site. We'll be ready to leave around midnight. And . . . I'm going to have to take the creature with me."

"She's my daughter." Jessie's voice was weak, but gaining strength again. "She's not a *creature!*"

Rhodes sighed; they'd already been over this several agonizing times. "We have no choice but to take the creature to Webb, and from there to a research lab in Virginia. There's no way we can let such a thing run loose; we don't know what its intentions are, or anything about its biology, chemistry, or—"

"Psychology," Tom finished for him; he put his glasses back on with trembling fingers. His wits had clicked back into gear, though everything still seemed hazy and dreamlike.

"Right. That too. So far, she—I mean, *it*—has been nonthreatening, but you never know what might set it off."

"Gnarly, man!" Ray said. "My sister the alien!"

"Ray!" Jessie snapped, and the boy's grin faded. "Colonel Rhodes, we're not going to let you take Stevie." Her voice cracked. "She's still our daughter."

"Still *looks* like your daughter."

"Okay! So whatever's in her might leave! If her body's fine, then her mind might come back—"

"Colonel!" Gunniston appeared in the doorway between the living room and den. His freckled face had paled even more, and he looked like what he was: a scared twenty-three-year-old kid in an air-force uniform. "She's on the last volume."

"We'll talk about this later," Rhodes told Jessie, and stood up. He hurried into the den, with Ray at his heels. Tom put his arm around Jessie and they followed.

But Tom stopped as if he'd been struck when he came through the door. Ray stood and stared, openmouthed.

The volumes of their encyclopedia lay all over the room. The *Webster's Dictionary, World Atlas, Roget's Thesaurus,* and other reference books lay on the floor as well, and right in the center of the disarray sat Stevie, holding the WXYZ volume of the *Britannica* between her hands. She sat on her haunches, perched forward like a bird. As Tom watched, his daughter opened the book and began to turn the pages at a rate of about one every two seconds.

"She's already gone through the dictionary and the thesaurus," Rhodes said. Call it an alien, or a creature, he reminded himself—but she looked like a little girl in blue jeans and a T-shirt, and those cold terms didn't seem right. Her eyes were no longer lifeless; they were sparkling and intense, directed at the pages with all-consuming concentration. "It took her about thirty minutes to figure out our alphabet. After that, it was open season on your bookcase."

"My God . . . this morning she could barely read," Tom said. "I mean . . . she's not even in the first grade yet!"

"That was this morning. I think she's about ready for college by now."

The pages continued to turn. There was a dripping noise, and Tom saw liquid soak into the carpet beneath his daughter.

"Evidently the body's still carrying out its normal functions," Rhodes told him. "So we know that at least one portion of a human brain's at work, if just unconsciously."

Jessie grasped her husband's arm and held on tightly; she'd seen him waver, and was afraid he was about to pitch onto his face. Stevie was still totally absorbed by the book, and the turning of the pages was getting faster, becoming almost a blur.

"She's goin' into overdrive!" Ray said. "Man, look at that!" He stepped forward, but the colonel caught his shirt and prevented him from going any closer. "Hey, Stevie! It's me, Ray!"

The child's head lifted. Swiveled toward him. The eyes stared, curious and penetrating.

"Ray!" he repeated, and thumped himself on the chest.

Her head cocked. She blinked slowly. Then: "Ray," the voice said, and she thumped her own chest. Returned to her reading.

"Well," Rhodes observed, "maybe she's not ready for college just yet, but she's learning."

Tom looked at all the books scattered about. "If . . . she's really not Stevie anymore . . . if she's something different, then how does she know about books?"

Jessie said, "She found them and must have figured out what they were. After she went through the alphabet, she walked around the house, examining things. A lamp seemed to fascinate her. And a mirror too—she kept trying to reach into it." She heard herself talking and realized she was sounding detached, like Rhodes. "That *is* our daughter. It is." But as she watched the encyclopedia's pages turning, she knew that wherever Stevie was—and what made Stevie? Her mind? Her soul?—it was no longer inside the body that crouched before them, absorbing information over a puddle of urine.

The last page was reached. The volume was closed and set gently, almost reverently aside. Tom now truly knew it wasn't Stevie; their daughter flung things instead of carefully putting them down.

The creature stood up, with a smooth and controlled motion, no longer unsteady on her feet. It was as if she'd gotten accustomed to the weight of gravity. She looked at the five people who stared back at her, her gaze carefully examining their faces. She lifted her hands and studied them, comparing their size to those on the arms of the others. Particularly intrigued by the glasses both Tom and Ray wore, she touched her own face as if she expected to find a pair there.

"She's got the alphabet, a dictionary and thesaurus, a world atlas, and a set of encyclopedias in her head," Rhodes said quietly. "I think she's trying to learn as much about us as she can." The creature watched his mouth moving and touched her own lips. "I guess this is as good a time as any, huh?" He took a step toward her, then stopped, so as not to get too close and scare her. "Your name," he said, trying to enunciate as clearly as possible. His heart was fluttering like a caged bird. "What is your name?"

"Your name," she answered. "What is your name?"

"*Your* name." He pointed at her. "Tell us yours."

She seemed to be thinking, her eyes fixed on him. She glanced at Ray and pointed. "Ray."

"Jeez!" the boy shouted. "An alien knows my name!"

"Hush!" Jessie almost pinched a plug out of his arm.

Rhodes nodded. "Right. That's Ray. What's *your* name?"

The creature swiveled around and walked with a graceful gliding gait to the hallway. She halted, turned toward them again. "Name," she said, and walked on into the hall.

Jessie's heart jumped. "I think she wants us to follow."

They did. The creature was waiting in Stevie's room. Her arm was lifted, her index finger pointing to something.

"Your name," Rhodes repeated, not understanding. "Tell us what we can call you."

She answered: "Dau-fin."

And all of them saw that her finger was aimed at the picture of a dolphin on Stevie's bulletin board.

"Double gnarly!" Ray exclaimed. "She's Flipper!"

"Dau-fin." It was said with the inflections of a child. Her arm stretched up; the fingers touched the picture, moved over the aquamarine water. "Dau-fin."

Rhodes was unsure if she actually meant the dolphin or the ocean. In any case he was certain the creature before them was much more than a dolphin in human skin: much, much more. Her eyes asked if he understood, and he nodded; her fingers lingered for a few seconds on the picture, making a gentle wavelike motion. Then her interest drifted to another picture, and Rhodes saw her flinch.

"Sting-er," she said, like she had tasted something nasty. She touched the scorpion, drew her fingers quickly back as if afraid she might be stung.

"It's just a picture." Rhodes tapped it. "It's not real."

She studied it for a moment longer—then she removed the little colored pins that fastened the picture to the cork and looked at it closely, her finger traveling the length of the segmented tail. Finally, her hands began to work at the paper. Folding it, Rhodes realized. Making it into a different shape.

Jessie's hand gripped Tom's. She watched as Stevie—or Daufin, or whatever—folded the paper and folded it again, the fingers now fast and supple. It took the creature only a few seconds to produce a paper pyramid; she twirled the pyramid away, and it flew across the room and bounced against the wall.

Gunniston picked it up. It was the damnedest paper airplane he'd ever seen.

The creature faced them; there was expectation in her eyes, and a questioning, but no one knew what the question might be.

She took a step toward Jessie, who in turn retreated a pace. Ray backed against the wall.

Daufin lifted her hand, placed it to Stevie's chest. "Yours," she said.

Jessie knew what the creature was asking. "Yes. My daughter. *Our* daughter." Her grip was about to break Tom's fingers.

"Daugh-ter," Daufin repeated carefully. "A fe-male off-spring of hu-man be-ings."

"Straight from Webster's," Gunniston muttered. "Think she knows what it means?"

"Quiet!" Rhodes told him. Daufin glided to the window, her chin uptilted. She stayed that way without budging for over a minute, and Jessie realized she was entranced by a sliver of blue sky through the drawn blinds. Jessie got her legs unfrozen and went to the window, pulling the blinds up by their cord. The afternoon sunlight streaming over the sill held a hint of gold, and the cloudless sky was brilliantly azure.

Daufin stood staring. She reached up with both hands and stood on tiptoes, the entire body straining for the sky. Jessie saw a change come over the face: it was no longer a blank, emotionless mask. In it was a yearning, a mingled joy and sadness that was beyond Jessie's emotions to comprehend. The face was at once Stevie's, with its innocence and fresh curiosity, and at the same time it was an ancient face—the face, perhaps, of an old woman, careworn and dreaming of what might have been.

The little hands stretched for the glass, but Stevie's body was way too short to get there. Daufin gave a snort of impatience, glided past Jessie, and dragged the chair over from Stevie's desk; she climbed up on it, leaned toward the window, and immediately smacked her forehead against the glass. Her fingers probed at the invisible barrier, pattering like moths trying to get through a screen. Finally, Daufin's arms lowered, the hands hanging limply at her sides.

"I . . ." Daufin said. "I . . . de-sire . . ."

"What'd she say?" Gunniston asked, but Rhodes put a finger to his lips.

"I de-sire. To." Daufin's head turned, and the eyes —something ancient behind them, something in dire need —found Jessie's. "I de-sire to o-rate your aur-i-cles."

No one spoke. Daufin blinked, awaiting a reply.

"I think she wants to be taken to our leader," Ray said, and Tom elbowed him none too gently in the shoulder.

Daufin tried again: "Os-cill-ate your tym-pan-um."

Jessie thought she understood. "You mean . . . talk to us?"

Daufin frowned, mulling over what she'd heard. She made a little chirping, weirdly musical noise, climbed down off the chair, glided past Jessie and out of the room. Rhodes and Gunniston hurried after her.

And by the time Jessie, Tom, and Ray got to the den, Daufin was crouched on the floor intent on rereading the dictionary from cover to cover.

15
Dark Karma

At the moment Daufin was trying to learn the nuances of English, Cody Lockett was operating the hydraulic lift in a garage stall of Xavier Mendoza's gas station, cranking up a Ford that needed new brake drums. He was wearing old, faded jeans and an olive-green workshirt that had his name beneath the Texaco star; his hands were greasy, his face streaked with grime, and he knew he was a long way from resembling the well-scrubbed gas jockeys in TV commercials, but staying clean didn't get the job done. In the last hour, he'd changed the oil in two cars and the spark plugs and points in a third. The garage was his territory, its tools hanging in orderly rows on the walls and gleaming like surgical instruments, a rack of tires giving off the smell of fresh rubber and an assortment of cables, radiator belts, and hoses hanging from the metal beams overhead. The garage door had been hoisted up and a big box fan kept the air circulating, but it was still plenty hot anywhere chrome reflected the sunlight and engines were continually turned over.

Cody got the lift as high as he wanted and locked it in place. He plugged in the electric gun that unscrewed lug nuts and began to take the tires off. Working here helped him forget about the old man. There was more than enough to keep him busy today—including hoisting out the destroyed engine of that sea-green pickup in the next stall —and sometime this afternoon he wanted to find time to tinker with his motorcycle's carb and smooth out the kinks.

The signal bell rang as a car pulled up to the pumps outside, but he knew Mr. Mendoza would take care of the gas customers. Sonny Crowfield had knocked off just before Cody came in for work—which was just as well, since Cody couldn't stand him; Crowfield, in Cody's opinion, was a crazy half-breed and a Rattler to boot, always talking shit about how he was going to someday stomp Jurado and become president. From what Cody heard, even the Rattlers didn't have much to do with Crowfield, who lived on the edge of the autoyard, all alone except for a collection of animal skeletons—and where and how he got those bones, no one knew.

A car horn honked. Cody looked up from his work.

At the pumps sat a silver-blue Mercedes convertible, its paint glossed to a high shine. Behind the wheel was a man wearing sunglasses and a straw Panama hat. He lifted a hand in a brown leather driving glove, motioning for Cody to come out. In the seat beside him was a husky Doberman, and another one crouched in the backseat. Mendoza emerged from his office and went around to speak to the driver. Cody returned to his job—but the Mercedes's horn rapped out an impatient tattoo.

Mack Cade was as persistent as a tick. Cody knew what he wanted. The horn honked again, though Mendoza was standing right there trying to tell Cade that Cody had work to do. Mack Cade was paying him zero attention. Cody said, "Shit!" under his breath, put aside the lug-nut gun, and wiped his hands off on a rag, taking his time about it; then he walked out into the glary sunlight.

"Fill 'er up, Cody!" Mack Cade said. "You know what she drinks."

"You've got garage work to do, Cody!" Mr. Mendoza told him, trying his best to cover for the boy—because he, too, knew Cade's game. "You don't have to come out and pump the gas!" His eyes were black and fearsome, and with his silver hair and bushy silver mustache he resembled an aged grizzly ready for a final tooth-and-claw battle; if those damned dogs weren't there he might have snatched Cade out of that fancy car and beaten him bloody.

"Hey, I'm particular about who touches my car." Cade's voice was a silky-smooth drawl; he was used to being obeyed. He smiled at Mendoza, showing a line of small white teeth in his deeply burnished face. "Bad vibes round here, man. You've got a real dark karma."

"I don't need your business, or your bullshit either!" Mendoza's shout made Typhoid, the dog in the passenger seat, stiffen and snarl. The dog in the rear, whose name was Lockjaw, was frozen and staring, his single ear laid back along his skull; that and the fact that Typhoid was a little larger through the shoulders was the only difference between the two animals.

"You sure about that? I can bring in my own gas trucks, if you want."

"Yeah, maybe that'd be just fi—"

"Hold it," Cody interrupted. "You don't need to be my watchdog," he said to Mendoza. "I can look out for myself." He walked to the diesel pump, withdrew the hose, and primed the numbers back to zero.

"Let's give peace a chance, Mendoza," Cade said as Cody started feeding the fuel in. "Okay?"

Mendoza snorted angrily and glanced at Cody; the boy nodded that everything was under control. Mendoza said, "I'll be in my office. You don't take no shit from him, understand?" He turned on his heel and strode away, and Cade revved up the volume on his tape deck. Tina Turner's raspy voice thundered, *"Better be good to me!"*

"You can clean the windshield, too," Cade told Cody as soon as Mendoza was in the office.

Cody went to work with the squeegee; he could see a distorted image of himself in the reflective lenses of the man's sunglasses. Cade's hat was held on by a leather chinstrap, he wore a silk short-sleeved shirt the color of sangria, and tie-dyed jeans. Around his neck dangled a few golden chains, among them one with an old peace sign on it, and one of those small gold ingots with foreign words. On his left wrist was a Rolex watch with diamonds set in its dial, and on the right was a gold bracelet with "Mack" engraved in it. Both of the Dobermans were watching with keen interest as Cody's squeegee went back and forth over the glass.

Cade lowered the music. "Guess you heard about the meteor. Far out, huh?"

Cody didn't reply. Of course he'd seen the helicopter sitting in Preston Park, but he hadn't known what was going on until Mr. Mendoza had told him. If Mr. Hammond had heard his wife's truck had been hit by a meteor, Cody mused, he sure as hell wouldn't have dicked around school so long after the bell rang.

"Yeah, I hear the meteor's hot too. Radioactive. That's supposed to be a secret, but I heard it from Whale Tail at the Brandin' Iron, and she heard it from the deputy. Seems to me a little radiation might spark this damned town up some, huh?"

Cody concentrated on getting the guts of a smashed moth off the windshield.

"I'm picking up some more bad vibes, Cody. There's a real purple haze around this place today, man."

"You're buyin' gas, not talk."

"Whoa! The stone face speaks!" Cade rubbed Typhoid's skull and watched the boy work. He was thirty-three years old, with a soft, cherubic face—but beneath the sunglasses his eyes were cold blue and cunning. Cody had seen them before, and they made him think of the hard steel of rabbit traps. Under his Panama hat, Cade's hair was pale blond and thinning, combed back from a high, unlined forehead. Two diamond studs glittered in his left earlobe. "Tomorrow's your last schoolday," he said; the shuck-and-jive had dropped from his voice. "Big day for you, man. Important day." He scratched beneath Typhoid's muzzle. "I guess you've been thinking about your future. About money too."

Don't answer him! Cody thought. Don't fall for it!

"How's your father doing? I missed him last time I stopped in for a doughnut."

Cody finished the windshield and glanced at the diesel pump. The numbers were still clicking.

"Hope he's okay. You know, with the town shutting down and all, it probably won't be too long before the bakery goes under. What's he going to do when that happens, Cody?"

Cody walked over to stand by the pump. Mack Cade's head turned to follow him, the smile as white as a scar. "I've got an opening for a mechanic," he said. "A good, fast mechanic. The opening won't last but for a week or so. Pay starts at six hundred a month. Do you know anybody who could use the money?"

Cody was silent, watching the numbers change. But inside his head *six hundred a month* kept repeating itself, gaining power with every repetition. God A'mighty! he thought. What I couldn't do with that kind of money!

"But it's not just the money," Cade pressed on, smelling blood in the boy's silence. "It's the benefits too, man. I can get you a car just like this one. Or a Porsche, if you want. Any color. How about a red Porsche, five on the floor, top speed a hundred and twenty? You name the options, you got them."

The numbers stopped. Cade's tank was full. Cody unhooked the nozzle, closed the gas port, and returned the hose to the diesel pump. Six hundred a month, he was thinking. A red Porsche . . . top speed a hundred and twenty . . .

"It's night work," Cade said. "The hours depend on what's in the yard, and I'll expect you to work sixteen hours straight if there's a rush on. My connections pay high green for quality work, Cody—and I think you can deliver it."

Cody squinted toward Inferno. The long fall of the sun had started, and though it wouldn't be dark until after eight, he could already feel the shadows creeping up behind him. "Maybe I can, maybe I can't."

"I've seen the work you do here. It's tight. You're a natural, and you shouldn't throw away a God-given talent on junkers, should you?"

"I don't know."

"What's to know?" Cade took a solid gold toothpick from

his shirt pocket and dug at a lower molar. "If it's the law you're skittish of . . . well, that's under control. This is a *business,* Cody. Everybody understands the language."

The boy didn't reply. He was thinking of what six hundred dollars a month could buy him, and how far away from Inferno he could get in a red Porsche. To hell with the old man; he could rot and turn into a maggot farm as far as Cody cared. Of course he knew what Mack Cade's business was. He'd seen the tractor-trailer trucks turn off Highway 67 and pull into Cade's autoyard in the middle of the night, and he knew they were hauling stolen cars. He knew, as well, that when the big trucks headed north again they were carrying vehicles without histories. After Cade's workmen had finished, the engines, radiators, exhaust systems, most of the body parts, even the hubcaps and paint jobs would have been changed, swapped around, made to look like cars sweet from the showroom floor. Where those finished chopshop specials went, Cody didn't know, but he figured they were resold by crooked dealers or used as company cars by organized gangs. Whoever used them paid heavy money to Cade, who'd found Inferno the perfect place to stash such an operation.

"You don't want to wind up like your old man, Cody." The boy saw his face reflected in Cade's sunglasses. "You want to do something with your life, don't you?"

Cody hesitated. He didn't know what he wanted. Though he didn't give a shit about the law, he'd never really done anything criminal, either. Maybe he did smash a few windows and raise some hell, but what Cade offered was different. A whole lot different. It was like taking a step beyond a line that Cody had balanced on for a long time—yet to cross that line meant he couldn't come back. Not ever.

"Offer's open for one week. You know where to find me." Cade's smile had clicked back on, full wattage. "How much do I owe you?"

Cody checked the numbers. "Twelve seventy-three."

The man popped open his glove compartment, and Typhoid licked his hand. In the glove box there was a .45

automatic and an extra clip. His hand came out holding a rolled-up twenty; he snapped the glove compartment shut. "Here you go, man. Keep the change. And there's a little something extra in there for you too." He started the engine, the Mercedes giving a clean, throaty growl. Agitated, Lockjaw stood stiff-legged on the backseat and barked in Cody's face. He smelled raw meat.

"Think on these things," Cade said, and accelerated out of the station with a shriek of flayed rubber.

Cody watched him speed away, heading south. He unrolled the twenty. Inside it was a small, capped glass vial holding three yellowish crystals. Though he'd never cooked the stuff before, Cody knew what crack looked like.

"You okay?"

Startled, Cody slipped the vial into his breast pocket, nestling the cocaine crystals under the Texaco star. Mendoza was standing about six feet behind him. "Yeah." Cody gave him the twenty. "He said to keep the change."

"And what else did he say?"

"Just chewin' air." Cody walked past Mendoza toward the garage stalls, trying to sort things out in his mind. He felt the pull of six hundred dollars a month on his soul, like a cold hand from the midst of a blast furnace. What's the problem? he asked himself. A few hours of work a night, the cops already paid off, a chance to move up in Cade's operation if I wanted. Why didn't I say yes right then and there?

"You know where his cars go, don't you?" Mendoza had followed Cody, and now leaned against the stall's cinder-block wall.

"Nope."

"Sure you do. About two or three years ago, a DA up in Fort Worth was found in the trunk of a car with his throat cut and a bullet between his eyes. The car was parked in front of City Hall. Of course it had no ID numbers. Where do you think it came from?"

Cody shrugged, but he knew.

"Before that," Mendoza continued, his burly brown arms folded over his chest, "a bomb went off in a pickup truck in

Houston. The cops figured it was supposed to kill a lawyer who was workin' on a drug bust—but it blew a woman and her kid to pieces instead. Where do you think that truck came from?"

Cody picked up the lug-nut gun. "You don't have to lecture me."

"I don't mean to sound like I am. But don't you believe for one minute that Cade doesn't know how his cars are used. And that's just in Texas—he sends them all over the country!"

"I was just talkin' to him. No law against that."

"I know what he wants from you," Mendoza said firmly. "You're a man now, and you can do as you please. But I have to tell you something my father told me a long, long time ago: a man is responsible for his actions."

"You're not my father."

"No, I'm not. But I've watched you grow up, Cody. Oh, I know all about that Renegade shit, but that's small compared to what Cade could drag you in—"

Cody pressed the gun's trigger, and its high squeal echoed between the walls. He turned his back on Mendoza and went to work.

Mendoza grunted, his gaze black and brooding. He liked Cody, knew he was a smart young man and could *be* somebody if he put his mind to it. But Cody had been crippled by that bastard father of his, and he'd let his old man's poison seep into his veins. Mendoza didn't know what was ahead for Cody, but he feared for the young man. He'd seen too many lives tossed away for the glint of Cade's fool's gold.

He returned to the office and switched on the radio to the Spanish music station in El Paso. Around nine o'clock the Trailways bus from Odessa would come through on its way south to Chihauhau. The driver always stopped at Mendoza's station to let the passengers buy soft drinks and candy from the machines. Then, except for an occasional truck, Highway 67 would lie empty, its concrete cooling under the expanse of stars, and Mendoza would shut down for the night. He would go home in time for a late dinner and a couple of games of checkers with his uncle Lazaro, who lived with him and his wife on Bordertown's First Street, until the ticking of the clock eventually urged the time for bed. Tonight he might dream of being a racecar driver, roaring around the dirt tracks of his youth. But, most likely, he would not dream.

And that would be another night gone, and another day approaching, and Mendoza knew that was the way a man's life ran out.

He turned the radio up louder, listening to the strident trumpets of a mariachi band, and he tried very hard not to let himself think about the boy in the garage, who stood at a crossroads that no one on earth could help him travel.

16

Inferno's Pulse

The shadows grew.

In front of the Ice House, the old-timers sat on benches smoking their cigars and corncob pipes and talking about the meteor. Heard it from Jimmy Rice, one of them said. Jimmy got it straight from the sheriff's mouth. Hell, I didn't get to be seventy-four years old to be kilt by no damned rock from out yonder in space, I'm tellin' you! Damn thing just about fell right on our heads!

They all agreed it had been a near miss. They talked about the helicopter, still sitting in the middle of Preston Park, wondering how such a thing could fly, and would *you* get up in one? Hell no, I ain't crazy! was the unanimous answer. Then their talk drifted to the new baseball season, and when was a southern team going to win a series? When time runs back-assward and horses stand on two legs! one of them growled, and kept chewing on his cigar butt.

In the House of Beauty on Celeste Street, Ida Younger frosted Tammy Bryant's mouse-brown hair and talked not about the meteor or the helicopter but about the two handsome men who had gotten out of it. The pilot's a hunk too, Tammy said. She'd seen him when he went into the Brandin' Iron for a hamburger and coffee—and, of course, she and May Davis just *had* to go in there for a bite of lunch

151

too. And you should've seen the way that damn Sue Mullinax flounced herself all over the cafe! Tammy confided. I mean, it was a disgrace!

Ida agreed that Sue was the nerviest bitch who ever tied a mattress to her back, and Sue's butt just kept getting bigger and bigger and that's what so much sex'll do to you too.

She's a nymphomaniac, Tammy said. A nympho, plain and simple.

Yeah, Ida said. Plain-lookin' and simpleminded.

And they both laughed.

On Cobre Road, past the Smart Dollar clothing store, the post office, the bake shop, and the Paperback Kastle, a middle-aged man squinted through his wire-rimmed spectacles and concentrated on inserting a pin through the abdomen of a small brown scorpion, found dead of Raid inhalation in the kitchen this morning. His name was Noah Twilley, and he was slender and pale, his straight black hair lank and going gray. His skinny fingers got the pin through, and he added the scorpion to his collection of other "ladies and gentlemen"—beetles, wasps, flies, and more scorpions, all pinned to black velvet and kept under glass. He was in the study of his white stone house, thirty yards behind the brick building with a stained-glass front window, a stucco statue of Jesus standing between two stucco cacti, and a sign that read INFERNO FUNERAL HOME.

His father had died six years ago and left the business to him—a dubious honor, since Noah had always wanted to be an entomologist. He had made sure his father was buried in the hottest plot on Joshua Tree Hill.

"Nooooaaaahhh! *Noah!*" The screech made his backbone stiffen. "Go get me a Co-Cola!"

"Just a minute, Mother," he answered.

"Noah! My show's on!"

He stood up wearily and walked down the corridor to her room. She was wearing a white silk gown, sitting up against white silk pillows in a bed with a white canopy. Her face was a mask of white powder, her hair dyed flame red. On the color TV, the Wheel of Fortune was spinning. "Get me a

Co-Cola!" Ruth Twilley ordered. "My throat's as dry as dust!"

"Yes, Mother," he answered, and trudged toward the staircase. Better to do what she wanted and get it over with, he knew.

"That meteor's doin' somethin' to the air!" she hollered after him, her voice as high as a wasp's whine. "Makin' my throat clog up!" He was on his way down the steps, but that voice followed him: "I'll bet old Celeste heard it hit! Bet it made her shit pickles!"

Here we go, he thought.

"That prissy-pants bitch livin' out there high and mighty, not carin' a damn about anybody else, just suckin' the guts out of this town. She did it, y'know! Prob'ly killed poor Wint, but he was too smart for her! Yessir! He hid all his money so she couldn't get none of it! Foxed her, he did! Well, when she comes to Ruth Twilley askin' for money and down on her hands and knees, I'm gonna snub her like she's a snail! You listenin' to me, Noah? *Noah!*"

"Yes," he answered, down in the depths of the house. "I'm listening."

She kept babbling on, and Noah let himself ponder what life might be like if that meteor had struck smack dab over the ceiling of her bedroom. There was not a plot on Joshua Tree Hill that was hot enough.

Across Inferno and Bordertown, other lives drifted on: Father Manuel LaPrado listened to confessions at the Sacrifice of Christ Catholic Church, while Reverend Hale Jennings put a pencil to paper at the Inferno Baptist Church and worked on his Sunday sermon. On his porch, Sarge Dennison napped in a lawn chair, his face occasionally flinching at unwelcome memories, his right arm hanging down and his hand patting the head of the invisible Scooter. Rick Jurado stacked boxes in the stockroom of the hardware store on Cobre Road, the Fang of Jesus heavy in his jeans pocket and his mind circling what Mr. Hammond had said today. Heavy-metal music blared from a ghetto blaster through the corridors of the 'Gades' fortress at the end of

Travis Street, and while Bobby Clay Clemmons and a few other 'Gades smoked reefers and shot the shit, Nasty and Tank lay on a bare mattress in another room, their bodies damp and intertwined in the aftermath of sex—the one activity for which Tank removed his football helmet.

The day was winding down. A postal truck left town, heading north to Odessa with its cargo of letters—among which were a high percentage of job applications, inquiries for employment, and supplications to relatives for extended visiting privileges. Of all people, the postman knew the pulse of Inferno, and he could see death scrawled on the envelopes.

The sun was sinking, and on the First Texas Bank the electric-bulb sign read 93°F. at 5:49.

17
The Baseball Fan

"I know this is an open line," Rhodes said to the duty officer at Webb Air Force Base. "I don't have closed comm equipment, and I don't have time, either. My ID is Bluebooker. Look it up." He held on to the phone as the duty officer verified his code. From the den he heard the television channel being changed again: the canned laughter of a sit-com. About six seconds passed, and the channel was changed once more: a baseball-game commentator, and this time the TV was left alone for a little longer.

"Yes sir. I copy you, Bluebooker." The duty officer sounded young and nervous. "What can I do for you, sir?"

"I need a transport aircraft waiting with a number one priority. I need it fueled for cross-country, and I'll be giving the destination in the air. Alert Colonel Buckner that I'm coming in with a package from our incident site. I need videotape equipment on board too. My ETA into Webb will be between two and three hundred hours. Got that?"

"Yes sir."

"Read it back to me." He heard the channel change: a news broadcast, something about hostages in the Middle East. The duty officer read everything back correctly, and Rhodes said, "Fine. I'm signing off." He hung up the phone and strode into the den.

Daufin sat on the floor—cross-legged this time, as if it had figured out that its crouching posture put strain on a human's knee joints. The creature's face was about twelve inches from the TV screen, watching a news story about floods in Arkansas.

"I wish we'd get some of that rain," Gunniston said, drinking from a can of Pepsi.

Daufin reached out and touched the TV screen. The entire picture warped out of shape; there was a *crack!* and the channels changed: Woody Woodpecker cartoons.

"Neat-o!" Ray was sitting on the floor, not too close to Daufin but not so far away, either. "She's got a remote control in her fingers!"

"Probably some kind of electromagnetic pulse," Rhodes told him. "It may be using the electricity in Stevie's body, or maybe it's generating its own."

Crack! Now there was a western movie on TV: Steve McQueen in *The Magnificent Seven.*

"Man, that's about the coolest thing I've ever—"

"Shut up!" Jessie's control had finally snapped, and she could stand it no longer. "You shut up!" Her eyes were bright with tears and anger, and Ray looked stunned. "There's nothing 'cool' about this! Your sister's *gone!* Don't you understand that?"

"I . . . didn't mean to—"

"She's *gone!*" Jessie advanced on Ray, but Tom quickly stood up from his chair and grasped her arm. She pulled free, her face strained and agonized. "She's gone, and there's just *that* left!" She pointed at Daufin; the creature still stared at the TV screen, oblivious to what Jessie was saying. "Jesus Christ . . ." Jessie's voice faltered. She put her hands to her face. "Oh my God . . . oh God . . ." She began to sob, and Tom could do nothing but hold her while she wept bitter tears.

Crack! A surfing competition appeared, and Daufin's eyes widened slightly, following the rolling blue waves.

Rhodes turned toward his aide. "Gunny, I want you to get out to the crash site and hurry them up. We need to get out of here as soon as we can."

"Right." He finished his drink, dropped the can into the trash, and put on his cap as he went out the door, heading for the helicopter.

Rhodes wished he were anywhere else but here, and his mind drifted to the farm where he lived with his wife and two daughters, near Chamberlain, South Dakota. On clear nights he studied the stars in his small observatory, or made notes for the book he was planning on life beyond earth; he wished he was doing either, right now, because he had no recourse but to take the creature to a research lab, no matter that it wore a little girl's face. "Mrs. Hammond, I know this is tough on you," he said. "I want you to know th—"

"Know *what?*" She was still enraged, her face streaked with tears. "That our daughter's still alive? That she's dead? Know *what?*"

Crack: a "Mork and Mindy" rerun. *Crack:* a financial news show. *Crack:* another baseball game.

"That I'm sorry," he went on resolutely. "For what it's worth, I've got two daughters myself. I can imagine what you must be feeling. If anything happened to either of them . . . well, I don't know what Kelly and I would do. Kelly's my wife. But at least you understand now that she—it—isn't your daughter. When the crew finishes up at the crash site, we'll be leaving. I'll take her—it—Daufin —to Webb, and from there to Virginia. I'm going to ask Gunny to stay with you."

"Stay with us? Why?" Tom asked.

"Just for a short while. A debriefing, I guess you'd call it. We'll want to get statements from all of you, go through the house with a Geiger counter, try to find that black sphere again. And we don't want this information leaking out. We want to control—"

"You don't want it leaking out," Tom repeated incredulously. "That's just great!" He gave a short, harsh laugh. "Our daughter's been taken away by some kind of damned alien *thing*, and you don't want the information leaking out." He felt the blood charge into his face. "What are we supposed to do? Just go on like it never happened?"

Crack: not a channel changing this time, but a bat connecting with a baseball. The crowd roared.

"I know you can't do that, but we're going to try to ease you away from this situation as best we can, with counseling, hypnosis—"

"We don't need that!" Jessie snapped. "We need to know where Stevie is! Is she dead, or is she—"

"Safe," Daufin interrupted.

Jessie's throat seized up. She looked at the creature. Daufin was staring at the baseball game, where a runner had slid into home plate. The ball was thrown back to the pitcher, and Daufin's eyes followed its trajectory with intense interest.

And then Daufin's head racheted toward Jessie: a slow, halting motion, as if she was still unsure of how the bones fit together. "Safe," she repeated. Her gaze locked on to the woman. "Ste-vie is safe, Jes-sie."

She managed a soft exhalation of breath: *"What?"*

"Safe. Freed from in-ju-ry or risk, al-so se-cure from dan-ger or loss. Is that not a cor-rect in-ter . . ." Daufin paused, scanning dictionary pages in the massive, perfectly organized library of her memory banks. "In-ter-pre-ta-tion?"

"Yes," Rhodes replied quickly. His heart had jumped; this was the first time the creature had spoken for over an hour, since that stuff about "oscillating tympanum." The TV channels had occupied her, and she'd been going through them again and again like a child with a new toy. "That's correct. How is she safe? Where is she?"

Daufin stood up awkwardly. She touched her chest. "Here." Touched her head. "Somewhere else." Her fingers fluttered in a gesture of distance.

No one spoke. Jessie took a step forward; her little girl's face watched her, eyes shining. "Where?" Jessie asked. "Please . . . I've got to know."

"Not far. A safe place. Trust me?"

"How . . . can I?"

"I am not here to hurt." It was Stevie's voice, yes, but it

158

was whispery and ethereal as well, the sound of cool wind across reeds. "I chose this one . . . but not to hurt."

"Chose her?" Rhodes asked. "How?"

"I call-ed this one. This one answer-ed."

"How do you mean, 'called'?"

A hint of frustration passed over the face. "I . . ." She spent a few seconds finding the proper term. "I sang-ed."

Rhodes felt close to pissing in his pants. An alien in the skin of a little girl stood before him, and they were talking. My God! he thought. What secrets she must know! "I'm Colonel Matt Rhodes, United States Air Force." He heard his voice shake. "I want to welcome you to planet Earth." Inwardly he cringed; it was corny as hell, but it seemed like the right thing to say.

"Pla-net Earth," she repeated carefully. Blinked. "In-sane forms here, par-don my terms." She motioned toward the TV screen, where a baseball manager had his face right up in an umpire's and was giving him a royal chewing out. "Ques-tion: why are these beings so small?"

Tom realized what she meant. "No, those are just pic-tures. On TV. The pictures come through the air from a long way."

"From oth-er worlds?"

"No. This one. Just other places."

Her eyes seemed to pierce him. "Are not the pic-tures true?"

"Some of them are," Rhodes said. "Like that baseball game. Some of them are just . . . playacting. Do you know what that means?"

She thought. "Pre-tend. A false show."

"Right." It had dawned on Rhodes, and the others too, how strange everything must appear to Daufin. Television, taken for granted by humans, would merit explanation, but along the way you'd have to explain about electricity, satellite transmissions, TV studios, news broadcasts, sports, and actors; the subject could be talked about for days, and still Daufin would have more questions.

"Don't you have TV?" Ray asked. "Or somethin' like it?"

"No." Daufin studied him for a few seconds, then looked at Tom. She touched the air around her eyes. "What are these? In-stru-ments?"

"Glasses." Tom removed his and tapped the lenses. "They help you see."

"See. Glasses. Yes." She nodded, putting the concepts together. "Not all pre-sent can see?" She motioned to Rhodes and Jessie.

"We don't need glasses." Again, Rhodes realized that the idea of eyeglasses was a tricky subject involving magnification, the grinding of lenses, optometry, a discussion of visual sense—another day-long conversation. "Some people can see without them."

She frowned, her face briefly taking on the appearance of a nettled little old lady's. She understood absolutes, yet there seemed to be no absolutes here. Something was, and yet it was not. "This is a world of play-act-ing," she observed, and her attention drifted back to the TV set. "Base-ball game," she said, locating the term in her memory. "Play-ed with a bat and ball by two teams on a field with four bases ar-rang-ed in a di-a-mond."

"Hey!" Ray said excitedly. "They must have baseball in outer space!"

"She's reciting the definition from the dictionary," Rhodes told him. "She must have a memory like a sponge."

Daufin watched another pitch. She couldn't comprehend the purpose of this game, but it seemed to be a contest of angles and velocities based on the planet's physics. She lifted her right arm in imitation of the pitcher's, feeling the strange tug and weight of alien anatomy. What appeared to be a simple motion was more complex than it appeared, she decided. But the game's apparently mathematical basis interested her, and it would merit further thought.

Then she began to walk around the room, her hands occasionally touching the walls or other objects as if making sure they were real and not figments of playacting.

Jessie was still balanced on a thin wire, and to fall would be frighteningly easy. Watching a creature wearing Stevie's skin, hair, and face, strolling around the den as if on a

Sunday visit to a museum, battered feverishly at her mind. "How do I know my daughter's safe? Tell me!"

Daufin touched a framed photograph of the family that sat on a shelf. "Be-cause," she said, "I pro-tect."

"You protect her? How?"

"I pro-tect," Daufin repeated. "That is all to know." Her interest went to another picture, then she drifted out of the den and into the kitchen.

Rhodes followed her, but Jessie had had enough; she slumped into a chair, mentally exhausted and fighting off fresh tears. Tom stood by her, his hands rubbing her shoulders and trying to get his own mind straight, but Ray hurried after the colonel and Daufin.

The creature stood watching the cat-clock's eyes tick back and forth. Rhodes saw her smile, and she made a sound like a high, clear chime: laughter.

"I think we've got a lot to talk about," Rhodes said, his voice still shaky. "I guess there are quite a few things you'd like to know about us—our civilization, I mean. And of course we'll want to know all about yours. In a few hours we'll be taking a trip. You'll be going to—"

Daufin turned. Her smile was gone, the face serious again. "I de-sire your aid. I de-sire to ex-it this plan-et, poss-i-ble if soon. I shall need a . . ." She pondered her choice of words. "A ve-hi-cle ca-pa-ble of ex-it-ing this plan-et. Be arrang-ed, can it?"

"A vehicle? You mean . . . a spaceship?"

"Wow," Ray breathed, standing in the doorway.

"Space-ship?" The term was unfamiliar, did not register in her memory. "A ve-hi-cle ca-pa-ble of ex-it—"

"Yes, I know what you mean," Rhodes said. "An interstellar flight vehicle, like the one you came in on." Something occurred to him to ask her. "How did you get out of that vehicle before it crashed?"

"I . . ." Again, a pause to consider. "I e-ject-ed."

"In the black sphere?"

"My pod," she explained, with a note of resigned patience. "May I ex-pect to ex-it, when?"

Oh, great! Rhodes thought; he saw where this conversation was leading. "I'm sorry, but it won't be possible for you to exit . . . I mean, leave."

She didn't reply. Just stared holes through him.

"We don't have interstellar flight vehicles here. Not anywhere on our planet. The closest we've got is called a space shuttle, and that only orbits the planet before it has to come back."

"De-sire to ex-it," she repeated.

"There's no way. We don't have the technology for that kind of vehicle."

She blinked. "No . . . way?"

"None. I'm sorry."

Her expression changed in an instant; the face contorted with pain and dismay. "Cannot stay! Cannot stay!" she said emphatically. "Cannot stay!" She began to circle the room restlessly, her eyes wide and shocked, her steps halting. "Cannot! Cannot! Cannot!"

"We'll take care of you. We'll make you comfortable. Please, there's no reason to—"

"Cannot! Cannot! Cannot!" she repeated, shaking her head back and forth. Her hands twitched at her sides.

"Please, listen . . . we'll find a place for you to live. We'll—" Rhodes touched her shoulder, and saw her head swivel toward him and her eyes fierce as lasers. He had time to think: Oh, shit—

And then he was knocked back, skidding on his heels across the linoleum, a charge of energy pulsing up his arm, searing through his nerves, and making his muscles dance. His brain buzzed as the cells heated up, and he witnessed a nova explode behind his eyeballs. He went off his feet, crashed into the kitchen table, and scattered the contents of a bowl of fruit everywhere as the table broke beneath his weight. His eyelids fluttered, and his next conscious image was Tom Hammond bending over him.

"She knocked the shit out of him!" Ray was saying excitedly. "He just touched her, and he sailed across the room! Is he dead?"

"No, he's coming around." Tom glanced up at Jessie, who stood watching the creature. Daufin had frozen in the center of the room, mouth half open, eyes glazed, as if the entity had gone into suspended animation.

"Knocked him on his ass!" Ray babbled on. "Wiped him out!"

A stream of urine came from Stevie's body and ran down the legs to the linoleum.

"What *are* you?" Jessie shouted at the thing; it remained rock-steady, impassive.

"Gunny, I want you to get out to the crash site," Rhodes said, trying to sit up. His face was bleached of color, a thread of saliva dangling from his lower lip. Tom saw that his eyes were bloodshot. "I've got two daughters myself. A debriefing, I guess you'd call it. Chose her? How?" His brain was skipping tracks with violent speed. "I want to welcome you to planet Earth. We don't need glas—*huh?*" He shook himself like a wet dog, his muscles still bunching and writhing like worms under his flesh. The urge to vomit almost overcame him. "What is it? What happened?" He had a headache fit to break his skull, and his legs were twitching with a will of their own.

Jessie saw Daufin come back from wherever she'd been; the face grew expression again, one of urgent concern. "I hurt-ed. I hurt-ed." It was said fretfully, and in a human might have been accompanied by the wringing of hands. "Still friends? Yes?"

"Yeah," Rhodes said; a cocked grin hung to his face, which looked moist and a little swollen. "Still friends." He got to his knees and that was all he could do without Tom helping him up.

"Cannot stay," Daufin said. "Must ex-it this plan-et. Must have ve-hi-cle. I de-sire no hurt to come."

"No hurt to come?" Jessie had hold of her senses now. For better or worse, she had to trust this creature. "Come from where? You?"

"No. From . . ." She shook her head, not finding the proper terms. "If I can not ex-it, there will be great hurt-ing."

"How? Who'll be hurt?"

"Tom. Ray. Rhodes. Jes-sie. Ste-vie. All here." She

opened her arms in a motion that seemed to include the entire town. "Dau-fin too." She went to the kitchen window, reached up for the blind's cord as she'd seen Jessie do, and gave a tentative pull, then reeled the blinds up. She squinted, seemed to be scanning the reddening sky. "Soon the hurt-ing will start," she said. "If I cannot ex-it, you must. Go far a-way. Very far. Now." She released the cord, and the blinds clattered back with the sound of dry bones clacking.

"We . . . we can't," Jessie said, unnerved by Daufin's matter-of-fact warning. "We *live* here. We can't go."

"Then take me a-way. Now." She looked hopefully at Rhodes.

"We're going to. Like I said, after the crew finishes up at the crash site."

"Now," Daufin repeated forcefully. "If not now . . ." She trailed off, unable to put into words what she was trying to convey.

"I can't. Not until the helicopter gets back. My flying vehicle. Then we'll get you to the air-force base." He still felt like electricity was jumping through his nerves. Whatever had hit him, it was one hell of a concentrated energy bolt, probably a more powerful version of what she'd used to flip through the TV channels.

"It must be now!" Daufin had come close to shouting, her face streaked with red light from the blinds. "Do you not un-der-stand"—she struggled for a term, found what she needed—"Eng-lish?"

"I'm sorry. We can't leave here until my aide gets back."

Daufin trembled, with either anger or frustration. Jessie thought the creature was going to pitch a fit, just as any child—or elderly woman—might. But in the next second Daufin's face froze again, and then she stood motionlessly, one hand gripped into a fist at her side, the other outstretched toward the window. Five seconds passed. Ten. She did not move. Thirty seconds later, she was still in her statue trance.

And she stayed that way.

Maybe that was how she pitched a fit after all, Jessie

thought. Or maybe she'd just checked out to do some heavy thinking. In any case, it didn't appear she was coming back for a while.

"Can I touch her and see if she falls over?" Ray asked.

"Go to your room," Jessie said. "Right now. Stay there until you're called for."

"Come on, Mom! I was just foolin'! I wouldn't really—"

"Go to your room," Tom commanded, and Ray's protests ceased. The boy knew that when his father said for him to do something, he'd better do it in a hurry.

"Okay, okay. I don't guess we're going to be eatin' any dinner tonight, huh?" He picked up an apple and an orange from the floor and started for his room.

"Wash those before you eat them!" Jessie told him, and he dutifully went into the bathroom to run water over the fruit before he disappeared, an outcast sentenced to solitary.

Daufin, too, remained in solitary confinement.

"I think I need to sit down." Rhodes picked up a chair and eased into it. Even his spine felt bruised.

Tom approached the creature and slowly waved his hand in front of her face. The eyes did not blink. He detected the rise and fall of her chest, though, and he started to reach for her pulse, but he thought about Rhodes flying through the air and he checked his motion. She was still alive, of course, and Stevie's bodily functions seemed to be operating just fine. A light sheen of sweat glistened on the cheeks and forehead.

"What did she mean? That about the hurting?" Jessie asked.

"I don't know." Rhodes shook his head. "My ears are still ringing. She just about sent me through the damned wall."

Jessie had to cross in front of Daufin to reach the window; Daufin didn't budge. Jessie pulled the blinds up to peer at the sky. The sun was setting, and to the west the sky had become a blast-furnace scarlet. There were no clouds.

But a movement caught Jessie's eye. She saw them then, and counted their number: at least a dozen vultures, circling Inferno like dark banners. Probably searching for carrion in the desert, she figured. The things could smell impending death several miles off. She did not like the sight, and she let the blinds fall back into place. There was nothing to do now but wait—either for Daufin to return from her isolation, or for Gunniston to come back in the helicopter.

She gently touched her daughter's auburn hair. "Careful!" Tom warned. But there was no shock, no brain-jarring bolt of energy. Just the feel of hair she'd brushed a thousand times under her fingers. Daufin's—Stevie's—eyes stared sightlessly.

Jessie touched the cheek. Cool flesh. Put her index finger against the pulse in the throat. Slow—abnormally slow —but steady. She had no choice; she had to trust that somewhere, somehow, the real Stevie was alive and safe. To consider any other possibility would drive her crazy.

She decided then that she was going to be okay. Whatever happened, she and Tom would see it through. "Well," she said, and pulled her hand away from the pulse. "I'm going to make a pot of coffee." She was amazed she could sound so steady when her guts felt like Jell-O. "That suit everybody?"

"Make it strong, please," Rhodes requested. "The stronger the better."

"Right." And Jessie began to move about her kitchen with a purpose again as the frozen alien gestured toward the window and the cat-clock ticked off the seconds and the vultures silently gathered over Inferno.

18
New Girl in Town

Darkness began to claim the sky, and the sign on the First Texas Bank read 88°F. at 8:22.

Under the incandescents of the garage stall, Cody had finished his work for the day and was assembling tools to tune up his motorcycle. Mr. Mendoza would close the station around nine o'clock, and then Cody would be faced with his usual decision: to sleep at home and have to face the old man sometime during the night; to crash at the fortress, which was as rowdy as a fraternity house in hell and reeked of marijuana fumes; or sleep atop the Rocking Chair, not the most comfortable roost but surely the most peaceful of his choices.

He leaned over to pull some clean rags from a cardboard box and the little glass vial fell from his pocket, making a merry tinkling note as it hit the concrete. The vial didn't break, and Cody quickly picked it up, though Mr. Mendoza was in his office reading the newspaper and waiting for the Trailways bus to pull in.

Cody held the vial up and looked at the crystals. He'd tried cocaine once, on a dare from Bobby Clay Clemmons, and once was enough; he didn't like the shit, because he understood how people could get hooked on it and feel like they couldn't live without it. He'd seen several 'Gades go off the deep end because of it, like Tank's older brother Mitch, who four years ago had driven his Mustang onto the railroad tracks and crashed into an oncoming train at seventy miles an hour, killing not only himself but two girls and Mayor Brett's son. Cody didn't drink, either; the most he'd do is some low-powered zooming on a weed or two, but never when anybody's life depended on his decisions. It was chickenshit to let drugs do your thinking for you.

But he knew people who'd give their right arms for an inhale of what those crack crystals would put out. It would be an easy thing to go up to the fortress, cook them over a flame, and toke until his brains turned blue. But he knew they wouldn't help him see the world any clearer; they'd just make him think that Mack Cade was the only way out of Inferno and he ought to jump at the sound of the master's voice.

He set the vial down atop the worktable, pondering the crystals for a moment and what Mr. Mendoza had said about a man being responsible for his actions. Maybe that was tired old bullshit, and maybe there was truth to it too.

But he already knew what he'd decided.

He lifted his right hand. In it was a ballpeen hammer. He brought it down on the vial, shattering it to pieces and crushing the yellow crystals. Then he used his left hand to brush the mess off the table and into a garbage pail, where it sank amid greasy rags and empty oil cans.

Six hundred dollars a month was not the price of his soul.

Cody put aside the hammer and continued gathering the wrenches and sockets he needed for his Honda.

A horn rapped twice: deep bass hoots. The Trailways bus from Odessa. Cody didn't look up, just kept at his task, and Mr. Mendoza went out to speak to the driver, who was from a town near his own in central Mexico.

The passengers, most of them elderly people, filed off the bus to use the bathroom or the candy and soft-drink machines. But one of them was a young girl with a battered brown suitcase, and when she left the bus it was with finality; this was the end of her journey. She glanced over at the driver, saw him talking to a husky man with silver hair and a mustache. Then her gaze fell on the blond boy who was working in the garage stall, and she lugged the suitcase with her as she walked in his direction.

Cody had all the tools he needed, and the new spark plugs were laid out. He knelt down to start in when a girl's voice said, from behind him, "Excuse me."

"Bathroom's through the door in the office." He motioned with a nod of his head, used to being interrupted by the bus passengers.

"Gracias, but I need some directions."

He looked around at her, and instantly stood up and wiped the grease from his hands onto the front of his already-grimy shirt.

The girl was sixteen or maybe seventeen, with jet-black hair cut to her shoulders. Her tawny eyes, set in a high-cheekboned, oval face, made a thrill run along Cody's backbone. She stood about five-six, was slender, and, in Cody's lingo, a smash fox. Even if she *was* Mexican. Her skin was the color of coffee and cream, and she wore hardly any makeup except for some pale lip gloss. Her eyes surely didn't need any artificial help, Cody thought; they were soulful and steady, if a little red-rimmed from a long bus trip. She was wearing a red-checked blouse and khaki trousers, black sneakers, and a small silver chain and heart that lay in the hollow of her throat.

"Directions," Cody repeated. There seemed to be too much saliva in his mouth; he was afraid he might drool, and then what would this smash fox think of him? "Uh . . . sure." He imagined he must smell like a combination grease factory and barnyard. "Directions to where?"

"I'm looking for a house. Do you know where Rick Jurado lives?"

He felt as if a bucket of freezing water had been thrown into his face. "Uh . . . yeah, I do. Why?"

"He's my brother," the smash fox said.

And he answered, in a small voice, "Oh."

The blond boy didn't say anything else. She'd seen his eyes narrow slightly when she'd mentioned Rick's name. Why was that? A spark of light jumped from his skull earring. He was handsome in a rough kind of way, she decided. But he looked like trouble, and something deep in his eyes was dangerous too, something that might snap fast at you if you weren't careful. She had the sensation that he was taking her apart and then fitting her back together again, joint by joint. "Well?" she prodded. "How do I get there?"

"That way." He motioned south. "Across the bridge, in Bordertown. He lives on Second Street."

"Gracias." She knew the address from the letters he'd been sending. She began to walk away, carrying the suitcase that held all her belongings in the world.

Cody let her go a few paces, couldn't help but watch her tight rear end as she walked. Smash fox, he thought, even if she was Jurado's sister. Damn, what a panic! He hadn't even known Jurado had any brothers or sisters. Must take after their mother, he reasoned, because she sure doesn't look anything like that wetback bastard! He knew other good-looking girls, but he'd never seen such a fine Mexican fox before; it was just kind of an added kick that she was a Jurado. "Hey!" he called after her, and she stopped. "Kinda long walk from here."

"I don't mind."

"Maybe not, but it's rough over there too." He emerged from the stall, wiping the rest of the grease from his hands. "I mean, you never know what might happen."

"I can take care of myself." She started off again.

Right, he thought. Get yourself raped by some of those crazy fuckers too. He looked up, saw stars coming out. A dark red slash cut the western horizon, and a yellow full moon was on the rise. From the Inferno Baptist Church he heard wobbly piano chords and a few voices struggling for harmony at choir practice. Inferno's lights had come on: the red flicker of neon at the Brandin' Iron, the white lights around the roof of the bank building, the garish multicolored bulbs over Cade's used-car lot. Houses showed squares of yellow and the faint blue glows of TVs. The town had turned the power off at the apartment building, but the 'Gades had used money from their treasury to buy portable incandescents at the hardware store, and those illuminated the corridors. Cody saw a blue pulse of light and a spiral of sparks from the junkyard, and he knew the night work had begun, somebody cutting metal with a blowtorch.

He watched Jurado's sister striding away, just about to reach the limits of the gas station's lights. Looked as if the suitcase was going to win the battle of wills at any second. He smiled thinly as an idea crept into his thoughts. Jurado would scream so hard the grease would fly off his hair if he did what he was thinking. Why not do it? What did he have to lose? Besides, it would be fun. . . .

He decided. Got on the motorcycle and kickstarted the engine.

"Cody!" Mr. Mendoza called, from where he stood jawing with the bus driver. "Where're you goin'?"

"To do a good deed," he replied, and before the man could speak again Cody accelerated away. He swung the Honda in front of Jurado's sister just at the edge of the lights, and she looked at him with puzzlement that became a flash of anger. "Hop on," he offered.

"No, I'll walk." She sidestepped the Honda and kept on going, the suitcase tugging mightily at her arm.

He followed at her side, the engine putt-putting and Cody in the saddle but more or less walking the machine along. "I won't bite."

No answer. Her steps had gotten faster, but the suitcase was holding her back.

"I don't even know your name. Mine's Cody Lockett."

"You're bothering me."

"I'm tryin' to *help* you." At least she'd answered that time, which meant progress of a kind. "If you hold that suitcase between us and hang on, I'll get you across the bridge and to your brother's house in about two minutes."

She'd come this far alone, in a groaning bus with a man snoring noisily in a seat two rows behind her, and she knew she could make it the rest of the way. Besides, she didn't know this boy and she didn't accept rides with strangers. She glanced back, noting uneasily that there was no more light until she reached the protection of the glass orbs that illuminated the bridge. But the houses were close, and she didn't really feel in any danger. If he tried anything, she could either swing the suitcase at him or drop it and claw at his eyes.

"So what's your name?" he tried again.

"Jurado," she answered.

"Yeah, I know that. What's your first name?"

She hesitated. Then: "Miranda."

He repeated it. "That's a nice name. Come on, Miranda; hop on and I'll take you across the bridge."

"I said *no.*"

He shrugged. "Okay, then. Don't say I didn't warn you about the Mumbler." It came to him, just like that. "Good luck gettin' across the bridge." He revved the engine, as if about to speed away.

She took two more determined steps—and then her determination faltered. The suitcase had never felt so heavy. She stopped, put the suitcase down, and rubbed her shoulder.

"What's wrong?"

"Nothing."

"Oh. I thought somethin' was wrong from the way you stopped." He read it in her eyes. "Don't worry about the Mumbler. He's not usually creepin' around before eight-thirty."

She stuck her wrist in front of the Honda's headlight. "It's *after* eight-thirty," she said, looking at her watch.

"Oh. Yeah, so it is. Well, he's not real *active* before nine."

"Who exactly are you talking about?"

"The Mumbler." Think fast, he told himself. "You're not from around here, so you wouldn't know. The Mumbler's dug himself a cave somewhere along the Snake River; at least that's what the sheriff thinks. Anyway, the Mumbler comes out of his cave at night and hides under the bridge. Sheriff thinks he might be a big Indian guy, about six feet eight or so, who went crazy a few years back. He killed a bunch of people and"—think fast!—"and got acid thrown in his face. Sheriff's been tryin' to catch him, but the Mumbler's quick as a sidewinder. So that's why nobody crosses the bridge on foot after dark; the Mumbler might be underneath it. If you don't cross over real quick, the Mumbler's up on that bridge like greased smoke, and he takes you down with him. Just like that." He paused; she was still listening. "You'd do better if you ran across the bridge. 'Course, that suitcase looks mighty heavy. You set it down on the bridge, and he's likely to hear the thump. The trick is to get across before he knows you're there." He gazed for a moment at the bridge. "Looks longer than it is, really," he said.

She laughed. The boy's expression during the telling had gone from cool to mock sinister. "I'm not a dumb kid!" she said.

"It's the truth!" He held up his right hand. "Honest Injun!"

Which made her laugh again. He realized he liked the sound of her laughter: it was clean, like what Cody envisioned the sound of a mountain stream over smooth stones must be like, someplace where snow made everything white and new.

Miranda hefted her suitcase again. Her shoulder protested. "I've heard some tall tales before, but that one wears elevator boots!"

"Well, go on, then." He feigned exasperation. "But don't stop once you start across. Just keep goin', no matter what you hear or see."

She regarded the bridge. Not much to look at, just gray concrete and pools of light and shadow. One of the glass globes had burned out, so there was a larger shadow pool about ten feet from the far side. She found herself thinking that if there really *was* a Mumbler, that would be the place he might strike. She hadn't come all the way from Fort Worth, changing buses in Abilene and again in Odessa, to get killed by a big scar-faced Indian. No, it was a made-up story, just to get her scared! Wasn't it?

"Full moon," Cody said. "He likes full moons."

"If you touch one place you're not supposed to," she told him, "I'll knock you cross-eyed." She held the suitcase upright, close to her chest, and sat behind Cody.

Bingo! he thought. "Grab my sides." She took his dirty shirt between tentative fingers. "We're gonna give it some gas to clear the bridge before the Mumbler knows we're there. Hold tight!" he warned—and then he let the engine rev until it howled. He kicked it into first gear.

The motorcycle shuddered and reared back, and for an instant Cody felt his heart leap into his throat and he thought the extra weight was going to tip them over. He leaned forward, fighting gravity. Miranda clenched her teeth on a scream. But then the Honda was shooting along Republica Road, the front end bounced down and burned rubber, and they were heading toward the bridge with the wind in their faces.

Miranda's hands gripped into his sides, about to claw the meat from his ribs.

They shot onto the bridge, cocooned in a roar. The bridge's ornate lampposts with their smoked-glass globes flashed past. Here came the biggest pool of shadow; it seemed as large as a tarpit to Miranda.

And then Cody had a wild hair. He just *had* to do it.

He yelled, *"There's the Mumbler!"* and jerked the Honda into the left lane as if to escape something slithering over the bridge's right side.

She shrieked. Her arms clutched at his chest, the suitcase pinned between them and about to blow the breath out of both of them. Her hair was flying around her shoulders, and for a gut-wrenching second she imagined something had plucked at it with an oozy hand, trying to tear her right off the cycle. Her shriek kept spilling out, her eyes about to jump from their sockets—but suddenly the shriek reached its limit and gurgled into laughter, because she knew there was no Mumbler and there never had been, but they were through the shadow and off the bridge and now Cody was cutting his speed on the streets of Bordertown.

She couldn't stop laughing, though she didn't know this boy—this gringo—and didn't trust his hands not to wander down to her legs. But they did not. She loosened her grip on his sides, holding on to his shirt again, and Cody relaxed because she'd just about pinched hunks of skin off him. He laughed with her, but his eyes were wary and flicking from side to side. He had entered the kingdom of the Rattlesnakes, and he had to watch his ass. But at least for the moment, he figured he sure had a pretty insurance policy perched behind him.

Cody swerved onto Second Street, avoided a couple of roaming dogs, and powered toward Jurado's house.

19
One Night

While Cody had been spinning his yarn about the Mumbler, Ray Hammond stared from the window of his room and let himself think what might happen if he was to go AWOL.

I'd get my butt beat, that's what, he decided. And I'd deserve it too.

But still . . .

He'd been in his room for about two hours, had plugged the headphones into his boom box and listened to Billy Idol, Clash, Joan Jett, and Human League tapes while he worked on a plastic model of a SuperBlitzer Go-Bot. His mother had come in about twenty minutes ago, bringing him a ham sandwich, some potato chips, and a Pepsi, and had told him that Daufin was still motionless in the kitchen. It was best that he stay here, out of the way, until the air-force men took the creature away, she'd said—and Ray had seen how that idea tore his mother up inside, but what was her choice? The thing in the kitchen was no longer Stevie; that was a bone-dry fact.

Thinking about his sister being gone, while her body stood in the kitchen, was a weird trip. Ray had always thought of Stevie as a little monkey, getting into his tape collection, his models, even once almost finding the cache of *Penthouse* magazines at the back of his closet, but of course he loved the brat; she'd been around for six years, and now . . .

And now, he thought, she was gone but her body remained. But what had Daufin meant about Stevie being protected? Was Stevie gone forever, or not? Weird, weird trip.

From his window he could see a blue neon sign farther down Celeste Street, between the Boots 'n Plenty shoestore and the Ringwald Drugstore; the sign read WARP ROOM. That was where everybody would be hanging out tonight, playing the arcade games and buzzing about the helicopter landing in Preston Park. They'd be cooking up rumors right and left, really throwing the tales around, and the place would be full of smash foxes. And of everybody there—all the 'Gades and jocks and party animals—only he would know the truth.

Right, he told himself. My sister got dusted today, and I'm thinking about girls. X Ray, you're the king turd, man.

But his mother had said something to him about twenty minutes ago that he heard a lot: *Stay out of the way.*

That seemed to be his middle name. Ray *Stay out of the way* Hammond. If it wasn't the older guys saying it to him at school, it was his own folks. Even Paco LeGrande, today, had been telling him to stay out of the way. Ray knew he was a zero with girls and not too sharp on looks, his talent in sports was nonexistent, and all anybody like him could do was stay out of the way.

"Dammit," he said, very softly. The Warp Room beckoned him. But he was supposed to stay here, and he knew for sure that Colonel Rhodes didn't want him going outside and telling everybody that an alien had come to visit Inferno. Forget it, he thought. Just stay here, out of the way.

But for one night—one night—he could stroll into the Warp Room and *be* somebody, even if he didn't tell a soul.

Before he knew what his fingers were doing, he unhooked the window's latch.

Going AWOL was a serious offense, he thought. Like Dad-would-blow-his-top kind of offense. Indefinite-grounding offense.

One night.

He pushed the window up about three inches; it made a faint skreeking noise.

Still can change your mind, he told himself. But he figured his folks wouldn't check in with him for a while; he could go to the Warp Room and come back before they ever knew he was gone.

He pushed the window up another few inches.

"Ray?" A knock at his door, and his father's voice.

He froze. He knew his dad wouldn't come in without being invited. "Yes sir?"

"You all right?"

"Yes sir."

"Listen . . . sorry I jumped you. It's just, you know, that this is kind of a trying time for everybody. We don't know what Daufin's doing, and . . . we want Stevie back, if that's possible. Maybe it's not. But we can hope, huh?" Tom paused, and in that pause Ray almost slid the window back down, but the Warp Room's blue neon burned in his eyeglasses. "You want to come out? I think it'd be okay."

"I'm . . ." Oh, Lord, he thought. "I'm . . . just gonna listen to some music, Dad. On my headphones. I'll just stay in here, out of the way."

There was a silence. Then: "Sure you're all right?"

"Yes sir. I'm sure."

"Okay. Well, come on out when you want." Ray heard his father's footsteps, moving along the corridor to the den. Murmured voices, Dad and Mom talking.

It was time to go, if he was going. He slid the window all the way up, climbed out with his heart pounding a fugitive rhythm; he slid the window down when he was out, and he ran along Celeste Street toward the Warp Room. If there was one thing he could do well, it was run.

But he found the Warp Room not nearly as crowded as he'd expected; in fact, only six or seven kids were inside, milling around the pinball machines. The Warp Room's walls were painted deep violet, with sparkly stars dashed here and there. Day-Glo painted planets dangled on wires from the ceiling, being stirred into small orbits by the fans. Arcade machines—Galaxian, Neutron, Space Hunter, Gunfighter, and about ten more—stood bleeping and burping for attention. Every so often the speaker atop the Space Hunter machine boomed out a metallic challenge: "Attention, Earthlings! Do you dare do battle with Space Hunter? Prepare for action! Prepare to be destroyed!"

At the back of the place, its manager—an elderly man named Kennishaw—sat on a folding metal chair reading a copy of *Texas Outdoorsman* magazine. A change-making machine stood next to him, and on the wall was a sign demanding NO CURSING, NO BETTING, NO FIGHTING.

"X Ray! How's it hangin', man?"

Ray saw Robby Falkner standing with Mike Ledbetter over by the Galaxian machine. Both of them were freshmen, and both of them were Nerd Club members in good standing. "Yo, Ray!" Mike called, in a voice that hadn't yet lost its childhood squeak. Ray walked to them, glad to see anybody he knew. He noted a 'Gade standing near the back, playing pinball; the boy's name was Stoplight, because his hair was dyed red on top and green on the sides.

"How's it goin'?" Robby gave Ray a high five while Mike concentrated on beating a few more points out of Galaxian.

"Okay. How about you?"

"I'll do. Man, that was neat about the chopper, huh? I saw it take off. Man, that was neat!"

"I saw it too," Mike commented. "Know what I heard? It wasn't any meteor that fell, no way! It was a satellite the Russians put up. One of those death satellites, and that's why it's radioactive."

"Yeah, well you know what Billy Thellman heard?" Robby leaned in closer, gathering the other boys together to share a secret. "It wasn't any meteor *or* a satellite."

"So what was it?" Ray kept his voice cool.

"It was a jet. A super-secret jet that crashed. Billy Thellman said he knew somebody who drove out there to see it, only the air-force men have got Cobre Road blocked off. So this guy started out on foot, and he walked and walked until he came across this crane scoopin' pieces of somethin' off the ground, and all these men in radiation suits. Anyway, they stopped this guy out there and they took his name and address and they got his fingerprints on a little white card too. They said they could take him to jail for sneakin' around out there."

"Gnarly," Mike said.

"Right. So they asked him what he'd seen, and he told 'em, and that's when they let him in on the secret. Billy says he heard it was an F-911, and that was the only one the air force had."

"Wow," Ray said.

"Man, look at *her!*" Mike whispered, furtively motioning to a lean blond girl who hung on the shoulder of a boy playing Gunfighter. "That's Laurie Rainey. Man, I hear she can just about suck the chrome off a fender!"

"Smash fox," Robby observed. "She's got skinny legs, though."

"Man, you wouldn't think they were skinny if they were wrapped around your ass! Shit!" Mike thumped the Galaxian machine with his fist, because the game had ended and he hadn't beat his best score. Old Eagle Eyes Kennishaw saw it, and hollered, "Hey, boy! Don't you hit on the machines!" His ire vented, he returned to his magazine.

The three boys drifted past Laurie Rainey for a closer look, and were rewarded with a whiff of her perfume. She was holding on to her date's belt, which Mike pointed out in a whisper was a sure sign that a girl was hotter than a short-fused firecracker.

"How come you're so quiet?" Robby asked Ray when they'd wandered over to the row of pinball machines.

"Me? I'm not quiet."

"Are so. Man, you're usually jawin' up a storm. Folks on your case?"

"No."

"So what it is, then?" Robby leaned against a machine and cleaned his fingernails with a match.

"Nothin'. I'm just quiet, that's all." It burned in him, but he knew he must not spill it.

Mike jabbed him in the ribs. "I think 'ou're hidin' somethin', cockhead."

"No, I'm not. Really." Ray dug his hands into his pockets and stared at a spot on the discolored linoleum. That crap about an F-911 had almost brought a laugh out, and he struggled not to smile. "Forget it."

"Forget *what?*" Robby asked, fired up by the idea that a secret was being kept. "Come on, X Ray! Let's hear it!"

It was so close to being told. In one more minute, he might be the most sought-after kid in Inferno. All kinds of smash foxes would be crowding around to hear. But no, he couldn't do it! It wasn't right! Still, his mouth was starting to open, and what would come out of it he didn't know. He was forming the words in his mind: *Let's just say I know it wasn't any damned F-9—*

"Looky here, looky here! Where's your girlfriend, fuckmeat?"

Ray knew that slurred, dark-toned voice. He whirled toward the doorway.

Three of them were standing there: Paco LeGrande, a plastic splint along the bridge of his nose and bandages stuck to his cheeks and forehead to secure it; Ruben Hermosa, grinning and damp-faced, his eyes bloodshot on weed; and Juan Diegas, another husky Rattlesnake.

Paco limped just a little as he took two steps forward, his combat boots clunking on the floor. All conversations within the Warp Room had ceased, all attention riveted to the invaders. "I asked you where your girlfriend was," Paco repeated, smiling thinly, his face swollen and purple circles ringing his eyes. He cracked his knuckles. "She's not around to save your skinny ass, is she?"

"Attention, Earthlings!" the Star Hunter's speaker boomed. "Do you dare do battle with Star Hunter? Prepare for action! Prepare to be destroyed!"

"Oh, shit," Mike Ledbetter whispered, and quickly backpedaled from Ray's side. Robby stood his ground a few seconds longer before he, too, abandoned Ray to his fate.

"You'd better get out, man!" It was Stoplight. "You're on 'Gade territory!"

"Was I talkin' to you? Shut your hole, you fuckin' freak!"

Stoplight wasn't nearly as big as the boys who blocked the door, and he knew he had no chance against them. "We don't want any trou—"

"Shut up!" Juan Diegas roared. "Your ass is *mine,* fucker!"

Kennishaw was on his feet. "Listen here! I won't have that kind of language in—"

With one quick, enraged motion, Paco turned and grasped a pinball machine. Muscles twitched in his forearms, and he threw the entire thing over on its side. Tilt bells rang madly, glass shattered, and sparks shot from the machine's innards.

The other kids trembled like live wires in a high wind. Kennishaw's face reddened, and he reached for the pay phone on the wall, his hand digging for a quarter.

"You want to keep that hand, you sonofabitch?" Paco asked him—not loudly, just matter-of-factly. Kennishaw saw the fury in the boy's eyes, and fear lanced him; he blinked, his mouth working but making no noise. The red cast of his face was fading to gray. He pulled his hand out of his pocket, quarterless.

"Muchas gracias." Paco sneered. His gaze jerked back to Ray Hammond. "You had a real good laugh at me today, didn't you?"

Ray shook his head. Paco's eyes were inflamed, and Ray knew all three Rattlers had to be in the stratosphere on maryjane or they wouldn't have dared come to the Warp Room.

"You callin' me a liar, you li'l fruit?" Two more strides, and Paco was within strike range.

"No."

Juan and Ruben laughed. Ruben leapt up, grabbed a

papier-mâché model of Saturn and yanked it off its wire. Juan slammed into the Aqua Marines machine like a mad bull and crashed it to the floor.

"Please . . . don't . . ." Kennishaw begged, plastered against the wall like a butterfly.

"I say you are," Paco prodded. "I say I heard you laughin' at me, and now you're callin' me a liar."

If his heart beat any harder, Ray figured he was going to sound like a human drum. He almost retreated from Paco, but what was the point? There was nowhere to run. He had to stand and deal with it, and hope that some 'Gades would walk through the door real soon.

"Nobody wants to fight, man!" Stoplight said. "Why don't you take off?"

Paco grinned. "*I* want to fight." And there was a crash and sizzle of sparks as Juan threw over another machine. Paco stared fixedly at Ray. "I told you, didn't I? I told you to stay out of my way."

Ray swallowed. Laurie Rainey was watching, and Robby, and Mike, and all the others. He knew he was about to be beaten; that was a fact. But there were worse things, and one of them was cringing. He felt a tight grin ripple across his mouth, saw that it puzzled even Paco for a second. Ray stepped forward to meet him, and said, "Fuck *you.*"

The blow was so fast he didn't even see it coming. It hit him in the jaw, lifted him off his feet, and knocked him into the Neutron machine. He went down on his knees, his glasses hanging from one ear and the taste of blood in his mouth. Paco's fist closed on his shirt, began to reel him to his feet.

Stoplight ran for the door, but Juan Diegas was quick; he aimed a kick that hit Stoplight in the shoulder and brought a yell of pain from him. Stoplight fell, and at once Juan was on him, flailing with his fists.

Ray saw Paco's leering face above him. He raised his fist to strike that face, but his arm was caught and pinned. Behind Paco, Ruben was leaping up, whooping with glee every time he plucked a planet off its wire.

Paco's fist lifted. It looked giant-sized, the knuckles scarred and rough.

Ray thrashed to escape, balanced on the toes of his sneakers. He could find no traction.

The fist reared back, hesitated—then whammed forward.

His mouth bleeding, Ray skidded backward under a pinball machine.

20
Wreckage

"Safe and sound," Cody said as he pulled the cycle to the curb in front of Rick Jurado's house. Miranda got off clutching her suitcase, her hair wild and windblown.

"Anybody ever tell you you drive too fast?"

"Nope." He glanced around; no Rattlers on the street, not yet at least. The sound of hammers rang from Cade's junkyard.

"Well, I'm telling you. You could've gotten us killed."

"You can get killed by breathin' around here," he answered. "Better get on inside." He nodded toward the house; the yellow porch light was on. In the air he could smell onions and beans. "I'll wait till you make it in."

"You don't have to."

"No sweat," he said, but he was sweating under his arms.

"Thanks for the ride. And for saving me from the Mumbler too." She smiled faintly, then started for the house.

"Anytime." Cody revved the engine, watching as she climbed the steps and knocked at the door. She was okay, he decided. Too bad that . . . well, just too bad.

The door opened. Cody saw Rick Jurado's face in the yellow light. "Brought you a present, Ricky!" he shouted. and as Rick stared, bewildered and shocked, Cody spun the

Honda around in a tight circle and rocketed away along Second Street.

"Damned crazy fool!" Rick raged, in Spanish—and then he looked at the girl who stood at his front door with a suitcase in her hand.

"Hi," she said.

He answered, "Hi," not recognizing her; but in the next second the bottom dropped out of his composure. The last picture she'd sent him had been over two years ago, and in those two years she had changed from a little girl to a woman. *Miranda?*

Her suitcase thumped to the porch's boards, and she reached for her brother. He put his arms around her, lifted her off her feet, and squeezed; he heard her make a small sob, and his eyes were burning too. "Miranda . . . Miranda, I can't believe this! How'd you get here? I just can't—" And then it hit him: Cody Lockett, with his sister. He almost dropped her, and as he set her down his eyes had gone maniacal. "What were you doin' with Lockett?"

"Nothing. He just gave me a ride."

"Did he touch you? I swear to God, if he touched you—"

"No, no!" His expression was scaring her. It was not the face of the gentle brother who wrote her letters with a graceful, precise hand. "He didn't do anything except bring me from the bus stop!"

"You stay away from him! He's trash! You understand?"

"No, I don't!" But she did, in that moment; she saw Rick's metal-studded bracelets—the macho fashion of many of the boys who ran with the gangs in Fort Worth —and she remembered how Cody had reacted when she'd mentioned Rick's name. Bad blood, she thought. "It's all right. I'm fine."

He was trembling with anger. How *dare* that bastard touch Miranda! It was yet another score that must be settled. But he forced the rage off his face and coiled it up inside, to wait. "I'm sorry. I didn't mean to get hot. Come inside!" He picked up her suitcase and took her hand. Once inside the house, he closed and bolted the door. "Sit down, please!" He started bustling around, trying to straighten up the dusty room.

"Where's Paloma?"

"Sleeping." His street inflections were gone. He brushed off the sofa's pillows and plumped them up. "I'll go wake her—"

"No, not yet. First I have to talk to you alone."

He frowned. That sounded serious. "What is it?"

Miranda walked across the room to Paloma's shelf of ceramic birds. She picked up a cardinal and ran her fingers over its wings. "I'm not going back to Fort Worth," she said finally. "Not ever."

"Bash him!" Ruben shouted merrily. "Bash the li'l fucker!"

Paco had hold of Ray's ankles and was trying to pull him out from underneath the pinball machine, but Ray grasped one of its legs and wasn't about to let go. His glasses had spun away, and blood drooled from his mouth. Still, his mind was clear; he thought he knew what it must be like to be a wounded animal set upon by vultures.

Robby Falkner screwed up his guts and charged, but Paco whirled upon him and smashed him in the face—one, two, three quick blows. Robby's nose burst open, and the boy gave a small weak cry as he fell.

On the floor Stoplight scrabbled away from Juan Diegas, who began to attack the arcade machines again. "Stop it! Please stop it!" Kennishaw hollered, crouching in a corner. Stoplight saw the open door in front of him and, one eye swollen shut and a gash across his cheek from a signet ring, he got up and ran onto the street. Behind him, Juan roared, "Wreckage!" and threw over the Gunfighter machine, which shot blue sparks and began to vomit forth its quarters.

Stoplight kept going past the sheriff's office. This was Renegade business, and he knew exactly what to do.

"It's her, isn't it?" Rick's eyes were black and fierce. "What's she done to you?"

"It's not that. I just had to get—"

He took her right hand. The palm was dry and cracked, the fingernails broken—she had the hands of a laborer instead of a Fort Worth high school junior. "I see," he said tautly. "She's had you scrubbing floors."

Miranda shrugged. "I did some work for a few people, after school. It wasn't much. Just sweeping, washing dishes, and—"

"Carting some fat gringo's garbage to the street?"

"It was a job." She pulled her hand away from his. "It wasn't her idea. It was mine."

"Yeah." Rick smiled bitterly. "And there you were being a maid while *she* sat around waiting for her pimp to call, huh?"

"Stop." Her gaze met his. "Just stop. You don't know, so you can't say."

"I *do* know! Hell, I read your letters! I kept them all! Maybe you never spelled it out, but I can read between the lines pretty good! She's a worthless *puta,* and I don't know why you stayed with her this long!"

Miranda was silent. She returned the cardinal to its place on the shelf. "No one's worthless. That's why I stayed."

"Yeah, well thank Mother Mary you got away before she could turn you into a whore too!"

She pressed a finger to his lips. "Please," she implored. "Let's talk nice, all right?"

He kissed her finger, but his eyes remained brooding.

"Look what I still have!" Miranda went to her suitcase, unlatched it, and dug through clothes until she found a many-times-folded piece of paper. She began carefully unfolding it, and Rick saw where it had been taped at the seams to keep it from falling apart. He knew what it was, but he let her open it and display it to him. "See? It looks almost new."

On the paper was a self-portrait, done in pastel crayons about three years ago. His face—a lot younger then, he thought—was drawn with thick and aggressive lines, lots of black shadow, and red highlights. It looked damned amateurish to him now. He'd done it in about an hour or so, while staring into a mirror in his room.

"Do you still draw?" Miranda asked him.

"A little." In his room, in a box under the bed, were dozens of pastel studies, most of them on lined notebook paper, of Bordertown, the desert, Rocking Chair Ridge, and the face of his grandmother. But it was a private thing he did, and no one but Miranda and Paloma knew about it. He refused to put any of his drawings up in the house for fear that the other Rattlers might see.

"You should do something with your talent," Miranda persisted. "You should go to art school or—"

"No more school. Tomorrow's my last day, and then I'm through."

"What are you going to do, then?"

"I've already got a good job, at the hardware store." He hadn't mentioned in any of his letters that he was a lowly stockboy. "I'm . . . uh . . . in inventory control. I figure maybe I can start painting houses on weekends. A fast house painter can make a lot of money."

"You can do better than that, and you know it. This says you can." She held up the self-portrait.

"No more school," he said firmly.

"Mama always said you were—" She stopped, knowing she was treading near a minefield, and then continued: "As hard to move as a mule train."

"She was right. For once." He watched as Miranda gently refolded the drawing and put it away. "So what happened?" he asked her, and waited to hear the whole story, even though he knew it was going to tear him apart.

"Cody! Cody!"

He looked up from putting the tools away in the garage stall. Stoplight was staggering toward him, nearly falling, his face a mask of blood. "They're killin' him, Cody!" Stoplight said, struggling for breath. He bent over, about to puke, and drops of blood spattered on the concrete. "Mr. Hammond's kid. X Ray. The Rattlers. They're at the Warp Room, and they're killin' him, man!"

"How many?" Ice water had flooded his veins, but a hard hot pulse beat in his skull.

"I don't know." He thought his brains must be knocked loose. "Five or six. Seven, maybe." Mendoza had been counting money from the register, and now he came out and saw the boy's bloody face; he stopped short, his mouth gaping.

Cody had no hesitation. He reached for the wall and lifted off a leather tool belt that held an array of wrenches, drawing it tight around his waist and buckling it. "Go find Tank, Bobby Clay, Davy, anybody and everybody you can. Move it!" Stoplight nodded, mustered his strength, and ran away, an obedient soldier. At once Cody was astride his motorcycle, and Mendoza's cry of "Cody! Wait!" was drowned out by the engine firing. Cody sped off into the darkness.

"Dammit!" Mendoza ran for the telephone in his office and hurriedly dialed the sheriff. One of the night deputies, Leland Teal, answered and Mendoza started telling him there was going to be a gang fight but Teal spent precious seconds fumbling for a pencil and paper to take down the information.

Cody skidded to a stop in front of the Warp Room. His insides cold and his eyes aflame, he strode through the doorway and saw the carnage.

Arcade machines had been overturned, spitting sparks across the floor. Ruben Hermosa was kicking the glass out of one of them, and from the back old Kennishaw was in a corner moaning "No . . . please . . . no . . ." Juan Diegas had hold of some kid—Robby Falkner, Cody thought it was—and was methodically rubbing the boy's face on the floor, leaving bloody streaks. Other kids cringed at the rear of the Warp Room.

And there was Paco LeGrande, splinted nose and all, kicking at Ray Hammond, who had curled up under a pinball machine and was desperately trying to protect his testicles. Cody heard the breath hiss between X Ray's teeth as one of those big combat boots struck his shoulder, and Cody said, "That's enough."

Paco stopped kicking, turned and grinned. Ruben Hermosa ceased his destruction, and Juan Diegas released Robby Falkner, who lay sobbing.

"Hey, man!" Paco said, and showed his palms. "We're jus' havin' us a li'l party."

"Party's over," Cody told him. He glanced quickly around. Only three Rattlers; what was that shit about five of them being here? Well, maybe LeGrande and Diegas made two apiece.

"I think the party's jus' startin'," Paco replied; his grin froze into a rictus, and he began striding forward, his boots clumping, his body getting ready to launch itself at Lockett.

Cody let him come on, and didn't move.

But when Paco was almost upon him, Cody's hand blurred to his tool belt. It came away with a wrench, and he flung it before Paco could register what was going to happen.

The wrench hit Paco's collarbone with a solid crunch. Paco yelled in pain and staggered back into Ruben, his face contorted even further. The wrench clattered to the floor.

Juan Diegas charged, was too fast for Cody to dodge. The Rattler hit him, head to belly, knocked the air from his lungs, and lifted him off his feet. He crashed into the Commando machine, and Juan pummeled wildly at his ribs. Cody jabbed an uppercut at Juan's chin, only grazed it, hooked his fingers into the Rattler's eyes, and twisted. This time Juan screamed and backpedaled, madly rubbing his scratched eyeballs. Cody wasted no time; he took a step forward, planted himself, and kicked Juan in the stomach. The other boy wheezed and went down.

Ruben Hermosa swung at Cody, caught him in the jaw, and rocked him back. Another blow grazed Cody's forehead. He lifted his arms, warded off a third punch, gripped Ruben's T-shirt, and slammed his fist into the boy's face; it was an instinct shot, and hit Ruben smack in the nose. Blowing blood, Ruben tried to retreat but Cody was all over him, hitting him in the face with pistonlike blows. Ruben staggered, his knees buckled—and then Paco leapt over the Solar Fortress machine and hit Cody with a bodyblock that knocked him sprawling.

Ruben scurried for the door on his hands and knees. Once outside, he got up and ran for Bordertown.

Cody had blood in his mouth, and his vision was hazed. He could hear the big boots coming, and he thought, Get up or you're buzzard bait! He tried to stand, but he knew he was too late. One of Paco's boots hit him under the right arm, sending jolts of pain shooting through his ribs. "Stomp him!" he heard Juan shout. Cody twisted, and the next kick caught his shoulder. His vision was clearing but his legs wouldn't move fast enough. He looked up, saw Paco towering over him and another kick about to be delivered. He had the mental image of it hitting his chin, knocking his head back, and snapping his neck like a chicken's. He had to move, and *quick*.

But before he could, a figure leapt upon Paco LeGrande's back and knocked the Rattler off balance. The kick never came. Cody saw X Ray's bleeding face—and the little sonofabitch was snarling.

Paco shouted with rage and reached back to tear X Ray off—but the smaller boy grabbed Paco's nose splint and gave it a mighty yank.

"I love her." Miranda's voice was quiet, her hands folded before her as she sat on the sofa. "But I couldn't stay with her anymore. I couldn't stand it."

Rick waited without pressing her, because he knew there was more and it had to come out.

"It got worse with the men," Miranda went on. "She started bringing them to the apartment. Those apartments . . . they have such thin walls." She picked at a broken fingernail, unable to look at her brother. "She met this guy. He wanted her to go to California with him. She said he"—a tortured smile flickered across her mouth—"made her feel pretty. And do you know what else she said?" She forced herself to meet his solemn gaze. He was waiting to hear it. "She said . . . we could make a lot of money in California. The both of us. She said that now I was old enough to start making some real money."

Rick sat without moving, his eyes deep ebony and his face like chiseled stone, but inside he was writhing. Their mother had left him here with Paloma when he was five years old and taken three-year-old Miranda with her; their father had abandoned them just after Miranda was born. Where Esteban Jurado was, Rick didn't know, nor did he particularly care, but over the years his mother had written him and Paloma chatty letters about her "modeling" career. There always seemed to be a big break on the horizon that never materialized, and gradually the letters were written more and more by Miranda. Rick had gotten very good at reading between the lines.

"I know what you're thinking, but you're wrong," Miranda said. "She was giving me a choice. I could either leave, or go to California with her. But I don't believe she really wanted me to. I believe she wanted me to pack my bag and go to the bus station and buy a ticket to Inferno, just like I did. That's what I believe." Her expression was as firm as his, but the glitter of tears had begun to show. "Please, Rick . . . please don't try to make me think that isn't true."

"Ricardo?" Paloma's voice drifted from the hallway. Before he could get up to help her, Paloma walked into the room, dressed in her cotton nightgown and her white hair disarrayed from sleep. "I heard you talking to someone."

"Grandmother," Miranda said—and Paloma abruptly halted, angling her head toward the dimly seen figure who stood up from the sofa.

"Who . . ."

"It's me, Grandmother." The girl approached her, gently took one of her thin, age-spotted hands. "It's—"

"Miranda," the old woman whispered. "Oh . . . Miranda . . . my little Miranda!" She touched the girl's hand, ran trembling fingers over Miranda's features. "All grown up!" The last time she'd seen the child was as a three-year-old,

being carried north in a Trailways bus. "Oh! So lovely! So lovely!" Miranda began to cry, tears of joy this time, and hugged her grandmother. And what Paloma would never tell either Miranda or Rick was that she'd been standing in the hallway for a long while, and had heard everything.

"*Guerra! Guerra!*" someone was shouting out in the street. Dogs started barking like crazy.

"What's that?" Paloma asked sharply. The shout kept coming: "*Guerra! Guerra!*" They all knew what it meant: gang war.

Rick had a knot in his throat; he turned away from his grandmother and sister and ran out to the porch. Ruben Hermosa was standing in the middle of Second Street, his T-shirt splattered with blood and his jeans wet and muddy from crossing the Snake River's putrid ditch. He was hollering at the top of his voice, and Rick saw Zarra come out of his house, and then Joey Garracone from his house up the street, followed by Ramon Torrez from next door. Other Rattlers were responding, and dogs barked frantically and raced across the yards, raising whirlwinds of dust.

Rick sprinted down the steps. "Shut up!" he yelled, and Ruben did. "What are you babblin' about, man?"

"The 'Gades!" Ruben said, his nose oozing blood. "At the Warp Room, man!" He clutched at Rick's shirt. "An ambush . . . Lockett hit Paco with a hammer . . . Juan got his eyes clawed, man. Oh Jesus . . . my nose got busted."

"Talk sense!" Rick gripped his arm, because the boy looked as if he were about to keel over. "What's goin' on? What were you doin' across the bridge?"

Pequin came running up, gleefully shouting "*Guerra!*" in imitation of the voice that had roused him onto the street.

"*Shut up!*" Rick commanded, right in his face, and Pequin's eyes flared with indignant anger but he obeyed.

"Jus' fuckin' around . . . not tryin' to hurt nobody," Ruben explained. "Jus' went over there for a kick, that's all. They jumped us." He looked around at the other Rattlesnakes. "They're killin' Paco and Juan! Right now!" He felt his wits get away from him like wild horses. "Maybe six or seven 'Gades, maybe more . . . it happened so fast."

"War!" Pequin shouted. "We're gonna stomp some 'Gade asses!"

"I said shut up!" Rick grasped Pequin's collar, but the smaller boy jerked away and ran toward Third Street, hollering his war chant to alert the Rattlers who lived over there. "Somebody stop him!" Rick demanded, but Pequin was drunk with the smell of violence and running like the wind.

"We've gotta get Paco and Juan out of there, Rick," Zarra said; his bullwhip was coiled and ready around his arm. "We've gotta save our brothers, man."

"Wait a minute. Let me think." But he couldn't think. His blood was on fire, and Pequin's shrill cry penetrated the walls of every house in Bordertown. There was no time to reason this thing out, because here came J. J. Melendez and Freddie Concepcion, followed by Diego Montana, Tina Mulapes, and a big red-haired girl everybody knew as "Animal."

"Those fuckers are gonna kill our bloods!" Sonny Crowfield had appeared, his face sweating and stained by the yellow porch light. "You gonna go over there or not, Jurado?" he challenged, and Rick saw that he gripped a length of lead pipe in his hand and his eyes were hungry for a fight.

Rick had to decide, and the decision was clear. The words came out: "We go."

As the others whooped and shouted, Rick looked at Paloma and Miranda, standing together on the porch. He saw his grandmother say *No* but he couldn't hear her voice for all the noise, and maybe that was best. Miranda wasn't sure what was happening, but she saw chains and baseball bats appearing as other kids came running up and she knew it had to be a gang fight. Rick touched his pocket, felt the Fang of Jesus there. Already some of the others were running for their cars and motorcycles, or sprinting toward the river's embankment as if rushing to a fiesta. It was all out of control now, Rick realized, and before this night was done a lot of blood was going to be spilled. Pequin's cry for war echoed across Bordertown.

Mrs. Alhambra was across the street, shouting for Zarra to come home, but he said urgently to Rick, "Let's move it!"

Rick nodded, started to go up the porch steps to his grandmother and sister, but there was no time. His hard mask settled into place. Wreckage, he thought, and he turned his back on them and strode like vengeance to his car.

21
Fireball

Paco's scream still lingered. He was down on the floor, writhing and holding on to his jerked and freshly bleeding nose.

Gotcha, Ray thought—and then Juan Diegas hit him in the side of the head with a swinging fist and he slid across the floor like a crumpled sack of laundry.

Cody struggled to stand. He got to his knees, and Juan grasped his collar and hauled him up the rest of the way. Juan slammed a fist into Cody's mouth, splitting his lower lip. Cody's legs sagged. Juan hit him again, opening a cut under his right eye with that signet ring.

"Stop it! Stop it!" Kennishaw yelled, still too scared to move.

Juan lifted his fist for another smash.

"Hold it right there!" Deputy Leland Teal—middle-aged and potbellied, with a face like a weary weasel's—stepped into the doorway. The other nightshift deputy, Keith Axelrod, was right behind him.

Juan just laughed. He started to deliver the punch that would break Cody's nose to pieces.

Headlights stabbed through the Warp Room's plate-glass window. There was a squeal of tires and the wailing of a supercharged engine, and Juan shouted, *"Oh madre!"*

A pickup truck painted in mottled camouflage grays and greens roared up onto the curb, narrowly missing Cody's Honda, clipped away a parking meter, and crashed through the window in a glittering spray of glass and an ear-popping explosion. The deputies dove for their lives, and the truck smashed a couple of arcade machines to kindling before it stopped. At once, Bobby Clay Clemmons leapt from the truck's bed onto Juan Diegas, swinging at him with a chain. Tank jumped from behind the wheel, roared like an enraged beast, and kicked at Paco's ribs. "Party time!" Jack Doss shouted as he tumbled out of the truck; he was armed with a baseball bat; he attacked the machines in a marijuana-fueled frenzy. Nasty was there too, urging on the violence. Davy Summers stood atop the truck, looking for somebody to stomp, and Mike Frackner drank down a beer, crumpled the can, and hurled it at Juan's head.

In the Hammonds' kitchen, Tom was pouring himself another cup of coffee when he thought Daufin might have moved. Just a fraction, a twitching of a muscle perhaps. Jessie and Rhodes were in the den, talking about what was to be done. Tom put a spoonful of sugar in his coffee. Again, he thought he caught a movement from the corner of his eye. He approached Daufin; her face—Stevie's face—was still frozen, the eyes staring straight ahead. But—yes! There it was!

Her right hand, motioning toward the window, had begun to tremble.

"Jessie?" he called. "Colonel Rhodes?" They came at once. "Look at that." He nodded toward the right hand. The shaking seemed to have gotten more severe just in the last few seconds.

Daufin's chest hitched, a sudden motion that made Jessie jump.

"What is it?" Tom asked, alarmed. "Can't she breathe?"

Jessie touched the chest. The breathing was shallow and fast. She felt for a pulse at the throat. It was racing. "Heartbeat's way up," she said tensely. Peered into the eyes;

the pupils had dilated to the size of dimes. "There's some kind of reaction going on, for sure." Her voice was steady, but her stomach flipflopped. The outstretched hand kept trembling, and now the tremors were coming up the arm as well.

Daufin's breath rattled in the lungs. It exhaled from her mouth, and made what Jessie had thought might have been a word.

"What was that?" Rhodes kept his distance from the creature. "What'd she say?"

"I'm not sure." Jessie looked into her face, was shocked to see the pupils rapidly contract to pinpoints and then begin to open up again. "Oh, Christ! I think she's having a seizure!"

Daufin's lips moved, just barely. This time Jessie was close enough to hear the raspy word that emerged in a bated breath. Or thought she heard it, because it made no sense.

"I . . . think she said *Stinger*," Jessie told them.

Stevie's—Daufin's—face had begun to bleach of color, taking on a waxy, grayish cast. Her little girl legs had started trembling, and she whispered it again: *"Sting-er."*

And in that whisper was the sound of utter terror.

As Juan Diegas begged for mercy from Bobby Clay Clemmons and Tank joined Jack Doss in tearing up the machines, Cody crawled over to Ray Hammond. The kid was on his hands and knees, shaking his head back and forth to clear it, blood dripping from his nose and burst lips to the floor.

"You okay?" Cody asked him. "Hey, X Ray? You hear me, man?"

Ray looked at him, could tell who it was even without his glasses. "Yeah," he croaked. "Think I . . . shoulda . . . stayed out of the way."

"No," Cody said, and grasped his shoulder. "I think you were right where you were supposed to be, bro."

Ray's bloody mouth grinned.

Horns blared from the street, and headlights flashed.

"We've got company!" Nasty shouted, reaching down into the truckbed for a length of wood with nails driven through it. "More Rattlers! A ton of 'em!"

Cody got to his feet. The wrecked Warp Room spun around him, and Tank kept him from falling again.

"Come on out, you shitkickers!" came the first taunt. The horns kept blasting. "Let's get it on, assholes!"

The two deputies backed away, knowing this was more than they'd bargained for. Their meager salaries weren't enough to make them face a riot. Four cars, two pickup trucks, and a couple of motorcycles carrying Rattlesnakes had converged upon the Warp Room. Deputy Teal had called Sheriff Vance at home before they'd left the office, but if Vance wasn't here yet, Teal decided not to risk his own blood and bones. The Rattlers, some of them armed with broken bottles and chains, began to get out of their vehicles. Deputy Axelrod shouted, "You kids break this up and go on—" but a bottle shattered against the wall near his head and his attempts at law enforcement were done as he ducked and ran.

"Help me!" Juan shrieked. "Get me outta here!" Bobby Clay silenced him with a boot to the gut.

"Come on!" Ramon Torrez, wielding a chain, shouted at the other Rattlers. "Let's rush the fuckers!"

"Rush 'em! Stomp their asses!" Sonny Crowfield motioned everybody on, but he was standing behind the safety of a car. At that moment Rick's Camaro pulled up and he and Zarra got out.

"I want *you*, bitch!" Animal pointed at Nasty, and in her other hand held a sawed-off bat. More taunts were flung back and forth, and inside the Warp Room Cody knew they were going to have to battle their way out.

Tank was breathing like a bellows, his face gorged with blood in the shelter of his helmet. "Fuckin' wetbacks! You want some?" he shouted. "Let's *party!*" And, bellowing, he propelled himself out of the Warp Room and into the enemy's midst.

* * *

Daufin's trance broke. The color rushed back into her face. She was trembling wildly, and she sank to her knees saying, "Sting-er. Sting-er. Sting-er . . ."

Over the noise of car horns, Jessie heard the glasses rattle in the cupboard.

A beer bottle exploded off Tank's helmet. He drove a fist into Joey Garracone's face, was hit across the back by a chain, and staggered. Somebody leapt off a car at him; two more bodies landed on him and drove him down, still swinging.

"Get 'em!" Bobby Clay's eyes shone with homicidal fury. He jumped through the Warp Room's shattered window, followed by Jack Doss, Nasty, and the other 'Gades who'd ridden the truck in. Fists and chains flailed; bottles sailed through the air. Rick ran into the melee, with Zarra at his side. Cody pulled another wrench from his tool belt and staggered outside, his muscles aching but his blood singing for violence.

And in his patrol car about twenty yards away, Ed Vance sat gripping the steering wheel with wet palms, hearing a singsong *Burro! Burro! Burro!* at the place in his mind where a frightened fat boy lived.

He felt the car shudder. No, he realized in another second. It was not the car—it was the ground.

"Sting-er. Sting-er. Sting-er," Daufin repeated, her eyes wide with terror. She drew herself across the floor toward a corner, under the ticking cat-clock, and began to try to fold her body up like a contortionist.

The glasses were jumping in the cupboards. Now Jessie, Tom, and Rhodes could all feel the floor starting to vibrate. A cupboard popped open, and coffee mugs spilled out. The house's walls were creaking and popping, little quick firecracker sounds.

"Oh . . . my . . . God," Rhodes whispered.

Jessie bent down in front of Daufin, who had squeezed herself into a position that must be about to snap Stevie's joints. "What is it?" The floor vibrations were getting worse. "Daufin, what is it?"

"Sting-er," the creature repeated, staring past Jessie, eyes fixed and glazed. "Sting-er. Sting-er . . ."

The light fixtures swung.

The patrol car's horn began blaring, without Vance touching it. God A'mighty! he thought, and scrambled out. He could feel the ground shaking through the soles of his boots, and now there was a low rumble that sounded like heavy plates of stone grinding together.

Tank was fighting for his life. Animal swung a bat at Nasty, who dodged and backpedaled, spitting curses. Rick saw figures fighting all around him, and his hand went to the Fang of Jesus but his fingers would not close on it. He heard tires squeal, looked over his shoulder, and saw two more cars full of 'Gades barreling along the street; before the cars had stopped, their passengers jumped out and joined the clash. A misthrown bottle crashed against his shoulder, and he tripped over two fighters and fell. He was about to struggle up when he felt the concrete shaking, and he thought, What the hell . . . ? His eardrums had started aching, his bones throbbing to a deep bass tone. He looked up, and his breath caught.

There was a fireball in the sky, and it was coming down on Inferno.

Rick got to his feet. The fireball was getting larger. Somebody—a 'Gade—grabbed his shirt and started to deliver a punch, but Rick flung the boy away with furious disdain. The street trembled, and Rick shouted, "Stop it! Stop it!" but the fighting was too fierce around him, nobody was listening. He looked up again, being jostled as a Rattler with a bleeding face staggered past him. The fireball's orange light licked the street.

Behind him, Vance had seen the fireball too. He squinted in its glare, felt his heart rise to his throat and lodge there like a lemon. It's the end of the world, he thought, unable to run or cry out. The fireball looked to be coming down right on top of him.

"Listen!" Rick yelled. He plunged into the thickest of the fighting, trying to separate the battlers for a second.

And there he came face-to-face with Cody Lockett.

Cody's bones throbbed, his eardrums pounding with pressure, but he'd thought it was his injuries catching up with him. Now, though, he saw an orange glow, but before he could look up he ran right into Rick Jurado. His first thought was that Jurado would be carrying a knife, and he had to strike before Jurado did; he lifted the wrench to bash the other boy across the skull.

Rick seized his wrist. "No!" he shouted, his eyes wild. "No, listen to—"

Cody kneed him in the stomach, driving the wind out of him, then he pulled his wrist loose to smash the weapon down on the back of Jurado's head.

Daufin screamed.

The fireball—almost two hundred feet across—roared down and crashed into Mack Cade's autoyard, throwing sheets of dust and pieces of cars into the air. Its shock wave heaved the earth, sent cracks scurrying along the streets of Inferno and Bordertown, blew out windows, and flung Cody Lockett off his feet before the wrench could fall. The metal fence around Cade's autoyard was flattened, and parts of it sailed off like deadly kites. The west-facing windows of the First Texas Bank exploded, followed a split second later by the east-facing windows as the shock wave roared through. The electric-bulb sign blew out as it registered 85°F. at 9:49.

The Hammonds' house shuddered, the floor jumping with a squall of stressed joints. Jessie went down, and so did Tom, and Rhodes was flung against the wall as the southern windows imploded and the shock hit him like a giant-sized hot skillet.

Paloma and Miranda were inside the house when the blast and wind came, and they gripped each other as the floorboards danced and the walls puffed dust. Glass flew around them, Paloma's shelf of ceramic birds crashed down, and both of them were knocked flat as the bass boom passed through.

Some of the sun-bleached roofs of Bordertown houses ripped off and took flight. Atop the Catholic church's spire, the cross was knocked crooked.

Ruth Twilley was thrown out of her bed, and screamed *"Noooaaaahhhh!"* as her son shielded his face from flying glass in his study. In the chapel, coffins rocked like cradles.

On his porch, Sarge Dennison cried out, "Incomin' mail!" and jerked awake to find himself sitting in a dust storm, his eardrums ringing and the steel plate in his skull pounding like Satan's anvil. Scooter had jumped into his lap and sat there shaking; Sarge rubbed the dog's invisible black-and-white-spotted hide with nervous fingers.

Burglar alarms were shrilling all along Cobre Road and Celeste Street. Dogs howled, and Inferno's three remaining caution lights creaked on their cables; the fourth, at the intersection of Oakley and Celeste, had crashed to the pavement.

The shutters had banged open in Curt Lockett's house, and he lay in the dark in a sweat-damp bed, his eyes wide as the walls moaned.

The shock passed on in phantom waves, and the night things darted into their holes.

22
The Skygrid

Vance stood up. Dust swirled around him, and through it he saw the sputtering of broken neon signs along Celeste Street. Most of the bulbs over Cade's used-car lot had exploded, some still spitting sparks. His cowboy hat was gone, and he felt wetness on his skull; he touched his hair, and his fingers came away smeared with scarlet. Glass got me, he thought, too stunned to feel any pain. But it wasn't a serious cut, just enough to leak some blood. He heard a boy wailing and somebody else sobbing, but the other combatants had been knocked dumb.

Flames leapt high over the autoyard. Cade's paint supply was going up. Black smoke whirled from a fiery pile of tires, where drums of gasoline had landed and exploded. Where was the fire truck? he wondered. Not enough time yet for the volunteer firemen to get their drawers on. And in the flash and coil of red fire Vance saw that something else now occupied Cade's property.

Vance fell back against the patrol car, his face turning pasty white. The car's horn was still blaring, but he hardly heard it. A thin trickle of red crept down his forehead.

Rick Jurado was standing, his shirt hanging in tatters. Dust clung to the sweat on his face and chest, and splinters of glass glittered in his hair. He saw Zarra lurching around a few feet away, the boy's hands still clamped to his ears. Around him, the Rattlers and Renegades were fighting different battles—not against each other, but against their rioting senses.

Rick saw it then too, amid the flames in the autoyard. He gasped, whispered, "My God," though he could barely hear his own voice.

Cody lay on his knees about ten feet away, fading in and out of consciousness. Bombed us, he thought. Fuckin' Rattlers set off dynamite . . .

The patrol car's horn finally got through to Vance; he thought the noise was going to push him over the edge, and he shouted, *"Shut up!"* and hammered the hood with his fist. The horn stuttered and ceased.

A minute later a siren shrieked. The fire truck, racing along Republica Road past Mendoza's Texaco station. It crossed the Snake River Bridge, lights flashing. Gonna need more than one damned hose, Vance thought—but one was all the fire department had. He knew he should do something, but he didn't know what. Everything seemed dreamy, edged with gauze. So after another moment he simply sat on the patrol car's dented hood, in a *Thinker* pose, and watched the fires burn around the thing that stood in Cade's chopshop.

"I don't know what it was, but it hit across the river." Tom was standing at a broken window, looking south. "Something's on fire over there. Wait a minute." He took his glasses off and cleaned the lenses on his shirt; one lens had cracked in a clean diagonal. He put them back on, and then he saw it. "What is *that?*"

Jessie peered over his shoulder, her hair gray with dust. She saw it too, and felt the back of her neck prickle. "Rhodes! Look at this!"

He stared for a minute, his mouth half open. His brain was pounding, and even his teeth ached. "Jesus," he managed to say. "Whatever it is, it's *big.*"

Jessie glanced down at Daufin—still contorted in the corner, trembling, her eyes darting from side to side like a trapped rabbit. "What came down?" Jessie asked. Daufin didn't answer. "Do you know what it is?"

Slowly, Daufin nodded. "Sting-er," she said, her voice strained from the scream.

"Stinger? What's that mean?"

Her face mirrored inner turmoil. She was trying to formulate the terms and express them from her memory of the dictionary and thesaurus, but they were difficult. These life forms towering before her had such limited vocabularies and technologies that communication was all but impossible. And their architecture was insane too; what they called walls, with their straight lines and flat, horrible surfaces, were enough to drive any civilized being to suicide.

All this went through Daufin's mind in a language as melodic as wind chimes and intangible as smoke. Some things would not translate into the snarling roars that came out of this daughter form's throat, and such an untranslatable thing was the event that had just taken place. "Please," she said, "take me a-way. Please. Very far a-way."

"Why are you so afraid?" Jessie pressed on. "Because of that?" She motioned to the object in the junkyard.

"Yes," Daufin replied. "Afraid, very much. Sting-er life is hurt."

The syntax wasn't proper, but the message was clear. Whatever had just landed across the river made Daufin quake with terror.

"I've got to get a closer look!" Rhodes said. "My God . . . I think it's another ETV!" He searched the sky; Gunniston would've seen that thing fall, and should be coming soon in the helicopter. "It should've shown up on the radar scopes at Webb—unless it slipped through the cracks somehow." He was thinking aloud. "Man, I can see those flyboys scrambling right now! Two UFOs in the same day! Washington's going to bust their nuts!"

"Ray," Tom said suddenly, "Where's Ray?"

Jessie followed him to Ray's room. He knocked. There was no answer, and both of them knew there was no way Ray's headphones could be turned up loud enough to have masked that object's crash. Tom opened the door, saw the empty bed, and walked straight to the window. His shoes crunched on broken glass. Tom touched the frame's unhooked latch; he was bristling with anger, but scared also that Ray had been in harm's way when . . .

Hell, he thought, getting a good view of the smoke and fire. *Everywhere's* in harm's way.

"Let's go find him," he said.

A bright red dune buggy shrieked to a halt on Celeste Street. "Get off your ass, Vance!" shouted the man who jumped out of the vehicle. "What in the name of cock-eyed Judas is goin' on here?"

"I don't know," Vance said listlessly. "Somethin' came down."

"I can see that! What *is* it?" Dr. Early McNeil's face was almost as red as his dune buggy; he had shoulder-length white hair, his scalp bald and age-spotted on top, a white beard, and blazing blue eyes that pierced the sheriff like surgical lasers. A big-boned and big-bellied man, he wore an oversized green scrub shirt and jeans with patches on the knees.

"That I don't rightly know, either." Vance watched an ineffectual stream of water arc toward the center of the flames. *Pissin'* would do just as well, he mused.

People were coming out of their houses, the younger ones running across the park, the older ones hobbling the best they could. Most of the Renegades and Rattlers had recovered, and all the fighting was done; they simply stood and stared, their bruised and sweating faces washed with firelight.

Cody was on his feet, his brain still murky and one eye swollen almost shut; through his good eye he saw the object as well as anyone else.

A black pyramid stood in the center of Mack Cade's junkyard. Cody figured it as maybe a hundred and thirty feet tall, maybe more. The fires reflected off its surface, yet the pyramid didn't exactly look like it was made of metal; it appeared to have a rough, scaly surface—like snakeskin, or armor plate segmented in a tight, overlapping pattern. Cody saw the firehose water hit it and turn to steam.

Someone touched his shoulder. A bruised place. Cody winced and saw Tank beside him. Tank's helmet had protected him from most of the beating, but creepers of blood gleamed at his nostrils where a lucky punch had landed. "You okay, man?"

"Yeah," Cody said. "I think."

"You look like mighty hell."

"Reckon I do." He glanced around, saw Nasty, Bobby Clay, Davy Summers . . . all the Renegades were on their feet, at least, though some of them looked as bad as he knew he did. His eye also found Rick Jurado, standing not ten feet away and watching the flames. The wetback bastard didn't seem to have a scratch on him. And there he was, and most of the Rattlers too, standing on Inferno's concrete after dark. Any other time, and Cody would have attacked him in a frenzy; but suddenly all of that seemed so much wasted energy, like shadowboxing. Jurado's head turned, and they faced each other.

Cody still gripped the wrench. He stared back at Rick Jurado.

"What're we gonna do, Cody?" Tank asked. "What's the score, man?"

"Even," Cody said. "Let's leave it like that." And he threw the wrench; it took out more glass from the Warp Room's shattered window.

Rick nodded and looked away. The battle was over.

"X Ray," Cody remembered. He began walking toward the Warp Room, saw that his Honda had blown over but was still okay, and then he entered the ruins. Ray Hammond was sitting with his back against the wall, his lips pulped and purple, streaks of blood all over his shirt. "You gonna live?" Cody asked him.

"Maybe." Ray could hardly talk. He'd bitten his tongue during the fight, and it felt the size of a watermelon. "What's burning?"

"Damned if I know. Somethin' fell and hit over in Cade's

place. Come on, try to stand up." He offered Ray his hand, and the smaller boy took it. Cody heaved him up, and instantly Ray's legs folded. "Just don't puke," Cody warned him. "I have to wash my own clothes."

They had just made it out when Jessie saw her son and almost screamed. Behind her, Tom swallowed a choke. Colonel Rhodes walked through the onlookers, his gaze riveted to the black pyramid, and the creature with Stevie's face stayed close to the Civic they'd driven up in.

"Ray! Oh my God!" Jessie cried out as she reached him; she didn't know whether to hug him or slug him, but he looked as if he'd had enough of the second so she did the first.

"Aw, Mom," he protested, pushing free. "Don't make a scene."

Tom saw Cody's bruised face, looked around at the other 'Gades and Rattlers, and had a pretty good idea of what must have happened. His anger had dissipated, and now he stared in awe at the towering pyramid as the fires leapt around it.

"Ain't gonna put that out with a hose, no sir!" It was Dodge Creech, wearing a yellow coat with blue plaid, slacks just a shade off the plaid's hue, and an open-collared pearl-gray shirt. He hadn't had time to choose a tie from his vast collection of eye-knockers; the shock wave had thumped his house and knocked both him and his wife, Ginger, out of their beds. His head shook, his jowls quivering. "Man, I'm gonna be on the telephone for a solid month tryin' to get this mess cleaned up with the central office! Tom, what the ever-lovin' hell is that thing?"

"I think . . . it's a spacecraft," Tom said, and Creech's eyes widened for a second.

"Excuse my ear wax," Creech tried again, "but I thought you said—"

"I did. It's a spacecraft."

"A *what?*" Vance had been standing close enough to hear. "Tom, you gone crazy?"

"Ask Colonel Rhodes what it is." Tom nodded toward the air-force officer. "He'll tell you."

Rhodes scanned the sky—and suddenly saw what he'd been looking for. An F-4E Phantom jet from Webb Air Force Base streaked over Inferno from east to west, its wingtip lights blinking; Rhodes followed it, saw it begin to turn for another pass over the black pyramid. Its pilot was probably even now radioing back what he was looking at, and in a short while the air would be full of jets circling Inferno. He glanced back at Daufin, saw her still standing near the car, her eyes tracking the jet. Wondering if that was enough to get her off the planet, he thought. She just appeared to be a scared little girl, auburn-haired and jittery as a colt.

It occurred to him that she'd just learned to walk. She probably didn't know how to run yet, or she would've already taken off.

"You know somethin' about this, Colonel?"

Rhodes pulled his attention away from Daufin. The sheriff and another man, dressed in a god-awful yellow-and-blue-plaid sportscoat, had approached him. "What the shit is that thing?" Vance asked, his face marked with a solitary creeper of blood. "Where'd it come from?"

"I don't know any more about it than you do."

"That's not what Tom Hammond just said, mister!" Dodge Creech challenged. "Look at this damned mess! Half the town's tore up! And you know who's gotta pay for it? *My* insurance company! Now what the hell am I supposed to tell 'em?"

"It ain't a meteor this time, for sure." Vance smelled a whiff of deceit. "Hey, listen here! Is this the same kinda thing that fell out in the desert?"

"No, it's not." Of that, Rhodes was certain; the color was different, and the ETV that had crashed out there was about a fifth the size of this one. He watched the Phantom return for another low pass. Where the hell was Gunny and the chopper? Rhodes had been trained in "fact guarding," as the Bluebook Project manual put it, but how could you hide something as big as that—

There was a low, reverberating sound over the noise of the flames; it sounded to Rhodes like a wet, husky gasp.

And in the next second a thin column of glowing violet light shot from the pyramid's apex, ascending another two hundred feet or so into the sky.

"What's it doin'?" Vance hollered, taking a backward step.

Daufin knew, and her hands curled into tight fists that left the marks of fingernails in her palms.

The column of light began to rotate like a stationary cyclone. The stream of water from the firehose ceased as the firemen fled. Strands of light coiled from the column, as it rotated faster and faster, and the strands began to interweave. Lines of violet darted off, crossing the horizon to the east, west, north, and south, gridding the sky over Inferno and pulsing with silent, steady power.

"Looks like a damn bug zapper!" Cody heard Tank say—and then he saw the jet go into a sharp upward angle, intending to pierce the violet mesh.

The Phantom's nose hit the grid and crumpled inward. The jet exploded in an orange ball, and Rhodes shouted, "No!" Pieces of the aircraft struck the grid and all of them burst into flame, the burning fragments spinning down to land in the desert three or four hundred yards south of Bordertown.

The grid continued to grow, covering the sky with sickly purple light.

Roughly seven miles in a circle around Inferno and Bordertown, the grid bent and plunged toward earth. It sliced through the telephone and power lines that marched along Highway 67, and a truck driver who was too slow on the brakes hit the grid at sixty miles an hour; the truck mashed inward like an accordion, tires blowing and engine hurtling backward through the cab. The truck bounced off the grid and blew up, as surely as if it had plowed into a wall of stone. A jackrabbit on the grid's other side panicked and tried to run through it to his hole, but he was fried and sizzling before his brain registered pain.

The grid's lines sank through the earth, anchoring deep, and on the way down they cut the water pipeline that snaked south and ended it in an underground roar of steam.

Along Celeste Street the lights went out without a flicker. Houses darkened. Television sets died, and electric clocks ceased ticking. Refrigeration pumps in the Ice House moaned and stopped. The caution lights went out, and so did the three unbroken glass globes on the Snake River Bridge.

Jessie heard it, and so did Tom, and Rhodes and Vance, Cody and Rick: the whine of power failing, the huge everyday network of machinery that ran Inferno and Bordertown now lurching in a lockstep, everything from the air conditioning in the funeral chapel's embalming room to the bank's electronic vault locks running down their final seconds.

And then, just like that, it was over.

Inferno and Bordertown lay under the violet glow of the skygrid, and there was silence but for the snarl of flames.

Rhodes's mouth had gone dry. To the east, another spark of flame erupted against the inside of the grid—probably a second jet trying to escape and exploding. It faded quickly, and what appeared to be cinders fell to earth. Rhodes realized he was looking at a force field, generated by a power source inside the pyramid.

"Oh . . . Lordy," Dodge Creech moaned.

The *chutchutchut* of rotors made Rhodes turn toward the southwest. From that direction came an air-force helicopter, flying about seventy feet from the ground. It gave the black pyramid a wide berth, slowly circled Inferno, and set down again in Preston Park. The colonel ran to it and saw Gunniston getting out in a crouch. Jim Taggart, the lanky, red-haired pilot, cut the chopper's engine and the rotors whined to a halt.

"We saw the fire!" Gunniston said when Rhodes reached him. "We were flying when the sky lit up with that . . . whatever it is. What happened to the lights?"

"Power's out. That's a force field, Gunny. I just watched two Phantoms get dusted when they haloed into it. Damn thing must go on for miles!"

Gunniston stared at the pyramid, his cheeks flushed with

excitement and the red glare of the autoyard's fire shining in his eyes. "Another ETV," he said.

"Right. The other choppers on the way?"

"No sir. We were the only ones who lifted off. Sanders and O'Bannon are still out at the site."

"I'd say this site has just become our number-one priority, wouldn't you? Follow me." He strode toward Sheriff Vance, with Gunniston right behind him. "We have to talk," Rhodes told Vance, whose bewildered eyes still begged for an explanation he could understand. "Send somebody to find the mayor. Better get your church pastors too, and anybody else who can help with crowd control. We'll meet in your office in fifteen minutes, and we'll need flashlights, candles, whatever you can round up."

"Fifteen minutes," Vance repeated. He nodded numbly. "Yeah. Right." He gazed up at the grid and his Adam's apple bobbled as he swallowed. "We're . . . we're caught in a *cage,* ain't we? I saw that plane blow to pieces. That damned cage goes right over the hori—"

"Listen to me very carefully," Rhodes said in a low, controlled voice, pushing his face toward the sheriff's. He could smell the man's sour sweat. "I expect you to be clearheaded and thinking straight. Next to myself and Captain Gunniston, you're in charge here. Do you understand?"

Vance's eyes bulged; never in his wildest nightmares had he ever really believed he'd be in charge of a crisis situation in Inferno. The most worrisome problem he'd ever faced was keeping the Rattlers and Renegades from killing each other. But now, in the space of seconds, his whole life was changed. "Y-yes sir," he answered.

"Go!" Rhodes ordered, and Vance hurried away. Now to round up Tom and Jessie and get them to the meeting too. Have to check the phones—though he already figured they were going to be dead, disrupted by the same force that had severed the power lines—and try the sheriff's battery-powered CB radio. There was the chance a radio transmission might get through to Webb AFB, but Rhodes had no idea what the limitations of the force field might be or, indeed, if there were any. *Caught in a cage,* Vance had said. "You've got that right," he said under his breath.

He glanced toward Tom's Civic and suffered another shock.

Daufin was not there.

Nor was she anywhere in sight.

Jessie had seen at about the same time, and her first cry was "Ste—" She checked it. "Tom, Daufin's gone!" she said, and Tom saw the empty space where Daufin had been just a moment or two before. They began to search through the onlookers as Ray sat down on the curb and counted his teeth. All of them remained, but he felt right on the edge of passing out.

In a few minutes Tom and Jessie found that Daufin was no longer on Celeste Street.

The flames were roaring through the supplies of paint and lubricant in Cade's autoyard, and black billows of smoke rose from burning tires and oil. The smoke rose to the top of the grid and collected there like thunderclouds, and overhead the moon turned ebony.

23
After the Fall

"Say *what?*" Early McNeil asked, his husky voice slow and deliberate.

"Inside the child's body is an alien life form," Rhodes repeated. "From where, I don't know. Just out there somewhere." He wiped sweat from his forehead with a damp paper towel. His shirt was plastered to his back. The electric fan was, of course, dead, and heat hung heavy in the sheriff's office. Several battery-powered lamps had been "requisitioned" from the hardware store and provided glary illumination. Gathered in the office, along with Dr. McNeil, Rhodes, and the sheriff, were Jessie and Tom, the Reverend Hale Jennings from the Baptist church, Father Manuel LaPrado, and his younger assistant, Father Domingo Ortega. Xavier Mendoza had been asked to come by LaPrado as a representative of Bordertown, and Mayor Brett stood gnawing on his fingernails next to Mendoza.

"So this creature came out of a ball and got into Stevie Hammond? Is that what you're askin' us to swaller?" Early continued, sitting on a hard bench brought from one of the cells.

"It's a little more complicated than that, but you've got the gist. I think the creature occupied her sphere—and I'm referring to 'it' as female because that simplifies things

216

too—until she was able to make the transference. How that happened, or the physics of it, I can't say. Obviously, we're dealing with some pretty strange technology."

"Mister, that's the damnedest tale I've ever heard. Pardon me, *padres.*" McNeil flicked a glance at Jennings and La Prado and lit a cigar with a kitchen match scraped across his boot sole, and if anybody didn't like the smoke, they could lump it. "Tom, what do you and Dr. Jessie have to say about this?"

"Just one thing: it's true," Tom said. "Stevie's . . . not Stevie anymore. The creature calls herself Daufin."

"Not exactly," Rhodes corrected. *"We* call her Daufin. I think she saw something in one of Stevie's pictures that she identified with. Whether it was a dolphin, or the ocean, I don't know. But I don't really believe that's the creature's name, or she'd have a better command of our language."

"You mean she can't talk?" Father LaPrado's voice was soft and frail. He was a reed-thin man of seventy-one, with large, sparkling hazel eyes and a headful of snowy hair. His shoulders were stooped, but he carried himself with great dignity. He occupied the chair at Danny Chaffin's desk.

"She can communicate, but only as much as a crash course in English allows her to. She's got to be highly intelligent and retentive, because it took her only a few hours to learn the alphabet, the dictionary, and to read through an encyclopedia. But I'm sure there are still a lot of concepts she can't understand, or translate to us."

"And she's missin'?" Vance asked. "A monster from another world's loose on our streets?"

"I don't think she's dangerous," Jessie asserted, before Vance's speculations got out of hand. "I think she's scared and alone, and I *don't* think she's a monster."

"That's mighty white of you, considerin' how she got inside your little girl." Vance realized what he'd just said, and he darted a glance at the Bordertown representatives, then back to Jessie. "Listen, she—it, or whatever—might *look* like a little girl and all, but how do we know she ain't got . . . like, y'know, *powers.* Like readin' minds—"

Then you don't have anything to worry about, Jessie thought. Your pages are blank.

"—or controllin' em, even. Hell, she might have a death ray or—"

"Cut the hysterics," Rhodes said firmly, and Vance immediately silenced. "First of all, Captain Gunniston and my chopper pilot are out searching for Daufin right now; secondly, I agree with Mrs. Hammond. The creature doesn't seem threatening." He didn't use the word *dangerous*—he recalled shaking hands with a lightning bolt. "As long as we're not threatening to *her*," he added.

"What are you plannin' on doin' when you find her? How you gonna get her back in her ball?" A shroud of cigar smoke floated around Early's head.

"We don't know yet. The sphere's missing, and we think she hid it somewhere. If it's any consolation, I don't think she meant to land here. I think her vehicle malfunctioned, and she was on her way to somewhere else."

"By vehicle I reckon you mean spaceship." Reverend Hale Jennings was standing at the window, his acorn-shaped bald head tinged violet by the skygrid. He was a stocky, broad-chested man in his late forties, built like a fireplug, and had been a boxing champ during his days in the navy. "How'd she pilot a spaceship if she was inside a sphere?"

"I don't know. We can only find out from her."

"Okay, but what about *that?*" Jennings's head tilted toward the black, scale-covered pyramid. "I don't know about you gents, but that particular visitor makes me a mite nervous."

"Yeah," Vance agreed. "How do we know Daufin didn't call it down to help her invade us?"

Colonel Rhodes measured his words carefully. To tell them that Daufin was terrified of that pyramid would not help their peace of mind, but there was no longer any use in hiding the truth. "There's no proof she brought it down, but she must know what it is. Just before it landed, she kept repeating something: Stinger."

There was a silence, as the possible meanings of that word

sank in. "Might be the name of the planet she comes from," Vance suggested. "Maybe she looks like a big ol' wasp under that skin."

"As I said," Rhodes continued doggedly, "she just learned English. Evidently the word *stinger* was suggested to her by something she saw." He remembered the picture of the scorpion on Stevie's bulletin board. "What she intended it to mean, I don't know."

"There's much you don't know, young man," Father LaPrado said, with a wan smile.

"Yes sir, but I'm working on it. As soon as we find Daufin, maybe we can clear some of these questions up." He glanced quickly at his wristwatch; it was 10:23, a little more than thirty minutes since the pyramid had come down. "Now: about the power failure. All of you have seen the smoke clouds hanging at the top of the grid. We're in some sort of force field, generated from inside the pyramid. Just as it keeps the smoke from getting out, it's cut the power and telephone lines. The thing is solid, though it appears transparent. It's just as if a big glass bowl was plopped on top of us. Nothing can get in and nothing can get out either." He'd tried the sheriff's CB radio and gotten a squeal of static as the radio waves were deflected.

"A force field," Jennings repeated. "How far out does it go?"

"We're going to take the chopper up and find out. My guess is that it's limited to the immediate area around Inferno and Bordertown—maybe ten miles at the most. We don't have to worry about the air giving out"—I hope, he thought—"but the smoke from those fires isn't going to go away." The blazes were still burning, and black smoke from burning heaps of tires was not only thickening at the top of the grid but beginning to haze the streets too, and the air was permeated with a scorched smell.

Early grunted, took one more long draw on his cigar, puffed the smoke away, and crushed the stogie out on the floor. "Reckon I'll do my part against air pollution," he grumbled.

"Right. Thanks."

"One moment." Father Ortega, a slim, somber-faced man with swirls of gray at his temples, stood next to LaPrado. "You say this field of force prevents entering and escape, *si*? Is it not clear that it has a particular purpose?"

"Yeah," Vance said. "To keep us caged up while we get invaded."

"No," the priest went on, "not to keep *us* caged. To imprison Daufin."

Rhodes looked at Tom and Jessie; all of them had already warily circled that conclusion. If the black pyramid—or something inside it—had come for Daufin, she obviously did not want to be taken. He returned his attention to Ortega, his expression studiously composed. "Again, we can only find that out from her. What we need to talk about now is crowd control. I doubt if anybody's going to be getting much sleep tonight. I think it would be best if people knew they had places to congregate, where there were lights and food. Any suggestions?"

"The high school gym might do," Brett offered. "That's big enough."

"Folks want to be closer to their homes," Jennings said. "How about the churches? We've got a ton of candles already, and I reckon we can get some kerosene lamps from the hardware store."

"Sí." LaPrado nodded assent. "We can share food from the bakery and the grocery store."

"Probably a pot of coffee or two still at the Brandin' Iron," Vance said. "That might help."

"Good. The next question is, how do we get people off the streets?" Rhodes looked to suggestions from LaPrado and Jennings.

LaPrado said, "We have bells, up in the steeple. If they haven't been knocked loose, we can start them ringing."

"That's a problem for us," Jennings answered. "We've got electronic bells. Took the real ones out four years ago. I reckon I can find some volunteers to go house to house, though, and let folks know we're open."

"I'll leave that and the food for both of you and the mayor to organize," Rhodes said. "I doubt if we can get everybody off the streets, but the more people indoors the better I'll feel about things."

"Domingo, will you see me back, please?" LaPrado stood up with Ortega's help. "I'll get the bells started, and ask some of the ladies to round up food." He shuffled to the door, and paused there. "Colonel Rhodes, if someone asks me what's happening, do you mind if I use your explanation?"

"What's that?"

"'I don't know,'" the old priest replied, with a grim little chuckle. He allowed Mendoza to open the door for him.

"Don't go too far, Father," Early said. "I may be needin' you pretty soon. You too, Hale. I've got four of Cade's workmen who aren't gonna last the night, and I imagine the fireboys'll be pullin' more bodies out when it gets cool enough to go in."

LaPrado nodded. "You know where to find me," he said, and left the office with Ortega and Mendoza.

"Fella don't have half his marbles," Vance muttered.

Early stood up. His time for lollygagging was spent. "Folks, this has been real educational, but I've got to get back to the clinic." Eight of the kids from the gang fight, including Cody Lockett and Ray Hammond, had been taken to the Inferno Clinic for stitches and bandages, but the seriously injured workers from Cade's junkyard—and only seven of a crew of forty-six had come staggering, burned, and bleeding over the mashed-down fence—were being attended to first. Early's staff of three nurses and six volunteers were treating shock and glass-cut patients by the glare of the emergency lights. "Dr. Jessie, I sure could use you," he said. "I've got a fella with a piece of metal scrapin' his backbone and another who's gonna have to part with a crushed arm pretty soon. Tom, if you can hold a flashlight steady and you don't mind a little blood, I can use you too." It occurred to him that Noah Twilley was going to be just as busy before long, when the firemen brought the rest of the corpses out.

"I can handle it," Tom said. "Colonel, will you let us know when you find her?"

"As soon as. I'm on my way to meet Gunny right now."

They followed Early out into the violet-hued street. A few knots of people remained on the street, gawking, but most of the onlookers had melted back to their homes. Rhodes walked toward Preston Park, Tom and Jessie went to their Civic, and Early climbed nimbly into his dune buggy.

As the buggy roared away, it was narrowly missed by a battleship-sized yellow Cadillac that stopped in front of the sheriff's office. Celeste Preston, wearing a scarlet jumpsuit, got out and stood with her hands on her hips, looking at the massive pyramid across the river. Her sharp-featured face angled up, her pale blue eyes examining the skygrid. She'd already seen the helicopter sitting in Preston Park; one of the three that had buzzed her house this morning, she thought with a resurgence of righteous anger. But the anger collapsed soon enough. Whatever that big bastard was over in Cade's autoyard, and that purple mesh covering the sky, they took precedence over her concern for her lost beauty sleep.

Mayor Brett and Hale Jennings emerged from Vance's office on their way to Aurora Street, where the Quik-Check Grocery's owner lived. Brett almost ran into Celeste, and his heart gave a violent kick because he was scared to death of her. "Uh . . . Miz Preston! What can I do for—"

"Howdy, Pastor," she interrupted, then turned her cold glare on the mayor. "Brett, I hope to God you can tell me what that thing is over there, and why the sky's all lit up and why my power and phones are out!"

"Yes ma'am." Brett swallowed thickly, his face beaded with sweat. "Well . . . see . . . the colonel says it's a space-ship, and it's got a force field comin' out of it that's stopped the electricity, and—" There was no way to explain all of it, and Celeste watched him like a hawk poised over a mouse.

"Mrs. Preston, I think it'd be best if you asked Sheriff Vance," Jennings advised. "He'll tell you the whole story."

"Oh, I can't wait for this!" she said, and as the two men walked to the pastor's blue Ford she squared her shoulders, lifted her chin, and almost took the door off its hinges when she stormed inside.

She caught Vance with his hand up the office Coke machine's innards, working a can free. "I've got some questions that need answerin'," she said as the door shut behind her.

Vance had hardly jumped when she came in; his nervous system had reached its quota of shocks. He kept at the can, which was still deliciously cool under his fingers. One more good twist and he'd have it out. "Sit down," he offered.

"I'll stand."

"Suit yourself." Damn, why wouldn't it come out? He did this all the time, and usually the cans popped out with no trouble. He jiggled it, but it seemed to be hung on something.

"Oh, for Christ's sake!" Celeste stalked toward him, shoved him none too gently aside, reached her arm up the vent, and grasped the can. She twisted her wrist sharply to the left and pulled the can out. "Here! Take the damned thing!"

Suddenly he didn't want it so much. Her arm was skinny as a rail, and he figured that's how she'd done it. "Naw," he said, "you can have it."

Normally she only drank diet colas, but the air was so hot and stifling she didn't care to be choosy. She popped the tab and drank several cool swallows. "Thanks," she said. "My throat was kinda dry."

"Yeah, I know what you mean. The water fountain's not workin', either." He nodded toward it, and when he did he caught a strange scent: like cinnamon, or some kind of fragrant spice. He realized a second later that it must be coming from Celeste Preston, maybe the scent of her shampoo or soap. Then the aroma drifted away, and he could smell his own sweaty self again. He wished he'd put on some more of his Brut deodorant, because it was wearing off fast.

"You've got blood on your face," she said.

"Huh? Yeah, reckon I do. Glass cut me." He shrugged. "Don't matter none." His nose searched for another sniff of cinnamon.

Just like a man! Celeste thought as she finished off the

drink. Damn fools get cut and bleed like stuck pigs, and they pretend they don't even notice it! Wint was the same way, slashed his hand open on barbed wire once and acted like he'd gotten a splinter in his finger, tryin' to be tough. Probably wasn't a dime's worth of difference between Wint and Vance, if you could shave about fifty pounds of fat off him.

She jerked herself back to reality. Either the heat was getting to her, or it was the smoke in the air; she'd never felt an iota of compassion for Ed Vance, and she sure didn't intend to start. She flung the can into a wastebasket and said stridently, "I want to know what the hell's goin' on around here, and I want to know *now!*"

Vance stopped sniffing. It wasn't cinnamon, he decided; it was probably witch hazel. He went to his desk and got the patrol car's keys.

"I'm talkin' to you!" Celeste snapped.

"I've gotta go over to Danny Chaffin's house and pick him up. My night deputies have vamoosed. You want to hear about it, you'll have to go with me." He was already on his way to the door.

"Don't you walk out on me!"

He paused. "I've gotta lock up. You comin', or not?"

Her idea of hell was to be in that patrol car with Vance's blubber shaking behind the wheel, but she saw she'd have to endure it. "I'm comin'," she said through gritted teeth, and followed him out.

24

Act of God

"Lord have mercy!" Dodge Creech peered out a cracked window at the pyramid. He was still wearing his yellow-and-blue-plaid sport coat, his red lick of hair damp with sweat and glued to his sparkling scalp. "Ginger, I'm tellin' you: if that thing had come down two hundred yards more north, we'd be laying in our graves right now. How in *hell* am I gonna explain this to Mr. Brasswell?"

Ginger Creech thought about it. She was sitting in a rocking chair across the pine-paneled living room, wearing her plain blue robe, her feet in Dearfoam slippers and pink curlers in her graying hair. Her brow furrowed. "Act of God," she decided. "That's what you'll tell him."

"Act of God," he repeated, trying it out. "No, he won't buy that! Anyway, if it was a meteor or somethin' that fell without a mind to it, then it would be an act of God. If it's somethin' that's got a mind, you can't call it an act of God." Harv Brasswell was Creech's supervisor, based in Dallas, and he had a powerfully tight fist when it came to damage claims.

"You sayin' God doesn't have a mind?" she inquired, her rocking coming to a halt.

"No, 'course not! It's just that an act of God has to be like a storm, or a drought, or somethin' only God could cause."

225

That still sounded lame, and he didn't want to stir Ginger up; she was a PTL, Ernest Angsley, Kenneth Copeland, and Jimmy Swaggart fanatic. "I don't think God had anythin' to do with this."

The squeaking of her chair continued. The room was illuminated by three oil-burning lanterns that had been hung from the wagon-wheel light fixture at the ceiling. A couple of candles burned atop the television set. Bookshelves were packed with *Reader's Digest Condensed Books,* stacks of *National Geographics,* insurance law and motivational salesmanship books, as well as Ginger's collection of religious tomes.

"I'll bet that thing threw every house in town off its foundations," Dodge fretted. "I swear, ninety percent of the windows must be broken. Streets all cracked too. I never believed in spaceships before, but by God if that's not one, I don't know what is!"

"I don't want to think about it," Ginger said, rocking harder. "No such thing as spaceships."

"Well, it sure ain't the Big Rock Candy Mountain out there! Lord, what a mess!" He rubbed the cool glass of iced tea he was holding across his forehead. The refrigerator had quit along with the power, of course, but the freezer unit still held a few trays of cubes. In this heat, though, they weren't going to last very long. "That Colonel Rhodes is havin' a meetin' with the sheriff and Mayor Brett. Didn't ask me, though. Guess I'm not important enough, huh? I can sell everybody in town their insurance and wait on 'em hand and foot, but I'm not important enough. There's thanks for you!"

"The meek shall inherit the earth," Ginger said, and he frowned because he didn't know what she was talking about and he didn't think she knew, either.

"I'm *not* meek!" he told her. She just kept rocking. He heard the deep, rhythmic tolling of the bell at the Sacrifice of Christ Catholic Church across the river, calling the parishioners. "Sounds like LaPrado's openin' up for business. Guess Reverend Jennings will too. It's gonna take more than church bells to keep folks—"

There was another sound, one that stopped him midsentence.

It was a sharp, cracking noise: bricks being wrenched apart.

Under my feet, Dodge Creech thought. Sounds like the basement floor's rippin' to—

"What's that noise?" Ginger cried out, standing up. The rocking chair creaked on without her.

The wooden floor trembled.

Dodge looked at his wife. Her eyes were glassy and wide, her mouth open in a straining O. Above their heads the wagon-wheel fixture shook, the oil lamps beginning to swing.

Dodge said, "I . . . think we're havin' an earthqu—"

The floor heaved upward, as if something huge had battered it from below. Nails leapt loose, glittering in the lamplight. Ginger staggered backward and fell, shrieking as Dodge toppled to his knees.

She saw the floor split open underneath him with a scream of tortured wood, and her husband's body dropped into the seam up to his neck. Dust billowed around him and filled the room, but she could still see his face: chalky pale, eyes holes of shock. He was looking at her as she crawled away from the collapsing floor on her back.

"Somethin's got me," he said, and his voice was a thin, awful whine. "Help me, Ginger. Please . . ." He lifted his hand out of the hole for her, and what looked like gray snot was drooling from his fingers.

Ginger wailed, curlers dangling from her hair.

And then Dodge was gone, down the hole in the living-room floor. The house shook again, the walls moaning as if in pain at giving up their master. Plaster dust welled through cracks in the pinewood like ghost breath—and then there was silence but for the creakings of the rocking chair and the wagon-wheel fixture. One of the lamps had fallen and lay unbroken on the round red throw rug.

Ginger Creech whispered, "Dodge?" She was shaking, tears running down her face and her bladder about to pop. Shouted it: *"Dodge!"*

There was no answer, just the chuckling of water down below, running from a broken pipe. The water soon ran out, and the chuckling ceased.

Ginger pushed herself toward the hole, her muscles sluggish as cold rubber bands. She had to look down it—did not want to, must not, should not—but she had to, because it had taken her husband. She reached the jagged edge and her stomach threatened eruption, so she had to squeeze her eyes shut and ride it out. The sickness passed, and she looked over into the hole.

Just dark.

She reached out for the oil lamp and turned up the wick. The flame guttered and rose to a knifelike orange point. She thrust the lamp down into the hole, her other hand gripping the splintered edge with white-knuckled fingers.

Yellow dust sifted and stirred in small, cyclonic whorls. She was peering down into the basement eight feet below; and in the basement floor was another hole that looked —yes, she thought, oh Jesus son of God Holy Christ yes—*gnawed* through the concrete bricks. Beneath the basement floor lay more darkness.

"Dodge?" she whispered, and it echoed *Dodge? Dodge? Dodge?* Her fingers spasmed; she lost the oil lamp, and it fell through the hole in the basement floor, kept falling, maybe ten or twenty more feet, finally shattered against red Texas dirt and the flames gouted as the rest of the oil caught. Down in that hole, Ginger could see the glimmering of ooze where something had dragged her husband to hell.

Her senses left her altogether, and she lay trembling on the warped floor, her body drawn up in a tight fetal position. She decided to recite the Twenty-third Psalm seven times, because seven seemed like a holy number and if she recited loud enough and wished hard enough she would lift her head and see Dodge sitting in his easychair across the room, reading one of his motivational salesmanship books, and the TV set would be tuned to PTL and the thing that could not possibly be a spaceship would be gone. She began to recite, but she almost gagged with terror; she'd forgotten the words.

A church bell was ringing.

It must be Sunday, she thought. Sunday morning, bright and new. She sat up, listening to the bell. What was that violet glow coming through the window? Where was Dodge, and why was that hole—

She had always loved the sound of a church bell, summoning her to worship. It was time to go now, and Dodge could come along later. And if he wore that red suit today, she'd skin him, just skin him alive. She stood up, her eyes empty and tear tracks glistening through the dust on her face. She left the house, walked out of her Dearfoams, and kept going barefoot along Brazos Street.

25
Sarge's Best Friend

"Don't you be scared now, Scooter. I'm not gonna let anythin' bad happen to you, no siree!" Sarge Dennison patted Scooter's head, and the invisible animal curled up against his leg. "Don't you worry. Ol' Sarge'll protect you." He was sitting on the edge of the bandstand in the middle of Preston Park, and had just witnessed the helicopter take off with the pilot and two men aboard. The aircraft reached a height of sixty feet and zoomed to the east, the chatter of its rotors rapidly fading.

Sarge watched it go, until its blinking lights were lost to sight. The bell of the Catholic church across the river was tolling, and a few people stood out on Celeste Street and Cobre Road, looking at the black pyramid and talking, but most had retreated to their homes. He observed the column of violet light, rotating slowly around and around; it reminded him, more than anything, of a barbershop pole. The top of the purple grid was lost in motionless clouds of ebony smoke, and the air smelled burnt. It was a smell he didn't like, because it made dark things in his mind start to move again.

Scooter whimpered. "Uh-uh, don't you cry." Sarge's voice was soothing, his fingers gentle as they stroked the air. "I'm not leavin' you."

There was a movement beneath him, and suddenly he was looking down at a little girl's face, washed with violet light, her auburn hair full of dust. She had poked her head out from the small crawlspace underneath the bandstand, and now watched him with eyes full of puzzlement.

"Howdy," Sarge said. He recognized the child. "You're Mr. Hammond's daughter. Stevie."

She said nothing.

"You know me, don't you? Sarge Dennison? Your mama brought you to school one afternoon. Remember?"

"No," Daufin said tentatively, ready to draw herself back into the protection of the shell she'd found.

"Well, I surely do. Guess it was last year, though. How old are you now?"

Daufin pondered. "Old," she said.

She's got a funny voice, he thought. Kinda raspy, or whispery, or somethin'. Sounds like she could use a cough drop. "What're you doin' under there?" Again, no answer. "Why don't you come on up and say hello to Scooter? I 'member he liked you."

She hesitated. This creature didn't seem threatening, and there was a pleasant . . . what was it termed? A pleasant smile on his cliff of features. Wasn't that a symbol of nonaggression? And she was curious as well; she'd seen him approach, heard him sit on the surface above her head. He'd been solitary; why was it, then, that he was communicating with an entity he kept referring to as Scooter?

Daufin crawled out. Sarge saw that her clothes were covered with dust, her hands and arms dirty, her sneaker laces untied and dragging. "Your mama's gonna tan your hide!" he told her. "You're a walkin' dustball!"

"I thought I was a daugh-ter," Daufin said, newly puzzled.

"Well . . . yeah, you are. I just meant . . . aw, forget it." He touched the whitewashed plank at his side. "Take a seat."

Daufin didn't fully understand what he meant, since she saw no chair, bench, or stool for the purpose of resting the rump of the human body, so she simply decided he was inviting her to imitate his position. She started to sit down.

"Hold it! Don't sit on Scooter!"

"Scoot-er?" she inquired.

"Sure! He's right here! Scooter, move your butt and give the little girl room. You 'member her, don't you? Stevie Hammond?"

Daufin tracked Sarge's line of sight, saw he was talking to what she perceived as empty space.

"There y'go," Sarge said. "He's moved now."

"I pre-fer to . . ." What was the term? "To take the up-right po-si-tion."

"Huh?" Sarge frowned. "What kinda talk is that?"

"Web-ster," came the reply.

Sarge laughed, scratched his head. His fingers made a grainy noise in the stubble of his hair. "You're a card, Stevie!" She watched the fingers move across his skull, then she plucked up a bit of her own hair and examined the difference. Whatever these life forms called human beings were composed of, they certainly had very few common characteristics. "So why are you hidin' under the band-stand?" Sarge asked, his right hand rubbing Scooter's muz-zle; Daufin's eyes followed the wavelike movements. He took her silence as sullen. "Oh. Did'ja run away from home?"

No reply.

He went on. "Ain't much to run *to* when you run away from home around here, is there? Bet your folks are kinda worried about you, huh? 'Specially with that big booger sittin' over there?"

Daufin gave the towering object a quick, cold glance, and a shudder passed through her host body. "Is that what you call it?" she asked. "A big . . ." This term was not in Webster language. "Boo-ger?"

"Sure is, ain't it?" He grunted, shook his head. "Never seen the like. Scooter ain't either. You could just about put the whole town inside that thing and still have room left over, I'll bet."

"Why would you?" she asked him.

"Why would I what?"

She was patient, sensing that she was dealing with a life form with minimal capabilities. "Why would you want to put the whole town in-side that big boo-ger?"

"I didn't mean *really*. I just meant . . . y'know, for in-stance." He regarded the skygrid. "I saw a plane hit up there and blow—*boom!*—just like that and gone. Sittin' on my porch, I saw it happen. Talkin' to the reverend a little while ago. The reverend says it's like a glass bowl turned upside down over Inferno. Says nothin' can get in, and nothin' can get out. Says it's somethin' from . . ." He motioned with a wave of his hand toward the night. "Out there, a long ways off." His hand reached back to touch Scooter. "But me and Scooter'll make out all right. Yessir. We've been together a long time. We'll make out all right."

De-lu-sion, she thought. A persistent belief in something false (opposite of true) typical of some mental (of or relating to the mind) disorders. "What is Scoot-er?" she asked.

He looked up at her, as if startled by the question. His mouth opened; for a few seconds his face seemed to sag on the bones, and his eyes glazed over. He stayed that way as she waited for an answer. Finally: "My friend," he said. "My best friend."

There was a growl, a noise of a kind Daufin had never experienced before. It seemed to gain volume, a harsh rolling and tumbling of tones that she could feel at her very center.

"You must be hungry." Sarge's eyes had cleared. He was smiling again. "Your stomach's talkin'."

"My . . . sto-mach?" This was a new and astounding revelation. "What mes-sage does it send?"

"You need food, that's what! You sure talk funny! Don't she, Scooter?" He stood up. "Better get on home now. Your folks'll be huntin' you."

"Home," Daufin repeated. That concept was clear. "My home is . . ." She searched the sky. The grid and the smoke clouds blocked off her reference points, and she could not see the star corridor. "Out there, a long way off." She mimicked his gesture, because it seemed an appropriate way to demonstrate great distance.

"Aw, you're joshin' me now!" he chided her. "Your house is just up the street. Come on, I'll walk you home."

His intention was to escort her back to the box where Stevie, Jessie, Tom, and Ray dwelled, she realized. There was no reason to hide anymore; there was no exiting this planet. The next move was not hers. She stood up on stalks that still felt gangly and precarious, and began to follow this creature across a fantasy landscape. Nothing in her deepest dreams had prepared her for the sights on this planet: rows of insanely built boxes brooding on either side of a flat, brutally hard surface; towering, ugly-hued growths studded with fearsome-looking daggers; the people's means of conveyance smaller boxes that jarred along the hard surfaces with sickening gravitational pressures and made noises like the destruction of worlds. She knew the terms—houses, cactus, automobiles—from that nightmarish collection called *Britannica,* but absorbing the written descriptions and flat images was far less disturbing than the realities. As they walked along and Daufin struggled with gravity, she heard the Sarge Dennison creature talking: "Come on, Scooter! Don't run off and get all dirty, now! No, I ain't gonna throw you a stick!" She wondered if there was a dimension here of which she was unaware—another world, hidden beyond the one she saw. Oh, there was much here to study and contemplate, but there was no time.

Her head swiveled back over her shoulder. The pain of unyielding structures stopped her head from a full rotation. Bones, she knew they were termed. The bones of her host body's arms and legs still throbbed from her contortions. She understood that bones were the framework of these creatures, and she recognized them as marvels of engineering to withstand this gravity and absorb the stunning punishment that came with "walking." These creatures, she mused, must have a deep kinship with pain, because it was ever-present. Surely they were a hardy species, to endure such tortures as "automobiles" and "streets" and "sneakers."

She stared for a moment at the big booger and the violet grid, and if Sarge Dennison had seen the angle of her neck, he would've thought, correctly, that it was on the verge of snapping. The trap is set, she thought in her language of chimes. Already there had been hurting. Soon the trap would spring, and here in this lifepod called In-fer-no there would be extinction. Much extinction.

In her chest there was a crushed sensation, more painful than even the gravity. These human beings were primitive and innocent, and they did not know what was ahead.

Daufin's steps faltered. It will happen because of me, she thought. Because I came here, to this small planet on the edge of the star corridor—a young civilization, still a distance away from the technology to take them into deep space where a million worlds and cultures yearned for freedom.

She'd hoped to learn their language, stay long enough to tell them about herself and why she was racing along the star corridor, and leave long before this; it had never occurred to her that they wouldn't have interstellar vehicles, since most of the civilizations she was familiar with did. The trap is about to spring, she thought—but I must not throw myself into it. Not yet, not until there is no more chance. She had promised this daughter would be safe, and she kept her promises.

Her head swiveled away from the skygrid and the black pyramid, but they remained as ugly as open wounds behind her eyes.

They reached the Hammond house. Sarge knocked at the door, waited, knocked again when there was no response. "Nobody to home," he said. "Think they're out lookin' for you?"

"I am here," she answered, not fully understanding. This Sarge creature was a disrupter of language.

"*I* know you're here, and *Scooter* knows you're here, but . . . little lady, you sure know how to throw a curveball, don't you?"

"Curve-ball?"

"Yeah. Y'know. Fastball, curveball, spitball—baseball."

"Ah." A smile of recognition skittered across her mouth. She remembered the spectacle on the teeah-veeah. "Safe!"

"Right." Sarge tried the doorknob, and the door opened. "Looky here! They must've left in a mighty big hurry!" He poked his head in. "Hey, it's Sarge Dennison! Anybody to home?" He didn't figure there was going to be a reply, and there was none. He closed the door and looked up and down the street. Candles flickered in a few windows. There was no telling where the Hammonds might be, with all the confusion of the last hour. "You want to go lookin' for your folks?" he asked her. "Maybe we can track 'em do—"

His voice was drowned out by the rotors of the helicopter as it flashed past overhead, going west, sixty or seventy feet off the ground. The noise shot Daufin off her feet and propelled her forward. She clamped both hands to one of Sarge's and stood close, her body shivering.

Child's scared to death, Sarge thought. Skin's cold too, and . . . Lord, she's got a strong grip for a kid! He could feel his fingers prickling with a needles-and-pins sensation, as if his hand was snared by a low-voltage electric cable. The feeling wasn't unpleasant, just strange. He saw Scooter running around in circles, also spooked by the 'copter's passage. "Ain't nothin' to be scared of. Just a machine," he said. "Your folks oughta be home pretty soon."

Daufin hung on to his hand. The electric tingling was moving up Sarge's forearm. He heard her stomach growl again, and he asked, "You had any dinner?" She was still too skittish to speak. "I don't live too far from here. Just up Brazos Street a ways. Got some pork 'n beans and some 'tater chips." The tingling had advanced to his elbow. She wouldn't let go. "You want to have a bowl of pork 'n beans? Then I'll bring you back here and we'll wait for your folks?" He couldn't tell if that was okay by her or not, but he took the first step and she did too. "Anybody ever tell you you walk funny?" he asked.

They continued toward Brazos, Daufin's hands latched to

Sarge's. The steady pulse of energy she emitted continued through Sarge Dennison's nerves, into his shoulder and neck, along his spine, and up into his cerebral cortex. He had a mild headache; the steel plate's playin' its tune again, he thought.

Scooter trotted alongside. Sarge said to the animal, "You're a mighty prancy thing, ain't—"

There was a pain in his head. Just a little one, as if a spark plug had fired.

Scooter vanished.

"Uh-uh-uh . . ." Sarge muttered; the spark plug short-circuited.

And there was Scooter again. A mighty prancy thing.

Sarge's face was sweating. Something had happened; he didn't know what, but *something*. The child's hand clung tight, and his head was hurting. Scooter ran ahead, to wait on the front porch, pink tongue hanging out.

The door was unlocked; it always was. Sarge let Scooter in first, and then Daufin finally released his hand as he searched for an oil lamp and matches. But the spark plug kept sputtering in his brain, and one side of his body—the side she'd been standing on—was full of prickly fire. Sarge got the lamp lit, and the glow chased some of the shadows away—but they were tricky shadows, and sometimes Scooter was there and the next second he wasn't.

"Little lady," he said as he sank into a chair in the immaculate room with its swept and mopped floor, "I'm . . . not feelin' so good." Scooter jumped into his lap and licked his face. He put his arms around Scooter. The little girl was watching him, standing just at the edge of the lamplight. "Lord . . . my head. Really beatin' the band in—" He blinked.

His arms were enfolded around nothing.

His brain sizzled. Cold sweat trickled down his face. "Scooter?" he whispered. His voice cracked, went haywire; his face contorted. "Scooter? Oh Jesus . . . oh Jesus . . . don't bring the stick." His eyelids fluttered. "Don't bring the stick. *Don't bring the stick!*"

Daufin stood at his side. She realized he was seeing into that dimension that she could not, and she said, very softly, "Tell me. What is Scoot-er?"

He moaned. The spark plug fired, sputtered, fired; ghostly images of Scooter faded in and out on his lap, like scenes caught in a strobe light. His hands clutched at empty air. "Oh dear God . . . don't . . . don't bring the stick," he pleaded.

"Tell me," she said.

His head turned. Saw her there. Scooter. Where was Scooter? The dark things in his mind were lurching toward the light.

Tears burned his eyes. "Scooter . . . brought the stick," he said—and then he began to tell her the rest of it.

26

The Creech House

"Found her walkin' right in the middle of the street, a block south of the church," Curt Lockett explained. "Just about knocked her flyin', but I put on the brakes in time."

Sheriff Vance regarded Ginger Creech again; she was standing barefoot in his office, and from the door she'd left bloody prints. Must've slashed her feet on broken glass, he figured. Lord, she's ready for the funny farm!

Ginger's eyes stared straight ahead, a few remaining curlers drooping in her hair, her face a pale mask of dust.

"Swear to God, she scared shit out of me," Curt said, glancing at Danny Chaffin. The deputy made another circle of Ginger. "I was on my way to the liquor store. Know where a man can get a drink?"

"Liquor store's locked up," Vance told him, rising from his chair. "That was one of the first things we did."

"Reckon so." Curt rubbed his mouth and gave a nervous smile; he felt as if he were shaking to pieces, and finding Ginger Creech walking like a brain-blasted zombie hadn't helped his jitters any, either. "It's just . . . y'know, I kinda need somethin' to take me through the night." From the open collar of his wrinkled white shirt hung his newly discovered necktie.

"Ginger?" Vance waved his hand in front of her face. She blinked but did not speak. "Can you hear me?"

"I'm lookin' for my boy," Curt said. "Either of you seen Cody?"

Vance had to laugh. He felt like he'd gone ten rounds with Celeste Preston thirty minutes ago, when he'd driven over to the Chaffin house on Oakley Street to pick up his deputy. He'd wound up explaining about the spaceship to Vic and Arleen Chaffin too, and Arleen had begun crying and moaning about it being the end of the world. Vance had returned Celeste to her car, and the last he'd seen of her she was driving westward in that big yellow Cadillac. Probably headin' for her hacienda and gonna hide under her bed, he thought. Well, nobody wanted her hangin' around here anyway!

"Curt," he said, "if you didn't sleep twenty hours out of the day, you'd be dangerous. Your boy raised hell at the Warp Room around nine-thirty, started a gang fight that put a bunch of kids in the clinic—which, with all these hurt people we've got, Doc McNeil sure as shit don't need."

"Cody . . . in a fight?" Time was all screwed up for Curt. He glanced at the clock, saw it had stopped at two minutes after ten. "Is he all right? I mean . . ."

"Yeah, he's okay. Busted up some, though. He headed over to the clinic."

Which meant a doctor's bill, Curt thought. Damned fool kid! He didn't have the sense God gave a bug!

"Ginger? It's Ed Vance. Danny, hand me that flashlight on the desk." He gripped it, flicked it on, and aimed it at the woman's sightless eyes. She flinched just a fraction, her arms stiffening at her sides. "Ginger? What happened? How come you're—"

She gave a terrible shudder, and her face strained as if its muscles were about to burst through the flesh.

"She's having a fit!" Curt squalled, and backed across the woman's bloody tracks toward the door.

Her gray lips trembled and opened. "'The . . . Lord . . . is my shepherd, I shall not want,'" she whispered. "'He maketh me lie down in green pastures. He . . . He leadeth me beside still waters . . .'" Tears broke and ran, and she stumbled on through the Twenty-third Psalm.

Vance's heart was pounding. "Danny, we'd better get over to Dodge's house. I sure as hell don't like the looks of this."

"Yes sir." Danny glanced at the glass-fronted cabinet that held the assortment of firearms, and Vance read his mind because he was thinking the same thing.

"Break out a shotgun for me," Vance said. "A rifle for you. Get 'em loaded." Danny took the key ring from him and unlocked the cabinet.

"'I will . . . fear no . . .'" The words gripped in her throat. "'Fear no . . . fear no . . .'" She couldn't make herself say it, and fresh tears streamed down her face.

"Curt, I want you to get Ginger to the clinic. Find Early and tell him—"

"Hold on!" Curt protested. He wanted nothing to do with this. "I ain't a deputy!"

"You are now. I'll swear you in later. Right now I want you to do what I say: take Ginger over there and tell Early how you found her." He took the shotgun Danny gave him and put a few extra shells in his pockets.

"Uh . . . what do you think happened?" Curt's voice trembled. "To Dodge, I mean?"

"I don't know, but we're gonna find out. Ginger, I want you to go with Curt. Okay? Can you hear me?"

"'Fear no . . .'" She squeezed her eyes shut, opened them again. "'Fear no . . .'"

"Ed, I don't know about this," Curt said. "I'm not deputy material. Can't you get somebody else to take her over?"

"Oh, Christ!" Vance shouted as his own raw nerves stretched toward the breaking point. Ginger jumped and whimpered and retreated from him. "Here! I'll pay you to do it!" He dug into his back pocket, brought out his wallet, and flipped it open. The only thing in there was a five-dollar bill. "Go on, take it! Go buy yourself a damned bottle at the Bob Wire Club, just move your ass!"

Curt's licked his lower lip. His hand burrowed into the wallet and came out five dollars richer.

Vance gently took Ginger's arm and led her out. She came

241

along docilely, her feet leaving bloody prints and her strained whisper of "'Fear no . . . fear no . . .'" sending shivers down the sheriff's backbone. Danny locked the door behind them and Curt guided the madwoman to his Buick, got her inside, and drove away toward the clinic, the tailpipe dragging and scratching sparks off the pavement.

Vance drove the patrol car while Danny sat in silence on the passenger side with his hands clamped like vises around the rifle. Dodge Creech's house, made of sand-colored stucco with a red slate roof, stood near the corner of Celeste and Brazos streets. The front door was wide open. The sheriff and deputy could see the faint glow of candles or lamps within the house, but there was no sign of Dodge. Vance pulled the car to the curb, and they got out and started up the pebbled walk.

About eight feet from the door, Vance's legs seized up. He'd seen one of Ginger's slippers lying on the dry lawn. A coldness was writhing in his belly, and the doorway looked like a mouth, ready to crunch down on him as he entered. From a great distance he thought he heard brutal young voices taunting *Burro! Burro! Burro!*

"Sheriff?" Danny had stopped at the door. "You okay?" In the dim violet light Vance's face glittered with sweat.

"Yeah. Fine." He bent over and rubbed his knees. "Just old football knees. Sometimes they flare up on me."

"I didn't know you ever played football."

"It was a long time ago." He was perspiring everywhere: face, chest, back, ass. A cold, oily sweat. His career as a sheriff had been limited to breaking up fights, investigating traffic accidents, and hunting down lost dogs. He'd never had to fire a gun in the line of duty, and the idea of going into that house and seeing what had made Ginger Creech go crazy made his balls crawl as if they were packed full of spiders.

"Want me to go on in?" Danny asked.

Yes, he almost said. But as he stared at the doorway, he knew he had to go in first. He had to, because he was the sheriff. Besides, he had a shotgun and Danny had a rifle.

Whatever it was in there, it could be shot full of holes just like anything else. "No," he said huskily. "I'll go first."

It took all his flabby willpower to start walking again. He entered the Creech house, flinching as he cleared the hungry doorway. A loose floorboard mewled under his right boot.

"Dodge!" he called. His voice cracked. "Dodge, where are you?"

They walked toward the light, through a foyer and into the living room, where a couple of oil lamps threw shadows and dust floated in layers from floor to ceiling.

"Sheriff, look at that!" Danny had seen it first, and he pointed to the jagged-edged hole in the floor. Vance approached it, and he and Danny stood over the hole peering down into darkness.

Squeak squeak. Squeak squeak.

Both of them looked up at the same time, and both of them saw it.

A figure sat in the rocking chair in the far corner of the room, slowly rocking back and forth, back and forth. A scatter of *National Geographics* lay on the floor beside the chair.

Squeak squeak. Squeak squeak.

"D-Dodge?" Vance whispered.

"Howdy," Dodge Creech said. Most of his face was in shadow, but he was still wearing his yellow-and-blue-plaid coat, dark blue slacks, pearl-gray shirt, two-toned loafers. His red lick of hair was greased back on his pate, and his hands were folded in his lap as he rocked.

"What's . . . what's goin' on?" Vance asked. "Ginger's about out of her—"

"Howdy," the other man said again, still rocking. There was no color in his face, and his eyes glittered in the light of the two remaining lamps that hung from the ceiling's wagon-wheel fixture. The wagon wheel was crooked. *Squeak, squeak* went the chair's runners.

His voice, Vance thought: his voice is funny. Raspy, like air through the bass pipes of a church organ. It sounded like Dodge's voice, yes, but . . . different too.

The glittering eyes were watching him carefully. "You're a person of authority, ain't you?" the voice asked, with a humming of sinus cavities.

"I'm Ed Vance. You know me. Come on, Dodge, what's this all about?" His knees were freezing solid again. Something was wrong with Dodge's mouth.

"Ed Vance." Dodge's head tilted slightly to one side. "Ed Vance," he repeated, as if he'd never heard the name before and he was making sure not to forget it. "Yessir, I knew they'd send a person of authority. That'd be you, wouldn't it?"

Vance looked at Danny; the boy was about a hair away from jumping out of his shoes, his hands clutching the rifle to his chest. The cadence of Dodge Creech's voice, the flat phrasing, the drawl: all of it was the same, yet there was that low church-organ undertone, and a rattling like loose phlegm in Dodge's throat.

"So let me pose a question to you, pardner," the figure in the rocking chair said. "Who's the guardian?"

"The . . . guardian?"

"I didn't stutter. Who's the guardian?"

"Dodge . . . what're you talkin' about? I don't know anythin' about a guardian."

The rocking ceased. Danny gasped and took a backward step, and he might have plunged into the hole if he hadn't checked himself.

"Maybe you don't at that," the man in the chair replied. "Maybe you do, and maybe you're handin' me bullshit on a platter, Ed Vance."

"No, I swear it! I don't know what you're talkin' about!" The thought hit him like a bullet between the eyes: This isn't Dodge anymore.

The figure stood up. Its clothes made a stiff crackling noise. Dodge Creech seemed two or three inches taller than Vance remembered, and much larger around the shoulders too. There was something funny about the way he moved his head—something like the jerky motion of a puppet on strings, guided by an unseen hand. The figure walked toward Vance, with that strange puppet's gait, and Vance backed away; it stopped, looked from Vance to Danny and back again, and then the white face with its wormy gray lips smiled—a teeth-clenched salesman's smile.

"The guardian," he repeated, and the light gleamed off teeth that were no longer teeth, but thousands of close-packed, blue metallic needles. "Who is it?"

Vance couldn't seem to get his breath. "I swear . . . don't know . . ."

"Well sir, maybe I believe you." The figure in the garish sport coat slowly rubbed its thick, colorless hands together, and Vance saw that the fingernails were about an inch long, made of that same blue-tinged metal and edged with tiny saw-blade-like teeth. "You bein' a person of authority and all, I ought to believe you, right?" the thing in Dodge's skin asked.

Vance had lost his voice.

Danny's back hit the wall, and a framed picture of Dodge receiving an award at an insurance salesmen's convention clattered to the floor.

"So I'll give you the benefit of the doubt. See, I've come a long way, and I've already spent a lot of time and effort." The metal-nailed hands kept rubbing together, and Vance realized that a swipe from one of them could rip his face off right down to the skull. "I can find the guardian my-self if I have to." The head suddenly whipped to the left with violent motion, and the thing's gaze followed the helicopter through a broken window as it circled the pyra-mid. "I don't like that thing. Not the least bit. I don't want it flyin' around my property." Its attention returned to Vance, and the sheriff saw that there was no life in Dodge's eyes; they looked wet and dead, like false eyes stuck into a grinning mask. "But I'll tell you true, Ed Vance: if I don't find out who the guardian is real soon, I'm gonna have to lay down the law. *My* kind of law."

"Who . . . what are you?" Vance rasped.

"I'm an . . ." The figure paused for a few seconds. "An exterminator. And you're a big fat bug. I'll be around, Ed Vance, and I want you to remember me. Okay?"

Vance nodded, a drop of sweat hanging from the tip of his nose. "Oka—"

One of Dodge's hands rose. The fingers probed the left eye and wrenched it from its socket. There was no blood, just strands of oozing fluid. The eyeball went into the needle-filled mouth and burst apart like a hardboiled egg as the jaws clamped down.

Danny moaned, fighting against a faint, and madness clawed at Vance's brain.

"When I want you, I'll find you," the creature said. "Don't try to hide. You can't. We square on that, pardner?"

"Sq-sq-square." The word came out in a choke.

"Good bug." And then the figure turned away from Vance, took two long strides, and dropped into the hole in the living-room floor.

They heard it thump to the bottom after a long fall. There was a quick scuttling sound. Then silence.

Danny screamed. He sprang to the edge of the hole, lifted his rifle and began firing into it, his face contorted with horror. Gunsmoke whirled through the dusty air, and spent cartridges flew. He came to the end of his bullets, but he kept frantically trying to feed shells into the chamber.

"Stop it," Vance said, or thought he had. "Stop it, Danny. *Stop it!*"

The deputy shuddered and looked at him, his finger still jerking on the trigger, his nose running, and the wind whooshing in his lungs.

"It's gone," Vance told him. "Whatever it was . . . it's gone."

"I saw it—I saw it looked like Dodge but it wasn't no way no way in hell was it Dod—"

Vance gripped his collar and shook his hard. *"Listen to me, boy!"* he roared, right in Danny's face. "I don't want you goin' as crazy as Ginger Creech, you hear me?" He felt a wetness at his crotch and knew he'd peed his pants, but right now he had to keep Danny from losing his mind. If the boy went over the edge, Vance would be right behind. "You hear me?" He gave another hard shake, which served to loosen the cobwebs of shock in his own brain as well.

"Wasn't Dodge. Wasn't," Danny mumbled. Then, with a gasp of breath: "Yes sir. I hear you."

"Go to the car." The boy blinked dazedly, still staring into the hole. "Go on, I said!"

Danny staggered out.

Vance swung his shotgun up and aimed it at the hole. His hands shook so hard he figured he couldn't hit a barn door in broad daylight, much less an alien who ate eyeballs and had a thousand needles for teeth. Because that's exactly what it had been, he realized: an alien, dug itself a tunnel from the pyramid across the river and crawled inside Dodge Creech. *My property*, it had said. And what was that shit about a guardian, and how come it could speak English with a Texas accent?

He backed away from the hole, his nerves sputtering. Tendrils of dust and gunsmoke broke, drifted, connected anew around him. He felt like a scream trapped in concrete, and right then he swore that if he got out of this, God willing, he was going to lose fifty pounds by Christmas.

One step out of the house and he turned and ran to the patrol car, where Danny Chaffin sat gray-faced and staring at nothing.

27
Scooter Brought the Stick

In a house at the far end of Brazos Street, Daufin listened while Sarge remembered.

"Scooter brought the stick," he whispered as the dark things moved in his mind. Over the steady tolling of the Catholic church's bell, he thought he heard gunshots: the rapid cracks of a carbine, like brittle sticks being trod upon. The memories were coming to life, and one half of his brain itched like a wound that must be torn open and scratched.

"Belgium," he said. His hands kneaded the air where Scooter had been, just a minute before. "Three-ninety-third infantry regiment, Ninety-ninth Infantry Division, Sergeant Tully Dennison, all present and accounted for, sir!" His eyes were wet, his face strained with internal pressures. "Diggin' in, sir! Hard ground, ain't it? Mighty hard. Froze almost solid. They heard some noise out over the ridge last night. Down there in the deep woods. Recon heard trucks movin' around. Maybe tanks too. Get that telephone cable laid down, yes sir!" He blinked, lifting his chin as if startled by the presence of Daufin. "Who . . . who are you?"

"Your new friend," she said quietly, standing between the light and the dark.

"Little girl shouldn't be out here. Too cold. Snow in them clouds. You speak English?"

"Yes," she said, aware that he was staring right through her, into that hidden dimension. "Who is Scoot-er?"

"Old dog just took up with me. Crazy ol' thing, but Lord can he run. I throw a stick, and he scoots after it. Throw it again, off he goes. Scooter, that's what he is. Can't be still. Skinny thing, about half dead when I found him. Gonna take good care of you, Scooter. You and me, we'll gonna be all right." He crossed his arms over his chest and began to rock. "Put my head on Scooter's side at night. Good ol' pillow. Keeps the foxhole warm. Man, he loves to chase those sticks. Run fetch it, Scooter! Lord, can he run!"

Sarge's breath had quickened. "Lieutenant says if there's any action we won't see it. No way. Says it'll be to the north or the south. Not our position. I just got here, I ain't killed nobody yet. I don't want to. Scooter, we're gonna keep our heads low. We're gonna bury our heads in the ground, ain't we? Just let all that metal fly right over us, huh?"

He shuddered, curled his knees up, stared past Daufin. His mouth worked for a few seconds, his eyes full of violet light, but no sound came out. Then a whisper: "Incomin' mail. Artillery openin' up. Long way off. Gonna go over our heads. Over our heads. Should've dug my foxhole deeper. Too late now. Incomin' mail." He moaned as if struck, squeezing his eyes shut. Tears crept from them. "Make it stop. Make it stop. Please oh Jesus make it stop."

Sarge's eyes flew open. "Here they come! Ready on the right, sir!" It had been a hoarse cry. "Scooter! Where's Scooter? God A'mighty, where's my dog? *Here come the Krauts!*" He was shaking now, his body curled up in the chair, the pulse throbbing at his temple like the rhythm of a runaway machine. "They're throwin' potato mashers! Get your heads down! Oh Jesus . . . oh Christ . . . help the wounded . . . his arm's blown off. Medic . . . *Medic!*" He clasped his hands to his skull, fingers gripping into the flesh. "Got blood on me. Somebody's blood. Medic, move your ass! They're comin' again! Throwin' grenades! Get your heads down!"

Sarge stopped his frantic rocking. His breath caught.

Daufin waited.

"One fell short," he whispered. "Fell short, and still smokin'. Potato-masher grenade. Got a wooden handle. And there he is. Right there." He stared at a point on the wall: the point where the past's shadows were emerging, ghostly scenes coagulating and rippling through the grenade smoke of more than forty years before. "There's Scooter," Sarge said. "Gone crazy. I can see it in his eyes. Gone crazy. Just like me."

He slowly thrust his hand forward, fingers outspread. *"No,"* the whisper came. "No. Don't bring the stick. Don't . . ."

A hiss of breath between his teeth: "I haven't killed yet . . . don't make me kill . . ."

His hand contorted; now it was clenched around an invisible pistol, the finger gripping the trigger. "Don't bring the stick." The finger twitched. "Don't bring the stick." Twitched again. "Don't bring the stick." A third and fourth times.

He was crying, silently, as the finger continued to twitch. "Had to stop him. Had to. Would've fetched me the stick. Dropped it right into my foxhole. But . . . I killed him . . . before the grenade went off. I know I did. I saw his eyes go dead. And then the grenade blew. Didn't make a loud noise. Not loud. And then there was nothin' left of him . . . except what was all over me." His hand lowered, dangled at his side. "My head. Hurts." Slowly, his hand relaxed, and the invisible gun went away.

His eyes had closed again. He sat without moving for a

time, just the rise and fall of his chest and the tears that crawled through the lines on his face.

There was nothing more.

Daufin walked to the front door and looked through the screen at the skygrid. She was trying to put her thoughts together, analyze and categorize what had just been said; she could make no sense of it, but pain and loss lay at its core, and those things she understood very, very well. She sensed a weariness coming over her, enfolding her; it was a weakness of muscles, sinews, and bones—the fabric that held this daughter's body together. She clicked through her memory and came up with the symbol N and, behind it, among the neatly assembled subjects: Nutrition. This daughter's body needed nutrition; it was running down and soon would approach collapse. The Sarge creature had mentioned food. She focused on F and found flat images of Food in her memory: Meat Groups, Vegetable Groups, Cereal Groups. All of them appeared sickening, but they would have to do. The next problem was locating these food groups. Surely they must be close at hand, stored somewhere in the Sarge creature's box.

She walked to his side and plucked at his sleeve. He didn't respond. She tried again, a little harder.

His eyes opened. The last firing of the spark plug in his brain was going out; he felt whole again, the cold tingling sensation gone. He thought he remembered having a terrible nightmare, but that was all gone too.

"Food," she said. "Do you have food here?"

"Yeah. Pork 'n beans. In the kitchen." He placed his hand against his forehead. He was trembling all over, and in his mouth there was a taste like bitter smoke. "Get you somethin' to eat, and then I'll take you home." He tried to stand up, had difficulty at first, then got to his feet. "Lord, I feel funny. Shakin' like a wild weed."

Terror gripped him. Where was Scooter?

There was a movement in the corner, behind Mr. Hammond's little girl. Over where the shadows lay.

Scooter padded out of the corner and looked expectantly at him, like old friends do.

"Mighty prancy, aren't you?" Sarge asked, and smiled. "Let's crack open a can of pork 'n beans for our new friend, okay?" He picked up the oil lamp and headed to the kitchen.

Daufin followed behind, thinking that sometimes the hidden dimension was best left unfathomed.

28

The Drifting Shadow

Working in the glare of a wall-mounted emergency light, Jessie made the last of six stitches and pulled the sutures tight under Cody Lockett's right eye. He winced just a fraction.

"If I was a horse," he drawled, "I'd already have kicked you across the barn."

"If you were a horse, I'd have already shot you." She gave a little extra tug on the filament, tied the sutures off, and snipped the excess. She swabbed another dash of disinfectant on the wound. "Okay, that does it."

Cody stood up from the treatment table and walked to a small oval mirror on the wall. It showed him a face with a left eye purple and swollen almost shut, a gashed lower lip, and the stitch ridges less than an inch below his right eye. His Texaco shirt was ripped and splattered with bloodstains —his own and Rattlesnake blood too. His head had stopped its drumrolls, though, and all his teeth were still in their sockets. He figured he'd been lucky.

"You can admire yourself somewhere else," Jessie said tersely. "Call the next one in as you leave." She had four more teenagers to see, waiting in the hall, and she went to the sink to wash her hands. When she turned the tap, a thin trickle of sandy water spooled out.

"Pretty good job, doc," he told her. "How's X Ray? He gonna be all right?"

"Yes." Thank God, she thought. Three of Ray's ribs were badly bruised, his left arm had been almost dislocated, and he'd come very near biting a piece out of his tongue, not to mention the other cuts and bruises. Right now he was resting in a room down the hall. A few of the other kids had lost teeth and been cut up, but there were no broken bones—except for Paco LeGrande, whose nose had been shattered. "Somebody could've been killed." She dried her hands on a paper towel, feeling grains of sand between her fingers. "Is that what you were trying to do?"

"No. I was tryin' to keep X Ray from gettin' his clock cleaned." He regarded his own skinned knuckles. "The Rattlers started it. The 'Gades were protectin' our own."

"My son's not a member of your gang."

"It's a club," Cody corrected. "Anyway, X Ray lives on this side of the bridge. That makes him one of us."

"Club, gang, whatever the hell you call it—it's a pile of shit." She crumpled the paper and tossed it into the wastebasket. "And my son's name is Ray, *not* X Ray. When are you and the Rattlesnakes going to stop tearing this town to pieces?"

"It's not the 'Gades who're tearin' things up! We didn't ask 'em to jump X Ray and bust up the Warp Room! Besides"—he motioned toward the window, at the black pyramid—"that sonofabitch did more damage in about two seconds than we could've done in two years."

Jessie couldn't dispute that fact. She grunted, realizing she'd come down pretty hard on the boy. She didn't know much about Cody Lockett: just what Tom had told her, and that his father worked at the bakery. She recalled that she had smelled alcohol on the man's breath one day when she'd gone in for some sweet rolls.

"Damn, it's *big.*" Cody went to the window. Some of the roughness had left his voice, and it held a note of awe. A few fires were still burning in Cade's junkyard, spiraling sparks into the sky. Up at the top of the glowing violet grid was a massive dark cloud of smoke and dust, hanging motionlessly over Inferno and blanking out the moon. Cody had never put much stock in the idea of UFOs and aliens before this, though Tank swore that when he was nine years old he'd seen a hovering light in the sky that had scared his underpants brown. He'd never thought much about life on other worlds, because life on this one was tough enough. All that stuff about UFOs and extraterrestrials seemed too distant to be concerned about, but now . . . well, this was a horse of a different shade. "Where do you think it came from?" he asked, in a quiet voice.

"I don't know. A very long way from here, I'm sure."

"Yeah, I reckon so. But why'd it come down in Inferno? I mean . . . whatever's inside it could've landed anywhere in the world. Why'd it pick Inferno?"

Jessie didn't answer. She was thinking about Daufin, and where the little girl—no, she corrected herself—where the creature might be. She looked out the window at the pyramid, and a single word came to her mind: *Stinger*. Whatever that was, Daufin was terrified of it, and Jessie was feeling none too easy herself. She said, "Better tell the next one to come in."

"Okay." Cody tore himself away from the window. He paused at the door. "Listen . . . for whatever it's worth, I'm sorry X Ray got hurt."

She nodded. "So am I, but he'll be all right. I guess he's tougher than I thought." She stopped short of thanking him for helping her son, because the details were still unclear and she saw him and Rick Jurado as the instigators of a gang fight that could've ended in kids getting killed. "You'll probably need something for a headache," she said. "If you ask Mrs. Santos at the front desk, she'll get you some aspirin."

"Yeah, thanks. Hey, maybe I'll have a neat little railroad track to remember tonight by, huh?"

"Maybe," she agreed, though she knew the scar would be hardly noticeable. "Anybody here to take you home?"

"I can walk. Gotta pick up my motor, anyway. Thanks for the patch-up job."

"Try to stay out of trouble, okay?"

He started to flip a witticism at her, but her eyes were honest and he let his swaggering pose drop. "I'll try," he said, and left the room. In the hallway, also lit by the harsh emergency lights, he told the next boy waiting on the bench to go in; the guy was a Rattler, with sullen eyes and a lower lip that looked as if it had lost a tangle with a meat grinder. Then he walked along the hall, passing rooms on either side. From one of them wailed a man's voice, a sound of pure agony. The smell of burned meat hung in the air, and Cody kept going. People were bustling around, throwing long shadows in the half-light. A Hispanic woman with blood all over the front of her dress hurried past him. A man on crutches and with a large bandage stuck to the side of his face stood in a doorway, staring blankly and muttering. Cody saw Doc McNeil coming, supporting a woman with dusty gray hair from which pink curlers dangled. She was wearing a blue robe, her face dead white and her eyes as wide as if she'd just stuck a finger into an electric socket. McNeil helped her into a room on the left, and Cody couldn't help but notice the bloody footprints on the carpet.

Then he was through the gauntlet of suffering and had reached the front desk, where he asked the round-faced nurse, Mrs. Santos, for his aspirin. She gave him a few tablets in a little plastic bottle, made sure she had his name and address down on the records sheet, and said he could go home. The waiting room was full of people too, most of them Bordertown residents who'd been shaken up by the concussion or who were waiting for word on injured relatives.

As Cody crossed the waiting room and headed for the door, his father stood up from a chair in the corner and said, "Boy? Hold on a minute."

Cody glimpsed the garish necktie and almost burst out laughing. No wonder the old man didn't wear ties; the thing emphasized his sinewy neck and made him look like a geek. Cody had had enough of the medicinal odors and anguished noises of the clinic, and he kept striding out the door without waiting for his father. His motorcycle was still parked in front of the Warp Room, and he meant to claim it. Behind him, his father called, "Cody! Where're you goin'?"

Cody might have slowed a step or two; he didn't realize it if he had. But then his old man was catching up with him, really stretching out those long legs. Curt walked to the side with the length of a man separating them. "I'm talkin' to you. Don't you understand English no more?"

"Just go away," Cody said, his voice clipped and tight. "Leave me alone." Over the smells of scorched metal and burning rubber, the aromas of Vitalis and body odor reached him.

"I came to see about you. Heard you got yourself in a fight. Lord, you look like you got your ass busted for sure!"

"I didn't."

"Looks must be deceivin', then." Curt watched the helicopter slowly circling over Cade's autoyard, making tentative approaches to the black pyramid and then veering away through the smoke. "I'm tellin' you," he said, "hell has sure come to Inferno. Ain't that about the weirdest sumbitch you ever saw?"

"I guess so."

"It's spooky. Somethin' like that shouldn't be. You know, I almost ran over Ginger Creech awhile ago. She was just strollin' down the street in her nightgown. God knows what's happened to Dodge. Whatever's goin' on, it's knocked Ginger right off her tracks."

The woman in the blue robe, Cody thought. Mrs. Creech. Sure, he should've recognized her. But then again, he'd never seen her looking like a crazy woman before.

"Guess what?" Curt asked when they'd gone a few more strides. "I'm a deputy. Don't that beat all? Yessir! Sheriff Vance said that if I was to take Ginger to the clinic, he'd make me a deputy. Bet I'll get me a badge. A silver badge, all shiny and nice." The helicopter zoomed overhead, stirring a storm of dust off the street, and turned toward the pyramid again. Curt gazed up at the skygrid. He didn't know what the thing was, but it was something else that should not be. It reminded him of jail bars, and started a crawling sensation of claustrophobia at the back of his neck. Without lights, Inferno resembled a ghost town, all the swirling dust and running tumbleweeds adding to the sense of desolation. Curt's thirst was getting stronger, and he thought it was somehow right that just as he was given some responsibility, Inferno was falling to pieces. He looked at Cody, walking beside him, and he saw how close that cut was to the boy's eye. Tomorrow morning he was going to feel as if he'd stuck his head into a blender. "You all right?" Curt asked.

"What the fuck do you care?" It came out before Cody could stop it.

Curt grunted. "Hell, I didn't say I *cared*. Just asked, that's all." He let silence reign for a few seconds, then tried again: "I got busted up like that once. A Mexican did it, in a bar. Fast little bastard, he was. Man, I couldn't see straight for a week!"

"I'm okay," Cody told him grudgingly.

"Yeah, you're a tough pair of nuts, ain't you? That shirt's a goner, though. Guess old Mendoza'll pitch a fit, huh?"

"No. Mr. Mendoza won't."

Curt decided to let that "mister" lie. What was the point? It amazed him, though, that Cody could still speak of that old wetback with respect after a Mexican had just about bashed his fool head in. Well, Cody had a lot to learn about Mexicans yet. "I found a tie," he said. "See?"

"Yeah. It looks awful."

Curt's first impulse was to snarl and clip him on the back of his skull, but he figured the boy had had enough punishment; anyway, Cody's comment made a faint smile steal across his mouth. "I reckon it does, at that," he admitted. "Never said I had good taste in ties, did I?" Cody glanced at him, and Curt looked away to hide the smile; it wouldn't do for Cody to see it, he decided. It was time to go collect on that bottle of Kentucky Gent. The five dollars was burning a hole in his pocket, and he hoped the Bob Wire Club was still open. If not, he'd kick the damn door down himse—

His thoughts were interrupted by a low rumbling noise that made his bones throb like a mouthful of bad teeth. Curt stopped in his tracks, and Cody halted because he'd both heard and felt the vibration. The noise continued, like the sound of heavy concrete plates grinding. "You hear that?" Curt asked. "What is it?" The sound drifted across Inferno and set the dogs howling again.

Cody looked at the pyramid and pointed. "There!"

A thin vertical crack of muddy violet light had appeared about thirty feet below the pyramid's apex. The grinding noise went on, and the crack of light was widening.

In the clinic, Jessie heard it and went to the window. Rick Jurado came out of his house, and stood on the front porch with Miranda beside him. Mack Cade was standing on Third Street next to his Mercedes, watching the volunteer firemen futilely trying to coax water pressure back into the limp hose, and his first thought was that the rumbling sounded like a massive crypt opening. Typhoid and Lockjaw ran around in a circle, yapping.

Others peered out their windows, and some of the seventy-eight people who had gathered in the Catholic church came out to the front steps to see. Sheriff Vance, who had returned only a few minutes before from Dodge Creech's house, emerged from his office into Celeste Street while Danny sat shaking inside.

The vertical line was about fifteen feet long and stretching open like a cyclopean eye. In the helicopter, Captain Taggart swooped past the fissure. Rhodes, who occupied the copilot's seat, and Gunniston in the observer's seat just behind him were shoved against their backrests by the g-forces. They saw the reptilian plates sliding away from the aperture, and the glow that drifted through was more like luminous mist than earthly light. The aperture's edges appeared moist, rimmed with gray like diseased gums. "Stay away from that grid," Rhodes warned as Taggart took the 'copter up again, but he knew Taggart understood the consequences of hitting that thing as well as he did. The rumbling noise continued as the plates unhooked and slid away from each other. The opening was now about forty feet wide, and Taggart lined the 'copter up with it and used his two control sticks to angle the blades so the machine hovered. Streams of liquid were oozing down from the sides and edges of the opening, running over the plates beneath it. Rhodes leaned forward, the seat belt tightening across his chest. He could see nothing but murk inside the fissure; it was like trying to peer through slimy water.

"Want me to get closer?" Taggart asked.

"Hell, no!" Gunniston yelped, his hands clenched to the armrests.

"Just hold this position," Rhodes told him. Several more plates moved apart, and then the noise abruptly ceased.

Mist curled from the opening and was tattered by the rotors. Taggart checked his gauges: fuel was getting low. They'd followed the grid from east to west and north to south and found that it extended just over seven miles in all directions. Its highest point was about six hundred feet directly above the pyramid, sloping away to spear through the earth at the grid's limits. Below the helicopter were dull red centers of flame amid the wreckage of Cade's autoyard, and the rising of heated air made the machine shudder.

"Thing looks like it's got skin," Gunniston said, staring with revulsion at the slick ebony plates.

Rhodes watched the opening. Banners of black smoke moved past the canopy, and for a few seconds his vision was obscured. When it cleared, he thought he saw something move inside the aperture: a drifting shadow, approaching through the mist. He didn't know what it was, but he realized they were far too close to the pyramid for comfort. "Move us away," he said tautly.

Taggart changed the rotors' pitch, started to slip the helicopter to the left.

As he did, the thing that Rhodes had seen emerged from the mist. Gunniston gasped, "Oh, Christ!" and Taggart throttled the engine up, veering away with such speed that the men were lifted off their seats. Never in his wildest nightmares had he witnessed such a thing as now cleared the pyramid's opening and hovered in the turbulent air.

29
The Duel

A helicopter had emerged from the black pyramid—but it was unlike any machine ever created on earth. Instead of rotors, triangular metallic wings like those of a giant dragon-fly beat rapidly along the sleek black body. Its cockpit—the shape an exact duplicate of the compartment in which Taggart, Rhodes, and Gunniston sat—was made of what appeared to be blue-green, opaque glass, multifaceted like the eye of an insect. Most startling of all, and what had caused Taggart to grip the throttle and veer away so fast, was the craft's tail section: it was made of intertwined, ropy black muscles, and at its end was a bony ball of spikes like a knight's mace. The tail was whipping violently back and forth, the muscles alternately clenching and relaxing.

"A doppelganger," Rhodes said.

Taggart was concentrating on working the cyclic control stick with his right hand and the twistgrip throttle with his left, backing the 'copter away without crashing into the bank building or drifting into the grid. Smoke swirled in front of the cockpit. The dragonfly machine held its position, but slowly angled as if its insect eye was following the earth craft. Gunniston said, *"What?"*

"A doppelganger," Rhodes repeated, thinking aloud. "A mirror image. At least . . . maybe that's how an alien sees us." Another thought struck him. "My God . . . there must be a *factory* in there!" But was it a machine, or was it alive? It was a double of their own helicopter, yes, but the way those wings and muscles worked, the thing might be a living creature—or more bizarre still, a combination of machine and alien life. Whatever it was, the sight held Rhodes in a thrall of horrified wonder.

The trance snapped, very suddenly, when the dragonfly darted forward, soundlessly and with a deadly grace.

"Go!" Rhodes shouted, but the breath was wasted. Taggart's hand on the throttle made the engine scream. The helicopter shot backward and up, missing the overhanging ledge of the bank building's roof by about eight feet. Gunniston's face was a bleached-out shock mask, and he gripped the armrests of his seat like a cat on a roller coaster. The dragonfly made a quick, twitching correction of flight, angled up, and came after them.

The 'copter rose into clouds of smoke and dust. Taggart was flying blind; he eased off on the throttle and spun the machine in a tight circle, the engine spitting through dirty air. As Taggart made the second rotation Gunniston yelled, "At starboard!"

The dragonfly plunged through the murk on their right, twisted violently around in imitation of their own maneuver, and the tail with its ball of spikes came at them. Taggart jerked the 'copter to the left; as the machine heeled over, the dragonfly's tail flashed past so close both Rhodes and Gunniston could see the razor-sharp edges of the spikes. Then clouds enveloped it, and as the 'copter kept falling Rhodes realized that a few blows from that damned tail could tear the aircraft to pieces. He didn't care to think about what it would do to flesh. Taggart let the helicopter plummet until his stomach lurched, and as they dropped through the clouds and leveled off he saw the houses of Bordertown about sixty feet below, people standing in the streets and the glow of candles through windows. He made another tight turn, zooming over the autoyard—and there was the dragonfly, emerging from the clouds and gaining speed at it hurtled at them.

"Head for the desert!" Rhodes said. Taggart nodded, his face sparkling with sweat, and gunned the throttle. As soon as the helicopter leapt forward, the dragonfly changed direction and maneuvered in front of them, cutting them off. "Dammit!" Taggart said, and altered course. The dragonfly did too. "Bastard's playing games with us!"

"Get us on the ground!" Gunniston pleaded. "Jesus Christ, set us *down!*"

The dragonfly pitched downward, came up again with terrifying speed at the helicopter's underbelly. Taggart had time only to rear the helicopter back on its tail rotor and pray.

In the next second came an impact that knocked the men breathless and rattled their brains. There was a shriek of tortured metal, even louder than Gunniston's scream. Everything not bolted down in the cabin—flight log, pencils, extra helmets, and flight jackets—flew around their heads like bats. The cockpit's glass shattered into a crazy quilt, but the glass was reinforced with metal filaments and did not explode into their faces. Acting on instinct, Taggart jerked the machine to the left again, the engine stuttering against a stall. The dragonfly swept upward and away, whirling around and around in a deadly pirouette, bits of the helicopter's metal flying off its tail like miniature comets.

The red landing-gear malfunction light blinked on the instrument panel, and Rhodes knew the skids were either mangled or torn away. "Clipped our skids!" Taggart shouted, panic starting to close around his throat. "Bastard clipped us!"

"Here it comes!" Gunniston had seen the thing through the unbroken window at his side. "At three o'clock!" he yelled.

Taggart felt the helicopter's blades respond to the stick, and the machine swung up as his feet worked the tail rotor pedals. They were on an even keel again, and he laid on the throttle and arrowed straight for the desert to the east of Inferno.

"It's closing!" Gunniston warned, daring to look back

through the rear observation port. "The thing's hauling ass!"

Rhodes saw the low-fuel warning light come on. The airspeed indicator was nosing toward a hundred and twenty, violet-washed desert flashing past about ninety feet below and the grid's eastern boundary in sight. Gunniston made a choked sound of terror as the dragonfly pulled up even with them at a distance of twenty or thirty yards to the right, its triangular wings a whirring blur. It hung there for about five seconds before it darted ahead, rapidly gained altitude, and vanished into the haze at the top of the grid.

Taggart could no longer see it through the cracked glass. He whipped the 'copter around in a spiraling turn that shoved Rhodes and Gunniston into their seats and dropped twenty feet lower to the desert, speeding back in the direction of Inferno. "Where is it? Where'd the bastard go?" he babbled. "You see it, Colonel."

"No. Gunny?"

Gunniston could hardly speak. He got out a weak "No, sir."

Taggart had to cut his speed before the reserve fuel drained. The speed-indicator needle trembled at sixty. "She's handling like a tractor!" Taggart said. "Must have a mess hanging down underneath! Damn sonofabitch just pulled away like we were sitting still!" Air was shrilling in through the cockpit's cracks, the control stick was sluggish, and they were flying on fumes. "I've got to set her down!" Taggart decided. "Gotta belly her in, Colonel!"

They were almost over Inferno again. "Clear the town first!" Rhodes said. "Slide her in on the other si—"

"*Jesus!*" Taggart screamed, because the dragonfly was dropping down from above, almost on top of them, and for an instant he thought he could see a distorted image of himself—an alien image—reflected in the multifaceted glass. He turned the 'copter over on its right side, trying to whip past—but the thing was too close, and its tail was swiping toward him. He drew a breath.

The tail smashed through the cockpit's glass, filling the compartment with a thousand stinging hornets. Fragments slashed into Rhodes's cheeks and forehead, but he'd flung his arms up and saved his eyes. He saw what happened to Taggart.

The spikes on the end of the tail buried themselves in Taggart's chest. His head, left arm, and most of the upper half of his torso disappeared in a blizzard of blood, metallic sparks, and flying glass. The dragonfly's tail continued through the pilot's backrest like a can opener, and Gunniston saw the clenching ebony muscles and the ball of spikes pass him with the velocity of a freight train before it tore through the 'copter's side and out again. He laughed hysterically, his face covered with Taggart's blood.

Irrevocably damaged, the helicopter reeled across the sky. It spun in a wide, fast circle, and through the broken glass Rhodes dazedly watched as the north face of the bank building grew larger.

He couldn't move. Couldn't think. Somebody's blood was everywhere. There was a lump in the pilot's seat that had no business being there, yet clenched to the control stick was a gray hand that should belong to someone. Red lights flashed all over the instrument panel and alarms buzzed. The roofs of Inferno were coming up fast, and Rhodes had the eerie sense of sitting still while the world and the wind were in terrifying motion. The bank building loomed ahead. We're going to crash, he thought calmly. He heard laughter, and its incongruous sound amid all the carnage made the slipping gears of his brain latch into place again. Within seconds they would smash into the bank building.

Rhodes reached for the pilot's control stick, but the gray hand was locked on it and the dead arm's muscles had seized up; the stick was immobile. He blinked, saw the copilot's stick in front of his own seat, a twistgrip throttle to the right. He grasped the stick. No reaction from the rotors. Dead controls, he thought. No, no . . . the transfer switch . . .

Rhodes reached over Taggert's corpse and hit the controls-transfer toggle on the instrument panel. The warning lights lit up on his side. He hadn't flown a helicopter for more than two years, but there was no time for a checkout course; he slipped his feet onto the pedals that operated the rear rotor and angled the control stick with his left hand, at the same time cutting the speed with his right. The building stood before him like a mountain, and even as the 'copter responded to a tight turn Rhodes knew there wasn't going to be enough room. "Hold on!" he shouted to Gunny.

As the 'copter swerved, its tail rotor smashed one of the few remaining windows on the building's second floor and chopped a desk to kindling. The main rotors scraped bricks and threw off a shower of sparks, and as the tail rotor slammed against the wall there was a rupture of lubrication lines and fluids exploded into flame. The helicopter kept turning, all control gone and bucking like an enraged bronco.

Rhodes saw the dragonfly hurtling at them, its wings swept tightly back along its body and the spiked tail flailing. He twisted the throttle to full power; the 'copter shuddered violently, hung waiting to be crushed against the building.

There was a gasp like air being sucked into laboring lungs, and the 'copter dropped another twenty feet and lurched forward.

The dragonfly zoomed over Rhodes's head, hit the bank building, and smashed itself like an insect against a flyswatter. It crumpled with a wet splatting sound, and pieces of dark matter burst over the bricks. Rhodes was engulfed in a squall of amber fluid, and then the helicopter was stuttering through the rain of alien liquid and he saw Cobre Road rising up to take them.

The craft bellied onto the pavement, bounced and slammed down again, skidding along Cobre Road, past Preston Park and caroming off a parked brown pickup truck. It kept going about sixty more feet, its engine dead but its bent rotors still whirling, and stopped just short of the Smart Dollar's plate-glass window, where a red-lettered sign proclaimed GOING OUT OF BUSINESS SALE.

"Well," Rhodes heard himself say, just to verify that he was still alive. He couldn't think of anything else, so he said it again: "Well." But now he smelled burning oil and heard the crackling of flames at the tail rotor, and he knew the fuel tank was probably torn open and they'd better get their asses clear. He twisted around to make sure Gunniston was all right; the younger man was splattered with blood and amber juice, but his eyes were wide open and he wasn't laughing anymore. Rhodes said, "Let's go!" and unbuckled his seat belt. Gunny didn't react, so Rhodes popped the seat belt off him, took his arm, and jerked the hell out of him. *"Let's go!"*

They clambered out. Rhodes saw four figures running toward them, and he shouted, "Stay back!" They obeyed, and Rhodes and Gunniston staggered away from the wreckage. About eight seconds later the 'copter's tail section exploded. A piece of metal the size of a pie pan shot through the Smart Dollar's window.

Three seconds after the first explosion, the helicopter went up in an orange blast, and more black smoke rose to join the clouds at the top of the grid.

Gunniston fell to the curb in front of the Paperback Kastle, and curled up into a shivering ball. Rhodes remained on his feet, watching the helicopter burn. The death of Taggart seemed unreal, something that had happened too quickly to apprehend. He looked at the bank building, could see the dragonfly's glittering slime oozing down the bricks; when he turned his attention to the black pyramid, he saw that the aperture had sealed itself.

"You sonofabitch," he whispered—and he thought that somewhere inside the pyramid a creature—or creatures —might be saying the same thing about him in the language of another world.

"I seen it!" said a leathery old man with white hair and a gold tooth, jabbering right in the colonel's face. "I seen it fly outta there, yessir!"

A rotund woman in overalls prodded Gunniston's ribs with the toe of a tennis shoe. "Is he dead?" she asked. Gunniston suddenly sat up, and the woman leapt backward with the speed of a gymnast.

Other people were coming, drawn by the burning helicopter. Rhodes ran a hand through his hair—and then he was sitting down, his back against the rough stone of the Paperback Kastle's wall though he didn't remember his knees bending. He smelled Taggart's blood all over himself, and there was another, acidic odor too: it took him back to his youth in the green hills of South Dakota, and the image of catching grasshoppers on a sunny summer afternoon. He remembered the sharp tang of the nicotine-brown juice the grasshoppers sprayed on his fingers: hopper pee, he called it. Well, he was covered with it now, and the thought stirred a grim smile—but the smile faded very quickly as the memory of Taggart's body being ripped apart came back to him.

"Your bird's had it," the old coot observed sagely, and another gout of flame leapt from the charred machine.

"Give 'em room, dammit! Step back, now!" Ed Vance pushed his way through the knot of gawkers. He'd trotted over from Celeste Street, and just that short distance had left him puffing and red-faced. He stopped when he saw the gore-covered Rhodes and Gunniston. "Holy Keerist!" He looked around for a couple of able-bodied men. "Hank! You and Billy come on and help me get 'em to the clinic!"

"We're all right," Rhodes said. "Just cut up a little, that's all." He saw tiny bits of glass glittering in his forearms, and he figured he was going to have a long bout with a pair of tweezers. There was a gash on his chin and another across his forehead that felt wicked, but they would have to wait. "Our pilot didn't make it." He turned to Gunniston. "You okay?"

"Yeah. Think so." Gunny had been protected from most of the glass by being behind the front seats, but there were several cuts in his hands and a sliver about two inches long was stuck in his left shoulder. He grasped it, yanked it out, and tossed it away.

Rhodes tried to stand, but his legs betrayed him. A younger man in a red-checked shirt helped him up, and Rhodes said, "I'm getting too old for this shit."

"Yeah, and I'm agin' more every piss-cuttin' minute!" Vance had watched the aerial duel and had thought for sure that the helicopter was either going to slam into the houses of Inferno or hit the First Texas Bank. He glanced at the building, saw the ooze where the flying monstrosity had impacted, and he recalled the creature in Dodge Creech's skin peering out the window and saying *I don't like that thing.* "Listen, Colonel, we've got to talk. Like right now."

Rhodes gingerly worked the kinked muscles in his arms. "I hope you'll understand when I say it'll have to wait."

"No sir," Vance said. *"Now."*

There was an urgency in the sheriff's voice that commanded his attention. "What is it?"

"I think we'd best take a little walk down the street." Vance motioned for him to follow, and Rhodes limped on stiff legs along Cobre Road. The helicopter was still belching black smoke and red licks of flame, and Rhodes thought he could smell Jim Taggart's body burning. When they were beyond earshot of the crowd, Vance said, "I think I had myself one of them close encounters. About twenty minutes ago I met somebody who looked like Dodge Creech . . . only he didn't, and he sure as hell wasn't."

Rhodes listened to the story without interrupting and shook off the shock that kept taking his mind back to the memory of a gray hand and arm and a mangled body. It was the living who were important now, and if the thing in the black pyramid could dig under the river and the houses of Inferno, it could come up wherever it pleased. Whatever it was, it had just turned this piece of Texas badland into a battleground.

"What the hell are we gonna *do?"* Vance asked at the end of his story.

"We sure can't run," Rhodes said quietly. "There's nowhere to run to." *I de-sire to ex-it,* he remembered Daufin saying, and how frantic she'd gotten when she'd understood there were no interstellar vehicles here. She'd begged to be taken away, and he hadn't done it; she must have known the other spaceship was after her. But for what reason? And who—or *what*—was the thing that Daufin called Stinger?

He touched his chin and looked at the blood on his fingers. His beige knit shirt was a patchwork of bloodstains —mostly Taggart's. He felt all right, maybe a little weak-headed. No matter, he had to keep going and think about rest and stitches later. He said, "Take me to Creech's house."

30
Coffin Nails

A silence settled over Inferno in the wake of the helicopter's crash. People who had been roaming the streets, talking about the pyramid and wondering if it was the Last Days, went home, locked their doors and windows, and stayed there in the violet-tinged gloom. Others went to the safety of the Baptist church, where Hale Jennings and a few volunteers passed out sandwiches and cold coffee in the light of the altar candles. Renegades were drawn to the lights of their fortress at the end of Travis Street; Bobby Clay Clemmons passed around some marijuana but mostly everybody just wanted to sit and talk, drink a few beers, and swap ideas about where the pyramid had come from and what it was doing here. At the Brandin' Iron, Sue Mullinax and Cecil Thorsby stayed on duty, making sandwiches out of cold luncheon meat for some of the regulars who wandered in, afraid to be alone in the dark.

In the clinic, Tom Hammond was holding a flashlight steady over an operating table as Early McNeil and Jessie worked on the mangled arm of a Hispanic man named Ruiz, who had stumbled across the river a few minutes after the pyramid had crashed down. The arm was hanging by red threads of muscle, and Early knew it had to come off. He said behind his surgical mask, "Let's see if I've still got it in me, kiddies," and reached for the bone saw.

Across the river, the fire fighters had given up. The wreckage of workshops and storehouses still smoldered in Cade's autoyard, tangled heaps of debris opening scarlet eyes of flame. Mack Cade cursed and promised to have their asses on keychains, but without water pressure the hoses were just so much flabby canvas and none of the firemen wanted to go any closer to the pyramid than they had to. They packed their gear into the fire truck and left Cade ranting with impotent rage beside his Mercedes, the two Dobermans barking in furious counterpoint.

Smoke suffused the air, lay low in the gash of the Snake River, and hung like gray fog in the streets. Overhead, the moon and stars were blanked out. But time continued to move, and the hands of wristwatches and battery-run clocks crept toward midnight.

Mrs. Santos left the clinic on Dr. McNeil's orders to find volunteers to give blood, and her attention was caught by the large yellow Cadillac that was parked just down Celeste Street, with a view across the river. A white-haired woman sat behind the wheel, staring at the pyramid as if mesmerized. Mrs. Santos approached the car, knowing who it belonged to; she tapped on the window, and when Celeste Preston lowered it, the chill of air conditioning drifted out. "We need blood at the clinic," Mrs. Santos said matter-of-factly. "Dr. McNeil says I'm not supposed to come back until I find six volunteers. Will you help us?"

Celeste hesitated, her mind still dazed by the thing out in Cade's autoyard, the skygrid, and the creature she'd watched crash into the bank building. She'd been on her way home after leaving Vance, but she'd had the urge to slow down, turn right on Circle Back Street, and drive through what remained of Wint's dream. Ol' Wint's rolling in his grave up on Joshua Tree Hill by now, she thought. Wasn't enough for Inferno to die with a whimper, like a hundred other played-out Texas towns. No, God had to give the coffin nails another twist. Or maybe it was Satan's work.

The air sure smelled like hell. "What?" she asked Early's nurse, not understanding.

"We need blood real bad. What type do you have?"

"Red," Celeste answered. "How the hell do I know?"

"That'll do. Will you let us have a pint?"

Celeste grunted. Some of the steel had returned to her eyes. "Pint, quart, gallon: what the hell? My blood feels mighty thin right now."

"It's thick enough," Mrs. Santos said, and waited.

"Well," Celeste said finally, "I don't reckon I've got anything better to do." She opened the door and got out. The seat was lumpy, and her ass had been falling asleep anyway, just sitting out here for the last fifteen or twenty minutes. "Will it hurt?"

"Just a sting. Then you'll have a rest and get a dish of ice cream." If it wasn't melting in the freezer, she thought. "Go tell Mrs. Murdock you want to give blood. She'll be at the front desk." Mrs. Santos was amazed at herself, a Bordertown resident giving orders to Celeste Preston. "I mean . . . if that's all right?"

"Yeah. Whatever." Celeste stared at the pyramid for a moment longer, and then she started walking to the clinic; Mrs. Santos continued along the street in the opposite direction.

In Sarge Dennison's house, across from where Reverend Jennings was leading a group of townspeople in prayer at the Baptist church, Daufin stood next to the chair in which Sarge was sprawled.

Now this was a curious thing, Daufin mused: the creature had been consuming the tasteless material called pork 'n beans from a round metallic receptacle, using a four-pronged tool, when he'd suddenly made an explosive noise from the depths of his chair, leaned his head back, and closed his eyes. "Gonna rest for a few minutes," he'd told her. "Ain't what I used to be. You keep Scooter company, hear?" And it wasn't very much longer before the creature's mouth had begun making a low buzzing sound, as if there were an efficient machine tucked away somewhere within.

Daufin had approached him and peered into the half-open mouth, but could see nothing except the strange bony appliances called teeth. It was another mystery.

Her stomach felt weighed. The receptacle of pork 'n beans that Sarge had opened and given to her was empty, and lay on a table along with the tool she'd used to eat it. The act of feeding on this world was a repetitive labor of balance, visual acuity, and sheer willpower. She was astounded that the beings could force such sludgy fodder into their systems. Lying beside Sarge's chair was a long yellow envelope made of a tough, slick material, and on the envelope was written the cryptic word "Fritos." Sarge had shared the crunchy food curls with her, and Daufin had found them at least palatable, but now the inside of her mouth was dry. It seemed there was always some discomfort on this world; perhaps, in some strange way, discomfort was this species' prime motivation.

"I am go-ing to try to find an ex-it now," she told him. "Thank you for the ed-i-bles."

Sarge stirred, drowsily opened his eyes. He saw Stevie Hammond and smiled. "Bathroom's in the back," he said, and settled himself in for a long nap.

This alien language was a puzzlement. The Sarge creature's buzzing began again, and Daufin walked out of the house into the warm dark.

Haze hung in the air, thicker than it had been when she'd come out here not long ago and seen the two flying machines whirling across the sky. She'd watched their duel, didn't really know what was happening, but reasoned it wasn't a common sight; there'd been humans watching from the street, and some of them had made high shrieking noises that she construed as sounds of alarm. Then, when the battle was over and the surviving machine fell with fire chewing its tail, Daufin was left with a single thought: *Stinger*.

Sarge had been kind to her, and she liked him; but now the need to find an exit called her. Her gaze swept the sky, scanning the violet mesh that trapped her and the humans in the same huge cage. She knew where it came from, and what powered it. Inside her there was a pressure as if some part of her was on the verge of breaking, and the pumping muscle at her center picked up speed. Hopeless! she thought as she scanned the skygrid from horizon to horizon. There is no exit! Hopeless!

A low gleam of light caught her eye, through the haze that clung close to the street. It was made of many colors, and it was an inviting light. If light could carry hope, Daufin thought, this light did. She began to walk toward the Inferno Baptist Church, where candlelight filtered through a stained-glass window.

The door was open. Daufin slid her head around its corner to peer inside.

Small white sticks with tips of light illuminated the interior, and at the opposite end from Daufin stood two metallic structures that each held six of the light-tipped sticks. Daufin counted, in the crude Earth mathematics, forty-six humans sitting on long high-backed benches, facing an upraised dais. Some of the humans had their heads bent over and their hands clasped. A man with a shiny head stood at the dais, and appeared to be dispensing liquid from a large receptacle into tiny ones held in a metallic tray.

And above the dais was a curious sight: a suspended vertical line crossed by a shorter horizontal line, and at its center the figure of a human being hung with arms outstretched. The figure's head was capped with a circle of twisted vegetation, and its face angled up toward the ceiling; the painted eyes were imploring, and seemed to be fixed on a distance far beyond the confines of this structure. Daufin heard a painful sound from one of the people on the benches: a "sob," she thought it was called. The hanging figure indicated this might be a place of torture, but there were mixed feelings here: sadness and pain, yes, but something else too, and she wasn't quite certain what it was. Perhaps it was the hope that she'd thought was lost, she decided. She could feel a strength here, like a collection of minds turned in the same direction. It felt like a sturdy place, and a safe shelter. This is an abode of ritual, she realized as she watched the man at the dais preparing the receptacles of dark red liquid. But who was the figure suspended at the center of two crossed lines, and what was its purpose? Daufin entered the building, going to the nearest bench and sitting down. Neither Hale Jennings nor Mayor Brett, who sat with his wife Doris on the first pew, saw her come in.

"This is the blood of Christ," the reverend intoned as he finished pouring the sacramental grape juice. "With this blood we are whole, and made new again." He opened a box of Saltines, began to crush them, and the pieces fell into an offering plate. "And this is the body of Christ, which has passed from this earth into grace so that there should be life everlasting." He turned to the congregation. "I invite you to partake of holy Communion. Shall we pray?"

Daufin watched as the others bowed their heads, and the man at the dais closed his eyes and began to speak in a soft rising and falling cadence. "Father, we ask your blessing on this Communion, and that you strengthen our souls in this time of trial. We don't know what tomorrow's going to bring, we're afraid, and we don't know what to do. What's happening to us, and to our town, is beyond our minds to comprehend. . . ."

As the prayer continued, Daufin listened closely to the man's voice, comparing it to the voices of Tom, Jessie, Ray, Rhodes, and Sarge. Each voice was unique in a wonderful way, she realized. And the correct enunciation was far different from her halting tongue. This man at the dais almost turned speaking into song. What she'd first considered a rough, guttural language—full of barbarity and made of unyielding surfaces—now amazed her with its variety. Of course a language was only as good as the meaning behind it and she still was having trouble understanding, but the sound fascinated her. And saddened her a little, as well; there was something indescribably lonely about the human voice, like a call from darkness into darkness. What an infinity of voices the human beings possessed! she thought. If each voice on this planet was unique, just that alone was a marvel of creation that staggered her senses.

". . . but guard us, dear Father, and walk with us, and let

us know that thy will be done. Amen," Jennings finished. He took the plate holding the little plastic cups of juice in one hand and the cracker crumbs in the other, and began to go from person to person offering Communion. Mayor Brett accepted it, and so did his wife. Don Ringwald, owner of the Ringwald Drugstore, took it, as did his wife and their two children. Ida Slattery did, and so did Gil and Mavis Lockridge. Reverend Jennings continued along the aisle, giving the Communion and saying quietly, "With this you accept the blood and body of Christ."

A woman sitting in front of Daufin began to cry, and her husband put his arm around her shoulder and drew her closer. Two little boys sat beside them, one wide-eyed and scared and the other staring over the back of the pew at Daufin. Across the aisle, an elderly woman closed her eyes and lifted a trembling hand toward the figure above the dais.

"With this you accept the blood and—" Jennings stopped. He was staring at the dusty face of Tom and Jessie's little girl. A thrill of shock went through him; this was the alien creature Colonel Rhodes was searching for. "—the body of Christ," he continued, offering the grape juice and cracker crumbs to the people on the pew in front of her. Then he stood beside her, and he said gently, "Hello."

"Hello," she answered, copying his dulcet voice.

Jennings bent down, and his knees creaked. "Colonel Rhodes is looking for you." The little girl's eyes were almost luminous in the golden candlelight, and directed at him with intense concentration. "Did you know that?"

"I sus-pect—" She stopped herself, wanting to try again with more of a human's smooth cadence instead of the halting Webster's pronunciation. "I suspected so," she said.

Jennings nodded. His pulse rate had kicked up a few notches. The figure sitting before him resembled Stevie Hammond in every way but for her posture: she sat rigidly, as if uncomfortable with the way her bones fit together, and her right leg was drawn up underneath her. Her arms hung limply by her sides. The voice was almost Stevie's, but with a reedy sound beneath it, as if she had a flute caught in her throat. "Can I take you to him?" he asked.

There was a quick expression of fear on her face, like a glimpse of dark water through white ice; then gone, frozen over again. "I must find an exit," she said.

"You mean a door?"

"A door. An escape. A way out. Yes."

A way out, he thought. She must be talking about the force field. "Maybe Colonel Rhodes can help you."

"He cannot." She hesitated, tried again: "He can't help me find an exit. If I am unable to exit, there will be much hurting."

"Hurting? Who'll get hurt?"

"Jessie. Tom. Ray. You. Everyone."

"I see," he said, though he did not. "And who'll do this hurting?"

"The one who's come here, searching for me." Her eyes were steady. Jennings thought something about them looked very old, as if a small ancient woman was sitting there wearing a little girl's skin. "Stinger," she told him, the word falling from her mouth like something hideously nasty.

"You mean that thing out there? Is that its name?"

"An approx-i-ma-tion," she said, struggling with the stubborn fleshy slab inside her mouth. "Stinger has many names on many worlds."

The reverend thought about that for a moment, and if anybody had ever told him he'd be talking to an alien and being told firsthand that there was life on "many worlds" he would have either decked the fool with a good right cross or called for the butterfly wagon. "I'd like to take you to Colonel Rhodes. Would that be all right?"

"He can't help me."

"Maybe he can. He wants to, like we all do." She seemed to be thinking it over. "Come on, let me take you to—"

"That's her!" someone shouted, startling the trays of grape juice and cracker crumbs out of the reverend's hands. Mayor Brett was on his feet, standing halfway up the aisle, his wife right behind him and shoving him into action.

Brett's finger pointed at Daufin. "That's her, everybody!" he yelled. "That's the thing from outer space!"

The couple in front of Daufin recoiled. One of the little boys jumped over the pew to get away, but the one who'd been watching her just grinned. Other people were standing up for a good look, and nobody was praying anymore.

Jennings rose to his feet. "Hold on now, John. Don't make a fuss."

"Fuss, my ass! That's her! That's the monster!" He took a backward step, collided with Doris; his mouth was a shocked O. "My God! In *church!*"

"We don't want to get all riled up," Jennings said, making an effort to keep his voice soothing. "Everybody just take it easy."

"It's because of *her* we're in this fix!" Brett howled. His wife's pinched face nodded agreement. "Colonel Rhodes said that thing got inside Stevie Hammond, and there she sits! God only knows what kinda powers she's got!"

Daufin looked from face to face and saw terror in them. She stood up, and the woman in front of her snatched her grinning little boy and backed away. "Get her out of here!" the mayor went on. "She don't have no right to be in the Lord's house!"

"Shut up, John!" Jennings demanded. People were already heading to the door, getting out as fast as they could. "I'm about to take her over to Colonel Rhodes. Now why don't you just sit down and put a lid on—"

The floor shook. Daufin saw the light sticks waver. One of the metallic holders toppled, and burning light sticks rolled across the crimson carpet.

"What was that?" Don Ringwald yelled, his owlish eyes huge behind his wire-rimmed spectacles.

There was a crackling noise. Concrete breaking, Jennings thought. He felt the floor shudder beneath the soles of his shoes. Annie Gibson screamed, and she and her husband Perry ran for the door with their two boys in tow. Across the aisle, old Mrs. Everett was jabbering and lifting both hands toward the cross. Jennings looked at Daufin, saw the fear slide into her eyes again, and then fall away, replaced by a blast-furnace glare of anger beyond any rage he'd ever witnessed. Daufin's fingers gripped the pew in front of her, and he heard her say, "It's Stinger."

The floor bulged along the aisle like a blister about to pop open. Brett staggered back, and his elbow clipped Doris solidly in the jaw and knocked her sprawling to the floor. She didn't get up. Someone screamed on the other side of the sanctuary. Stones were grinding together, timbers squealed, and the pews rolled as if on stormy waves. Jennings had the sense of something massive under the sanctuary's floor, something surfacing and about to burst through. Cracks shot up the walls, and the figure of Jesus on the cross broke loose and crashed down upon the altar in a flurry of rock dust.

A section of the church on the left collapsed, the pews splitting apart. Dust whirled through the last of the candle-light, and Daufin shouted, "Get out! Get out!" as people surged toward the doorway, trailing screams. Jennings saw the carpet rip apart, and a jagged fissure opened along the aisle. The floor heaved, shuddered, began to collapse inward as dust billowed up from the earth. Ida Slattery almost knocked Jennings off his feet as she barreled past him, shrieking. He saw Doris Brett fall through the floor, and the mayor was climbing over the twisting pews like a monkey to get to the doorway.

Gil Lockridge fell through, and his wife Mavis a second afterward as the floor opened under her feet. The Ringwalds' oldest boy pitched through, and hung screaming to its side as Don reached down for him. "Praise be to Jeeeesus!" Mrs. Everett was shouting insanely.

Pews were splitting with gunshot cracks as the floor pitched wildly, fissures snaking up the walls. Overhead, the wooden rafters began breaking and plummeting down, and the stained-glass windows shattered as the walls shook on their foundations.

Some of the candles had set fire to the carpet up near the altar, and the nibbling flames threw grotesque shadows as people fought to get out the door or climb through the windows. Jennings scooped Daufin up and held her, as he would any child, and he could feel her heart pounding at furious speed. Mrs. Everett fell as the floor collapsed beneath her; she hung to the splintered edge of a pew, her feet dangling over darkness, and Jennings grasped her arm to haul her up.

But before he could, Mrs. Everett went down with such force that his own arm was almost wrenched from its socket. He heard her scream turn into strangling, and he thought, Something pulled her down.

"No! No!" Daufin was shouting, twisting to get out of the human's grip. Her insides were aflame with rage and terror, and she knew that what was happening in this place was because of her. The screams pierced her with agony. *"Stop it!"* she cried out, but she knew the thing beneath the floor would not hear her, and it knew no mercy.

Jennings turned, started for the door.

He took two strides—and then the floor broke open in front of him.

He fell, both arms scrabbling for a grip as Daufin held around his neck. He caught the broken edge of a pew, splinters driving into his palms. His legs searched for a foothold, but there was nothing there. A rafter slammed down so close he felt its breeze on his face. He sensed more than felt something moving sinuously underneath him —something huge. And then he *did* feel it—a cold, gluey wetness around his feet, closing over his ankles. In another second he was going to be jerked down as Mrs. Everett had been; his shoulder muscles popped as he heaved himself and Daufin up, and the suction on his ankles threatened to tear him apart at the waist. He kicked frantically, got one leg loose and then the other, and he latched his knees on the pitching floor. Then he was up again and running, and as the roof began to sag he cleared the doorway, tripped over a crawling body, and pitched onto the sandy lawn. His right side took most of the impact; he let go of Daufin and rolled away to keep from crushing her. He lay on his back, stunned and gasping, as the church's walls were riddled with cracks and sections of the roof crashed inward. Dust plumed up through the holes like dying breath. The church's steeple fell in, leaving a broken rim of stones. The walls trembled once more, wooden beams shrieked like wounded angels, and finally the noise of destruction echoed away and faded.

Slowly the reverend sat up. His eyes were itchy with grit and his lungs strained air from the whirling dust. He looked to his side, saw Daufin sitting up with her legs splayed beneath her like those of a boneless doll, her body jerking as if her nerves had gone haywire.

She knew how close the hunter had been. Maybe it had sensed the gathering of creatures in that abode and had struck as a demonstration of its strength. She didn't think it had known she was there, but it had been so very close. And *too* close for some of the humans; she looked around, quickly counting figures through the dust. She made out thirty-nine of them. Stinger had taken seven. The knot of muscle at her center would not cease its hammering, and her face felt gorged with pressure. Seven life forms gone, because she had crashed on a small world where there was no exit. The trap had closed, and all running was useless. . . .

"You did this!" Someone's hand closed around her shoulder and yanked her to her feet. There was rage in the voice, and rage in the touch. Her legs were still wobbly, and the human hand shook her with maddened fury. "You did this, you little . . . alien bitch!"

"John!" Jennings said. "Let her go!"

Brett shook her again, harder. The little girl felt as if she were made of rubber, and her lack of substance further infuriated him. "You damned *thing!*" he shrieked. "Why don't you go back where you came from!"

"Stop it!" The reverend started to rise, but a pain shot from his shoulder down his back. He stared numbly at his feet; his shoes were gone, and gray slime clung to his argyle socks.

"You don't belong here!" Brett shouted, and shoved her roughly away. She stumbled backward, all balance lost, and gravity took her to the ground. "Oh God . . . oh Jesus," the mayor moaned, his face yellow with dust. He looked around, saw that Don and Jill Ringwald and their two sons had made it out, as well as Ida Slattery, Stan and Carmen Frazier, Joe Pierce, the Fancher family, and Lee and Wanda Clemmons among the others. "Doris . . . where's my wife?" Fresh panic hit him. *"Doris! Hon, where are you?"*

There was no reply.

Daufin stood up. Her center felt bruised, and the foul taste of pork 'n beans soured her mouth. The anguished human being turned, started staggering back toward the ruined abode of ritual. Daufin said, "Stop him!" in a voice that reverberated with power and made Al Fancher clasp his hand on Brett's arm.

"She's gone, John." Jennings tried to stand again, still could not; his feet were freezing cold, and seemed to have been shot full of novocaine up to his ankles. "I saw her go down."

"No, you didn't!" Brett pulled free. "She's all right! I'll find her!"

"Stinger took her," Daufin said, and Brett flinched as if he'd been struck. She realized the human had lost a loved one, and again pain speared her. "I'm sorry." She lifted a hand toward him.

Brett reached down and picked up a stone. "You did it! You killed my Doris!" He took a step forward, and Daufin saw his intention. "Somebody oughta kill *you!*" he seethed. "I don't care if you're hidin' in a little girl's skin! By Jesus, I'll kill you myself!" He flung the stone, but Daufin was faster by far. She dodged aside, and the stone sailed past her and hit the pavement.

"Please," she said, offering her palms as she retreated to the street. "Please don't . . ."

His hand closed on another rock. "No!" Jennings shouted, but Brett threw it. This time the rock clipped Daufin's shoulder, and the pain made her eyes flood with tears. She couldn't see, couldn't understand what was happening, and Brett hollered, "Damn you to hell!" and advanced on her.

She almost stumbled over her legs, righted herself before she fell; then she propelled herself away from the human being in the complex motion of muscles and bones called running. Pain jarred through her with every stride, but she kept going, cocooned in agony.

"Wait!" Jennings called, but Daufin was gone into the haze of smoke and dust.

Brett took a few paces after her, but he was all used up and his legs gave out on him. "Damn you!" he shouted after her. He stood with his fists clenched at his sides, and then he turned back toward what was left of the church and called for Doris in a voice racked with sobbing.

Don Ringwald and Joe Pierce helped Jennings up. His feet felt like useless knobs of flesh and bone, as if whatever had grasped him had leeched all the blood out and destroyed the nerves. He had to lean heavily on the two men to keep from going down again.

"That does it for the church," Don said. "Where do we go now?"

Jennings shook his head. Whatever had broken through the church floor would have no trouble coming up through any house in Inferno—even through the streets themselves. He felt a tingling in his feet; the nerves were coming back to life. He caught lights through the haze and realized where they were coming from. "Up there," he said, and motioned toward the apartment building at the end of Travis Street. That place, with its armored first-floor windows and its foundation of bedrock, would be a tougher nut for Stinger to crack. He hoped.

Other people were coming from the houses nearby, alerted by the noise and screams. They followed as the two men helped Jennings along the street, and the rest of the congregation moved toward the only building that still showed electric lights.

After a few minutes, Mayor Brett wiped his nose on his sleeve, turned away from the ruins, and walked after them.

31
Below

"Flashlight," the colonel said, and Vance gave it to him.

Rhodes bent down, his knees on the basement's cracked concrete floor, and aimed the light into the hole. There was a drop of about ten feet, and the red dirt glistened as if a huge snail had tracked over it.

"He was sittin' in a rockin' chair up there," Vance repeated for the third time, motioning toward the hole in the den floor above their heads. "It, I mean. Whatever it was—'cause it sure as hell wasn't Dodge." He was whispering; his gut churned, and the skin had drawn tight at the back of his neck. But the flashlight beam had shown them that nothing was hiding in the Creech basement except a little green lizard over by the washing machine. "It knew *English,*" Vance said. "Spoke it like a Texan. How the hell could it know the way we talk?"

Rhodes shone the light around and saw a broken pipe, slick with some kind of gelatinous excretion. A bittersweet chemical smell—not unlike the odor of peaches rotting under a high summer sun—drifted up from the hole to sting his nostrils. "I've got two theories, if you want to hear them," he said.

"Shoot."

"One, that the creature monitored earth's satellites and

figured out our language. But that wouldn't account for it speaking with a Texas accent. Two, that it somehow got into the man's language center."

"Huh?"

"It might've tapped the brain's language center," Rhodes explained. "Where an individual's dictionary is stored. That way it would pick up the accent too."

"Jesus! You mean . . . it like got into Dodge's *brain?* Like a worm or somethin'?" Vance's hand tightened around the loaded shotgun at his side. He and Rhodes had gone by the office to pick up the flashlight, and the sheriff also wore a shoulder holster with a fully loaded Snubnose .38 in it. Lying on the concrete within easy reach of Rhodes's right hand was one of the repeating rifles from the sheriff's gun cabinet.

"Maybe. I don't know what the process might be, but it could've read the language center like a computer reading a program." He angled the light in another direction, saw more gleaming red dirt and darkness beyond. "Whatever this thing is, it's highly intelligent and it works *fast.* And one other thing I'm fairly sure of: it's not the same kind of creature as Daufin."

"How do you figure that?" He jumped; that damned green lizard was scurrying around again.

"Daufin had to learn our language from scratch, starting with the alphabet," Rhodes said. "The other creature—the one Daufin calls Stinger—uses a much more aggressive process." Understatement of the year, he thought. "I believe it killed Dodge Creech—or stored him somewhere—and what you saw was its simulation of him, just like that flying bastard simulated our helicopter."

"Simulated? Is that like a mutant or somethin'?"

"Like a . . . a replicant," Rhodes explained. "An android, for want of a better word, because I think part of that weird chopper was alive. Probably the thing you saw was alive too—but just as much of a machine as a living creature. Like I say, I don't know how it works, but I think one thing's particularly interesting: if Stinger did create a replicant of Dodge Creech, it screwed up on the teeth and fingernails."

"Oh. Yeah. Right," Vance agreed, recalling that he'd told Rhodes about those metallic needles and the blue saw-edged nails.

"There are probably other differences too, internally. Remember, to it *we're* the aliens. If somebody showed you a blueprint of a creature you'd never seen before, and gave you the raw materials to make it with, I doubt if the final result would look much like the real thing."

"Maybe so," Vance said, "but it seems to me the sonofabitch has just figured out a better way to kill."

"Yeah, that too." One more revolution of the light's beam in the hole, and he knew what had to be done. "I've got to go down in there."

"Like hell! Mister, your head must be screwed on with rusty bolts!"

"I won't argue that point." He shone the light around the basement and stopped it at a coil of garden hose hanging from a wall hook. "That'll have to do for rope." His light found a water pipe on the wall nearby. "Help me secure it around there."

They got the hose tied and knotted and Rhodes threw its free end into the hole. He pulled at it a few times to make sure it would bear his weight, and then he balanced on the hole's edge for a minute until his heartbeat calmed down. He tossed Vance the flashlight. "Drop that and the rifle to me when I get to the bottom." He felt a flagging of his courage. He still had Taggart's blood up his nose and brown streaks of gore and grasshopper pee all over him.

"I wouldn't do it," Vance advised soberly. "Ain't worth gettin' yourself killed."

Rhodes grunted. He'd just as soon mark this off as a sorry misadventure, but Vance sure as hell wasn't going to do it; there was no one else but him, and that was how things were. His testicles crawled, and he had to go before all his courage ebbed away. "Here goes," he said, and swung his weight out over the hole. The pipe creaked ominously but remained bolted to the wall. Rhodes climbed down into the darkness, and a few seconds later his shoes squished as they touched bottom. "Okay." His voice echoed back to him, doubled in volume. "Drop the light."

Vance did—reluctantly—and Rhodes caught it though his palms were already slick with sweat. He shone the light around in a quick circle. A film of pale gray ooze maybe an inch deep covered the red dirt; it was still fairly fresh and crept down the walls in rivulets. To Rhodes's right, a tunnel had been bored through the dirt and extended beyond the light's range. His mouth dried up as he realized the size of the thing that had dug it; the tunnel was almost six feet high and about four or five feet in width.

"The rifle," he said, and caught that too as it fell.

"You see anythin'?"

"Yeah. A tunnel's ahead of me. I'm going in."

"Lord God!" Vance said under his breath. He felt as defenseless as a skinned armadillo without the flashlight, but he figured the colonel was going to need it more. "Anythin' moves in there, you blow the bejeezus outta it and I'll haul you up!"

"Check." Rhodes hesitated, looked at his wristwatch in the glare of the light. It was almost eighteen minutes until midnight. The witching hour, Rhodes thought. He took the first step into the tunnel, having to bend over only a few inches; the second step was no easier, but he kept going with the flashlight in his left hand and the rifle stock braced against his right shoulder. His finger stayed close to the trigger.

As soon as the light was gone, Vance heard the lizard rustle over in its corner and came within a bladder's squeeze of wetting his trousers.

Step by slow step, the colonel moved away from beneath the Creech house. About ten feet in, he paused to examine the substance on the walls, floor, and ceiling. He tentatively touched a drool of it and jerked his hand back; the stuff was slick and as warm as fresh snot. Some kind of natural lubricant, he decided. Maybe an alien equivalent of saliva or mucus. He would've liked to have gotten a sample of it, but he couldn't bear to carry any of it back with him. Anyway, the gunk was all over his shoes. He went on, following the tunnel as it made a long curve to the right. The walls were slowly dripping and the dirt was blood red. He had the weird sensation of walking deeper into a nostril, and at any second he expected to see damp hairs and blood vessels.

The tunnel went straight for about thirty feet before it snaked slowly to the left. Was Stinger a part-machine, part-living hybrid like the dragonfly had been? Rhodes wondered. Or was Stinger Daufin's term for not a single creature, but a collection of them?

He stopped. Listened. A strand of ooze dripped from the ceiling and clung to his shoulder.

There was a distant rumbling noise, and a slight vibration in the tunnel floor. It ceased after a few seconds—and then there it was again, a rumbling like a subway train somewhere beyond the walls. Or a subterranean bulldozer, he thought grimly. Little scurryings of fear ran in his belly. The noise seemed to be coming from somewhere to his left. Maybe it was the sound of something digging, or the sound of a massive thing moving through an already-dug tunnel. Heading where, and for what reason? If Stinger was digging tunnels like this one under the entire town, then it was either wasting a lot of energy or preparing for a major assault. There was no way to know what its intent and capabilities were until Daufin explained why it was after her. And first of all, she had to be found—he hoped by himself and not by Stinger.

The noise of either digging or tunnel travel again faded away. There was no telling how far this tunnel went —probably all the way under the river to the black pyramid —but Rhodes had seen and heard enough. He could feel the slimy excretion in his hair, and a strand of it was sliding slowly down his neck. It was time to get the hell out.

He retreated, the light's beam spearing along the tunnel in front of him.

And the light caught something: a figure, jerking in and then out of the beam, way down at the far end of the tunnel.

Rhodes's legs locked up. The breath froze in his lungs.

There was silence, except for a slow dripping noise.

Something's down there, he thought. Watching me. I can feel the sonofabitch. Just beyond the light. Waiting.

He couldn't move, and he feared that if he did break his legs loose from their terror lock and start running, whatever was down there would be on him before he could make it the sixty feet back to where Vance waited.

Still silence.

And then a voice. An old woman's voice, singing: "Jeeesus loves the little chilllldren, alllll the chilllldren in the worrrlllld. . . ."

"Who's there?" Rhodes called. His voice shook. Smart move! he thought. Like it's really going to answer!

The singing had a metallic undertone, and it drifted past him like a half-remembered Sunday school song from a tinny record player. After a few more seconds, it stopped in midphrase, and the silence descended again.

The flashlight's beam trembled. He aimed the rifle's barrel down the tunnel.

"Praise the Lord!" the old woman's voice called. "Glory be!"

"Step into the light," Rhodes said. "Let me see you."

"Hot hot hot! You're a very naughty boy and you'll get a switchin'!"

It occurred to him that it might really be an old woman, fallen down here and gone crazy in the darkness.

"I'm Colonel Matt Rhodes, United States Air Force!" he said. "Who are you?"

The silence stretched. He sensed a figure, standing just beyond the light. "God don't like naughty boys," the old woman's voice answered. "Don't like liars, neither. Who's the guardian?"

It was the question that Vance had told Rhodes the Dodge Creech creature had asked, and now the colonel knew for sure it was no crazy old lady down there in the dark.

"What guardian?" Rhodes asked.

"God chews up liars and spits 'em out!" the voice shouted. "You know what guardian! Who is it?

"I don't know," he said, and he began to back away again. The ooze squished underfoot.

"Colonel?" It was Vance's voice, echoing through the tunnel from behind him. "You okay?"

"You okay?" the awful voice in front of him mimicked. "Where you goin', Colonel Matt Rhodes United States Air Force? Love thy neighbor as thyself. Put out that hot wand of hell and let's have us a tea party."

The flashlight, Rhodes realized. It's afraid of the flashlight.

"Naughty, naughty boy! Gonna switch you good and proper!" The thing sounded like a demented grandmother on speed.

He kept backing away, moving faster now. The thing didn't speak again, and all Rhodes wanted to do was to get out of this tunnel, but he dared not turn his back and run. The light was holding it at bay; maybe something in the wavelength of electric light, he reasoned. If alien eyes had never been exposed to electric light before, then . . .

He stopped. Why wasn't the thing still taunting him? Where the hell was it? He glanced over his shoulder, quickly shone the light behind him. Nothing there. A bead of sweat crawled into his eye and burned it like a torch.

And in the next instant there was the crack of earth splitting open and he whirled to see a flurry of dirt erupt in front of him and two gaunt arms with metallic saw-edged fingernails coming up from the floor. The thing scuttled up like a roach, white hair red with Texas dirt and flower-print press hanging in slimy tatters, the old woman's face slick and shining. Needle teeth glinted like blue fire in its mouth as Rhodes thrust the flashlight right into the dead and staring eyeballs.

"Naughty boy!" the thing shrieked, throwing up one arm over its face and the other swinging viciously at Rhodes.

He backpedaled and fired the rifle. It bucked against his shoulder and almost knocked him flat; the bullet tore a gash across a gray cheek. He fired again, missed, and then the creature that looked like an old woman was charging him, an arm still covering its eyes and its head thrashing with what was either rage or pain.

The thing's other hand closed on his left wrist. Two metal nails winnowed into his skin, and he knew that if he lost the light he was finished. He heard himself scream; the hand had a terrible, crushing power in it, and his wrist felt as if it was about to break.

He jammed the rifle barrel right up against the crook of the thing's elbow and pulled the trigger. Pulled it again. And again, and this time wrenched his arm away from her. There was a roar coming from the creature's mouth like air through a cracked steampipe.

The thing abruptly turned and, its eyes shielded and back bowed with a dowager's hump, scurried away from Rhodes down the tunnel. It flung itself to the floor, began to frantically dig itself down with feet and fingers, throwing damp dirt backward upon Rhodes. In about five seconds it had burrowed halfway into the earth.

Rhodes could stand no more. His nerve snapped, and he fled.

Vance had heard an old woman's shout, the sound of rifle fire, and a scream that had made the hairs on the back of his neck do the jitterbug. Now he heard someone running down there—shoes squishing on that shit in the tunnel—and then the choked thunder of Rhodes's voice: *"Get me out!"* The rifle was flung up, but Rhodes held on to the flashlight.

Vance started hauling up the hose, and Rhodes climbed up it as if the devils of hell were snapping at his ass. The colonel fought upward the last three feet, grabbed the broken concrete, and pulled himself out of the hole, scrabbling away from it on his hands and knees; he lost the flashlight, which had been clamped under his arm, and it rolled away across the floor.

"What happened? God A'mighty, what happened?" Vance reached down for the light and turned it on the colonel's face; it was a mask of chalk with two gray-ringed cigarette burns where the eyes had been.

"I'm all right. All right. I'm all right," Rhodes said, but he was cold and clammy and the sweat was running off him and he knew he was one giggle away from the funny farm. "The light. Doesn't like it. Nope! Shot it. Shot it, sure did!"

"I heard the shots. What were you shootin' a—" His voice clogged and stopped. He had seen something, there in the light, and he felt his stomach heave.

Rhodes lifted his left arm. A gray hand and forearm was hanging on to his wrist, two metal nails dug into his skin and the other fingers clamped tight. At the end of the forearm, where the elbow's crook had been, was a mass of torn tissue that oozed pale gray fluid.

"Shot it!" Rhodes said, and a terrible grin flickered across his mouth. "Shot it, sure did!"

32

Landscape of Destruction

Rick Jurado stood in the front room of his house, staring through a cracked window toward the smoldering junkyard. Candles burned around the room, and his Paloma was softly crying.

Mrs. Garracone, from a few doors down, was crying too, and her son Joey stood with his arm around her shoulders to steady her. Zarra was in the room, his bullwhip coiled around his arm, and Miranda sat on the sofa beside her grandmother, Paloma's hands in her own.

Father Ortega waited for an answer to the question he'd just posed. Mrs. Garracone had come to him about twenty minutes before. She'd been to the clinic, had waited anxiously for word about her husband, Leon. But Leon Garracone, who labored in one of the machine shops in Cade's autoyard, had not been found.

"I know he's alive," she repeated, speaking to Rick. "I know it. John Gomez came out alive, and he worked right beside my Leon. He said he crawled out and he could hear other people in there callin' for help. I know my Leon's still in there. Maybe he's pinned under somethin'. Maybe his legs are broken. But he's alive. I *know* it!"

Rick glanced at Father Ortega, saw that the priest believed as he did: that the odds of finding Leon Garracone alive in the debris of the autoyard were very, very slim.

But Domingo Ortega lived on Fourth Street, two doors down from the Garracones, and he had always counted Leon as a good friend. When Mrs. Garracone and Joey had come to him, begging him to help, he'd had to say yes; he'd been trying to find other volunteers, but no one wanted to go into the autoyard with that outer-space machine sitting in there and he didn't blame them. "You don't have to go," he told Rick. "But Leon was . . . Leon's my friend. We're going to go in and try to find him."

"Don't do it, Rick," Paloma begged. "Please don't."

"Help us, man," Joey Garracone said. "We're brothers, right?"

"There's been enough death!" Paloma tried shakily to stand, but Miranda restrained her. "It's a miracle anybody got out of that place alive! Please don't ask my son to go in there!"

Rick looked at Miranda. She shook her head, adding her opinion to Paloma's. He was ripped between what he knew was the sensible thing and what he considered to be his duty as leader of the Rattlers. Gang law said that if one of the brothers needed help, you gave it without question. He took a deep breath of smoke-tainted air and released it. The whole town smelled like scorched metal and burning tires. "Mrs. Garracone," he said, "will you take my grandmother and sister to the church with you? I don't want them being alone."

"No!" This time Paloma did stand up. "No, for the love of God, no!"

"I want you to go with Mrs. Garracone," he said calmly. "I'll be all right."

"No! I'm begging you!" Her voice broke, and new tears ran down her wrinkled cheeks.

He walked across the crooked floor to her and put his arm around her. "Listen to me. If you believed I was still out there, and alive, you'd want someone to go in after me, wouldn't you?"

"There are others who can do it! Not you!"

"I have to go. You know that, because you taught me not to turn my back on my friends."

"I taught you not to be a fool, either!" she answered, but Rick could hear in her voice that she had grudgingly accepted his decision.

He held her for a moment longer, and then he said to Miranda, "Take care of her," and he let his grandmother go. Paloma seized his hand, squeezed it tightly, and the cataract-covered eyes found his face. "You be careful. Promise it."

"I promise," he said, and she released him. He turned toward Father Ortega. "All right. Let's get it done."

Mrs. Garracone left with Paloma and Miranda, heading to the Catholic church on First Street. Armed with a flashlight, Father Ortega led Rick, Zarra, and Joey Garracone in the opposite direction, along smoky Second Street toward the blown-down fence of the autoyard and the fires beyond.

At the yard's edge, they stopped to survey a landscape of destruction: car parts had been thrown into tangled heaps of metal, piles of tires billowed dense black smoke, and what had been either wooden or brick buildings were either smashed flat or turned to rubble.

And overshadowing all was the black pyramid, its base sunken into the earth.

"I wouldn't do what you're thinking," someone warned. Sitting on the hood of his Mercedes was Mack Cade, smoking a thin cheroot and regarding the ruins like a fallen emperor. Typhoid crouched at his feet, and Lockjaw sat in the backseat. Cade still wore his Panama hat; his tanned face, wine-red shirt, and khaki trousers were streaked with soot. "Nothing in there worth going after."

"My dad's in there!" Joey answered adamantly. "We're gonna bring him out!"

"Sure you are." Cade spewed a thread of smoke. "Kid, there's nothing left but bones and ashes."

"You shut your filthy mouth!"

Typhoid stood up and growled darkly, but Cade rested

one booted foot on the dog's back. "Just telling it like it is, kid. There are some drums of paint and lubricant that haven't blown up yet. That's what I'm waiting on. You want to get yourselves killed, you go right ahead."

"You know where Leon Garracone was working," Ortega said. "Why don't you do something worthwhile for once in your life and help us find him?"

"Garracone, Garracone . . ." He thought for a moment, trying to place a face with the name. They all looked alike to him. "Oh, yeah! Garracone was always bitching for a raise. He worked in the engine shop. That's what's left of it." He pointed, and through the haze they could make out a heap of broken bricks about fifty yards in.

"John Gomez got out," Ortega said, undaunted. "He's cut up and burned, but he's alive. Leon could still be—"

"Sure. Dream on, *padre*. Anyway, what the hell is Garracone to *you?*" He removed the cheroot from his mouth and flicked it away. The gold chains around his neck made a tinkling noise as he moved.

"Leon is my friend. Which is something I don't suppose you understand."

"I've got all the friends I need, thanks." Cade had a staff of five Mexican servants at his house, a live-in teenage mistress—a little coked-up go-go dancer from San Antonio —and a fat-bellied cook named Lucinda, but his real friends were always with him. The two dogs never judged him, or pressured him, or gave him bad vibrations. They were always ready to rip the throats out of his enemies, and they obeyed without question: to him, that was true friendship. "Jurado, you've got more sense than this. Tell 'em how crazy they are, man."

"We've got to see for ourselves."

"You'll see, all right! Man, didn't you get a look at that flying bastard? There's something *alive* in that fucker!" He motioned toward the pyramid. "You go out there and it'll chew your asses up too!"

"Let's go," Ortega urged. "This leech is useless."

"My mama didn't raise any fools!" Cade retorted as the others started into the autoyard, watching their steps over the twisted sheet-metal fence and the wicked coils of concertina wire. "I'll tell Noah Twilley where to find your bodies!" But they paid him no more attention and moved into the yard past heaps of razor-sharp metal and smoking debris. Soon afterward, they heard the blare and crash of Cade's tape deck, cranked up loud enough to blast God's eardrums: Alice Cooper, wailing about dead babies in a cupboard.

The sandy ground was littered with parts of engines and cars, charred wooden planks, bricks, and other junk. Zarra lagged behind to poke around the warped chassis of what appeared to have been a Porsche, thrown upside down by the concussion. Father Ortega saw a man's bloodstained shirt lying nearby, but he didn't call attention to it. The dark smoke of smoldering tires hung close to the earth, unstirred by a breeze, and piles of wreckage glowed fierce red at their centers. The black pyramid loomed frightening-ly close. Rick hesitated, looking up toward the column of light that whirled around and around with hypnotic effect at its apex, then got his legs moving again.

But he couldn't shake the feeling of being watched. It was a sense he'd developed by necessity, to guard against a 'Gade coming up behind him at school and taking him down with a kidney punch. The back of his neck prickled and he kept glancing around, but nothing moved through the smoke. It was more than being watched, he decided; it was a sensation of being taken apart, measured, dissected like a frog in biology class. "Creepy in here," Zarra mut-tered, walking just to Rick's right, and Rick knew Zarra must be feeling it too.

They crossed the yard to the jumble of bricks and metal beams that Cade had pointed out. Not far away was a mound of cars and pickup trucks that had been crunched together like a bizarre sculpture. Joey Garracone got down on his knees in the sand and started tossing broken bricks aside and calling for his father.

"You and Zarra start on the other side," Ortega sug-gested, and they went around the collapsed building —where they came face-to-face with a burned-up corpse lying next to a crumpled sky-blue Corvette. The corpse's head was smashed in, and broken teeth gleamed in the gaping mouth. Whoever he was, he had reddish-blond hair; a white man, not Joey's father. The heavy, sickly-sweet odor of burned meat reached them, and Zarra gasped. "I'm gonna volcano, man!" He turned and ran away a few yards, bending his head toward the ground. Rick clamped his teeth together, walked past the dead man, and stood waiting for the dizzy sickness to pass. It did, mercifully, and then he was ready to work. Zarra came back, his face yellow.

They began to search through the ruins of the engine shop, clearing away some of the mountain of bricks. After about ten minutes of work, Ortega uncovered another dead man: it was Carlos Hermosa—Ruben's father—and the way the man's body was contorted Ortega knew the spine and neck must be broken. Joey stared for a moment at the corpse, his face covered with dust and sweat, and then he silently continued his labor. Ortega made the sign of the cross and kept tossing bricks aside.

The work was hard. It looked to Rick as if the whole building—which had been a flat-roofed structure about forty feet long—had caved in on itself. He moved a length of pipe, and broken bricks tumbled down along with a charred sneaker that he at first thought might have a foot in it but was empty, its owner either buried or blown out of his shoe by the concussion.

He came to a metal beam that Zarra helped him shift with back-wrenching effort, and after the beam was laid aside Zarra looked at him and said quietly, "Do you hear that?"

"Hear what?"

"Listen!"

Rick did, but all he could hear was Cade's tape deck playing.

"Hold it. I don't hear it anymore." Zarra walked into the wreckage, searching for the sound he'd heard. He bent down, tossed more bricks and rubble away. Then: "There! You hear that, man? Over this way!"

"I didn't hear anything." Rick went to where Zarra was and waited. A few seconds passed—and then, muffled and indistinct, came the clink of metal against metal. It was a steady rhythm, coming from somewhere deep within the ruins, and Rick realized somebody was signaling. "Hey! Father!" he shouted. "Over here!"

Ortega and Joey came running, their clothes and skin filmed with dust. Zarra picked up a piece of pipe and hit it against a brick a few times, and they all heard the answering knocks from below. Ortega got down on his knees, shining the flashlight in amid the bricks in search of an airspace. Zarra kept signaling, and the clinking noise came back to him.

"It's Domingo Ortega!" the priest shouted. "Can you hear me?"

They waited, but heard no response. "Help me," Ortega said, and he and the boys began to work at a fever pitch, digging their way down through three or four feet of rubble. Within minutes their hands were scraped raw, and blood seeped from cuts in Rick's palms. Ortega said, "Hold it," and leaned forward, listening. There was the sound of metal on metal again, someone hammering at a pipe. "Can you hear me down there?" Ortega hollered.

A weak, raspy shout drifted up: "Yeah! Oh Christ, yeah! Get us outta here!"

"Who are you? How many are with you?"

"Three of us! I'm Greg Frackner! Will Barnett and Leon Garracone are down here too!"

"Papa!" Joey yelled, tears streaming down his cheeks. "Papa, it's Joey!"

"We're down in the work pit, and there's all kinds of shit wedged in on top of us," Frackner continued. "I can see your light, though!"

"Are you hurt?"

"Broken arm, I reckon. Ribs don't feel too swift either. Will's coughin' up blood, and Leon's passed out again. I think his legs are busted. What the hell hit us, man? A bomb?"

Ortega avoided the question. "Can you move at all?"

"A little bit, but it's mighty tight in here. We're breathin' okay, though."

"Good." It was clear to Ortega that they were going to need more muscle power to get the three men out. "Just take it easy, now. We're going to have to go back for some picks and shovels."

"Whatever it takes, man! Listen . . . can you leave the light where I can see it? I keep thinkin' I hear somethin' diggin' down here. Like *underneath* us. I'm scared of rats. Okay?"

"Okay," Ortega said, and wedged the flashlight in between two bricks so its beam would shine down into the airspace. "We'll be back!" he promised, and he grasped Joey's shoulders and pulled the boy up too.

They started back across the autoyard, under the violet glow and the motionless black clouds, and Rick had that crawly sensation of being watched again. He turned toward the pyramid.

A man was standing about twenty feet away. He was lean, tall, and broad around the shoulders; he stood slightly hunchbacked, and his arms dangled limply at his sides. Rick was unable to tell much about the man's face, other than that it looked to be wet. The man wore dark pants and a striped short-sleeve shirt, the clothes covered with dirt. He was just standing there, his head cocked slightly to one side, watching them. "Father?" Rick said, and Ortega heard the raw nerves in Rick's voice and stopped; he looked back, and then all of them saw the hunchbacked man who stood like a statue.

Ortega's first thought was that it was one of Cade's workmen who'd just dug himself out of the ruins. He stepped forward. "You all right?"

"Who's the guardian?" the man asked, in a thick, slow drawl that had an undercurrent like the whistle of steam from a teakettle.

The priest's steps faltered. He couldn't see much of the man's face—just some slicked-down gray hair and a damp and gleaming slab of forehead—but he thought he recognized the voice. Only the voice usually said *What can I fit you for, padre?* It was Gil Lockridge, Ortega realized. Gil and his wife Mavis had owned the Boots 'n Plenty shoestore for over ten years. But Gil wasn't so tall, Ortega thought. And he wasn't so large around the shoulders, nor was he hunchbacked like this man was. But . . . it was Gil's voice. Wasn't it?

"I asked you a question," the man said. "Who's the guardian?"

"Guardian?" Ortega shook his head. "Guardian of *what?*"

The man drew in a long lungful of air and released it—a long release—with a noise that reminded Rick of the way that sidewinder had rattled when he'd reached into the box for the Fang of Jesus. "I don't like bein' . . ." There was a hesitation, as if he were searching for the correct phrase. "Bein' trifled with. I don't like it a'tall." He took two strides forward, and Ortega backed away. The man stopped, and now Ortega could see some kind of ooze sliding off the man's lantern-jawed face. Gil's eyes were black, sunken, terrible. "I know the one I'm lookin' for is here. I know there's a guardian. Maybe it's you." The eyes fixed on Zarra for a second. "Or maybe it's you." A glance at Rick. "Or is it you?" The gaze returned to Father Ortega.

"Listen . . . Gil . . . how'd you get out here? I mean . . . I don't understand what you're—"

"The one I'm seekin' is a subversive criminal," the man went on. "An enemy of the collective mind. I don't know how you deal with criminals on this"—he looked around with a sinuous movement of the neck and said contemptuously—"*world,* but I'm sure you understand the concepts of law and order. I intend to bring the creature to justice."

"What creature?" It hit him then: what Colonel Rhodes had said about Stevie Hammond. "The little girl?" he asked before he could think about what he was saying.

"The little girl," the voice repeated. The eyes had taken on a keen glint. "Explain."

Ortega stood very still, but his insides had twisted into knots. He damned his tongue; there was an awful hunger on the wet and waxy face of the man-thing that stood before him. It was not Gil Lockridge; it was a mocking imitation of humanity.

"Explain," the thing commanded, and took a gliding step forward.

"Run!" Ortega shouted to the boys; they were frozen with shock, couldn't move. "Get away!" he yelled, and as he backed up he saw a length of pipe lying on the ground beside his left foot. He picked it up and held it threateningly over his head. The thing was almost upon him, and he had no choice; he hurled the broken pipe at the Gil Lockridge face with the strength of panic.

The pipe smashed into the moist features with a noise like a hammer whacking a watermelon. The right cheek split open from eye to corner of mouth, and gray fluid dripped out. The face showed no reaction, no pain. But there was a slight smile on the crooked mouth now, and needlelike teeth glinted inside the cavity. The rattling voice said with a hint of pleasure, "I see you speak *my* language."

There was a ripping sound: the tearing of brittle cloth. Little crackling noises like a hundred bones breaking and rearranging themselves within seconds. Joey Garracone screamed and ran, but Rick and Zarra stood their ground, transfixed with terror. The man's hunched back was swelling, bowing his spine downward; his eyes were riveted to Ortega, who moaned and retreated on trembling legs.

The thing's shirt split open, and a bulbous lump rose at the end of the spine. It tore through the pale counterfeit skin and revealed black, interlocking scales similar to those on the pyramid. From its lower end uncoiled a dripping, segmented tail about five feet long and triple the thickness of Zarra's bullwhip; the tail rose into the air with a clicking, bony sound, and at its tip was a football-sized nodule of metallic spikes.

"No," Rick heard himself croak—and the grinning, split-open face ticked toward him.

Father Ortega turned to run; he got two strides away before the monster leapt after him. The spiked tail whipped forward in a deadly blur, caught the side of the priest's head, and demolished it in an explosion of bone and brains. Ortega fell to his knees, his face a crimson hole, and slowly, with exquisite grace, toppled into the sand.

The monster whirled around, crouched and ready, the tail flicking back and forth with fragments of Ortega's head clinging to the spikes.

Zarra let out a choked shriek, backed away, and stumbled over a pile of rubble. He went down hard on his tailbone, sat there gaping as the creature took a step toward him.

Rick saw automotive parts scattered all around him; there was no time to judge if he should run or not, because in another few seconds that spiked tail would be within range of Zarra. Rick picked up a twisted hubcap and flung it, and as it sailed at the monster's head the tail flicked out almost lazily and knocked the piece of metal aside.

Now Rick had the creature's undivided attention, and as it stalked toward him Rick hefted a car's door from the sand and held it before himself like a shield. "Run!" he shouted to Zarra, who started crawling frantically on his hands and knees. *"Go!"*

The tail swept at Rick. He tried to dance out of its way, but the thing hit his makeshift shield and threw off a shower of sparks; the impact lifted him off his feet and hurled him onto his back on the ground. His hands still gripped the dented-in car door, which lay on top of him, and as he struggled up, his head ringing, the monster advanced in a crouch and the tail swung again.

This time the car's door was ripped away from him and flung through the air. Rick twisted, scurrying toward the unpainted frame of a Jaguar sedan that sat near a pile of rusted metal six feet away. As he flung himself into the doorless and windowless car, he heard the bony rattling of the monster's tail right behind him; he pulled his legs in just as the ball of spikes whammed against the Jaguar's side, making the frame shudder and moan like a funeral bell. He scrambled through the opposite door hole, got his feet under him, and ran.

He didn't know where Zarra was, or if he was heading out

of the autoyard or deeper into it. The hanging layers of dark smoke accepted him, and fitful fires glowed red through the gloom. On all sides stood heaps of car parts, chassis, rows of BMWs, Mercedes, Corvettes, and other high-ticket vehicles awaiting transformation. The place was a maze of metal walls, and Rick didn't know which way to run; he looked over his shoulder; he couldn't see the thing behind him, but that didn't mean it wasn't there. He ran on, his lungs straining for air through the smoke, and in another moment found his way blocked by a steep ridge of scrap metal. He turned back, ran past a collapsed building where a dead man in a blue shirt lay sprawled amid the bricks.

Rick stopped below a pile of flattened car bodies, his lungs heaving, to try to get his bearings. He'd never been in here before, the smoke seared his eyes, and he couldn't even think straight. What had happened to Father Ortega seemed unreal, a pull from a bad dose of weed. He was shaking now, his body out of control. He was going to have to start running again, but he feared what might be waiting for him out there in the smoke. He slid his hand into his pocket to grasp the Fang of Jesus.

But before he could get his fingers on the switchblade, something dark dropped down like a noose and tightened around his throat.

He knew what it was, because he heard the bony clicking of the tail's segmented joints. The monster was above him, sitting on one of the flattened cars. Rick's heart stuttered, and he felt his face freeze as the blood left it. Then he was being lifted off his feet, the pressure just short of strangling him, and he thrashed until a hand gripped·his hair.

"The little girl," the awful, hissing voice said. The thing's mouth was right beside Rick's ear. "Explain."

"I don't . . . I don't . . . know. I swear . . ." His feet were about six inches off the ground. He didn't know anything about a guardian, or a little girl, and he felt the gears of his brain start to smoke and slip.

The tail tightened. Rick squeezed his eyes shut.

Maybe five seconds passed; to Rick it was an eternity he

would never forget. And then the voice said, "I have a message for the one called Ed Vance. I want to meet with him. He knows where. Tell him."

The tail went slack—*click click click*—and Rick fell to his knees as it released him.

At first he could only lie huddled up, waiting for the spikes to smash his head in, unable to move or think or cry for help. But gradually he realized that the thing was going to let him live. He crawled away from it, still expecting a blow at any second, and finally he forced himself to stand. He could sense the thing watching him from its perch, and he dared not turn around to look at it; the slick, bony feel of the tail remained impressed in the flesh of his throat, and he wanted to scrub that skin until it bled.

Rick almost broke into a run, but he feared that his legs were too weak and he'd fall on his face. He started walking, retracing the way he thought he'd come; the smoke parted before him and closed at his back. He was dimly aware that his legs were moving on automatic, and in his mind the images of the monster killing Father Ortega and pursuing him through the autoyard darted like a cageful of shadows.

He came out of the autoyard about forty yards north of where they'd gone in, and how long that journey had taken he had no idea. He kept walking south along the collapsed fence, and finally he saw Cade's Mercedes sitting in front of him.

Instantly Lockjaw began barking furiously, rearing up in the backseat. Zarra was sitting on the pavement, shivering, his knees drawn up to his chin and both arms clutching the bullwhip to his chest. He looked up, saw Rick, and scrambled to his feet with a grunt of surprise.

Mack Cade stood at the edge of the autoyard, the .38 in a white-knuckled grip in his right hand. He whirled around, aiming the pistol at the figure that had just lurched out of the smoke. About fifteen minutes ago, Joey Garracone had raced past him, trailing a scream that had even overpowered Cade's tape deck. Soon afterward, Zarra had come out babbling about something with a tail that had killed Domingo Ortega. "Hold it!" Cade shrieked, his blue eyes wide. "Stop right there!"

Rick did. He wavered, almost fell. "It's me," he said.

"Where's Ortega?" Cade's false cool had cracked like cheap plastic, and underneath it was a little boy's terror. "What happened to the priest, man?" He kept his finger on the trigger.

"Dead. Out there somewhere." Rick motioned with a leaden arm.

"I told you not to go in there!" Cade shouted. "Didn't I? I told you not to, you stupid shits!" He peered into the haze, searching for Typhoid; the dog had raced out there a few minutes ago, barking and growling at something, and hadn't returned. "Typhoid!" he hollered. "Come on back, boy!"

"We've got to tell Vance," Rick said. "It wants to see him."

"Typhoid!" Cade took three steps into the autoyard, but could make himself go no farther. The concertina wire snagged his trousers, and oily beads of sweat rolled down his face. "Typhoid, come on!"

Lockjaw kept barking. Cade prowled along the wire, calling for Typhoid in a voice that began to strain and quaver.

"I said we've got to tell Vance!" Rick repeated. "Right now!"

"I've gotta find my dog!" Cade shouted, his face stricken. "Something's happened to Typhoid!"

"Forget the dog! Father Ortega's dead! We've got to tell the sheriff!"

"I told you not to go in there! I said you were all crazy as hell!" Cade felt a weakness falling over him, like a sun in eclipse. The yard and its fortune of cars were reduced to true junk, and in that smoke Cade could smell the burning of syndicate money and his own skin. "Typhoid!" he yelled, his voice rasping. "Come back!" His voice echoed over the ruins. There was no sign of the Doberman.

"You going to take us to Vance or not?" Rick asked him.

"I can't . . . leave my friend," Cade said, as something

that had been nailed in place for a long time broke inside him. "Typhoid's out there. I can't leave him." He stared at the boy for a few seconds, to make sure he understood, and then Cade said thickly, "You can take the car. I don't give a shit." He started walking into the yard, and Lockjaw saw his master going and leapt out of the Mercedes to follow.

"No!" Rick shouted. "Don't!"

Cade went on. He looked back, a terrible smile on his sweat-damp face. "You gotta know who your friends are, kid. Gotta stick up for them. Think on these things." He gave a short, sharp whistle to Lockjaw, and the Doberman walked at his side. Cade began to call for Typhoid again, his voice getting weaker, and the two figures vanished into the haze.

"Get in the car," Rick told Zarra, and the other boy stumbled dazedly toward it. Rick slid behind the wheel, turned the keys in the ignition, and laid rubber in reverse.

33

The Flesh

"Howdy, Noah," Early McNeil said as Tom escorted Noah Twilley into the clinic lab. "Shut the door behind you, if you please."

Twilley blinked in the glare of the emergency lights and looked around. His eyes were used to the funeral chapel's candlelight. In the lab were Sheriff Vance, Jessie Hammond, and a dark-haired man with a crewcut and blood all over his shirt. The dark-haired man was sitting on a stainless-steel table, holding his left wrist. No, Twilley realized in another second; no, that was not the man's hand on his wrist. It was a hand and arm that ended at a mutilated elbow.

"Lord," Twilley whispered.

"Kinda thought you might say that." Early sneaked a grim smile. "I asked Tom to fetch you over 'cause I figured you'd want to see this thing, you bein' on a speakin' acquaintance with bodies and all. Come take a closer look."

Twilley approached the table. The dark-haired man kept his head down, and Twilley saw a syringe lying nearby and realized the man had been sedated. Also on the table, lying in a little plastic tray, was an arrangement of scalpels, probes, and a bone saw. Twilley took one look at the nub of the elbow and said, "That's not bone."

"Nope. Sure as hell isn't." Early picked up a probe and

tapped what appeared to be a tight coil of flexible, blue-tinged metal that had erupted from the wound. "That's not muscle, either." He indicated the ripped red tissue, which had oozed a spool of gray fluid onto the floor. "But it's pretty close. It *is* organic, though it's not like anythin' I've ever seen before." He nodded toward a microscope set up on the counter, with a slide that held a smear of the tissue. "Take a gander at it, if you like."

Twilley did, his pale, slender fingers adjusting the lens into focus. "Lord A'mighty!" he said, which was about the strongest language he used. He had seen what all of them already knew: that the muscle tissue was part organic and part tiny metallic fibers.

"Too bad you didn't shoot the head off this shitter, Colonel," Early told him. "I sure would like to get a look at the brain."

"You go down in that hole!" Rhodes's voice was a harsh rasp. "Maybe you'll have better luck."

"No thankee." Early picked up a pair of forceps and said, "Doc Jessie, will you shine that light a bit this way, please?"

Jessie clicked on a small penlight and aimed it where the metallic fingernails had pierced the colonel's flesh. One of the fingers had crunched into the face of Rhodes's wrist-watch and stopped it at four minutes after twelve, about a half hour ago. The colonel's hand had taken on a blue tinge from the pressure. "Well, let's start with this one," Early decided, and started trying to withdraw the little saw blade from the man's flesh.

By the penlight, Jessie could see age spots scattered over the top of the false hand. There was a small white scar on one knuckle—maybe a burn scar, she thought. A knuckle's brush against a hot pan. Whatever had created this mechanism had gotten the texture and color of an elderly woman's flesh down to perfection. On the ring finger was a thin gold band, but strands of the pseudo-skin had grown over and around it, entrapping it as if the thing that had made this replica had assumed the ring was somehow an organic part of the hand.

"Thing don't want to come out." The finger was resisting

Early's forceps. "It's gonna take some skin out of you, Colonel. Hope you don't mind."

"Just do it."

"I told him not to go down there." Vance felt woozy, and he sat on a stool before his legs gave way. Thin creepers of blood had intertwined around Rhodes's wrist. "What the hell are we gonna *do?*"

"Find Daufin," Rhodes said. "She's the only one who knows what we're up against." He flinched and drew a breath as Early pulled the first fingernail loose. "That tunnel . . . probably goes all the way under the river." He stared at the penlight in Jessie's hand. His brain gears were thawing out, and he remembered the creature protecting its eyes from the flashlight's beam. "The light," he said. "It doesn't like light."

"What?" Tom asked, coming closer to the table.

"It . . . tried to shield its eyes. I think the light was hurting it."

"That damned thing with Dodge's face didn't mind the light," Vance said. "There were oil lamps hangin' from the ceilin'."

"Right. Oil lamps." Rhodes was getting some of his strength back, but he still couldn't bear to look at the gray hand clamped to his wrist. Early was struggling to extract the second fingernail. "You didn't have a flashlight, did you?"

"No."

"Maybe it's just electric light that hurts it. Firelight and electric light have different spectrums, don't they?"

"Spectrums?" Vance stood up. "What the hell's that?"

"A fancy word for the strength of wavelengths in light," Early told him. "Hold still, now." He gripped the forceps hard and jerked the finger's metal saw blade out of Rhodes's skin. "That one just about grazed an artery." The other fingers still held on to Rhodes's wrist like the legs of a spider.

"So maybe the wavelengths in electric light do something to its eyes," Rhodes went on. "It said 'hot,' and it had to tunnel underneath me because it didn't like the light. If it screwed up on the bones and the teeth, maybe it screwed up on the eyes too."

"Hell, light's just light!" Vance said. "Ain't nothin' in it to hurt anythin'!"

"A bat would disagree with you, Sheriff." Noah Twilley turned toward them from the microscope. "So would a whole encyclopedia of cave-dwelling rodents, fish, and insects. Our eyes are used to electric light, but it blinds a lot of other species."

"So what are you sayin'? This thing lives in a cave?"

"Maybe not a cave," Rhodes said, "just an environment where there's no electric light. That could be a world full of tunnels, for all we know. From the speed it digs, I'd say Stinger's used to traveling underground."

"But electric lights don't bother Daufin," Jessie reminded him. "All the lights were on in our house before the pyramid came down."

He nodded. "Which goes along with what I think is true: Daufin and Stinger are two different forms of life, from different environments. One transfers itself in and out of a black sphere, and the other travels underground and makes replicants like this one"—he glanced distastefully at the false hand—"so it can move above ground. Maybe it makes copies of life forms on whatever world it lands on. I can't imagine what the process is, but it must be damned fast."

"Damned strong too." Early was doing his best to pry the fingers loose with the forceps and a probe. "Noah, reach in that bottom drawer down there." He motioned to it with a lift of his chin.

Noah opened it. "Nothing in here but a bottle of vodka."

"Right. Open it and hand it here. If I can't smoke, I can sure as shit drink." He took the bottle, swigged from it, and offered it to Rhodes, who also took a swallow. "Not much, now. We don't want you keelin' over. Doc Jessie, get me some cotton swabs and let's mop up some of this bleedin'."

Early had to ask Tom to take another pair of forceps and help him twist each finger out of Rhodes's flesh. It took the strength of both men, working hard, to do the job. The fingers broke with little metallic cracking sounds, and the hand finally plopped to the table. On Rhodes's wrist was a violet bruise in the shape of a hand and fingers, and he immediately doused his flesh with vodka and scrubbed it with a paper towel, opening up the cuts again. He poured more vodka on it, wincing with the pain, and kept rubbing until the paper towel came apart and Early clutched his shoulder with a pressure that would have made a Brahma bull pay attention.

"Settle down, son," Early said calmly. He took the fragments of paper from Rhodes and tossed them into the wastebasket. "Tom, will you help the colonel to a room down the hall, please? I believe he could do with some rest."

"No." Rhodes waved Tom away. "I'm all right."

"I don't think you are." Early took the penlight from Jessie and used it to examine the man's pupils. Their reaction was sluggish, and Early knew Rhodes was tottering right on the edge of serious shock. "I'd say you've had kind of a rough night, wouldn't you?"

"I'm all right," Rhodes repeated, pushing the light aside. He could still feel those damned cold fingers on his wrist, and he didn't know if he would ever stop shaking inside. But he had to put up a brave front, no matter what. He stood up, averted his gaze from the false hand. "We've got to find Daufin, and I don't have time to rest." He smelled the blood and acrid juice that had spurted out of the dragonfly. "I'd like to change shirts. This one's had it."

Early grunted, watching the younger man below beetling brows. Rhodes didn't fool him for a second; the colonel was holding himself together with spit and gristle. "I can get you a scrub shirt. How about that?" He walked over to a closet, opened it, and pulled out one of the lightweight sea-green shirts. He tossed it to Rhodes. "They come in two sizes: too small and too large. Try it on."

The shirt was a little too large, but not by much. Rhodes's blood-smeared knit shirt followed the paper towel into the wastebasket.

"I left my mother alone," Noah Twilley explained. "I'd better get back."

"Ought to get yourself and ol' Ruth to a place with electric lights—like here," Early said, motioning toward the emergency floods. "If the colonel's right, that damned Stinger'll stay away from 'em."

"Right. I'll go get her and bring her back." He paused for a moment to jab a probe at the hand that lay palm up, fingers curled like the legs of a dead crab, on the table. The probe touched the center of the palm, and the fingers gripped into a fist, the sudden movement almost shooting all of them—especially Rhodes—out of their shoes. "Reflex action," Noah said, with a sickly half smile, and he tried to pull the probe free but the fingers had locked around it. "I'll go get my mother," he told them as he hurried out of the lab.

"Just what we need: that crazy loudmouth woman runnin' around here," Early groused when Noah was gone. He picked up a towel and wrapped the hand in it, probe and all, and when he was done he took another swig from the vodka bottle.

Someone knocked on the door. Mrs. Santos looked in without waiting for an invitation. "Sheriff, there're two boys here to see you."

"What do they want?"

"I don't know, but I think you'd better come quick. They're pretty torn up about something."

"Take 'em to my office," Early said. "Ed, you can talk to 'em in there."

Mrs. Santos left to get them, but Vance hesitated because he smelled more trouble and he knew Doc Early did too. "How are we gonna find Daufin?" he asked Rhodes. "There are plenty of places she could be hidin'."

"She can't have gotten out of the force field, but that's still a seven-mile radius," the colonel answered. "I don't think she's left town, though. At least she knows she can hide here, and she doesn't know anything about what's beyond Inferno and Bordertown."

"There are a lot of empty houses around," Tom said. "She could be in any one of them."

"She's not going to get very far from the sphere." Jessie

couldn't remember if she'd locked the front door or not; that detail had been lost in the hurry to find out what had come down in Cade's autoyard. "Either Tom or I ought to go back to our house and wait there. She might show up."

"Right. I can get Gunny to round up some volunteers and start combing the streets." The search was not going to be an easy task, he knew, with all that haze out there and the visibility eroding more every hour. "If we go door to door, maybe we can find someone who's seen her." He tried to rub warmth into his left wrist, but the feel of the cold fingers would not go away. "I need some black coffee," he decided. "I've got to keep going."

"Probably some left over at the Brandin' Iron," Vance said. "They keep a pot full until the stuff gets out and walks off."

Jessie stared at Colonel Rhodes for a moment. He was still pale, but some of the color had resurfaced in his face and his inner fires were lit again. A question had been hanging in her mind: a question that she knew she shared with Tom. It had to be asked, and now was the time. "If . . . when . . . we find Daufin, what are we going to do with her?"

Rhodes already knew where the question was aiming. "It looks to me as if Stinger's a lot stronger than she is—and a hell of a lot stronger than any of us too. Stinger must know Daufin's out of her sphere and in a host body, and that's what it means by 'guardian.' It's not going to drop the force field until it has her, so I'll jump ahead and tell you that I don't know what's going to happen to Stevie."

"If there *is* a Stevie anymore," Tom said quietly. Jessie had been thinking that too, and she felt a clench of anguish inside her. But Daufin had said Stevie was safe, and Jessie realized she was clinging to the word of a creature she hadn't even dreamed existed twenty-four hours ago. "I'm going to check on Ray," she told them, and she tore her mind away from the alien that lived in her little girl's skin, walked out of the lab and down the hall to Ray's room.

"I'd best see what those boys want." Vance moved toward the door, dreading the news that waited for him in Doc

Early's office. When it rains it pours! he thought, merrily going crazy. He stopped just shy of the door. "Tom, will you come with me?"

Tom said he would, and they left the lab.

McNeil's cluttered office was decorated with bullfight posters and thickets of potted cacti sat on the windowsills. Vance took one look at the strained faces of Rick Jurado and Zarra Alhambra, their eyes sunken and ringed with gray, and he knew the shit had just deepened to about neck level.

"What happened?" Vance asked Rick, who kept shivering and rubbing his throat.

Rick told him, speaking in a halting, brain-blasted voice. He and Zarra had gone to the sheriff's office, where Danny Chaffin had told them where Vance was. The deputy had been sitting at the CB radio, calling for help into a sea of static and surrounded by loaded weapons from the gun cabinet.

When Rick reached the part about the thing's body bursting a spiked tail, Vance made a soft, choking moan and had to sit down.

"It killed Father Ortega," Rick continued. "Hit him in the head. Just like that." He stopped, drew in a breath and let it out. "It went after me. Caught me, with that . . . that tail. It wanted to know about the little girl."

Tom said, "Oh, Jesus."

"I thought it was going to kill me. But it said . . ." Rick's eyes found the sheriff's. "It said for me to take a message to you. It wants to see you. It said you'd know where."

Vance didn't reply, because the room was spinning too fast and the emergency lights threw gargoyle shadows on the walls.

"Where?" Tom asked him.

"The Creech house," he answered finally. "I can't go back in there." His voice broke. "Oh God, I can't." A brutal echo drifted to him: *Burro! Burro! Burro!* Cortez Park and pantherish faces swirled around him, and he clenched his hands into fists.

He was the sheriff of Inferno: a joke job. A chaser of lost dogs and traffic offenders. One hand out to Mack Cade and the other over his eyes. The little fat boy inside him quivered with terror, and he saw the door of the Creech house stretching to engulf him.

A hand touched his shoulder. He looked up, wet-lashed, into Tom Hammond's face.

"We need you," Tom said.

No one had ever said that to him before. *We need you.* The sound of it was shockingly simple, and yet it was strong enough to tatter the long-ago, distant taunts like cobwebs in the desert wind. He lowered his head, the fear still jabbing at his guts. Only it didn't seem as bad as it had been a few seconds before. He had been alone for a long time—way too long, and it was time for that weakling fat boy who carried a Louisville Slugger onto the streets of Bordertown to grow up. Maybe he couldn't make himself walk into the Creech house again; maybe he'd get to that door and scream and keep running until he dropped or a monster with a tail full of spikes reared up before him.

Maybe. Maybe not. He was the sheriff of Inferno, and they needed him.

And knowing it was true made the taunts drift away, like bullies who had realized the fat little boy walking across Cortez Park cast a man-sized shadow.

Vance lifted his head and wiped his eyes with the back of a pudgy hand. "All right," he said. No promises. The doorway still had to be dealt with." He stood up, and said it again: "All right."

Tom left to get Colonel Rhodes.

34

Worm Meat

"Typhoid! Here, boy!" Mack Cade's voice was giving out from shouting, and at his side Lockjaw was whining and jumping in a jangle of nerves, stopping to fire rapid barks in the direction of the pyramid. Cade let the dog bark, hoping the sound would attract Typhoid.

There was no sign of the Doberman. Smoke from burning tires drifted slowly around him, and he walked through a dark wonderland of destruction. The .38, gripped in his right hand, was cocked and ready for whatever might be waiting.

Each step took him deeper into the yard. He knew every inch of the place, and now he feared all of them. But Typhoid had to be found, or no amount of coke in the world would ease his brain tonight. The dogs were his friends, his good-luck charms, his bodyguards, his power translated into animal form. Screw humans, he thought. None of them were worth a shit. Only the dogs mattered.

He saw the black pyramid, its damp-looking plates washed with violet light, looming terrifyingly close, and he veered away from it. His polished Italian boots stirred up ashes and dust, and when he looked back he could no longer see any of the houses of Bordertown, just dark upon dark.

The yard's familiar buildings—its workshops and storage

structures—had been flattened and blasted by the concussion and the explosion of drums of gasoline and lubricants. The sleek rebuilt Porsches, BMWs, Corvettes, Jaguars, and Mercedes that had been lined up ready for pickup and delivery to Cade's masters had been scorched, warped, and tossed like Tonka Toys.

My ass is grass, he thought. No: lower than grass. My ass is worm meat.

The troopers would come, eventually. Then the reporters. It was all over, and the sudden change of his fortunes unhinged him a little further. He'd always expected that if the end came it would be an undercover bust by the federals, or some wild-hair lawyer who decided the money wasn't enough, or one of the fringe players who sang to save his own skin. No scenario of disaster had ever had a sonofabitching black pyramid from outer space in it, and Cade figured that would be really funny if he were on the shore of a Caribbean island where there were no extradition treaties.

"Typhoid! Come on, boy! Please . . . come back!" he shouted. Lockjaw whined, nudged his leg, raced off a few yards, and then darted back to him.

Cade stopped. "It's you and me, buddy," he said to Lockjaw. "Us two against the world."

Lockjaw yipped. A small sound.

"What is it?" Cade knew that sound: alarm. "What do you h—"

Lockjaw growled, deep in his throat, and his ears lay back.

There was a splitting noise in the earth, like a seam of stone breaking. The sand swirled around Cade's boots like a whirlpool, and he was twisted around in a violent corkscrew motion. The ground beneath him collapsed, and his legs disappeared up to the knees.

He drew a sharp breath, tasted bitter smoke at the back of his throat. Something moist and lurching had his legs, was drawing him under. He was almost down to his waist within seconds, and he thrashed and screamed but his legs were held fast. Lockjaw was barking fiercely, running in circles around him. Cade fired into the ground, the bullet kicking up a spray of sand. Whatever had him continued to pull him down, and he kept firing until the bullets were gone.

The earth was up to his chest. Lockjaw darted in, and Cade's flailing arms grabbed the dog, pulled the Doberman against him, and tried to use its weight to pull himself free. Lockjaw scrabbled wildly, but the sand began to take the dog's body along with Cade's. He held on, and when he opened his mouth to scream again, sand and ashes filled it, slithering down his throat.

The man and his dog disappeared together. Mack Cade's Panama hat whirled in the eddies of the sand, then lay half buried as the earth's circular motion slowed and stopped.

35

The Open Door

While Rick and Zarra had been waiting in McNeil's office, Cody Lockett opened his eyes to candlelight and sat up with a jolt that made the hammering in his skull start up again.

He held his Timex up to the candle stuck on the plywood table beside his bed: 12:58. It had been about an hour since he'd come to the house, swallowed two aspirin with a swig of Seven-Up from a half-drained can in the refrigerator, and laid down to rest his brain. He wasn't sure he'd actually been sleeping, maybe just drifting in and out of an uneasy twilight, but his head did feel a little better and his muscles had unknotted some too.

Cody didn't know where his father was. The last he'd seen of Curt, the old man was hightailing it down the street as the helicopter and that other flying thing had battled above Inferno. Cody had watched it all, and after the 'copter had crashed on Cobre Road, he figured he'd zombied out, somehow walking to his motorcycle in front of the Warp Room and winding up here.

He was still wearing the bloody rags of his Texaco shirt. He stood up from the bed, steadied himself against its iron frame as the walls swelled and slowly rotated. When they stopped turning, he unlatched his fingers and walked across the room to his chest of drawers, opened the top drawer, and got out a fresh white T-shirt. He threw aside the Texaco tatters and worked the T-shirt on over his head, wincing at a stitch of pain along his rib cage. His belly growled, and he uprooted the candle from its little puddle of dried wax and followed its light into the kitchen.

The refrigerator held a few mold-ravaged TV dinners, some brown meat wrapped up in foil, a chunk of Limburger cheese that Cody wouldn't have offered to a dog, and assorted bowls and cups full of leftovers. He didn't trust any of them, but the candlelight found a grease-stained paper sack in there and he pulled it out and opened it; inside were four stale glazed doughnuts, booty from the bakery. They were as tough as lawnmower tires, but Cody ate three of them before his stomach begged for mercy.

In the back of the refrigerator was a bottle of Welch's grape juice. He reached in for it, and that was when he felt the floor tremble.

He stopped, his hand gripping the bottle's neck.

The house creaked. There was a polite clink of dishes and glasses in the cupboards. Then the rude bang of a pipe breaking deep in the earth.

Something's under the house, he realized. His heart picked up hot speed, but his mind was cold and clear. He could feel the tremor of the boards under his sneakers, like the way the floor used to shake when slow-moving freight trains passed, heavy-laden, on the copper company's tracks.

The floor's vibration ebbed and stopped. A whiff of dust floated through the candlelight. Cody was holding his breath, and only when his lungs jerked for air did he gasp. The kitchen smelled of burning rubber; the stink of Cade's autoyard was sliding through the cracks. Cody brought the grape juice out, unscrewed the cap, and washed down the last of a glazed doughnut that had lodged in his craw.

The world had gone freak-o since that damned bastard had crashed down across the river. Cody didn't care to speculate about what might have passed underneath his feet; whatever it was, it had been maybe ten or twelve feet below the ground. He wasn't planning on waiting around to see if it came back, either. Wherever the old man was, Cody thought, he'd have to cover his own ass this time. Anyway, God always looked out for fools and drunks.

He blew the candle out, laid it on the kitchen counter, and left the house, getting astride his motor at the bottom of the steps and putting on his goggles. The street was tinged with violet, layers of smoke lying close to the concrete and making Inferno look and smell like a battle zone. Through the pall, Cody could see the shine of the lights up at the fortress. That was the place to go, he decided; there was too much dark everywhere else. First he wanted to run past Tank's house, over on Circle Back Street, to see if the dude was there with his folks before he went up to the apartment building. He stomped a couple of times on the starter before the engine cranked, and drove toward Celeste Street.

His headlamp's glass had been broken during the fight —beer bottle probably clipped it, he reckoned—but the bulb was still working. The light stabbed through the dirty haze, but Cody kept his speed down because Brazos Street was riddled with cracks and in some places buckled upward as much as six inches. His tires told his backbone that whatever had gone under his house had passed this way too.

And then he was almost upon her.

Somebody standing in the middle of the street.

A little girl with auburn hair, her eyes glowing red in the headlamp's beam.

"Look out!" Cody shouted, but the little girl didn't budge. He jerked the wheel to the left and hit the brakes; if he'd passed any closer to the child he could've flicked her earlobe. The Honda flashed past her and the front tire hit a bulge in the pavement that made the frame shudder; Cody wrestled the handlebars and brakes to keep from crashing into a stand of cactus. He pulled up about two feet short of porcupine city and skidded the Honda around in a flurry of sand. Its engine coughed and quit.

"Are you crazy?" Cody hollered at the child. She was just standing there, holding something in cupped hands. "What's *wrong* with you?" He whipped off his goggles, beads of sweat burning his eyes.

She didn't answer. She seemed not to even know how

close she'd been to kissing a tire. "You almost got yourself killed!" He chopped down the kickstand, got off, and strode toward her to pull her out of the street.

But as he reached her, she lowered her arms and he could see what was cradled in her hands. "What is this?" she asked.

It was an orange-striped kitten, probably only a month or so old. Cody glanced around to get his bearings and saw they were standing in front of the Cat Lady's house. A few feet away, the orange mama tabby sat on her haunches, patiently awaiting the return of her own.

"You know what it is," he snapped, his nerves still raw. "It's a kitten. Everybody in the world knows what a kitten is."

"A kit-ten," the child repeated, as if she'd never heard the word before. "Kitten." It was easier that time. Her fingers stroked the fur. "Soft."

Something weird about this kid, Cody thought. Mighty weird. She didn't talk right, and she didn't stand right either. Her back was too rigid, as if she were straining against the weight of her bones. Her face and hair were dusty, and her blue jeans and T-shirt looked as if she'd been rolling on the ground. Her face was familiar, though; he'd seen her somewhere before. He remembered where: at school one afternoon in April. Mr. Hammond's wife and the kid had come to pick him up. The little girl's name was Sandy, or Steffi, or something like that.

"You're Mr. Hammond's kid," he said. "What're you doin' wanderin' out here alone?"

Her attention was still focused on the kitten. "Pretty," she said. She'd reasoned it was the younger form of the creature that waited not far away, just as the form she occupied was the young female form of the human beings. She stroked its body with a gentle touch. "This kitten is a fragile construction."

"Huh?"

"Fragile," she repeated, looking up at him. "Is that not the correct term?"

Cody didn't reply for a few seconds. He couldn't; his

voice was lost. Mighty, mighty weird, he thought. Warily, he replied, "Kittens are tougher than they look."

"So are daughters," Daufin said, mostly to herself. She carefully leaned over and placed the kitten on the ground in the exact spot she'd found it. Immediately the older quadruped picked it up by the scruff of the neck and bounded away with it around the corner of the house.

"Uh . . . what's your name?" Cody's heart had begun slamming again, and a trickle of sweat crept down the middle of his back. Already wet rings were coming up under his arms, and the night's heat was stifling. "It's Sandy, isn't it?"

"Daufin." She stared steadily at him.

"I think I'm about ready for a rubber room." He pushed a hand through his tangled hair. Maybe he'd suffered a worse punch than he'd thought, and his brains had been knocked loose. "You *are* Mr. Hammond's little girl, aren't you?"

She pondered a correct response to his question. This one had strange discolorations on his cliff of features, and she could see that bewilderment had taken the place of anger. She knew he would think she was as alien as she thought him to be. What was that strange extension dangling from the hearing cup called an "ear"? Why was one visual orb smaller than the other? And what was the now-silent monster that had roared down on her through the murk? Puzzles, puzzles. Still, she felt no terror in him, as there had been in those others when she'd fled the destroyed abode of ritual. "I have chosen to . . ." What would the proper translation be? "To clothe myself in this daughter." She lifted her hands, as if she were showing off a new and wonderful dress.

"Clothe yourself. Uh-huh." Cody nodded, one eye large and the swollen eye twitching. "Man, you've looped the loop for damn sure!" he told himself. This looked like Mr. Hammond's kid standing before him, but she sure didn't use a kid's words. Except maybe if she was out of her mind, which he wasn't doubting. One of them had to be. "You ought to be at home," he said. "You shouldn't be walkin' around by yourself, not with that thing sittin' over there."

"Yes. The big booger," she said.

"Right." Another slow nod. "You want me to take you home?"

"Oh!" It had been a quick intake of breath. "Oh, if you could," she whispered, and she looked up at the gridded sky. The darkness claimed all reference points.

"You live on Celeste Street," Cody reminded her. He pointed toward the vet's office, just a couple of blocks away. "Over there."

"My home. My home." Daufin reached toward the sky, her hands open. "My home is very far from here, and I can't see the way." Her host body trembled, and she felt a heat behind her own cliff of features. It was more than the increase in the rush of that vital fluid through the miraculous network of arteries, more than the muscle pump's brain-timed beating. It was deeper, a yearning that burned at the center of her being. Within it, her memories of home began to unfold. They came to her in her own language of chimes, but they were synthesized through the human brain and left her tongue in human speech. "I see the tides. I feel them: rising, falling. I feel life in the tides. I feel whole." Cody saw her body begin to undulate slightly, as if in rhythm with the currents of a spectral ocean. "There are great cities, and groves of peace. The tides move over mountains, through valleys and gardens where every labor is love. I feel them; they touch me, even here. They call me home." The movement of her body abruptly stopped. She stared at her hands, at the frightening appendages of alien flesh, and the memories fled before the horror of reality.

"No," she said. "No. That's how my world *was*. No more. Now the tides carry pain, and the gardens lie in ruins. There is no more singing. There is no more peace, and my world suffers in the shadow of hate. *That* shadow." She reached toward the pyramid, and Cody saw her fingers clench into a claw, her hand trembling. She closed her eyes, unable to endure the visions behind them. When they opened again, they were blurred and burning. There was a wetness around them, and Daufin put a hand to her cheek to investigate this new malfunction. She brought her hand away, the fingers glistening and a single unbroken drop of liquid suspended on the tip of the longest digit.

Another drop ran down her cliff of features and into the corner of her mouth. In it she could taste the tides of her world.

"You won't win," she whispered, staring fixedly at the pyramid. Cody felt something inside him shrink back; her eyes were blazing with a power that made him fear he might explode into flame if they were aimed at him. "I won't let you win."

Cody hadn't moved. At first he'd been sure either he or the little girl had leapt headlong into the Great Fried Empty, but now . . . now he wasn't sure. The black pyramid must have a pilot or crew of some kind. Maybe this kid was one of them, and she'd made herself—itself—resemble Mr. Hammond's daughter. On this sweltering, crazy night it seemed that all things were possible. And so he blurted out a question that on any other night of his life would have sealed his permanent residence in the Great Fried Empty: "You're not . . . from around here, are you? I mean . . . not . . . like . . . from this *planet?*"

She blinked away the last of the searing wet, and her head swiveled toward him with smooth grace. "No," she said, "I'm not."

"Wow." There was a knot in his throat the size of a basketball. He didn't know what else to say. It made more sense now that she was wandering around in the dark and hadn't known what a kitten was; but why would the same creature who was so gentle with a kitten destroy the helicopter? And if this was an alien from the pyramid, what was the thing burrowing under the streets? "Is that yours?" He pointed at the pyramid.

"No. It belongs to . . . Stinger."

He repeated the name. "Is that . . . like . . . the captain or somebody?"

She didn't understand what he meant. She said, "Stinger is . . ." There was a hesitation as her memory scanned the volumes of the *Britannica* and the dictionary. After a few seconds, she found a phrase that was accurate in Earth language: "A bounty hunter," she said.

"What's he hunting?"

"Me."

This was too much for Cody to comprehend all at one time. Meeting a little girl from outer space in the middle of Brazos Street was weird enough, but a galactic bounty hunter in a black pyramid was one brainblaster too many. He caught movement from the corner of his eye, looked over, and saw two cats nosing around the wilted shrubs in Mrs. Stellenberg's yard. Another cat was standing on the porch steps, wailing forlornly. Kittens scampered from the brush and chased each other's tails. It was after one o'clock in the morning; why were Mrs. Stellenberg's cats out?

He walked to the Honda, angling the headlight so it shone at the Cat Lady's house. The front door was wide open. The cat on the steps arched its back, spitting in the headlight's glare.

"Mrs. Stellenberg!" Cody called. "You all right?"

Coils of smoke meandered past the light. "Mrs. Stellenberg!" he tried again, and again there was no reply.

Cody waited. The open door both beckoned and repelled him. What if she'd fallen in the dark and knocked herself out? What if she'd broken a hip, or even her neck? He was no saint, but he couldn't pretend he didn't care. He walked to the foot of the steps. "Mrs. Stellenberg! It's Cody Lockett!"

No answer. The cat on the steps gave a nervous yowl and shot past Cody's feet, heading for the brush.

He started up. He had taken two of the steps when he felt a quick tug at his elbow.

"Careful, Cody Lockett," Daufin warned, standing right beside him. Stinger had passed this way and its reek lingered in the air.

"Yeah." She didn't have to tell him twice. He continued up the steps and paused at the doorway's dark rectangle. "Mrs. Stellenberg?" he called into the house. "Are you okay?"

Nothing but silence. If the Cat Lady was in there, she couldn't answer. Cody took a deep breath and stepped over the threshold.

His foot never found the floor. He was tumbling forward, falling through darkness, and Daufin's restraining hand was a half second too late. Cody's mouth opened in a cry of terror. It came to him that the front room of the Cat Lady's house had no floor, and he was going to keep falling until he crashed through the roof of hell.

Something whammed underneath his right arm, knocking the wind out of him, and he had the sense to grab hold of it before he slid off. He gripped both hands to a swaying thing that felt like a horizontal length of pipe. Dirt and stones cascaded into the darkness beneath him. He didn't hear them hit bottom. Then the pipe's swaying stopped, and he was left dangling in midair.

His lungs heaved for breath, and his brain felt like a hot pulse of overloaded circuits. He locked his fingers around the pipe, kicked out, could find nothing there. The pipe began swaying again so he ceased his struggling.

"Cody Lockett! Are you alive?" Daufin's voice came from above.

"Yeah," he rasped. He knew she hadn't heard him, so he tried again, louder: "Yeah! I guess . . . I wasn't careful enough, huh?"

"Can you"—her memory banks raced for the terminology, and she leaned over the gaping hole but couldn't see him—"climb out?"

"Don't think so. Got hold of a pipe." He kicked out again, still could find no walls. The pipe made an ominous, stressed creaking, and more gobbets of dirt hissed down. "I don't know what's under me!" The first bite of panic sank deep. His hands were slick with sweat. He tried to pull himself up, to swing a leg onto the pipe for support, but his bruised ribs daggered him with pain. He couldn't get his leg up, and after three futile attempts he stopped trying and concentrated on conserving his strength. "I can't get out!" he shouted.

Daufin measured the sound of his voice at being, in Earth

distance, approximately thirteen-point-six feet down, though the echoes gave a distortion of up to three inches more or less. She hung in the doorframe and looked around the floorless room, searching for anything she might use to reach him. The only things left were a few pictures hanging on the cracked walls.

"Listen to me!" Cody called. "You've got to find somebody to help! Understand?"

"Yes!" The knot of muscle in her chest labored furiously. She saw the pattern now: Stinger was searching for her by invading these human abodes and seizing whoever it found within. "I'll find help!" She turned from the doorway and ran down the steps. Then she was on the street, running toward the center of town, fighting the planet's leaden gravity and her own clumsy appendages.

Cody squeezed his eyes shut to keep out the beads of sweat. If he let his fingers relax just a fraction, he would slide off the pipe and plummet down God only knew how far. He didn't know how long he could hold on. "Hurry!" he called up, but Daufin had gone. He hung in darkness, waiting.

36
Mouth of the South

"Mother!" Noah Twilley shouted as he came in the front door. "We're going to the clinic!" He had left an oil lamp burning on a table in the foyer, and now he picked it up and headed toward the staircase. "Mother?" he called again. Ruth Twilley had remained in her white bedroom, the bedcovers pulled up to her chin while he'd gone with Tom Hammond to the clinic. He reached the stairs and started up.

They ended after six risers. Noah stood gripping the broken banister and peering into a dark chasm that had taken down the rest of the staircase. Below, in the depths of the hole, was a little flicker of fire. A broken lamp, Noah realized. Puddle of oil still burning.

"Mother?" he called; his voice cracked. His light ran along fissures in the walls. Ruth Twilley, the Mouth of the South, was silent. The ruined staircase swayed and moaned under Noah's weight, and he slowly retreated to the bottom of the steps.

Stood there, numbed and shaking. "Mother, where are you?" It came out like the wail of an abandoned child.

The lamplight gleamed off something on the floor. Footprints. Slimy footprints, coming down the stairs from that awful hole. Smears and splatters of a gray, snotlike substance trailed along the steps and through the hallway toward the rear of the house. Somebody needs a Kleenex, Noah thought. Oh, Mother's going to blow a gasket about this mess! She was upstairs in bed, with the sheet pulled to her chin. Wasn't she?

He followed the trail of slime drips into the kitchen. The floor was warped and crooked, as if something huge had destroyed the very foundations of the house. He shone the lamp around, and there she was. Standing in the corner by the refrigerator, her white silk gown wet and gleaming, strands of slime caught in her red hair and her face a pale gray mask.

"Who's the guardian?" she asked, and her eyes had no bottom.

He couldn't answer. He took a step back and hit the counter.

"The little girl. Explain." Ruth Twilley drifted forward, the glint of silver needles between her fleshy scarlet lips.

"Mother. I . . . don't . . ." His hand spasmed and opened, and the oil lamp fell to the floor at his feet. The glass broke, and streamers of fire snaked across the linoleum.

She had almost reached him. "Who's the guardian?" she repeated, walking through the fire.

It was not his mother. He knew there was a monster behind Ruth Twilley's slick face and it was almost upon him. One arm came up, and a hand with metallic, saw-blade fingernails reached toward him. He watched it coming like the head of a sidewinder, and he pressed back against the counter but there was nowhere to go.

His arm brushed something that clattered on the Formica. He knew what it was, because he'd left it out to spray in the corners. You never knew what might creep in from the desert, after the lights were out.

She was a step away, and her face pressed toward his. A little thick rivulet of slime oozed from her chin.

Noah's hand closed around the can of Raid on the countertop, and as he picked it up he flicked the cap off and thrust the nozzle at her eyes. His index finger jabbed down on the spigot.

White bug-killing foam jetted out and covered the Ruth Twilley face like a grotesque beauty mask. It filled her eyes, shot up her nostrils, ran through the rows of needle teeth. She staggered back, whether hurt or just blinded he didn't know, and one of her hands swung at Noah's head; he lifted his arm to ward it off, was struck on the shoulder as if by a brick wrapped up in barbed wire. The shock of pain knocked the Raid can from his fingers, and as he was thrown against the kitchen wall he felt warm blood running down his hand.

She whirled like a windup toy gone berserk, crashing over the kitchen table and chairs, caroming off the refrigerator, her serrated nails digging at her own face and eyes. Noah saw gobbets of gray flesh fly, and he realized she was trying to strip the skin to the bone. She made a roaring sound that became the scream he had heard every day of his life, four or five times a day, like a regal command issued from the white bedroom: *"Noooaaahhhhh!"*

Whether the thing in his mother's skin knew that was his name or not didn't matter. In that sound Noah Twilley heard the slam of a jail cell's door, forever locking him to a town he hated, in a job he hated, living in a hated house with a crazy woman who screamed for attention between soap operas and "Wheel of Fortune." He smelled his own blood, felt it crawling over his hand and heard it pattering to the floor, and as he watched the red-haired monster crashing around the kitchen he lost his mind as fast as a fingersnap.

"I'm here, Mother," he said, very calmly. His eyeglasses hung by one ear, and blood flecked the lenses. "Right here." He walked four steps to a drawer as the creature continued to flail its face away; he opened the drawer and pulled out a long butcher knife from amid the other sharp utensils. "Noah's right here," he said, and he lifted the knife and went to her.

He brought the knife down in the side of her throat. It slid into the false flesh about four inches before it met resistance. He pulled it out, struck again, and one of her hands caught him across the chest and hurled him off his feet against the counter. He sat up, his glasses gone but the bent-bladed knife still clenched in his hand, blood rising through the rips in his chest. His lungs gurgled, and he coughed up crimson. The monster's hands were swiping through the air, seeking him, and Noah could see that she had clawed her eyes and most of the facial flesh away. Metallic veins and raw red tissue jittered and twitched in the craters. Chemicals burned her, he thought. Good old Raid, works on all kinds of insects. He stood up, in no hurry, and walked toward her with the knife upraised and the merry shine of madness in his eyes.

And that was when the thing's spine bowed out and there was a crackling sound of bones popping. The back of her gown split open and from the dark, rising blister at the base of her backbone uncoiled a scaly, muscular tail that ended in a ball of spikes.

Noah stopped, staring in stupefied wonder as the burning oil flamed around his feet.

The tail whipped to the left, smashing through a cupboard and sending pieces of crockery flying like shrapnel. The monster was crouched over almost double, the network of muscles and connective tissues damp with oozing lubricants at the base of the tail. The ball of spikes made a tight circle, bashed a rain of plaster from the ceiling, and whirled past Noah's face with a deadly hiss.

"My God," he whispered, and dropped the knife.

Her eyeless face angled toward the noise. The half-human, half-insect body scuttled at him. The hands caught his sides, saw-blade nails winnowing into the flesh. The tail reared back, curving into a stately arc. Noah stared at it, realized that he was seeing the shape of his death. He thought of the scorpions in his collection, pierced with pins. Revenge is mine, sayeth the Lord, he thought. He gave a strangled laugh.

The tail jerked forward with the velocity of an industrial piston, and the ball of spikes smashed Noah Twilley's skull into a thousand fragments. Then the tail began whipping back and forth in quick, savage arcs, and in another moment the quivering mass gripped between alien hands no longer resembled anything human. The tail kept slashing away pieces until all movement had ceased, and then the hands hurled what was left against the wall like a sack of garbage.

The blind thing flailed its way out of the kitchen, following the odor of its spoor, returned to the broken staircase, and dropped into darkness.

37

Bob Wire Club

"Set 'em up again, Jacky!" Curt Lockett banged his fist on
the rough-topped bar. The bartender, a stocky gray-bearded
man named Jack Blair, looked at him from down the bar
where he was talking to Harlan Nugent and Pete Griffin.
The light of kerosene lanterns hung in Jack's round eyeglasses, and above the lenses his brows were as shaggy as
caterpillars.

"Almost a half bottle gone, Curt," Jack said in a voice like
a bulldozer's growl. "Maybe you ought to pack up your
tent."

"Hell, I wish I could!" Curt replied. "Wish I could pack
up and light out of this shithole and by God I wouldn't
never look back!" He pounded the bar again. "Come on,
Jacky! Don't cut your ole buddy off yet!"

Jack glared at him for a few seconds. He knew how Curt
acted with more than a half bottle lighting his wick. Over at
a table, Hal McCutchins and Burl Keene were smoking
cigarettes and talking, and others had come and gone. The
one thing everybody in the Bob Wire Club had in common
was that they had nowhere else in particular to go, no wives
waiting for them, nothing to do but kill some time drinking
at one-fifteen in the morning. Jack didn't care much for
Curt Lockett, but the man was a steady customer. He came

down the bar, opened the half-drained bottle of Kentucky Gent—the cheapest brand in the house—and poured him another shotglass full. When Jack started to draw it away, Curt gripped the bottle's neck in a lockhold.

"Mighty thirsty," Curt said. "Mighty, mighty thirsty."

"Keep the fucker, then," Jack said, giving in to the inevitable.

"Yessir, I seen it!" Pete Griffin went on with what he'd been saying. He was a leathery cowboy with blue eyes sunken in a wrinkled, sunbaked face. "Damn thing's blockin' the highway 'bout five miles north." He swigged from his lukewarm bottle of Lone Star beer. "I was about to hit the pedal and try to tear ol' Betsy right through it, and then I seen somethin' else." He paused for another drink. Ol' Betsy was his rust-eaten red pickup truck, parked in the sandy lot out front.

"What'd you see?" Jack prodded.

"Dead things," Pete said. "I got out and took me a closer look. There was burned-up rabbits and a couple of dead dogs lyin' right where the thing went into the ground. You can see through it, and it don't look as sturdy as a spiderweb, but . . . well, I seen somethin' on the other side too. Looked to have been a truck, maybe. It was still smokin'. So I got in ol' Betsy and decided to mosey back thisaway."

"And I'm sayin' ain't such a thing possible," Harlan contended, his voice slurred from four boilermakers. "Cain't such a thing be solid!"

"It is, by God! Hell, my eyes ain't gone yet! That thing's solid as a stone wall and it burned them animals up too!"

Curt laughed harshly. "Griffin, you're crazy as a three-legged toadfrog. You cain't see through anythin' solid. I'm dumb as a board, and even *I* know that!"

"You drive on up there and try to get through it, then!" Pete's face bristled with indignant anger. "I'll come along behind and sweep up your ashes—not that that boy of yours would want 'em!"

"Yeah!" Harlan gave a dry chuckle. "We'll put them ashes

in a whiskey bottle for you, Curt. That way you can rest in peace."

"Rest pickled is more like it," Jack said. "Curt, why don't you go on home? Don't you care about your boy?"

"Cody can take care of himself. Always has before." Curt swigged down the whiskey. He was feeling okay now. His nerves had steadied, but he was sweating too much to get drunk. The Bob Wire Club was stiflingly hot without power to run the fans, and Curt's shirt was plastered to his skin. "He don't need me, and I sure as hell don't need him."

"If I had a family, I'd sure be with 'em at a time like this." Out of habit, Jack took a rag and cleaned the bartop. He lived alone in a trailer behind the Bob Wire Club, and he'd kept the place open after the electricity had gone out because he couldn't have slept anyway. "Seems only right a father ought to be with his boy."

"Yeah, and a wife ought to be with her husband too!" Curt snapped. It had come out of him before he'd had time to check it. The others stared at him, and he shrugged and sipped from the bottle. "Just forget it," he said. "Cody ain't a kid no more."

"Well, still don't seem right," Jack continued, following the swirls of his rag. "Not with that damn bastard sittin' across the river and all hell breakin' loose."

"I hear there's an air-force colonel in town," Hal McCutchins said. "He was in the chopper that went down, but he got out okay. Sumbitch flew out of that pyramid and knocked it down like it was made out of paper!"

"Thing's a spaceship." Burl Keene, his bulging belly quivering against the table's edge, reached for a handful of peanuts from a bowl. "That's the talk. Thing's come from Mars."

"Ain't nobody on Mars." Jack stopped cleaning. "The scientists proved that. No, that thing's come from somewhere a long ways off."

"Scientists don't know nothin'," Burl countered, chomping on peanuts. "Hell, they don't even believe there was a Garden of Eden!"

"Mars is nothin' but rocks! They took pictures on Mars and that's all you can see!"

Curt scowled and tipped the bottle to his mouth again. Whether the black pyramid had brought invaders from Mars or cat people from Pluto didn't matter much to him; as long as they left him alone, he didn't care. He listened as Jack and Burl went on about Mars, but his mind was on Cody. Maybe he ought to find out if the boy was all right. Maybe he was a fool for sitting here thinking that Cody could handle himself in every kind of jam. No, he decided in the next second, Cody was better off on his own. The boy was a damn idjit sometimes, but he was tough as nails and he could make do. Besides, he was probably up at the apartments with that gang of his. They all hung thick as thieves and took care of each other, so what was there to worry about?

Besides, rough treatment was good for Cody. That made a boy into a man. It was the way Curt's father had raised him, bullying and beating. Cody would be stronger for it.

Yeah, Curt thought. His knuckles bleached around the bottle's neck. Strong, just like his old man.

He couldn't remember the last time he'd talked to Cody without blowing his top. Maybe it was because he didn't know how to, he thought. But the kid was so headstrong and wild, nobody could get through to him. Cody walked his own path, right or wrong. But sometimes Curt thought he saw Treasure in Cody's face, clear as day, and his heart ached as if it had been kicked.

There was no use in thinking these thoughts. Nothing good came out of them, and they made Curt's head hurt. He looked into the amber bottle, at the liquid that lay within, and he smiled as if seeing an old friend. But there was a sadness in his smile, because full bottles always ran empty.

"Maybe they've got caves," Burl Keene was saying. "Under Mars. Maybe they just went into their caves when the pictures got took."

Curt was about to tell him to stop shoveling the horseshit when he heard the bottles clink together on the shelves behind the bar.

It was not a loud sound, and neither Jack nor Burl stopped their jabbering. But Curt had heard it clearly enough, and in another few seconds he heard them clink again. He set his own bottle on the bar and saw a tremor on the whiskey's surface. "Jack?" he said. Blair paid no attention. "Hey, Jack!" Curt said, louder.

Jack looked at him, fed up with Curt Lockett. "What is it?"

"I think we're havin' a—"

The Bob Wire Club's floor suddenly buckled upward, timbers squealing as they snapped. The two pool tables jumped a foot in the air, and billiard balls were flung out of their racks. Bottles and glasses crashed down behind the bar. Jack was knocked off his feet, and Curt's barstool went over. He landed on his back on the floor, and under him he could feel the boards pitching and heaving like a bronco's shoulder blades.

The floor's motion eased, then stopped. Curt sat up, stunned, and in the lamplight saw a horrible thing: the last of the Kentucky Gent spilling from the overturned bottle.

Harlan and Pete were on the floor too, and Burl was coughing up peanuts. Harlan got to his knees and shouted, "What hit us?"

There was a bang like a sledgehammer on wood. Curt heard the squall of nails popping loose. "Over there!" He pointed, and all of them saw it: about ten feet away, a board was being knocked upward from the floor. The second blow sent it flying up to hit the ceiling, and Curt caught sight of a slim human hand and arm reaching through the cavity. Another timber was knocked loose, then the fingers of that hand gripped the edge of a third board and wrenched it down. Now there was a gap large enough for a person to crawl through, and about three seconds later a figure began to emerge from the floor.

"Holy Jesus and Mary," Jack whispered, standing up behind the bar with sawdust in his beard.

The figure got its head and shoulders through, then worked its hips free. A long pair of bare legs pulled out, and the figure rose to its feet.

340

It was a slender and pretty blond girl, maybe sixteen years old, wearing nothing but a lacy bra and a pair of pink panties with "Friday" stitched across the front. She stretched to her full height, her ribs showing under her pale skin and her hair shining wetly in the lamplight. Her face was as calm as if she came up through barroom floors every night of her life, and her gaze went from one man to the next with cold attention.

"I'm dead," Burl gasped. "I've gotta be dead."

Curt tried to stand up, but his legs weren't ready. He knew who she was: her name was Laurie Rainey, and she worked afternoons at the Paperback Kastle near the bakery and came in sometimes for grape jelly doughnuts. She was a pretty thing, and he liked to watch her chew. He tried to stand again, and this time he made it all the way up.

She spoke. "Ya'll are gonna tell me about the little girl," she said, in a thick whangy Texas accent with a rattling metallic undertone. Her skin gleamed, as if she were coated with grease. "Ya'll are gonna tell me right *now.*"

None of the men spoke, and no one moved. Laurie Rainey looked around, her head slowly racheting as if her neck and spine were connected by gear wheels.

"The little girl," Jack repeated dumbly. "What little girl?"

"The one who's the guardian." Her eyes found him, and Jack had the sensation of peering into a snakepit. There were things slithering around in there that he would not care to know. "Ya'll are gonna tell me, or I'm done bein' nice."

"Laurie . . . " Curt's mind stuttered like a blown-out engine. "What were you doin' under the *floor?"*

"Laurie." The girl's head notched toward him. "Is that the guardian's name?"

"No. It's *your* name. Christ, don't you know your own name?"

The girl didn't reply. She blinked slowly, processing the information, and her mouth tightened into an angry line. "What we have here," she said, "is a failure to communicate." She turned to her left, walked about three strides to the nearest pool table, and placed her hands under its edge. With a quick, blurred motion, she flipped her hands forward and the pool table upended as if it had the weight of a corn husk. It came off the floor and crashed through the Bob Wire Club's front window into the parking lot, throwing glass all over Curt's Buick and Pete Griffin's pickup truck.

She strode purposefully to the second pool table, balled up her right fist, and smashed it through the green felt covering. Then she picked up one end of the table and flipped it across the barroom into a couple of pinball machines. All the men could do was gawk, openmouthed, and Jack Blair almost fainted because he knew it took three men to lift those pool tables.

The girl's head racheted, surveying the destruction. There was no damage to her hand, and she wasn't even breathing hard. She turned toward the men. "Now we'll have us a nice little talk," she said.

Burl Keene yelped like a whipped dog and scrambled for the door, but he was way too slow. The girl leapt forward and was on him even as he reached for the knob. She caught his wrist and twisted it sharply. Bones popped, and their jagged edges ripped through the meat at Burl's elbow. He screamed, still thrashing to get out the door, and she wrenched at his broken arm and chopped a blow at his face with the edge of her free hand. Burl's nose exploded, and his teeth went down his throat. He fell to his knees, blood streaming down his mangled face.

Jack reached beside the cash register and pulled his shotgun from its socket. The girl was turning toward him as he cocked the gun and lifted it. He didn't know what kind of monster she was, but he didn't plan on sharing Burl's fate. He squeezed the trigger.

The shotgun boomed and bucked. A fist-sized hole appeared in the girl's belly, just above the panty line, and bits of flesh and gray tissue exploded from her back. She was knocked off her feet, her body slamming against the wall. She went down, trailing gray slime.

"God A'mighty!" Curt shouted in the silence after the blast. "You done killed her!"

Hal McCutchins picked up a cue stick and prodded the twitching body. Something writhed in the belly wound like a mass of knotted-up worms. "Lord," he said in a choked voice. "You blew the hell out of—"

She sat up.

Before Hal could jump back, the girl grabbed the cue stick and pulled it from his hands so fast his palms were scorched. She hit him across the knees with the heavy end of it, and as his kneecaps shattered Hal fell on his face.

She stood up, her belly oozing and a malignant grin stretching her mouth. Red lamplight glinted off a mouthful of needles. "Ya'll want to play rough?" the rattling voice asked. "Okey-dokey."

She slammed the stick's blunt end down on Hal McCutchins's head. The stick snapped in two, and Hal's skull broke open like a blister. His legs kicked in a dance of death, his brains exposed to the light.

"Shoot it!" Curt screamed, but Jack's finger was already pulling the trigger again. The creature was hit in the side, spun around, and flung backward. A gray mist hung in the air, and Curt screeched because there was sticky wet matter on his shirt and arms. The creature fell over a table but righted herself and did not go to the floor. In the wound her ribs looked to be fashioned from blue-tinged metal, but a thorny coil of red intestines protruded from the hole. She advanced toward the bar with the splintered piece of cue stick in her hand.

Jack fumbled to shove another shell into the breech. Curt scrabbled on his hands and knees for cover under a table, and Harlan and Pete had mashed themselves against a wall like bugs trapped to a screen.

Jack cocked the shotgun and lifted it to fire. As he did, the creature hurled the cue stick like a javelin. Its sharp end penetrated Jack's throat and emerged from the back of his neck in a bloody spray, and Jack's finger twitched on the trigger. The buckshot tore the right side of the monster's face off, peeled away gray tissue and red muscle right down to the blue metallic cheek and jawbone. Her eye on that side rolled back to show the white. Jack clawed at his throat, strangling, and fell behind the bar.

"Get away! Get away!" Pete was shouting hysterically, but

Harlan picked up a chair and flung it at the creature. The thing shrugged off the object and charged at him, gripping both hands around his neck and picking him up off the floor. She twisted his head as easily as a chicken's, and Harlan's face turned blue just before his neck snapped.

Pete fell to his knees, his hands upraised for mercy. "Please . . . oh God, don't kill me!" he begged. "Please don't kill me!"

She tossed Harlan Nugent aside like an old sack and gazed down into Pete's eyes. She smiled, fluid running from the wound in her face, and then she gripped Pete's wrists, put her foot against his chest, and yanked.

Both arms ripped out of their sockets. The jittering torso collapsed, Pete's mouth still working but only a whisper of shock coming out.

Under the table, Curt tasted blood. He'd bitten his tongue to keep from screaming, and now he felt a darkness pulling at his mind like a deep, beckoning current. He watched as the creature held Pete Griffin's disembodied arms before her, as if studying the anatomy. Pete's fingers still clenched and relaxed, and blood pattered to the boards like a rainstorm.

I'm next, Curt thought. God help me, I'm next.

He had two choices: stay here or make a run for it. It wasn't much of a choice. He thrust his hand into his pocket and pulled out his car keys. They jingled, and he saw the monster's head rotate around on its neck at an impossible angle so that the face was where the back of the head ought to be. The single, inflamed eye found him.

Curt shot out from under the table and raced for the broken window. He heard two thumps as she dropped Pete's arms, then the crash of a table going over. The thing was leaping after him. He jumped through the window like diving into a hoop, hit the ground on his hands and knees, and crawled madly toward the Buick. A hand caught the back of his shirt, and he knew she was right there with him.

He didn't think. He just did. His left hand gripped sand, and he twisted around and flung it into Laurie Rainey's savage, ruined face.

Her eye blinded, she tore the shirt off his back and swiped at him with her other hand. He ducked, saw the glint of little saw blades as her fingers flashed past his face. Curt kicked out at her, hit her in the breastbone, and pulled his leg back before she could grab it. Then he was up and running, and he reached his car and slid behind the wheel, his fingers jamming the key home.

The engine made that knocking noise like it did every time it didn't want to start, only this time it sounded like a fist on a coffin's lid. Curt roared, "Start, damn you!" and sank his foot to the floorboard. The tailpipe belched dark smoke, the engine's muttering turned into a growl, and the Buick jerked in reverse. But not fast enough: Curt saw the creature racing after him, coming like an Olympic sprinter across the Bob Wire Club's lot. He battled the wheel as the tires hit Highway 67's pavement, trying to get the car turned in the direction of Inferno. But the monster was almost to the car, and he forced the gearshift into first and shot forward to run her over. She jumped just before the Buick hit her, grabbing hold of the roof's edge and scuttling up onto it on her belly.

He swerved the car, trying to throw her off. She held on, and Curt laid on the accelerator. He turned on the head-lights; in the green glow of the dashboard the speedometer needle edged past forty. He realized he was going north instead of south but he was too scared to do anything but keep his foot on the pedal. At fifty the vibration of the bald tires all but jerked the wheel out of his hands, and at sixty the old engine was wheezing at the gaskets.

Something slammed down over his head and a blister of metal bloomed in the roof. Her fist, he thought. She was trying to beat through the roof. Another slam, and a second blister grew beside the first. Her hand crept into the car, fingers wrenching at the roof's joints. Screws popped loose. There was a shriek of rusted metal; she was bending the roof back like the lid of a sardine can. A crack zigzagged across the windshield.

Screaming at its limits, the engine hit seventy miles an hour and rocketed Curt along Highway 67.

38
The Streets of Inferno

In the seven minutes since Daufin had left Cody Lockett, she'd seen no other humans on the streets of Inferno. She had gone back to the house of Tom, Jessie, and Ray, and though the doorway was unlocked, the abode was empty of life. She tried the doors of two other abodes, found the door to the first sealed and the second house also empty. The murk was getting thicker, and Daufin found that human eyes had a radically limited field of vision. The brown haze made her host eyes sting and water, and she could see less than forty feet in all directions as she continued along Celeste Street in search of help.

Two lights were coming through the smoke. Daufin stopped, waiting for them to get closer. She could hear an engine: the crude, combustion-powered conveyance called a car. But the car slowed and turned to the right before it reached her, and she saw the red smears of its taillights drawing rapidly away. She ran after it, crossing the sandy plot of earth where she'd hidden under the protective shell and met the Sarge Dennison creature. Another set of headlights passed on Celeste Street, going east, but the vehicle was moving too fast for Daufin to catch and by that time she'd reached Cobre Road. She kept running in the direction of the first car she'd seen and in another moment she saw the red points of the taillights again, just up the street. The car wasn't moving, but the engine still rumbled. She approached it, saw that the vehicle's doors were open but no one was in sight. A little rectangle fixed to the back of the car had letters on it: CADE-1. It was parked in front of a structure with shattered light apertures—"windows," she knew they were termed—and the doorway hung open as well. A square with writing above the doorway identified the structure as INFERNO HARDWARE.

"Place has been ripped off," Rick said to Zarra as they stood at the rear of the store. He'd found a flashlight and batteries, and he shone its beam into the broken glass counter where the pistols had been locked up. Out of an assortment of eight guns on display, not one remained. "Somebody cleaned Mr. Luttrell out." He pointed the light at the racks where six rifles had been; they were gone, hacked right out of their locks by an ax or machete. Boxes of ammunition had been stolen from the storage shelves, and only a few cartridges gleamed in the light.

"So much for findin' a piece, man," Zarra said. "Let's get our butts across the bridge."

"Hold on. Mr. Luttrell keeps a pistol in his office." Rick started back, through a swinging door into the storeroom, and Zarra followed the light. The office was locked, but Rick bashed open the door with two kicks and went to the manager's paper-cluttered desk. The drawers were locked too. He went out to the storeroom, found a box of screwdrivers, and returned to the job at hand. He and Zarra levered the drawers open with screwdrivers, and in the bottom drawer, under a pile of dog-eared *Playboy* magazines, was a loaded .38 pistol and an extra box of bullets. At the clinic Rick and Zarra had listened to Colonel Rhodes's story about the two spaceships and the creatures called Daufin and Stinger. Rick could still feel the slick scales of that thing's tail around his throat, and damned if he was going to go back to Bordertown without a gun. The Fang of Jesus paled before Smith & Wesson firepower.

"Let's go, man!" Zarra urged nervously. "You got what you came for!"

"Right." Rick left the office with Zarra right behind him. They went through the storeroom door again, and suddenly from the front of the store there was a crash and clatter that almost made their hearts seize up. Zarra gave a little moan of terror, and Rick snapped the .38's safety off and cocked it. He probed around with the light, following the beam with the gun barrel.

He couldn't see anyone. Somebody in here after guns, just like us, he thought. He hoped. "Who's there?" he said.

Something moved to his left. He swung the light in that direction, toward shelves where coils of rope and wire were kept. "I've got a gun!" he warned. "I'll shoot your damned —" He stopped speaking when the light found her.

She was standing there holding a coil of rope between both hands. A bundle of copper wire had fallen off the shelf, upsetting a display of jars of nails. She was wearing just what Colonel Rhodes had said: a dusty Jetsons T-shirt and blue jeans, and her face was that of Mr. Hammond's child. Except behind that face, according to Rhodes, was an alien called Daufin and this was the little girl the thing in Cade's autoyard was looking for. "Don't move." His throat clogged up. His heart was beating so hard he could hear the blood roaring in his ears. "I've got a gun," he repeated, and his gunhand trembled.

"Cody Lockett needs help," Daufin said calmly, squinting into the harsh light. Her memory banks found the term *gun* and identified it as a primitive percussion-cap weapon. She could tell from the human's voice that he was terrified, so she stood very still.

"It's *her*," Zarra whispered. His legs were about to fold up. "Oh Christ, it's her!"

"What are you doing in here?" Rick asked, and kept his finger on the trigger.

"I saw your vehicle. I followed you," Daufin explained. "Cody Lockett is in need of help. Will you come with me?"

It took a few seconds for him to register what she'd said. "What's happened to him?"

"He fell. To below."

"Below where?"

She remembered the name Cody Lockett had called into the house, and pronounced it with difficulty: "Mrs. Stell-enberg's abode. I'll guide you there."

"No way!" Zarra said. "We're goin' back to Bordertown! Right, Rick?"

The other boy didn't answer. He wasn't exactly sure where Lockett was, but the creature seemed to be saying that he'd fallen under a house. "Do you know how far down he is?"

"Thirteen-point-six Earth feet. An approximate calculation, plus or minus three inches."

"Oh."

"By visuals I calculate this tether to be fifteen Earth feet in length." She struggled to lift up the heavy coil of rope she'd dragged off a shelf. The muscles of the daughter's arms strained with the weight. "Will you help me?"

"Forget Lockett, man!" Zarra objected. "Let's get back to our own people!"

Daufin didn't understand the tone of refusal. "Is Cody Lockett not one of your own?"

"No," Rick said. "He's a 'Gade, and we're Rattler—" He stopped, realizing how dumb that must sound to somebody from another planet. "He's different."

"Cody Lockett is a human being. You are human beings. What is the difference?"

"Our kind lives across the river," Zarra said. "That's where we're goin'." He walked on along the aisle toward the door paused in the doorway when he saw Rick wasn't following. "Come on, man!"

Rick kept the flashlight on the little girl's face. She stared fixedly at him, waiting for his response. Cody Lockett was nothing to him, but still . . . it seemed like they were all in this together, and the violet skygrid had caged both Renegades and Rattlers alike.

"Please," Daufin implored.

He sighed and lowered the .38. "You go on back to the church," he told Zarra. "Tell Paloma I'm okay."

"You're off your bird! Lockett wouldn't do shit for *you!*"

"Maybe he wouldn't, but I'm not Lockett. Go ahead, take the car. I'll come when I can."

Zarra started to protest again, but he knew that once Rick's mind was made up, he couldn't be swayed. "Damn stupid!" he muttered, then, in a louder voice: "You watch your ass. Got it?"

"Got it," Rick answered, and Zarra went out to Cade's Mercedes, got in, and wheeled it toward the bridge.

"Okay," Rick said to Daufin when the Mercedes was gone and it was too late for second thoughts. "Take me to him."

39
Highway 67

The creature's fist banged down like an anvil on the top of Curt Lockett's Buick. The metal dented in over his skull, and now the underside of the roof was as crumpled as a crushed beer can. The car was shuddering, just on the edge of going out of control, and the speedometer needle trembled on the wild side of seventy.

Curt screamed, "Get off!" and jerked the car to right and left. The Buick roared around a curve, slipped off the road, and threw up a boil of dust and stones. When he got the tires back on the pavement, he saw a shape before him in the headlights: a pickup truck going about twenty miles an hour, its bed loaded down with a mattress and junk furniture and a little dark-haired Mexican child sitting atop a stack of crates. The child's eyes had widened with terror, and as Curt fought the wheel the Buick grazed past the pickup and left it in a swirl of dust.

The road wound between red boulders the size of houses. Over the engine's shriek Curt heard the squeal of the roof peeling back; the metal-nailed fingers were at work, gripped along the top of the passenger door. More screws popped out, and she kept battering the roof in with her other fist. He jerked the car violently left and right again, but the monster held on as tight as a tick.

The roof broke loose from the rim of the windshield. Cracks jigsawed across the glass. Her hand folded around the rusted metal at the top of the driver's door, and Curt beat at the fingers with his fist. She reached in, groping for him, and almost snagged his hair before he could slide across the seat. The car slewed to the right, left the road, and bounced over ruts that whammed Curt's skull against the roof dents. And suddenly the creature lost her grip, slid backward over the roof with a skreek of metal nails and down the rear windshield. She tried to catch hold, found nothing to grip. In the rearview mirror, Curt saw her slide over the fishtailing trunk, saw her half-mangled, half-beautiful face glisten in the red glare of the taillights. Her face disappeared over the trunk's bulbous slope, and Curt whooped with joy.

"To hell with you!" he shouted hoarsely as he veered the car back up on the road. "Teach you to mess with a cowboy!"

Highway 67 straightened out to meet more desert. In the distance, maybe two miles ahead, the purple grid plunged into the earth all along the horizon. It blocked the road, but beyond it was a sea of flashing blue-and-red lights: state trooper cars.

Cain't such a thing be solid, he remembered Harlan saying. Ain't such a thing possible.

Curt glanced at the speedometer. Seventy-five. I can bust through it, he told himself. Bust right through like it's made out of glass. And if I can't . . . well, I won't never know it, will I?

His hands clenched the wheel to hold the jittering tires steady. Curt kept the pedal flat, and he could feel the engine's heat bleeding through the firewall on his legs.

And then there was a hollow boom like a bomb going off and steam shot from under the hood. Black smoke burst from the tailpipe. The Buick hitched, and metal clanged like Chinese gongs in the engine. That did her, Curt thought. Somethin' busted bad. Instantly the speedometer began falling: through seventy . . . sixty-five . . . sixty . . .

But the grid was looming up fast. I can make it, he

reasoned. Sure thing. I can bust right through that sonofabitch, because can't such a thing be solid . . . .

I'm leavin' my boy behind.

The realization of it knocked him breathless. I'm hightailin' like a yellow-assed coward, and I'm leavin' my son back there.

My son.

The speedometer had fallen to fifty. The grid was less than a half mile away. I can still make it, he thought.

But his left foot poised over the brake. Hesitated, as the yards swept past.

Damn kid can't take care of himself, Curt thought. Everybody knows that.

He jammed his foot down. The brake pedal popped, went loose, and sparks jumped from the brake shoes. The inside of the car was full of scorch smell, and the brakes were gone.

The grid grew in the windshield, and beyond them the flashing sea of lights.

He wrenched up the parking brake and fought the gearshift from fourth into second; there was a deep grinding and machine-gun chatter as the gears were stripped. The car jolted, kept going at forty miles an hour the last two hundred yards. He twisted the wheel, but the slick tires had their own mind and even as they started to turn he knew the grid was going to take him.

A hand and arm suddenly reached through the open window of the passenger door. The creature's head and shoulders pulled through, and Curt realized the thing had been hanging on to the Buick's side like a leech. The good eye fixed on him with cold rage, the hand straining toward his face.

He screamed, lost the wheel. The Buick angled off the road, heading for the grid fifty yards away. He had time to see that the speedometer needle hung at just over thirty miles an hour, and then the creature with blond hair had pulled half her body into the car.

There was only one way out. Curt wrenched upward on the door's handle and jumped. He landed in yielding sand, but the impact was rough enough to send constellations reeling through his brain. The wind bellowed out of his lungs, but he had enough sense left to roll away from the car and keep on rolling.

The Buick traveled another fifteen feet and hit the grid. Where the car impacted, the violet weave pulsed a fierce incandescent red, like the eye of a stove. The hood caved inward, the engine block bursting through the rusty firewall like a red-hot fist. Daggers of metal flew into the creature with Laurie Rainey's face, and she was caught under the dashboard as it folded upon her.

The car bounced back, the crumpled hood glowing scarlet as if it had absorbed heat from the grid. The tires were melting, black smoke belched as oil caught fire, and with an orange flash and an ear-cracking explosion, the Buick tore apart at its seams and debris spun into the air. All of it had taken about three seconds from contact to blast.

Pieces of the car banged down around Curt, who lay on his belly puking up Kentucky Gent. The smell sickened him further, and he kept heaving until there was nothing left but air.

He sat up on his knees. The way his nose was bleeding, it was broken for sure. Not a lot of pain, though. He figured that would come later. He looked at his left arm—the side he'd landed on—and saw tatters of skin hanging down. From the shoulder to the elbow was a red mass of friction burns, and the flesh over his ribs on that side was scorched raw too. Blood tainted his mouth, and he spat out a tooth and stared at what used to be his car.

The remains of the Buick were on fire, but what was left looked like black twists of melting licorice. Fearsome heat lapped at Curt's face. The grid's red glow was fading, returning to cool violet. Another blast leapt up from the Buick's chassis, throwing molten metal like a spray of silver dollars.

Curt stood up. His legs were a little wobbly, but otherwise all right. His tongue found another tooth hanging by a strand of flesh on the left side of his jaw, and he reached in and jerked the bit of broken enamel out.

Something emerged, running, from the Buick's wreckage.

It was coming right at Curt, but he was too shocked to move.

The thing was charred ebony, humpbacked and twisted. It looked to be a headless, burned-up body with one remaining arm writhing at its side like an injured snake —and at the base of its spine was another burned thing, about five feet long, that whipped wildly back and forth.

Still Curt didn't move. He knew he ought to, but his brain couldn't get the order through to his legs.

The horror lurched past about ten feet in front of Curt. He could smell a sickly-sweet reek that might have been burning plastic, and he heard a high, terrible hissing noise. The thing stumbled, went on six more strides, then fell to its knees in the loose sand and began to frantically dig with its remaining hand. Sand flew; it shoved its headless neck and shoulders into the burrow, its feet kicking up spirals of sand. In another few seconds the creature had gotten in up to its waist and then it began to shudder uncontrollably. Its legs twitched, burned pads of its feet pushing with feeble effort.

And finally it lay still, all of it hidden beneath the sand except for the blackened legs.

Whatever it was, Curt wouldn't have gone a step closer to it for a million dollars and a truckload of Kentucky Gent; in fact, whiskey was the last thing he wanted right now. A sip of water to cleanse the foulness from his mouth was what he craved. He backed away from the charred creature; it did not move again, did not rise from the sand, and he prayed to God that it was dead.

Curt turned, everything hazy and dreamlike, toward the grid.

Beyond it were not only state trooper cars, but several dark blue cars, unmarked vans, and a couple of white panel trucks. And a lot of people over there too: men in trooper uniforms and men in dark blue uniforms and caps. Government men, Curt reckoned. Looked like air-force blue.

He walked nearer the grid to get a better look. The grid made a faint humming noise that pricked pain in his eardrums, and the air smelled of lightning storms. A helicopter was landing beyond the cars; Curt could see the rotors whirling around but could hear no engine sound. Over on the right were two large trailers and more trucks. Off in the distance along Highway 67 were a lot of headlights. Roadblock up ahead, he figured. He blew blood and snot from his nose, wiped his nostrils with his skinned forearm, and saw the excitement on the grid's other side.

A group of eight or nine men had gathered, and several of them were motioning for Curt to come closer. They seemed to be shouting, from the strained expressions on their faces, but Curt couldn't hear a word.

He approached to within six feet of the grid and stopped. On the ground just to his left was what looked like half of a burned-up coyote.

A man in khaki trousers and a sweat-stained gray knit shirt waved for his attention. The man cupped his hands around his mouth and began obviously shouting. Curt shook his head and pointed at his ears. There was a hurried conference among some of the men, then one of them sprinted off toward a panel truck.

Another man, wearing an air-force uniform and visored cap, came through the group and stood staring at Curt with dark, deep-set eyes in a hawk-nosed face. Curt could see the name tag on his jacket: "Col. Buckner." Curt didn't know what to do, so he gave the officer a jaunty little salute, and Buckner nodded grimly.

The one who'd gone to the panel truck returned with a clipboard and black marker. Buckner took it from him and scribbled something, then held it up for Curt to see: IS COLONEL RHODES ALIVE?

Curt remembered what he'd heard about an air-force officer at the Bob Wire Club, and he shouted, "I think so!" but realized they couldn't hear him either. He nodded in reply. Buckner ripped off the clipboard's first sheet of paper and wrote another question: CAN YOU FIND RHODES AND BRING HIM HERE?

Curt mouthed *How?* and motioned toward the Buick's wreckage. The man in the khaki trousers pointed to something beyond Curt, and he turned to look.

The pickup truck full of furniture was just groaning to a stop. Its driver, a heavyset Hispanic man, got out and gaped at the grid. On the passenger side was a woman holding a baby, and the little boy in the truck's bed climbed up on top to get a better view. The man came forward, babbling rapidly in Spanish.

"Forget it, *amigo*," Curt said, getting the gist of what the man meant. "There's no way out." He turned back to the officers. Buckner had written a statement on the clipboard: VITAL TO FIND RHODES. WE MUST KNOW SITUATION.

"The situation is real shitty," Curt answered, and gave a hollow laugh.

"We tryin' to get out!" the pickup's driver said, his voice on the edge of panic. "My wife and childrens! We gotta get out!"

"Not by this road." Curt scanned east and west. The grid was unbroken in both directions. "Might as well head back to town."

"No! We gotta get out!"

"That used to be my car." Curt jerked a thumb toward the flaming ruin. "It hit this damned cage." He bent down, picked up a fist-sized rock, and tossed it into the grid. There was a quick popping noise and the stone exploded into fiery particles. "I don't think you want your family endin' up in a grease spot, do you?"

The man hesitated, his seamed face stricken. Looked at his wife and son, then back at the grid. "No," he said at last. "I don' want that."

Curt glanced at the air-force officers. Buckner was still holding up the clipboard, and Curt made an okay sign with his hand. "I'd appreciate a ride to town," he told the Mexican. "Ain't nobody gettin' out by this road tonight."

"Sí." The man stood for a moment, not knowing what to do, then went to tell his wife they would not be going to Odessa after all.

Curt walked to where the burned creature lay in the sand. It still wasn't moving. He gathered bloody saliva in his mouth and spat it out. The spit sizzled when it hit the thing's leg. Curt retreated to the pickup and climbed into the truck's bed, wedging himself between the crates and a cane table. The little boy, dark eyes as big as walnuts, sat cross-legged on the other side and regarded him studiously. Four chickens in a cage cackled and fretted, and the truck vibrated on the verge of breakdown as the Mexican reversed it away from the grid. He cranked the wheel around, turned the truck, and headed for Inferno. Curt watched the rotating trooper lights until the road curved and they were lost to sight, and then he rested his chin on his skinned knees and tried to keep his mind from going back to the Bob Wire Club, where five men lay mutilated. It was an impossible task. A fit of shivering hit him, and tears came to his eyes. He felt himself cracking to pieces. Got to find Cody, he thought. Got to find my boy.

Something tugged at the cuff of his trousers. The little boy had slid forward, and he said, "Be okay, mister. Be okay." The child reached into a pocket of his dirty blue jeans and brought out a half-gone pack of peppermint Life-Savers. He offered the next ring of candy to Curt, and Curt saw a tie rack in his son's hand and his heart almost broke.

He lowered his head, and the child removed a Life-Saver and laid it beside the man.

40
The Hole

Cody's arms had gone dead. All the blood had run out of them, and his legs felt like they each were hundred-pound sacks of concrete. Maybe it had been ten minutes since Daufin had gone, at the most fifteen, but his strength was giving out fast. All he could do was hang, as sweat slipped down his face and his hands cramped into claws around the pipe.

"Help me, somebody!" he shouted, and instantly regretted it. The pipe swayed again, and a rush of dirt cascaded into the hole. She left me, he thought. She's not comin' back. Hell, she probably didn't even understand I was in trouble! No, no, he corrected himself as the panic gnawed his guts again. She went to get help. Sure. She'll be back. He had no choice but to hold on, as the chill of shocked nerves and blood-drained muscles began to spread through his shoulders.

And then he heard something that made the hairs stir at the nape of his neck.

It was a quiet sound, and at first he thought it must be dirt falling to the bottom—but the longer he listened the more he was sure it was not. This was a furtive, scuttling sound, a moist sound.

Cody held his breath. It was the noise of something moving in the darkness below.

"Lockett! You down there?"

The shout had almost jolted Cody's fingers loose. He peered up, could make out someone leaning over the hole. "Yeah! I'm here!" A flashlight came on, the beam probing down.

"Man, you got yourself in a deep hole this time, didn't you?"

The voice had a Mexican accent. He knew that voice, heard its taunts in his sleep. But he said, "Who is that?"

"Rick Jurado, *su buen amigo,*" came the sarcastic reply. *Your good friend.* "We've got a rope. Hang on."

"Who's up there with you?"

"Your other good friend," Rick told him, and Cody knew who he meant.

Rick laid the .38 down on the porch. Daufin reached for it, out of curiosity, but Rick said, "Better leave that alone. Thing'll blow a hole right through you," and she nodded and pulled her arm back. He looked for a place to anchor the rope, had to settle for the white wrought-iron railing that went around the porch.

"The tether is not going to be long enough," Daufin said as she visually measured the distance from where Rick was knotting the rope to the doorway and the hole. "There will be a shortage of three feet."

"Can't help that. We'll have to do with what we've got." He uncoiled the rope and went back to the doorway, standing on the threshold. "Rope's coming down!" he called, and dropped it in. He aimed the flashlight down, and saw that Daufin was right: the rope's end dangled three feet above the pipe where Lockett's fingers gripped.

Cody looked up at the rope, and three feet had never seemed so far. He tried to hoist himself up on the pipe, but again pain shot through his bruised ribs and the pipe swayed and creaked. "I can't make it!" he shouted. He let himself hang once more, and his arms felt as if they were about to tear loose from the sockets. By the flashlight's beam, he saw rivulets of gray ooze sliding down the hole's walls and dripping into the darkness below.

Rick knew what had to be done. He said quietly, "Damn it to hell," and then he gave the light to Daufin. "Hold this. Keep it aimed at him. Understand?" She nodded, and Rick gripped the rope, eased himself over the side, and started down.

He hung a few inches over the pipe, unwilling to put his weight on it. The way that thing shimmied, he figured a few more pounds of pressure might snap it loose from the walls. "Lockett!" he said. "This is as close as I can get! You'll have to reach up and grab my legs!"

"No way, man. I'm tired. Can't do it." It was all he could do to hang on without moving. Any more swaying and his slippery palms might betray him, or the pipe might break. "Oh Jesus, my arms . . ."

"Don't give me that jive! Just reach up and grab my legs!"

The soles of Rick's shoes were about five inches above Cody's grip on the pipe. Cody knew the only way out of here was to do as the Rattler said, but his strength was draining fast and the effort seemed enormous. The muscles of his shoulders were cold chunks of agony, a stabbing pain spreading across his rib cage. Reach up, he told himself. Just reach up. One hand at a time. He started to, but his willpower collapsed like wet cardboard. His fingers clenched harder, and just that little movement made the pipe moan and tremble. His guts clutched and writhed. I'm scared shitless, he thought, and he said, "I can't do it."

Rick's biceps bulged, his arms ready for the shock of Lockett's weight. "Come on, tough gringo!" he mocked. "You gonna start cryin' for your mama?" Lockett didn't reply. Rick sensed he had given up. "Hey, I'm talkin' to you, fuckhead! Answer me!"

A few seconds' pause. Then: "Get bent."

"I'll bend your redneck ass, you shitkicker! Maybe I ought to leave you down here and forget it, huh?"

"Maybe you ought to." Cody heard it again: a scuttling

from below. His heart was racing as he tried to get his muscles revved up for another effort, but his mind told him the pipe would collapse if he moved.

"Man, my sister's got more guts than you! So does my grandmother!" Taunting might get him mad enough to reach up, Rick figured. "If I'd known you were such a pussy, I would've whipped your tail a long time ago!"

"Shut up," Cody croaked.

He's almost through, Rick thought. He said the first thing that came to him: "I told my sister you weren't worth lizard crap."

"Huh? What about your sister?"

That had perked him up. "Yeah, Miranda was askin' me all about you. Who you were and everythin'. She thought you were okay. *Just* okay."

"She said that?"

"Yeah." He figured it was a necessary lie. "Don't let it go to your head, man. She needs glasses."

"She's pretty," Cody said. "A smash fox."

Any other time, that remark would have called for a punch to the teeth. Now, though, Rick saw it as a way to get Cody off that pipe. "You like my sister, huh?"

"Yeah. I guess I do."

"You want to see her again, you've gotta get out of here. Only way to do that is reach up."

"I can't, man. I'm done."

"What I'm gonna do," Rick said, "is let myself down a little more. I'm gonna put my feet on that pipe, and I figure it'll probably break in two. Either you go down or you grab hold. Understand?"

"No. Wait, man. I'm not ready."

"Yeah you are," Rick told him, and he lowered himself another hand grip down the rope and placed his right foot on the pipe first.

There was a squall of stressed metal. The pipe shook violently and began to bend inward, and Rick shouted, "Grab hold!"

Cody's face sparkled with sweat in the flashlight's beam. He gritted his teeth, felt the swaying pipe about to collapse.

It was now or never. His fingers wouldn't open. A bead of sweat dropped into his eye and seared it shut.

Rick placed his left foot on the pipe and let his weight settle. "Do it!" he urged as the pipe began to rip loose from the wall and dirt and rocks streamed down.

"You sonofabitch!" Cody shouted, and the fingers of his right hand let go. His shoulder muscles screamed as he dangled by one arm, his right hand reaching up for Rick Jurado's ankle. He gripped it, clenched his fingers tight —and suddenly the pipe buckled, ripped loose in a shower of dirt, and fell.

Rick's hands scorched along the rope to the bitter end before they locked shut. Now all the pressure was on Rick's arms and shoulders as Cody held on by one ankle and tried to snag the other. They swung between the slimy walls, and there was a muffled crash as the pipe hit bottom another fifteen feet below.

Cody caught Rick's left leg. Pulled himself up to the other boy's waist. Rick heard the rope groan with their weight, and if that railing up there gave way, they were both in for a long fall. He hauled them up a couple of feet, the muscles and veins standing out in his arms and the blood roaring in his head, and then Cody grabbed hold of the rope's end and took some of his weight off Rick.

"Come up!" Daufin called. "Come up!"

Rick started climbing, hand over hand, his shoes slipping off the oozing wall. Cody tried to follow, got about four feet nearer the top before his arms gave out. He hung while Rick clambered up and hauled himself through the doorway.

"Pull him up!" Daufin said, and she made an effort at reeling the rope up with her free hand while the other fixed Cody in the flashlight's beam. "Hurry!" The urgency in her voice roused Rick off his belly and made him look over the hole's edge.

Something was coming up the wall about six feet below Cody. It was a human figure with white hair, but its face was averted from the light. Its hands were plunged into the slime and dirt, and the thing was pulling itself smoothly up like a mountaineer.

Cody hadn't seen it. He squinted in the dusty beam. "Come on, man! Help me up!"

Rick placed his feet against the doorframe, grasped the rope with both hands, and started pulling. His own strength was almost gone, and Lockett felt like dead weight.

Cody came up another fourteen inches and tried to find traction against the wall, but the slime was too thick.

A hand closed around his left ankle, and he looked down into the Cat Lady's grinning face.

Except now she had a mouthful of silver needles, and her skin was a mottled grayish yellow like a dead snake that had begun to rot in the sun. She was trying to keep Cody between herself and the light, her belly pressed against the wall. Her eyes were full of cold fire.

She spoke, in a voice like a rush of steam through a ruptured pipe: "Sloowww dowwwnnn, youuu gerrrmmmmm . . ."

He was frozen for about three seconds, and in that space of time he knew the meaning of terror. She was pulling him toward her, the cold fingers drawing tighter, her free hand clawed into the ooze and dirt. Rick's frantic tug on the rope thawed his senses, and he acted on instinct: he kicked her in the face with his right foot. It was like kicking a brick but a spray of broken needles flew from the mouth and her nose burst like a snail.

He jerked his ankle free, felt a blaze of pain as her nails scraped through the boot to flesh, and then he was climbing that rope hand over hand like a born monkey. Rick reeled him up, and Cody came out of the hole so fast he barreled into Daufin and knocked her flat. The flashlight rolled across the porch.

Cody scurried away from the hole on his hands and knees, and Rick let go of the rope and pushed himself back from the doorway. He could hear the wet squishing of the white-haired thing coming up. "The light!" he shouted. "Get the light!"

Daufin, her head ringing, saw the flashlight lying on the edge of the porch. She crawled after it.

A hand and arm emerged from the hole. Metallic nails.

dug into the wooden doorframe, and the monster began to pull itself out. The other hand flailed up, reaching for Rick's legs, and he kicked frantically at it.

Daufin picked up the flashlight and aimed it at the doorway. The beam hit the creature's wrinkled, glistening face, and it gave a gurgling cry of what might have been mingled rage and pain and threw a hand up over its eyes. But it was almost free of the hole now, and with a muscular lurch the body flopped out onto the porch and squirmed toward Rick.

It was almost upon him when Cody stepped forward and thrust his hand into the Cat Lady's face. The hand had an extra finger of metal: the barrel of the .38 he'd picked up from the porch. He fired, point-blank, and part of Mrs. Stellenberg's jaw caved in. The second bullet plowed into an eye, the third shell took away a hunk of white hair and flesh and exposed not bone but a knotty, grayish-blue metallic surface that writhed like a bagful of snakes.

The mouth stretched open; the sinewy neck elongated and the head came up to snap at Cody's gunhand. He fired into the mouth, showering silver needles and punching a hole that splattered gray liquid from the back of the head. A hand flashed at him, narrowly missed his knees as he retreated. Rick got his legs out of the monster's reach, rolling away to the porch's edge. Daufin stood where she was beside Cody, holding the light steady with both hands.

The Cat Lady's body shivered. The arms and legs began to lengthen with brittle cracking sounds. Dark, scaly pigment rose through the yellowish skin. The spine bowed, humped up, and the flesh split along the backbone. Daufin grasped Cody's arm and pulled him back as the thing's tail uncoiled and hammered upward into the porch's ceiling. Now the Cat Lady's limbs were muscular, insectile stalks streaked with bands of leathery scales, and the grotesque body lifted off its belly and shambled forward, leaving a trail of slime.

Cody extended the pistol and fired twice. One bullet hit the center of the thing's face and caved it in, rocking the head back. The second knocked out more needles and broke the lower jaw loose from its hinges. And then Cody squeezed the trigger and the hammer fell on an empty chamber.

The thing flailed at the flashlight's beam, fingers trying to grip hold of it as if it were solid. The tail thrashed out, the bony spikes whipping back and forth through the light in a vicious frenzy. The single eye in the ruined, dripping face twitched in its socket. Rick had already jumped over the porch railing, and Daufin and Cody backed down the steps away from the tail.

The creature made a high, hissing sound that was a weird combination of human shriek and insectile droning, and then the body retreated to the doorway and scuttled into the hole. The darkness took it. A long way down there was the solid *thump* of the body hitting, then a skittering noise like a crab burrowing back to its nest.

"Gone," Daufin said. Her throat had constricted. "Stinger is gone."

"Jesus," Cody rasped. Oily sweat was leaking down his face, and he felt close to a faint. *"That* was Stinger?"

"Stinger's creation. All the creations are Stinger."

Rick walked away and bent over the gutter. His stomach seethed, but nothing would come up. Cody said, "You all right?"

Rick spat out saliva that tasted like battery acid. "Oh yeah," he managed. "I see freaks like that every day, man. Don't you?" He straightened up, drew in air that reeked of burning rubber, and held out his hand toward Cody. "The gun. Give it here."

Cody gave it to him, and Rick broke open the extra box of bullets in his pocket and reloaded the chambers. Daufin aimed the flashlight at her face and looked into the light until her eyes were dazzled, then she waved her hand through the beam. "It's a flashlight," Cody told her. "Works on a battery, like my motor's headlamp."

"I understand the principle. A portable power source, yes?"

"That's right."

She nodded and returned her attention to the light. She

was used to the harsh illumination by now, but when she'd first seen it—in the house of Jessie, Tom, and Ray—the light had had a startlingly ugly underglow that lit the human faces in nightmare colors. This hard incandescence was very much different from the soft light in the abode of ritual. She placed her fingers close to the bulb and could feel a prickly heat sliding into her skin—a sensation the human beings probably paid little attention to. *"This* drove Stinger away," she said. "Not the percussion-cap weapon."

"What?" Cody asked.

"This power source drove Stinger away," she repeated. "The flashlight."

"It's just a light, that's all." Rick pushed the last bullet in and snapped the cylinder shut. "It can't hurt anybody."

"Can't hurt a human, maybe not. I know this power source is designed to aid human visual perception, but it blinded Stinger. Maybe gave physical pain too. I saw the reaction."

"Only thing it was reactin' to was bullets," Cody told her. "Pump enough shells into its damned head, and it'll sure as hell react!" He kept watch on the doorway, where a pool of slime shimmered on the porch's boards.

Daufin didn't answer. There was something in the light that hurt Stinger, something that didn't affect humans. Maybe it was the heat, or the composition of the light itself, something in the physical and microscopic disturbance of matter along the illuminating beam. The humans might not realize it, but this light was a weapon much more powerful than the flimsy percussion-cap noisemaker.

"What did you mean, 'Stinger's creation'?" Rick asked the little girl. The street inflections had dropped from his accent. "Was it Stinger or wasn't it?"

"It was . . . and was not," she answered. "It was created and is controlled by Stinger, but Stinger remains underground."

"You mean Stinger built that thing and made it look like Mrs. Stellenberg?" Cody asked.

"Yes. What you saw was a living mechanism. Stinger will construct what is needed."

"Needed for what?" Rick clicked on the .38's safety and eased the pistol into his waistband.

"Needed to find me," Daufin said. "Stinger will use whatever raw materials are available for the constructions. Stinger's digging underneath the streets, coming up into the abodes, and gathering raw materials."

"Human bodies," Rick said.

"Correct. When Stinger seizes the necessary raw material, sensory signals are returned through organic filaments that connect Stinger with machines on the interstellar vehicle." She motioned through the haze toward the pyramid. "The machines were built by Stinger's masters, and they translate the signals into physical reality." She realized from their blank stares that they weren't comprehending, so she made a fast mental scan through the *Britannica's* pages again. "Like a baseball game on teeah-veeah," she said. "The pictures are taken apart at their source, and put back together again at their destination. Only, in this case, Stinger has a choice of how to recombine the signals, to make creations that are stronger and faster than the originals."

"Yeah," Cody said, beginning to understand. "Uglier too."

"The creations are powered by Stinger's lifeforce," she went on. "In essence, they are Stinger, because they think with the same brain. Like a hundred teeah-veeah sets in a hundred different rooms, all tuned to the same baseball game. Stinger remains physically underground, but the creations allow Stinger's sight and brain to be in many places at the same time."

"You never told me why it's after you," Cody prodded.

"I escaped from a prison world," she said. "I entered the body of a guard and stole a garbage scow. That's what they construct there. Stinger's masters want me returned to"—here she encountered another difficulty of translation—"Rock Seven," was the best she could do.

"Sounds like a radio station," Rick said.

"Rock Seven is an approximate name. It does not translate. Nothing can live there outside the prison." A grim smile crept across her mouth, and the eyes in the child's face looked very old. "It's a caldron of murderers, the diseased, plunderers, and pirates—and even criminals like me."

Cody wasn't sure he wanted to know, but he had to ask: "What crime did you do?"

"I sang. Stinger's masters decreed that to be against the law on my world."

"You *sang?* Is that all? What's so bad about that?"

"It was the song." Now Daufin's eyes had a glint of steel in them. "The song stirred destruction. It was an old song, one almost forgotten. But I knew it, and I had to sing it. If I didn't, all my tribe would die." Her eyes narrowed, and the flesh seemed to tighten across the facial bones. For an instant Cody and Rick thought they could see another face behind Stevie Hammond's; this one was leather tough, frightening in its intensity. It was the face of a warrior, not a child. "I'll get home," she vowed quietly. "I'm not a savior, and I never asked to be. But I'll get home or I'll die trying, and Rock Seven will never hold me. *Never.*" She sensed a cold pulse of power sweep slowly past her, and she turned toward the pyramid. Cody and Rick had felt it too, but to them it was just a little cool breath of air. Her heartbeat thudded faster, because she knew what it was, and what it searched for.

"It ends here," Daufin said. "Right here. I've escaped from Rock Seven twice before. Twice before they sent Stingers after me and took me back. They kept me alive because they wanted to 'study' me." She smiled bitterly, and there was rage in it too. "An indignity—a needle to watch your bowels move, a chemical to malform your dreams. Nothing is sacred, nothing is private. Your life is measured in reactions to pain, freezing, and burning." Her hands curled into fists at her sides. "You are twisted until the screams run out. And all that time of 'studying' you know your world is being eaten away to the heart." Her voice cracked, and for a few seconds she trembled but could not speak. Then: "When they're done, they'll search for new worlds to ravage. One of them might be Earth." She glanced at Cody and Rick, then back through the murk at Stinger's ship. "It ends here, with my death or Stinger's."

"What do you mean, 'one of them might be Earth'?" Cody asked.

She drew in a long breath, and had to tell the humans what she knew to be true. "Stinger is not only a bounty hunter of escaped criminals. Stinger hunts planets for bounty as well. When Stinger returns to Rock Seven, a report will be given on this planet's inhabitants, technological levels, and defense systems. According to that report, Earth may be added to the list of planets scheduled for invasion by"—a translation problem—"the House of Fists. Stinger's masters. I don't think it will be very long before they send the first fleet."

"Christ!" Cody said. "What do we have that they want?"

"Life," Daufin answered bluntly. "All life but their own is repugnant to the House of Fists. They can't stand knowing that somewhere a life form flourishes without their permission. They will come here, take prisoners for study, gather whatever minerals might strike their interest, and either introduce a disease into the ecosystem or conduct mass executions. That is their pleasure and purpose of existence."

"Sounds like real party-down dudes." Rick looked around, his hand on the .38's grip. The smoke had closed in, and he could see no cars nor people anywhere. "Lockett, you'd better get her off the street. You don't want any more surprises popping up."

"Right. But if that damned thing can bust up through the ground, where can I take her that's safe?"

"What is that?" Daufin pointed, and Cody and Rick saw the faint glow of the apartment building's lights through the haze.

"The 'Gade fortress. It's built pretty tough," Cody said. "About the only place around here that's worth a damn."

"Stinger won't like those lights," Daufin told them. "I think that's a safe structure." If any Earth structure was really safe, she thought.

Rick said, "I'm heading back across the river. A lot of people over there are holed up in the church." He looked at Daufin again; the defiant face-behind-the-face had gone away, and she looked like an ordinary little girl again. "Colonel Rhodes and the sheriff are looking for you. They were over at the clinic about twenty minutes ago, but I heard them say they were going to the Creech house. Know where that is?" he asked Cody.

"Yeah. Dodge Creech's house. It's not too far from here." Without any weapons, though, he didn't care to go cruising the streets with her. There was no telling what might slither out of one of the dark houses. "I'm gonna get her up to the fort first. Then I'll hunt Vance down."

"Okay. You two watch your backs."

Rick started to stride away, but Cody called, "Hey! Hold on!" and Rick paused. "You didn't have to come down in that hole," Cody said. This was one of the strangest moments of his life, standing on Renegade territory after dark with the leader of the Rattlers about eight feet away and a creature from another world beside him. He felt a drifty, dreaming sensation, and if there wasn't a puddle of slime on the Cat Lady's porch and blood squishing in his boot from his clawed ankle, he might not believe it had ever happened. "I appreciate it."

Thanks from a 'Gade—especially from Cody Lockett —was in its own way even more bizarre than the circumstances. Rick shrugged. "Wasn't a big thing." His rope-scorched hands would tell him later that it had been.

"I think it was. Hey, did you mean what you said about your sister?"

"No," Rick said firmly. A spark of the old anger resurfaced. "You get Miranda out of your head. Understand?"

"Maybe I will, maybe I won't." Back to business, Cody thought.

"You *will*. Shitkicker." They locked stares for a few seconds, like two bulldogs that refused to give an inch of ground, and then Rick backed away into the cracked street. He turned abruptly, disdainfully, and walked into the haze.

"I won't. Spitball," Cody said quietly. Then he glanced at Daufin. "Bet they don't have motorcycles where you come from, huh?"

"Undoubtedly," she answered.

"Then you can tell your people all about 'em, 'cause that's what you're about to ride on." He went to the Honda, got on, and kickstarted the engine. "Climb on behind me and hold tight." She did, nervous about the machine's vibration and the noise, and Cody wheeled the cycle away from the Cat Lady's house and sped toward Travis Street.

41
Blue-eyed and Smiling

"Maybe it didn't mean this place," Vance whispered shakily. "Maybe it meant somewhere else."

"No, I don't think so." Rhodes spoke in a normal voice. There was no need for whispering, because Stinger had to know they were waiting in Creech's den. He aimed his flashlight at the hole in the floor. There was no movement, no sign of life—in whatever form—down in the darkness. "What time is it?" he asked Tom.

"Almost twenty till two," Tom answered, checking his watch in the beam of his own flashlight. Jessie stood beside him, her hair in sweat-damp curls and a fine layer of dust on her face. Rhodes had asked them to come, to see what they were dealing with, but he'd warned them not to say anything about Daufin. David Gunniston stood on the other side of the colonel, the younger man's face still ashen with shock but his eyes alert and his hand on the butt of the .45 he'd taken from Vance's gun cabinet. Vance had a Winchester repeating rifle, and Rhodes held the shotgun loaded with tear-gas shells at his side.

"Bastard's making us wait," Rhodes said. They'd been here for almost thirty minutes, long enough to drink the thermos of cold coffee they'd gotten from Sue Mullinax at the Brandin' Iron. "Trying to make us sweat a little."

"It's doing a damned good job," Jessie said as she wiped her face with her forearm. "One thing I want to know: if Stinger's somehow making . . . what did you call them?"

"Replicants."

"If Stinger's making replicants, what's happening to the real people?"

"Killed, most likely. Maybe stored like lab specimens. I don't know." He glanced at her and managed a faint smile. "We'll have to ask when it shows up."

"*If* it shows up." Vance had backed away from the hole, and stood pressed against the wall. His shirt stuck to him like glue-dipped wallpaper, and sweat dripped from his chin. "Listen . . . if it looks like Dodge, I'm gonna have to be excused. I don't think I can take that again."

"Just don't start blasting with that rifle. I'm not sure it'd do much good anyway." Rhodes kept rubbing the hand-shaped bruise on his arm.

Vance snorted. "Mister, it'd do *me* a hell of a lot of good!"

"Colonel?" Gunniston bent down at the rim of the hole. "Listen!"

They all heard it: a thick, wet sound, like boots slogging in a swamp. Something moving through the slime-walled tunnel, Rhodes knew. Coming closer. "Get back," he told Gunny, and the younger man scrabbled away from the edge. Vance cocked the Winchester, and Rhodes darted a warning glance at him.

The sounds stopped. Silence fell.

Rhodes and Tom kept their lights aimed at the hole. From below, a man's voice drifted up: "Put your lights out, folks. I'm picking up some real bad vibes."

It was a mellow, laid-back voice. No one recognized it but Vance, who had heard it often enough. His face bleached fishbelly gray, and his body mashed harder against the wall.

"Do it," Rhodes said. He turned off his flashlight, and so did Tom. Now the only illumination in the room was the dusty yellow glow of the remaining oil-burning lanterns. "All right. You can come up now."

"Oh no. Not yet, pardner. Throw them down to me."

It can't stand electric light, Rhodes thought. No, more

than that: it's *afraid* of electric light. He tossed his flashlight into the hole and nodded for Gunniston and Tom to do the same. A moment later there came the snapping sounds of the flashlights being broken apart.

"That's it. You can come up," Rhodes said.

"I can come up anywhere and anytime I fucking please," the voice replied. "Haven't you figured that out by now?" There was a pause. "If you have any more of these up there, you'll be very sorry."

"Those are all we brought."

"They're little pieces of nothing anyway, aren't they? I can break them with my breath." The voice was jaunty, confident now that the flashlights were destroyed. A quiet *thud* and a scuttling noise followed. Rhodes figured the thing had just leapt up and pulled itself into the basement. Then another *thud,* and one hand caught the edge of the hole. Saw-blade fingernails gouged into the broken wood, and the creature's head rose into view.

Jessie gripped Tom's hand with a strength that popped his knuckles. Vance gave a feeble moan.

It was Mack Cade's face, blue-eyed and smiling like a choirboy. He was hatless, his thin blond hair plastered to his skull. His tan had faded to a sickly yellow hue. He pulled himself up with one-armed ease, got his knees on the hole's edge, and stood up.

Vance almost passed out, and the only reason he did not was the knowledge that he would be unconscious on the floor with that god-awful thing standing ten feet away.

"Oh . . . Jesus," Gunniston whispered.

"Everybody stay where you are," Rhodes said, as calmly as he could. He swallowed; his insides had given a savage twist. "Just take it easy."

"Yeah," the creature with Mack Cade's smile said. "Hang loose."

In the lamplight, they all could see it much too clearly. Mack Cade had a left arm, but his right one was squashed and melted into something that had grown from his chest. It was a black-streaked lump of meat with a flat, almost reptilian head on a squat and muscular neck. In that head were slanted amber eyes, and two stubby, deformed legs dangled from the bony wedges of its shoulders.

Jessie knew what it was: a dog. One of Cade's Dobermans, implanted in the thing's chest like a bizarre Siamese twin.

The gold chains around Cade's neck were now part of his flesh too, braided in and out of his skin. The cold blue eyes moved slowly from one figure to the next. The dog's head, splotched with patterns of human flesh and Doberman hide, writhed as if in profound agony, and around the lump of its body the folds of Cade's wine-red shirt crackled like waxy paper. "Wow," the Cade mouth said, and lamplight sparked off the close-packed rows of needle teeth. "You came to party, didn't you, Ed Vance?" The thing's gaze speared him. "I thought you were the head honcho."

Vance couldn't speak. Rhodes took a deep breath and said, "He's not. I am."

"Yeah?" The eyes fixed on him. The dog's mouth stretched open and showed more silver needles. On each paw were two serrated metal hooks. The creature took two strides toward Rhodes, and the colonel felt panic rise up like a scream but he locked his knees and did not retreat.

Stinger stopped about three feet away. The eyes narrowed. "You. I know you, don't I?" The squashed Doberman's head made a low groan, and the jaws snapped wantonly. "You're Colonel Matt Rhodes United States Air Force. Right?"

"Yes."

"I remember you. We met before, down there." A jerk of the head toward the hole. Still smiling, Stinger lifted its left arm and extended the index finger. The arm glided forward, and the metal nail pressed against Rhodes's cheek. "You hurt me," Stinger said.

There was a quiet *click* as Gunniston eased back the .45's hammer.

"Hold your fire." The saw-blade edge had cut his cheek, and a drop of blood coursed slowly down to his jawline. He met Stinger's intense stare without flinching. The thing was talking about the old woman down in the tunnel. Wherever the true Stinger was—most likely in the pyramid—it must have a direct sensory bond with the replicants, including reaction to pain. "We came here in good faith," Rhodes said. "What do you want?"

"I want to deal."

Rhodes knew what Stinger meant, but he wanted it spelled out. "Deal for what?"

"The superfine, high-quality, grade-double-A package you've got stashed somewhere in this joint." The fingernail withdrew, taking a smear of human blood with it. "You know: the guardian. The little girl."

Jessie's heart kicked. Vance shivered; the thing had Cade's slick salesman's drawl down to perfection.

"What little girl?" The drop of blood fell from Rhodes's chin and hit the green scrub shirt with a soft *plop*.

"Don't shit me, *amigo.*" The dog's head growled hoarsely, its neck straining. "I've been . . . like . . . asking around, if you get my drift. Kicking back, seeing the sights. You've got a real trippy world here, dude. But I know the guardian's a little girl, and I know she's somewhere close. I want her, and I mean to take her. So do we deal or not?"

Rhodes knew dangerous ground lay ahead. He said, carefully, "Maybe we know who you're talking about and maybe we don't. *If* we do, what do we get from the deal?"

"You get to keep your asses," Stinger said, the eyes bright—almost merry—with the prospect of violence. "That clear enough?"

"You've already killed quite a few people. That's not good business."

"Sure it is. My business is squashing bugs."

"A professional killer?" Rhodes's throat felt dry enough to crack. "Is that what you are?"

"Man, you people are *dense!* Ugly too." Stinger looked down at the twitching mass hanging from its chest. "What *is* this shit?"

"I'd like to know where you came from," Rhodes pressed on. "What planet?"

Stinger hesitated, the head cocked over to one side. "The planet Moondoggie, in the constellation Beach Blanket Bingo," the thing said, and cackled. "What the fuck does it matter? You wouldn't know where it is, anyway. Face it. man: I'm not leaving without the guardian, so you might as well hand her over and let's be done with it."

Jessie could stand being silent no longer. It was the wrong, stupid thing to do, and she knew that, but it burst out of her anyway: *"No!* We're not giving her up to you!"

Rhodes twisted around and his stare burned holes through her. She got control of herself again, but the damage was done. The counterfeit Mack Cade face watched her impassively, while the dog's jaws snapped at the air as if ripping off hunks of fresh meat. Stinger said quietly, "Now we've got it clear who we're talking about, so we can quit dicking around. First off, I know my bounty's here. I tracked her ship to this world, and my sensors are picking up the pod's energy. Exactly where it is, I'm not sure—but I'm narrowing it down, and I know she won't be too far from it." A metallic smile flashed. "Technology's a great thing, huh?"

"What do you mean, your 'bounty'?" Rhodes asked. "Are you being paid for this?"

"'Paid' is a relative term, man. I'm being rewarded for carrying out a mission."

"To find her and kill her?"

"To find her and take her where she belongs. She—" Stinger stopped, a grimace of annoyance rumpling the face. "You don't know a damned thing, do you? This is like trying to talk to my asshole and expecting it to"—there was a pause and a slow blink, and Rhodes could almost see the thing searching at mind-boggling speed through the man's language center for the correct analogy—"sing like Aretha Franklin. Man, this is *primitive* shit!"

"Sorry we're so uncivilized," Rhodes said, "but we're not invading other worlds trying to kidnap children, either."

"'Invading,'" Stinger repeated after a few seconds of reflection. The eyelids had slid down to half mast. "There's another relative term. Listen, I couldn't care less about this dump. I'm just passing through. As soon as I get my prisoner, I'm history."

"What makes her so important?" Tom spoke up, and the creature's head twisted toward him.

"I see the problem around here," Stinger announced. "Too many chiefs and not enough ensigns . . . engines . . . Indians," the thing corrected itself. "You ought to know 'she' isn't what you'd call female. And she's not male, either. Where she comes from, that doesn't matter. All the screwing on her world's done by the tides or something. 'She' could just as easily take a man to be a guardian; the guardian's a shell for her to walk around in. But since I don't find any description of the creature in your lingo, I guess it's okay to call it a 'she.'" Stinger sneered the word. "And for her to take a little girl as a guardian is a real laugh, because she's as old as dirt. But she's smart, I'll give her that much, and she's sure run me a chase." The thing's gaze slid back to Rhodes. "It's over now: where is she?"

"I never said we knew who you're talking about."

Silence stretched, and the replicant's gray lips twitched like cankerworms. "What you can't seem to figure out is that I'm on the side of law and order. My assignment is to find the criminal and return her to a maximum-security penal world—from which she escaped. She got into a guard and stole a garbage scow. I figure the ship went haywire, sailed off course, and got sucked into the gravity field here. She must've jettisoned her guardian and gotten back into her pod before the crash; she ejected, and that's the story."

"Not all of it," Rhodes said. He kept a poker face. "Why is she a criminal?"

"After her planet was liberated, she decided to disobey the new prime directives. She started urging her kind to resistance, violence, and sabotage. She's nothing but a wild animal."

"'Liberated'?" Jessie didn't like the sound of that. "Liberated from what?"

"From waste and stupidity. See, there's a natural chemical on her world that's poisonous as all hell anywhere else. What you folks don't know is that all kinds of little wars are going on out there—alliances breaking up, new ones forming, one group deciding it wants a planetary system and another kicking sand about it. Goes on all the time." The thing's shoulders shrugged. "Well, suppose some up-and-comer decides to get hold of the poison and start spreading it around. I'm telling you, the shit is *deadly.* That stuff gets out in space, and it might even drift this way. It cuts right through body armor and dissolves the bones and guts into mush. That's why we liberated the planet—so we can keep that shit from getting into the arsenals of fruitcakes. Everything was going fine until 'she' started raising hell. Made herself out to be a 'revolutionary' and all that crap." The head shook back and forth, the face puckered with a scowl. "She's trying to get back so she can stir up more trouble—maybe sell that poison to the highest bidder."

Rhodes didn't know whether to buy the story or not. "Why didn't you tell us this before now?"

"Because I didn't know anything about you. As far as I knew, you were helping her. Everybody seemed like they'd rather fight than talk like sensible folks." Stinger's eyes bored into Rhodes's. "I'm a forgiving kind of dude. Let's be friends. Okay?"

Just like Mack Cade would've done it, Vance thought. Sucker 'em in with a glad hand and squash 'em with a fist. He found his voice, and he said, "Colonel? I inkthay it ielays."

Rhodes saw Stinger blink with incomprehension, saw the gears of language start turning behind the manufactured face; they slipped on the grease of pig Latin. *I think it lies,* Vance had said.

"Explain," Stinger demanded, the metallic voice all business again.

"We've got to talk about this. The others and myself."

"Nothing to talk about, man. Either we deal or not."

"We need some time."

Stinger didn't move, but the dog's head thrashed angrily.

Seven or eight seconds crept past. Rhodes felt sweat trickling from his armpits. "You dudes are playing games with my brain," the creature said. "Trying to fuck me up." It advanced on Rhodes, and was right there in his face before he could back away. Gunniston lifted the .45 and aimed it at the monster's head, and Vance hefted the rifle up and put his finger on the trigger.

"You listen," Stinger hissed. The thing was breathing —its imitation lungs doing the job of the originals. The breath was a faint rumbling, like the noise of a blast furnace going at full burn miles distant, and the air from Stinger's mouth washed into Rhodes's face and reeked of hot plastic and metal. The dog's teeth snagged Rhodes's shirt. "Playtime's over. I want the guardian and the pod."

"We need . . . more time," Rhodes said. If he retreated one step or otherwise flinched, he knew those saw-blade nails would be on his throat. "We'll have to find her."

"I tried to be friendly, didn't I?" The index finger rose up and glided across his chin. "You know, I create things. Out in my ship. I've got a workshop in there. Just give me the flesh, and I can create . . . wonders." The smile came up again, and the needle teeth glittered inches away from the colonel's face.

"I've seen one of your creations. The flying thing."

"Pretty, huh? If you'd like to see my workshop, I could snatch you under my arm and take you there right now. I could make you over, better than you are. A lot stronger . . . and a lot meaner too."

"I'm already mean enough."

Stinger cackled; there was a sound like grind wheels turning in its throat. "Maybe you are, at that," the creature agreed, and lifted its left wrist. Embedded in the flesh was the diamond-studded face of a Rolex watch with a tiny inset second hand. "I figure this is a tool to mark the passage of time. I've been watching it work. What's the time right now?"

Rhodes was silent. Stinger waited. "Three minutes before two," the colonel said.

"Good boy. When that long spear rotates again, I'll be back here. If you don't have the guardian and the pod, I'm going to create a real *special* bug squasher."

"That's only one hour! We can't find her in that short a time!"

"It's all you've got. You understand, Colonel Matt Rhodes United States Air Force?"

"Yes," he answered, and felt doom settle on his shoulders like a cold shroud.

"One hour," Stinger said. The thing's head turned, and Stinger stared at Gunniston and the .45 the man aimed. "Would you like to eat that?"

Gunniston's hand shook. Slowly he lowered the pistol.

"I think we understand each other now." Stinger walked to the edge of the hole and hesitated with one foot over empty space. The dog's eyes shone red in the lamplight. "One hour," the voice emphasized. "Think on these things."

The replicant dropped into darkness. They heard it hit bottom, followed by the smack of its boots as it raced away through the tunnel's ooze. The noise faded, and Stinger was gone.

42

The Fortress

No one spoke for a long moment. Smoke drifted through the light. Then Vance jabbered, "I was ready to shoot the bastard! I was just waitin' for the word, and I could've blown its head off!"

"Right," Rhodes said. He wiped the creeping line of blood from his cheek, his eyes hollowed out and scared. "And gotten yourself and the rest of us torn to pieces too. Tom, what time is it?"

"One minute till two."

"Which means we've got fifty-eight minutes to find Daufin and her pod. We're going to have to split up and start searching."

"Hold on!" Jessie said. "What are you saying? That we're going to give Daufin up?"

"That's right. Have you got a better idea?"

"We're talking about my little girl."

"We're talking about an *alien*," Rhodes reminded her. His insides were still quaking. The smell of hot metal remained in his nostrils. "No matter what it looks like. We've gotten into something here that I think we'd better get our asses out of real fast."

"I'm not handing my little girl over to that sonofabitch!" Jessie vowed. Tom started to touch her shoulder to calm her, but she pulled away. "Do you hear me? I'm not doing it!"

"Jessie, it's either Daufin or a lot of people—your friends —who die. I'm not doubting for one second that Stinger could lay waste to this whole town. Right now I don't care why Stinger wants Daufin, or what she's done; I just want to find her and save some people's lives, if I can."

"What about Stevie's life?" Tears scorched Jessie's eyes. Her heart was pounding wildly, and she couldn't seem to draw a full breath. "My God, we'll be throwing my daughter's life away!"

"Not if we can find Daufin and get her to go back into her pod. Maybe that'll release Stevie." He couldn't stand this house any longer; the walls were closing in on him. "I'm sorry, but we don't have any choice. Sheriff, I say we go get your deputy and break into teams for a house-to-house search. Go up and down the streets and pick up some volunteers, if we can find any." He knew that a street search in all this smoke and dust was going to be almost impossible, but there was no other way. "Maybe somebody at the clinic's seen her, or she might've gone across the bridge into Bordertown. Tom, will you and Jessie go check your house and start searching east along Celeste Street from there?"

Tom stared at the floor. He felt Jessie watching him. "Yes," he said. "We will."

"Thank you. We need to meet somewhere in thirty minutes and map out where we've been. How about the Brandin' Iron?"

"Fine," Tom said.

"All right. Let's get started." Without waiting for the others, he left the house and went out to the patrol car, parked in front of the Hammonds' Civic at the curb. Vance and Gunniston followed, then Jessie and Tom. Vance said, "Better take this," and gave Tom the Winchester. "I'll pick up the other rifle at the office. You two be careful, hear?"

"We will be," Tom told him, and Vance got behind the wheel, pulled the car away from the curb, and drove back toward the center of town.

Jessie watched the car's lights move away and be swallowed by the murk. She felt faint and she stumbled, but Tom caught her and she held on to him. Tears tracked through the dust on her cheeks. "I can't do it," she said weakly. "Oh Jesus, I can't give her up."

"We have to. Listen to me." He put a finger under her chin and lifted her head. "I want more than anything in the world to have Stevie back, just like you do. But if Stevie's gone—"

"She's not! Daufin said she was safe!"

"If she's gone," Tom continued, "our world's not going to end. We have Ray, and we have each other. But if we don't find Daufin and turn her over to that thing, a lot of people are going to die." Jessie was almost blinded by tears now, and she put her hands to her face. "We have to," he repeated, and he opened the door for her and then went around to the driver's side. Jessie was about to slide in when she heard the muttering of an engine, coming closer. A single headlight showed brownish yellow through the smoke. Somebody on a motorcycle, she realized.

Tom hesitated, gripping the door handle, as Cody Lockett stopped beside the car. Cody pushed his goggles back up on his forehead. Attached to the handlebars with a strip of electrical tape was a sawed-off baseball bat with nails protruding from it: a weapon from the 'Gade arsenal. "I'm lookin' for Vance and Colonel Rhodes," Cody said. "They're supposed to be here."

"You just missed them. They're on their way to the sheriff's office." Tom opened the door and put the Winchester into the backseat. "Who told you they were here?"

"I . . . uh . . . ran into Rick Jurado. Listen . . ." He glanced at Jessie, could see from her red and puffy eyes that she'd been crying. He didn't know exactly how to say this, so he just plowed on ahead. "I found your little girl."

Tom was speechless. Jessie choked back a sob and said, "Where is she?"

"Up at the fort. The apartments, I mean. There's a whole lot of people up there, so she's okay." Cody would never forget the faces of Tank, Nasty, and Bobby Clay Clemmons when he'd told them that the little girl wasn't what she appeared to be. They hadn't believed him until she'd started to talk, and then their jaws had fallen to the floor. Along with most of the Renegades, there were about two hundred or more people in the building who'd been drawn by the electric lights. Cody had gotten the creature settled in, poured warm beer over the two gashes on his ankle, and taped a cloth around it, then come hunting for Vance and the colonel. "Uh . . . there's somethin' else you ought to know," he said. "I mean . . . she looks like your little girl and all, but . . . she's not."

"We know that," Tom replied.

"You do? Man, I thought I was goin' off the deep end when she told me who she was!"

"Same here." He glanced at Jessie, and saw she knew what he was about to say. "We have to tell Rhodes. We can catch him before he leaves the sheriff's office."

"Tom . . . please. Wait," Jessie said. "Why don't we talk to her first? Try to make her understand that we've got to get Stevie back?"

Tom looked at his wristwatch. It was four minutes after two, and he'd never thought a second hand could move so fast. "We've got less than thirty minutes before we're supposed to meet at the Brandin' Iron."

"That's time enough for us to talk to her! Please . . . I think we might be able to make her understand better than Rhodes could."

His gaze lingered on the racing second hand, but his mind was already made up. "All right," he said: "Take us to her," he told Cody, and got behind the wheel as Cody lowered his goggles and swung the motorcycle around.

At the end of Travis Street, a dozen cars and pickup trucks were parked haphazardly in the apartment building's lot; a couple of them had run right up to the front door. Cody waited for Tom and Jessie to get out of their Civic, and then he threaded his motorcycle through the vehicles and to the door, which was covered with gray sheet metal and had a narrow view slit like all the first-floor windows. "Open up, Bobby!" he called, and heard the sound of the many latches being thrown back. Bobby Clay Clemmons pulled the heavy door open, its hinges groaning like the entrance to a medieval castle, and Cody powered the motorcycle on through and into the stark white glare of the wall-mounted incandescents.

He popped the kickstand down and left the Honda near the stairway that ascended to the second floor, and a moment later Tom—carrying the Winchester—and Jessie came in. "Lock it," Cody said, and Bobby Clay pushed the door shut and shot all four of the bolts home.

Neither Jessie nor Tom had ever been in the Winter T. Preston apartment building before. A long corridor lined with doors—some of them torn off their hinges—went the length of the first floor, and the cracked plaster walls screamed with graffiti in a blaze of Day-Glo orange and purple. The place smelled of marijuana, stale beer, and the ghost aromas of the mine workers and their families who'd lived here: a commingling of sweat, dry heat, and scorched food. For the first time in almost two years, voices other than those of Renegades echoed through the building.

"This way." Cody led them up the stairs. The second floor was a mirror image of the first, except a ladder ascended through a trapdoor to the roof. People were sitting in the hallway, and bare mattresses had been dragged out of some of the apartments for them to rest on. They were mostly Inferno people, with only seven or eight Hispanic faces among them. As they followed Cody, Tom and Jessie had to step over and around the refugees; the lights revealed familiar faces: Vic Chaffin and his wife Arleen, Don Ringwald and his family, Ida Slattery, the Craziers, Jim and Paula Cleveland and many others. The apartments were full too, and a few infants keened a discordant chorus. There was some talking, but not a lot; most people were numbed, and some of them were sleeping sitting up. The heat from all these close-packed bodies was tremendous, and the air was tainted with smoke.

Cody took them to a closed door that had HQ and KNOCK FIRST scrawled on it in red spray paint above a Billy Idol poster. Cody did knock, and a little sliding aperture opened. Nasty's green eyes, outlined with glittery gold mascara, peered out. Then the aperture shut, the door was unlocked, and they went in.

This was Cody's home whenever he came here. The front room held a cot, a stained plaid sofa with the stuffing leaking out through knife rips, a scarred pinewood table and chairs, and a small, battered refrigerator saved from the dump and forced to gasp out a few more months. The floor was covered with faded brown linoleum that was curling up in the corners, and on the cheaply paneled walls hung motorcycle and rock-star posters. A window, cracked open to admit smoky air, faced south. A short hallway went past a busted-up bathroom and into what used to be a bedroom, now the 'Gades' armory where a variety of weapons like brass knuckles and pellet rifles hung on wall hooks.

Tank had been sitting on the sofa, and now he quickly stood up as he saw Mr. Hammond and his wife come in. His camouflage-daubed football helmet was snug around his skull. Cody relocked the door, and Nasty stepped back to let the Hammonds see who stood at the window, facing them.

"Hello, Tom and Jessie," Daufin said, and smiled wanly.

The moment enfolded Jessie. That was Stevie's body, Stevie's face, Stevie's dimpled smile. Even the voice was Stevie's, if you chose not to hear the fragile undertone like wind chimes in the cradle of a breeze. Inside that body was Stevie's heart, lungs, veins, and organs; all of it belonged to Stevie except the unknown center where Daufin lived. Jessie took a step forward, and fresh tears broke. Another step, and Tom saw where she was going and he reached for her but let his hand fall short.

Jessie walked across the room to the body of her daughter, and she started to place her hands on the little shoulders with the intention of picking the child up and holding her close—just for a moment, to feel the beating of Stevie's heart and know that somewhere, in whatever way she couldn't even begin to fathom, Stevie was alive.

But in the child's face the eyes sparkled with intelligence and fire—intense and even frightening—that was far beyond Stevie's years. The face was Stevie's, yes, but the spirit was not.

That was clear to Jessie in an instant, and her hands poised over Daufin's shoulders.

"You're . . . you're *filthy!*" Jessie said, and blinked away the tears. "You must've been rolling in the dust!"

Daufin looked down at her own dirty clothes. Jessie's hands lowered, and brushed loose dust off the T-shirt. "Don't they teach you to be clean where you come from? My God, what a mess!" The auburn hair was full of tangles, bits of weed and spiderweb strands. Jessie saw Nasty's buckskin shoulderbag on the table; the bag was open, and the pink handle of a hairbrush protruded. She took the brush out and started going through the child's hair with the dirt-hating vengeance of a mother.

Puzzled, Daufin started to back away. Jessie snapped, "Hold still!" and Daufin stood at attention while the brush strokes puffed dust into the air.

"We're glad to see you," Tom said. He knelt down so his eyes would be on a level with Daufin's. "Why'd you run away?"

"I went whack-o," she said.

"Uh . . . we've been . . . like . . . teachin' her Earth lingo," Tank explained. "She's been tellin' us about her planet too. It sounds mighty gnarly, man!" For once, his grim, hatchet-nosed face had taken on a childlike shine of excitement.

"I guess so." Tom watched his wife brushing their child's hair with determined strokes, and he thought his heart might break. "Daufin, we just had a talk with . . . something. I can't say it was a man, and I can't say it was a machine."

Daufin knew. "Stinger."

"Yes." He looked up at Cody Lockett. "It took Mack Cade's body and made him into a . . . ." Again, words failed him. "Part man, part dog."

"One of Cade's Dobermans is growing out of his chest." Jessie's hand continued to guide the brush.

"Freakacreepy!" Nasty said. Her love of danger was stoked and burning. "Man, I'd like to see *that!*"

"You're crazy as hell too!" Cody snapped. "It got the Cat

389

Lady," he said to Tom. "Mrs. Stellenberg. It made her into something with a tail full of spikes, and I shot the bitch full of holes but she just kept comin'."

"All are Stinger," Daufin said quietly, standing rigid while she endured whatever it was Jessie was doing. It seemed to be giving Jessie pleasure. "Stinger creates them, and they become Stinger."

Tom didn't quite follow that. "Like robots, is that right?"

"Living mechanisms. They think with Stinger's brain, and they see with Stinger's eyes. Stinger hears and speaks through them. And kills through them too."

"Somethin' mighty big's been roaming around under the streets," Cody said. "Is that one of Stinger's machines too?"

"No," Daufin said. "That is Stinger itself. Stinger captures and stores bodies for duplication. Signals—you would call them blueprints—pass from Stinger to machines on the ship and there the replicants are made."

"So we know it got Dodge Creech, Cade, Mrs. Stellenberg, and whoever that was in the autoyard. Plus the thing that left its arm with Rhodes." Tom stood up and laid the Winchester on the table. "Stinger's probably taken a lot of others we don't know about too."

"There!" Jessie finished her battle with the last snarl and stepped back. She felt light-headed and drifty, and she'd caught a hint of the apple-scented shampoo she'd washed Stevie's hair with last night. "Now you look pretty again!"

"Thank you," Daufin said; it was obviously a compliment, and deserved a reaction, though why these people lavished such attention on strands of limp cellular matter was another mystery of the human tribe. Her gaze went to Tom. "You said you talked to Stinger. About me, of course."

"Yes."

"Stinger wants me and my lifepod, and an ultimatum was given."

Tom nodded. "It said it wants you in one hour"—a glance at the racing hands of his watch—"and we've got about forty minutes left."

"Or Stinger will continue the destruction," Daufin said. "Yes. That's Stinger's way."

"The sonofabitch wants to take her back to prison!" Cody spoke up. "And all she did was *sing!*"

"Sing? That's not what Stinger said. He—it—told us about the chemical on your world," Tom recounted. "The poison, I mean. Stinger said you . . ." It was crazy, looking at his little girl's face and saying these things. "Said you were a wild animal."

"I am," she answered without hesitation. "To Stinger and the House of Fists, I deserve a cage and a frozen sleep."

"The House of Fists? What's that?"

"Stinger's masters. A race that worships violence; their religion is the conquest of worlds, and their entrance into the afterlife is determined by the deaths of what they consider lower beings." A faint, gritty smile surfaced. "Wild animals like me."

"But if they're trying to control this chemical, isn't that for the good of—"

Daufin laughed: a mixture of a child's laugh and the sound of coins thrown to the floor. "Oh yes!" she said. "Yes, they *are* trying to control the chemical!" The fires ignited in her eyes again. "But not for the good of their brother creatures, no matter what Stinger told you. They want the chemical for their weapons! They want to build deadlier fleets and more ways to kill!" The little body shook with fury. "The more of the chemical they steal from my planet, the closer my tribe comes to destruction! And the closer *all* worlds come to being destroyed, as well—including this one! Do you think Stinger will leave here and *not* tell the House of Fists about your planet?" She searched for words, stumbled over the tangle of human speech, grasped hold of a phrase the humans named Tank and Nasty had taught her: "Get *real!*"

The flesh of Daufin's face had drawn tight, showing the sharp angles of the bones. Her eyes blazed with anger, and she began to pace back and forth in front of the window. "I never meant to come here. My ship lost power, and I had to put it down where I could. I know I've brought hurting to you, and to others here. For that I will carry a burden for the rest of my life." She stopped suddenly, looking back and forth between Tom and Jessie. "Stinger *will* tell the House of Fists about you, and about this world. Stinger will say you are soft, defenseless life forms who were born to be caged, and they'll come here. Oh yes, they'll come here —and they might bring their weapons full of the 'poison' they've stolen from *my* planet! Do you know what that 'poison' is?"

Tom thought she was about to start spouting steam from her nostrils. "No," he said warily.

"Of course you don't! How could you?" She shook her head, exasperated. A fine sheen of sweat glistened on her cheeks. "I'll do more than tell you; I'll show you."

"Show us?" Jessie said. "How?"

"Through the inner eye." Daufin saw no comprehension on their faces; they were blank slates, waiting to be written on. She lifted both hands toward them. "If you want to know, I'll take you there. I'll show you my world, through the eye of my memory."

The humans hesitated. Daufin didn't blame them. She was offering a glimpse of the unknown, and what was home to her would be to them an alien realm. "Take my hands," she urged, and her fingers strained for contact. "If you want to know, you have to see."

Tom took the first step forward, and when it was done, the hardest part was over. He walked to Daufin and slid his hand into hers. The flesh was oven hot, and as her fingers gripped tight he could already feel the prickling of an electrical charge passing from her into him.

"Jessie?" Daufin asked.

She came to her daughter's outstretched hand, and took it.

43

Waiting for the Spacemen

At twelve minutes after two, Tyler Lucas sat on the front porch of his house with a rifle beside him and waited for the spacemen to come.

The sky was covered with a hazy violet grid. After the power had gone out, he and Bess had driven into Inferno, had seen the black pyramid and gotten the lowdown from Sue Mullinax and Cecil at the Brandin' Iron. "The spacemen have landed, sure's shootin'!" Sue had said. "Cain't nobody get in or out, and the phones are dead too! I swear to God, when that thing hit, it lifted this whole block and me off my feet too, so you know it must've packed a punch!"

Then she'd given that giggly laugh of hers—the laugh that had made her so popular when she was a slim-waisted Preston High School cheerleader—and bustled off to fix Tyler and Bess cold hamburgers.

"Ty? Here y'go." Bess had come out and offered her husband a glass of iced tea. The tea had been made that morning, which was a good thing because the faucets wouldn't pull up a drop of water. "That's the last of the ice cubes." They were small half-moons, and everything in the refrigerator was thawing out quick in this sullen heat.

"Thanks, hon." He rubbed the cold glass over his sweating face, sipped at the tea, and gave it back to her when she'd sat down on the edge of the porch next to him. She drank with a deep thirst. Off in the desert a chorus of coyotes howled, their voices jagged and nervous. Tyler watched the road.

They'd decided that when the spacemen came, they would die right here, defending their home. The air-force people had been wandering all over the place before the sun went down, scooping up little fragments of blue-green metal and putting them in weird bags that folded up like accordians. Where were the air-force men now?

Tyler and Bess had driven their pickup west along Cobre Road. A little less than half a mile had cranked off the odometer before they'd come to where the violet grid had entered the earth and blocked their way. Around the grid's glowing prongs Cobre Road's asphalt was still bubbling. Tyler had thrown a handful of sand into the grid, and little grains of molten glass had come back at them.

"Well," Tyler drawled, laying the rifle across his knees, "I never thought there'd come a time when you couldn't see the stars out here. I reckon progress has caught up with us, huh?"

She started to answer, but could not. She was a tough old bird, and she hadn't cried for a long time. There were tears in her eyes now, and her throat had constricted. Tyler eased an arm around her. "Kind of a pretty light, though," he said. "If you like purple."

"I hate it," she managed.

"Can't say I cotton to it much, either." His voice was soft, but he was mulling over some hard questions. He didn't know how they would come, or when, but he didn't mean to give up without one hell of a fight. He was going to drill as many as he could, and go down fighting like Davy Crockett at the Alamo. But the worst question gnawed at him: should he save a bullet for Bess, or not?

He was thinking about it, his gaze on the road, when he heard a woman scream.

He looked at Bess. They stared at each other for a second. The woman's scream came again.

They both realized what it was at the same time. Not the scream of a woman, but the shrieking of Sweetpea, back in the barn.

"Get a flashlight! Hurry!" he told her, and as she ran inside he sprinted on his wiry legs off the porch and around the house. The barn was about thirty yards back, next to Bess's cactus garden. He heard the frantic thump of Sweetpea's hooves hitting the sides of his stall, and Tyler's palms were wet around the rifle. Something was at the horse.

He threw back the crossbeam and hauled the doors open. Everything was as dark as sin in there. The big palomino was still screaming, about to bash the boards loose. Tyler shouted, "Whoa there, Sweetpea! Settle down, boy!" but the horse was going wild.

Tyler's first thought was that a sidewinder or scorpion must've gotten into the stall—but suddenly there was a cracking noise and the barn's floor shook under his boots.

Sweetpea grunted as if he had been kicked in the belly. There followed a thrashing, panicked sound coupled with Sweetpea's high screams. Tyler looked over his shoulder, saw Bess running with a flashlight's beam spearing ahead. She gave it to him, and he aimed it at the horse's stall.

The palomino was sunk up to his flanks in the sandy earth, broken floorboards jutting up around him. Sweetpea's eyes were red with terror, and foam snorted from his nostrils as he fought. His hind legs had disappeared into the hole, the front legs pawing at the air. Muscles rippled along his body as he tried to tear loose from whatever was pulling him through the barn floor.

Tyler gasped, the sense knocked out of him. The horse sank another two feet, and the barn echoed with Sweetpea's cries.

"The rope!" Bess shouted, and reached for the lariat coiled near the door. There was a slipknot already on it, and she widened the noose, swung the rope twice around to play it out, and let fly for Sweetpea's head. Her aim was off by six inches, and she quickly reeled it back to try again as the horse was jerked down to his shoulders in a spray of sand.

On the next attempt, the rope slipped over Sweetpea's skull and tightened around the base of the neck. The rope pulled taut between them, started smoking a raw groove through Bess's hands. Tyler dropped the rifle, wedged the flashlight into the joint of two beams, and grabbed the rope, but both he and Bess were wrenched off their feet and dragged across the splintery floor. Sweetpea disappeared into the earth up to his throat.

Tyler struggled up, the rope entwined around his hands and his shoulder muscles popping. He planted his boots and fought it, his fingers turning blue, but he was being pulled steadily toward the stall. Now only Sweetpea's muzzle was still visible, and the sand was starting to slide over it.

"No!" Tyler yelled, and heaved backward on the rope so hard the raw flesh of his fingers split open like blood-gorged sausages. The sand eddied around like a whirlpool, there was a last feeble thrashing, and Sweetpea was gone.

But the rope continued to be drawn downward by a tremendous strength. Bess grabbed her husband's waist, and they went to the floor again. "Let go!" Bess screamed, and Tyler opened his bloody fingers but the rope was tangled around his hands.

Bess held on, splinters piercing her arms and legs. Tyler was trying to shake the rope loose, and they were almost pulled under the railing into Sweetpea's stall before he felt the tension go slack.

Tyler lay on his belly, tears of pain crawling down his cheeks. Bess rolled over on her side, softly moaning.

He sat up, forced his hands to close around the rope and started pulling it from the depths. "Bess, bring the light," he told her, and she silently went to get it.

The rope came up, foot after foot. Bess retrieved the flashlight. Its bulb had dimmed, in need of a fresh battery. She pointed it toward the empty stall.

Tyler walked into the stall, continuing to draw the rope

up. It was wet, and glistened in the murky light. Everything was dreamlike to him, this couldn't possibly be real, and in a minute or so he would awaken to Bess's call that breakfast was on the table. He sank to his knees beside the broken floorboards and watched the rope slither from the sand.

Its other end emerged. Tyler picked it up. Held it toward the light. Strands of thick gray ooze dripped from the ragged edge.

"Looks like . . . it's been sawed clean through," he said.

And a shape came corkscrewing up in a whirl of sand, so fast Tyler had no time to react.

A pair of jaws opened. Silver-blue needles snapped shut on Tyler's throat.

The flat, reptilian head flailed viciously from side to side, the needle teeth ripping through tissue and arteries. Tyler's mouth filled with blood. He realized that the rope had not been sawed; it had been chewed.

That was his last thought, because with the next savage twist the creature broke his neck. It kept twisting, and Tyler's head with its bulging, sightless eyes began to crack from the spinal column.

Bess screamed, dropped the flashlight as her hands pressed to her mouth. She saw what the creature was: a large dog—a Doberman concocted from a madman's nightmare. Instead of hair, its hide was covered with leathery, interlocking scales, and beneath it the knots of muscle bunched and rippled.

Its amber eyes found her. The thing gave Tyler's neck one last ferocious shake and began to stretch its jaws impossibly wide, like the unhinging jaws of a snake. It flung the dead man aside.

Bess backpedaled, tripped, and fell on her tailbone. The monster scrabbled up over the top board of Sweetpea's stall, dropped to the floor, and advanced on her, its mouth trailing Tyler's blood.

The Winchester had tripped her up. Her legs were lying across it. She swung the rifle up and started shooting at the approaching shape. One bullet furrowed across its skull, a second entered its shoulder, a third slammed into its ribs. But then it was upon her, and its mouthful of needles clamped shut on her face.

She kept fighting. Her finger continued to spasm on the Winchester's trigger, sending bullets through the walls while the other fist beat at the thing's scaly hide. She was a Texas woman, and she didn't give up easily.

The issue was settled in another five seconds. Bess's skull broke with a noise like that of a clay jar cracking, and rows of needle teeth sawed into her brain.

Blood ran through the hay. The monster released the crushed mass and turned upon the flashlight, tearing it to pieces with teeth and metal-nailed claws. Then it crouched in the darkness, belly to the floor, and listened eagerly for the sounds of any other humans nearby; there were none, and the thing gave a low grunt of what might have been disappointment. It climbed back into Sweetpea's stall and began to dig down through the sand where the horse had gone. The monster's front and hind legs moved in a blur of synchronized power, and in another moment it had burrowed into the earth and the sand shifted over it like a whisper.

44

Through the Inner Eye

"Don't be afraid," Daufin said. "Seal your external visualizers."

"Huh?" Tom asked.

"Close your eyes."

He did. And promptly opened them again. "Is this . . . going to hurt?"

"Only me, because I'll see my home again."

"What are you going to do?" Jessie's arm was tight, ready to pull away.

"I'm going to take you on a journey, backward through the inner eye. I want to answer your questions about why I'm called a criminal. These things can't be told; they must be experienced."

"Wow!" Nasty stepped forward, the light sparkling off the bits of golden glitter in her Mohawk. "Can I . . . like . . . go with you?"

"I'm sorry, no," Daufin said. "There's only room for two." She caught Nasty's wistful expression. "Maybe some other time. Close your eyes," she repeated to Tom and Jessie, and they did. Cody came closer to watch, and his heart was beating hard but he didn't have a clue as to what was about to happen.

Daufin's eyes shut. She waited, as the energy cells of her memory began to charge like complex batteries.

Jessie feared that Stevie's body temperature was getting too high, and that the heat would damage her brain and organs. But Daufin had said that Stevie was safe, and she had to trust this creature or she would lose her mind. Still, the hand she held continued to heat up; Stevie's body could tolerate such a fever for more than a few minutes without breaking down.

Tom said, "I feel like we're getting ready to go play hide-and-see . . . *damn!*" He jumped, because what had seemed like a thunderbolt had snapped along his spine. He opened his eyes but the light was a brutal shock, with a hard yellow-green underglow, and he shut them again.

"Tom? What is it?" Jessie asked. To him her voice was a slow, underwater slur, and he thought, My brain's getting scrambled.

"Silence," Daufin whispered, and in her voice chimes echoed.

Jessie kept her eyes closed, waiting for she didn't know what. Though the hand she held seethed with heat, cold currents were beginning to run through her arm and up her shoulder; an electrical power being generated within Stevie's body, steadily gaining strength and entering Jessie through the connection of flesh.

The cold pulse had entered Tom's bones too, and he shivered. He thought he could no longer feel the floor beneath his feet; he seemed to be drifting, his body slowly skewing to right and left, held only by Daufin's grip. "What's happen—" He stopped speaking, because the harshness of his own voice, the alien quality of it, terrified him.

Jessie had heard a hoarse grunt that may have been the semblance of a human voice. The cold had enfolded her, from scalp to toes, like a breeze from the Ice House on a blistering July day. Another sensation was coming upon her: movement at a tremendous speed. She thought that if she could force her eyelids up, she might see the atoms in the wall in motion like patterns of static on a television screen and her own body moving so fast it found an opening between them and slipped through. There was no panic, only exhilaration. It was what she thought a night sky-dive might be like, freefalling through darkness except there was no up or down—just out, beyond what she knew of life.

Something glinted on her left, on her right, above and below. Blurred points and clusters of light passing at incredible velocity. But her eyes were still closed—or at least she sensed they were. Stars, she realized. My God . . . I'm in the middle of a universe!

Tom had seen them too. Constellations wheeled across the heavens, ringed worlds luminous with distant sunlight, gas clouds rippling like the wings of manta rays.

And then they were almost upon it: a world as white as a pearl, surrounded by six white moons that crossed each other's orbit with unerring precision. The planet loomed before them, citadels of clouds covering its surface and in their midst storms spinning with silent ferocity.

Too fast! Jessie thought as the clouds came up at her. Too fast! We're going to—

They pierced the clouds, descending through whirlwinds. A smell of ammonia filled Jessie's nostrils. There was another breath-stealing shock of cold, followed by utter darkness. They were still traveling at high speed, slanting downward. Warmth touched Tom and Jessie, chasing away the cold. The darkness lightened to royal blue, then a rich, aquatic blue-green. Silken liquid pressed at Tom's face, and claustrophobia gripped him. We're going to drown! he thought, and tried to pull free from Daufin's hand but her grip strengthened, would not release him. He wanted to thrash loose and get to the surface, but he realized he was still breathing just fine. We're not really in an alien ocean, he told himself as they continued down. This is a dream . . . we're still standing in the apartment building, back in Inferno . . .

With an effort, he twisted his head to look at Daufin for reassurance.

He was no longer holding the hand of a little girl.

The hand was ghostly gray, as transparent as mist, with

two slender fingers and a short, flattened thumb. It was a small thing that looked as fragile as blown glass, and attached to that hand was a stalk that trailed four or five feet to Daufin's real form.

Beside Tom in the gliding aquamarine was a body shaped like a torpedo, perhaps eight feet in length and full of iridescence like trapped stars. More stalks—tough, tentaclelike arms—drifted with the motion of the liquid around them, each with a similar two-fingered, single-thumbed hand. The body ended in a thick flat paddle of muscle that effortlessly propelled them onward, and attached to a protrusion just short of the tail was a silver filament that linked the body with its small black sphere.

Electrical energy sparked through Daufin's translucent flesh. Organs were visible in there, anchored by a simple framework of gray cartilage. Tom looked at where he thought Daufin's head should be, and saw a curved knob with a sickle-shaped mouth and a trunklike appendage about two feet long. He could see one of the eyes: a yellow orb the size of a baseball, with a vertical green pupil. The eye cocked in his direction. There was peace in its gaze, a languid power. The head nodded, and Tom inhaled sharply at the sign of recognition; air filled his lungs instead of liquid. The ghostly, electric-charged fingers squeezed his hand, and another arm drifted up and touched Tom's shoulder in a gesture of comfort.

Daufin took them deeper. Warm currents slid around their bodies and the light was growing stronger, as if this planet's sun lay at its center.

Rising up from the depths like flickers of moving neon were more of Daufin's tribe. Jessie recoiled, felt Daufin's strong grip, and then she looked and saw Daufin as Tom had. Her first impulse was to pull away from the spindly hand, but she checked it. Of course Daufin was a different form; what else could she have expected? Daufin was a creature designed for an oceanic world, even though the "ocean" might be composed of ammonia and nitrogen.

The other creatures propelled themselves in joyous spirals, leaving phosphorescent wakes and their pods weaving at the ends of the tethers. They were oblivious to the human presence, but both Tom and Jessie knew that this was Daufin's memory—her inner eye—and they were only visitors here, the alien ghosts of the future. Hundreds of the creatures made a formation around Daufin, sailing with the precise movements of birds through untroubled air, and Jessie realized Daufin must be a leader of some kind to merit such an escort.

Now the impressions of Daufin's world, filtered through her inner eye, came in rapid succession to Jessie and Tom: shimmering outlines of Everest-sized mountains and deep valleys between them, huge orchards where rows of kelplike vegetation were tended, crevasses showing cracks of fierce white glare—a glimpse into the immense power source that lay at the heart of this world. The vermiform towers of a city—sloping, curved, and ridged shapes that resembled the intricacies of seashells—stood beyond the mountains, and thousands of Daufin's tribe moved in currents above their walls.

Time shifted, or Daufin's memory skipped tracks. In a valley below was a miles-long chasm of white fire that shot up whiplashes of electricity. The tides had changed too; they were no longer gentle, but swirled with restless energy. Daufin began to roll over and over, still gripping Tom and Jessie, and underneath what might have been the throat a series of small gill-like flaps vibrated; from them issued a compelling chiming sound.

In response came Daufin's tribe, struggling against the currents. They rolled like Daufin, and from the underside of their bodies emerged round pink nipples. Other shapes, also summoned by Daufin's song, rose from the valley's chasm; they were disk-shaped creatures, blue electrical impulses sparkling around their rims and at their centers a knot of pulsing fire. As Daufin's song continued, the new creatures began to attach themselves to the pink underbelly nipples. Dark fluids jetted, shimmering with iridescence. Wheels of creatures danced, rose, and fell in the turbulence. Three of them fixed to nipples on Daufin's belly, spasmed, and spun away like dead leaves. It was a mass mating ritual, Jessie realized; a ballet of life and death.

Another blink of time. Something was approaching from beyond. Something alien, and horribly cold.

It arrowed through the sea with a chatter of circuits, expelled a black harpoon, and sped downward into the valley of fire. More came, following the first. The new arrivals were connected to long clear hoses that snaked up to the surface. Machinery began to grind and pumps hissed, and through the hoses were drawn hundreds of the disk-shaped creatures that lived at the center of Daufin's world.

Down came more dark spears, more greedy hoses. The brutal harvest continued, suctioning up seed-giving creatures older than time itself, that were a vital part of the planet's power source. When the wild currents called Daufin and she sang again, there weren't enough seed-givers to impregnate even half the tribe; they were being harvested faster than the unknown creation processes of the planet could produce them.

Daufin's inner eye revealed the first stirrings of fear, and with them the knowledge of balances in decay. And now a clear sign of crisis: the planet's central fires dimming, the great engine of light and warmth wearing itself out as it tried to manufacture more seed-givers to replace those being lost. Tom and Jessie saw the image of a peace mission—four of Daufin's tribe swimming the long distance to the surface, to communicate to the aliens above why the harvesting must stop. Time passed, and they did not return.

Death had come. Daufin swam with her new calf amid the forest of hoses; her study of mathematics, used in the building of the tribe's cities, would allow her to calculate the time remaining from the number of seed-givers being suctioned up a single hose, but that was a statistic she didn't wish to know. The orchards, the city, the entire tribe—all had been sentenced to death by a cold executioner. The calf played innocently between the hoses, unaware of the terrible reality—and the sight of that blind innocence amid the carnage cracked something within Daufin, made her thrash and wail with anguish. Aggression was evil, buried in the long-ago legends of a war that had evolved the tether and sphere as part of the tribe's natural defenses, but a chasm of fire had opened within Daufin and wild tides summoned her. Her wail became a song of rage, like the urgent tolling of alarm bells—and then her body hurtled forward, and her fingers gripped the nearest hose. Too strong to tear, which further enraged her. The sickle-slash mouth opened, and the flat teeth of a vegetarian clamped on the hose and ground into it. A shock of agony and shame coursed through her, but the song of rage powered her on; the hose ripped, and seed-givers spilled out, whirled around her, began to drift downward again into the valley. The next hose was easier, and the one after that easier still. A storm of seed-givers flowed from the tears.

And through that storm Daufin saw two of the tribe, hovering, watching with a mixture of horror and reawakened purpose. They hesitated, on the verge of sacrilege, and as Daufin's song rose in intensity they propelled themselves forward and joined her task.

A dark cloud approached from the city. Adrift in the inner eye, Tom and Jessie saw it just as Daufin had: thousands of the tribe, responding to this almost-forgotten song. Many saw the violence and stayed back, unable to give themselves to aggression, but many more attacked the hoses in a frenzy. A timeshift: more machines and hoses streaked down from the surface, harpooning into the planet's heart, but swarms of Daufin's tribe followed as she sang—a turbulence of rage as raw as a scream.

Finally, the battleground lay silent, and broken hoses drifted in the current.

But the peace was short, the nightmare just beginning. A blink of the inner eye, and Tom and Jessie felt a vibration in their bones. From the surface's darkness descended four rotating metallic spheres; they roamed over the city, issuing sonic blasts like Earth thunder magnified a millionfold. The walls and towers shivered and cracked, shock waves destroyed the towers, the city crumpled, and the bodies of dead and wounded spun in the debris. Daufin's calf was torn away from her; she reached for it, missed, saw the calf instinctively withdraw into its lifepod in a shimmer of contracting organs and flesh. The pod sailed away, mingling with hundreds of others buffeted in the savage tides. A piece of jagged wall flew out of the murk at Daufin. There was a crackling of energy, a shrinking of flesh and internals, the skin turned to smoke, the organs merged into a small ball of electrical impulses, and in the next instant there was nothing but the black sphere, hitting the fragment of wall and ricocheting away.

A current took them—Daufin, Tom, and Jessie, bodiless and floating in an armored shell—and the darkness closed in. There was a rapid ascent, as if they were being hurled upward in an Earth tornado. Something glimmered ahead: a blue webbing—a net, full of entrapped creatures from the upper regions, things that resembled fluorescent starfish, flat gasping membranes, and aquatics with eyes like golden lamps. The sphere hit it, was enfolded in the webbing. And hung there, along with the other helpless life. A thudding of machinery came from above. The net was being hauled up. The sphere broke the surface like a sheet of black glass, and in that realm between the ocean and the low white clouds spidery structures squatted like malignant growths. Nightmarish figures stood on them, watching the net come up. One of them reached out a talon, and gripped the pod.

Daufin's inner eye cringed. The power of memory was not strong enough to hold her, and she fled.

Stars swept past Jessie and Tom—an outward journey, away from Daufin's world. Each had glimpses of hallucinatory scenes: massive, scuttling creatures with voices like doomsday trumpets; space machines bristling with weapons; a gargantuan pyramid with mottled yellow skin and two scarlet suns beating down on a tortured landscape; a floating cage and amber needles that punctured the pupils of Daufin's eyes.

She moaned, and her hands opened.

Tom and Jessie were grasped by an abrupt deceleration, as if they were aboard a high-speed elevator shrieking to the bottom of a mile-long shaft. Their insides seemed to squeeze with compression, their bones bending under gravity's iron weight. And then the stop came: a whisper instead of a crash.

Tom lifted his eyelids. Three monsters with bony limbs and grotesque fleshy heads were standing before him. One of them opened a cavity full of blunt little nubs and grunted, "Yu-hoke, Mstyr Hamynd?"

Jessie heard the guttural growl, and her eyes opened too. She was supported on unsteady stalks, the light was glary and hostile; she was about to topple, and as she cried out the sound daggered her brain. One of the aliens, a thing with a horrid angular face topped with coiled pale sprigs and a totem of some kind dangling from a flap on the side of its head, moved forward and caught her with snaky arms.

She blinked, momentarily stunned. But the creature's face was changing, becoming less monstrous. Features —hair, ears, and arms—became familiar again, and then she could recognize Cody Lockett. Relief rushed through her, and her knees sagged.

"I've got you," Cody said. This time she could understand the words.

Tom wavered on his feet, his palms pressed to his eye sockets. "You okay, Mr. Hammond?" Tank asked again. Tom's brain ached as if deeply bruised. He managed to nod. "If you're gonna puke, you'd better do it out the window," the boy advised.

Tom lowered his hands. He squinted in the light and looked at the three Renegades; their faces were human again—or, in Tank's case, nearly so.

"I can stand by myself," Jessie said, and when Cody let her go, she sank wearily to her knees. She didn't know if all of herself had returned from the void yet, and maybe it never would. Cody offered to help her up, but she waved him off. "I'm all right. Just leave me alone for a minute." She looked to her side, into the face of her little girl.

Tears had streamed down the cheeks. The eyes were tormented. "Now you know me," Daufin said.

Tom lifted his left wrist, had a few seconds of difficulty in deciphering the numerals, as if he'd never seen such symbols before. It was two-nineteen. Their "journey" had taken less than three minutes.

"You two look *sick!*" Nasty observed. "What happened?"

"We got an education." Jessie tried to rise, but still wasn't ready. "The chemical," she said to Daufin. "It's reproductive fluid, isn't it?"

"Yes." Daufin's gaze was impassive, and a final tear trickled slowly down her left cheek. "What the House of Fists calls 'poison' is the same chemical that gives my tribe life."

Jessie remembered the jetting of dark fluid during the mating ritual. The same chemical vital to the reproduction process on Daufin's world was a weapon of destruction for the House of Fists.

"I have to get home," Daufin said firmly. "I don't know how many are still alive. I don't know if my own child still is. But I led them. Without me, they won't fight. They'll slip back into the dream of peace." She drew a long breath, and for a few seconds she allowed herself to feel the caress of the tides again, rising and falling. "It was a dream that lasted too long," she said, "but it was a wonderful dream."

"Even if you could get home, how would you fight them? They'd just keep coming, wouldn't they?"

"Yes, they would, but our world is a long way from theirs. We have to stop them from building a permanent base, and destroy everything of theirs we can. Their treasury isn't bottomless; they spend all they have on weapons. So there has to be a breaking point beyond which they can't go."

"That sounds like wishful thinking," Tom said.

"It is, unless I can get home to act on it. We know the planet. They don't. We can strike and hide in places they can't reach." Her eyes shone with a glint of steel again. "The House of Fists has been studying me to find out why my body resists the 'poison.' I've escaped Rock Seven before. This time they'll kill me. I can't give myself to Stinger—not yet. Do you understand that?"

"We do. Colonel Rhodes might not." Another glance at the wristwatch. "Jessie, he's going to be waiting for us by now at the Brandin' Iron."

"Listen, I don't get all this," Cody said, "but I believe one thing for sure: if we let Stinger take Daufin and leave here, that won't be the end of it. Like she said, he'll send those House of Fist sumbitches after us—and that won't be just Inferno in deep shit, man! That'll be the whole *world!*"

"Maybe so, but we've still got to let Rhodes know we've found her."

"Tom's right," Jessie agreed. She stood up, still felt light-headed and stretched, and she had to lean against the table for support. "We'll go get the colonel and bring him back here," she said to Daufin. "He can help us figure out what to do."

"You two better stay here with her." Cody fished the Honda's keys out of his pocket. "I'll go down to the Brandin' Iron and get him."

"Yeah, and I've gotta go find my folks," Tank said. His camouflage-painted pickup truck, one headlight and the radiator grille smashed from its rude entry into the Warp Room, was in the parking lot. "I ain't seen 'em since I left the clinic."

"Just stay in here and hang tight," Cody told Tom and Jessie. He left the apartment, and Nasty followed Tank to the door. She paused, looked at Daufin with something like admiration, and said, "Bi*zarre!*" Then she strode after Tank, and the door closed behind her.

45

Spit 'n Gristle

Vance parked the patrol car in front of the Brandin' Iron, peeled his sweat-sopped shirt off the seat back, and walked in. The plate-glass window had been shattered, but a sheet had been nailed up over it to keep most of the smoke out. A few kerosene lamps cast a fitful glow, and the place was empty except for a back booth where three old-timers sat talking quietly. Vance avoided their stares and bellied up to the counter. Sue Mullinax, still wearing her gold-colored waitress uniform and her heavy makeup still more or less where it ought to be, came down the counter with a cup about a quarter full of cold coffee. "This is the last of the java," she said as she gave it to him, and he nodded and swigged it down.

He angled his wrist toward a nearby lamp and checked the time. Twenty-three minutes after two. The Hammonds were late, and so were Rhodes and Gunniston. Didn't matter much, he thought. Nobody was going to find that little critter, at least not in the time they had left. You couldn't see a thing for all that smoke out there. He and Danny had checked houses all along Aurora, Bowden, and about a third of Oakley Street. Nobody had seen the little girl, and several of the houses had no floors, just holes into darkness. Danny had started going to pieces again, and

Vance had to take him back to the office. Inferno had always seemed like such a small place, but now the streets had elongated and the houses had become shadow mansions, and with all this smoke and dust there was just no damned way to find somebody who didn't want to be found.

"Rough night," Sue said.

"Better believe it. Cecil gone home?"

"Yeah, he lit out awhile back."

"Why don't you shut down and head out too? Not much use stayin' open, is there?"

"I like to have somethin' to do," she said. "Better stay here than go to a dark house."

"Reckon so." The low light was flattering to her. He thought that if she didn't wear enough makeup to pave a road, she'd be real pretty. 'Course, Whale Tail was as chunky as a fire plug, but who was he to consider size with all the spare tires he was trucking around? Maybe she did wear a mattress on her back, but maybe there was a reason for that too. "How come you never left Inferno?" he decided to ask, to keep his mind off the inexorable tick of time. "Seems like you were real smart in high school and all."

"I don't know." She shrugged her fleshy shoulders. "Nothin' ever came along, I reckon."

"Hell, you can't *wait* for things to come along! You gotta go after 'em! Seems like you could've found yourself a good job somewhere, got yourself hitched up, maybe have a houseful of kids by now." He upturned the cup and caught the last bitter drop of coffee.

"Just never happened. Anyways"—she smiled faintly, a sad smile—"the men I've been seein' don't exactly want to get married and have kids. Well, I probably wouldn't have been too good at that, either."

"You're still just a kid yourself! What are you, twenty-eight, twenty-nine?" He saw her grimace. "That's not old! Hell, you've still got"—his voice faltered, but he kept going—"plenty of time yet."

She didn't answer. Vance looked at his watch again.

Another minute had gone. "Danny's sweet on you," he told her. "You know that, don't you?"

"I like Danny. Oh, I don't mean for marryin'. Not even for . . . y'know." A blush rose in her round cheeks.

"I thought you and Danny were . . . uh . . . real close."

"We are. Friends, I mean. Danny's a *gentleman,*" she said with dignity. "He comes over to my place, and we talk. That's all. It's rare to find a man to talk to. Seems like men and women have a hard time just talkin', don't it?"

"Yeah, I guess so." He felt a pang of shame for making fun of her, and it occurred to him that maybe Danny was more of a man than he'd thought.

She nodded. Her head turned toward the doorway. Vance saw her eyes; they seemed to be fixed on a great distance. "Maybe I could've gone," she said. "I was the best in my typin' class. Reckon I could've been a secretary. But I didn't want to leave. I mean . . . Inferno ain't the best place in the world, but it's my home. That makes it special, no matter how much it's broke down. I've got real good memories of Inferno . . . like when I was head cheerleader at the high school, and one night we were playin' the Cedartown Cavaliers." Her eyes shone with the blaze of ten years past. "It was rainin' that night, just pourin' down, but me and my girls were out there. And right when Gary Pardee threw that forty-yard touchdown the girls lifted me up and I did a monkey flip and everybody on that field let out a holler like I hadn't never heard before. Ain't heard one like it since, either. Folks came up to me later and said it was amazin', how I could do a monkey flip in all that rain without breakin' my neck, and they said I came down light as an angel's feather." She blinked; just like that, the spell broke. "Well," she said, "I'm *somebody* here, and out there . . ." She motioned toward the rest of the world. "I wouldn't be nobody." Her eyes found his, and looked deep. "This is my home. Yours too. We've gotta fight to keep it."

The taste of ashes was in Vance's mouth. "We will," he said, but the words had a hollow ring.

Headlights shone through the sheeted window. A car

pulled up beside Vance's. The headlights were cut, and then a solitary figure approached the door. Not Rhodes or Gunniston, Vance knew. They'd gone off on foot. Celeste Preston sauntered in as if she owned every crack in the tiles, sat down at the far end of the counter, and said, "Gimme a beer and an egg."

"Yes ma'am." Sue got a lukewarm Lone Star out of the cooler and went to the refrigerator for the egg.

Celeste's gaze wandered down the counter. She nodded at Vance. "Kinda past your bedtime, ain't it?"

"Kinda." He was too tired to trade punches with her. "I wouldn't sleep very good, anyways."

"Me neither." She took the egg Sue gave her, broke its shell against the counter's edge, and swallowed the yolk whole, then chased it down with a chug-a-lug of beer. "I gave blood a couple of hours ago," she explained, and wiped a yellow strand off her mouth with the back of her hand. "Wint used to say a raw egg and beer was the quickest way to get your vitamins."

"Quickest way to puke too," Vance said.

She swigged down more beer, and Sue went to check on the old-timers at the back. "How come you're not out protectin' the town, Vance? Maybe drag that sonofabitch outta his spaceship and sit on him till he calls uncle?"

Vance took his pack of Camels from his breast pocket and lit a cigarette, mulling her questions over. He snorted smoke, looked at her, and said, "And why don't you crawl up your ass and pull the hole in after you?" She just stared at him, her eyes like bits of cold flint and the beer bottle short of her lips. "You're an almighty high bitch to be sittin' in here tellin' me what I oughta do. You don't think I give a shit about this town, do you? Well, maybe I screwed up some—screwed up a *lot*—but I've always done what I thought was best. Even when I was takin' money from Cade. Shit, what *else* was gonna keep Inferno alive but that little bastard's business?" He felt blood ballooning his face, and his heart was pounding. "My wife hated every inch of this town and ran off with a truck driver, but I stayed. I've got two sons that went with her, and they only know enough about me to cuss me over the telephone, but I stayed. Every day I eat dust and get cursed in two languages, but I stayed. I've paid my *dues,* lady!" He jabbed the cigarette at her. "So don't you sit there in your joggin' suit and your diamond rings on your fingers and say I don't care about this town!" And then he said something he'd always known, but never dared to admit: "It's all I've got!"

Celeste stayed motionless for a moment. She sipped from the Lone Star and set the bottle softly down on the counter. Lifted her fingers to display the rings. "They're fake," she said. "Sold the real ones." A brittle smile played across her mouth. "I reckon I deserved that, Ed. Spit 'n gristle's what we've been needin' around this cemetery. How about sharin' your smokes?" She picked up her beer and slid over the seats, sitting down with two between them.

Ed, he thought. That was the first time she'd ever used his first name. He skidded his pack of Camels and his lighter toward her, and she scooped them up. She lit a cigarette and inhaled with pure pleasure. "Figure if I'm gonna die, I might as well go happy," she said.

"We're not gonna die. We'll get out of this."

"Ed, I like you better when you tell the truth." She spun the pack and lighter back to him. "Our hides are worth about as much as Kotex in a men's prison, and you know it."

They heard the growl of an engine outside. Cody Lockett came in through the smoke and lifted his goggles. "I'm lookin' for Colonel Rhodes," he said to the sheriff. "He's supposed to be here."

"Yeah, I'm waitin' for him too. He's about ten minutes late." He didn't care for another glance at his watch. "What do you want him for?"

"The little girl's up at the 'Gade fort. You know who I mean: Daufin."

Vance almost came up off his seat. "Right now? She's there right now?"

"Yeah, Mr. Hammond and his wife are with her. So where's the colonel?"

"He and Captain Gunniston were goin' across the bridge into Bordertown. I guess they're still over there."

"Okay. I'll go hunt 'em. If they show up here, you tell 'em the news." He put the goggles back over his eyes and sprinted out to the Honda, got on, pumped the kickstarter, and headed east on Celeste Street. Two things hit him: he'd just given an order to the sheriff—and been obeyed—and that was Celeste Preston herself sitting in there. He turned onto the bridge and throttled up, the engine making a choked roar in the dirty air.

He was halfway across when two headlights stabbed through the haze. A car was racing over from Bordertown, straddling the center line. Cody and the car's driver hit their brakes at the same time, and both vehicles swerved with a scream of tires and stopped almost abreast of each other. The car's engine rattled and died.

Cody saw it was Mack Cade's silver Mercedes. There were two men in it, the driver a rugged-looking dude with close-cropped dark hair and a streak of dried blood on his face. "You Colonel Rhodes?" Cody asked, and the man nodded. "Mr. Hammond and his wife sent me. Their little girl's up at the apartment building." He motioned to it, but its lights couldn't be seen from this distance. "At the end of Travis Street."

"We already know." Rhodes started the engine again. "A boy at the church told us." He and Gunniston had gone into the Catholic church on First Street and asked Father LaPrado if they could address from the podium the people who'd come in for shelter. Along with the information, Rick Jurado had given them the keys to the Mercedes. "We haven't got much time," Rhodes said, and he backed the car up, straightened it out, and sped away.

Cody knew who he'd found out from. Jurado was the only one who could've told him. He started to turn his bike around, but he realized he was only about thirty yards from Bordertown. The church was maybe another fifty or sixty yards along First Street. If Jurado was there, his sister would be too. He decided he might maybe even go in if he felt like it. What were the Rattlers going to do, jump him right in church? It would be worth seeing the shock on Jurado's face—and, besides, he wouldn't mind another look at Miranda.

Everything was going to hell anyway, and this seemed like the right time to dare fate. He gunned the engine and headed south, and in another few seconds the tires bit Bordertown pavement.

46
Time Ticking

A figure walked through the haze, favoring a right leg that folded up at the knee joint. "Come on, Scooter!" he said, and paused for the dog to catch up. Then he walked on, up to the front door of the Hammond house on Celeste Street. He knocked on the door, waited, and knocked again. "Nobody here!" he told Scooter. "Do we go home or set up camp?"

Scooter was undecided too. "She might show up," Sarge said. "This is where she lives." He tried the doorknob; it turned, and the door opened. "Anybody home?" he called, but there was no answer from within. Scooter sniffed around the doorframe and took the first step inside the house. "Don't you go in there! We ain't been invited!" Sarge protested. Scooter had his own mind, though, and the dog trotted on in as fancy as you please.

But the decision was made. They would wait here for either the little girl or the Hammonds. Sarge walked in, shut the door, and found his way into a room where a lot of books lay on the floor. He wasn't much for reading, but he remembered a book his mother used to read to him: something about a little girl who went down a hole after a rabbit. His bad knee bumped a chair, and he let himself spill into it.

Scooter crawled up into his lap, and the both of them sat together in the dark.

About a quarter mile from the Hammond house, Curt Lockett entered his own front door. The raw left side of his face was covered with gauze, and adhesive strips held a pad of iodine-smeared cotton to the flayed skin over his ribs. He'd passed out in the back of the pickup truck and awakened as he was being carried over the Mexican's shoulder like a grain sack into the clinic. A nurse had given him a couple of painkilling shots and tended to his wounds, all the time while he was babbling like a crazy fool about the massacre at the Bob Wire Club. The nurse had called Early McNeil in to listen, and Curt had told him about the trooper cars and the air-force men out on Highway 67. McNeil had promised to let the colonel know and wanted to put Curt in a room, but Curt couldn't stand that. The reek of disinfectant and alcohol was too much like Kentucky Gent; it reminded him of Hal McCutchins's brains gleaming in the lamplight and made him sick to his stomach.

He'd already seen that Cody's motorcycle wasn't here. The boy was probably up at the apartment building, like he figured. Darkness used to be no problem for him, but he had trouble going through the front room while visions of a charred black thing with a whipping tail dug into his brain. But he made the kitchen, fumbled in a drawer for candles and matches. He found a single stubby candle and a matchbook and lit the wick. The flame grew, and he saw that the matchbook advertised the Bob Wire Club.

There was evidence that Cody had been here: a candle was stuck to a saucer on the countertop. Curt opened the refrigerator, got out a bottle of grape juice—just a few swigs left in it—and finished it. The coppery taste of blood was still in his mouth, and two empty sockets where teeth had been pounded with his heartbeat.

He relit the candle in the saucer and took it with him to the bedroom. His best shirt, the red cowboy number, was lying on the floor and he gingerly shrugged into it. He sat on the bed, sweat crawling down his face in the rank heat.

He noticed that the little picture of Treasure on the bedside table had fallen over. He picked it up, stared at her face in the low yellow light. Long time gone, he thought. Long time.

The bed pulled at him. It wanted him to crawl into the damp sheets, hold Treasure's picture to his chest, curl up, and sleep. Because sleep was next to death, and he realized that was what he'd been waiting for. Treasure was in a place beyond his reach, and she still had golden hair and a smile like sunshine and she would be forever young while he just wore out a little more every day.

But by the candlelight he saw something in the picture that hadn't been evident to him before: Treasure's face had Cody in it. The thick, curly hair was the same as Cody's, yes, but there were other things too—the sharp jawline, the full eyebrows, the angular shape of the face. And the eyes too: even smiling, there was steel in Treasure's eyes, just like there was in Cody's. Treasure had to be mighty strong to put up with me, Curt thought. Mighty strong.

Cody was in Treasure. Right there he was, right in the picture. He'd been there all along, but Curt had never seen it until this moment.

And Treasure was in Cody too. It was as clear as a shaft of sunlight breaking through storm clouds, and darkness began to unlock in Curt's mind.

His hand pressed to his mouth. He felt as stunned as if he'd just taken a punch in the teeth. Treasure was in Cody. She had left him part of herself, and he'd tossed the gift aside like a snotty rag. "Oh Lord," he whispered. "Oh my Lord." He looked at the splintered tie rack that hung on the wall, and a moan ached for release.

He had to find Cody. Had to make the boy understand that his eyes had been blind and his heart sick. That wouldn't make up for things, and there was a lot of dirty water under the bridge—but it had to start somewhere, didn't it? He carefully removed the picture of Treasure, because he wanted Cody to see himself in her, and he gently folded it and put it in his back pocket.

His boots clumped across the crooked boards with the noise of someone who has found a destination. The screen door slammed at his back, and he walked to Sombra Street and turned north where it met Travis.

At the Inferno Clinic, Ray Hammond finished putting on his clothes, blood-splattered shirt and all, and left his room. His glasses were gone and everything was blurry around the edges, but he could see well enough to walk without bumping into walls. He had almost made it to the nurses' station when a nurse—Mrs. Bonner, he thought it was —suddenly came out of a door on his right and said, "Where do you think you're going, young man?"

"Home." His tongue was still swollen and the hinges of his jaw ached when he talked.

"Not until Dr. McNeil gives you the okay."

She had that rough authority in her voice, like Cross Eyes Geppardo. "I'm giving myself the okay. I can't sleep, and I'm not going to lie in there and stare at the ceiling."

"Come on." She took his arm. "You're going back to bed."

Somebody else trying to get me out of the way, he thought, and a flash of anger lit him up inside. "I *said* I'm going home." Ray jerked his arm free. "And I didn't say you could touch me, either." Even without his glasses he could see her mouth purse with indignation. "Maybe I'm a kid, but I've got *rights*. Like going to my own house if I want to. Thanks for patching me up, and *adios*." He walked past her, limping a little bit. He expected her hand to grasp his shoulder, but he was three strides away before he heard her start calling for Dr. McNeil. He went past the front desk, said good night to Mrs. Santos, and kept on going out the door. Dr. McNeil didn't come after him. He figured the doc had more important things to do than chase him down. He could barely see ten feet ahead for all the haze and his own bad eyes, and the air smelled like a chem lab stinkbomb, but

420

he kept on trudging along Celeste Street, his sneakers crunching on bits of glass from the shattered windows.

As Ray was starting home, Cody Lockett pulled his motorcycle to the steps of Bordertown's Catholic church. He lifted his goggles and sat for a moment with the engine popping under him. Candlelight shone through the church's stained-glass windows, and he could see people moving around in there. On any other night, his ass would be grass for being over here, but tonight the rules had changed. He cut the engine and headlight and got off, and that was when he saw the figure standing in a yard just across First Street, less than fifteen feet away. His hand settled on the nail-studded bat taped to the handlebar.

Cody couldn't make out the face, but he could see that the black hair hung over the figure's shoulders in oily ringlets. "Crowfield?" he said. Louder: "That you, Crowfield?"

Sonny Crowfield didn't move. Maybe there was a smile on his face, or maybe it was more of a leer. His eyes gleamed wetly in the church's candlelight.

"Better get off the street, man!" Cody told him. Still Crowfield didn't respond. "You gone deaf or somethi—"

A hand closed on his arm. He hollered, "Shit!" and whirled around.

Zarra Alhambra stood on the steps. "What're you doin' over here, Lockett? You gone crazy?" Rick had put him on guard at the door, and he'd heard Lockett's motorcycle and then the boy talking to somebody.

Cody pulled his arm free. "I came over to see Jurado." He didn't say which one. "I was tryin' to tell Crowfield he'd better find some cover." He motioned across the street.

Zarra looked in that direction. "Crowfield? Where?"

"Right *there*, man!" He pointed—and realized his finger was aimed at empty space. The figure was gone. "He was standin' over there, in that yard," Cody said. He looked up and down the street, but the smoke had taken Sonny Crowfield. "I swear it was him! I mean . . . it *looked* like him."

The same thought hit both of them. Zarra retreated a couple of steps, his eyes wide and darting. "Come on," he said, and Cody quickly followed him into the church.

The sanctuary was packed full of people, sitting on the pews and in the aisles. Father LaPrado and six or seven volunteers were trying to keep everyone calm, but the babble of frightened voices and the wail of babies was like the din of a madhouse. Cody figured there were at least two hundred Bordertown residents inside the sanctuary, probably more in other parts of the church. At the altar a table had been set up with paper cups and bottled water, sandwiches, doughnuts, and other food from the church's kitchen. Dozens of candles cast a tawny glow, and a few people had brought kerosene lamps and flashlights.

Cody was about four strides through the doorway when someone planted a palm against his bruised breastbone and shoved him backward. Len Redfeather, an Apache kid almost as big as Tank, snarled, "Get your ass *out*, man! *Now!*"

Somebody else was beside Cody, shoving him too, and at the sign of a ruckus three more Rattlesnakes pushed their way to the back of the church like a human wedge. Redfeather's next thrust slammed Cody up against the wall. "Fight! Fight!" Pequin started yelling, jumping up and down with excitement. "Hey, I don't want any trouble!" Cody protested, but Redfeather kept shoving him, banging his back up against the cracked plaster.

"Stop that! There'll be no fighting in here!" Father LaPrado was coming up the aisle as fast as he could, and Xavier Mendoza stood up from his seat beside his wife and uncle and tried to get to Cody's defense.

Now there were Rattlesnake faces all around Cody, taunting and shouting. Redfeather's hand gripped the front of Cody's T-shirt, started to rip it off him, and Cody whacked his arm into the Apache's elbow and knocked the hand away. "No fighting in my church!" the priest was hollering, but the knot of Rattlesnakes had closed around Cody, and neither LaPrado nor Mendoza could break through. Redfeather grabbed Cody's shirt again, and Cody saw the boy's battle-scarred fist rise up and he knew the punch was going to pop his lights out. He tensed, just about to block the blow and drive a knee into Redfeather's groin.

"Stop."

It was not a shout, but the command was spoken with absolute authority. Redfeather's fist paused at its apex, and his rage-dark eyes flickered to his left. Rick Jurado pushed past Pequin and Diego Montana, stared intensely at Cody for a few seconds. "Let him go," Rick said.

Redfeather gave Cody one more hard shove for good measure, then released his handful of T-shirt and uncocked his fist.

Rick stood right in front of Cody, not allowing him any room to move. "Man, you've gone around the bend for sure. What're you doin' over here?"

Cody tried to look around the sanctuary, but he couldn't see Miranda amid all the people and Rick shifted to block his view. "I thought I'd come say thanks for savin' my skin. No law against that, is there?"

"Okay. Thanks accepted. Now get out."

"Rick, he says he saw Sonny Crowfield outside, standin' across the street." Zarra pushed his way next to Rick. "I didn't see him, but I thought . . . you know . . . that it might not be Sonny anymore."

"Right," Cody said. "It might be one of those things, like the Cat Lady. He was across from the church; maybe he was watchin' the place."

Rick didn't like that possibility. "Anybody seen Sonny Crowfield?" he asked the others.

"Yeah!" Pequin spoke up. "I saw him about an hour ago, man. He said he was headin' home."

Rick thought for a moment. Crowfield lived in a shack down at the end of Third Street; he wasn't among Rick's favorite people, but he was a Rattler and that made him a brother too. All the other Rattlers were accounted for, except the five who were laid up at the clinic. Rick's Camaro was still parked in front of his house on Second Street. "Your motor outside?" he asked Cody.

"Yeah. Why?"

"You and me are gonna take a ride over to Crowfield's house and check it out."

"No way! I was just leavin'." Party time was over, and Cody edged toward the door, but a crush of Rattler bodies hemmed him in.

"You came in here to show how brave you are, didn't you?" Rick asked. "Maybe another reason, too." He'd seen Cody rubbernecking around, and he knew who the boy was searching for. Miranda sat with Paloma in a pew about halfway along the center aisle. "You owe me. I'm collecting, right now." He pulled the reloaded .38 out of his waistband and spun the cylinder a few inches in front of Cody's face. "You up to it, macho man?"

Cody saw the haughty defiance in Rick's eyes, and he smiled grimly. "Have I got a choice?"

"Stand back," Rick told the others. "Let him go if he wants to." They moved away, and a path was open to the door.

Cody didn't give a kick about Sonny Crowfield. He didn't care for another meeting with Stinger, either. He started to head for the door—but suddenly there she was, standing just behind her brother. Sweat sparkled on her face, her hair lay in damp curls, and dark hollows had gathered under her eyes, but she was still a smash fox. He nodded at her, but she didn't respond. Rick saw the nod and turned. Miranda said, "Paloma's afraid. She wants to know what's going on."

"We're about to throw some garbage out on the street," he answered. "It's okay."

Her gaze returned to Cody. He was about the most bedraggled and beat-up thing she'd ever seen. "Hi," he said. "Remember me?" And then Rick pressed the pistol's barrel up against Cody's cheek and leaned forward. "You don't talk to my sister," Rick warned, his eyes boring into Cody's. "Not one word. You hear me?"

Cody ignored him. "Your brother and I are gonna go for a little spin on my motor." The gun barrel pressed harder, but Cody just grinned. What was Jurado going to do, shoot him right here in front of the priest, his sister, God, and everybody? "We won't be too long."

"Leave him alone, Rick," Miranda said. "Put the gun down."

Never in Rick's wildest nightmares had he ever envisioned anything like this: Cody Lockett not only on Rattler turf, but in the *church!* And talking to Miranda like he actually *knew* her! His guts writhed with fire and fury, and it was all he could do not to smash his fist into Lockett's grinning face.

"Rick!" Now it was the snap of Mendoza's voice as he pushed people out of his way and came forward. "Cody's all right! Leave him alone!"

"It's okay," Cody said. "We're on our way out." He reached up, grasped Jurado's gunhand, and eased it aside. Then, with a last lingering glance and a smile at Miranda, he walked through the Rattlesnakes and paused at the door. "You comin', or not?" he asked.

"I am," Rick said. Cody slid the goggles over his eyes and went down the steps to the motorcycle.

In another few seconds Rick followed, the .38 in his waistband again. Cody got on the Honda and started the engine, and Rick straddled the passenger seat behind him. Over the motor's snarl, Rick said, "When we get out of this, I'm gonna beat you so bad you'll wish I'd left you down in that ho—"

Cody throttled up, the engine screamed, and the front tire reared up off the pavement, and Rick held on for dear life as the machine shot forward.

47
Firepower

"We've got seven minutes," Tom said in answer to the colonel's question about how much time remained before Stinger's deadline.

Rhodes returned his attention to Daufin. "You know Stinger can destroy this town. You know he'll do it if we don't give you over."

"If we *do* give her up," Jessie said, "it's not just our child's body we're talking about. If Stinger gets back to his masters and tells them about us, they'll come here with an invasion fleet."

"I can't think about that right now!" Rhodes ran his forearm across his face. The apartment was thick with heat, and smoke was creeping in through the cracked-open window. "All I know is, Stinger wants Daufin. If we don't hand her over in less than seven minutes, a lot of people are going to die!"

"And more people are going to die if we do!" She caught the faintest breeze, and offered her throat to it.

Daufin was staring out the window into the haze. There: she felt it again. A cold current of power. She knew what it was: a seeker beam from Stinger's ship, probing for the lifepod. It had passed on now, continuing its slow rotation across Inferno. Daufin's host skin prickled in its wake. The

426

pod had its own natural defense system that would deflect the beam for a short time, but Daufin had learned enough about Stinger's technology to know that sooner or later the seeker would pinpoint its target.

"What's Stinger going to make? Do you know?" Rhodes asked her.

She shook her head. Death and destruction crowded into her brain; she saw this lifepod called Inferno ablaze and crushed—if not by Stinger, then by the House of Fists. She glimpsed a fragment of the force field, glowing through the clouds of smoke, then her view was obscured again. She knew that many innocents were about to die, and too many had already perished because of her. The old rage seethed inside her. She saw the towers of her city crack and fall, saw mangled bodies spinning in the debris. The same brutality was about to happen here. "I must exit this world," Daufin said. "I've *got* to get home."

"There's no way!" Rhodes countered. "We told you: Earth doesn't have interstellar vehicles!"

"You're incorrect." Daufin's voice was quiet, and she continued to stare to the southwest, in the direction of Mack Cade's autoyard.

"Do you know something I don't?"

"There *is* an interstellar vehicle on Earth." Her eyes shone as if brilliant with fever. "Stinger's ship."

"What good will that do you?"

"I'm going to take Stinger's ship," she answered. "That's how I'm going to get home."

As the voice of a warrior came from a little girl's throat, Cody guided the motorcycle to the curb where Rick directed him. Sonny Crowfield lived alone in a gray clapboard shack on the edge of Cade's autoyard, and Cody drove up onto a trash-strewn yard and stopped with the headlight aimed at the closed front door. The house's porch sagged, the windows were broken out, and the place appeared deserted —but then again, so did the other houses on Third Street. Cody cut the engine but left the headlight burning. Rick got off, withdrew the .38, and walked to the bottom of the porch's three cinder-block steps before he realized Cody wasn't with him.

"I said I'd come with you," Cody told him. "I didn't say I'd go in."

"Muchas gracias." Rick snapped the pistol's safety off and started up the steps. He rapped on the door with the barrel. "Hey, Crowfield! It's Rick Jurado!"

No one came to the door. Cody shifted uneasily in his seat and glanced around. The pyramid stood to his right; he could see its vague, violet-washed outline through the murk.

"Answer up, Sonny!" Rick called. He knocked with his fist—and suddenly the door fell in with a scream of splintered wood and hung by one hinge. Rick jumped back, and Cody's hand leapt to the baseball bat.

"I don't think he's home," Cody said.

Rick peered inside, could see nothing. "You got a light?"

"Forget it, man! Crowfield's gone!"

"You got a light or not?" Rick asked, and waited. Cody snorted and dug his Zippo lighter out of his pocket. He flipped it to Rick, and the other boy caught it. Rick popped the flame up and started to cross the threshold.

"Watch your step!" Cody warned. "I don't want to be pullin' you up on a rope!"

"Front room's got a floor," Rick said, and he went in.

The house had a cemetery smell. The lighter's flame told Rick why: skeletons hung on the cracked walls. The bones had belonged to vultures, armadillos, coyotes, and snakes, and they were all over the place. He followed the flame through the front room into a hallway where bat and owl skeletons dangled on wires. He'd heard about Crowfield's "collection" from Pequin, but he'd never been here before and he was glad he hadn't. He came to another room off the corridor and thrust the lighter into the doorway.

"Shit," he whispered. Most of the room's floor had collapsed into darkness.

He walked carefully to the edge of the broken floorboards and looked down. He couldn't see a bottom, but the light glinted off something lying a few feet to his left, up against the wall's baseboard. He reached for it, and found a copper-jacketed bullet in his hand. And there were more of them: nine or ten bullets, lying on the other side of the hole. If Crowfield had bullets, there must be a gun around here, Rick thought. There was a closet within reach, and he opened it.

The lighter was beginning to scorch his hand, but the flame revealed another of Crowfield's collections: inside the closet, amid half-assembled skeletons and plastic bags full of assorted bones, were two rifles, four boxes of ammunition, a rusty .45 pistol, a case of empty Coke bottles, and two red tin cans. Rick caught the reek of gasoline. Sonofabitch had an arsenal, he realized. There were other items too: a bayonet, a couple of hunting knives, some of those morningstar blades that karate fighters threw, and a camouflage tarpaulin. Rick moved the tarp aside, and underneath was a small wooden box. He bent down. In faded red letters on the box was written DANGER! HIGH EXPLOSIVES! PROPERTY OF PRESTON COPPER MINING COMPANY.

He lifted the lid—and instantly pulled the lighter's flame back.

Nestled in waxed paper inside were five mustard-yellow sticks, each about nine inches long. The dynamite sticks had fuses of varying lengths, the longest maybe twelve inches and the shortest four inches. A couple of the sticks were scorched like hot dogs that had cooked too long on a grill, and Rick figured they were duds that had failed to ignite the first time around. How they'd ended up here he didn't know, but it was obvious that Sonny Crowfield had been getting ready to wage war—maybe on the Renegades, or maybe to take over the Rattlesnakes. He looked again at the Coke bottles and the gasoline tins. Easy to make a firebomb that way, he thought. Easy to set fire to a house or two and let the 'Gades take the blame, try to stir up a war so all this firepower could be useful.

"Sonofabitch," Rick said. He let the lid drop back and stood up. A little plastic bag fell open, and rat bones spilled out.

Outside, Cody felt the hairs on the back of his neck prickle—and just that quick he knew someone was behind him. He looked over his shoulder.

Sonny Crowfield was standing at the curb, eyes like dead black stones, mouth a thin gray gash, and the face damp and pallid. "I know you." The voice sounded like a warped, slowed-down recording of the real Crowfield. "You gave me some pain, man." The figure took a step forward. Its grin widened, and now Cody could see the rows of needle teeth. "I want to show you somethin' real pretty. You'll like it." The metal-nailed hand reached out.

Cody stomped down on the kickstarter. The engine rattled, backfired, but wouldn't catch.

The hand glided toward him. "Come on, man. Let me show you what I've made."

Another stomp, with all of Cody's strength behind it. The engine coughed and fired, and as the fingers started to clench into his shoulder Cody twisted the throttle and shot the motorcycle up the cinder-block steps and through the doorway into Crowfield's house.

The headlamp splayed onto Rick, who was just coming out of the corridor. He threw himself against a wall and a coyote skeleton fell off its hooks and crumpled to the floor. He shouted, "What the hell are you doing?" as Cody stopped the cycle just short of a collision.

"Get on!" Cody shouted right back. "Hurry!"

"Get on! Why?" He thought Cody had tumbled into the Great Fried Empty—and then a figure with long black hair filled up the doorway.

"Time's up," Stinger said, in its manufactured Sonny Crowfield voice.

Rick lifted the .38 and fired twice, the gunshots deafening. Both bullets hit the creature's chest, and it grunted and stumbled back a step, then righted itself and stormed across the threshold again.

"Get *on!*" Cody demanded, and Rick planted himself on the passenger seat. Cody guided the cycle into the corridor and powered up. Skeletons of flying things swung on wires over their heads. The Honda emerged from the corridor into a boxy kitchen, and Cody skidded it to a stop over the dirty yellow linoleum. He twisted the handlebars, seeking a way out with the headlight. "Where's the back door?" he yelled, but both of them saw that there was none, and the kitchen's single window was boarded up.

"Time's up! They didn't do what I told 'em!" Stinger raged, in the darkness between the kitchen and the house's only door. "Gonna smash some bugs!" There was the noise of combat boots clumping through the corridor. "I'll show you what I've made! It's gonna be here real soon!"

Cody switched off the headlight, and now the darkness was complete.

"Are you crazy? Keep the light on!" Rick protested, but Cody was already turning the motorcycle in a tight circle so that they were aimed into the corridor.

"Hang on," Cody told him. He revved the engine, and it responded with a throaty roar. "I want to be on him before the bastard knows what's hit him. If you fall off, you're dead meat. Got it?"

"Got it." Rick clamped one arm around Cody's waist and kept his finger on the .38's trigger.

The clump of boots was about halfway along the corridor. There were little rattling sounds: the thing's head and shoulders brushing skeletons.

Three more steps, Cody thought. Got to hit that thing and keep on going. His palms were wet, and his heart was slamming like a Beastie Boys drumbeat. One more step.

It came. The monster was almost in the kitchen. Cody revved the engine until it shrieked and released the brakes.

The rear tire spun on the linoleum, and there was the smell of scorched plastic. But in the next instant the motorcycle reared up and shot forward on its back tire. Rick hung on, and Cody hit the headlight switch.

Stinger was right there, framed in the corridor. The wet gray face convulsed as the light fell upon it, and both Rick and Cody saw the eyeballs smoke and retreat into their sockets. There was a roar of pain that shook the walls, and

Stinger's hands rose up to shield the eyes; its body was already starting to curl up, the spinal cord bulging with the pressure of the spiked tail beneath it.

The front tire hit the thing's face and the machine kept going over Stinger's body as if trying to claw its way out. Stinger went down to the floor. The motorcycle shuddered, careened to the side, and ricocheted off the wall, and the headlight's bulb blew out. Rick was lifted off his seat and almost lost hold of Cody, and something that no longer had a human shape was flailing wildly underneath the motorcycle.

But then they had broken clear of it and Cody powered the Honda through the doorway and down the porch steps. They went across the yard in a spray of sand as Cody fought to turn the machine—and in front of them they saw the pavement of Third Street at the edge of Cade's autoyard start to crack apart and buckle upward. A shape was struggling up from the street. Cody got the cycle under control and skidded to a stop about ten feet from the emerging creation.

"Here it comes!" a hunchbacked thing with a weaving tail rasped as it slithered down the steps of Crowfield's house. "Gonna smash *allllll* the little bugs!"

"Go!" Rick shouted. Cody didn't have to be told twice. He couldn't tell what was digging itself out of the ground, but he didn't care for a closer look. He laid on the throttle and the motorcycle arrowed east. Behind them, Third Street broke open and Stinger's new creation began to crawl free.

48
Nasty's Hero

Walking east on Celeste Street, Ray saw his shadow thrown before him by a single headlight, and he turned to wave down a ride. It was Tank's one-eyed truck, and it slowed to a stop in front of him.

Tank was at the wheel, his face daubed green by the instrument panel, and Ray could make out Nasty sitting on the passenger side. Tank leaned his helmeted head through the window. "You goin' up to the fort?"

"No. Home."

"Your folks are at the fort. So's most everybody else. Your sister too."

"Stevie? They found her?"

"Not exactly Stevie," Nasty told him. "Come on, we're headed up there." She opened the door for him, and he slid in beside her. Tank put the gearshift into first and started forward, turning left onto Travis Street. The tires bounced roughly over fissures in the pavement. Tank stared grimly ahead, trying to see through the smoke by the remaining light. He and Nasty had gone to his parents' house on Circle Back Street and found the place leaning on its foundations, a hole in the den floor big enough to drive a tractor through. Of his mother and father there was no sign, but some kind of slimy stuff was streaked on the walls and carpet.

"They're probably all right," Nasty repeated for the third or fourth time. "They probably went to a neighbor's house."

Tank grunted. They'd checked the other four houses on Circle Back Street; there'd been no answer at three of them, and at the fourth old man Shipley had come to the door with a shotgun. "Maybe they did," he said, but he didn't believe they'd gotten out of the house alive.

Ray shifted his position. The warmth of Nasty's thigh was burning into his leg. This would be one hell of a time to get a hard-on, and of course as soon as he thought about it the miraculous, unstoppable process began. Nasty looked at him, her face just a few inches away, and he thought, She can read my mind. Maybe it was because they were touching, and if he pulled away, she wouldn't know what he was thinking, but there was no room to maneuver in the cramped, greasy-smelling truck cab.

"You look different without your glasses," she decided.

He shrugged. Couldn't help but notice how her breasts thrust against the thin cotton of her sweat-damp T-shirt. He could see the nipples, which didn't help his condition any. "Not so different," he said.

"Yeah you do. Older."

"Maybe I just feel older."

"Hell, we all do," Tank said. "I feel like I'm ninety fuckin' years ol——" He felt the truck shudder. The wheel trembled in his hands. He leaned forward, had seen something out in the haze, wasn't sure what it had been but his heart was jammed in his throat.

"What is it?" Nasty asked him, her voice rising with alarm.

He shook his head and started to plant his foot on the brake pedal.

And that was when he saw the concrete of Travis Street buckle upward about fifteen feet in front of the pickup truck and rise like a gray wave. Something huge was moving just under the surface, as if swimming through Texas earth, and its motion lifted Tank's truck on the crest of the land wave, raised it amid chunks of broken and grinding pavement.

Nasty screamed and gripped the dashboard, and Ray had his fingers on the door handle. As the truck angled sharply downward and slid off the concrete swell toward a sea of cracks, something rose up from a fissure and into the headlight's beam: a snaky coil as wide as the truck, covered with mottled greenish-gray scales.

Then the coil went down as the creature dove deeper, spewing up a spray of red dirt and sand like the spume of a whale. The pickup truck turned sideways, and the wheel spun out of Tank's grip. The concrete was still in motion under the tires, splitting and separating, and as Tank threw his door open and started to jump the truck hit a jagged edge of pavement, heeled to the left, and crashed down on top of him. He made no sound of pain, but Ray heard the crack of his helmet breaking. The truck's weight continued to slide forward as the pavement settled, smearing Tank's body beneath it. And then the hood slid into a fissure that slammed down on it like a shark's jaws. Metal groaned and crumpled, sparks shot off the edges, and flames began to lick around the hood.

It had only taken five or six seconds. Ray blinked, smelled burning oil and paint, and heard Nasty's wounded moaning. She was lying underneath him, half on and half off the seat. The earth was still trembling in the wake of the monster's passage, and metal shrieked as the truck sank deeper into the chasm. Something popped in the engine—a surprisingly gentle sound—and red tendrils of flame gnawed toward the shattered windshield. He felt the fearsome heat on his face, and he knew then that if they sat there much longer they were going to be fried. The truck sank down another three or four inches. He pulled himself up toward the passenger door and forced it open with the strength of the doomed, then he hung to the doorframe and reached down to Nasty. "Take my hand! Come on!"

She looked up at him, and he could see the blood crawling out of her nostrils. He figured she must have banged her head against the dashboard when the truck had turned over. She was embracing the steering wheel with both arms. The truck lurched and slid down another couple of inches, and now the heat was getting savage. Ray shouted, "Grab my hand!"

Nasty unhooked the fingers of her right hand from the wheel, wiped her nose, and stared at the blood. She made a half giggle, half moan, and Ray strained down and grasped her wrist. He tugged mightily at her. "We've got to get out!"

It took her a few precious seconds to register that fire was coming through the windshield and that Ray was trying to help her. She released her hold on the wheel and pushed herself up, pain thrumming through her skull from the knock she'd taken to her forehead. Ray pulled her out of the pickup's battered cab, and they fell together to the broken concrete. Her body went limp, but Ray got to his feet and started hauling her up. "Come on!" he said. "We can't stay here!"

"Tank," she said, her voice slow and slurred. "Where's Tank? He was right here just a minute ago."

"Tank's gone. Come on! Up!" He got her to her feet, and though she was several inches taller, she leaned against his shoulder. He looked around, his eyes stinging from the smoke, and saw that Travis Street—at least the small section he could see of it—had become a ridged and gullied battlefield. Whatever that thing was, it had folded the concrete back and split it to pieces like a bone-dry riverbed.

Flames bellowed around the truck. Ray didn't like the idea of staying so close to it; the thing might blow up or whatever had passed under the street might be drawn to the light. In any case, he craved some shelter. He pulled Nasty with him across the street, mindful of the cracks around them, the largest about three or four feet wide. "Where'd Tank go?" she asked. "He was drivin', wasn't he?"

"Yeah. He went on ahead," was all he could think to say. The outline of a house came out of the murk, and Ray guided Nasty toward it. How far they were from the fort he didn't know, but he wasn't sure they'd passed the intersection of Sombra and Travis, and that was a good hundred yards from the apartment building's parking lot. Just short of the house's porch steps, Ray felt the earth tremble: the creature passing somewhere close by. From the next street over came the splintering crash of a house being lifted off its foundations.

They went up the steps. The front door was locked, but the nearest window was glassless and Ray reached into it, snapped the jamb's lock off, and pushed the window up. He slid in first, then helped Nasty through. She stumbled, her strength used up, pitched forward, and they both fell to the hardwood floor.

Her mouth was right up against his ear, and she was breathing hard. Any other time this would have been a fantasy come true, he thought—but his mind couldn't focus on sex at the moment, though her body was molded into his and her breasts pressed against his chest. God had a mighty wicked sense of humor, he decided.

The house creaked at the joints. Under them the floor rolled like a slow wave, and cracks shot up the walls. Along Travis Street the houses moaned as the creature tunneled beneath them, and Ray heard the scream of timbers caving in as a structure collapsed two or three houses away.

Nasty, tough as nails and swigger of tobacco spit, was shivering. Ray put his arms around her. "You're going to be all right," he said. His voice didn't quaver too much, which surprised him. "I'll protect you."

She lifted her head, looked at him face-to-face, and her eyes were scared and dazed but there was a grim hint of a smile on her mouth. "My hero," she said, and then she let her head rest on his shoulder and they lay there in the dark as Inferno ripped apart at the seams.

Across the bridge, Cody skidded the cycle to a stop in front of the Catholic church, and Rick jumped off. He looked back along First Street, couldn't see anything through the haze. But that thing would be out of the ground by now, and probably heading this way. Zarra, Pequin, and Diego Montana had been waiting at the door for Rick's return, and now they came down the steps. Cody got off the Honda, looked at the church, and knew those people jammed in there wouldn't have a rat's ass of a chance. If electric light hurt Stinger—and the way the monster in Crowfield's house had reacted showed that Daufin was right—then there was only one safe place he could think of.

"We've gotta move these people out before that thing gets here!" Cody said to Rick. "We're not gonna have much time!"

"Move them! *Where?*"

"Across the bridge. To the fort." All of them gaped at him as if he'd gone totally off his bird. "Forget that gang shit!" he said, and felt as if the words split an old skin that had been shriveling tighter and tighter around him. He saw there were a lot of cars and pickups parked around the church, on both sides of the street, and most of them were broken-down heaps, but they could each carry five or six people. The pickup trucks could carry more. "We get 'em loaded and out as fast as we can!" he said. "The fort's the only place Stinger won't try to dig into, because of the lights!"

Rick wasn't sure he believed that, but the apartment building was a lot sturdier than the church. He made his decision fast. "Diego, where's your car?" The boy pointed to a rusted brown Impala across the way. "I want you to drive it up the street about fifty yards." He motioned west. "Pequin, you go with him. Keep your lights on, and if you see anything or anybody coming, you haul ass back."

Diego sprinted to the car, and Pequin started to protest, but he obeyed the order like a good soldier.

"Zarra, you get the Rattlers together. Tell them where we're going, and that we'll need all the cars we can find. I want every Rattler car loaded. Go!"

Zarra ran up the steps into the church. Rick turned to Cody. "I want you to . . ." He hesitated, realizing he was talking to the enemy just like he would a Rattler. "I'll find Father LaPrado and start getting everybody out," he amended. "I could use another scout."

Cody nodded. "I reckon so. I could use that gun on your hip too."

Rick gave it to him, handle first, and Cody slid it into his waistband. "Four bullets left," Rick said. "Don't pull a John Wayne if you see it coming. Just get back here in one piece."

"Man, you like givin' orders, don't you?" Cody stomped down on the kickstarter and the hot engine fired. He offered a sly smile. "You just take care of your little sister. I'll be back." He turned the Honda around in a tight circle and sped west on First Street, and Rick ran up the steps into the sanctuary.

Diego Montana's car was just creeping along, and Cody flashed by it about forty yards away from the church; he veered into the center of the headlights' beam but had to cut his speed to a glide as the Impala stopped and he outran the lights. The violet-tinged gloom closed around him, and he pulled to the curb to wait for his night vision to sharpen.

At the church, Rick had convinced Father LaPrado that they had just a short time to evacuate almost three hundred people. The problem was how to do it without creating a panic, but there was no time to deliberate; Father LaPrado stood up before the congregation and explained in a voice as tough as brine-dipped leather that they had to leave quickly and everything they'd brought—pillows, clothes, food, possessions—would have to remain behind. They would clear the aisles first, then leave row by row starting from the rear. Everyone who had a car or truck should go to it and wait for it to be filled before driving off. They were heading across the bridge, he told them, to take shelter in the apartment building at the end of Travis Street.

The evacuation started, and cars carrying Bordertown residents began crossing the Snake River Bridge.

A hundred yards west, Cody wheeled the motorcycle into a dirt alley and drove through it onto Second Street. He cut the engine and coasted, listening. Could hear the noise of cars hightailing toward Inferno. Dark houses stood in the smoke, not a candle showing anywhere. Over toward Third Street a couple of dogs were howling. He guided the Honda over the curb and in between two houses, and there he stopped to listen again. His heartbeat drummed in his ears.

He walked the motorcycle ahead, came out from between the houses—and froze when he saw a formless thing standing about ten feet in front of him. It didn't move, either. Cody was afraid to draw a breath. Slowly he pulled the .38 out and his thumb found the safety catch. Clicked it off. He lifted the gun, steadied his hand. The thing still didn't budge. He took a step closer, his finger lodged on the trigger, and that was when he realized he was aiming at a discarded washing machine standing in somebody's backyard.

He almost laughed. Some John Wayne! He was glad none of the 'Gades were around to see this, or his reputation would be lower than ant pee.

He was about to put the .38 away when he heard a slow, scraping noise.

He tensed, stood rigid and stock-still. The sound repeated —metal across concrete, he thought it was—but where it was coming from he wasn't sure. Was it ahead, on Third Street, or behind him on Second? He bellied down in the dust and crawled back into the space between the houses, and he lay there trying to pinpoint the sound's direction. The haze was playing tricks with him. The scraping noise was first ahead, then behind him. Was it moving toward him, or away: he couldn't be sure, and not knowing made his guts twist. Whatever it was, it sounded like something that was just learning how to walk and dragging its feet—or claws. The good part was that it was moving slowly and clumsily; the bad part was that it sounded heavy.

He caught movement through the murk: a shape on Second Street, lumbering past Cody's hiding place. No damned washing machine this time. The sonofabitch was big and alive and it passed with a noise like razor blades scraping a chalkboard. The haze swirled around it and spun in its wake, and then whatever it was had gone on, striding inexorably toward the church.

Cody gave it about ten more seconds, and then he scrambled up, got on the motorcycle, and started the engine; it roared like hellfire in the narrow space, and Cody gunned it toward Third Street, saw clothes flagging from a line, and ducked just in time to keep his head. He turned left on Third with a shriek of tires and rocketed east all the way to Republica Road. Then straight to the intersection of First Street again, where cars were turning toward the bridge. He took another left, deftly dodged a pickup truck full of people, and wound his way through the refugees to the steps of the church.

Inside, Mendoza was helping Paloma Jurado along the aisle. Over a hundred people had already gone, and the cars had been leaving as fast as they could get packed. But only two cars and Mendoza's pickup truck were left, and it was clear a lot of people were going to have to make it on foot.

"Take my grandmother with you," Rick told him. He looked around, saw twenty more elderly people who couldn't make it over without a ride. His Camaro was still parked in front of his house on Second Street, and there wasn't time to go after it. "You go with them," he said to Miranda, and motioned toward Mendoza.

She'd already grasped the situation. "There's not enough room left for me."

"You can *make* room! Go!"

"What about you?"

"I'll find a way. Go on, take care of Paloma!"

She was about to follow Mendoza and her grandmother to the door when Cody Lockett came along the aisle. He glanced quickly at her, his face gray with dust except for the area around his eyes where the goggles had rested, then directed his attention to Rick. She saw that his swagger and cockiness had dissolved. "It's headed this way," he said. "I saw it on Second Street. I couldn't tell much about it, but the thing's *huge.*"

Rick saw Mendoza guiding Paloma out the door, with a few other old people in tow. It wouldn't take but a couple of minutes for Mendoza's truck to fill up. "I said *go!*" he snapped at Miranda.

"I'm staying with you," she said.

"The hell you are! Come on!" He grasped her arm, and she just as stubbornly pulled away.

"There you go, spoutin' out orders again," Cody said.

"You shut up!" Rick looked around, trying to find a Rattler to help him, but the rest of them had already gone; Father LaPrado was herding the remaining thirty or so people out. A car horn began blaring in the distance, getting louder, and Rick knew what that meant: Diego and Pequin had seen something and were racing back. He pushed his way through the door and out to the steps, with Cody and Miranda following.

The Impala had pulled up to the curb, and already people were jamming into it. Others had decided to run, and they were heading north toward the riverbank. Pequin got out of the car just as Rick reached the street. "We saw somethin', man!" Pequin pointed west, and his hand trembled. "Out there, maybe thirty or forty yards!"

"What'd it look like?" Cody asked him.

Pequin shook his head. "I don't know, man. We just saw somethin' movin' out there, and we hauled ass back! It's comin' this way!"

"Rick, I'm ready to go!" Mendoza was behind the wheel of his pickup, with Paloma and his wife in the cab beside him. Eight others were loaded into the truck bed. "Bring your sister!"

"When you go, I go," she told Rick before he could speak. He glanced into the haze to the west, then back to Mendoza. Time was ticking past, and the creature was getting closer. "Take off!" he said. "I'll bring Miranda over myself!" Mendoza nodded, waved a hand, and drove toward the bridge. Diego's car was jammed so full it was dragging the pavement, and the last car was loaded down too. More than eighty people were going north on foot. Diego put the Impala into reverse and it shot backward, throwing sparks off its hanging tailpipe. "Wait for me, you bastard!" Pequin shouted, running after him.

"Hey, Jurado," Cody said quietly, "I think we've got company."

The haze swirled before the thing's approach. They could hear the scrape of metal on concrete. The last car, carrying seven or eight people and a couple hanging to the doors, backfired and sped away.

The shape came out of the smoke and lurched into the candlelight that streamed from the church's windows.

49
Stinger's New Toy

Rick laughed. He couldn't help it. All that hurrying to get people evacuated, and what had emerged from the murk was a horse. A palomino, broad-shouldered and muscular, but just a damned horse. It took another clumsy step forward and stopped, tottering as if it had been sipping from a trough laced with whiskey.

"It's a drunk horse!" Rick said. "We were scared shitless of a drunk horse!" The thing must've gotten away from somebody's farm or ranch, he figured. Surely this wasn't what had come out of that hole in the street. At least now he and Miranda had a ride across the bridge. The horse was just standing there, staring at them, and Rick thought it might be in shock or something. He started toward it, his hand offered. "Easy, boy, Take it ea—"

"Don't!" Cody gripped his arm. Rick stopped, less than ten feet from the horse.

The animal's nostrils flared. Its head strained backward, showing the cords of muscle in its throat, and from the mouth came a noise that mingled a horse's shrill whinny and the hiss of a steam engine.

Rick saw what Cody had seen: the horse had silver talons—the claws of a lizard—instead of hooves.

His legs were locked. The creature's deep-socketed eyes

ticked from Cody to Rick and back again—and then its mouth stretched open, the rows of needles sparkling in the low light, and its spine began to lengthen with the cracking sounds of bones breaking and re-forming.

Cody stepped back and bumped into Miranda. She clutched at his shoulder, and behind her the last dozen people to emerge from the church saw the thing in the street and scattered. But the final person to come out stood in the doorway, his backbone straight as an iron bar; he drew a deep breath and started purposefully down the steps.

The creature's body continued to lengthen, muscles thickening into brutal knots under the rippling flesh. Dark pigment threaded through the golden skin, and the bones of its skull popped like gunshots and began to change shape.

Rick retreated to the curb. His heart was beating wildly, but he couldn't run. Not yet. What was being born in front of him held him like a hallucination, a fascinating fever dream. The head was flattening, the lower jaw unhinging and sliding forward as gray drool dripped from the corners of the mouth. The spine bowed upward, the entire body hunched, and with a sound of splitting flesh, a thick, segmented black tail uncoiled from the base of the vertebrae. A wicked cluster of metallic spikes, each one almost six inches long, pushed out of the black wrecking ball at the end of the tail.

The monster had doubled its length, the legs splaying out like those of a crab. And now spinier legs, each with three silver talons, were bursting through the skin of its sides. The body settled, its belly grazing the pavement. The flesh was splitting open, revealing a hide of interlocked black scales like the surface of the pyramid, and the thing thrashed as if trying to escape a cocoon. Flakes of golden skin flew like dead leaves.

Cody had the .38 in his hand. His motorcycle was just beside him, and he knew he should get on and go like a bat out of hell, but the spectacle of transformation held him fast. The creature's elongated, knotty skull was now somewhere between that of a horse's and an insect's, the neck squat and powerful, muscles bunching and writhing as the body threw off pieces of dead flesh. It hit him that this was unlike anything he'd ever seen in any sci-fi or Mexican horror flick for one simple and terrible reason: this thing seethed with life. As the old skin ripped away, the creature's movements were no longer clumsy but quick and precise, like those of a scorpion scuttling from the wet dark under a rock. The flesh of its head burst open like a strange fruit and dangled in tatters. Beneath it was a nightmare visage of bone ridges and black scales. The convex eyes of a horse had been sucked inward, and now amber eyes with vertical black pupils gleamed in the armored overhang of the brow. Two more alien eyes emerged from the holes where the horse's nostrils had been, and diamond-shaped vents along the sides of its body gasped and exhaled with a bellows' *whoosh.*

The monster shrugged off the last scraps of horseflesh. Its narrow body was now almost fifteen feet long, each of its eight legs six feet in length and the ball of spikes quivering another twenty feet in the air. The two sets of eyes moved independently of each other, and as the thing's head turned to follow the flight of a Bordertown resident across First Street toward the river, Rick saw a third set of eye sockets just above the base of the skull.

"Get back," Cody said to Miranda. Said it calmly, as if he saw creatures like this every day of his life. He felt icy inside, and he knew that either he was about to die or he was not. A simple dare of fate. He lifted the .38 and started to squeeze off the four bullets.

But someone walked into the pistol's path. Someone wearing black, and holding up with both hands a staff with a gilt crucifix atop it. Father LaPrado walked past Rick. Rick was too stunned to stop the priest but he'd gotten a look at LaPrado's ashen face and he knew the Great Fried Empty had just swallowed him.

Father LaPrado began shouting in Spanish: "Almighty God casts you out! Almighty God and the Holy Spirit sends you back to the pit of hell!" He kept going, and Rick took two steps after him, but the quadruple eyes on the creature's skull locked on LaPrado and it rustled forward like a black, breathing locomotive. LaPrado lifted the staff in demented defiance. "I command you in the name of God to return to the pit!" he shouted. Rick reached for him, about to snag his coat. "I command you! I command—"

There was a banshee shriek. Something whipped past only inches in front of Rick, and the wind of its passage whistled around his ears. His hand had blood all over it, and suddenly Father LaPrado was gone. Just gone.

Blood on my shirt, Rick realized. The unreality of a dream cloaked him. He smelled musty copper.

Drops of crimson began to shower down on him. And other things and parts of things. A shoe hit the pavement to his left. An arm plopped down on the right, six or seven feet away. The remains of Father LaPrado's body, hurled high and torn to shreds by the ball of spikes, fell to the earth around him. The last thing down was the staff, snapped in two.

The monster's tail, dripping with blood and bits of flesh, lifted up into the air again. Cody saw the thing quiver, about to strike. Rick just stood there, paralyzed. There was no time to weigh the past against the present: Cody started running toward him, got off two shots, and saw a pair of the amber eyes fix on him. The tail hesitated for a vital three seconds, the creature choosing between double targets, then whipped in a vicious sideswipe, the air shrieking around the bony spikes.

Cody hit Rick with a bodyblock and knocked him sprawling over the curb, heard the ball of spikes coming, and flattened himself against the bloody pavement.

It passed less than a foot over him, came back again in a savage blur, but Cody was already twisting away like a worm on a hot plate and the tail struck sparks off the street. The tail was retracted for another slash, and Cody saw Rick sit up, the boy's face splattered with LaPrado's blood. "Run!" Cody shouted. "I'll get Miranda across!" Still Rick didn't respond, but Cody couldn't help him anymore. Miranda was crouched down on the church steps, calling for her brother. Cody got up, took aim at one of the thing's eyes, and fired the last two bullets. The second shot gouted gray fluid from the top of the skull, and the creature made a sharp hissing noise and scuttled backward.

Cody sprinted back across the street, zigzagging to throw off the thing's aim. He dropped the pistol, leapt onto the motorcycle's seat. The key was already in the ignition, and Cody yelled "Get on!" to Miranda as he stomped on the starter. The engine racketed, popped, would not catch. The creature started striding forward again, getting within striking range. Cody came down on the starter a second time; the engine backfired, caught and faded, fired up again with a throaty growl. The back of his neck prickled. He sensed the tail curling up into the air. Cody looked over his shoulder, saw the monster's black head with its underslung jaws full of needles thrusting toward him. And then a figure ran from the right, shouting and waving its arms, and one set of eyes darted at Rick. A foreleg lifted, the silver claws slashing so fast Rick hardly saw it coming. He flung himself backward, the talons streaking past his face.

But Miranda was on the motorcycle, clinging tight to Cody's waist. She screamed "Run!" to Rick, and Cody throttled up. The machine shot away from the curb and sped toward Republica Road.

Rick scrambled on his hands and knees up over the curb. He heard the slithering of the thing coming after him, the scrape of the talons on the concrete. He got to his feet and ran north, across a yard and in between two houses. And in that narrow space he stepped on a loose stone and his left foot slid, the ankle twisting with a pain that jabbed all the way to his hipbone. He cried out and fell on his face in the sand and weeds, clutching at his ankle.

The houses on either side of him shuddered and moaned. Boards cracked, plaster dust puffing from the walls. Rick looked back, and saw the dark shape trying to squeeze its body into the space after him, its strength breaking the houses off their foundations.

Eighty yards away, Cody and Miranda were almost across

the bridge when something—a human figure—rose up from the smoke directly in front of them. Cody instinctively hit the brakes, started to swerve the machine aside, but there wasn't enough time. The motorcycle smacked into whoever it was, skidded out of control, and flung both of them off. It crashed into the side of the bridge, the frame bending with a low moan like guitar strings breaking and the front tire flying up into the air. Cody landed on his right side and slid in a fury of friction burns.

He lay curled up and gasping for breath. Fate bit my ass this time, he thought. No, no; must've been the Mumbler, he decided. Old fuckin' Mumbler just crawled up on the bridge and gave us a whack.

Miranda. What had happened to Miranda?

He tried to sit up. Not enough strength yet. There was an awful pain in his left arm, and he thought it might be broken. But he could move the fingers, so that was a good sign. His ribs felt like splintered razors; one or two of them were snapped, for damn sure. He wanted to sleep, just close his eyes and let it all go, but Miranda was somewhere nearby—and so was whatever they'd crashed into. Some protector I turned out to be, he thought. Not worth a damn. Maybe the old man was right after all.

He smelled gasoline. Motor's tank ruptured. And about two seconds later there was a *whump!* of fire and orange light flickered. Pieces of the Honda clattered down around him and into the Snake River's gulley. He got up on his knees, his lungs hitching. Miranda lay on her back about six feet away, her arms and legs splayed like those of a broken doll. He crawled to her. Saw blood on her mouth from a split lower lip and a blue bruise on the side of her face. But she was breathing, and when he spoke her name her eyelids fluttered. He tried to cradle her head, but his fingers found a lump on her skull and he thought he'd better not move her.

Cody heard footsteps—two boots: one clacking, one sliding.

He saw someone lurching toward them from the Bordertown side. Rivulets of gasoline had run from the smashed motorcycle, and the figure kept coming through the fire. It was hunchbacked, with a spiked tail, and as it got nearer Cody could see a grin of needles.

Half of Sonny Crowfield's head had caved in. Something that shone like gray pus had leaked through the empty left eye socket, and the imprint of a motorcycle tire lay across the cheek like a crimson tattoo. The body jittered, one leg dragging.

It came on across the streams of flame, the cuffs of its jeans smoking and catching fire. The grin never faltered.

Cody crouched over Miranda. He looked for the nail-studded baseball bat but it was gone. The clacking boot and dragging boot closed in, the hunchbacked body and tail of spikes silhouetted by fire. Cody started to rise; he was dead meat now, and he knew it, but maybe he could get his fingers in that remaining eye and jerk it off its strings. Pain shot through his ribs, stole his breath, and hobbled him. He fell back to his side, wheezing for air.

Stinger reached Miranda. Stood over her, staring down. Then a metal-nailed hand slid over her face.

Cody was all used up. There was nothing more. Tears were in his eyes, and he knew Miranda's head was about to be crushed and there was only one chance to save her life. The words were out of him before he could think twice: "I know who you're lookin' for."

The dripping head lifted. The hand remained clasped to Miranda's face. She moaned, still mercifully unconscious, and Stinger gripped her hair with the other hand. "The guardian." The voice was a gurgle of fluids. "Where is she?"

"I . . . can't . . ." Cody felt close to a faint. He didn't want to tell, and tears burned his eyes but he saw the fingers tighten on Miranda's face.

"You'll tell me," Stinger said, "or I'll tear this bug's head off."

Lying between the two houses on First Street, Rick hugged the ground and started crawling. The monster couldn't get its body into the space, and neither would the arm reach Rick. He heard a crash that seemed to shake the earth. Timbers flew around him, and he realized the thing was beating the two houses to pieces with its tail. He struggled up, hobbling on his good leg, as roof shingles and shards of wood exploded like bomb blasts. Ahead was a chest-high chainlink fence and on the other side the river's gulley. He saw fire on the bridge but he had no time to concern himself with what was burning; he clambered over the fence, slid down a slope of red dirt, and lay in the muddy trickle of water. From Bordertown he could hear the crash and shatter of the houses coming apart. In another couple of minutes the creature was going to break through and come across the river. He roused himself, shunting aside the pain in his swollen ankle, and started climbing up the opposite slope toward the rear of the buildings on Cobre Road.

On the bridge barely fifty yards from Rick, Cody Lockett knew his luck—and possibly Daufin's too—had finally run out. Stinger would destroy the town and everyone in it, starting with Miranda. But the fort was protected from Stinger not only by its foundation of bedrock and its armored windows, but by its electric light. Even if he knew where Daufin was, there was still no way he could get to her. Cody sat up, his brain doing a slow roll, and smiled grimly. "She's up there," he said, and pointed to the faint smudge of light. He saw an expression of dismay flicker across the ruined face. "Pretty, huh? Better wear your sunglasses, fuckhead."

Stinger released Miranda. Both hands gripped Cody's throat, and the tail thrashed above the boy's head. "I won't need sunglasses," the gurgling voice replied. The face pressed toward Cody's. "I'm gonna earn my bounty by scoopin' up some live bugs to take on a little trip. I'm real close to findin' her pod too. If she doesn't want to go, that's fine: she can rot in this shithole. *Comprende?*"

Cody didn't answer. The thing's breath smelled like burned plastic. And then it let go of his throat, put an arm around his waist, and lifted him off the concrete as easily as if he were a child. The pain in his rib cage savaged him, brought cold sweat to his pores. Stinger lifted Miranda with the other arm. Cody tried to thrash loose, but the pain and effort were too much. He passed out, his hands and legs dangling.

Stinger tucked the bodies to his sides and continued walking across the bridge toward Inferno, dragging the malfunctioning leg. He entered a sky-blue house near the intersection of Republica and Cobre roads. The living room had no floor, and Stinger dropped into darkness with his cargo of bugs.

50

High Ground

Ed Vance and Celeste Preston were sharing a third bottle of Lone Star at the Brandin' Iron and waiting for the end of the world when they heard the shriek of tires turning onto Travis Street. Several times in the past fifteen minutes the Brandin' Iron's floor had shuddered, and a stack of plates had crashed down in the kitchen with a noise that had almost shot Sue Mullinax out of her sneakers. The old-timers who'd been sitting at the back had fled, but Vance didn't budge off his seat because he knew there was nowhere to run to.

Now, though, it sounded like a lot of cars were heading north up Travis. Sounded like some of them were banging into each other, they were in such a hurry. Vance got off the counter stool and went out to the street. He could see the headlights and taillights of vehicles roaring along Celeste Street, turning onto Travis, some running up over yards and adding more dust to the thick air. Looked like a mass exodus, but where the hell were they going? He could barely make out the glow of the 'Gade fort, and he figured that was drawing all the cars. They were racing like the devil himself was snapping at their fenders.

He realized Celeste had followed him out. "I'd better get

453

up there and find out what's goin' on," he told her. "Seems that'd be a safe place for you too."

"I'm gettin' my ass out of here." She still had hold of the Lone Star bottle, about three swigs left in it, and she dug into her jumpsuit pocket for her Cadillac keys. "Best thing about that big ole house is, it's got one hell of a strong basement." She started around to the driver's side, but paused before she slid under the wheel. "Hey, Vance!" she called. "Basement's got a lot of room. Even enough for a fat sumbitch like you."

It was a tempting offer. Maybe it was the beer sloshing in his belly, or maybe the fact that the light wasn't worth a damn, but Vance thought at that instant that Celeste Preston was . . . well . . . almost pretty.

He wanted to go. Wanted to real bad. But this time the monsters of Cortez Park would not win. He said, "I reckon I'll stick here."

"Suit yourself, but I think you've seen *High Noon* too many times."

"Maybe so." He opened the patrol-car door. "You take care."

"Believe it, pardner." Celeste got into the Cadillac and plugged the key into the ignition.

Vance heard a sound like clay plates cracking. Celeste Street seemed to roll like a slow wave, fissures snaking across the concrete. Sections of the street collapsed, and human figures began to crawl out of the holes. Vance made a choking sound.

Something burst up out of the street next to Celeste's Cadillac. She looked into the seamed face of a heavy-set Mexican woman, and the woman's hand darted in through the open window and closed on Celeste's wrist. Celeste stared dumbly at the brown hand, at the saw-blade-edged fingernails digging into her flesh. She had a split second choice of whether to scream or act.

She picked up the beer bottle beside her on the seat and smashed it into the creature's face. Gray fluid splattered from the slashed cheek. Then she let the scream go, and as she jerked loose, ribbons of flesh flayed off her arm. The thing reached for her again, but Celeste was already squirming out the passenger door. The claws ripped across the back of the driver's seat.

Celeste tumbled to the curb. The creature hopped nimbly up onto the hood, was about to leap at her—and then Vance shot it point-blank in the head with the Winchester rifle he'd pulled out of the patrol car.

The bullet went through its skull and shattered the windshield; now Vance had the creature's full attention. He put the next bullet between its eyes, the third one knocking its lower jaw out of joint and fountaining broken needles into the air. It made a shrieking noise and jumped off the hood, its spine bowing and the scorpion tail bursting loose. Its arms and legs elongated, mottled with black scales, and before Vance could fire again the thing scrabbled off and dropped into a hole in the street.

Another hunched and misshapen replicant, its spiked tail weaving like a cobra's head, rushed out of the smoke at Vance. He had time to see it wore the ooze-wet face of Gil Lockridge and then he started shooting. A bullet ricocheted off the pavement, but the next thunked into the body, staggering the creature, and Vance shot it in the forehead. The tail crashed against the front of Celeste's Cadillac, caving in the radiator grille, but it backed off and retreated.

An acidic, sickly-sweet smell was in the air. Vance saw other figures scuttling in the haze, and he ran the four strides to the patrol car, popped out the spent clip of bullets, and shoved a fresh one in. He had two more, each holding six cartridges, and those he jammed into his pocket. A third figure lurched toward him. Vance fired twice at it, didn't know if he did any damage or not but the thing—a scorpion's body with the dark-haired head of a man —hissed and darted away. "Come on!" Vance shouted, his gaze sliding from side to side and his heart slamming. "This is *Texas,* you sonsofbitches! We'll kick your asses!"

But no more of the things rushed him. There were others out there, maybe five or six of them, emerging from the holes like scorpions stirred up from a nest. They were racing toward Travis Street.

Oh Jesus, Vance thought. Stinger's found out where Daufin is.

There was a crashing sound and the thud of falling bricks. Vance looked to his right, saw the smoke and dust swirling around a shape as long as a train's engine moving along Celeste Street. He caught a glimpse of a massive spiked tail, and then it slashed from one side to another and the storefronts exploded as if hit by a demolition ball. The thing's tail swept aside the chainlink fence that surrounded Mack Cade's used-car lot, hit a car, and knocked it onto its side. Then the thing was clambering through the cars like a roach over food crumbs, and as the tail kept smashing cars Vance saw sparks fly. A pickup truck upended and slid into the street. The creature got amid the cars and madly flailed left and right, and there was a hollow boom of gasoline going up, followed by a leap of red flame that let Vance and Celeste see the black, eight-legged body and the narrow head that was a bizarre combination of horse and scorpion. The thing flung cars in all directions, more fires started up and fed on the ruptured gas tanks, and then it continued its progress through the heart of Inferno.

Vance grasped Celeste's bleeding arm and pulled her up. Sue Mullinax was standing in the cafe's doorway, her freckled face milky white as she watched the monster coming. Vance saw that it would be on them in seconds, and its tail was battering everything on both sides of the street. "Get inside!" he yelled at her. She backed into the cafe, and Vance pulled Celeste with him through the door. Sue scrambled over the counter, huddling down beside the refrigerator. Vance heard stones crash into the street: a wall toppling. He dropped the rifle, hefted Celeste Preston and shoved her over the counter, and he was climbing over too when the entire front wall of the Brandin' Iron imploded in a storm of white stones and mortar. The patrol car slewed in, smashing chairs and tables out of its path. Three fist-sized pieces of rock slammed into Vance's shoulder and side and knocked him over the counter like a bowling pin.

The roof sagged, the air white with rock dust. Pools of fire burned around the broken oil lamps. The Brandin' Iron's front wall was a gaping cavity. Outside, the creature veered to the right, its tail whipping through the front of the House of Beauty, and then it crawled north along the buckled wreckage of Travis Street. In its wake, five more of the smaller things came up out of holes and followed like scavengers after a shark.

In the Hammonds' house, Scooter was barking fit to bust. Sarge lay on the den floor, his hands covering his head and his body trembling violently. About a minute before, something had hit the wall that faced Celeste Street and the entire house had jumped off its foundations in a shatter of glass and breaking stone. Sarge sat up, his nostrils stung by dust and his eyes wide and glassy with the memories of incoming artillery rounds. Scooter was right beside him, still barking furiously. "Hush," Sarge said; his voice was a husky rasp. "Hush, Scooter," he said, and his best friend obeyed.

Sarge stood up. The floor had been knocked crooked. He'd gone into the kitchen ten minutes before to raid the refrigerator and had found a pack of wooden Fire Chief matches, and now he struck one of them and followed its light to the front door.

There was no front door. Most of the wall was gone too. Antitank gun, Sarge thought. Blew a hole clean into the house. He could see the red leap of fires in the direction of Cade's used-car lot. And something else out there, gliding through the smoke and flames. Tiger tank, he thought. No, no. Two or three Tigers. Maybe more. But he couldn't hear the clank of treads, and the thing didn't lumber like a machine. It had the fluid, terrifying power of life.

Celeste Street had broken open. Sarge could see other shapes—human-sized, but hunchbacked things that moved with the quick purpose of ants swarming toward a meal.

The match burned his fingers. He shook it out and let it drop, and he retreated from the collapsed wall. Struck another match, because the darkness had claws. Scooter circled his legs, whining nervously. The house was no longer safe; it was laid open like a wound, and at any moment those things in the street might scurry in. Sarge dared not leave the house, but he knew he and Scooter couldn't stand out in the open like shell-shocked fools, either. He backed out of the den and into a hallway. There was a door on his left; he opened it, faced a closet full of boxes, a vacuum cleaner, other odds and ends. It was too narrow for both himself and Scooter. The match went out, and he struck a third one. Panic was eating into him. He remembered a captain's face, the man saying, *Always take the high ground.* He looked up, lifted the match, and found what he was seeking.

At the hallway's ceiling there was a little recessed square and a cord hanging down about six inches. Sarge reached up, grasped the cord, and pulled it. The square opened, and a folding metal stairway came down. Just as in his own house, there was a small attic. The high ground, Sarge thought. "Go on, Scooter!" he said, and the dog scampered up the steps. Sarge followed. The space was a little larger than the attic in his house, but still there was just enough room to lie flat on his belly. He got himself turned around, pulled the steps back up, and the attic door clicked shut.

The match died. He lay for a moment in the dark. The attic smelled of dust and smoke, but he could breathe all right. Scooter nudged up against him. "Ain't nobody can find us here," Sarge whispered. "Nobody." He scraped another match along the Fire Chief box and held it up to see what was around them.

He was lying on a mat of pink insulation, and the storage space was jammed with cardboard boxes. A broken lamp leaned against the eaves, and what appeared to be sleeping bags were rolled up within Sarge's reach. The insulation was already itching his skin. He grasped one of the sleeping bags and pulled it toward him to lie on. He got it spread out, but there was something lumpy in it. Something round, like a baseball.

He reached into it, and his hand found a cool sphere.

The match went out.

51

Scuttle and Scrape

Daufin had seen the red burst of explosions from the center of Inferno, and she knew the time had come.

Cars and pickup trucks had careened into the parking lot, people rushing to the safety of the apartment building, and Gunniston had gone to find out what was happening. Jessie, Tom, and Rhodes remained with Daufin, watching as the alien paced back and forth at the window like a desperate animal in a narrowing cage.

"I want my daughter back," Jessie said. "Where is she?"

"Safe. In my pod."

Jessie stepped forward and dared to grasp Daufin's shoulder. The alien stopped her pacing and looked up at the woman's face. "I asked you where she is. You're going to tell me."

Daufin glanced at the others. They were waiting for her to speak, and Daufin knew it was time for that too. "My pod is in your house. I put it through the upper hatch."

"Upper hatch?" Tom asked. "We don't even have an upstairs!"

"Incorrect. I put my pod through the upper hatch of your house."

"We looked through every inch of that place!" Rhodes told her. "The sphere's not there!"

But Jessie searched the child's face, and she remembered the flecks of pink insulation in the auburn hair. "We looked everywhere we thought you could reach. But we didn't check the attic, did we?"

"The *attic?* That's crazy!" Rhodes said. "She couldn't even *walk* when we found her! How could she have gotten into the attic?"

Jessie knew. "You'd already learned how to walk by the time we'd gotten there, hadn't you?"

"Yes. I did the teeah-veeah thing." She saw they didn't comprehend. "I playacted," she explained, "because I didn't want you to look through the upper hatch."

"You couldn't have reached the trapdoor by yourself," Jessie said. "What did you stand on?"

"A bodily-support instrument." She realized that hadn't translated as she'd intended. "A chair. I made sure it was back in place, exactly where it had been."

Jessie recalled the little girl pulling the chair to the window and standing up on it to press her hands against the glass. It had never occurred to her that Daufin could have used a chair once before, to reach the trapdoor's cord. She looked out at the fires and saw they were on Celeste Street, very close to their own house. "How do you know Stevie's safe?"

"My pod is . . . how do you say . . . in-de-struc-ti-ble. Nothing can break it open, not even Stinger's technology." Daufin had felt the chill sweep of the seeker beam two minutes before, and she calculated that it made a complete rotation once every four hundred and eighty Earth seconds. "What is the time, please?" she asked Tom.

"Eighteen minutes after three."

She nodded. The seeker beam should return in approximately three hundred and sixty seconds. She began a mental countdown, using the rigid Earth mathematics. "Stinger's searching for my pod with a beam of energy from his ship," she said. "The beam's been activated since Stinger landed. It's powered by a machine that's calculated the measurements and density of my pod, but the pod has a protective mechanism that deflects the beam."

"So Stinger won't be able to find it?" Jessie asked.

"Stinger hasn't found it yet. The beam's still activated." She watched the dance of the fires, and she knew she had to tell them the rest of it. "The beam's very strong. The longer I'm out of the pod, the weaker the defense mechanism becomes." She met Jessie's gaze. "I never thought I'd be out of it this long."

"You mean Stinger's got a good chance of finding out it's in our attic," Tom said.

"I can calculate the odds, if you like."

"No." Jessie didn't care to hear them because they'd be in Stinger's favor, like everything else seemed to be.

Rhodes walked to the window to get a breath of air. The last few cars were barreling into the parking lot. He wasn't sure he wanted to know what those people were running from. He turned toward Daufin. "You said you could get away in Stinger's ship. How is that possible?"

"I've escaped from Rock Seven twice before. I was hunted and taken back by Stinger both times. I know the ship's systems, and the machines that operate the controls. And I know how to use the star corridor to get home."

"If you got inside, you could find a way to shut off the force field?"

"Yes. The force field comes from the auxiliary power supply. That power is rerouted to start the . . ." There were no Earth words to describe the pyramid's flight system. "The main engines," was the best she could do.

"So the force field has to be shut down before the engines can start? How long does that take?"

"A variable amount of time, depending on how much power's been drained. I'd calculate roughly fifteen to twenty of your minutes."

He grunted, trying to clear his mind enough to think. "Sun'll be coming up in about an hour and a half. There're probably several hundred state troopers, air-force people, and reporters around the force field's perimeter by now." A faint smile touched his mouth. "I'll bet old Buckner's in charge. Bet that bastard's going crazy trying to keep the news hounds from taking pictures. What the hell: this'll be

461

all over the newspapers and TV within twelve hours and there's not a damned thing anybody can do about it." The smile faded. "If the force field was down, we'd have a chance to get out of here with our skins still on." He lifted his arm and looked at the bruise in the shape of a hand imprinted around it. "Most of us, I mean. I want you to think hard: is there *any* way to get into that ship?"

"Yes," she answered promptly. "Through Stinger's tunnels."

"I mean another way." The mention of those tunnels had sent a dagger of fear into Rhodes's heart. "How about the portal the flying thing came out of? Are there other passages into the ship?"

"No. Only the tunnels."

The breath hissed from between his teeth like air from a pierced tire, and his hope deflated with it. There was no way on God's green earth he could go back into those tunnels.

Gunniston returned from the corridor, and with him was Zarra Alhambra. "Tell them what you told me," he urged.

"Somethin' came up out of the street over in Bordertown," Zarra said to the colonel. "All of us were in the church. Cody Lockett and Rick saw it, and we cleared everybody out of the church and herded 'em over here. That's all I know, man."

"Where're Cody and Rick now?" Tom asked.

"I don't know. Everythin' was happenin' so fast. I guess they're on the way here."

Daufin felt the seeker beam rotate past, its chill prickling her skin. Her calculation had been off by four seconds.

The door opened again. It was Bobby Clay Clemmons, who'd been up on the roof keeping watch with Mike Frackner and a couple of other 'Gades. He glanced quickly at the Rattlers; any other time he would have attacked them in a blind rage for intruding on 'Gade territory, but all that was forgotten. "Hey, Colonel!" he said. "Somethin's movin' around down there!" He strode to the window, and Rhodes went with him.

Two of the cars down in the maze of vehicles still had their headlights on. At first Rhodes couldn't see much through the smoke and dust—and then he caught sight of a shape moving quickly over on the right, and another one on the left. A third shape, running low to the ground, skittered under a car and stayed there. And now more of them were coming along Travis Street. He heard the scuttle and scrape of claws as the things climbed up over the cars. He shuddered; he was reminded of walking into the kitchen of the farmhouse he'd grown up in, switching on the lights, and seeing a dozen roaches scurry off a platter of birthday cake.

Dark, scaly backs darted through the headlight beams. A spiked tail swung, and one of the lights smashed out. Another tail rose up, quivered with tension, and broke out first one headlight and then a second. The fourth and last headlight was smashed. Down in the murk, the things began to swarm toward the apartment building, their tails beating haphazardly at the sides of the cars, but they stopped at the edge of the parking lot.

"Stinger's afraid of the electric light." Daufin was standing beside Rhodes, peering over the windowsill. "It hurts him."

"Maybe it hurts Stinger, but maybe it doesn't hurt all *those* things."

"All are Stinger," she said. Her eyes followed the twitching of the spiked tails. Their hammering was becoming a regular rhythm now, like a brutal taunt. "He won't get in here while these lights are on."

Tom had already picked up his rifle from the table. Beside it was the tear-gas shotgun that Rhodes had brought in, and Gunniston still had his .45 automatic. Rhodes looked at Bobby Clay Clemmons. "Have you got any weapons here?"

"Arsenal's this way." Bobby Clay led him into the next room and switched on the battery lamp mounted to the wall. Its light revealed racks where a variety of objects hung: sawed-off baseball bats, a couple of pellet rifles, and two pairs of brass knuckles. "This all you've got?"

"That's about it." The boy shrugged. "We never . . . like . . . wanted to *kill* anybody, man. Few other things in here." He walked to a green footlocker and opened it. Inside were tools—a hammer, two or three screwdrivers, assorted jars of nails, and other junk. There were only two items that Rhodes thought might be of use: a battery-powered bull's-eye lantern and a flashlight. He pulled them out and turned them on to check the batteries. The lantern was strong enough, but the flashlight was almost dead. He took the lantern back to the other room, just in case—God forbid —something should happen to the wall lights.

The crashing of spikes against metal was steady and insistent. The noise got to Tom; he crossed the room, slid the rifle's barrel through the window, and fired at one of the dark shapes. The slug, if it hit, did not stop the rhythmic pounding.

"Save your bullets!" Rhodes told him. "Stinger's trying to psych us out." He heard more gunshots, from other windows. Bullets scratched sparks off the concrete, but the noises went on. It sounded like the tramping of an army over broken glass.

Tom was about to pull the rifle barrel back in when he saw something else out there. It was a large shape, coming steadily across the parking lot toward them, but he couldn't make out anything else. "Rhodes!" he said. "Look at—"

There was the sound of metal crumpling. And in the next second what might have been a car door crashed against the side of the building. Glass shattered in a window three or four away from the one where Tom stood. A fusillade of gunfire erupted. Rhodes came to the window, could only see the vague outline of something huge out there—and then the mashed bulk of a red Mustang hit the wall about ten feet away and slid down with a shriek of metal. Whatever it was, the bastard was strong enough to hurl a car twenty or thirty feet. "Get down, everybody!" he said, ducking below the window. The others got down too, and before she could think about what she was doing, Jessie grasped her little girl's body and pulled her close.

"Gunny!" Rhodes said. "Go down the hall and keep everybody away from the windows!" The other man hurried out. Rhodes peered up over the sill. The shape was moving closer, but not yet in the wash of the building's lights. Another piece of metal—a hood, he thought it might be—sailed out and bounced off one of the first-floor windows, but the crash and echo sounded like the place was coming to pieces. A tire followed within seconds, shattering the window two apartments to the left. Someone cried out in pain as flying glass hit them, and Daufin broke free from Jessie's grip.

She rushed to the window before anyone could stop her, and she grabbed the rifle out of Tom's hands and struggled to balance it on the sill. Even as Rhodes was reaching for her, she lodged two fingers on the trigger and squeezed. The recoil threw her backward, skidding her across the floor, but instantly she was up again and trying to drag the rifle with her. Her eyes were wild, wet with rage and frustration. Tom clutched the rifle before Daufin could get it up on the sill, and as he pulled her away from the window the wall exploded inward over their heads.

Rhodes saw the thing's tail burst through in a shower of rubble and dust. Stones clattered down around Jessie, Zarra, and Bobby Clay, and Tom protected Daufin with his body. The tail darted out again, leaving a hole as big around as a washtub. Rhodes looked out the window, got a nerve-shredding glimpse of the creature's head as it scuttled back from the light's edge. As it retreated, it slashed out with its tail again and the spikes shrieked past the wall.

Daufin squirmed away from Tom, her skin radiating little shocks like an electric eel, and leapt up onto the windowsill. Rhodes thought she was going to jump through, and he dared to grab her arms. A shock coursed through him, rattling his teeth, but he hung on. *"No!"* he shouted, trying to hold her back as she thrashed like an animal.

Her attention was only on one thing: getting out of this box and leading Stinger away from the humans trapped here. But suddenly she saw the huge shape coming through the smoke; the white light washed onto its head, glinting off the needle teeth in its thick, elongated jaws. Two of the eyes ticked toward her, while two aimed at another window, and for a second she thought she could see her face reflected on the thin black pupils. Whether those eyes knew her or not, she didn't know: they were as cold and impassive as the icy vaults of deep space. Stinger kept scurrying forward, the tail rising up behind it like a deadly question mark. The full glare of the electric light fell onto its head. There was a sizzling sound that made Rhodes think of bacon on a grill; he saw the creature's eyes blistering and oozing where the light touched them. The tail whipped forward, and Rhodes yanked Daufin out of the window and to the floor. The spikes crashed into the wall of the apartment next door. There was a cacophony of screams, and the entire second level shook.

Brick dust filled the room. Rhodes sat up, peered out, but the thing had retreated from the light. In the parking lot the tails of the other Stingers kept up their steady, martial drumbeat. Daufin was lying on her side, breathing heavily, knowing that Stinger was trying to smash out the lights. Then something hit her like a physical blow: the seeker beam had been due to pass twelve seconds ago. Her mental countdown was still progressing. Where was the seeker beam? If it had been turned off . . .

She didn't want to think about what that might mean.

"Hang on," Rhodes said tersely. "It's coming back." He reached for Tom's rifle.

In the close darkness of the Hammonds' attic, Scooter began growling. Sarge lit another match and held it to the ebony sphere in his hand. Couldn't see anything in it, but when he shook it he thought he could hear the quiet slosh of liquid. Thing was as cool as if it had just come out of a refrigerator. He pressed it against his cheeks and forehead like a piece of ice. Scooter got up off the sleeping bag and gave a nervous yip, and Sarge said, "Don't you fret, now. Ol' Sarge'll take care of—"

The house trembled, and from downstairs came the scream of splitting wood.

"—you," he finished thickly.

There was a crash of furniture either falling or being thrown over, then silence. Scooter whined and pressed against Sarge's side, and Sarge put his arm around his best friend. The match went out, but he didn't try to light another because the scrape on the box would be too loud.

The silence stretched. Then came the sound of footsteps, entering the hallway. They stopped just below the attic's hatch.

The hatch was jerked open, and the steps unfolded.

Sarge crawled away from it, his hand clenching the black sphere.

"Come down," a man's voice said. "Bring the pod with you."

Sarge didn't move. Scooter growled softly.

"If you have a light, I want you to throw it down to me." An impatient pause. "You don't want to get me super pissed, do you?"

The voice had a Texan accent, but there was something wrong with it. Around the words was a rattling, as if whoever was speaking had a nest of snakes in his throat. And now there was another noise too: a low moan that sounded like a dog in agony.

Sarge tossed the box of matches down the hatch. A hand caught and crumpled it. "Now you and the pod."

He didn't know what the man meant about a "pod," but he whispered shakily to Scooter, "We're gonna have to go down there. Ain't no way around it." He slid toward the hatch, and Scooter followed.

A man-sized shape stood in the hallway. As Sarge reached the bottom of the steps, a hand grabbed the sphere away from him so fast it was only seconds later that Sarge felt pain and the welling of blood from his fingers. Fella's got sharp nails, he thought. Scratched the fool out of me. He could see the man lift the sphere up before his face. There was something writhing at the man's chest, where nothing ought to be but skin and shirt.

The man whispered, *"I've got you."* And the way he said that made the flesh crawl at the back of Sarge's neck.

The hand placed the sphere down in that writhing mass on his chest. Sarge heard the click of fangs as the sphere was accepted.

And then the man's arm—as damp and slimy as a centipede's belly—hooked around Sarge and lifted him off the floor, squeezing the breath out of him. Sarge was too stunned to fight back, and before he knew what was happening the man was striding toward a gaping hole in the den's floor. Sarge tried to call for Scooter, couldn't summon up his voice, and then the man had walked into the hole and they were falling. Sarge wet his pants.

The man's legs hit bottom like shock absorbers, but the impact traveled through Sarge's body and made his head feel like a sack of shattered glass. Sarge gave a muffled groan. The man began running through the winding dark, boots making a *shuckshuckshuck* noise in the ooze, and carried Sarge away.

52
The Trade

The creature's tail slammed through the wall into the room where Curt Lockett and four other people hugged the floor. Bricks flew, and one of them hit the battery lamp that hung on the wall near the door and broke it to pieces. The light went out. Curt heard the boom of a shotgun from the next room. The tail thrashed over his head and exited in a boil of dust, and Curt crabbed out of the room into the corridor as fast as he could move.

The hall was packed full. Dozens of Inferno and Bordertown people crouched close to each other in the sharp glare of the lights, so tight they looked like they were melded together. Dust was billowing through the corridor, babies were crying and so were a few full-grown men. Curt felt pretty near tears himself. He'd come here hunting Cody, but one of the Renegades had told him that Cody was gone. So Curt had stayed to wait for him, and then all hell had broken loose. He crawled away from the door, getting another wall in between himself and that big sonofabitch with the spiked tail. Somebody was babbling in Mexican right next to his ear, but the bodies shifted to give him shelter.

The floor heaved. More bricks caved in, and screams swelled. An old woman was sobbing next to him, and

469

suddenly her hands were on his arm, moving along the forearm until they locked with his fingers. He looked into her wrinkled face and saw that her eyes were clouded with cataracts. She kept rocking back and forth, and the man beside her put his arm around her shoulders.

Curt and Xavier Mendoza stared at each other. "Where's Cody?" Mendoza asked.

"Still out there somewhere."

The old woman began speaking frantically in Spanish, and Mendoza tried to comfort her as best he could. Paloma Jurado was desperate to find out what had happened to Rick and Miranda, but as far as Mendoza knew they hadn't gotten to the building yet.

Curt saw the fat bulk of Stan Frazier squeezed up against the wall not far away. The man was sweating buckets, and he had a shiny hogleg Colt pistol clamped in his hands. When the building shook again, Curt pulled his hand free and crawled to his neighbor. "Hey, Frazier! You usin' that?"

Frazier made a little gasping noise, his tongue lolling around in a shocked white face. Curt said, "Don't mind if I do," and worked the gun out of the sausagey fingers. Then he crawled back on his belly into the room he'd just vacated, where there were two holes in the walls the size of truck wheels. He crouched at the shattered window, pulled the Colt's hammer back, and waited for that battering ram on legs to come out of the smoke again. He would've given his left nut for one sip of Kentucky Gent, but there was no time to let the craving take him because the smoke parted and there was the creature's shape again, skittering forward. The tail whipped out, hit the wall somewhere to Curt's right, and hurled a storm of bricks. Curt started firing, heard two of the bullets ricochet off body armor but two more made a satisfying *splat* as if they'd hit softer tissue. The tail swung in his direction, passed the window, and crashed into the wall of the room next to him. The floor shuddered as if a bomb had gone off. Curt fired the last two shots and saw gray fluid spray from a foreleg—then the thing had withdrawn into the murk again and there was a crunching noise as it backed over cars.

"Here."

Curt looked around. Mendoza had left Paloma Jurado with his wife and uncle and crawled into the room. He offered his palm, and in it were four more bullets. "He had these in his pocket," Mendoza said. "I thought you might need them."

"I reckon so." Curt hastily dumped the empty cartridges and reloaded. His hands were shaking. "Bitch of a night, huh?"

Mendoza grunted, allowed himself a grim smile. "*Sí*. You look like somebody stepped on you."

"Feel like it too." A bead of sweat swung from the tip of Curt's nose. "Got in a little scrape up on Highway Sixty-seven awhile back. You don't have a cigarette on you, do you?"

"No, sorry."

"Gotta be some smokes around here somewhere." He clicked the cylinder back in true and lined up a bullet under the hammer. "You seen my boy tonight?"

"He was over in Bordertown about twenty minutes ago. That was the last I saw of him."

"He'll be all right. Cody's tough. Like his old man." Curt laughed harshly. Mendoza began to crawl back to his family, but Curt said, "Hold on. I want to say somethin' to you, and I reckon this is the time to do it. Cody seems to think you're okay. He's a damn fool about a lot of things, but judgin' people ain't one of 'em. You must've given him a pretty fair deal. Guess I appreciate that."

"He's a good boy," Mendoza said. He found it hard to look into Curt's watery, sick-dog eyes. "He's going to be a better man."

"Better than me, you mean."

This time Mendoza met Curt's gaze. "*Sí*," he answered. "That's exactly what I mean."

"Ain't no skin off my ass what you think of me. You've been decent to my boy, and I said thanks. That's it." He turned his back on Mendoza.

The other man had a hard knot of anger in his stomach. He didn't know what gave Curt the right to call Cody his "boy." From what he'd seen, Curt only had use for Cody to clean up the house or bring money and cigarettes home to him. Well, a dog couldn't change his smell. Mendoza said, "You're welcome," through gritted teeth and returned to his wife and uncle.

One thing that old wetback forgot to say, Curt thought. Cody'll be a better man *if he's still alive*. No telling what was roaming around out there in the dust and smoke, and where Cody might be. Why that damn kid went over to Bordertown I'll never figure out, he told himself. But one thing I know for sure: I'll kick his butt till it sings Dix—

No. No you won't.

Curt leaned his chin against his gunhand. Those long-tailed bastards out there were still playing a tune on metal, like they knew they were taunting everybody in the building. He started to squeeze off a bullet and then figured he'd better save them. It was a damned funny thing: his head was clear, and he felt all right. His raw flesh was still leaking and hurting like hell, but he could stand the pain. He wasn't scared—at least, not petrified. Maybe it was because Treasure was with him. If the boy showed up—*when* he showed up—Curt was going to . . . well, he didn't exactly know what he would do, but it wouldn't be violent. Maybe he'd tell the boy how nice that tie rack looked on the wall, and how he hoped the boy would do more work like that. Say it and mean it. Maybe try to lay off the juice too; that wouldn't be too hard, considering that for the rest of his life he would hear bones crack when he had a whiff of whiskey. But there was a long way to go, a lot of bad things in between him and Cody. They would have to be shoveled aside, one by one. And that, he figured, was how everything on God's earth got done.

Someone touched his shoulder, and he spun around and put the pistol's barrel into a young man's face. "What the hell you doin', sneakin' up like that?"

"Colonel Rhodes says he wants everybody away from the windows," Gunniston told him, and eased the pistol aside.

"Too late in here, fella. Window's done busted."

"Better clear out and stay in the hallway, though."

Gunniston started to crawl out and head for the next room down.

"Hey!" The name had just clicked through to Curt. "Who'd you say? Colonel Rhodes?" When Gunniston nodded, Curt said, "I've got a message for him. Where is he?"

"Six doors up the hall," Gunniston said, and moved on.

Curt crawled out, past Stan Frazier, stood up, and made his way through the corridor without stepping on more than seven or eight people. He counted off five apartments and at the sixth, the door that had HQ and KNOCK FIRST spray-painted on it in red, he went in without knocking. Inside, crouched on the floor, were two boys Curt recognized as friends of Cody's, the lady vet and her husband and little girl, and a man with a black crewcut who was on his knees at the window. The man had a rifle, and he'd swung it up at Curt just as the door had opened.

Curt lifted his hands. "You Colonel Rhodes?"

"That's right. Put your gun on the table."

Curt did. Rhodes looked like a man you didn't argue with. His eyes were sunken in dark hollows, and his face was puffy and speckled with glass cuts. "I'm Curt Lockett. Can I put my hands down?" Rhodes nodded and lowered the rifle, and Curt eased his arms to his sides. "I was up on Highway Sixty-seven, right at the edge of where that purple cage comes down. There's a whole bunch of trooper cars and people on the other side of it. Lot of government brass too. You know a Colonel Buckner?"

"Yes."

"He's up there with 'em. He was writin' on a pad and showin' it to me, 'cause I could see 'em but I couldn't hear 'em. Anyway, he wanted to make sure you were okay and find out what was goin' on. I was supposed to take you the message."

"Thanks. I guess it's a little late."

"Yeah." Curt looked at the battered wall. "I guess it is." His gaze went to the little girl. She was trembling, and he knelt down beside her. "Don't fret none, little darlin'. We're gonna get out of this, sure as—"

"Thank you for your concern," she said, and her ancient,

white-hot eyes went through him like lasers through tissue paper, "but I am *not* a little darling."

Curt's smile hung by a lip. "Oh," he said—or thought he did—and stood up.

"Colonel, listen!" Tom said. The rhythmic beating of the creatures' tails on metal was slowing. The noise stopped. He peered out the window, could see the smaller shapes moving away amid the cars. The larger one had drawn back into the murk and disappeared. "They're leaving!"

Rhodes looked out, verified that the creatures were indeed retreating. "What's going on?" he asked Daufin. "Is this some kind of trick?"

"I don't know." She came forward to see. The seeker beam still hadn't returned, and that could mean only one thing: her pod had been found. But maybe not; maybe the beam had malfunctioned, or maybe its power drain was too severe. She knew she was, as these humans might say, grasping at cylindrical drinking tubes.

Tom and Rhodes watched the creatures moving away until the haze swallowed them. Fires still burned on Celeste Street, and from off in the distance there was a crash of timbers exploding into the air: maybe the monster's wrecking-ball tail knocking a house to fragments. A silence fell, except for the noise of crying babies and adult sobbing.

"Those sonsofbitches gonna come back?" Curt asked.

"I'm not sure," Rhodes answered. "Looks like they might be calling it quits."

Daufin strung the meaning of that term together in about three seconds. "Incorrect," she said. "Stinger does not call it quits."

"You sure talk funny for a little girl," Curt told her. "No disrespect meant," he said to Jessie. And then he remembered something he wished he could forget: Laurey Rainey rising out of the Bob Wire Club's floor, and her rattling voice saying *Ya'll are gonna tell me about the little girl. The one who's the guardian.* Whatever was going on here, he wasn't sure he wanted to know about it. "Anybody got a cigarette and a match?" Bobby Clay Clemmons gave him the last six Luckies in the pack and a little plastic Bic lighter. Curt lit up and inhaled down to the depths of his lungs.

"Daufin? I know you're in there!"

The voice came from the parking lot. The heart hammered in Daufin's chest, and she wavered on her feet: but she knew it had only been a matter of time, and now the time had come.

"Daufin? That's what they call you, isn't it? Come on, answer me!"

Tom and Jessie recognized Mack Cade's voice. Rhodes thought he could make out a figure standing atop a car just beyond the edge of the light, but he wasn't sure. The voice might be coming from anywhere.

"Don't make this any harder than it has to be! My time is money!"

Curt sat on the floor, the cigarette clenched in a corner of his mouth and his eyes narrowed behind a screen of smoke. He watched the little girl that he knew was no longer truly human. Tom started to pull her away from the window, but she said, "No," and he let her alone.

"You want me to stomp a few more bugs in the dirt, I will!" Stinger promised. "It's up to you!"

The chase was over. Daufin knew it, and all her hiding was done. "I'm here!" she called back, and her voice drifted through the smoke to the figure she could just barely see.

"Now that wasn't so hard, was it? You gave me a good run, I'll say that for you. Gave me the slip in that asteroid field, but you knew I'd find you. A garbage scow's not built for speed."

"They're not built for reliability, either," she said.

"No, I guess not. You want to come on now? It'll take awhile for my engines to warm up."

Daufin hesitated. She could feel the walls of Rock Seven closing around her, and a torture of needles and probes awaited.

"I don't really need you anymore," Stinger said. "I've got your pod. That's enough to secure my bounty. When I take off, there's no way for you to get back to your planet. But I thought maybe—just maybe—you might like to trade."

"Trade for what?"

"I've got three live bugs in my ship. Their names are Sarge Dennison, Miranda Jurado, and Cody Lockett."

Curt sat very still. He stared straight ahead, and wisps of smoke curled from his nostrils. Belly-down on the floor, Zarra whispered, *"Madre de Dios."*

Daufin looked at Tom and Jessie, and they saw Stevie's features pinched with agony. Jessie felt faint; if Stinger had the pod, he had Stevie too. She lowered her head, tears beginning to creep down her cheeks.

"I'm waiting," Stinger prompted.

Daufin drew a deep breath. Another Earth phrase, one taught her by Tank and Nasty, came to mind: *up shit creek.* The humans had done all they could for her; now she would have to do all she could for *them.* "Let them go and I'll come to you," she said.

"Right!" Stinger laughed dryly. "I didn't get to be this old by being stupid. You come to me first, then I let them go."

She knew Stinger would never set them free. They would bring him a bonus from the House of Fists. "I need time to think."

"You have no more time!" It was an angry shout. "Either you come out right now or I take your pod and the three bugs! Understand?"

Curt smiled grimly, but his eyes were glazed. "God-damned Mexican standoff," he muttered, with no apologies to Zarra.

"Yes," Daufin answered. Her voice cracked. "I understand."

"Good. Now we're getting somewhere, right? Lot of bad vibes in this dump, Daufin. At least you could've crashed on a planet that *smells* better."

Rhodes eased the rifle's barrel out the window, but Daufin said quietly, "Don't," and he took his finger off the trigger. Daufin raised her voice: "Take them. I'm not coming."

There was a shocked silence. Jessie pulled her knees up to her chin and began to rock like a child. Curt watched the cigarette smoke drift toward the ceiling.

"I don't think I heard you," Stinger replied.

"Yes you did. Take them. My pod and the three humans. I'd rather die here than live in a prison." She felt the blood rushing into her face. With it came a torrent of rage, and she leaned precariously out the window and shouted, *"Go on and take them!"*

"Well, well," Stinger said. "I misjudged you, didn't I? You sure that's how you want to play it out?"

"I'm sure."

"So be it. I hope you like this place, Daufin; you're going to be here for a mighty long time. I'll think about you when I jingle my change." The figure, which had been shielding its eyes with its single arm, got down off the car and strode away.

As Stinger left the parking lot, another figure rose up from between two cars over on the far left, almost to the red boulders that ended Oakley Street, and hobbled toward the fortress.

"Stevie . . . oh my God . . . Stevie," Jessie moaned, her hands cupped to her mouth.

There was stark terror in the woman's voice: an emotion that translated in any language. Daufin pivoted from the window, walked to Jessie, and knelt down in front of her. "Listen to me!" Daufin said urgently. Looked at the others, her eyes blazing. "All of you listen! Stinger would never let them go! They're worth more of a bounty to him!"

"So that's it." Rhodes let the rifle rest at his side. He felt a hundred years old. "Stinger's won."

53
One Way

"No!" Daufin said fiercely. "Stinger has *not* won!" She peered into Jessie's eyes. "I won't let Stinger win. Not now. Not ever." Jessie didn't speak, but she wanted desperately to believe.

Daufin stood up. "The process of systems checks will have already begun, all regulated by machines. There'll be other duties, like the freezing of sleep tubes for his prisoners. Stinger will be busy monitoring the machines; the procedure should take between twenty to thirty Earth minutes. When the force field is turned off, the engines will start to energize. I calculate another fifteen to twenty minutes for the power system to reach lift-off capacity. So: I have roughly thirty-five to fifty minutes to breach Stinger's ship, find the prisoners, and get them out."

Rhodes stared at her with utter disbelief. "No way."

"One way: through the tunnels. I've got to find the entrance nearest Stinger's ship. I presume that would be somewhere across the bridge."

With an effort, Jessie spoke. "Even . . . if you could get them out . . . what about Stevie? How are we going to get Stevie back?"

"Find the pod. Take it from Stinger. As I've said, I've been aboard a Stinger's ship twice before, and I know how the systems work. I can enter the navigational quadrants for my world into the guidance mechanism, put everything on automatic, place my pod in a sleep tube, and meld into it before the freezing process is finished. When I enter the pod, Stevie will be freed."

"But still in the pyramid," Tom said. "And how are you going to find the pod *and* those three people inside that thing? It must be huge!"

"I know from experience where the prisoners are being held: level three, where the cages are. The pod will be close to Stinger."

"So you find Stinger and you find the pod, is that what you mean?" Rhodes asked. He raised his eyebrows. "Have you considered that Stinger *wants* you to come after them?"

"Yes. I won't disappoint."

"That's crazy!" Rhodes insisted. "Maybe you're some kind of firebrand on your world, but on this one you're just a little girl! First thing, you'd have to get through the tunnels—and my guess is that Stinger's got replicants in there waiting for you; and secondly, you'd have to kill Stinger to take the ship. How are you going to do that?"

"I don't know," she answered. "I've never seen a Stinger killed before."

"Great!" Rhodes frowned and shook his head. "We don't have a chance, folks."

"I didn't say that Stinger *couldn't* be killed," Daufin continued, and the strength of her voice revitalized Jessie's waning hope. "Stinger must have a vulnerable spot, just like every other creature. If Stinger were invulnerable, there'd be no need for the replicants."

"A vulnerable spot," Rhodes repeated quietly. "Right. Well, I wouldn't go down into those tunnels without a grenade launcher and a few dozen napalm bombs. It'd be suicide."

"I'm willing to risk it." Tom grasped the rifle and retrieved it from the other man. His face was pale and sweating, his lips a tight gray line. "I'm going with Daufin."

"And get yourself killed? Forget it!"

Jessie reached up and took Daufin's hand. Little waves of

static electricity flowed between them. "Tell me the truth: can we get Stevie out of there?"

"We can try. I want to go home as badly as you want Stevie. If my tribe doesn't fight, they'll die. If the House of Fists returns here, your Earth will die. Neither of us has a choice."

Jessie nodded, and looked at Tom. "I'm going too." She stood up.

Before Tom or Rhodes could respond, the door opened and Gunniston came in. With him this time were Rick Jurado and Pequin. Rick's face was streaked with dust and grime and his swollen ankle was bound up as tight as he could stand with a strip of sheet from the Smart Dollar. He had come out amid the houses at the end of Oakley Street in time to hear Stinger's message, had checked with Mendoza and his grandmother, and then snagged Gunniston and Pequin. He nodded a greeting at Zarra, relieved to see his friend was still alive, then directed his attention to the colonel. Underneath the dust, Rick's skin had bleached a couple of shades but his eyes were hard and determined. "That thing's got my sister! What are we going to do about it, man?"

"Nothing," Rhodes said. "I'm sorry, but there's no—"

"Yes there is!" Rick had shouted it. "I'm not letting that bastard take Miranda!"

"We're going into the ship and get them back," Jessie told him. "Tom, Daufin, and me."

"Dream on." Rhodes wiped sweat out of his eyes. "You go into those tunnels, there's no way anybody's coming back again. Hell, even if you *did* get to the ship, what would you use for weapons? Maybe you could round up a few more guns, okay, but I don't think bullets are going to do Stinger much harm."

"We need electric lights." Daufin was aware of time ticking away. "Strong ones."

Tom said, "We could take some of the lamps off the walls and figure a way to carry them. Maybe wire three or four of them together. Plus we've got that." He motioned at the bull's-eye lantern.

"We've got a whole lot more." Rick turned to Pequin. "You hung around with Sonny Crowfield, didn't you? Did you know about the arsenal?"

"What arsenal?"

"Don't play dumb, man! I found all those guns and shit in Crowfield's closet! What was he about to try?"

Pequin started to deny it again, but he knew Rick would see the lie. "Sonny . . . was gonna start a war with the 'Gades. Gonna make it look like the 'Gades were burnin' down houses in Bordertown."

"But they weren't?"

"No. I was with him when he set the fires." Pequin shrugged. "We wanted some action, that's all."

"I want to know about the dynamite."

Pequin stared at the floor. He could smell the blood that was spattered over the front of Rick's shirt. "Sonny, me and Paco LeGrande went over the fence into the mine, couple of months ago. Just screwin' around. We found the shed where they used to keep the dynamite. We thought the place was just full of empty boxes at first, but Paco stepped on a loose board and his foot went through. We found the sticks in the dirt underneath, so we put 'em in a box and brought 'em out."

"To do what? Blow up somebody's house over here?"

"No." Pequin smiled sheepishly, showing his silver tooth. "To blow this place up, when the war started."

"There are five sticks of dynamite—with caps and fuses —in Sonny Crowfield's house over in Bordertown," Rick said to Colonel Rhodes. "And more guns and ammo too. Sonny's one of those things now: there's a hole in the floor, and how far down it goes I don't know."

"Where is this house?" Daufin asked.

"On Third Street." Like she would really know where that was, he thought. "Right next to where the spaceship's sitting."

"That would be the nearest way into the ship, with the least distance of tunnel to go through," she said. "Dy-na-mite." Her memory found the definition: an explosive compound usually formed into a cylinder and detonated by lighting a fuse. "What does it look like?"

"Like a ticket to hell, if you ain't careful," Curt replied. He drew on his cigarette and held it up. "Kinda like that, only bigger. Meaner too." He crushed the butt out on the floor. "You got capped and fused dynamite lyin' around untended for God knows how long, you're askin' to get blown to smithereens."

"Some of the sticks looked burned," Rick said. "Like they'd been lit before but hadn't gone off."

"Duds. A dud sometimes don't stay a dud, though. You can't tell about dynamite—especially not that cheap shit ol' man Preston shipped in. That stuff might go if you looked at it cross-eyed, or then again you might burn it with a flamethrower and it'd just sit there and sputter."

Daufin didn't follow most of what the man had said, but she knew even a crude explosive might be useful. "We'll need rope," she said to Rick.

"We can get plenty of that at the hardware store. And there's wire to tie the lamps together too."

"Then that's where we should go first." Tom moved to the wall and lifted one of the battery lamps off its hook. "Get ourselves organized and go from there."

"You mean get yourselves screwed up and slaughtered!" The power of Rhodes's shout silenced everyone. "My God, you're going at this thing like scouts on a field trip!" He advanced on Tom Hammond and gripped the rifle. "What are you going to do when something with metal claws comes out of the ground and grabs your gun? Or your throat? You'll wind up either getting slashed to pieces or blowing everybody else up! Will that get Stevie back for you?" He glared at Daufin. "Will that get you home?"

"Man, if you haven't got any balls just stay here!" Rick told him.

"You'll be the first to get your balls torn off," Rhodes said. He held Rick's stare for a couple of seconds, and then he pulled at the rifle. Tom resisted him. The colonel's face was gray, his eyes deep-sunken, but there was still a lot of strength in his grip and some of his fire had returned. "First," he said, "you need a leader."

"I can lead them," Daufin asserted.

"Not in the body of a little girl, you can't. Not in a body you don't *own*. Maybe you know a hell of a lot I don't, but flesh is flesh and if it gets flayed off there'll be nothing for Stevie to come back to." He pulled harder at the rifle. "Give it to me. With the lights and the dynamite, we might have a chance. *Might,* I said." Fear of those tunnels and the things that would be waiting in them clawed at his stomach, but Daufin was right: they had to try. "I'll lead you."

Gunniston said instantly, "I'm going too, sir."

"Negative. If I don't come out, you'll be needed to brief Colonel Buckner. You're staying here." The other man started to protest. "That's an order," Rhodes emphasized, and Gunniston remained silent.

Tom gave up the rifle. "All right." Rhodes looked around at the others. "If Daufin's right about the time factor, we've got to get moving. Who else is going besides Jessie and Rick?"

Bobby Clay Clemmons backed against the wall. Zarra started to speak, but Rick cut him short: "You're staying. You take care of Paloma, understand?" He waited until Zarra nodded.

"Mr. Lockett?" Rhodes asked. On the floor, Curt had taken a picture out of his pants pocket, unfolded it, and now stared fixedly at the girl's face. He didn't answer Rhodes, and a shadow lay across his eyes.

"That's it, then. We need to round up some more lamps and flashlights. Let's get to it," he said, before good sense could overrule his decision.

Curt stayed where he was as the others left. Rick paused to untie the strip of sheet, draw it as tightly as he could bear, and then knot it again. The pain was a deep, pulsing ache but no bones had been broken. He said, "You're Cody Lockett's father?"

"Yeah." Curt refolded the photograph and put it away. "Cody's my son."

"We'll get him out of there. Him and my sister both." Rick saw the hogleg Colt on the table and picked it up. "This yours?"

"Yes."

"Mind if I take it?"

Curt said, "Lordy, Lordy, Lordy," and fresh sweat sparkled on his face. He closed his eyes for a few seconds; when he opened them, the same old world was still there, and he thought he could feel it spinning on its axis like a runaway carnival ride. He had a thirst like a chunk of sun lodged down his throat. He stood up, a sneer warping his mouth. "The day I let a wetback kid do my job is the day I'm not fit to be pissed on," he said, and his hand closed around the Colt.

54

The Cage

Cody heard Miranda moan. She was coming to, and Cody crawled across the leathery floor to her.

"My head . . . my head," she whispered, pressing her hand against the blue bruise and knot on her forehead above her left eye. Her eyelids fluttered, and she tried to open them but they were just too heavy.

"She gonna be all right?"

Cody glanced over at Sarge, who sat about five feet away with his arms locked around his knees. Sarge's face had taken on a chalky cast in the violet glow of the cage's bars. "I don't know," Cody said. "She took a pretty hard knock." She was still moaning, her voice softer as she drifted off again. Cody had spat up a little blood, and he was breathing in gasps around the pain of a broken rib, but otherwise he was okay. He was more mad than scared, and his muscles were pumped full of adrenaline. Miranda lay still again. Cody checked her pulse for the sixth or seventh time; it felt a little slow to him, but at least it was strong. She was a lot tougher than she looked.

Cody stood up, holding his side, and made another circle of their cage. It was a cone about fifteen feet around, with bars of purple light. He'd already tested the bars by kicking at them, and the sole of his boot had been burned almost clean through, fiery speckles of melting rubber shearing off and those bits exploding again as they went into the bars. What those beams would do to flesh he didn't want to know. The entire cage was suspended about three feet off the floor, which was made of interlocked black scales.

He didn't know what he'd expected the inside of the spaceship to look like—maybe full of high-tech, polished chrome gizmos that whirred with mysterious purpose; but this place smelled like an overflowed cesspool and puddles of ooze shimmered on the floor. Pipes that looked as if they were made of diseased dinosaur bones hung from the ceiling and snaked along the walls, and from them came a rushing, thrumming sound of something liquid passing through. The musty air was so cold and damp that Cody could see his breath, but the chill had sharpened his senses. The impression he got of the spaceship was that it was not a marvel of alien technology, but rather the inside of a medieval castle that lacked heat, electricity, and sanitation. Slime festooned the bony pipes, and when it dripped, it made slithering sounds on the floor. One thing he thought he'd seen but couldn't be sure of: not only were the floor's scales absorbing the ooze, but every so often they seemed to swell an inch or two upward and deflate again, as if they were alive and breathing.

Cody stopped his circling. He stood close to the bars but could feel no sensation of heat; the beams burned with a cold fire. On the chamber's floor was a small black pyramid about the size of a shoebox. He'd seen Stinger's boot touch that pyramid when his head was dangling down and the thing's arm was about to crush him. The pyramid had glowed from within with dim violet light. There'd been a droning noise, and the next thing he knew he and Miranda were being dumped onto a black dish that turned out to be the cage's floor. As the cage's bars had illuminated, the cage itself had ascended.

Later—and how much later Cody didn't know because his brain was still jammed up—a creature with Mack Cade's face and the head and shoulders of a dog growing from its chest had entered the chamber carrying another body. Cody had watched as the creature's boot had touched the pyramid. The violet light had come on, the cage had begun to settle, and when it reached the floor the beams had extinguished. Then Sarge Dennison had been added to the cage, the creature had touched the pyramid once more, and the bars had flickered to life. Again the cage rose off the floor, and Stinger had looked at Sarge and asked his name, just as he'd asked Cody what the girl's name was. It had taken Sarge a few seconds to even understand what the question was, but finally he'd stuttered his name out and Stinger had left—but not before Cody had seen the black sphere gripped between the dog's jaws.

He stared at the small pyramid, now dark. An on–off switch, Cody assumed. Touching it would lower the cage and turn off the bars. But it was three feet below them and at least another three feet beyond the cage's edge. Way too far to reach, even if he could get his arm between the bars without burning it off up to the elbow. Still . . . that was the only way out he could see, and he didn't know what Stinger had planned for them but he figured it wouldn't be pleasant.

He dug into his pocket and came up with a dime, four pennies, and his lighter. How much pressure was needed to trip the switch? The weight of the lighter hitting it might be enough—but he quickly dismissed that idea, because if the lighter was punctured, the fluid would explode all over the cage. He put the lighter back in his pocket, lay down on his stomach, and stretched his flattened hand toward the bars edge-on while his thumb trapped the coins. The space between the bars was wide enough to accept his hand, and he kept gliding his wrist through, grateful for his slim build. The pain in his ribs flared up again; when he gasped for breath, the movement made his arm drift a fraction to the right.

The hair on his forearm crisped, burning away with faint crackling noises. Cody held himself as still as he could, but the effort was making his arm shake. Now his palm was sweating. He tried to get the coins in position to flick them at the small pyramid, and he promptly lost the dime and one of the pennies, which fell straight down to the floor. His hand was cramping, and he had no time to aim: he flung both coins out with a snap of his wrist, saw one hit beyond the pyramid and the other to the left.

"Shit!" he said, and pulled his arm and hand back through the bars. All the hair up to the middle of his forearm had been burned away, but his skin was untouched. Another fraction of an inch, though, and the cage would smell of burned meat. His arm was trembling right down into the shoulder socket, and he saw that tripping that switch was pretty much hopeless. He crawled away from the edge and sat back on his haunches, rubbing his shoulder. He looked up; overhead eight feet or so the violet beams merged together at the top of the cage, and the mechanism that hoisted the cage was somewhere above that. His gaze returned to the small pyramid on the floor. "Got to be some way to reach it," he said.

"Reach what?" Sarge asked.

"That thing there." Cody pointed down to it, and Sarge saw what he meant and nodded. "I think it controls the cage. If I could trigger it with somethin' I might be able to—"

"Cody?" Miranda's voice was a pained whisper. She was trying to sit up, her eyes wide and bloodshot. "Cody?"

He got to her side. "Take it easy. Come on, just lie still."

"What happened? Where are we?" She looked around, saw the violet bars that circled them. "Rick . . . where's Rick?"

"Rick's okay," he lied. She blinked up at him. "He made it over the bridge."

"We . . . hit something, didn't we? Oh . . . my head . . ." Her hand found the bruise and knot. She winced, fresh tears trickling from the corners of her eyes. Her memory was hazy; she remembered a figure in front of them on the bridge, a jarring collision, and a sensation of falling. Mercifully there was nothing after that. "Are you all right?"

"I've been better." Cody smoothed the damp curls away from her forehead. Concussion, he figured. "Can you feel this?" He rubbed her hands, and she said, "Yes." Then her ankles. "Yes," Miranda responded, and Cody relaxed some. She had friction burns on her arms and a split and swollen lower lip, but he figured it could've been a lot worse: a broken back, broken arms or legs—and surely a broken neck if Stinger hadn't been stopped.

"We hit . . . the Mumbler, didn't we?" she asked.

Cody smiled faintly. "We sure did. Knocked him on his ass too."

"I . . . thought you said you could drive that motor."

"I think I did a pretty good job. We're not dead, are we?"

"I'm not sure yet." Now it was her turn to offer him the hint of a tough smile, though her eyes were still vague. "I think I should've stayed in Fort Worth."

"Yeah, but then you would never have met *me.*"

"Bit shit," she said, and he knew she was going to be okay. The strength was coming back into her voice.

He decided Miranda wasn't going to pass out again, and he had to tell her what had happened and where they were. "We're inside the spaceship," he said. "In what looks like a dungeon, I think. Anyway, we're hangin' in Stinger's idea of a jail cell." He waited for her response, but there was none. "Stinger could've killed us. He didn't. He wants us alive, which is just fine with me."

"Me too," Sarge said, and Miranda lifted her head to see who'd spoken. "I'm Sarge," he told her. "This is Scooter right over here." He gestured into the empty space.

"Scooter's his dog," Cody quickly explained. "Um . . . Sarge doesn't go anywhere without Scooter, if you get my drift."

Miranda eased herself into a sitting position. Her head still pounded, but at least she could see straight now. She wasn't sure who was crazy and who wasn't, but then Sarge started rubbing an invisible dog and said, "Don't you worry none, Scooter. I'll take care of you," and she realized Sarge lived in a permanent twilight zone.

"Sorry I got you into this," Cody said to her. "You ought to be more particular who you ride with."

"Next time I will be." She tried to stand, but she felt so

weak she had to rest her head against her knees. "What's that thing keeping us for?"

"I don't know. I wouldn't want to guess, either." Cody thought that the noise of fluid rushing through the pipes had gotten louder. There was another sound too: a distant reverberation, like a muffled bass drum or a heartbeat. Whole damn ship's alive, he thought. "We've got to get out of here." He crawled over to the cage's edge, just short of the light bars, and stared down at the small pyramid again. Got to trip that switch, he knew. But how? "Don't happen to have a slingshot on you, do you?" he asked half jokingly, and of course she shook her head no. He lay on his belly, his chin resting on his hands, and just looked at the pyramid. His belt buckle was jabbing his stomach, and he shifted his position.

Belt buckle, he thought.

He abruptly sat up, unbuckled the belt, and reeled it out of the loops.

Sarge said, "Hey, don't do that in front of a lady!"

"How far would you say that thing is?" he asked Miranda, and pointed at the pyramid.

"I don't know. Seven feet, maybe."

"I peg it closer to six and a half. I wear a twenty-eight-inch belt, and . . ." He looked at Sarge, saw the scuffed black belt in the man's dungarees. "Sarge, hand me your belt."

"My *belt?* Boy, what's wrong with you?"

"Take it off, Sarge! Come on, hurry!"

Sarge did, reluctantly, and handed it to Cody. "What size is this?" Cody asked. Sarge shrugged. "The church ladies buy all that stuff for me. I don't keep up with it."

"Looks a good forty inches." Cody was already knotting the two belts together so the buckles were on opposite ends. "Maybe we've got us a long enough reach here. We'll find out." He gave the knot a tug to make sure it wouldn't come apart.

"What're you going to do?" Miranda asked.

"I'm pretty sure that thing down there is the control box for this cage. I think that if I trip it, it'll lower the cage. So I might be able to get us out of here."

"Don't mind him," Sarge whispered to Scooter. "He's crazy, that's all."

"Listen to me, both of you." The urgency in Cody's voice stopped Sarge's whispering. "I'm gonna slide my arm out through the bars as far as I can. If I can't keep steady, they'll burn my arm up real quick. Sarge, I want you to hold my legs. If my arm catches fire, I want you to pull me back as fast as you can. Got it?"

"Me? Why me?"

"Because you're a lot stronger than Miranda, and because she's gonna be keepin' an eye out if Stinger comes back. Okay?"

"Okay," Sarge answered, in a small voice.

Cody pushed the belt ahead of him between the bars, and the buckle on the other end went over the edge. Then Sarge grasped Cody's ankles as Cody slid forward with his face only inches from the beams. Slowly he eased his hand through, then his wrist, then up to the forearm where the hairs had been burned away. The buckle was lying on the floor just underneath the cage; now the trick was flicking his wrist to snap the buckle against the control box.

His face was right up on the beams, and he could hear their deadly hum. Now was the time to try it if he ever was. He snapped his wrist upward. The belt buckle scraped along the floor, stopped two or three inches short of the pyramid. He drew it back and flicked it forward again; once more, the buckle fell short.

Cody strained his arm another quarter inch between the bars. There was about enough room for a toothpick to fit in between them and his skin. A few hairs sparked and crisped away, in pinpoint flames. His heartbeat was making his body tremble. Steady . . . steady, he told himself. He flicked the belt forward. Still too short. A drop of sweat rolled into his right eye and blinded him, and his first impulse was to wipe it out, but if he moved without thinking, either his face or his arm would go into the bars. He said, "Sarge, pull me back. *Slow.*"

Sarge hauled him away from the edge, and Cody kept his arm rigid until the fingers had cleared. Then he rubbed his eye with his other hand, got on his knees, and pulled the belt up. "It's not long enough," he said. "We need another couple of inches." But he knew there was nothing else to be used, and he was about to toss the knotted belts aside in frustration when Miranda said, "Your earring."

Cody's hand went to his earlobe. The skull earring hung down a little more than two inches. He took it off, knotted the small chain to one of the buckles so the silver skull had as much play as possible, then gripped the other buckle and said, "Sarge, let's try it again."

Working slowly and carefully, Cody dropped the buckle with the tiny skull dangling from it over the cage's edge and let its weight pull the rest of the belt down. Then he slid forward, Sarge grasping his ankles again, and negotiated his hand, wrist, and forearm between the violet bars. When he was set and ready, he snapped his wrist upward. This time he thought the extension would reach; again it just barely fell short of contact. He had to push another quarter inch of skin through.

He started sliding his arm forward, millimeter by millimeter. Beads of sweat were heavy in his eyebrows, and one of them popped and sizzled as it touched a beam. A little more, he thought. Just a little more. The hairs on his arm were afire. A little more. Now he could see no room between his skin and the bars. A fraction more, that's all . . .

There was a soft *whuff* as a lock of his hair grazed the bar before his face and caught fire. The flames crawled toward his scalp. Miranda cried out, "Pull him back!" He felt Sarge's hands tighten on his ankles, and at the same time Cody flicked the belt with a quick jerk of his wrist.

He heard it: the metallic, almost musical *tring* of the silver skull hitting the control box. But whether that was contact enough to trip the switch he didn't know, and in the next second Sarge was hauling him away from the bars and Miranda was plucking away burning hair. The muscles in his forearm cramped rigid, and as the belt came up over the edge it wandered into one of the bars and was sliced in two as cleanly as by a white-hot blade. He lay on his back, rubbing the cramp out of his arm, the buckle still clenched in his hand.

And then he realized, with a start, that the cage was descending.

He sat up, a stubble of burned hair still smoking above his left eye. The pyramid glowed violet. The cage settled gently to the floor, and the circle of bars went dark.

55
Stinger's Realm

Matt Rhodes was the first down the rope into the hole beneath Sonny Crowfield's house. The bull's-eye lantern was tied to his waist and a fully loaded automatic rifle from Crowfield's arsenal was strapped around his shoulder. As soon as his shoes squished into the ooze at the bottom, he took the lantern off and aimed it into the tunnel ahead. Nothing moved in there but the slow dripping of gray slime. He looked up, saw Rick Jurado's light about twenty feet above. He pulled on the rope, and Rick started down.

Rick had the second of Crowfield's rifles, as well as one of the flashlights they'd gotten from people at the fortress. When Rick made it down, the rope was hauled up and a few seconds later came down again tied around the device Daufin had suggested they make: four of the bright battery lamps wired together and with a wire handle like a basket of light. It illuminated the tunnel with a powerful white glare, and Rhodes breathed a lot easier when it reached the bottom.

Jessie climbed down next, carrying a flashlight and the Winchester strapped to her shoulder. Tom followed, with Daufin clinging around his neck. The last down was Curt Lockett. Hanging at his chest was a hiker's backpack, brought from the hardware store, that held the five sticks of dynamite and the hogleg Colt.

Tom set Daufin down. The tunnel that stretched before them was about seven feet in height and another six or seven feet wide. In the muck around them were pieces of the house's floor, a mattress, and a broken-up bed. Crowfield was probably lying in it when the floor split open, Rick figured. He unstrapped the rifle, propped its stock against his hip, and kept the flashlight's beam pointed ahead. Rhodes gave his lantern to Tom and took the bundle of battery lamps. "Okay," Rhodes said quietly, his voice echoing. "I'll go first. Daufin behind me. Then Jessie, Tom, Lockett, and Rick brings up the rear. Lockett, I don't want you throwing those sticks without my order. Got it?"

A flame flared. Curt lit a Lucky with the Bic lighter. "Got it, boss man."

"Rick, make sure you watch our backs. And everybody keep as quiet as you can: we want to be able to hear anything digging." He swallowed thickly. The air was wet and heavy down here, and the rotten-peaches odor of the gray ooze stung his nostrils. The slime hung from the ceiling and sides of the tunnel like grotesque stalactites, pools of it shimmering an iridescent silver on the floor. "What's this wet shit all over the place?" Curt asked. It was about two inches deep underfoot, as slick as engine grease.

"Stinger digs these tunnels," Daufin answered. "It sprays them with lubricant so it can move faster."

"Lubricant!" Curt grunted. Little ants of fear were running figure eights in his belly. "Stuff looks like snot!"

"One thing I want to know," Rhodes said. "Does the power source that runs the replicants come from Stinger or the ship?"

"From Stinger." Daufin peered down the tunnel ahead, alert for any sign of movement. "The replicants are expendable, meant to be discarded after their use is finished."

The replication process must be incredibly fast, Jessie thought. The creation of living tissue bonded with metallic fibers, the inner organs, synthetic bones—all of it was too much for an earthbound mind to comprehend. Her own questions about what Stinger looked like, and how it created the replicants from human bodies, would have to wait. It was time to go.

"Everybody ready?" Rhodes waited for them all to reply, and then he started into the tunnel, careful of his footing in the slime and trying very hard not to think about the size of the monster that had drilled through the Texas dirt.

Rick shone the light behind them. All clear. Before leaving the 'Gade fort, he'd knelt down beside Paloma and held her hands between his. Had told her what he had to do, and why. She'd listened silently, her head bowed. Then she'd asked him to pray with her, and he'd rested his cheek against her forehead as she begged God's mercy on her grandson and granddaughter. She'd kissed his hand and looked at him with those sightless eyes that had always seen to his soul. *"Dios anda con los bravos,"* she'd whispered, and let him go.

He hoped she was right, and that God did indeed walk with the brave. Or at least watch over the desperate.

Since leaving the apartment building, they'd seen neither the creature that had grown out of the horse nor any of the human-sized Stingers. They'd found two fifteen-foot lengths of rope at the hardware store and had come across the bridge, where Rick's heart had sunk when he'd seen the battered remains of Cody Lockett's motorcycle still burning. He didn't know if Cody's old man recognized the machine too, but Curt Lockett hadn't made a sound.

The tunnel veered to the right. The lamps revealed an intersection of three passages, all going in different directions. Rhodes chose the center of the tunnels, which continued in what he thought was the way to the black pyramid, and Daufin nodded when he looked at her for reassurance. They went into it, their lights glinting off the wet walls. In another moment they could hear a steady pounding ahead, like the beating of a huge heart.

"Stinger's ship," Daufin whispered. "The systems are charging."

Rick kept his flashlight aimed behind them. And it happened so fast he had no time to cry out: a hunchbacked figure scurried into the beam about twenty feet away, lifted its hands before its face, and quickly retreated to the darkness.

Rick stopped. His knees were rubbery. He'd seen the weaving tail, and the thing had resembled a mottled eight-legged scorpion with a human head. "Colonel?" He said it louder: *"Colonel?"*

The others had gone on a few paces, but now Rhodes halted and looked back. "What's wrong?"

"It knows we're here," Rick answered.

From in front of them came a woman's Texan drawl: "I wouldn't come any closer if I were ya'll."

Rhodes swung around and held the lamps up. Twelve or fifteen feet ahead, the tunnel wound to the left and he knew the creature must be standing around that turn.

"You bugs sure like to live dangerous," Stinger said. "Is the guardian with you?"

Daufin took a step forward. "I'm here," she said defiantly. "I want the three humans set free."

There was a cold little laugh. "Lordy Mercy, was that an order? Honeychild, you're in *my* world now. You want to come on and give yourself up, I might think about lettin' the bugs go."

"Either you set them free," Daufin said, "or we will."

That brought another giggle. "Look behind you, honeychild. You can't see me, but I'm there. I'm in the walls. I'm up over you and down underneath. I'm *every-where.*" Anger was creeping in. "I've got your pod now, honeychild. That'll be good enough for my bounty. Plus I've found a whole world full of bugs that can't fight worth a damn, and I ought to thank you for leadin' me here."

"It doesn't matter. You're not going anywhere."

"No? Who's gonna stop me?"

"I am."

There was silence. Daufin knew Stinger would not rush forward into the glare. And then Stinger hissed: "Come on, then. I'm waitin' for you. Come on, let's see what color your guts are!"

"Get down," Curt said quietly, and he touched the fuse of

the dynamite stick he was holding to the red tip of his cigarette. The fuse smoked and sparked, began to burn, and Rhodes shouted, "I told you not to—"

"Fuck it," Curt said, and hurled the stick toward the bend in the tunnel.

Rhodes grabbed Daufin and threw both himself and her into the muck. The others hit the ground and two seconds later there was a blast like a dozen shotguns going off. The tunnel's floor shook, chunks of dirt flying through the air and showering down. Rhodes sat up, his ears ringing. Daufin struggled out from underneath him and got to her knees. She looked back in amazement at Curt, who was already on his feet and taking another puff from his bent cigarette. "That's what dynamite is," he said.

Stinger's voice did not return. But from around the bend there was a terrible gasping sound, like air being drawn into diseased lungs. Rhodes stood up, cocked his rifle, and held it as steady as he could, then began walking forward. He crouched and rounded the bend, ready to open fire.

Something was on the tunnel floor, trying to crawl away through the ooze. It had one arm, the other a blackened mass lying several feet away, and its head was a misshapen lump. In the torn face, the mouth full of broken needles gasped like the gill of a bizarre fish, and the single remaining eye flinched in the light. The spiked tail had risen from its backbone and thrashed weakly from side to side. The thing's hand started clawing frantically at the dirt, trying to dig itself in.

Rhodes held the bundle of lamps closer to its face, avoiding the twitching tail. The awful ruined mouth stretched open, spilling gray fluid, and the eye began to smoke and burn in its socket. A charred, acrid chemical odor hung in the air. The eye popped open, melted in a rivulet of ooze, and the body shuddered and lay still. The tail thrashed once more before it fell like a dead flower.

Electric light burns out the thing's eyes, Rhodes thought. And once they were blinded, Stinger had no more use for the replicants—which were, in essence, walking and talking cameras—so the power source that animated them was simply turned off. But if all the replicants were in some strange way part of Stinger—powered perhaps by Stinger's brainwaves—then it was likely Stinger could feel pain: the impact of a bullet, or the blast of dynamite. *You hurt me,* he remembered the creature saying to him in Dodge Creech's house. All the replicants were Stinger, and Stinger was vulnerable to pain through them.

Rhodes led the others past the burned shape on the ground, his pace faster. Daufin glanced only incuriously at the thing, but Jessie didn't let herself look at it. Curt tapped his ashes onto the mangled head, though he moved past as rapidly as everyone else.

And they were about ten feet past the dead replicant when dirt exploded from the tunnel wall to Rhodes's right. A hunchbacked shape lunged for the lamps, its tail breaking loose from the dirt and slamming into the ceiling. Rhodes twisted toward it, but the thing was on top of him before he could fire. He heard gunshots: Rick and Tom's rifles firing almost point-blank, and then his shoulder was hit by what felt like a runaway power saw and he was lifted off his feet. He was knocked against the other wall with a force that almost broke his back. Jessie screamed, and then there was more gunfire and Rhodes's knees were sagging, warm wetness spilling along his arm. He went down.

Rick saw the thing's face: dark eyes and gray hair—the face of Mr. Diaz, who owned the shoe repair shop on Second Street, on a scorpion's body. He thrust his rifle's barrel into that face and blew its lower jaw away. The creature reeled backward, one arm rising to shield its eyes from the light. Curt fired one of his four bullets, shot a chunk out of its head, and dark wormy things boiled from the wound. Its tail swung, narrowly missing Tom's head. Then the replicant turned and dove into the hole it had emerged from, scurrying back into the dirt and disappearing within seconds.

Gunsmoke drifted through the tunnel. Jessie was already on her knees beside the colonel, and she could see the glint of bone down in the wound on his shoulder. There was a lot of blood. Rhodes's face was ashen. He was still gripping his rifle and the lamps' handle in white-knuckled hands.

"Bastard clawed me," Rhodes said. "Trying to break out the lights."

"Don't talk." Jessie tore the shirt away from the ripped flesh. The wound was deep and nasty; slashed muscle tissue clenched and relaxed.

Cold sweat had welled up on Rhodes's face. He smiled faintly at Jessie's frown of concern. "Lady, talking's about all I can do right now. I'm a mess, huh?"

She looked up at Tom. "We've got to get him out."

"No! By the time you do . . . Stinger will have taken off." Rhodes's arm was, thankfully, still numb. He clasped his hand over the wound and gripped tightly, as if to hold back the pain before it hit. "Listen to me. If you want to get Stevie back . . . and the others too . . . you've got to do it for yourselves. I've gone as far as I can go." He found Daufin, who was standing next to Rick and watching him intently. "Daufin . . . you said you could lead them. Here's your chance."

"How bad's he hurt?" Daufin asked Jessie.

"No major artery's cut. Mostly muscle damage. It's the shock I'm worried about; he's already suffered too many traumas tonight."

"So who hasn't?" Rhodes was getting cold, and he felt unconsciousness pulling at him. "Leave me here and go! We've come this far, dammit! Go!"

"He's right," Rick said. "We've got to go on."

"I'm gettin' my boy out of there, by God," Curt vowed, though his stomach fluttered with fear. "No matter what."

"We have to go," Daufin agreed. The rhythmic pounding of the ship's systems drawing power from the reserves was getting louder. She knelt down beside Colonel Rhodes. "Stinger may come for you. You know that, don't you?"

"Yep. Here." He pushed the lamps toward her. "Somebody give me a flashlight." Tom did, and Rhodes propped the rifle up beside him with a bloody finger on the trigger.

"And dynamite too," Daufin suggested. Curt gave him a

stick, lit a cigarette for him, and put it between the colonel's gray lips.

"Thanks. Now I'm loaded for bear." Rhodes looked into Daufin's face. He no longer saw a little girl. A being impassioned and proud was kneeling next to him, and she had ancient eyes that had endured a world of pain but still had the shine of courage. "You're okay," he told her, in a weakening voice. "I hope you get back to your . . ." How had she put it? "Your tribe," he remembered. "I hope you teach them that life is worth fighting for."

"I will." She gently laid her hand against his grizzled cheek, and he could feel the tingle of electricity in her fingers. "You're not going to die." It was a command.

"I always planned on dying in South Dakota, anyway. In bed, when I'm a hundred and one." The pain was beginning to take him, but he didn't let his face show it. "You'd better go."

"We'll be back for you," Rick said.

"You sure as hell better be." He put the stick of dynamite across his chest, just in case.

Daufin gave Jessie the lamps and then started along the tunnel at a brisk pace. Jessie and the others followed. The metallic boom of the ship's pulse told Daufin that the systems were rapidly energizing. The tunnel wound to the left just ahead. They had to be almost under the ship by now, and soon they'd see the opening into it. The question was: would Stinger try to stop them from getting inside, or let them enter the ship?

As her eyes darted from side to side and she listened for the scurrying of claws digging in the dirt, Daufin knew Stinger was right: this warren of tunnels was his world, and he was everywhere.

Her legs moving like little pistons, the alien warrior in the body of a child advanced deeper into Stinger's realm.

56
The Chopshop

"Hold it," Cody whispered. Behind him, Miranda and Sarge stopped. "I see a light ahead."

To call it a light was for want of a better term: it was more of a luminous violet mist, hanging at the far end of the passage they'd been following for the last ten minutes. Cody figured it as being about forty feet away, though distance had become unreal. They'd been in the dark since leaving the chamber where they'd been caged, and they'd been feeling their way along a passage with walls and floor that felt like soggy leather. Cody thought they were gradually descending, going around in slow spirals. They'd seen no other openings, no other lights.

Cody held Miranda's hand, and cautiously led her forward. She had hold of Sarge's hand, pulling him along. They walked through two or three inches of a thick sludge that lay at the bottom of the corridor and dripped from above, and then they reached the luminous mist. By it they could see that the corridor wound to the right. Ahead was a circular portal into what looked like a large chamber, lit in a sickly violet glow.

"Come on, Scooter!" Sarge whispered over his shoulder. "You gotta keep up!"

They emerged from the corridor. Cody stopped, stunned by the sight.

Above them, perhaps a hundred feet in the air, was a huge ball of purple mist, radiating light like an otherwordly sun. Other portals and platforms advanced up the inner walls of the ship right up to its distant apex. It made Cody think of what the inside of an antbed must look like, but he could see no other sign of life. About sixty feet above hung another black pyramid, the size of a tractor-trailer truck, connected to the walls by two massive metal arms. A network of thousands of silver cables ran from the pyramid into the walls, but Cody was most astounded by what stood before them.

Across an area fifty yards wide and the same distance in length were hundreds of structures—spheres, octagons, bulky slabs, and some as graceful and puzzling as abstract sculptures. All of them were as black as ebony, and appeared to be covered with scales. They were arranged in long rows, connected by silver-blue rods; some of the structures were twenty or thirty feet tall.

"What are they?" Miranda asked fearfully.

"Machines, I think." Cody had thought at first that this must be the ship's engine room, but the rhythmic pulse was not coming from here but from a level below. One black wall was covered with thousands of dimly glowing, violet geometric shapes. Probably Stinger's language, Cody guessed. On another wall were rows of triangular screens, displaying what looked like X-ray images of human skeletons, skulls and organs from varying angles. A different set of images appeared every two or three seconds, like a visual encyclopedia of human anatomy.

"Good God A'mighty!" Sarge stared upward. "Got a fake sun in here!" But the ball of mist gave off a cold light, and the sight of it made his head throb.

"There's got to be a way out." Cody held Miranda's hand and started across the chamber's black, leathery floor. Pools of slime lay everywhere, as if a huge snail had recently crawled through. Cody reasoned that there had to be another portal, maybe on the opposite side of the ship.

They went between the rows of machines. Cody heard a slow *whooshing*, and he realized with a prickle of flesh at the back of his neck that some of the machines were breathing. But they couldn't be alive; they *couldn't* be! Still, their scaled surfaces expanded and contracted, each with a slightly different rhythm. Cody thought Miranda's grip was going to break his hand.

Hanging from one of the structures, a large slab studded with needles like an alien sewing machine, were scraps of what might have been human flesh—or a good imitation of it. Another structure held a huge spindle with a coil of finely meshed wires that fed into the next machine, and there was a chute with scraps of cloth, hair, and what might have been bones lying on it like discarded bits of trash. These were the machines that made Stinger's replicants, Cody realized. The chamber was a chopshop, eerily similar to Mack Cade's.

Beyond the machines was another portal. Cody walked toward it, but suddenly stopped.

"What is it?" Miranda asked, almost bumping into him.

"Look at those." He pointed. On the chamber floor, trailing into the passage before them, were thirty or more cords of what looked like stretched red muscle. Cody looked back to see what they were connected to; the fleshy fibers ran along the floor and into the largest of the breathing black machines. His next question was: what were those attached to on the other end?

They had no choice but to enter the passageway. "Let's go," Cody said, more to get himself moving than for any other reason. He took three steps onto the sludgy surface —and then he heard a high whining noise like the line on a fishing rod being rapidly reeled up.

The cords on the floor were vibrating. They were being pulled into the breathing machine, and Cody knew that something was coming through the passage ahead. He heard the noise of movement, the scuttling of claws against the passage surface. What sounded like an army of Stingers on the march.

"Back!" he told Miranda and Sarge. "Get back! Hurry!"

The noise of something massive was almost upon them. Cody guided them behind cover of a structure that resembled a gigantic blacksmith's anvil, and then he crouched down and watched the portal, his spine crawling as the cords continued to reel into the depths of the breathing machine.

And there it was, sliding through the opening into the chamber, its mottled flesh wet and gleaming under the violet sun. What had sounded like an army was only one creature, but the sight of such an ungodly thing speared terror through Cody. He felt as if his insides were shriveling, and he knew what he was looking at—not one of the replicants this time, but the thing that had crossed the void of space hunting Daufin, that had landed the spaceship here, dug tunnels under Inferno, and burst through the floors of houses in search of human bodies. There it was, twenty feet away from him.

In the tunnel outside the ship, Daufin was still advancing like a small juggernaut. Behind her, Jessie and the others were having trouble keeping pace. Curt slipped in the slime, got up cursing and slinging the stuff off himself. Daufin listened to the pulse of the ship's systems. She didn't know if the force field had been turned off yet, but when it was a huge amount of energy would be shifted to the engines.

At the rear of the group, Rick took four more strides and two hands burst from the dirt at his feet.

One of them locked around his swollen ankle, the claws piercing his skin. He cried out "Jesus!," pointed his rifle at the thing's head, and started shooting. Pieces of flesh flew off the face. "Back here!" Curt hollered. He put the Colt's barrel against the thing's dark-haired skull and pulled the trigger. The head broke open, spewing its insides. But the thing was still fighting its way out of the ground, one hand gripping Rick's ankle and the other flailing at Curt's legs. Curt jumped like he was barefoot on a hot griddle. Rick fell, aimed his light into the thing's face, and saw the eyes sucked back into hoods of flesh. They smoked and burst, the face contorting with either pain or rage. The claws released him, and the creature thrashed itself down into the ground again and disappeared.

"Everyone all right?" Daufin had stopped fifteen feet ahead. Jessie shone the lamps back to illuminate the others.

Curt was helping Rick up, both of them trembling. "Can you walk?" Curt asked. Rick tried weight on his ankle. Actually, the claw slashes had relieved some of the pressure, but his ankle was bleeding. He nodded. "Yeah, I can make it."

"Hold it." Tom had seen something, and he pointed his light along the tunnel in the direction they'd come. His eyes widened behind his glasses. "Oh my God," he said.

Four human scorpions were scuttling toward them, their spiked tails thrashing. The light hit them and they flinched, shielded their eyes, but kept coming.

Tom lifted his rifle and started to fire. Curt said, "Don't waste the bullets, man." He flicked his lighter, touched the flame to one of the dynamite fuses. It sparked and flared. "Everybody kiss the ground!" As the fuse was gnawed away, he flung the stick at the things and dove onto his face.

The seconds ticked past. No explosion.

"Christ!" Curt looked up. The creatures were right on the dynamite. Still no blast. "Must've been a damned du—"

It exploded. The four bodies were thrown against the tunnel's sides in the thunderclap glare of the concussion, and the shock wave passed Curt and the others like a searing desert wind. Daufin was on her belly too, the blast's breeze ruffling her hair.

Jessie held up the lamps and saw two of the figures digging themselves into the walls. A third was lying there twitching, and a fourth did not move at all.

"Bingo," Curt said.

Daufin stood up.

And that was when the figure that had rushed along the tunnel behind her seized her by the back of the neck and lifted her off her feet. Two of its claws sliced into the skin, bringing a cry of pain from her. She was held at arm's length, her legs dangling.

"It's over," Stinger whispered, in the voice of Mack Cade.

Jessie had heard Daufin's cry, and she started to turn around and shine the light ahead. But Mack Cade's voice was a harsh command: "Throw your weapons away! All of them! If you don't, I'll break her neck!"

Jessie hesitated. Glanced at Tom. He stared at her, gripping the rifle to his chest.

"Throw your weapons away," Stinger repeated. The replicant held the child between itself and the lights. The dog's head writhed in its chest. "Throw them down the passage as far as you can. *Do it!*"

"Oh, Jesus!" Curt fell to his knees in the muck, rocking back and forth. "Don't kill me! Please . . . I'm beggin' you!" His eyes were wild with terror. "Please don't kill me!"

"There's bug bravery!" Stinger shook Daufin, and droplets of blood fell from the cuts on the back of her neck. "Look at them! There're your protectors!"

Curt was still rocking back and forth, making sobbing sounds. "Get up," Rick said. "Come on, man. Don't let this piece of shit see you beg."

"I don't wanna die . . . I don't wanna die . . ."

"We're all going on a nice long trip," Stinger said. "I won't kill you if you do what I say. Throw your weapons down the passage. *Now.*"

Tom drew a deep breath, his head bowed, and tossed the rifle away. He winced when it splatted into the ooze. Curt threw the hogleg Colt down the tunnel. Rick's rifle went next. "The lights too!" Stinger shouted. "I'm not a fool!"

Curt's light went first. Then Rick's, and Tom's lantern. Jessie threw the wired-together lamps away, and it landed near the blown-up scorpion creature.

"You have something else," Stinger said quietly. "The weapon that shouts and burns. What's it called?"

"Dynamite," Jessie told him, one hand pressed to her face.

"Dy-na-mite. Dynamite. Where is it?"

No one spoke. Curt was still huddled over, but making no sound.

"Where?" Stinger demanded, and shook Daufin so hard it brought a grunt of pain from her.

"Give it to him, Curt," Tom said.

Curt straightened up, slowly took the knapsack off. "The dynamite's in here," he said, and tossed it toward Stinger. It landed at Jessie's feet.

"Take the dynamite out and let me see," Stinger said.

Jessie picked up the knapsack and reached in. Her hand found not the last two sticks of dynamite, but a pack of Lucky cigarettes.

"Let me see!" Stinger demanded.

"Go on." Curt's voice had a nervous edge. "Let him see what he wants to."

"But . . . this isn't—"

"Show him," Curt interrupted.

And then she understood, or at least thought she did. She brought out the pack of cigarettes and held them in her palm. Stinger's eyes watched her over Daufin's shoulder. "Here it is," Jessie said. Her throat was dust dry. "Dynamite. See?"

Stinger made no sound. The blue Mack Cade eyes stared at the pack of Luckies in Jessie's palm. Blinked. Then once more. Processing information, Jessie thought. Maybe searching through the language centers of all the brains it had already stolen. Would it know what dynamite was, and what the explosive looked like? A hissing sound came from Stinger's throat. "That's a package," Stinger suddenly said. "Open it and show me the dynamite."

Jessie's hands were trembling. She tore the pack open, and held up the remaining three cigarettes so he could see them.

There was a long moment in which she thought she would scream. If Stinger had any information on dynamite, it might be the same definition Daufin knew: an explosive compound usually formed into a cylinder and detonated by lighting a fuse. The cigarettes were cylinders, and how would Stinger know any differently? She could almost see the gears turning rapidly behind the creature's counterfeit face.

Stinger said, "Put the dynamite down. Step on it until it's dead."

Jessie dropped the cigarettes and pressed them deep into the slime.

A quick smile flickered across the thing's mouth, and Stinger lowered Daufin but kept his hand clenched on her neck. "Now I feel better! Good vibes again, ya'll! Everyone walk in front of me. *Go!*"

Jessie let out the breath she'd been holding. Curt Lockett had gambled on the fact that Stinger had never seen dynamite before. But where were the last two sticks?

Curt stood up. His red cowboy shirt had been buttoned almost to the throat. He followed Rick along the tunnel, his arms close to his sides and his back slightly stooped like a dog afraid of being beaten.

Stinger shoved Daufin into the muck. Hauled her up again, shoved her roughly forward. She'd already seen what was clamped between the dog's jaws: her lifepod. Stinger grabbed a handful of her hair. "I knew the bugs would draw you out. Oh, we're going to have a nice long trip together. You, me, and the bugs. Think on these things." He shoved her again, and followed the others into the dark with his spiked tail thrashing.

57
Stinger Revealed

Cody looked upon Stinger in the dank light of a violet sun, and the world seemed to freeze on its axis.

Stinger—the bounty hunter from a distant planet—was a snaky length of mottled dark and light flesh. Its body shone with slime, and it moved on hundreds of small silver-clawed legs, propelling the bulk forward with wavelike undulations. Like a fat, oily centipede, Cody thought; but it had two large hinged and clawed forelegs that looked like the shovels of a living bulldozer. It was those forelegs that had dug the tunnels and smashed through the floors of houses.

Its head was a duplicate of the thing that had burst out of the horse—thick, elongated jaws and four amber eyes with thin black pupils in a flattened, almost reptilian skull. Except the jaws did not hold needle teeth. The mouth was a large, wet gray suction cup, like the underside of a leech.

Stinger's body continued to glide into the chamber. Cords of elastic red muscle emerged from its sides and connected it to the breathing machine, which Cody figured must reel the cords in and out automatically; but it was clear that Stinger was tethered to the machine, and might even be part machine itself.

But the worst was that in some places Stinger's flesh was almost transparent, and Cody could see what was in there:

corpses, drifting as if in a macabre ballet. What looked like hundreds of ropy filaments had wrapped around the corpses and seemed to be feeding them into the organs. A horse floated in there, drifting as if on an obscene tide. Flashes of what might have been electricity jumped along the filaments, illuminating the dead in that corpse-swollen body as if by strobe lights. A woman's pickled face pressed up against the scaly flesh, red hair floating, and then she tumbled backward in terrible slow motion. More bodies moved in Stinger's internal currents, and there were other faces Cody recognized and wished he did not. He pressed a hand against his mouth, fighting on the edge of the Great Fried Empty.

It knows my name, he thought, and that almost sent him over.

Finally, Stinger's tail slid through the portal. It had a wrecking ball of spikes, just as the horse creature's tail had. The tail twitched with horrible life, and the hundreds of legs carried Stinger's bloated, twenty-foot-long body across the floor with a noise like sliding razor blades.

Cody couldn't move. The portal was clear now, though slimed with Stinger's ooze, and they might be able to make it. But what if they couldn't? The breathing machine was reeling fleshy cords out again as Stinger slithered toward the far side of the chamber. Cody looked over his shoulder at Miranda and Sarge; both of them were pressed against their shelter, and Sarge's eyes had bulged with terror. He motioned for them to stay where they were, then crawled out of cover on his stomach to see where Stinger had gone.

The thing had reached the wall of geometric symbols. It reared up, eight feet of its body leaving the floor, and the legs on its lower length pushed it onward. The flesh of its belly was smooth and white, like the flesh of a maggot. It looked vulnerable in comparison to the scaly upper body, Cody thought. Like you could punch a hole in it with a good shotgun blast.

But he had no shotgun, and all he could do was watch while the thing's small claws began to touch the symbols with blurred speed, each one moving independently. As the symbols were activated, their violet glow went out. Stinger's head lifted, the eyes peering up, and Cody looked up too. Far above, the spinning cyclone of the force field at the ship's apex had begun to slow its revolutions. As Stinger manipulated another series of symbols, the cyclone of light slowed . . . slowed . . . and extinguished.

The force field had been turned off. Instantly, the suspended violet sun brightened.

There was a bass grinding of machinery. The two metal arms were lowering the small pyramid to the floor. As it came down it opened, and within was a compartment that looked like a control center, full of rows of metallic levers. The pyramid settled to the floor with a slight jarring thump.

Stinger continued to touch the symbols, all its attention focused on the work. Mechanisms whined and whirred in the walls, and the entire ship vibrated with a pulse of power.

Cody crawled back to Miranda and Sarge. "We've got to get out *now!*" he whispered urgently. "I'm going first. I want you right behind me. Understand?"

"Yes." Miranda's face was still chalky, but her eyes were clear.

Sarge nodded. "We can't forget Scooter! Got to bring Scooter with us!"

"Right." Cody peered out again, marking Stinger's position, then at the portal. The time to go was now. He tensed, about to leap up and run like hell.

Before he could, Jessie Hammond staggered through the portal. This new shock froze Cody where he was. She was followed by Tom Hammond, Rick Jurado, and . . .

"Oh, Christ," Cody breathed.

His old man came in, stoop-shouldered. Right behind him was Daufin, her spine rigid and head uplifted defiantly . . . and then the spike-tailed nightmare that looked like Mack Cade with one arm and a dog's head growing from its chest. Miranda leaned forward, saw Rick and started to shout, but Cody pressed his hand over her mouth and pulled her back behind the machinery.

Rick's stomach lurched. He'd seen the thing standing at

the wall, and he felt the blood drain out of his face. Jessie glanced quickly back at Curt; beads of sweat glittered on his cheeks and forehead. Tom took Jessie's hand, and Daufin turned to the one-armed replicant.

"You have me now," she said. "And my pod. Let the humans go."

"Prisoners have no right to demand." The replicant's eyes were supremely confident and contemptuous. "The bugs wanted to help you so much, they can go to prison with you." Daufin knew it spoke with Stinger's thoughts, but Stinger was busy with the lift-off preparations and didn't turn away from the programming console. Evidently Stinger thought so little of her and the humans that it saw no need for more replicants to guard them.

"Where's my sister?" Rick forced himself to look into the creature's face. "What've you done to her?"

"Liberated her. And the two others, just as I've liberated all of you. From now on, there will be no more waste in your lives. Where you're going, every moment will be productive." The gaze slid to Daufin. "Isn't that right?"

She didn't answer. She knew what lay ahead of them: a torture of "tests" and, finally, dissection.

"You're going through there." The single claw motioned toward the portal on the chamber's other side. "Move." He reached out to shove Jessie.

Rick knew they were dead. All of them. Miranda too. There was nothing left for him to lose, and he'd rather die on Earth than in outer space or some prison world beyond the stars. His decision was made in an instant, and it freed him from the terror that had locked around him. He drove his hand into his pocket. His fingers closed on the object there, and he wrenched it out.

His other hand seized the creature's wrist.

The Mack Cade face twisted toward him, mouth opening in a gasp of indignation.

At Rick's side, the honed blade of the Fang of Jesus clicked out. "Eat this," Rick said.

He'd always been fast. Fast enough to grab the knife from

513

under a sidewinder's snout. And now he brought the Fang of Jesus up in a blur of motion and drove the blade into the replicant's left eye with all his strength behind it.

It went in up to the hilt. Gray fluid spurted from the wound over Rick's hand. The creature gave a grunt of surprise and the body staggered back, tail writhing, but Rick dared not let either the wrist or his knife go.

Across the chamber, Stinger's head turned, its claws still darting over the geometric symbols. It made a wet, enraged hissing sound, and its brainwaves directed the Mack Cade replicant like a master puppeteer.

Rick pulled the knife out, struck for the other eye. The thing's head jerked to one side and the blade ripped across the cheek. The dog's jaws opened wide, dropping the pod to the floor, and its needle teeth snapped at Rick's ribs. They caught a mouthful of shirt and tore the cloth away. Rick held on to the replicant's flailing arm with grim determination and kept knifing at the thing's face, cutting away chunks of false flesh.

The dog's neck strained, its teeth about to pierce the skin on Rick's side.

Tom lunged forward, latching his hands around the dog's throat. The neck had tremendous strength in it and the head thrashed, its jaws snapping at Tom's face. Tom hung on, even when its stubby forelegs came up and the two hooked claws raked bloody ribbons out of his arms.

The three figures staggered across the chamber. Daufin saw the pod bounce twice and roll in Stinger's direction. She ran after it, scurrying over the tendrils that delivered Stinger's encoding signals to the replicating machines, leapt onto the pod, and snatched it up.

Stinger was lowering itself from the programming console. One pair of its eyes still monitored the combatants, but the other pair was aimed at Daufin. Explosions of electricity flared inside the monster, and with a noise like a steam engine building power, the corpse-swollen body began to undulate toward her.

The replicant's spiked tail rose up over Rick's head, about to smash his skull.

But Cody had already shot from his hiding place and was sprinting forward. He reached up, grabbing the tail just below the ball of spikes. Its power lifted him off the floor, but Cody's weight stopped the blow before it fell. The replicant roared with anger, trying to shake Cody off.

The others saw Cody grappling with the tail, but there was no time to find out where he'd come from. Everything was happening too fast: the replicant's claw was flailing Rick from side to side as he kept stabbing right down to the metallic skull. Tom's arms were streaked with blood, savage pain thrumming through him, and he could only hold the dog's head a few seconds longer.

Jessie had run to Daufin's side. She picked her up, holding her protectively, as a mother would any child. Stinger was coming at them, gathering speed, the silver claws skittering across the floor.

Someone shoved her aside. Curt Lockett touched the lighter's flame to the first of the two dynamite sticks he'd taken from the knapsack and clasped under his arms. His face was bleached, a pulse beating rapidly at his temple. He saw his own death coming at him, and his legs shook but he stood facing the onrushing beast as the dynamite's fuse sparked and caught.

He hurled the stick. It fell short, but Stinger went over it like an oozing train.

There was no blast. Fuse got crushed, Curt thought. "Get back!" he shouted to Jessie. "Move your ass, la—"

His voice was drowned out by a hollow *whuuummmp!* like a huge shotgun going off in a mass of wet pillows. Stinger shuddered, its tail slamming against the wall. At the same instant, the mouth in Mack Cade's knife-slashed face bellowed with pain, and the dog's head howled. The Fang of Jesus slammed into the mouth and sent needles flying.

Some of Stinger's claws had crisped, and yellow flames gnawed at the underbelly flesh. A pool of liquid was spreading across the floor, and as Stinger writhed and rose up like a quaking mountain Curt saw a three-foot-long gash with charred edges on the soft white flesh. Inside, electricity sputtered along the veins and organs.

But Stinger kept coming, trailing slime and some of its guts behind it. Curt retreated, pulling out the last stick of dynamite. Jessie still clutched Daufin, and was backing away too. Curt flicked the lighter, touched the fuse to the flame with shaking hands.

"Hold it! Hold it!" Rick shouted to Tom, but the man's arms were scored with gashes and the dog's head got away from him. As Rick dodged the snapping jaws, the replicant flung him aside. It strode toward Curt, Cody straining against its tail. The dynamite's fuse was smoking, and Curt cocked his arm back to throw it.

"Dad!" Cody screamed. "Watch out!"

Curt whirled around. The replicant was upon him, its face hanging in tatters and the single eye glinting with fury.

The thing's claw flashed out in a vicious arc. Shreds of Curt's red cowboy shirt and pieces of flesh flew into the air, followed by streamers of blood. The dynamite's fuse popped a flame, but Curt's hand lost it and the stick fell to the floor. The replicant kept slashing at the ruins of his chest, and Curt tried to fight it off as blood clogged his lungs and welled up into his mouth.

Cody frantically jerked back on the tail, his own injured ribs driving agony through him. He hauled the monster back a few feet from his father. Curt went down, and the replicant's tail threw Cody from side to side but he gripped tight and held on.

Stinger loomed over them, the undulations of its body opening wider the charred and torn bellyflesh.

Cody saw the dynamite, its fuse sizzling down toward the cap. It lay less than ten feet from him, but he dared not let go of the spiked tail.

Daufin struggled loose from Jessie's grip; she hit the floor running and picked up the dynamite stick. A pair of Stinger's eyes twitched toward her, and almost simultaneously the replicant turned away from Curt Lockett and rushed at her. No! Cody thought. Can't let it get her! He dragged against the tail, his teeth clenched and tears of pain in his eyes; the replicant's aim was jarred, and the metal-nailed hand whipped past Daufin's head.

Daufin stood her ground as Stinger began to rear up before her.

She had a quick mental image: the pitcher in that mathematical game of safes and outs called baseball. Saw the pitcher's arm cocking back, then flashing forward again in a miracle of moving muscles, bones, and sinews. She cocked her own arm back in imitation of that pitcher, and with a split-second calculation of angles and velocities she threw the sizzling stick of dynamite.

It flew across the twelve feet between her and Stinger, and landed in the wound on Stinger's soft belly, exactly where she'd aimed. She dropped to her knees as the replicant's claw flailed where her head had been a second before and Cody strained to hold the thing back.

A heartbeat passed, as long to Daufin as an agonizing eternity.

Stinger's flesh quivered, its body contorting like a question mark; there was a hollow boom that made Jessie think of thunder caught in a bucket. Two things happened at once: a shower of sparks seemed to jump from Stinger's organs, and the monster's flesh swelled and stretched like a grotesque sausage about to burst apart. The tear at its belly split wider, rimmed with yellow flames, and as Stinger thrashed wildly, burning coils of intestines spilled out. Flares of electricity exploded within the body, as if the double blasts had set off an internal chain reaction.

The replicant with the ruined face of Mack Cade made a strangling, moaning sound and lurched to right and left, the claw swiping at empty air as Daufin scrambled beyond its reach. The dog's howling was hoarse and full of pain, its teeth gnashing so hard the needles were shearing off. Jessie bent down and pulled Daufin close to her, their hearts pounding in unison.

Stinger's head reeled; it began backing away, its sucker mouth oozing drool, and beneath its body was a spreading circle of ripped organs, things that looked like dark red matter with needle-teethed mouths. The organs themselves gasped and twitched like misshapen fish as they came out, and when Earth air hit them, they ignited with yellow flames and shriveled into leathery ashes. Stinger stretched upward, as if reaching for the violet sun. Something exploded with white fire inside it. The split widened further, more tides of thick inner matter streaming out. The upper portion of Stinger's body crashed to the floor.

The replicant toppled to its knees.

Cody let go of the tail, his arms bruised at their sockets, and got away from it; he slipped in his father's blood, and crawled to where Curt lay.

Stinger's body began to collapse like a torn-open gasbag. The tail kept hammering at the wall and floor, but it was getting weaker.

The replicant fell forward, and Mack Cade's face banged down.

"You'rrrre *out*," Jessie heard Daufin whisper.

Rick was trying to stand up, fighting the weight of shock. And then Miranda was beside him and he didn't know if he was dead or crazy or dreaming, but she put her arms around him and those were real enough. He laid his head against her shoulder.

Sarge Dennison had come out from hiding. He stood watching the creature slowly implode. Brackish tides rolled across the floor, and in it were what had once been human bodies. He reached down; Scooter licked his hand. "Good boy," he said.

Bursts of fire rippled through Stinger's gutted hulk. The tail was still feebly twitching, and some of the claws were still trying to crawl. One pair of eyes had rolled back into the head. The body kept shuddering, the sucker mouth rasping like an engine dying down.

"Lordy, Lordy," Curt managed to say. "What the hell did I do?"

"Don't talk. We're gonna get you out." Cody had pulled his father's shoulders off the floor, and Curt's head rested on Cody's leg. Where Curt's chest had been was a heaving mass of tissue. Cody thought he could see the heart laboring in there. He wiped a trickle of blood from his father's lips.

Curt swallowed. Too much blood, he thought. Could

hardly draw a breath for it. He looked up into his son's face, and he thought he saw . . . no, couldn't be. He'd taught his son that a real man never cries. "I hurt a little bit," he said. "Ain't no big thing."

"Hush." Cody's voice broke. "Save it for later."

"I got . . . a picture in my back pocket." He tried to shift, but his body was too heavy. "Can you get it for me?"

"Yes sir." Cody reached into the pocket and found it, all folded up. He saw who the picture was of, and his heart almost cracked. He gave it to Curt, who held it before his face with bloody fingers.

"Treasure," Curt said softly. "You sure did marry one hell of a fool." He blinked, found Cody again. "Your mama used to pack a lunch for me. She'd say, 'Curt, you do me proud today,' and I'd answer, 'I will, Treasure.'" His eyes closed. "Long time back. I used to be a carpenter . . . and . . . I took the jobs that came along."

"Please . . . don't talk," Cody said.

Curt's eyes opened. They were glassy, and his breathing was forced. He gripped his hand around the photograph. "I . . . did wrong with you," he whispered. "Mighty wrong. Forgive me?"

"Yes sir. I forgive you."

His other hand slid into Cody's. "You be . . . a better man than me," he said. Gave a grim little smile. "Won't be too hard, will it?"

"I love you, Dad," Cody said.

"I . . ." Something broke inside him. Something heavy fell away, and at the same time he realized life was short he felt light and free. "I . . . love you," he answered, and he wished to God he'd had the courage to say those simple words a long time ago. "Damn kid," he added. His hand tightened around his son's.

Cody was blinded by tears. He wiped his eyes, but the tears returned. He looked at the still-shuddering mass of Stinger, then back to Curt.

The man's eyes had closed. He might have been sleeping, any other time. But down in that morass of ripped flesh and lungs Cody could no longer see the heart beating. The grip on Cody's hand was loosening. Cody held on, but he knew the man had gone—escaped, really, to a place that had no dead ends but only new beginnings.

Daufin was standing next to him. She was clutching the sphere, her face dark-hollowed and weary. The strength in her host body was almost used up. "I owe him—and you—a debt I can never repay," she said. "He was a very brave human."

"He was my father," Cody answered.

Rick was on his feet. He limped with Miranda's help over to the fallen replicant, placed one foot on the thing's shoulder, and shoved the body over onto its back. The dog's head lolled, its eyes amber blanks.

But suddenly the body hitched. The single blue Mack Cade eye was still open, and it fixed on Rick with utter loathing.

The mouth stretched, and from between the needle teeth came a harsh, dying hiss: "You . . . *bugsssss . . .*" The eye rolled back into the head, and the mouth gave a final rattling gasp.

A death rattle came from Stinger's husk. The tail rose up, the ball of spikes quivering, and crashed down one last time as if in defiance.

And then the carcass lay still.

But the ship's pulse was thunderous now, and the violet sun crackled with energy. Daufin turned toward Jessie, who knelt at Tom's side. The man's arms had been flayed raw, and Jessie was tearing up strips of his shirt to bind the slashes. "The time is short," Daufin said. She scanned the programming console, seeking to decipher a code in the geometric shapes. "The engines are about to reach their lift-off threshold. If they go beyond that point, they might suffer damage." She peered at the banks of levers inside the smaller pyramid. "That's the control center. I can delay lift-off long enough for you to leave the tunnels—but there won't be time to change the navigational coordinants and get to the sleep tubes."

"Try that in English," Tom said.

"I can't keep the ship on the ground much longer," Daufin translated. "And I don't have time to meld into my pod. I need another guardian."

Jessie felt as if the breath had been punched out of her. *"What?"*

"I'm sorry. I need physical form to keep the ship from lifting off while you're in the tunnels. The shock wave would kill you."

"Please . . . give Stevie back to us." Jessie stood up. *"Please!"*

"I want to." The face was tormented, and the small hands clutched the black sphere to her chest. "I must have another guardian. Please understand: I'm trying to save all of you as well as myself."

"No! You can't have Stevie! I want my daughter back!"

"Uh . . . is 'guardian' kinda the same as 'custodian'?"

Daufin looked to her right, and up at Sarge Dennison. "What's a guardian do?" he asked cautiously.

"A guardian," she answered, "protects my body and holds my mind. I wear a guardian like armor, and I respect and protect the guardian's body and mind as well."

"Sounds like a full-time job."

"It is. A guardian knows peace, in a place beyond dreams. But there'll never be any returning to Earth. Once this ship takes off—"

"The sky's the limit," Sarge said.

She nodded, watching him hopefully.

"And if you get another guardian, you . . . like . . . shed your skin? And the Hammonds get their real daughter back? Right?"

"Right."

He paused, his face lined with thought. He looked at his hands for a few seconds. "Can we take Scooter?" he asked.

"I wouldn't dream of not taking Scooter," she said.

Sarge pursed his lips and hissed out air. "What'll we do for food and water?"

"We won't need them. I'll be in a sleep tube, and you'll be

here." She lifted the pod. "With Scooter, if that's as you wish."

He smiled wanly. "I'm . . . kinda scared."

"So am I," Daufin said. "Let's be brave together."

Sarge looked up at Tom and Jessie, then over at the others. Returned his gaze to the little girl's intense and shining eyes. "All right," he decided. "I'll be your guardian."

"Place your fingers against this," Daufin told him, and he gingerly touched the sphere. "Don't be afraid. Wait. Just wait."

Blue threads began to creep across the black surface. "Hey!" Sarge's voice was high and nervous. "Look at that!" The blue threads connected with each other, and floated like mist beneath their hands. Daufin closed her eyes, blocking out all externals and the insistent bellows' boom of the ship. She concentrated solely on opening the vast reservoir of power that lay within the sphere, and she felt it react to her like the ocean tides of her world, flowing over and around her, drawing her deeper into their realm and away from the body of Stevie Hammond.

Blue sparks jumped around Daufin's fingers. "Lord!" Sarge said. "What was—" They danced around his fingers too; he felt a faint tingling sensation that seemed to flow up and down his spine. "Lord!" was all he could say, and that in a stunned whisper.

And in the next instant currents of power snapped out of the sphere, coiled around Daufin's hands and Sarge's too. His eyes widened. The bright blue bands intertwined, braided around each other, and shot with an audible humming sound into the eyes of both Daufin and Sarge, into their nostrils and around their skulls. Daufin's hair danced with sparks. Sarge's mouth opened, and sparks were leaping off his fillings.

Tom and Jessie held on to each other, not daring to speak or move, and the others were silent.

The power surge snapped Sarge's head back. His legs buckled, and he fell to the floor. Daufin went down two seconds later. The energy flow ceased, and the pod fell out of the child's hands and rolled to Jessie's feet.

Daufin sat up. Blinked at Tom and Jessie. Started to speak but nothing came out.

Sarge's body trembled. He rolled over on his side, slowly got up on his knees.

Daufin rubbed her eyes. Sarge breathed deeply a few times, and then he spoke: "Take your daughter home, Tom and Jessie."

"Mama?" Stevie said. "I'm . . . so sleepy."

Jessie rushed to her daughter, picked her up, and hugged her, and Tom put his arms around both of them. "Why are you crying?" Stevie asked.

Sarge retrieved the sphere and stood up. His movements were quicker than before, and his eyes glinted with a fierce intelligence. "Your language . . . isn't big enough to tell you how grateful I am," he said. "I'm sorry I brought such pain to this world." He looked down at Curt's body, and placed his hand on Cody's shoulder. "It wasn't what I wanted."

Cody nodded, but was unable to reply.

"We know," Tom said. "I wish you could've seen a better part of our world."

"I think I saw a fine part of it. What's any world but its tribe? And the generations yet to be?" He reached out, gently touching Stevie's auburn hair with Sarge's work-gnarled fingers.

Stevie's eyes and brain were fogged with the need for sleep. "Do I know who you are?"

"Nope. But someday—maybe—your parents might tell you."

Stevie nestled her head against Jessie's shoulder. She didn't care where she was, or what was happening; her body was worn out. But she'd been having such a wonderful dream, of playing in the summer sun in a huge pasture with Sweetpea. Such a wonderful dream . . .

"The greatest gift is a second chance," the alien said. "That's what you've given my tribe. I wish there was something I could give in return—but all I can do is promise that on my world there'll always be a song for Earth." A smile touched the corners of Sarge's mouth. "Who knows? Someday we might even learn to play baseball."

Jessie grasped his hand. Words failed her, but she found some. "Thank you for giving Stevie back to us. Good luck to you—and you be careful, you hear?"

"I hear." He looked at the others, nodded farewell at Cody and Rick, then back to Jessie and Tom. "Go home," he told them. "You know the way. And so do I."

He turned and strode across the floor. One leg folded up at the knee joint like an accordian. He entered the small pyramid, paused only briefly as he studied the instruments, then began to rapidly manipulate the levers.

Tom, Jessie, Cody, Rick, and Miranda left the chamber, with Stevie clinging to Jessie's neck. They went the way they'd come in, through the passage that spiraled down to a wide black ramp in the tunnel below. The lights they'd thrown away were still burning in the distance.

And in the black sphere in the creature's hand, Sarge Dennison stood at a crossroads. He was a young man, handsome and agile, with his whole life before him. For some reason, and this was unclear, he was wearing an olive-green uniform. He had a suitcase in his hand, and the day was sunny and there was a nice breeze and the dirt road went in two directions. The signpost had foreign words on it: the names of Belgian villages. From one direction he thought he heard the dark mutter of thunder, and clouds of dark smoke were rising from the ground. Something bad was happening over that way, he thought. Something real bad, that should not ever have to happen again.

A dog barked. He looked the other way, and there was Scooter. A mighty prancy thing, waiting for him. The dog's tail wagged furiously. Sarge looked toward the clear horizon. He didn't know what was over that way, beyond the green trees and the soft hills, but maybe it was worth a walk.

He had all the time in the world to get there.

"Hold on!" he called to Scooter. "I'm comin'!" He started walking, and it was funny but the suitcase hardly weighed a feather. He leaned down and picked up a stick, and he flung it high and far and watched Scooter kick up dust as the dog ran to fetch it. Scooter got the stick and brought it back. It seemed to Sarge that they could play this game all day.

He smiled, and passed on along a dirt road into the land of imagination.

58
Dawn

Rick started up the rope, and twenty feet had never looked so deep. He made it up about eight feet before his arms gave out. He fell back, exhausted.

A voice came from above: "Tie a loop in the rope and put your foot in it! We'll haul you up!"

"Okay!" Tom shouted. "Hold on!" He got the loop tied, and Rick stepped into it. He was drawn steadily upward and a few seconds later was pulled onto the floor of Crowfield's house. He saw a smear of red early-morning sun in the sky. The force field was gone and the desert breeze was drifting the smoke and dust away.

Xavier Mendoza, Bobby Clay Clemmons, Zarra, and Pequin had come from the fortress. They dropped the rope back down and this time reeled Miranda up.

When Rhodes came up, he almost kissed the floor but he was afraid that if he got down on it he'd never get back up. He lurched to the front door, holding his mangled shoulder, breathed deeply of fresh air, and looked out at the world.

Helicopters roared back and forth over Inferno and Bordertown, cautiously circling the black pyramid. Higher up were the contrails of jet fighters, their pilots awaiting orders. On Highway 67 were hundreds of headlights: a convoy of trucks, jeeps, vans, and trailers. Rhodes nodded.

Now the shit was about to hit the fan. He could hear the noise of the pyramid: from here, it was a low-pitched rumble. Daufin—Sarge, now—was still holding the ship back, giving them time to get clear of the tunnels.

Ray Hammond heard the chatter of a 'copter overhead, and he opened his eyes. He was lying in a bathtub, Nasty's Mohawked head against his shoulder. Red stripes of sunlight slanted through a broken window. They had hidden here since Tank's truck had overturned, had heard the smashing of houses around them, but had stayed put. Climbing into the bathtub had been Ray's idea.

He started to climb out, but Nasty murmured and clutched at his chest. She was still pretty much out of it, he knew, and she needed to be taken to Doc Early. He looked at her face and smoothed some of her wild hair down—and then the ruddy light showed him what the dark had kept secret: Nasty's blouse had pulled open, and . . .

Oh my God! Ray thought. Oh my God there they are!

Both her breasts were exposed. There they were, nipples and everything, just inches away from his fingers.

He stared at them, mesmerized.

So close. So close. Crazy, he thought, how his mind could switch from almost getting killed to the idea of losing his virginity in a bathtub, but that was the Alien Sex Beam for you. Unpredictable.

Maybe just one touch, he decided. One quick touch, and she'd never know.

He moved his fingers toward them, and Nasty's eyes opened. They were red and swollen. Her whole face was puffy and bruised looking, but he still thought she was pretty. And maybe never prettier, her face against his shoulder and so close to him. Her eyes struggled to focus. She said, "Ray?"

"The one and only." He gave a nervous little laugh.

"Thought so." She smiled sleepily. "You're okay, kid. You're gonna make some girl feel real special someday. Like she's a lady." Her eyes closed again, heavy-lidded, and her soft breath brushed his throat.

He looked at her breasts for a while longer, but his fingers crept no closer. There would be a time, he thought. But not now. Not today. That time was in the future. Maybe not with Nasty, but with some girl he didn't even know yet. Maybe love would have something to do with it too. And maybe thinking about things like this was what they called "growing up."

"Thanks," he said to her, but she didn't answer. He gathered her blouse together and slipped a couple of buttons through their loops so when somebody found them she'd look like what she did to him: a sleeping Guinevere. And that was his chivalrous deed for the year, he decided. From here on out it was Wild Animal City. His body felt like a bag of knots, and he laid his head back and watched the red sun coming up.

Helicopters were flying over Celeste Street, their rotors stirring the haze away, as Ed Vance, Celeste Preston, and Sue Mullinax emerged from the Brandin' Iron. They'd stayed behind the counter after the wall had crashed in, flat on their faces in the debris. There had been more sounds of destruction, and Vance had figured it was the end of the world until Celeste had given an ungodly shriek and they'd all heard the helicopters. Now they saw that the force field was gone, and as the wind of 'copter rotors swirled along the street Vance couldn't help himself. He gave a whoop and hugged Celeste Preston, picking her up off her feet.

Something flapped past Vance's face like a green bat. Then more of them, running before the wind. Sue shouted, "What is it?"

Celeste reached out and snagged a handful as they rushed past. She opened her hand, and was looking at eight one-hundred-dollar bills.

Money was flying all over Celeste Street. "My God!" Sue snatched up two handfuls and shoved them down her blouse, and now other people were out in the street, amid all the wreckage, picking up money too. "Where's it comin' from?"

Celeste struggled out of the sheriff's bear hug and walked

over sliding masses of money. Her yellow Cadillac had gone over on its side, two tires flat, and in the red light she could see the bills whirling up out of the car when the helicopters passed overhead. She reached the car on wobbly legs, and she said, "Shit."

The hundred-dollar bills were coming from the ripped-open front seat, where the thing's claws had slashed. Vance came toward her, his wet shirt stuffed with money. "Have you ever seen the like of this?" he hollered.

"We've found where Wint hid his money," Celeste said. "Old crazy sonofabitch stuffed my seats full. He told me never to sell that car. Reckon I know why now."

"Well, start pickin' it up, then! Hell, it's flyin' all over town!"

Celeste grunted and looked around. The streets were riddled with chasms and cracks, stores appeared to have been hit by bombs, cars were smashed and many still on fire over in Cade's used-car lot, houses were fit for kindling. "Ain't much left of Inferno," she said. "Old town's 'bout done."

"Get the money!" Vance urged her. "Come on, it's yours! Help me get it!"

She stared at her handful of cash for a moment. And then she opened her fingers and the money took flight.

"Are you crazy? It's goin' *everywhere!*"

"Wind wants it," Celeste said. "Wind oughta have it." She regarded him with her icy blue eyes. "Ed, I'm damned grateful to be alive after what we just went through. I've lived in a shack and I've lived in a fancy house, and I'm not sure which suits me best. You want it, you go ahead and take it. All goin' to the tax man, anyhow. But I'm alive this mornin', Ed, and I feel mighty rich." She breathed deep of clean air. "Mighty rich."

"I do too, but that don't mean I've lost my mind!" He was busy stuffing his pockets, back and front.

"Ain't no matter." She waved his objections away. "Sue, you got any more beer in there?"

"I don't know, Mrs. Preston." Sue had stopped picking up money. Her blouse was full of bills, but her eyes were dazed and seeing Inferno all torn up made everything doubly unreal. "I think I'm . . . gonna go see if anything's left of my house. You help yourself to whatever you want." And then she walked away, through the bluster and scurry of cash, toward Bowden Street.

Celeste saw headlights up at the far end of the street. "Looks like we've gonna have company real soon. You want to share another beer with me 'fore they get here?"

Vance reached for another bill. As he grasped it three sneaked away from him. And he realized that he could never scoop up all of it, and trying to would make him crazy. He stood up. Money was already swirling out of his overstuffed pockets. It was a nightmare in the center of a dream nestled in a nightmare, and the only thing solid seemed to be the woman standing in front of him. The crackle of bills taunted him as they flew, and he knew he could work all his life and never have a bucket's worth of what was spinning in the breeze.

But he had never thought he'd live to see the sun rising, and there it was. Its heat touched his face. He blinked back tears.

"Come on, Ed," Celeste said, in a gentle voice. Just for a second, there in the rotors and the wind and the noise of flying money, she thought she'd heard Wint laugh. Or at least chuckle. She took the sheriff's arm. "Let's us rich folks get off the street," she said, and she guided him like a docile bear through the broken facade of the Brandin' Iron.

Other people came out of the houses where they'd been hiding and blinked in the early light. Inferno looked as if a tornado had zigzagged across it, craters here and there where the weakened earth had collapsed. And some people found more than destruction: on Oakley Street lay the horse creature, which had torn a swath of houses apart across Travis, Sombra, and Oakley but had fallen when Stinger did. Wedged in cracks were other things: scorpionlike bodies with human heads, their eyes blank, their lifeforce extinguished at the same instant as Stinger's. It would take weeks for all the bodies to be found.

Sue Mullinax was nearing her house at the corner of

Bowden and Oakley when somebody shouted, "Hey, lady! Stop!"

She looked up, at Rocking Chair Ridge. The light was strengthening, and the shadows were melting away. On top of the ridge was a small dune buggy, and there were two men standing beside it. One of the men had a videotape camera, aimed at the black pyramid. He swung it in her direction. The other man came down the ridge in a boil of sliding dust and rocks. He had a dark beard and wore a cap that said NBC. "What's your name, lady?" he asked, fumbling for a notepad and pen.

She told him. He shouted to the other man, "Get down here! We've got an interview!" The one with the videotape camera scrambled down the ridge, almost falling on his tail before he made it. "Oh Lord," Sue said, frantically trying to fix her hair. "Oh Lord, am I gonna be on TV?"

"National news, lady! Just look at me, now." A red light lit up on the camera, and Sue couldn't help but stare at the lens. "When did the UFO come down?"

"Almost quarter till ten. I remember, 'cause I saw the clock just before it hit." She pulled her dusty hair back from her face, aware that the money stuffed in her blouse was going to make her appear even heftier than she was. "I work at the Brandin' Iron. That's a cafe. Lord, I must look a mess!"

"You look fine. Get me a pan shot and come back to her face." The cameraman slowly swiveled, filming the houses of Inferno. "Lady, this is about to be the most famous town in the country. Hell, in the whole *world!*"

"Am . . . *I* gonna be famous?" she asked.

"You and everybody else. We've gotten a report that there might've been extraterrestrial contact. Can you verify that?"

She was aware of the importance of her answer. And just like that she saw her face and the faces of other people from Inferno and Bordertown on the newscasts, the covers of magazines, newspapers, and books, and she had a dizzy spell that was almost as heart-stopping as a monkey flip. She said, very clearly, "Yes." Said it again. "Yes. There were two creatures. Both different kinds. The sheriff—Sheriff Ed Vance is his name—told me one was after the other. When that ship came down, the whole town almost shook itself to—"

"Cut!" the man in the cap said. He was looking over his shoulder, and he'd seen what was coming. "Thanks, Mrs. Mullinax. Gotta go!" He and the cameraman began running up the ridge to the dune buggy.

She saw what had scared them: a jeep full of soldiers with MP on their helmets was turning onto Bowden, its driver swinging around the cracks and craters. Some of the soldiers leapt out and sprinted up the ridge after the two newsmen. "It's *Miss* Mullinax!" she shouted. The dune buggy's engine fired before the soldiers could get there, and the vehicle sped away down the other side of the ridge.

An unmarked dark blue car stopped at the north end of the Snake River Bridge. Two men in the uniforms of air-force colonels and another man in civilian clothes got out. They strode briskly toward the group of people who were coming from the south end of the fire-scarred bridge.

"My God!" The hawk-nosed officer with "Buckner" on a security-clearance tag at his breast pocket halted. He'd recognized one of the men approaching them, but if that was indeed Colonel Rhodes, Matt had aged ten years in one night. "I think we've found him." And another few steps closer brought an "Affirmative. It's Colonel Rhodes. Tell Central."

The other officer, a captain named Garcia, had a field telephone, and through it he said, "Able One to Central, we've found Colonel Rhodes. Repeat: we've found the colonel. We need a medic evac truck, on the double."

"Medic evac on the way, Able One," the dispatcher answered, routing traffic from the Central Command trailer parked in the Bob Wire Club's lot.

Rhodes was being helped along by Zarra Alhambra, and he saw Colonel Buckner of Special Intelligence coming toward him. "Morning, Alan," he said when the other man reached them. "You missed some excitement last night."

Buckner nodded, his dark eyes humorless. "I suppose I

did." He looked at the ragtag bunch of civilians. They appeared to have stumbled out of a battle zone: their clothes were covered with dust and grime, their eyes weary hollows in bruised and blood-streaked faces. One of them, a wiry young man with curly blond hair, was being supported between a Hispanic boy and girl, and all three of them had the thousand-yard stare of shell-shock victims. Another older man had bloody strips of shirt around his arms, and next to him was an ashen-faced woman holding a little girl who—amazingly—appeared to be asleep. The other people were more or less just as dazed and battered. But Matt Rhodes had left Webb AFB yesterday morning looking fairly young, and now dust lay in deep lines on his glass-cut face and much of his hair had seemingly turned gray overnight. Coagulated blood had oozed through the fingers of the hand clamped to his shoulder. He was smiling bravely, but his eyes were deep-socketed and there were things behind them that would haunt him for the rest of his life.

"This is Mr. Winslow. He's a coordination specialist." Buckner motioned to the civilian, a crewcut blond man in a dark blue suit. Mr. Winslow wore sunglasses and had a face like a slab of stone, and Rhodes caught a whiff of Washington. "Captain Gunniston's already been taken to Debriefing," Buckner said. It was actually a large trailer parked near the Texaco station. "We'll have a truck here for you in a few minutes to take you to Medical." He gazed around at the destruction. "Looks like this town took a hell of a beating. Can you estimate the casualties?"

"High," Rhodes said. His arm was no longer hurting now; it was just heavy, like a sack of freshly poured concrete. "But I think we came out on top." How to explain to this man standing before them that in the space of twenty-four hours—an iota of a second on the scale of the universe —the fate of two civilizations had been fought for in the Texas dust?

"Colonel Buckner?" Garcia said, the field phone's receiver to his ear. "I've got Perimeter Control. They're reporting intruders getting through security—probably newsmen.

Captain Ingalls says there's no way to stop them with all the open spaces out—"

"Tell him to keep them out of here!" Buckner snapped. In his voice there was a hint of panic. "Jesus Christ! Tell him to lock the bastards up if he has to!"

"Might as well forget it," Rhodes said calmly. "There's no way to keep this secret."

Buckner gaped at him as if Rhodes had just asserted that the American flag's colors were green, pink, and purple, and Winslow's reflective sunglasses held images of Rhodes's face.

The distant rumbling of the black pyramid suddenly stopped.

Cody, Rick, Rhodes, and the others looked back at it. The object's base had begun to glow a blue-orange color. Waves of heat shimmered in the morning light.

The bridge trembled. A vibration passed through the earth, and the upper three quarters of the pyramid began to rise, leaving the heated base below. Thin jets of white flame shot around the pyramid's rim, and those flames roared through the tunnels on the Bordertown side and melted red dirt and sand into clumps of ebony glass. Hot winds shrilled across the bridge.

The pyramid slowly rose four hundred feet in the air and paused there, golden sunlight hitting its black-scaled surface. The pyramid began a graceful rotation.

"Captain Redding reports Alpha Strike's Sidewinders are armed and ready," Garcia relayed to Buckner through the field phone.

Sidewinder missiles, Rhodes knew. He looked up, saw the contrails of jets gathering into strike formation. "Let it alone," he said.

Buckner grabbed the phone's receiver. "This is Team Leader, Alpha Strike. Hold your positions. Fire Sidewinders on my command, acknowledge?"

"No!" Tom protested, pushing forward. "Let the ship go!"

Whips of energy were flailing out from the pyramid's sides. "Ready on my command," Buckner repeated.

"Tell the fighters to disarm, Alan." Rhodes clutched the man's wrist. "I don't care what your orders are. Please let it go." The other man pulled free, splotches of red surfacing on his cheeks.

And now the pyramid's sides were compressing, as loops of power crackled from it like lightning and shot a hundred feet in all directions. The air fluttered with heat, making the pyramid shimmer like a mirage. In another few seconds the spacecraft had tightened itself into a shape akin to that of a sharpened spear.

It began to ascend again, faster now, rapidly gaining speed. In the space of two heartbeats it was an ebony streak moving upward into the blue.

"Go," Rick said. "Go!"

The fighters were waiting, circling above.

Buckner's mouth started to open.

Rhodes reached out, with deliberate strength, and jerked the phone's cable out of its field pack.

There was a sonic boom that knocked the first roving vultures out of the turbulent air and kicked up dust over thirty miles of Texas desert. The spacecraft seemed to elongate, a dark blurred streak arcing into the cloudless heavens like an arrow. It shot past the circling jets as if they were painted on the sky and vanished in a violet shimmer.

The wind blew across the bridge, ruffled clothes and hair and whistled over the remaining roofs of the town.

The ship and its pilot were gone. Far above, the jets were still going around and around like frustrated mosquitoes deprived of a good arm to bite.

"Sir?" Winslow's voice was slow and thick. Rhodes thought they must breed these high-level government security boys on farms somewhere. "I believe that was probably your last action as a member of the United States Air Force."

"You can kiss my ass," Rhodes said. To Buckner, "You too." He gazed up. The fighters were coming down. It was all over but the cleaning up.

A truck with a Red Cross on it pulled to the north end of the bridge. Its rear panel opened up and a ramp slid down.

Inside were cots, oxygen masks and tanks, medical supplies and a couple of attendants.

"Time to go." Buckner motioned Rhodes on.

The colonel took a few steps, Zarra helping him, but he stopped abruptly. The sun was a quarter up, the sky was turning blue, and it was going to be another scorcher. He turned to the others, looked at the faces of Cody, Rick, Miranda, Jessie, Tom, and the little girl. Even the sonic boom hadn't awakened her, and he figured they all would be sleeping like that pretty soon. Later there would be night-mares. But everyone would deal with those as best they could, because human beings knew nothing if not how to endure. We saved two worlds, Rhodes thought. Not a bad night's work for bugs.

He offered his face to the sun, and went on.

Jessie felt Stevie's heart beating, slowly and steadily, against her chest. She touched the child's face, ran her hand over the dusty auburn hair—and her fingers found two blood-clotted slashes under Stevie's hair, at the back of the neck. Stevie shifted her weight and made a pained face in her sleep. Jessie removed her fingers.

Someday the story would have to be told to her. Someday, but not this one.

Jessie clasped Stevie with one arm and her other hand found Tom's. They needed to get Ray at the clinic, but Ray would be all right. He was a born survivor, Jessie knew. That trait must run in the family. Tom and Jessie crossed the bridge, and Stevie dreamed of stars.

Trucks and jeeps were all over Inferno now. Several helicopters warily circled the starship's remaining base section, which engineer crews in the days ahead would find impossible to cut apart or otherwise move.

A figure lingered on the bridge as the others went across. Cody stared at the wreckage of his motorcycle, his hands hanging limply at his sides. The Honda—his old friend —was dead too, and it seemed like the bridge was a hundred miles long.

Rick glanced over his shoulder and stopped. "Take my

sister with you," he told Mendoza, and the man helped Miranda to the truck. Then Rick limped back and stood waiting.

Cody reached down, picked up a piece of scorched exhaust pipe. Let it clatter back to the pavement like so much useless junk.

"Heard you were good with tools," Rick said.

Cody didn't answer. He sat down, his knees pulled up close to his chest.

"You coming, or not?"

Cody was silent. Then, after a long shudder of breath: "Not."

Rick limped a few paces closer. Cody averted his face. Rick started to speak, but it was just filling space. He didn't know what to say. Then something hit him, right out of the blue: "It's the last day of school. How about that? Think we graduated?"

"Leave me alone. Go on." He motioned toward the Inferno side.

"No use sitting out here, Cody. Either you walk the distance or somebody'll come get you."

"Let 'em come!" Cody shouted, and when he turned his face, Rick saw the tears running down his cheeks. "My dad's dead, don't you get it?" The shout left his throat raw. His eyes was so full he couldn't see. "My dad's dead," he repeated in a quieter voice, as if grasping it fully for the first time. Everything that had happened in Stinger's spaceship was a jumbled blur, and it would take him a long time to sort it out. But he remembered clearly enough his father lying in front of him, holding on to life long enough to look at a faded picture. A hole yearned inside him, and never in his wildest dreams would he have thought he might ever miss his father.

"Yeah, he is dead," Rick agreed. He came two more paces nearer. "He saved our tails, I'll tell you that. I mean . . . I didn't know him too well, but . . . he sure came through for us. And for Daufin too."

"A hero," Cody said. He laughed in spite of the tears, and

he had to wipe his nose. "My dad's a hero! Think they'll put that on his tombstone?" His crazy smile fractured, because he realized there wasn't a body to bury.

"I think they might," Rick told him.

"Yeah. Maybe so." Cody watched the sun coming up. It had been almost twenty-four hours since he'd been sitting on the Rocking Chair, counting the dead ends; he felt older now, but not weaker. His dad was dead, yes, and he would have to deal with that, but the world seemed different today; it seemed larger, and offered second chances and new beginnings.

"We did something real important last night," Rick said. "Something that people might not ever understand. But we'll know it, and that may have to do."

"Yeah." Cody nodded. "I reckon so. What do you think's gonna happen to Inferno?"

"I think it'll be around for a while longer. Bordertown too. As soon as people find out what landed here—well, you never know about tomorrow." Rick stepped forward and offered his hand. "You want to go across now?"

Cody looked at the brown hand for a moment. The palm was rope-burned. He wiped his eyes and snuffled his nose. If any of the 'Gades saw him like this, he'd . . .

No, he thought. No 'Gades and no Rattlers. Not anymore. That was yesterday, and today began for both of them from right here, at the middle of this bridge.

Cody reached up and grasped the hand, and Rick helped him to his feet.

The sunlight strengthened, chasing away the last shadows, and two men crossed the bridge together.

About the Author

A modern master of horror, Robert R. McCammon is the author of seven previous novels, including *The New York Times* bestseller *Swan Song*. His short stories have been adapted for television's *Darkroom* and *Twilight Zone* series. A native of Birmingham, Alabama, McCammon is currently at work on a new collection of short fiction to be published soon by Pocket Books. "Horror writers," says McCammon, "are simply trying to make sense out of the chaos, and . . . ourselves as well. We have to go all the way in, to conduct exploratory surgery. And some surgery is done with a laser, and some with a saw. . . ."